THE VIKING PORTABLE LIBRARY

LOUISA MAY ALCOTT

LOUISA MAY ALCOTT was born in Germantown, Pennsylvania, in 1832, the second of four daughters of Abigail May Alcott and Bronson Alcott, the prominent Transcendentalist thinker and social reformer. Raised in Concord, Massachusetts, and educated by her father, Alcott came under the influence of the great men of his circle: Emerson, Hawthorne, the preacher Theodore Parker, and Thoreau. From her youth, she worked at various tasks to help support her family: sewing, teaching, domestic service, and writing. In 1862, she volunteered to serve as a nurse in a Union army hospital—an experience that provided her with material for her first successful book, *Hospital Sketches* (1863). Between 1863 and 1869, she published many anonymous and pseudonymous Gothic romances and lurid thrillers. But it was the publication of *Little Women* (1868–69), a novel based on the girlhood adventures of the four Alcott sisters, that brought her immense popular acclaim and financial security. In the wake of *Little Women*'s popularity, she brought out *An Old-Fashioned Girl* (1870), *Little Men* (1871), *Eight Cousins* (1875), *Rose in Bloom* (1876), *Jo's Boys* (1886), and other books for children, as well as three major works for adults: *Work* (1873), *A Modern Mephistopheles* (1877), and *Moods* (1882), a revised version of her 1864 novel. An active participant in the women's suffrage and temperance movements during the last decade of her life, Alcott died in Boston in 1888.

ELIZABETH LENNOX KEYSER teaches English at Hollins University and edits the journal *Children's Literature*. Her book *Whispers in the Dark: The Fiction of Louisa May Alcott* won the 1993 Children's Literature Association Book Award. She is also the author of the Twayne Masterworks volume *Little Women: A Family Romance*.

EACH VOLUME in The Viking Portable Library either presents a representative selection from the works of a single outstanding writer or offers a comprehensive anthology on a special subject. Designed for compactness and readability, these books fill a need not met by other compilations. All are edited by distinguished authorities, who have written introductory essays and included much other helpful material.

THE VIKING PORTABLE LIBRARY

LOUISA MAY ALCOTT

LOUISA MAY ALCOTT was born in Germantown, Pennsylvania, in 1832, the second of four daughters of Abigail May Alcott and Bronson Alcott, the [illegible] transcendentalist, thinker and social reformer. Raised in Concord, Massachusetts, she was educated by her father and came under the influence of the great men of his circle: Emerson, Theodore Parker and Thoreau. From her youth she worked [illegible] to support her family [illegible] teaching, sewing and writing. In 1862 she volunteered to serve as a nurse in a Union army hospital in Washington—an experience that [illegible] material for Hospital Sketches (1863). [illegible] Moods (1864) and [illegible] sensational romances and [illegible] thrillers. But it was the publication of Little Women (1868), a novel based on the childhood adventures of the four Alcott sisters, that brought her immense popular acclaim and financial security. In the wake of Little Women's popularity she brought out An Old-Fashioned Girl (1870), Little Men (1871), Eight Cousins (1875), Rose in Bloom (1876), Jo's Boys (1886) and other books for children, as well as books for adults, including Work (1873), A Modern Mephistopheles (1877) and Moods (1882), a revised version of her 1864 novel. An active participant in the women's suffrage and temperance movements during the last decades of her life, Alcott died in Boston in 1888.

ELIZABETH LENNOX KEYSER teaches English at Hollins University and edits the journal Children's Literature. Her book, Whispers in the Dark: The Fiction of Louisa May Alcott, won the 1994 Children's Literature Association Book Award. She is also the author of [illegible]

Each volume in The Viking Portable Library either presents a representative selection from the works of a single outstanding writer or offers a comprehensive anthology on a special subject. Averaging 700 pages in length and designed for compactness and readability, these books fill a need not met by other compilations. All are edited by distinguished authorities, who have written introductory essays and included much other helpful material.

The Portable

LOUISA MAY ALCOTT

Edited with an Introduction by

ELIZABETH LENNOX KEYSER

PENGUIN BOOKS

PENGUIN BOOKS
Published by the Penguin Group
Penguin Group (USA) Inc., 375 Hudson Street, New York, New York 10014, U.S.A.
Penguin Group (Canada), 90 Eglinton Avenue East, Suite 700, Toronto, Ontario, Canada M4P 2Y3 (a division of Pearson Penguin Canada Inc.)
Penguin Books Ltd, 80 Strand, London WC2R 0RL, England
Penguin Ireland, 25 St Stephen's Green, Dublin 2, Ireland (a division of Penguin Books Ltd)
Penguin Group (Australia), 250 Camberwell Road, Camberwell, Victoria 3124, Australia (a division of Pearson Australia Group Pty Ltd)
Penguin Books India Pvt Ltd, 11 Community Centre, Panchsheel Park, New Delhi – 110 017, India
Penguin Group (NZ), 67 Apollo Drive, Rosedale, North Shore, Auckland 0745, New Zealand (a division of Pearson New Zealand Ltd)
Penguin Books (South Africa) (Pty) Ltd, 24 Sturdee Avenue, Rosebank, Johannesburg 2196, South Africa

Penguin Books Ltd, Registered Offices: 80 Strand, London WC2R 0RL, England

First published in Penguin Books 2000

Grateful acknowledgment is made for permission to reprint two selections from *The Selected Letters of Louisa May Alcott*, editors, Joel Myerson and Daniel Shealy, associate editor, Madeleine B. Stern (Little, Brown). Copyright © the Estate of Theresa W Pratt, 1987. Used by permission.

LIBRARY OF CONGRESS CATALOGING-IN-PUBLICATION DATA

Alcott, Louisa May, 1832–1888.
The portable Louisa May Alcott / edited and with an introduction by Elizabeth Lennox Keyser.
p. cm. —(The Viking portable library)
Includes bibliographical references.
ISBN 978-0-14-027574-2
1. New England—Social life and customs—Fiction. 2.Alcott, Louisa May, 1832–1888—Correspondence. 3.Alcott, Louisa May, 1832–1888—Diaries. 4. Authors, American—19th century—Correspondence. 5. Authors, American—19th century—Diaries. 6.New England—Intellectual life—19th century. I. Keyser, Elizabeth Lennox, 1942– II.Title. III.Series.

PS1016.K49 2000
813'.4—dc21 99-057115

Printed in the United States of America
Set in Bembo
Designed by Sabrina Bowers

CONTENTS

III. MEMOIRS, JOURNALS, AND LETTERS

INTRODUCTION

TWENTY-FIVE YEARS AGO, a *Portable Alcott* would have been inconceivable. Although her name had been a household word since the publication of *Little Women* in 1868, and generations of young readers had enjoyed not only that book but also its sequels, Alcott had never been considered even a minor figure in the American literary canon. Now, at the end of the twentieth century, Alcott's fiction can be found in the adult literature section of any bookstore—not only familiar titles, formerly considered children's literature, such as *Little Women* and *Rose in Bloom,* but unfamiliar ones, such as *The Inheritance* and *A Long Fatal Love Chase.* The former was adapted for television shortly after its publication in 1997, the latter appeared on the *New York Times* best-seller list, and a 1994 film version of *Little Women* was a box office hit. Even more surprising, however, Alcott is now receiving serious and widespread scholarly attention. Alcott sessions are featured on the programs of academic conferences, doctoral candidates are producing dissertations on her work, and scholarly books, articles, and editions devoted to Alcott are being published at an ever-increasing rate. Selections from Alcott now appear in the major American literature anthologies used in college classrooms, and her work is taught in American literature, women's literature, and social history, as well as children's literature, courses. What accounts for this phenomenon?

First, it must be recognized that Alcott is not the only nineteenth-century American woman writer to enjoy a renaissance in the final quarter of the twentieth century. The women's movement of the 1960s and 1970s both encouraged more women to enter the college teaching profession and created a tremendous impetus within academe to recover forgotten, neglected, or underestimated women writers. Harriet Beecher Stowe, long depreciated as a writer of propaganda and/or sentimental fiction, was among the first to be rehabilitated. She and Susan Warner, author of the best-selling *The Wide, Wide World,* now stand shoulder to shoulder with such fictional giants of the 1850s as Herman Melville and Nathaniel Hawthorne. Catharine Maria Sedgwick and Lydia Maria Child, contemporaries of James Fenimore Cooper, are now lauded for their comparatively enlightened portrayal of Native Americans. Feminist Margaret Fuller is now placed alongside her Transcendentalist contemporaries Ralph Waldo Emerson and Henry David Thoreau. African-American women writers such as Harriet Jacobs and Frances Harper are studied along with Frederick Douglass and Charles Chesnutt, themselves beneficiaries of the movement toward a more-inclusive literary canon. Contemporaries of Alcott such as Rebecca Harding Davis and Elizabeth Stuart Phelps have also received considerable attention. The reassessment of late-nineteenth-century writers Mary E. Wilkins Freeman, Sarah Orne Jewett, and Kate Chopin has revealed the way in which the terms "regionalism" and "local color" had been used to marginalize important women writers. Begun in 1984 as a newsletter, *Legacy: A Journal of American Women Writers* documents the dramatic expansion of the rich scholarly field of nineteenth-century American women's writing.

Granted that nineteenth-century American women writers have become a growth industry for both academe and the book trade, the recent upsurge of interest in Louisa May Alcott remains almost unique. The only comparable figure that comes to mind is Edith Wharton, and the reason for the popular, media, and scholarly attention she has recently enjoyed is, I would argue, similar. Both authors, until the late 1970s, had images that assured that they would continue to be read by a limited audience but that encouraged large segments of their potential audience to dismiss them: Alcott was, as she had been dubbed upon her death in 1888, "the children's friend"; Wharton was the bloodless dissector of upper-class New York society. But both authors, it was dramatically revealed some twenty years ago, had lived double lives: Alcott had spent a decade publishing dozens of stories about mad, vengeful, and manipulating women in adulterous, bigamous, and incestuous relationships; the unhappily married Wharton had had a passionate affair with a bisexual journalist and projected a novel about incest, a graphic (some would say pornographic) fragment of which survives. The radical disparity between what were regarded, for different reasons, as rather staid authors and their newly revealed passion and intensity created the desire to find and read everything by and about them and to reread familiar texts in this new and richer context.

Credit for the Alcott revelation and revival must go in large part to

Madeleine B. Stern, who, with her friend Leona Rostenberg, discovered the first cache of Alcott "thrillers," as she calls them, more than fifty years ago. It was not until 1975, however, that a selection of these works were edited by her and published under the title *Behind a Mask*. That volume was followed the next year by a second collection, *Plots and Counterplots*. As Stern explains in her introductions to these and still later collections, Alcott wrote countless lurid tales during the 1860s, publishing them either anonymously or under the pseudonym A. M. Barnard. Most of these tales appeared serially in Frank Leslie's several weekly newspapers or in James R. Elliott's weekly *The Flag of Our Union*. From Alcott's letters and journals, edited by Stern, Joel Myerson, and Daniel Shealy, we can see that her motive in writing these tales was twofold: the money she earned (usually less than a hundred dollars per tale) helped support her and her family, but she also enjoyed the process of writing, falling into a "vortex," as she called it. The nightmares that Alcott records having suffered after an attack of fever (see her Georgetown journal in this volume) also suggest that writing sensational fiction gave her an outlet for emotions that she could not express in any other way. With the financial success of *Little Women* in 1868, and the approach of middle age, Alcott ceased to produce Gothic thrillers, but she did return at least once to the genre, providing the novel *A Modern Mephistopheles* for her publisher's No Name Series in 1877.

It was never a secret that Alcott had written racy stories early in her career: her autobiographical heroine Jo March does so in *Little Women*, Alcott herself later acknowledged authorship of *A Modern Mephistopheles* and in 1887 suggested reprinting it under her name together with the early Gothic tale "A Whisper in the Dark," and Ednah Dow Cheney, in her 1889 biography, reluctantly alluded to her having produced work that "she wisely renounced as trash" (395). Nonetheless, it was not until the republication of the stories themselves, coinciding as it did with the women's movement and the rise of feminist criticism, that Louisa May Alcott was cast in an entirely new light. How did one square the rebellious, assertive heroines of the sensation stories, some of whom would not blink at murder if it served their purposes, with the submissive, self-sacrificing heroines of *Little Women*, whose consciences torture them if they long for a pretty dress or utter an angry word? Does Jo remain undiminished and undaunted until the very last page or does she gain maturity by giving up unrealistic aspirations? Or does she immolate herself on the altar of her family? Which was the "real" or more subversive or more feminist Louisa May Alcott—the sensation writer or the children's author? These were the questions that feminist critics began almost immediately to ask in such groundbreaking essays as Judith Fetterley's "*Little Women*: Alcott's Civil War" (1979) and "Impersonating 'Little Women': The Radicalism of *Behind a Mask*" (1983).

But to solve the puzzle of the relationship between *Little Women* and the sensation fiction, one needed some missing pieces, namely what else she wrote and also more about her life. Thus in the years following Stern's first two collections of thrillers, Alcott's nonsensational writings for adults—*Hospital Sketches*, "Transcendental Wild Oats," and *Work*—reappeared. "Diana and Persis," a novella not published in her lifetime, and, finally, *Moods*, her first published novel, were edited by Sarah Elbert. These important works occupy a middle ground between the anonymous tales, which Alcott considered self-indulgent potboilers, and the children's fiction, in which Alcott apparently felt pressure to inculcate moral—and especially "family"—values as well as provide entertainment. In fact, Alcott's Civil War and domestic stories, published in periodicals such as *The Atlantic Monthly*; her adult novels *Moods* and *Work*, begun early in her career; and "Diana and Persis," which may have been an aborted attempt to write another, but still better, serious adult novel, probably represent the type of work for which the young aspiring author wished to become known. These, together with the publication of more thrillers (including the full-length novels *A Modern Mephistopheles* and *A Long Fatal Love Chase*), her juvenilia (*The Inheritance* and a play, *Norna*), and her letters and journals, reveal both a pragmatic writer, always intent on gratifying her audience, and a passionate artist, managing nonetheless to express her own strongest feelings and commitments. Not limited to the rendering of social surfaces with the liveliness and humor that endeared her to young readers, her art was fully capable of plumbing psychological depths, whether of the individual or the national consciousness. But because she explored these in the domestic settings where she first experienced them, her soundings have been late in gaining the recognition they deserve.

II.

It would not be an exaggeration to say that Louisa May Alcott's family was her life and work, for her fifty-six years were spent in the bosom of a family that she supported by writing and that provided the inspiration for her art. At the same time, however, that family was situated in the midst of and connected with most of the major social and intellectual movements of the day. Her mother, Abigail May, came from a prominent Boston family of judges, scholars, clergymen, and reformers, and her uncle, the Reverend Samuel May, became a leader of the antislavery cause. Alcott's father, Bronson Alcott, had more humble origins, but even before his marriage, he had gained a reputation as a progressive educator. When Louisa was a small child, her father founded the Temple School in Boston and was aided in his work by two remarkable women: bookseller Elizabeth Peabody, sister to Sophia, who was to marry Nathaniel Hawthorne and become the Alcotts' neighbor, and Margaret Fuller, soon to become editor of the *Dial*, the Transcendentalist journal, and to conduct her "conversations"—meetings that provided women (and, occasionally, men) with cultural and consciousness-raising opportunities. When the Temple School eventually failed, Bronson's friend Ralph Waldo Emerson invited him to move with his family to Concord. There, during her formative years, Louisa had daily contact with the Emerson family as well as with Henry David Thoreau. Inspired by the model of George Ripley's Brook Farm and other utopian communities, Bronson founded his own, smaller experimental community at Fruitlands. Back in Boston during the 1850s, Bronson participated in protests against the Fugitive Slave Law and held "conversations" of his own, attended by such figures as Wendell Phillips, William Lloyd Garrison, Thomas Wentworth Higginson, and Theodore Parker, a minister whom Louisa especially admired. When the Civil War broke out, the Alcotts hosted John Brown's daughters, and, during it, Louisa corresponded with and about the younger brothers of Henry James, one of whom was wounded at Fort Wagner, where he served with Robert Gould Shaw's all-black regiment. Thus, however claustrophobic and ingrown Alcott's family life appears to us today, it was never insulated from the ideological ferment and turbulent events of the mid-nineteenth century.

Louisa May Alcott's life was framed by that of her father: she was born on her father's birthday in 1832, and her death, in 1888, followed his by two days. He undoubtedly had a profound effect both on her work and work habits, but whether the influence was positive or negative, whether it represents emulation or rebellion, are questions much debated. During her childhood, her relationship with Bronson was stormy. He preferred her docile sister Anna, whereas Louisa felt a stronger bond with her mother, Abby. As a professional educator, Bronson took great interest in his children's development, keeping detailed journals of their intellectual and moral progress, and requiring them to keep their own journals as soon as they were able to do so. Both parents read and wrote in these journals, and Louisa appears to have cherished Abby's notes, even though they placed contradictory demands on her for purity and candor. The intense moral scrutiny to which Louisa was subjected, and her difficulties in withstanding it, may have taught her at an early age to write for two audiences—herself and others—simultaneously.

If, as biographer Martha Saxton has argued, Bronson's disapproval gave Louisa a sense of herself as dark, deviant, and demonic, his impecuniousness gave her a strong determination to be financially independent. The failures of the Temple School and Fruitlands, where mother and daughters did most of the physical labor and the family almost starved; the lecture tours from which Bronson returned penniless; and the family's dependence on the generosity of the Mays and Emerson, all instilled in Louisa a relentless work ethic that probably contributed to her relatively early death. From an early age, Alcott worked to support the family, whether with needle or pen, and gradually, in her twenties, she became its principal breadwinner. In the last decade of her life, after the death of her mother, she seems not only to have supplanted her father as head of the family but also to have supplanted her mother as his partner. Throughout her adult years, Alcott seems to have had a wry but genuine affection for her father, to have been both protective and proud of him as a wholly impractical but visionary thinker. Her use of his favorite *Pilgrim's Progress* in *Little Women*, her depiction of Plumfield and Professor Bhaer's educational practices in the sequels, have been interpreted variously as tributes to her father, unwitting betrayals, or conscious critiques of a well-meant but repressive regime. The involvement of her heroines with much older men—from Jo's marriage to the fatherly Professor Bhaer to the blatantly incestuous relationships in *The Marble Woman*, one of Alcott's most bizarre sensational stories—has prompted speculation about her Oedipal desire for her demanding, emotionally distant father.

The great love of Alcott's life, however, was doubtless her mother, whom she idealized as Marmee in *Little Women*. Alcott seems never to have contemplated the possibility of marriage, perhaps because of the obligation she felt to support her family, perhaps because she had witnessed her mother's marital difficulties, or perhaps because her emotional needs were better satisfied by her mother and, to a lesser degree, her sisters than they could have been by anyone else. From an early age, Alcott aspired to win her mother's approval, and even when she failed to achieve it, as she occasionally did, she felt that her mother understood the temperament that was similar to her own. Observing her mother's economic hardships, the embarrassment of her reliance upon her May relatives, and, especially, the physical and emotional toll taken by her labor at Fruitlands, where the family was almost destroyed by Bronson's infatuation with his disciple Charles Lane, Alcott resolved that as an adult she would make her mother's life secure and comfortable. But she did not simply regard her mother as a victim. Abigail May Alcott, when she found that her husband could not or would not support their family, attempted to do so herself. She undertook paid charitable work in Boston and opened an "intelligence service" or employment agency for women. And, shortly after the 1848 Seneca Falls convention, she embraced the suffrage cause and, for a time, was actively involved. The demands of marriage and motherhood, however, mitigated against any sustained commitment, and it remained to her daughter to bring that feminist legacy to fruition.

Louisa's relationship with her older sister, Anna, was a close one despite their initial rivalry for their father's affection. Bronson had always encouraged recitation as well as writing, and when the family returned from Fruitlands to Concord, Anna and Louisa transformed the barn of Hillside, their new home, into a theater where they performed melodramas like the one Jo writes in *Little Women* or scenes from Dickens. When the family moved again, to Boston, and then to Walpole, New Hampshire, Anna and Louisa continued to pursue their passion for the theater, joining the Amateur Dramatic Company of Walpole. On the Alcotts' third and final remove to Concord, they joined the Concord Dramatic Union, through which Louisa became close friends with Alfred Whitman, one prototype for Laurie, and Anna met her future husband, John Pratt, the model for Meg's John Brooke. A more melancholy event immortalized in *Little Women*, however, was in preparation for the family. Elizabeth Alcott, one of Louisa's two younger sisters, was slowly dying of consumption. The special relationship that obtains between Jo and Beth in *Little Women* has not been substantiated by Alcott biographers as having existed between Louisa and Lizzie. But her loss, coinciding as it did with the engagement of Anna and John, left Louisa feeling bereft, and it was not long after this that Alcott left Concord for Boston, where, despairing at her inability to find work, she was briefly tempted to throw herself into the water of the Mill Dam, a temptation that she later placed before her heroine, Christie Devon, in *Work*.

Alcott's most interesting and complicated sororal relationship was with her younger sister Abigail May, the Amy of *Little Women.* The baby of the family, as fair as Louisa was dark, May was predictably petted and spoiled. Too young to remember much of the demoralizing Fruitlands experience, May had a sunny disposition and seemed always able to dissociate herself from the family's problems. In important ways, however, she did resemble Louisa, for she was talented and willful. Louisa, when she began to support the family, gave May the advantages she had never had, sending her abroad to study art and sharing an apartment with her in Boston. May, unlike Amy, did not discover that "talent isn't genius" and marry young; instead, she cheerfully persisted in her career as a painter, enjoying some success in Paris. Finally, in her late thirties, May met and married a young Swiss businessman, only to die a year later shortly after giving birth to their daughter. Louisa was devastated by this loss, following fast upon the death of her beloved mother, and promptly volunteered to adopt her namesake, Louisa May Nieriker. Thus once again Alcott stepped in to assume a surrogate role, this time as mother. Not only had she, as breadwinner, been a surrogate husband to her mother, she had belatedly assumed the same role in regard to Anna, for when John Pratt died in 1871, she began supporting her and her two sons.

It is fascinating to see how these family relationships are transformed in *Little Women* as well as in other Alcott works. On the surface, at least, of Alcott's most famous novel, her parents and sisters, with the possible exception of May, are idealized. For one thing, the March family's poverty, which is attributed to the father's high-minded disinterestedness, is genteel, and he is physically distant—serving as a Union army chaplain—rather than emotionally withdrawn. Although it was Louisa, not her father, who went to Washington to work in an army hospital, where she fell ill, in *Little Women* Jo despairs at her inability to contribute to the war effort. And just as Alcott transfers her own participation in the war to Mr. March, so she shifts responsibility for her sister Lizzie's Illness from Abby to Jo. In *Little Women,* Jo's selfish refusal to visit the indigent Hummels exposes Beth to the fever that fatally weakens her constitution, whereas in fact, it was Abby who contracted the disease from one of her charity cases and thus infected the entire family. In the sequel *Little Men,* John Brooke's death leaves his wife, Meg, financially independent rather than another burden for her sister to bear.

Other aspects of the March saga, on the other hand, are lifted directly from life. Jo's play, *Norna,* was one of Louisa's; a poem Jo writes for

Beth was written by Louisa for Lizzie; Alcott, like Jo, did publish a story entitled "The Rival Painters"; and in *Little Men*, Professor Bhaer requires a student to ferule him just as Bronson Alcott is reported to have done. More significantly, Louisa, like Jo, did view Anna's marriage as a defection, and she often regarded May as Jo does Amy—as someone who always gets what she wants without effort. But a decade later, Alcott was to render a more flattering portrait of May in "Diana and Persis," the novel or novella on which she was working at the time of May's death. Portraying the Jo and Amy characters, Diana and Persis, as two friends and fellow artists, Alcott once again combines idealization with literalism—describing paintings of May's that can be seen in the Alcotts' Orchard House today and devoting a chapter to her virtually unaltered letters. And once again Alcott's sleight of hand, her mysterious alchemy, works. The story, though unpublished at the time and possibly left unfinished, constitutes a moving meditation on the obstacles—both external and internal—still confronting the woman artist and on the different ways the Alcott sisters chose to meet them.

III.

Any anthology necessarily represents a partial portrait and reflects the editor's interpretation of the author. In choosing selections for *The Portable Louisa May Alcott*, I wished to give an overview of her oeuvre, including samples of the various genres in which she worked in the course of her thirty-year career. In doing so, I wanted to convey both her wide range and the characteristic themes and techniques that consistently cross the boundaries of genre and audience. In addition to transcribing and transforming material from her own life, Alcott exploited her preoccupation—indeed her obsession—with the theater. As the narrator of her last novel, *Jo's Boys*, says, it was "impossible for the humble historian of the March family to write a story without theatricals in it." These theatricals range from the "Plays at Plumfield" presented in *Little Men* and *Jo's Boys* to amateur and professional performances of Shakespeare in her adult fiction. Most fascinating, perhaps, is the way in which Alcott's heroines, whether professional actresses or not, must perform offstage as though womanhood itself is a demanding role. This postmodern notion of gender as performance, surprising to find in a writer long deemed old-fashioned, is supported by other motifs in Alcott's fiction, such as the fluidity of gender roles and actual androgyny. Alcott's insights into the way in which gender is constructed, to use our modern parlance, strengthened her support for women's rights, which she overtly champions in such novels as *Work*, *Rose in Bloom*, and *Jo's Boys*. More subtle, however, is her exposure of women's wrongs, not only in her sensation fiction, such as *A Modern Mephistopheles*, but in realistic novels such as *Moods* and *Little Women*. An important way in which she does this is through her allusions to other writers, allusions that sometimes take the form of enactments of their work.

The 1881 edition of *Moods*, the centerpiece of this collection, embodies almost all of Alcott's preoccupations and illustrates many of her characteristic practices. Written between 1860 and 1864, when it was first published, and revised in 1881, it is a product of Alcott's early maturity later seasoned with the experience of more than fifteen years of successful authorship. The story of an ardent young girl who marries for lack of any other vocation and then suffers the consequences of her mistake, it understandably met with mixed reviews, including a scathing one by the youthful Henry James. Revising the novel in 1881, Alcott restored chapters she had omitted from the first edition, eliminated a melodramatic subplot, and substituted a happy ending for the original tragic one. As though anticipating a revival of the earlier criticism, she added a somewhat disingenuous preface, implying that the work had been written in her teens and that its faults were those typical of juvenilia. Given the amount of critical attention the work has received since its rediscovery and the important place it holds in Alcott's career, it is surprising that only one modern edition has become available, Sarah Elbert's reprint of the 1864 edition with the chapters added to the 1881 addition printed as an appendix at the end.

Moods is not as autobiographical as many of Alcott's other novels. The indulged and childlike heroine, Sylvia Yule, bears little resemblance to Alcott or her sisters. In one respect, however, the work more than any other evokes Louisa's Concord girlhood: Sylvia's friendship with and attraction to Geoffrey Moor and Adam Warwick replicates Louisa's feelings for her father's friends Emerson and Thoreau. The epigraph to the 1864 edition was a sentence from Emerson's essay "Experience," in which he likens life to "a train of moods like a string of beads; and as we pass through them they prove to be many colored lenses, which paint the world their own hue, and each shows us only what lies in its own focus." The comparison doubtless appealed to Alcott, who, as she recorded in her journal, suffered from moodiness throughout her youth, an affliction shared by Sylvia and attributed in part to her home, which, like Alcott's, is inharmonious. Seeking a friend upon whose stability and wisdom she can rely, Sylvia gravitates toward Moor, who, like Emerson, inhabits an "Old Manse." Just as Louisa did, Sylvia identifies herself with Bettina, whose correspondence with Goethe was supposedly published in Countess von Arnim's *Letters to a Child*, and thus prepares herself to become the protégée of a male mentor. Moor's home, especially his library and garden, provides a refuge for Sylvia, whereas the natural settings she explores in the company of Adam Warwick give her a seductive and, as it turns out, misleading sense of freedom. Warwick, the "strong, free, self-reliant man," rich "because he makes his wants so few," is obviously an idealized version of Thoreau; the river journey he conducts is doubtless based on Louisa's own outings with Thoreau and perhaps his published accounts of such journeys.

The contemplative and the active man, the poet and the hero, Moor and Warwick constitute a tribute to her father's friends, but at the same time each is weighed in the balance and found wanting. Only at the end of *Moods*, when they publish a book combining Moor's poetry with Warwick's prose, do the nurturing qualities of the one and the crusading qualities of the other offer the possibility of psychic wholeness. Alcott's androgynous vision, similar to Margaret Fuller's in *Woman in the Nineteenth Century*, is anticipated at the beginning of the 1864 edition, when Moor observes Sylvia working in her garden and takes her for a boy. Henry James in his condescending review seems to have interpreted Sylvia's male attire as a seductive ruse: "One of [Sylvia's] means of fascination is to disguise herself as a boy and work in the garden with a hoe and wheelbarrow" (Elbert, *Moods*, 219). Alcott, perhaps remembering this gibe, dressed Sylvia more conventionally in the 1881 edition. What James failed to see in the novel, however, is that Sylvia's cross-dressing points to a significant theme—that characteristics we consider male and female are not exclusive to one gender or the other. In the revision, Alcott retains the sense of Sylvia's androgynous potential: "If she had seemed strong-armed and sturdy as a boy before, now she was tender-fingered as a woman." But Sylvia, ironically advised by the self-reliant Warwick to forget herself and live more for others, sacrifices any opportunity she may have had to develop masculine strength and sturdiness, committing herself prematurely to the marital custody of Moor. Of the novel's major characters, only Faith Dane, the heroine of Alcott's earlier story "My

Contraband" and a figure possibly based on Fuller herself, combines, as Moor initially appears to do, the strength associated with a man with the tenderness associated with a woman.

Throughout the novel, Sylvia's plight is universalized by Alcott's literary allusions. As we have seen, Sylvia confesses to having envied Bettina her intimacy with Goethe, one of Alcott's favorite authors. Shortly thereafter, Moor compares Warwick, whom Sylvia has not yet met, to Goethe. Further, Sylvia borrows from Moor's library Goethe's *Wilhelm Meister*, in which the hero rescues Mignon, an elflike girl, who later dies of unrequited love for him. Soon Moor begins to regard Sylvia as "this modern Mignon." In an early scene, Moor shows Sylvia his herb garden, and in cataloging his herbs, he paraphrases Shakespeare's Ophelia. On the river journey Sylvia takes with Moor, Warwick, and her brother Max, Sylvia entertains her male companions by enacting roles from Shakespeare, including Ophelia as well as Lady Macbeth, Rosalind (another opportunity for cross-dressing), and Juliet. Max, a painter, later has Sylvia pose as Clytemnestra. The association of Sylvia with famous literary victims and villains suggests the power and passion pent up within her. Later, Warwick warns that further concealment of their love from Moor, to whom Sylvia is now married, would be tantamount to murder, and shortly thereafter Sylvia inadvertently reveals their secret by walking, like Lady Macbeth, in her sleep.

Other significant allusions are to Tennyson and Hawthorne. At the end of the idyllic river journey, in which Sylvia falls in love with Warwick and both men fall in love with her, Sylvia gazes back to the "charmed river," and the narrator explicitly compares her to the "fairy Lady of Shalott," who, "sick of shadows," left her web and loom only to die on contact with the real world. Henry James's indignant response to the river journey—"it is hard to say whether the impropriety of this proceeding is the greater or the less from the fact of her extreme youth"—lends support to Jennifer A. Gehrman's interpretation of "The Lady of Shalott" as a cautionary tale, admonishing woman not to "stray from her sphere, to seek direct interaction with the world beyond hearth and home" (Elbert, *Moods*, 220; Gehrman, 123). The river journey harms Sylvia because it offers only a temporary escape from the shadow life she has been living and to which she seems condemned; the men who appear to include her in their active, adventurous life ultimately encourage her to return to the loom. The Golden Wedding celebration at the heart of the river journey introduces Sylvia to the crippled "daughter Patience," "who seldom see[s] what's going on outside four walls," an admission that connects her with the Lady of Shalott and thus, ominously, with Sylvia. But perhaps the most telling allusion occurs late in the book when Sylvia, separated from both her husband and Warwick, is compared with Hawthorne's Hester Prynne. Although she has narrowly escaped Hester's sin of adultery, her searing experience has permitted her, like Hester, to detect a legion of fellow sufferers. Even Faith Dane, living in the "virgin loneliness" that Margaret Fuller saw as a necessary stage in women's struggle for equality, is reminiscent of Hester, who, upon returning to America, served as confessor to troubled women and prophesied a "brighter period, when . . . a new truth would be revealed, in order to establish the whole relation between man and woman on a surer ground of mutual happiness."

Margaret Fuller wrote in *Woman in the Nineteenth Century*, a work that seems to have influenced Alcott profoundly, that "the life of Woman must be outwardly a well-intentioned, cheerful dissimulation of her real life." On the river journey, Sylvia proves herself a gifted actress, but once the journey is over, she must begin acting in earnest. First, she must conceal her love for Warwick, after he leaves without declaring his love for her. As though seeking inspiration for the role that she must play, Sylvia finds the theater "both a refuge and a solace . . . and Shakespeare's tragedies became her study." Although she never affects a passionate love for Moor, she must, upon accepting his proposal, feign contentment. When, after her marriage, she learns that Warwick does indeed love her, dissimulation becomes still more difficult. Sensing her unhappiness, Moor encourages her to pretend that she is "little Sylvia" again, a role she finds it impossible to sustain. When Warwick and Faith visit unexpectedly, Sylvia must hide her emotion from both husband and friends. At first, she succeeds in deceiving Warwick, for "men seldom understand the subterfuges women instinctively use to conceal many a natural emotion which they are not strong enough to control, not brave enough to confess." He, in contrast, is described as one who "could act no part," "hating all disguises," for he has never been called upon to live the double life that, to a woman, becomes almost second nature. To escape her husband's detection, Sylvia rearranges her hair so as to hide her face, then, in a show of openness, tells him she has done so from a different motive. Coyly, she asks him, "Did you think I could be so artful?" and, unsuspectingly, he answers, "Your craft amazes me."

Sylvia's "craft" is one that she shares with most of Alcott's heroines. In the sensation story "La Jeune; or, Actress and Woman," reprinted in this volume, the private life of the heroine, a professional actress, proves to have been a more brilliant performance than any of her theatrical roles. In fact, in order to create the glamorous image necessary to succeed on the stage, "La Jeune" must conceal her nationality, marital status, financial need, physical condition, and, especially, her age. Her purpose in doing so, however, is not a matter of worldly ambition but of survival for herself and her dependent. The plight of Jean Muir, the heroine of *Behind a Mask*, is no less desperate than La Jeune's, and she too fabricates an identity for herself. Like La Jeune, she conceals a previous marriage and the ravages of time upon her aging body, but she also obliterates from the record any traces of her acting career. In her impersonation of an eighteen-year-old governess, Jean adopts many of the stratagems used for more innocent purposes by the young Sylvia Yule. In fact, so subtle is her performance that she even feigns adopting stratagems when she senses that they are expected of a woman in her position. But when asked by her employers to participate in an evening of amateur theatricals, Jean as the biblical Judith enacts her rage at those who both necessitate and condemn feminine duplicity.

The subtitles of "La Jeune" and *Behind a Mask*—"Actress and Woman" and *A Woman's Power* respectively—suggest that acting for Alcott and her heroines is paradoxical. The narrator of "La Jeune," on hearing her confession, declares that "never in her most brilliant hour, on stage or in *salon,* had she shone so fair or impressed me with her power as she did now. That was art, this nature. I admired the actress, I adored the woman." Acting implies an art or artfulness, a craft or craftiness, at odds with the feminine ideals of innocence, purity, and truth. Yet her vulnerability, dependence, and the impossible ideals themselves virtually mandate the development of a double consciousness. The narrator's belief that the actress can be readily distinguished from the woman is discredited by Alcott in tale after tale. Whereas he may believe that La Jeune's power derives from her conformity to an ideal of womanhood, he would never have become obsessed to discover what lay behind her mask had it not been for her consummate acting, both offstage and on. A similar obsession motivates Jasper Helwyze in Alcott's sensational novel *A Modern Mephistopheles*. The heroine, Gladys, dissembles her anxiety about her husband's mysterious relationship to Jasper and feigns contentment. Only under the influence of the hashish he administers does Gladys, in enacting scenes from Tennyson's *Idylls of the King*, express both her passion for her husband and her determination to free him from Jasper's toils. Free in the role of Vivien to cast off her guise of purity and innocence, Gladys reveals a sensuality that awakens her husband's dormant desire and serves notice to Helwyze that hers is a power with which he must reckon. Louisa May Alcott, now her many masks and disguises have been at least partially penetrated, must also be reckoned with as an author of craft and artistry. Whereas generations of children have long adored the woman who created *Little Women*, adult readers are now free to admire the actress who played that woman.

CHRONOLOGY

1830 Amos Bronson Alcott, an idealistic young schoolmaster, marries Abigail May ("Abby"), the daughter of a prominent Boston family and, later, the model for Marmee in *Little Women.*

1831 The Alcotts move from Boston to Germantown, Pennsylvania, where Bronson has been asked to found a school. In March, Anna, the model for Meg in *Little Women*, is born. Bronson begins the first of his three detailed infant journals.

1832 Louisa May Alcott is born November 29 in Germantown on her father's thirty-third birthday. From the first, Bronson, who takes an active role in their upbringing, finds Louisa much less tractable than her sister.

1834 The Alcotts return to Boston, where Bronson, with the help of well-known educator Elizabeth Peabody, launches his Temple School.

1835 Elizabeth Peabody Alcott ("Lizzie"), the model for Beth in *Little Women*, is born. Elizabeth Peabody publishes *Record of a School*, an account of Bronson's experimental pedagogy, much of which is reflected in Louisa's writing, especially *Little Men*, the sequel to *Little Women.*

1836 Ralph Waldo Emerson and others, including Bronson Alcott and Henry David Thoreau, found the Transcendentalist Club. Emerson publishes *Nature*, the movement's manifesto. Margaret Fuller, later to edit the Transcendentalist journal the *Dial* and write the feminist tract *Woman in the Nineteenth Century*, begins to teach at the Temple School. Early acquaintance with such figures is to have a profound effect on Louisa May Alcott's development as a writer.

1837 Bronson's *Conversations with Children on the Gospels*, published at the end of 1836, is attacked for its radical ideas. The Temple School fails. Emerson urges Bronson to abandon teaching for authorship.

1839 Bronson admits a black child to the school he is conducting in his home. As a result, virtually all the children are withdrawn, and Bronson's once-promising career as an educator is over.

1840 At Emerson's urging, the Alcotts move to Concord. Abigail May Alcott, the model for Amy in *Little Women* and several other of Alcott's heroines, is born. Bronson publishes his "Orphic Sayings" in the newly founded *Dial*, only to have them ridiculed and scorned. The family struggles with poverty.

1842 Emerson enables Bronson to travel to England, where a school at Ham Common, Surrey, founded upon his principles, had been named Alcott House. Sixth months later, he returns with a disciple, Charles Lane, and his son William.

1843 The Alcotts and Lane, forming a "consociate family," undertake a utopian experiment at Fruitlands in Harvard, a community fourteen miles from Concord. Bronson's impracticality inflicts hardship on his wife and children, and his relationship with Lane, who now preaches celibacy, threatens the already troubled marriage. Some of the family's distress is reflected in the ten-year-old Louisa's journal. Years later, she will satirize the Fruitlands experiment in "Transcendental Wild Oats."

1844 Bronson is severely depressed after Lane and his son leave Fruitlands to live with the Quakers. The Alcotts leave Fruitlands themselves but remain in Harvard.

1845 A legacy to Abby enables the Alcotts to buy a house in Concord, which Bronson names Hillside. Back in Concord, Louisa idolizes Emerson, the family benefactor, and her father's friend Thoreau. Both will become models for Alcott heroes. Louisa also begins to write, and she and her sister Anna, like Jo and Meg in *Little Women*, collaborate on a number of plays.

1848 Still impoverished, the family returns to Boston, where friends of Abby's create a position for her as a kind of social worker. The first women's rights convention is organized by Elizabeth Cady Stanton at Seneca Falls. Abby becomes a supporter. Louisa has a poem published.

1852 The Hawthornes purchase Hillside (which they rename the Wayside), enabling Abby to relinquish her role as breadwinner.

Louisa's story "The Rival Painters" is published in *The Olive Branch*. During these Boston years, Louisa continues to write poems, plays, and fiction, including her first novel, *The Inheritance*, which will not be published until 1997 (Dutton). Together, the Alcott girls, like the March sisters in *Little Women*, found a Pickwick Club and publish a newspaper. The older girls, like Meg and Jo in *Little Women* and Christie Devon, the heroine of a later adult novel, *Work*, contribute to the family income by teaching and sewing.

1854 Louisa's collection of fantasy stories, entitled *Flower Fables*, originally written for Emerson's daughter, Ellen, is published. At Christmas, Louisa presents her mother with a copy, accompanied by a note in which she determines "to pass in time from fairies and fables to men and realities."

1856 The family contracts scarlet fever "from some poor children Mother nursed." All recover, but Lizzie's health is permanently impaired.

1858 The family returns to Concord, this time to Orchard House (today a museum, open to the public). Lizzie dies, and Anna announces her engagement to John Pratt, the model for John Brooke in *Little Women*. Louisa, devastated by the loss of her two sisters, has suicidal fantasies.

1860 Anna and John are married. Louisa publishes "A Modern Cinderella," a story based on their courtship and a precursor of *Little Women*.

1862 In December, Louisa goes to Washington, D.C., as a Union army nurse. She soon contracts typhoid fever, is brought home by Bronson, and suffers lurid nightmares during her convalescence. The calomel with which she is treated will have a lasting deleterious effect upon her health.

1863 Louisa's sensation story "Pauline's Passion and Punishment" wins a prize, and *Hospital Sketches*, based on her nursing experience, is published to acclaim. During the next five years, she will publish anonymously or pseudonymously most of her sensation or Gothic stories. Similar to the ones Jo writes and eventually repudiates in *Little Women*, dozens of these are now available in modern collections, edited by their discoverer, Madeleine B. Stern.

1864 *Moods*, Alcott's first realistic novel for adults, is published to mixed reviews, including one by the youthful Henry James. Like much of Alcott's sensation fiction, but more directly, *Moods* protests the lack of opportunities for women to develop their full potential. Alcott's experience editing *Moods* and its reception will furnish the basis for the "Literary Lessons" chapter of *Little Women*.

1865 Alcott travels to Europe as a companion to the invalid Anna Weld. She meets a Polish youth, Ladislas Wiesniewski, who will become a model for Laurie in *Little Women*.

1866 Alcott returns to Concord. Her sensation story "A Modern Mephistopheles or The Long Fatal Love Chase" is rejected by her publisher as "too sensational" (*Journals*, 153). It will not be published until 1995 (Random House). Like many of Alcott's characters, the heroine, Rosamond, rebels against her restrictive female role, but in doing so, she falls prey to the obsession of a bigamist.

1868 Alcott assumes editorship of *Merry's Museum*, a periodical for children. Thomas Niles of Roberts Brothers asks her to write a girls' story. Alcott reluctantly agrees to do so, and the result is *Little Women* (known today as part 1). In response to her readers' enthusiasm, Alcott immediately begins writing a sequel. But she rejects their demands that she marry Jo to Laurie and marries her instead to Professor Bhaer.

1869 The second part of *Little Women* is published. Its popular and financial success persuades Alcott to give up writing sensation fiction for nearly a decade.

1870 Alcott publishes *An Old-Fashioned Girl* and goes abroad with her sister May (like Amy March, an aspiring artist). In Italy, she learns that John Pratt has died and immediately begins writing *Little Men* in order to support her sister Anna and two nephews.

1871 Alcott returns to Boston. *Little Men* is published.

1873 "Transcendental Wild Oats" and *Work* are published. This novel for adults, begun in the 1860s under the title "Success," is almost as autobiographical as *Little Women*. Christie Devon, the heroine, works at a series of jobs—household servant, actress, companion, seamstress; breaks down and contemplates suicide; is befriended by a minister (based on Theodore Parker, a well-known Boston minister whom Louisa much admired); marries a nurseryman on the eve of the Civil War; enlists as a nurse; and, after her husband's death and the birth of their child, becomes an advocate for women's rights. The book ends with Christie at forty, the same age as her creator.

1875 *Eight Cousins* is published.

1876 *Rose in Bloom*, the sequel to *Eight Cousins*, is published. Rose, the heroine of these two novels, is much more conventional than Jo, but she nonetheless seeks a vocation. Like many of Alcott's heroes, Rose's uncle Alec and cousin Mac (whom she eventually marries) seem modeled on the Transcendentalist friends of her father's. Alcott's feminism is especially manifest in these books, as in her last novel, *Jo's Boys*.

1877 Alcott publishes *A Modern Mephistopheles* in Roberts Brothers' No Name Series. While the novel has many connections with the 1866 manuscript of the same title, it is closer to a story Alcott actually published earlier, entitled "The Freak of a Genius." Aside from *A Long Fatal Love Chase*, this is Alcott's most ambitious work of sensation fiction. It is also, as far as we know, the only such writing she produced during this decade, and, according to her journal, she welcomed the respite from "providing moral pap for the young" (204). In November, Alcott's mother dies.

1878 *Under the Lilacs* is published. May Alcott, who has been studying art abroad, largely supported by Louisa, marries a Swiss businessman, Ernest Nieriker, in Paris. Alcott uses May's letters and romance with Nieriker as the basis for a novella, "Diana and Persis."

1879 May Alcott Nieriker dies in December, six weeks after the birth of her daughter, Louisa May. Alcott apparently abandons "Diana and Persis," which, though it appears to have been completed, will remain unpublished until 1978. She prepares to adopt her namesake, Louisa May Nieriker.

1881 *Jack and Jill* is published. Louisa May Nieriker ("Lulu") arrives. Alcott revises *Moods* for publication by Roberts Brothers. She restores several chapters omitted from the earlier edition and substitutes a happy ending for the original tragic one. Alcott will become increasingly unwell during the 1880s. Unable to sustain the effort needed to write longer works of fiction, she publishes a number of short story collections, which include many previously published stories.

1886 Alcott finally publishes *Jo's Boys*, the sequel to *Little Men*. Although she complains constantly in her journal about the drudgery of writing it, the work is actually one of her most interesting, combining as it does overt feminist statements with even stronger covert ones.

1888 Bronson Alcott dies, and Louisa May Alcott dies two days later, "in all probability of intestinal cancer" (*Letters*, xli).

PART I

SHORT FICTION

Louisa May Alcott is best known for her juvenile novels, but she was a prolific writer of short fiction for both children and adults. Not only did she write for different audiences, but she also wrote in at least two different genres for each audience. Her short fiction for children, which she wrote throughout her career, includes the fairy tales and fantasy stories of Flower Fables *(1854), her first book publication, and* Morning-Glories, and Other Stories *(1868), published the same year as* Little Women. *Thereafter, she continued to publish fantasy stories in such periodicals as* St. Nicholas *and* Harper's Young People *and to include new as well as previously published children's fantasy in the six volumes of* Aunt Jo's Scrap-Bag *and the three volumes of* Lulu's Library. *Alcott's genius in writing for children, however, lies in her realistic depictions of family life. Such stories dominate the* Scrap-Bag *and* Lulu *series as well as* A Garland for Girls *(1888). Whereas Daniel Shealy has collected all of Alcott's fantasy stories in* Fairy Tales and Fantasy Stories *(University of Tennessee Press, 1992), Alcott's realistic tales for children are not yet readily available. Claire Boose did publish a number of them in her 1982 volume* Works of Louisa May Alcott *(Avenel), and Joy A. Marsella has published a critical study of the* Scrap-Bag *volumes.*

Today, the best known of Alcott's short works are ones for which she was not recognized in her lifetime—her sensation stories or thrillers for adults. Thanks to the indefatigable sleuthing of Madeleine B. Stern, no fewer than thirty-three of these anonymously and pseudonymously published stories are now in print. These works, which range from the very short tale to the elaborately plotted novella, appeared in such publications as Frank Leslie's Illustrated Newspaper, The Flag of Our Union, Frank Leslie's Lady's Magazine, *and the* Ten Cent Novellettes *series. Almost all of these stories were first published in the 1860s and written before the success of* Little Women *in 1868–69. For more than a hundred years, they languished unread in moldering periodicals, and their reappearance in the 1970s, coinciding as it did with the revival of the women's movement, regained for Alcott an adult reading audience and made her a subject of interest to feminist scholars. But as these scholars have since demonstrated, Alcott, at the time she was cranking out sensation stories with clockwork regularity, was also aspiring to a more exalted position in the literary marketplace. During the 1860s, her short fiction appeared in that arbiter of taste* The Atlantic Monthly, *as well as in* The Commonwealth, *which published her first big success,* Hospital Sketches *(1863). Like Alcott's realistic stories for children, her realistic stories for adults deserve to be better known. Elaine Showalter's collection* Alternative Alcott *and Sarah Elbert's* Louisa May Alcott on Race, Sex, and Slavery *have made some of these short works available, and the stories and sketches dealing with race and the Civil War have begun to receive serious critical attention.*

The eight stories reprinted here represent the different genres in which Alcott worked, as well as different stages of her career. "My Contraband," first published under the title of "The Brothers" in The Atlantic Monthly *(November 1863), is one of several works based on Alcott's experience as a Civil War nurse and reveals her abolitionist sympathies (see "M. L.," "An Hour," and* Work*). Like her more autobiographical* Hospital Sketches, *"My Contraband" is told in the first person by a nurse who becomes attached to one of her patients, but whereas nurse Tribulation Periwinkle of* Hospital Sketches *comforts "a brave Virginia blacksmith" through his last hours, Faith Dane prevents a contraband quadroon from wreaking vengeance upon his white half-brother. Faith, in her ability to intercede and exercise moral suasion, anticipates her role in Alcott's full-length novel* Moods. *"A Whisper in the Dark," published the same year as "My Contraband," but in* Frank Leslie's Illustrated Newspaper, *is to the feminist reader an equally powerful political statement. Just as Robert, the slave, has no right to his wife, so Sybil, as a woman, has no right to determine whom and when she will marry. Robert is estranged by race from father and brother, Sybil is deprived of a mother's love by what men interpret as madness. Robert is enslaved, Sybil incarcerated, and both are deprived not only of freedom but also of the knowledge that would free them. The one statement, however, is straightforward, though not without its ironies and ambiguities; the other is oblique, muted, a veritable "whisper in the dark."*

"Thrice Tempted," which appeared anonymously in Frank Leslie's Chimney Corner *(July 1867), and "Psyche's Art," published by Loring in 1868, the same year as* Little Women, *part 1, also represent two different adult genres and suggest the fine, sometimes*

even nonexistent line between children's and adult literature. "Thrice Tempted" is unusual among Alcott's sensation stories in that the heroine, Ruth, is no femme fatale like her rival, Laura, but a lonely, diffident, not conventionally attractive, generous, and principled girl; in short, she resembles the heroine of many domestic novels, whether for children or adults. Nonetheless, she commits a crime perhaps more heinous than that of any other Alcott character. "Psyche's Art," on the other hand, bears a family resemblance to *Little Women*. Psyche could be one of the March sisters—an amalgam of Meg, Jo, and Amy, and her sister May could be Beth. But in this story, Alcott dares to do what she did not in the longer work: she permits readers to choose between two alternative endings, to decide whether Psyche marries or devotes herself to art.

Two short sensation stories, "La Jeune; or, Actress and Woman" (*Frank Leslie's Chimney Corner*, 1868) and "My Mysterious Mademoiselle" (*Frank Leslie's Lady's Magazine*, 1869), exemplify Alcott's fascination with the theater and its amorphous potentiality. Both stories employ an unreliable male narrator, unreliable in that he betrays even more about himself than he wishes to reveal. In "La Jeune," the narrator prides himself on not being taken in by the actress heroine, but he finds to his chagrin that her impersonation is entirely other than he suspects. In "My Mysterious Mademoiselle," the narrator plays a cat and mouse game with the sharer of his railway carriage. Like Sybil's uncle in "A Whisper in the Dark," he tries to take advantage of his confinement with a spirited young girl, but she frustrates his efforts and, in doing so, suggests, like Laurie and Jo, the fluidity of gender roles.

Finally, two children's stories represent the genres of domestic realism and fantasy, but they, like several of the adult stories, suggest a dual audience. "Cupid and Chow-chow," first published in *Hearth and Home* (May 1872), became the title story for the third volume of *Aunt Jo's Scrap-Bag* (1874). This story is especially interesting for its treatment of the suffrage movement. How does one reconcile the seemingly satiric treatment of Chow-chow and her mother, an avid suffragist, with Alcott's own support of suffrage and other women's rights? "Queen Aster," significantly, was first published in *The Woman's Journal* (February 1887), an organ of the women's rights movement to which Alcott had previously contributed. There it was entitled "A

Flower Fable," an allusion not only to Alcott's earlier Flower Fables *but also to the tale's allegorical nature. Although reprinted as a children's story in* Lulu's Library, *"Queen Aster" clearly can be read as a feminist fable, offering a utopian vision of social harmony and justice under matriarchal rule.*

My Contraband

DOCTOR FRANCK came in as I sat sewing up the rents in an old shirt, that Tom might go tidily to his grave. New shirts were needed for living, and there was no wife or mother to "dress him handsome when he went to meet the Lord," as one woman said, describing the fine funeral she had pinched herself to give her son.

"Miss Dane, I'm in a quandary," began the Doctor, with that expression of countenance which says as plainly as words, "I want to ask a favor, but I wish you'd save me the trouble."

"Can I help you out of it?"

"Faith! I don't like to propose it, but you certainly can, if you please."

"Then name it, I beg."

"You see a Reb has just been brought in crazy with typhoid; a bad case every way; a drunken, rascally little captain somebody took the trouble to capture, but whom nobody wants to take the trouble to cure. The wards are full, the ladies worked to death, and willing to be for our own boys, but rather slow to risk their lives for a Reb. Now, you've had the fever, you like queer patients, your mate will see to your ward for a while, and I will find you a good attendant. The fellow won't last long, I fancy; but he can't die without some sort of care, you know. I've put him in the fourth story of the west wing, away from the rest. It is airy, quiet, and comfortable there. I'm on that ward, and will do my best for you in every way. Now, then, will you go?"

"Of course I will, out of perversity, if not common charity; for some of these people think that because I'm an abolitionist I am also a heathen, and I should rather like to show them that, though I cannot quite love my enemies, I am willing to take care of them."

"Very good; I thought you'd go; and speaking of abolition reminds me that you can have a contraband for servant, if you like. It is that fine mulatto fellow who was found burying his rebel master after the fight, and, being badly cut over the head, our boys brought him along. Will you have him?"

"By all means,—for I'll stand to my guns on that point, as on the other; these black boys are far more faithful and handy than some of the white scamps given me to serve, instead of being served by. But is this man well enough?"

"Yes, for that sort of work, and I think you'll like him. He must have been a handsome fellow before he got his face slashed; not much darker than myself; his master's son, I dare say, and the white blood makes him rather high and haughty about some things. He was in a bad way when he came in, but vowed he'd die in the street rather than turn in with the black fellows below; so I put him up in the west wing, to be out of the way, and he's seen to the captain all the morning. When can you go up?"

"As soon as Tom is laid out, Skinner moved, Haywood washed, Marble dressed, Charley rubbed, Downs taken up, Upham laid down, and the whole forty fed."

We both laughed, though the Doctor was on his way to the dead-house and I held a shroud on my lap. But in a hospital one learns that cheerfulness is one's salvation; for, in an atmosphere of suffering and death, heaviness of heart would soon paralyze usefulness of hand, if the blessed gift of smiles had been denied us.

In an hour I took possession of my new charge, finding a dissipated-looking boy of nineteen or twenty raving in the solitary little room, with no one near him but the contraband in the room adjoining. Feeling decidedly more interest in the black man than in the white, yet remembering the Doctor's hint of his being "high and haughty," I glanced furtively at him as I scattered chloride of lime about the room to purify the air, and settled matters to suit myself. I had seen many contrabands, but never one so attractive as this. All colored men are called "boys," even if their heads are white; this boy was five-and-twenty at least, strong-limbed and manly, and had the look of one who never had been cowed by abuse or worn with oppressive labor. He sat on his bed doing nothing; no book, no pipe, no pen or paper anywhere appeared, yet anything less indolent or listless than his attitude and expression I never saw. Erect he sat, with a hand on either knee, and eyes fixed on the bare wall opposite, so rapt in some absorbing thought as to be unconscious of my presence, though the door stood wide open and my movements were by no means noiseless. His face was half averted, but I instantly approved the Doctor's taste, for the profile which I saw possessed all the attributes of comeliness belonging to his mixed race. He was more quadroon than mulatto, with Saxon features, Spanish complexion darkened by exposure, color in lips and cheek, waving hair, and an eye full of the passionate melancholy which in such men always seems to utter a mute protest against the broken law that doomed them at their birth. What could he be thinking of? The sick boy cursed and raved, I rustled to and fro, steps passed the door, bells rang, and the steady rumble of army-wagons came up from the street, still he never stirred. I had seen colored people in what they call "the black sulks," when, for days, they neither smiled nor spoke, and scarcely ate. But this was something more than that; for the man was not dully brooding over some small grievance; he seemed to see an all-absorbing fact or fancy recorded on the wall, which was a blank to me. I wondered if it were some deep wrong or sorrow, kept alive by memory and impotent regret; if he mourned for the dead master to whom he had been faithful to the end; or if the liberty now his were robbed of half its sweetness by the knowledge that some one near and dear to him still languished in the hell from which he had escaped. My heart quite warmed to him at that idea; I wanted to know and comfort him; and, following the impulse of the moment, I went in and touched him on the shoulder.

In an instant the man vanished and the slave appeared. Freedom was too new a boon to have wrought its blessed changes yet; and as he started up, with his hand at his temple, and an obsequious "Yes, Missis," any romance that had gathered round him fled away, leaving the saddest of all sad facts in living guise before me. Not only did the manhood seem to die out of him, but the comeliness that first attracted me; for, as he turned, I saw the ghastly wound that had laid open cheek and forehead. Being partly healed, it was no longer bandaged, but held together with strips of that transparent plaster which I never see without a shiver, and swift recollections of the scenes with which it is associated in my mind. Part of his black hair had been shorn away, and one eye was nearly closed; pain so distorted, and the cruel sabre-cut so marred that portion of his face, that, when I saw it, I felt as if a fine medal had been suddenly reversed, showing me a far more striking type of human suffering and wrong than Michael Angelo's bronze prisoner. By one of those inexplicable processes that often teach us how little we understand ourselves, my purpose was suddenly changed; and, though I went in to offer comfort as a friend, I merely gave an order as a mistress.

"Will you open these windows? this man needs more air."

He obeyed at once, and, as he slowly urged up the unruly sash, the handsome profile was again turned toward me, and again I was possessed by my first impression so strongly that I involuntarily said,—

"Thank you."

Perhaps it was fancy, but I thought that in the look of mingled surprise and something like reproach which he gave me, there was also a trace of grateful pleasure. But he said, in that tone of spiritless humility these poor souls learn so soon,—

"I isn't a white man, Missis, I'se a contraband."

"Yes, I know it; but a contraband is a free man, and I heartily congratulate you."

He liked that; his face shone, he squared his shoulders, lifted his head, and looked me full in the eye with a brisk,—

"Thank ye, Missis; anything more to do fer yer?"

"Doctor Franck thought you would help me with this man, as there are many patients and few nurses or attendants. Have you had the fever?"

"No, Missis."

"They should have thought of that when they put him here; wounds and fevers should not be together. I'll try to get you moved."

He laughed a sudden laugh: if he had been a white man, I should have called it scornful; as he was a few shades darker than myself, I suppose it must be considered an insolent, or at least an unmannerly one.

"It don't matter, Missis. I'd rather be up here with the fever than down with those niggers; and there isn't no other place fer me."

Poor fellow! that was true. No ward in all the hospital would take him in to lie side by side with the most miserable white wreck there. Like the bat in Æsop's fable, he belonged to neither race; and the pride of one and the helplessness of the other, kept him hovering alone in the twilight a great sin has brought to overshadow the whole land.

"You shall stay, then; for I would far rather have you than my lazy Jack. But are you well and strong enough?"

"I guess I'll do, Missis."

He spoke with a passive sort of acquiescence,—as if it did not much matter if he were not able, and no one would particularly rejoice if he were.

"Yes, I think you will. By what name shall I call you?"

"Bob, Missis."

Every woman has her pet whim; one of mine was to teach the men self-respect by treating them respectfully. Tom, Dick, and Harry would pass, when lads rejoiced in those familiar abbreviations; but to address men often old enough to be my father in that style did not suit my old-fashioned ideas of propriety. This "Bob" would never do; I should have found it as easy to call the chaplain "Gus" as my tragical-looking contraband by a title so strongly associated with the tail of a kite.

"What is your other name?" I asked. "I like to call my attendants by their last names rather than by their first."

"I'se got no other, Missis; we has our masters' names, or do without. Mine's dead, and I won't have anything of his 'bout me."

"Well, I'll call you Robert, then, and you may fill this pitcher for me, if you will be so kind."

He went; but, through all the tame obedience years of servitude had taught him, I could see that the proud spirit his father gave him was not yet subdued, for the look and gesture with which he repudiated his master's name were a more effective declaration of independence than any Fourth-of-July orator could have prepared.

We spent a curious week together. Robert seldom left his room, except upon my errands; and I was a prisoner all day, often all night, by the bedside of the rebel. The fever burned itself rapidly away, for there seemed little vitality to feed it in the feeble frame of this old young man, whose life had been none of the most righteous, judging from the revelations made by his unconscious lips; since more than once Robert authoritatively silenced him, when my gentler hushings were of no avail, and blasphemous wanderings or ribald camp-songs made my checks burn and Robert's face assume an aspect of disgust. The captain was the gentleman in the world's eye, but the contraband was the gentleman in mine;—I was a fanatic, and that accounts for such depravity of taste, I hope. I never asked Robert of himself, feeling that somewhere there was a spot still too sore to bear the lightest touch; but, from his language, manner, and intelligence, I inferred that his color had procured for him the few advantages within the reach of a quick-witted, kindly-treated slave. Silent, grave, and thoughtful, but most serviceable, was my contraband; glad of the books I brought him, faithful in the performance of the duties I assigned to him, grateful for the friendliness I could not but feel and show toward him. Often I longed to ask what purpose was so visibly altering his aspect with such daily deepening gloom. But I never dared, and no one else had either time or desire to pry into the past of this specimen of one branch of the chivalrous "F.F.Vs."

On the seventh night, Dr. Franck suggested that it would be well for some one, besides the general watchman of the ward, to be with the captain, as it might be his last. Although the greater part of the two preceding nights had been spent there, of course I offered to remain,—for there is a strange fascination in these scenes, which renders one careless of fatigue and unconscious of fear until the crisis is past.

"Give him water as long as he can drink, and if he drops into a natural sleep, it may save him. I'll look in at midnight, when some change will probably take place. Nothing but sleep or a miracle will keep him now. Good-night."

Away went the Doctor; and, devouring a whole mouthful of grapes, I lowered the lamp, wet the captain's head, and sat down on a hard stool to begin my watch. The captain lay with his hot, haggard face turned toward me, filling the air with his poisonous breath, and feebly muttering, with lips and tongue so parched that the sanest speech would have been difficult to understand. Robert was stretched on his bed in the inner room, the door of which stood ajar, that a fresh draught from his open window might carry the fever-fumes away through mine. I could just see a long, dark figure, with the lighter outline of a face, and, having little else to do just then, I fell to thinking of this curious contraband, who evidently prized his freedom highly, yet seemed in no haste to enjoy it. Dr. Franck had offered to send him on to safer quarters, but he had said, "No, thank yer, sir, not yet," and then had gone away to fall into one of those black moods of his, which began to disturb me, because I had no power to lighten them. As I sat listening to the clocks from the steeples all about us, I amused myself with planning Robert's future, as I often did my own, and had dealt out to him a generous hand of trumps wherewith to play this game of life which hitherto had gone so cruelly against him, when a harsh choked voice called,—

"Lucy!"

It was the captain, and some new terror seemed to have gifted him with momentary strength.

"Yes, here's Lucy," I answered, hoping that by following the fancy I might quiet him,—for his face was damp with the clammy moisture, and his frame shaken with the nervous tremor that so often precedes death. His dull eye fixed upon me, dilating with a bewildered look of incredulity and wrath, till he broke out fiercely,—

"That's a lie! she's dead,—and so's Bob, damn him!"

Finding speech a failure, I began to sing the quiet tune that had often soothed delirium like this; but hardly had the line,—

"See gentle patience smile on pain,"

passed my lips, when he clutched me by the wrist, whispering like one in mortal fear,—

"Hush! she used to sing that way to Bob, but she never would to me. I swore I'd whip the devil out of her, and I did; but you know before she cut her throat she said she'd haunt me, and there she is!"

He pointed behind me with an aspect of such pale dismay, that I involuntarily glanced over my shoulder and started as if I had seen a veritable ghost; for, peering from the gloom of that inner room, I saw a shadowy face, with dark hair all about it, and a glimpse of scarlet at the throat. An instant showed me that it was only Robert leaning from his bed's foot, wrapped in a gray army-blanket, with his red shirt just visible above it, and his long hair disordered by sleep. But what a strange expression was on his face! The unmarred side was toward me, fixed and motionless as when I first observed it,—less absorbed now, but more intent. His eye glittered, his lips were apart like one who listened with every sense, and his whole aspect reminded me of a hound to which some wind had brought the scent of unsuspected prey.

"Do you know him, Robert? Does he mean you?"

"Laws, no, Missis; they all own half-a-dozen Bobs: but hearin' my name woke me; that's all."

He spoke quite naturally, and lay down again, while I returned to my charge, thinking that this paroxysm was probably his last. But by another hour I perceived a hopeful change; for the tremor had subsided, the cold dew was gone, his breathing was more regular, and Sleep, the healer, had descended to save or take him gently away. Doctor Franck looked in at midnight, bade me keep all cool and quiet, and not fail to administer a certain draught as soon as the captain woke. Very much relieved, I laid my head on my arms, uncomfortably folded on the little table, and fancied I was about to perform one of the feats which practice renders possible,—"sleeping with one eye open," as we say: a half-and-half doze, for all senses sleep but that of hearing; the faintest murmur, sigh, or motion will break it, and give one back one's wits much brightened by the brief permission to "stand at ease." On this night the experiment was a failure, for previous vigils, confinement, and much care had rendered naps a dangerous indulgence. Having roused half-a-dozen times in an hour to find all quiet, I dropped my heavy head on my arms, and, drowsily resolving to look up again in fifteen minutes, fell fast asleep.

The striking of a deep-voiced clock awoke me with a start. "That is one," thought I; but, to my dismay, two more strokes followed, and in remorseful haste I sprang up to see what harm my long oblivion had done. A strong hand put me back into my seat, and held me there. It was Robert. The instant my eye met his my heart began to beat, and all along my nerves tingled that electric flash which foretells a danger that we cannot see. He was very pale, his mouth grim, and both eyes full of sombre fire; for even the wounded one was open now, all the more sinister for the deep scar above and below. But his touch was steady, his voice quiet, as he said,—

"Sit still, Missis; I won't hurt yer, nor scare yer, ef I can help it, but yer waked too soon."

"Let me go, Robert,—the captain is stirring,—I must give him something."

"No, Missis, yer can't stir an inch. Look here!"

Holding me with one hand, with the other he took up the glass in which I had left the draught, and showed me it was empty.

"Has he taken it?" I asked, more and more bewildered.

"I flung it out o' winder, Missis; he'll have to do without."

"But why, Robert? why did you do it?"

"Kase I hate him!"

Impossible to doubt the truth of that; his whole face showed it, as he spoke through his set teeth, and launched a fiery glance at the unconscious captain. I could only hold my breath and stare blankly at him, wondering what mad act was coming next. I suppose I shook and turned white, as women have a foolish habit of doing when sudden danger daunts them; for Robert released my arm, sat down upon the bedside just in front of me, and said, with the ominous quietude that made me cold to see and hear,—

"Don't yer be frightened, Missis; don't try to run away, fer the door's locked and the key in my pocket; don't yer cry out, fer yer'd have to scream a long while, with my hand on yer mouth, 'efore yer was heard. Be still, an' I'll tell yer what I'm gwine to do."

"Lord help us! he has taken the fever in some sudden, violent way, and is out of his head. I must humor him till some one comes"; in pursuance of which swift determination, I tried to say, quite composedly,—

"I will be still and hear you; but open the window. Why did you shut it?"

"I'm sorry I can't do it, Missis; but yer'd jump out, or call, if I did, an' I'm not ready yet. I shut it to make yer sleep, an' heat would do it quicker'n anything else I could do."

The captain moved, and feebly muttered "Water!" Instinctively I rose to give it to him, but the heavy hand came down upon my shoulder, and in the same decided tone Robert said,—

"The water went with the physic; let him call."

"Do let me go to him! he'll die without care!"

"I mean he shall;—don't yer meddle, if yer please, Missis."

In spite of his quiet tone and respectful manner, I saw murder in his eyes, and turned faint with fear; yet the fear excited me, and, hardly knowing what I did, I seized the hands that had seized me, crying,—

"No, no; you shall not kill him! It is base to hurt a helpless man. Why do you hate him? He is not your master."

"He's my brother."

I felt that answer from head to foot, and seemed to fathom what was coming, with a prescience vague, but unmistakable. One appeal was left to me, and I made it.

"Robert, tell me what it means? Do not commit a crime and make me accessory to it. There is a better way of righting wrong than by violence;—let me help you find it."

My voice trembled as I spoke, and I heard the frightened flutter of my heart; so did he, and if any little act of mine had ever won affection or respect from him, the memory of it served me then. He looked down, and seemed to put some question to himself; whatever it was, the answer was in my favor, for when his eyes rose again, they were gloomy, but not desperate.

"I *will* tell yer, Missis; but mind, this makes no difference; the boy is mine. I'll give the Lord a chance to take him fust; if He don't, I shall."

"Oh, no! remember he is your brother."

An unwise speech; I felt it as it passed my lips, for a black frown gathered on Robert's face, and his strong hands closed with an ugly sort of grip. But he did not touch the poor soul gasping there behind him, and seemed content to let the slow suffocation of that stifling room end his frail life.

"I'm not like to forgit dat, Missis, when I've been thinkin' of it all this week. I knew him when they fetched him in, an' would 'a' done it long 'fore this, but I wanted to ask where Lucy was; he knows,—he told to-night,—an' now he's done for."

"Who is Lucy?" I asked hurriedly, intent on keeping his mind busy with any thought but murder.

With one of the swift transitions of a mixed temperament like this, at my question Robert's deep eyes filled, the clenched hands were spread before his face, and all I heard were the broken words,—

"My wife,—he took her—"

In that instant every thought of fear was swallowed up in burning indignation for the wrong, and a perfect passion of pity for the desperate man so tempted to avenge an injury for which there seemed no redress but this. He was no longer slave or contraband, no drop of black blood marred him in my sight, but an infinite compassion yearned to save, to help, to comfort him. Words seemed so powerless I offered none, only put my hand on his poor head, wounded, homeless, bowed down with grief for which I had no cure, and softly smoothed the long, neglected hair, pitifully wondering the while where was the wife who must have loved this tender-hearted man so well.

The captain moaned again, and faintly whispered, "Air!" but I never stirred. God forgive me! just then I hated him as only a woman thinking of a sister woman's wrong could hate. Robert looked up; his eyes were dry again, his mouth grim. I saw that, said, "Tell me more," and he did; for sympathy is a gift the poorest may give, the proudest stoop to receive.

"Yer see, Missis, his father,—I might say ours, ef I warn't ashamed of both of 'em,—his father died two years ago, an' left us all to Marster Ned,—that's him here, eighteen then. He always hated me, I looked so like old Marster: he don't,—only the light skin an' hair. Old Marster was kind to all of us, me 'specially, an' bought Lucy off the next plantation down there in South Carolina, when he found I liked her. I married her, all I could; it warn't much, but we was true to one another till Marster Ned come home a year after an' made hell fer both of us. He sent my old mother to be used up in his rice-swamp in Georgy; he found me with my pretty Lucy, an' though young Miss cried, an' I prayed to him on my knees, an' Lucy run away, he wouldn't have no mercy; he brought her back, an'—took her."

"Oh, what did you do?" I cried, hot with helpless pain and passion.

How the man's outraged heart sent the blood flaming up into his face and deepened the tones of his impetuous voice, as he stretched his arm across the bed, saying, with a terribly expressive gesture,—

"I half murdered him, an' to-night I'll finish."

"Yes, yes—but go on now; what came next?"

He gave me a look that showed no white man could have felt a deeper degradation in remembering and confessing these last acts of brotherly oppression.

"They whipped me till I couldn't stand, an' then they sold me further South. Yer thought I was a white man once,—look here!"

With a sudden wrench he tore the shirt from neck to waist, and on his strong, brown shoulders showed me furrows deeply ploughed, wounds which, though healed, were ghastlier to me than any in that house. I could not speak to him, and, with the pathetic dignity a great grief lends the humblest sufferer, he ended his brief tragedy by simply saying,—

"That's all, Missis. I'se never seen her since, an' now I never shall in this world,—maybe not in t'other."

"But, Robert, why think her dead? The captain was wandering when he said those sad things; perhaps he will retract them when he is sane. Don't despair; don't give up yet."

"No, Missis, I 'spect he's right; she was too proud to bear that long. It's like her to kill herself. I told her to, if there was no other way; an' she always minded me, Lucy did. My poor girl! Oh, it warn't right! No, by God, it warn't!"

As the memory of. this bitter wrong, this double bereavement, burned in his sore heart, the devil that lurks in every strong man's blood leaped up; he put his hand upon his brother's throat, and, watching the white face before him, muttered low between his teeth,—

"I'm lettin' him go too easy; there's no pain in this; we a'n't even yet. I wish he knew me. Marster Ned! it's Bob; where's Lucy?"

From the captain's lips there came a long faint sigh, and nothing but a flutter of the eyelids showed that he still lived. A strange stillness filled the room as the elder brother held the younger's life suspended in his hand, while wavering between a dim hope and a deadly hate. In the whirl of thoughts that went on in my brain, only one was clear enough to act upon. I must prevent murder, if I could,—but how? What could I do up there alone, locked in with a dying man and a lunatic?—for any mind yielded utterly to any unrighteous impulse is mad while the impulse rules it. Strength I had not, nor much courage, neither time nor will for stratagem, and chance only could bring me help before it was too late. But one weapon I possesed,—a tongue,—often a woman's best defence; and sympathy, stronger than fear, gave me power to use it. What I said Heaven only knows, but surely Heaven helped me; words burned on my lips, tears streamed from my eyes, and some good angel prompted me to use the one name that had power to arrest my hearer's hand and touch his heart. For at that moment I heartily believed that Lucy lived, and this earnest faith roused in him a like belief.

He listened with the lowering look of one in whom brute instinct was sovereign for the time,—a look that makes the noblest countenance base. He was but a man,—a poor, untaught, outcast, outraged man. Life had few joys for him; the world offered him no honors, no success, no home, no love. What future would this crime mar? and why should he deny himself that sweet, yet bitter morsel called revenge? How many white men, with all New England's freedom, culture, Christianity, would not have felt as he felt then? Should I have reproached him for a human anguish, a human longing for redress, all now left him from the ruin of his few poor hopes? Who had taught him that self-control, self-sacrifice, are attributes that make men masters of the earth, and lift them nearer heaven? Should I have urged the beauty of forgiveness, the duty of devout submission? He had no religion, for he was no saintly "Uncle Tom," and Slavery's black shadow seemed to darken all the world to him, and shut out God. Should I have warned him of penalties, of judgments, and the potency of law? What did he know of justice, or the mercy that should temper that stern virtue, when every law, human and divine, had been broken on his hearthstone? Should I have tried to touch him by appeals to filial duty, to brotherly love? How had his appeals been answered? What memories had father and brother stored up in his heart to plead for either now? No,—all these influences, these associations, would have proved worse than useless, had I been calm enough to try them. I was not; but instinct, subtler than reason, showed me the one safe clue by which to lead this troubled soul from the labyrinth in which it groped and nearly fell. When I paused, breathless, Robert turned to me, asking, as if human assurances could strengthen his faith in Divine Omnipotence,—

"Do you believe, if I let Marster Ned live, the Lord will give me back my Lucy?"

"As surely as there is a Lord, you will find her here or in the beautiful hereafter, where there is no black or white, no master and no slave."

He took his hand from his brother's throat, lifted his eyes from my face to the wintry sky beyond, as if searching for that blessed country, happier even than the happy North. Alas, it was the darkest hour before the dawn!—there was no star above, no light below but the pale glimmer of the lamp that showed the brother who had made him desolate. Like a blind man who believes there is a sun, yet cannot see it, he shook his head, let his arms drop nervelessly upon his knees, and sat there dumbly asking that question which many a soul whose faith is firmer fixed than his has asked in hours less dark than this,—"Where is God?" I saw the tide had turned, and strenuously tried to keep this rudderless life-boat from slipping back into the whirlpool wherein it had been so nearly lost.

"I have listened to you, Robert; now hear me, and heed what I say, because my heart is full of pity for you, full of hope for your future, and a desire to help you now. I want you to go away from here, from the temptation of this place, and the sad thoughts that haunt it. You have conquered yourself once, and I honor you for it, because, the harder the battle, the more glorious the victory; but it is safer to put a greater distance between you and this man. I will write you letters, give you money, and send you to good old Massachusetts to begin your new life a freeman,—yes, and a happy man; for when the captain is himself again, I will learn where Lucy is, and move heaven and earth to find and give her back to you. Will you do this, Robert?"

Slowly, very slowly, the answer came; for the purpose of a week, perhaps a year, was hard to relinquish in an hour.

"Yes, Missis, I will."

"Good! Now you are the man I thought you, and I'll work for you with all my heart. You need sleep, my poor fellow; go, and try to forget. The captain is alive, and as yet you are spared that sin. No, don't look there; I'll care for him. Come, Robert, for Lucy's sake."

Thank Heaven for the immortality of love! for when all other means of salvation failed, a spark of this vital fire softened the man's iron will, until a woman's hand could bend it. He let me take from him the key, let me draw him gently away, and lead him to the solitude which now was the most healing balm I could bestow. Once in his little room, he fell down on his bed and lay there, as if spent with the sharpest conflict of his life. I slipped the bolt across his door, and unlocked my own, flung up the window, steadied myself with a breath of air, then rushed to Doctor Franck. He came; and till dawn we worked together, saving one brother's life, and taking earnest thought how best to secure the other's liberty. When the sun came up as blithely as if it shone only upon happy homes, the Doctor went to Robert. For an hour I heard the murmur of their voices; once I caught the sound of heavy sobs, and for a time a reverent hush, as if in the silence that good man were ministering to soul as well as body. When he departed he took Robert with him, pausing to tell me he should get him off as soon as possible, but not before we met again.

Nothing more was seen of them all day; another surgeon came to see the captain, and another attendant came to fill the empty place. I tried to rest, but could not, with the thought of poor Lucy tugging at my heart, and was soon back at my post again, anxiously hoping that my contraband had not been too hastily spirited away. Just as night fell there came a tap, and, opening, I saw Robert literally "clothed, and in his right mind." The Doctor had replaced the ragged suit with tidy garments, and no trace of the tempestuous night remained but deeper lines upon the forehead, and the docile look of a repentant child. He did not cross the threshold, did not offer me his hand,—only took off his cap, saying, with a traitorous falter in his voice,—

"God bless yer, Missis! I'm gwine."

I put out both my hands, and held his fast.

"Good-by, Robert! Keep up good heart, and when I come home to Massachusetts we'll meet in a happier place than this. Are you quite ready, quite comfortable for your journey?"

"Yes, Missis, yes; the Doctor's fixed everything! I'se gwine with a friend of his; my papers are all right, an' I'm as happy as I can be till I find"—

He stopped there; then went on, with a glance into the room,—

"I'm glad I didn't do it, an' I thank yer, Missis, fer hinderin' me—thank yer hearty; but I'm afraid I hate him jest the same."

Of course he did; and so did I; for these faulty hearts of ours cannot turn perfect in a night, but need frost and fire, wind and rain, to ripen and make them ready for the great harvest-home. Wishing to divert his mind, I put my poor mite into his hand, and, remembering the magic of a certain little book, I gave him mine, on whose dark cover whitely shone the Virgin Mother and the Child, the grand history of whose life the book contained. The money went into Robert's pocket with a grateful murmur, the book into his bosom, with a long look and a tremulous—

"I never saw *my* baby, Missis."

I broke down then; and though my eyes were too dim to see, I felt the touch of lips upon my hands, heard the sound of departing feet, and knew my contraband was gone.

When one feels an intense dislike, the less one says about the subject of it the better; therefore I shall merely record that the captain lived,—in time was exchanged; and that, whoever the other party was, I am convinced the Government got the best of the bargain. But long before this occurred, I had fulfilled my promise to Robert; for as soon as my patient recovered strength of memory enough to make his answer trustworthy, I asked, without any circumlocution,—

"Captain Fairfax, where is Lucy?"

And too feeble to be angry, surprised, or insincere, he straightway answered,—

"Dead, Miss Dane."

"And she killed herself when you sold Bob?"

"How the devil did you know that?" he muttered, with an expression half-remorseful, half-amazed; but I was satisfied, and said no more.

Of course this went to Robert, waiting far away there in a lonely home,—waiting, working, hoping for his Lucy. It almost broke my heart to do it; but delay was weak, deceit was wicked; so I sent the heavy tidings, and very soon the answer came,—only three lines; but I felt that the sustaining power of the man's life was gone.

"I tort I'd never see her any more; I'm glad to know she's out of trouble. I thank yer, Missis; an' if they let us, I'll fight fer yer till I'm killed, which I hope will be 'fore long."

Six months later he had his wish, and kept his word.

Every one knows the story of the attack on Fort Wagner; but we should not tire yet of recalling how our Fifty-Fourth, spent with three sleepless nights, a day's fast, and a march under the July sun, stormed the fort as night fell, facing death in many shapes, following their brave leaders through a fiery rain of shot and shell, fighting valiantly for "God and Governor Andrew,"—how the regiment that went into action seven hundred strong, came out having had nearly half its number captured, killed, or wounded, leaving their young commander to be buried, like a chief of earlier times, with his body-guard around him, faithful to the death. Surely, the insult turns to honor, and the wide grave needs no monument but the heroism that consecrates it in our sight; surely, the hearts that held him nearest, see through their tears a noble victory in the seeming sad defeat; and surely, God's benediction was bestowed, when this loyal soul answered, as Death called the roll, "Lord, here am I, with the brothers Thou hast given me!"

The future must show how well that fight was fought; for though Fort Wagner once defied us, public prejudice is down; and through the cannon-smoke of that black night, the manhood of the colored race shines before many eyes that would not see, rings in many ears that would not hear, wins many hearts that would not hitherto believe.

When the news came that we were needed, there was none so glad as I to leave teaching contrabands, the new work I had taken up, and go to nurse "our boys," as my dusky flock so proudly called the wounded of the Fifty-Fourth. Feeling more satisfaction, as I assumed my big apron and turned up my cuffs, than if dressing for the President's levee, I fell to work in Hospital No. 10 at Beaufort. The scene was most familiar, and yet strange; for only dark faces looked up at me from the pallets so thickly laid along the floor, and I missed the sharp accent of my Yankee boys in the slower, softer voices calling cheerily to one another, or answering my questions with a stout, "We'll never give it up, Missis, till the last Reb's dead," or, "If our people's free, we can afford to die."

Passing from bed to bed, intent on making one pair of hands do the work of three, at least, I gradually washed, fed, and bandaged my way down the long line of sable heroes, and coming to the very last, found that he was my contraband. So old, so worn, so deathly weak and wan, I never should have known him but for the deep scar on his cheek. That side lay uppermost, and caught my eye at once; but even then I doubted, such an awful change had come upon him, when, turning to the ticket just above his head, I saw the name, "Robert Dane." That both assured and touched me, for, remembering that he had no name, I knew that he had taken mine. I longed for him to speak to me, to tell how he had fared since I lost sight of him, and let me perform some little service for him in return for many he had done for me; but he seemed asleep; and as I stood re-living that strange night again, a bright lad, who lay next him softly waving an old fan across both beds, looked up and said,—

"I guess you know him, Missis?"

"You are right. Do you?"

"As much as any one was able to, Missis."

"Why do you say 'was,' as if the man were dead and gone?"

"I s'pose because I know he'll have to go. He's got a bad jab in the breast, an' is bleedin' inside, the Doctor says. He don't suffer any, only gets weaker 'n' weaker every minute. I've been fannin' him this long while, an' he's talked a little; but he don't know me now, so he's most gone, I guess."

There was so much sorrow and affection in the boy's face, that I remembered something, and asked, with redoubled interest,—

"Are you the one that brought him off? I was told about a boy who nearly lost his life in saving that of his mate."

I dare say the young fellow blushed, as any modest lad might have done; I could not see it, but I heard the chuckle of satisfaction that escaped him, as he glanced from his shattered arm and bandaged side to the pale figure opposite.

"Lord, Missis, that's nothin'; we boys always stan' by one another, an' I warn't goin' to leave him to be tormented any more by them cussed Rebs. He's been a slave once, though he don't look half so much like it as me, an' I was born in Boston."

He did not; for the speaker was as black as the ace of spades,—being a sturdy specimen, the knave of clubs would perhaps be a fitter representative,—but the dark freeman looked at the white slave with the pitiful, yet puzzled expression I have so often seen on the faces of our wisest men, when this tangled question of Slavery presented itself, asking to be cut or patiently undone.

"Tell me what you know of this man; for, even if he were awake, he is too weak to talk."

"I never saw him till I joined the regiment, an' no one 'peared to have got much out of him. He was a shut-up sort of feller, an' didn't seem to care for anything but gettin' at the Rebs. Some say he was the fust man of us that enlisted; I know he fretted till we were off, an' when we pitched into Old Wagner, he fought like the devil."

"Were you with him when he was wounded? How was it?"

"Yes, Missis. There was somethin' queer about it; for he 'peared to know the chap that killed him, an' the chap knew him. I don't dare to ask, but I rather guess one owned the other some time; for, when they clinched, the chap sung out, 'Bob!' an' Dane, 'Marster Ned!'—then they went at it."

I sat down suddenly, for the old anger and compassion struggled in my heart, and I both longed and feared to hear what was to follow.

"You see, when the Colonel,—Lord keep an' send him back to us!—it a'n't certain yet, you know, Missis, though it's two days ago we lost him,—well, when the Colonel shouted, 'Rush on, boys, rush on!' Dane tore away as if he was goin' to take the fort alone; I was next him, an' kept close as we went through the ditch an' up the wall. Hi! warn't that a rusher!" and the boy flung up his well arm with a whoop, as if the mere memory of that stirring moment came over him in a gust of irrepressible excitement.

"Were you afraid?" I said, asking the question women often put, and receiving the answer they seldom fail to get.

"No, Missis!"—emphasis on the "Missis"—"I never thought of anything but the damn' Rebs, that scalp, slash, an' cut our ears off, when they git us. I was bound to let daylight into one of 'em at least, an' I did. Hope he liked it!"

"It is evident that you did. Now go on about Robert, for I should be at work."

"He was one of the fust up; I was just behind, an' though the whole thing happened in a minute, I remember how it was, for all I was yellin' an' knockin' round like mad. Just where we were, some sort of an officer was wavin' his sword an' cheerin' on his men; Dane saw him by a big flash that come by; he flung away his gun, give a leap, an' went at that feller as if he was Jeff, Beauregard, an' Lee, all in one. I scrabbled after as quick as I could, but was only up in time to see him git the sword straight through him an' drop into the ditch. You needn't ask what I did next, Missis, for I don't quite know myself; all I'm clear about is, that I managed somehow to pitch that Reb into the fort as dead as Moses, git hold of Dane, an' bring him off. Poor old feller! we said we went in to live or die; he said he went in to die, an' he's done it."

I had been intently watching the excited speaker; but as he regretfully added those last words I turned again, and Robert's eyes met mine,—those melancholy eyes, so full of an intelligence that proved he had heard, remembered, and reflected with that preternatural power which often outlives all other faculties. He knew me, yet gave no greeting; was glad to see a woman's face, yet had no smile wherewith to welcome it; felt that he was dying, yet uttered no farewell. He was too far across the river to return or linger now; departing thought, strength, breath, were spent in one grateful look, one murmur of submission to the last pang he could ever feel. His lips moved, and, bending to them, a whisper chilled my cheek, as it shaped the broken words,—

"I'd 'a 'done it,—but it's better so,—I'm satisfied."

Ah! well he might be,—for, as he turned his face from the shadow of the life that was, the sunshine of the life to be touched it with a beautiful content, and in the drawing of a breath my contraband found wife and home, eternal liberty and God.

A Whisper in the Dark

As we rolled along, I scanned my companion covertly, and saw much to interest a girl of seventeen. My uncle was a handsome man, with all the polish of foreign life fresh upon him; yet it was neither comeliness nor graceful ease which most attracted me; for even my inexperienced eye caught glimpses of something stern and somber below these external charms, and my long scrutiny showed me the keenest eye, the hardest mouth, the subtlest smile I ever saw—a face which in repose wore the look that comes to those who have led lives of pleasure and learned their emptiness. He seemed intent on some thought that absorbed him, and for a time rendered him forgetful of my presence, as he sat with folded arms, fixed eyes, and restless lips. While I looked, my own mind was full of deeper thought than it had ever been before; for I was recalling, word for word, a paragraph in that half-read letter:

> *At eighteen Sybil is to marry her cousin, the compact having been made between my brother and myself in their childhood. My son is with me now, and I wish them to be together during the next few months, therefore my niece must leave you sooner than I at first intended. Oblige me by preparing her for an immediate and final separation, but leave all disclosures to me, as I prefer the girl to remain ignorant of the matter for the present.*

That displeased me. Why was I to remain ignorant of so important an affair? Then I smiled to myself, remembering that I did know, thanks to the willful curiosity that prompted me to steal a peep into the letter that Mme. Bernard had pored over with such an anxious face. I saw only a single paragraph, for my own name arrested my eye; and, though wild to read all, I had scarcely time to whisk the paper back into the reticule the forgetful old soul had left hanging on the arm of her chair. It was enough, however, to set my girlish brain in a ferment, and keep me gazing wistfully at my uncle, conscious that my future now lay in his hands; for I was an orphan and he my guardian, though I had seen him but seldom since I was confided to Madame a six years' child.

Presently my uncle became cognizant of my steady stare, and returned it with one as steady for a moment, then said, in a low, smooth tone, that ill accorded with the satirical smile that touched his lips, "I am a dull companion for my little niece. How shall I provide her with pleasanter amusement than counting my wrinkles or guessing my thoughts?"

I was a frank, fearless creature, quick to feel, speak, and act, so I answered readily, "Tell me about my cousin Guy. Is he as handsome, brave, and clever as Madame says his father was when a boy?"

My uncle laughed a short laugh, touched with scorn, whether for Madame, himself, or me I could not tell, for his countenance was hard to read.

"A girl's question and artfully put; nevertheless I shall not answer it, but let you judge for yourself."

"But, sir, it will amuse me and beguile the way. I feel a little strange and forlorn at leaving Madame, and talking of my new home and friends will help me to know and love them sooner. Please tell me, for I've had my own way all my life, and can't bear to be crossed."

My petulance seemed to amuse him, and I became aware that he was observing me with a scrutiny as keen as my own had been; but I smilingly sustained it, for my vanity was pleased by the approbation his eye betrayed. The evident interest he now took in all I said and did was sufficient flattery for a young thing, who felt her charms and longed to try their power.

"I, too, have had my own way all my life; and as the life is double the length, the will is double the strength of yours, and again I say no. What next, mademoiselle?"

He was blander than ever as he spoke, but I was piqued, and resolved to try coaxing, eager to gain my point, lest a too early submission now should mar my freedom in the future.

"But that is ungallant, Uncle, and I still have hopes of a kinder answer, both because you are too generous to refuse so small a favor to your 'little niece,' and because she can be charmingly wheedlesome when she likes. Won't you say yes now, Uncle?" And pleased with the daring of the thing, I put my arm about his neck, kissed him daintily, and perched myself upon his knee with most audacious ease.

He regarded me mutely for an instant, then, holding me fast, deliberately returned my salute on lips, cheeks, and forehead, with such warmth that I turned scarlet and struggled to free myself, while he laughed that mirthless laugh of his till my shame turned to anger, and I imperiously commanded him to let me go.

"Not yet, young lady. You came here for your own pleasure, but shall stay for mine, till I tame you as I see you must be tamed. It is a short process with me, and I possess experience in the work; for Guy, though by nature as wild as a hawk, has learned to come at my call as meekly as a dove. Chut! What a little fury it is!"

I was just then; for exasperated at his coolness, and quite beside myself, I had suddenly stooped and bitten the shapely white hand that held both my own. I had better have submitted; for slight as the foolish action was, it had an influence on my afterlife as many another such has had. My uncle stopped laughing, his hand tightened its grasp, for a moment his cold eye glittered and a grim look settled round the mouth, giving to his whole face a ruthless expression that entirely altered it. I felt perfectly powerless. All my little arts had failed, and for the first time I was mastered. Yet only physically; my spirit was rebellious still. He saw it in the glance that met his own, as I sat erect and pale, with something more than childish anger. I think it pleased him, for swiftly as it had come the dark look passed, and quietly, as if we were the best of friends, he began to relate certain exciting adventures he had known abroad, lending to the picturesque narration the charm of that peculiarly melodious voice, which soothed and won me in spite of myself, holding me intent till I forgot the past; and when he paused I found that I was leaning confidentially on his shoulder, asking for more, yet conscious of an instinctive distrust of this man whom I had so soon learned to fear yet fancy.

As I was recalled to myself, I endeavored to leave him; but he still detained me, and, with a curious expression, produced a case so quaintly fashioned that I cried out in admiration, while he selected two cigarettes, mildly aromatic with the herbs they were composed of, lit them, offered me one, dropped the window, and leaning back surveyed me with an air of extreme enjoyment, as I sat meekly puffing and wondering what prank I should play a part in next. Slowly the narcotic influence of the herbs diffused itself like a pleasant haze over all my senses; sleep, the most grateful, fell upon my eyelids, and the last thing I remember was my uncle's face dreamily regarding me through a cloud of fragrant smoke. Twilight wrapped us in its shadows when I woke, with the night wind blowing on my forehead, the muffled roll of wheels sounding in my ear, and my cheek pillowed upon my uncle's arm. He was humming a French *chanson* about "love and wine, and the Seine tomorrow!" I listened till I caught the air, and presently joined him, mingling my girlish treble with his flutelike tenor. He stopped at once and, in the coolly courteous tone I had always heard in our few interviews, asked if I was ready for lights and home.

"Are we there?" I cried; and looking out saw that we were ascending an avenue which swept up to a pile of buildings that rose tall and dark against the sky, with here and there a gleam along its gray front.

"Home at last, thank heaven!" And springing out with the agility of a young man, my uncle led me over a terrace into a long hall, light and warm, and odorous with the breath of flowers blossoming here and there in graceful groups. A civil, middle-aged maid received and took me to my room, a bijou of a place, which increased my wonder when told that my uncle had chosen all its decorations and superintended their arrangement. "He understands women," I thought, handling the toilet ornaments, trying luxurious chair and lounge, and ending by slipping my feet into the scarlet-and-white Turkish slippers, coquettishly turning up their toes before the fire. A few moments I gave to examination, and, having expressed my satisfaction, was asked by my maid if I would be pleased to dress, as "the master" never allowed dinner to wait for anyone. This recalled to me the fact that I was doubtless to meet my future husband at that meal, and in a moment every faculty was intent upon achieving a grand toilette for this first interview. The maid possessed skill and taste, and I a wardrobe lately embellished with Parisian gifts from my uncle which I was eager to display in his honor.

When ready, I surveyed myself in the long mirror as I had never done before, and saw there a little figure, slender, yet stately, in a dress of foreign fashion, ornamented with lace and carnation ribbons which enhanced the fairness of neck and arms, while blond hair, wavy and golden, was gathered into an antique knot of curls behind, with a carnation fillet, and below a blooming dark-eyed face, just then radiant with girlish vanity and eagerness and hope.

"I'm glad I'm pretty!"

"So am I, Sybil."

I had unconsciously spoken aloud, and the echo came from the doorway where stood my uncle, carefully dressed, looking comelier and cooler than ever. The disagreeable smile flitted over his lips as he spoke, and I started, then stood abashed, till beckoning, he added in his most courtly manner, "You were so absorbed in the contemplation of your charming self that Janet answered my tap and took herself away unheard. You are mistress of my table now. It waits; will you come down?"

With a last touch to that unruly hair of mine, a last, comprehensive glance and shake, I took the offered arm and rustled down the wide staircase, feeling that the romance of my life was about to begin. Three covers were laid, three chairs set, but only two were occupied, for no Guy appeared. I asked no questions, showed no surprise, but tried to devour my chagrin with my dinner, and exerted myself to charm my uncle into the belief that I had forgotten my cousin. It was a failure, however, for that empty seat had an irresistible fascination for me, and more than once, as my eye returned from its furtive scrutiny of napkin, plate, and trio of colored glasses, it met my uncle's and fell before his penetrative glance. When I gladly rose to leave him to his wine—for he did not ask me to remain—he also rose, and, as he held the door for me, he said, "You asked me to describe your cousin. You have seen one trait of his character tonight; does it please you?"

I knew he was as much vexed as I at Guy's absence, so quoting his own words, I answered saucily, "Yes, for I'd rather see the hawk free than coming tamely at your call, Uncle."

He frowned slightly, as if unused to such liberty of speech, yet bowed when I swept him a stately little curtsy and sailed away to the drawing room, wondering if my uncle was as angry with me as I was with my cousin. In solitary grandeur I amused myself by strolling through the suite of handsome rooms henceforth to be my realm, looked at myself in the long mirrors, as every woman is apt to do when alone and in costume, danced over the mossy carpets, touched the grand piano, smelled the flowers, fingered the ornaments on étagère and table, and was just giving my handkerchief a second drench of some refreshing perfume from a filigree flask that had captivated me when the hall door was flung wide, a quick step went running upstairs, boots tramped overhead, drawers seemed hastily opened and shut, and a bold, blithe voice broke out into a hunting song in a tone so like my uncle's that I involuntarily flew to the door, crying, "Guy is come!"

Fortunately for my dignity, no one heard me, and hurrying back I stood ready to skim into a chair and assume propriety at a minute's notice, conscious, meanwhile, of the new influence which seemed suddenly to gift the silent house with vitality, and add the one charm it needed—

that of cheerful companionship. "How will he meet me? And how shall I meet him?" I thought, looking up at the bright-faced boy, whose portrait looked back at me with a mirthful light in the painted eyes and a trace of his father's disdainful smile in the curves of the firm-set lips. Presently the quick steps came flying down again, past the door, straight to the dining room opposite, and, as I stood listening with a strange flutter at my heart, I heard an imperious young voice say rapidly, "Beg pardon, sir, unavoidably detained. Has she come? Is she bearable?"

"I find her so. Dinner is over, and I can offer you nothing but a glass of wine."

My uncle's voice was frostily polite, making a curious contrast to the other, so impetuous and frank, as if used to command or win all but one.

"Never mind the dinner! I'm glad to be rid of it; so I'll drink your health, Father, and then inspect our new ornament."

"Impertinent boy!" I muttered, yet at the same moment resolved to deserve his appellation, and immediately grouped myself as effectively as possible, laughing at my folly as I did so. I possessed a pretty foot, therefore one little slipper appeared quite naturally below the last flounce of my dress; a bracelet glittered on my arm as it emerged from among the lace and carnation knots; that arm supported my head. My profile was well cut, my eyelashes long, therefore I read with face half averted from the door. The light showered down, turning my hair to gold; so I smoothed my curls, retied my snood, and, after a satisfied survey, composed myself with an absorbed aspect and a quickened pulse to await the arrival of the gentlemen.

Soon they came. I knew they paused on the threshold, but never stirred till an irrepressible "You are right, sir!" escaped the younger.

Then I rose prepared to give him the coldest greeting, yet I did not. I had almost expected to meet the boyish face and figure of the picture; I saw instead a man comely and tall. A dark moustache half hid the proud mouth; the vivacious eyes were far kinder, though quite as keen as his father's; and the freshness of unspoiled youth lent a charm which the older man had lost forever. Guy's glance of pleased surprise was flatteringly frank, his smile so cordial, his "Welcome, cousin!" such a hearty sound that my coldness melted in a breath, my dignity was all forgotten, and before I could restrain myself I had offered both hands with the impulsive exclamation "Cousin Guy, I know I shall be very happy here! Are you glad I have come?"

"Glad as I am to see the sun after a November fog."

And bending his tall head, he kissed my hand in the graceful foreign fashion he had learned abroad. It pleased me mightily, for it was both affectionate and respectful. Involuntarily I contrasted it with my uncle's manner, and flashed a significant glance at him as I did so. He understood it, but only nodded with the satirical look I hated, shook out his paper, and began to read. I sat down again, careless of myself now; and Guy stood on the rug, surveying me with an expression of surprise that rather nettled my pride.

"He is only a boy, after all; so I need not be daunted by his inches or his airs. I wonder if he knows I am to be his wife, and likes it."

The thought sent the color to my forehead, my eyes fell, and despite my valiant resolution I sat like any bashful child before my handsome cousin. Guy laughed a boyish laugh as he sat down on his father's footstool, saying, while he warmed his slender brown hands, "I beg your pardon, Sybil. (We won't be formal, will we?) But I haven't seen a lady for a month, so I stare like a boor at sight of a silk gown and highbred face. Are those people coming, sir?"

"If Sybil likes, ask her."

"Shall we have a flock of people here to make it gay for you, Cousin, or do you prefer our quiet style better; just riding, driving, lounging, and enjoying life, each in his own way? Henceforth it is to be as you command in such matters."

"Let things go on as they have done then. I don't care for society, and strangers wouldn't make it gay to me, for I like freedom; so do you, I think."

"Ah, don't I!"

A cloud flitted over his smiling face, and he punched the fire, as if some vent were necessary for the sudden gust of petulance that knit his black brows into a frown, and caused his father to tap him on the shoulder with the bland request, as he rose to leave the room, "Bring the portfolios and entertain your cousin; I have letters to write, and Sybil is too tired to care for music tonight."

Guy obeyed with a shrug of the shoulder his father touched, but lingered in the recess till my uncle, having made his apologies to me, had left the room; then my cousin rejoined me, wearing the same cordial aspect I first beheld. Some restraint was evidently removed, and his natural self appeared. A very winsome self it was, courteous, gay, and frank, with an undertone of deeper feeling than I thought to find. I watched him covertly, and soon owned to myself that he was all I most admired in the ideal hero every girl creates in her romantic fancy; for I no longer looked upon this young man as my cousin, but my lover, and through all our future intercourse this thought was always uppermost, full of a charm that never lost its power.

Before the evening ended Guy was kneeling on the rug beside me, our two heads close together, while he turned the contents of the great portfolio spread before us, looking each other freely in the face, as I listened and he described, both breaking into frequent peals of laughter at some odd adventure or comical mishap in his own travels, suggested by the pictured scenes before us. Guy was very charming, I my blithest, sweetest self, and when we parted late, my cousin watched me up the stairs with still another "Good night, Sybil," as if both sight and sound were pleasant to him.

"Is that your horse Sultan?" I called from my window next morning, as I looked down upon my cousin, who was coming up the drive from an early gallop on the moors.

"Yes, bonny Sybil; come and admire him," he called back, hat in hand, and a quick smile rippling over his face.

I went, and standing on the terrace, caressed the handsome creature, while Guy said, glancing up at his father's undrawn curtains, "If your saddle had come, we would take a turn before 'my lord' is ready for breakfast. This autumn air is the wine you women need."

I yearned to go, and when I willed the way soon appeared; so careless of bonnetless head and cambric gown, I stretched my hands to him, saying boldly, "Play young Lochinvar, Guy; I am little and light; take me up before you and show me the sea."

He liked the daring feat, held out his hand, I stepped on his boot toe, sprang up, and away we went over the wide moor, where the sun shone in a cloudless heaven, the lark soared singing from the green grass at our feet, and the September wind blew freshly from the sea. As we paused on the upland slope, that gave us a free view of the country for miles, Guy dismounted, and standing with his arm about the saddle to steady me in my precarious seat, began to talk.

"Do you like your new home, Cousin?"

"More than I can tell you!"

"And my father, Sybil?"

"Both yes and no to that question, Guy; I hardly know him yet."

"True, but you must not expect to find him as indulgent and fond as many guardians would be to such as you. It's not his nature. Yet you can win his heart by obedience, and soon grow quite at ease with him."

"Bless you! I'm that already, for I fear no one. Why, I sat on his knee yesterday and smoked a cigarette of his own offering, though Madame would have fainted if she had seen me; then I slept on his arm an hour, and he was fatherly kind, though I teased him like a gnat."

"The deuce he was!"

With which energetic expression Guy frowned at the landscape and harshly checked Sultan's attempt to browse, while I wondered what was amiss between father and son, and resolved to discover; but finding the conversation at an end, started it afresh by asking, "Is any of my property in this part of the country, Guy? Do you know I am as ignorant as a baby about my own affairs; for, as long as every whim was gratified and my purse full, I left the rest to Madame and Uncle, though the first hadn't a bit of judgment, and the last I scarcely knew. I never cared to ask questions before, but now I am intensely curious to know how matters stand."

"All you see is yours, Sybil" was the brief answer.

"What, that great house, the lovely gardens, these moors, and the forest stretching to the sea? I'm glad! I'm glad! But where, then, is your home, Guy?"

"Nowhere."

At this I looked so amazed that his gloom vanished in a laugh, as he explained, but briefly, as if this subject were no pleasanter than the first, "By your father's will you were desired to take possession of the old place at eighteen. You will be that soon; therefore, as your guardian, my father has prepared things for you, and is to share your home until you marry."

"When will that be, I wonder?" And I stole a glance from under my lashes, wild to discover if Guy knew of the compact and was a willing party to it.

His face was half averted, but over his dark cheek I saw a deep flush rise, as he answered, stooping to pull a bit of heather, "Soon, I hope, or the gentleman sleeping there below will be tempted to remain a fixture with you on his knee as 'Madame my wife.' He is not your own uncle, you know."

I smiled at the idea, but Guy did not see it; and seized with a whim to try my skill with the hawk that seemed inclined to peck at its master, I said demurely, "Well, why not? I might be very happy if I learned to love him, as I should, if he were always in that kindest mood of his. Would you like me for a little mamma, Guy?"

"No!" short and sharp as a pistol shot.

"Then you must marry and have a home of your own, my son."

"Don't, Sybil! I'd rather you didn't see me in a rage, for I'm not a pleasant sight, I assure you; and I'm afraid I shall be in one if you go on. I early lost my mother, but I love her tenderly, because my father is not much to me, and I know if she had lived I should not be what I am."

Bitter was his voice, moody his mien, and all the sunshine gone at once. I looked down and touched his black hair with a shy caress, feeling both penitent and pitiful.

"Dear Guy, forgive me if I pained you. I'm a thoughtless creature, but I'm not malicious, and a word will restrain me if kindly spoken. My home is always yours, and when my fortune is mine you shall never want, if you are not too proud to accept help from your own kin. You are a little proud, aren't you?"

"As Lucifer, to most people. I think I should not be to you, for you understand me, Sybil, and with you I hope to grow a better man."

He turned then, and through the lineaments his father had bequeathed him I saw a look that must have been his mother's, for it was womanly, sweet, and soft, and lent new beauty to the dark eyes, always kind, and just then very tender. He had checked his words suddenly, like one who has gone too far, and with that hasty look into my face had bent his own upon the ground, as if to hide the unwonted feeling that had mastered him. It lasted but a moment, then his old manner returned, as he said gaily, "There drops your slipper. I've been wondering what kept it on. Pretty thing! They say it is a foot like this that oftenest tramples on men's hearts. Are you cruel to your lovers, Sybil?"

"I never had one, for Madame guarded me like a dragon, and I led the life of a nun; but when I do find one I shall try his mettle well before I give up my liberty."

"Poets say it is sweet to give up liberty for love, and they ought to know," answered Guy, with a sidelong glance.

I liked that little speech, and recollecting the wistful look he had given me, the significant words that had escaped him, and the variations of tone and manner constantly succeeding one another, I felt assured that my cousin was cognizant of the family league, and accepted it, yet with the shyness of a young lover, knew not how to woo. This pleased me, and quite satisfied with my morning's work, I mentally resolved to charm my cousin slowly, and enjoy the romance of a genuine wooing, without which no woman's life seems complete—in her own eyes at least. He had gathered me a knot of purple heather, and as he gave it I smiled my sweetest on him, saying, "I commission you to supply me with nosegays, for you have taste, and I love wild flowers. I shall wear this at dinner in honor of its giver. Now take me home; for my moors, though beautiful, are chilly, and I have no wrapper but this microscopic handkerchief."

Off went his riding jacket, and I was half smothered in it. The hat followed next, and as he sprang up behind I took the reins, and felt a thrill of delight in sweeping down the slope with that mettlesome creature tugging at the bit, that strong arm around me, and the happy hope that the heart I leaned on might yet learn to love me.

The day so began passed pleasantly, spent in roving over house and grounds with my cousin, setting my possessions in order, and writing to dear old Madame. Twilight found me in my bravest attire, with Guy's heather in my hair, listening for his step, and longing to run and meet him when he came. Punctual to the instant he appeared, and this dinner was a far different one from that of yesterday, for both father and son seemed in their gayest and most gallant mood, and I enjoyed the hour heartily. The world seemed all in tune now, and when I went to the drawing room I was moved to play my most stirring marches, sing my blithest songs, hoping to bring one at least of the gentlemen to join me. It brought both, and my first glance showed me a curious change in each. My uncle looked harassed and yet amused; Guy looked sullen and eyed his father with covert glances.

The morning's chat flashed into my mind, and I asked myself, "Is Guy jealous so soon?" It looked a little like it, for he threw himself upon a couch and lay there silent and morose; while my uncle paced to and fro, thinking deeply, while apparently listening to the song he bade me finish. I did so, then followed the whim that now possessed me, for I wanted to try my power over them both, to see if I could restore that gentler mood of my uncle's, and assure myself that Guy cared whether I was friendliest with him or not.

"Uncle, come and sing with me; I like that voice of yours."

"Tut, I am too old for that; take this indolent lad instead. His voice is fresh and young, and will chord well with yours."

"Do you know that pretty *chanson* about 'love and wine, and the Seine tomorrow,' cousin Guy?" I asked, stealing a sly glance at my uncle.

"Who taught you that?" And Guy eyed me over the top of the couch with an astonished expression which greatly amused me.

"No one; Uncle sang a bit of it in the carriage yesterday. I like the air, so come and teach me the rest."

"It is no song for you, Sybil. You choose strange entertainment for a lady, sir."

A look of unmistakable contempt was in the son's eye, of momentary annoyance in the father's, yet his voice betrayed none as he answered, still pacing placidly along the room, "I thought she was asleep, and unconsciously began it to beguile a silent drive. Sing on, Sybil; that Bacchanalian snatch will do you no harm."

But I was tired of music now they had come, so I went to him, and passing my arm through his, walked beside him, saying with my most persuasive aspect, "Tell me about Paris, Uncle; I intend to go there as soon as I'm of age, if you will let me. Does your guardianship extend beyond that time?"

"Only till you marry."

"I shall be in no haste, then, for I begin to feel quite homelike and happy here with you, and shall be content without other society; only you'll soon tire of me, and leave me to some dismal governess, while you and Guy go pleasuring."

"No fear of that, Sybil; I shall hold you fast till some younger guardian comes to rob me of my merry ward."

As he spoke, he took the hand that lay upon his arm into a grasp so firm, and turned on me a look so keen, that I involuntarily dropped my eyes lest he should read my secret there. Eager to turn the conversation, I asked, pointing to a little miniature hanging underneath the portrait of his son, before which he had paused, "Was that Guy's mother, sir?"

"No, your own."

I looked again, and saw a face delicate yet spirited, with dark eyes, a passionate mouth, and a head crowned with hair as plenteous and golden as my own; but the whole seemed dimmed by age, the ivory was stained, the glass cracked, and a faded ribbon fastened it. My eyes filled as I looked, and a strong desire seized me to know what had defaced this little picture of the mother whom I never knew.

"Tell me about her, Uncle; I know so little, and often long for her so much. Am I like her, sir?"

Why did my uncle avert his eyes as he answered, "You are a youthful image of her, Sybil"?

"Go on, please, tell me more; tell me why this is so stained and worn; you know all, and surely I am old enough now to hear any history of pain and loss."

Something caused my uncle to knit his brows, but his bland voice never varied a tone as he placed the picture in my hand and gave me this brief explanation:

"Just before your birth your father was obliged to cross the Channel, to receive the last wishes of a dying friend. There was an accident; the vessel foundered, and many lives were lost. He escaped, but by some mistake his name appeared in the list of missing passengers; your mother saw it, the shock destroyed her, and when your father returned he found only a motherless little daughter to welcome him. This miniature, which he always carried with him, was saved with his papers at the last moment; but though the seawater ruined it he would never have it copied or retouched, and gave it to me when he died in memory of the woman I had loved for his sake. It is yours now, my child; keep it, and never feel that you are fatherless or motherless while I remain."

Kind as was both act and speech, neither touched me, for something seemed wanting. I felt yet could not define it, for then I believed in the sincerity of all I met.

"Where was she buried, Uncle? It may be foolish, but I should like to see my mother's grave."

"You shall someday, Sybil," and a curious change came over my uncle's face as he averted it.

"I have made him melancholy, talking of Guy's mother and my own; now I'll make him gay again if possible, and pique that negligent boy," I thought, and drew my uncle to a lounging chair, established myself on the arm thereof, and kept him laughing with my merriest gossip, both of us apparently unconscious of the long dark figure stretched just opposite, feigning sleep, but watching us through half-closed lids, and never stirring except to bow silently to my careless "Goodnight."

As I reached the stairhead, I remembered that my letter to Madame, full of the frankest criticisms upon people and things, was lying unsealed on the table in the little room my uncle had set apart for my boudoir; fearing servants' eyes and tongues, I slipped down again to get it. The room adjoined the parlors, and just then was lit only by a ray from the hall lamp.

I had secured the letter, and was turning to retreat, when I heard Guy say petulantly, as if thwarted yet submissive, "I *am* civil when you leave me alone; I *do* agree to marry her, but I won't be hurried or go a-wooing except in my own way. You know I never liked the bargain, for it's nothing else; yet I can reconcile myself to being sold, if it relieves you and gives us both a home. But, Father, mind this, if you tie me to that girl's sash too tightly I shall break away entirely, and then where are we?"

"I should be in prison and you a houseless vagabond. Trust me, my boy, and take the good fortune which I secured for you in your cradle. Look in pretty Sybil's face, and resignation will grow easy; but remember time presses, that this is our forlorn hope, and for God's sake be cautious, for she is a headstrong creature, and may refuse to fulfill her part if she learns that the contract is not binding against her will."

"I think she'll not refuse, sir; she likes me already. I see it in her eyes; she has never had a lover, she says, and according to your account a girl's first sweetheart is apt to fare the best. Besides, she likes the place, for I told her it was hers, as you bade me, and she said she could be very happy here, if my father was always kind."

"She said that, did she? Little hypocrite! For your father, read yourself, and tell me what else she babbled about in that early *tête-à-tête* of yours."

"You are as curious as a woman, sir, and always make me tell you all I do and say, yet never tell me anything in return, except this business, which I hate, because my liberty is the price, and my poor little cousin is kept in the dark. I'll tell her all, before I marry her, Father."

"As you please, hothead. I am waiting for an account of the first love passage, so leave blushing to Sybil and begin."

I knew what was coming and stayed no longer, but caught one glimpse of the pair. Guy in his favorite place, erect upon the rug, half laughing, half frowning as he delayed to speak, my uncle serenely smoking on the couch; then I sped away to my own room, thinking, as I sat down in a towering passion, "So he does know of the baby betrothal and hates it, yet submits to please his father, who covets my fortune—mercenary creatures! I can annul the contract, can I? I'm glad to know that, for it makes me mistress of them both. I like you already, do I, and you see it in my eyes? Coxcomb! I'll be the thornier for that. Yet I do like him; I do wish he cared for me, I'm so lonely in the world, and he can be so kind."

So I cried a little, brushed my hair a good deal, and went to bed, resolving to learn all I could when, where, and how I pleased, to render myself as charming and valuable as possible, to make Guy love me in spite of himself, and then say yes or no, as my heart prompted me.

That day was a sample of those that followed, for my cousin was by turns attracted or repelled by the capricious moods that ruled me. Though conscious of a secret distrust of my uncle, I could not resist the fascination of his manner when he chose to exert its influence over me; this made my little plot easier of execution, for jealousy seemed the most effectual means to bring my wayward cousin to subjection. Full of this fancy, I seemed to tire of his society, grew thorny as a brier rose to him, affectionate as a daughter to my uncle, who surveyed us both with that inscrutable glance of his, and slowly yielded to my dominion as if he had divined my purpose and desired to aid it. Guy turned cold and gloomy, yet still lingered near me as if ready for a relenting look or word. I liked that, and took a wanton pleasure in prolonging the humiliation of the warm heart I had learned to love, yet not to value as I ought, until it was too late.

One dull November evening as I went wandering up and down the hall, pretending to enjoy the flowers, yet in reality waiting for Guy, who had left me alone all day, my uncle came from his room, where he had sat for many hours with the harassed and anxious look he always wore when certain foreign letters came.

"Sybil, I have something to show and tell you," he said, as I garnished his buttonhole with a spray of heliotrope, meant for the laggard, who would understand its significance, I hoped. Leading me to the drawing room, my uncle put a paper into my hands, with the request "This is a copy of your father's will; oblige me by reading it."

He stood watching my face as I read, no doubt wondering at my composure while I waded through the dry details of the will, curbing my impatience to reach the one important passage. There it was, but no word concerning my power to dissolve the engagement if I pleased; and, as I realized the fact, a sudden bewilderment and sense of helplessness came over me, for the strange law terms seemed to make inexorable the paternal decree which I had not seen before. I forgot my studied calmness, and asked several questions eagerly.

"Uncle, did my father really command that I should marry Guy, whether we loved each other or not?"

"You see what he there set down as his desire; and I have taken measures that you *should* love one another, knowing that few cousins, young, comely, and congenial, could live three months together without finding themselves ready to mate for their own sakes, if not for the sake of the dead and living fathers to whom they owe obedience."

"You said I need not, if I didn't choose; why is it not here?"

"I said that? Never, Sybil!" and I met a look of such entire surprise and incredulity it staggered my belief in my own senses, yet also roused my spirit, and, careless of consequences, I spoke out at once.

"I heard you say it myself the night after I came, when you told Guy to be cautious, because I could refuse to fulfill the engagement, if I knew that it was not binding against my will."

This discovery evidently destroyed some plan, and for a moment threw him off his guard; for, crumpling the paper in his hand, he sternly demanded, "You turned eavesdropper early; how often since?"

"Never, Uncle; I did not mean it then, but going for a letter in the dark, I heard your voices, and listened for an instant. It was dishonorable, but irresistible; and if you force Guy's confidence, why should not I steal yours? All is fair in war, sir, and I forgive as I hope to be forgiven."

"You have a quick wit and a reticence I did not expect to find under that frank manner. So you have known your future destiny all these months then, and have a purpose in your treatment of your cousin and myself?"

"Yes, Uncle."

"May I ask what?"

I was ashamed to tell; and in the little pause before my answer came, my pique at Guy's desertion was augmented by anger at my uncle's denial of his own words the ungenerous hopes he cherished, and a strong desire to perplex and thwart him took possession of me, for I saw his anxiety concerning the success of this interview, though he endeavored to repress and conceal it. Assuming my coldest mien, I said, "No, sir, I think not; only I can assure you that my little plot has succeeded better than your own."

"But you intend to obey your father's wish, I hope, and fulfill your part of the compact, Sybil?"

"Why should I? It is not binding, you know, and I'm too young to lose my liberty just yet; besides, such compacts are unjust, unwise. What right had my father to mate me in my cradle? How did he know what I should become, or Guy? How could he tell that I should not love someone else better? No! I'll not be bargained away like a piece of merchandise, but love and marry when I please!"

At this declaration of independence my uncle's face darkened ominously, some new suspicion lurked in his eye, some new anxiety beset him; but his manner was calm, his voice blander than ever as he asked, "Is there then someone whom you love? Confide in me, my girl."

"And if there were, what then?"

"All would be changed at once, Sybil. But who is it? Some young lover left behind at Madame's?"

"No, sir."

"Who, then? You have led a recluse life here. Guy has no friends who visit him, and mine are all old, yet you say you love."

"With all my heart, Uncle."

"Is this affection returned, Sybil?"

"I think so."

"And it is not Guy?"

I was wicked enough to enjoy the bitter disappointment he could not conceal at my decided words, for I thought he deserved that momentary pang; but I could not as decidedly answer that last question, for I would not lie, neither would I confess just yet; so, with a little gesture of impatience, I silently turned away, lest he should see the telltale color in my cheeks. My uncle stood an instant in deep thought, a slow smile crept to his lips, content returned to his mien, and something like a flash of triumph glittered for a moment in his eye, then vanished, leaving his countenance earnestly expectant. Much as this change surprised me, his words did more, for, taking both my hands in his, he gravely said, "Do you know that I am your uncle by adoption and not blood, Sybil?"

"Yes, sir; I heard so, but forgot about it," and I looked up at him, my anger quite lost in astonishment.

"Let me tell you then. Your grandfather was childless for many years, my mother was an early friend, and when her death left me an orphan, he took me for his son and heir. But two years from that time your father was born. I was too young to realize the entire change this might make in my life. The old man was too just and generous to let me feel it, and the two lads grew up together like brothers. Both married young, and when you were born a few years later than my son, your father said to me, 'Your boy shall have my girl, and the fortune I have innocently robbed you of shall make us happy in our children.' Then the family league was made, renewed at his death, and now destroyed by his daughter, unless—Sybil, I am forty-five, you not eighteen, yet you once said you could be very happy with me, if I were always kind to you. I can promise that I will be, for I love you. My darling, you reject the son, will you accept the father?"

If he had struck me, it would scarcely have dismayed me more. I started up, and snatching away my hands, hid my face in them, for after the first tingle of surprise an almost irresistible desire to laugh came over me, but I dared not and gravely, gently he went on.

"I am a bold man to say this, yet I mean it most sincerely. I never meant to betray the affection I believed you never could return, and would only laugh at as a weakness; but your past acts, your present words, give me courage to confess that I desire to keep my ward mine forever. Shall it be so?"

He evidently mistook my surprise for maidenly emotion, and the suddenness of this unforeseen catastrophe seemed to deprive me of words. All thought of merriment or ridicule was forgotten in a sense of guilt, for if he feigned the love he offered it was well done, and I believed it then. I saw at once the natural impression conveyed by my conduct; my half confession and the folly of it all oppressed me with a regret and shame I could not master. My mind was in dire confusion, yet a decided "No" was rapidly emerging from the chaos, but was not uttered; for just at this crisis, as I stood with my uncle's arm about me, my hand again in his, and his head bent down to catch my answer, Guy swung himself gaily into the room.

A glance seemed to explain all, and in an instant his face assumed that expression of pale wrath so much more terrible to witness than the fiercest outbreak; his eye grew fiery, his voice bitterly sarcastic, as he said, "Ah, I see; the play goes on, but the actors change parts. I congratulate you, sir, on your success, and Sybil on her choice. Henceforth I am *de trop,* but before I go allow me to offer my wedding gift. You have taken the bride, let me supply the ring."

He threw a jewel box upon the table, adding, in that unnaturally calm tone that made my heart stand still:

"A little candor would have spared me much pain, Sybil; yet I hope you will enjoy your bonds as heartily as I shall my escape from them. A little confidence would have made me your ally, not your rival, Father. I have not your address; therefore I lose, you win. Let it be so. I had rather be the vagabond this makes me than sell myself, that you may gamble away that girl's fortune as you have your own and mine. You need not ask me to the wedding, I will not come. Oh, Sybil, I so loved, so trusted you!"

And with that broken exclamation he was gone.

The stormy scene had passed so rapidly, been so strange and sudden, Guy's anger so scornful and abrupt, I could not understand it, and felt like a puppet in the grasp of some power I could not resist; but as my lover left the room I broke out of the bewilderment that held me, imploring him to stay and hear me.

It was too late, he was gone, and Sultan's tramp was already tearing down the avenue. I listened till the sound died, then my hot temper rose past control, and womanlike asserted itself in vehement and voluble speech. I was angry with my uncle, my cousin, and myself, and for several minutes poured forth a torrent of explanations, reproaches, and regrets, such as only a passionate girl could utter.

My uncle stood where I had left him when I flew to the door with my vain cry; he now looked baffled, yet sternly resolved, and as I paused for breath his only answer was "Sybil, you ask me to bring back that headstrong boy; I cannot; he will never come. This marriage was distasteful to him, yet he submitted for my sake, because I have been unfortunate, and we are poor. Let him go, forget the past, and be to me what I desire, for I loved your father and will be a faithful guardian to his daughter all my life. Child, it must be—come, I implore, I command you."

He beckoned imperiously as if to awe me, and held up the glittering betrothal ring as if to tempt me. The tone, the act, the look put me quite beside myself. I did go to him, did take the ring, but said as resolutely as himself, "Guy rejects me, and I have done with love. Uncle, you would have deceived me, used me as a means to your own selfish ends. I will accept neither yourself nor your gifts, for now I despise both you and your commands." And as the most energetic emphasis I could give to my defiance, I flung the ring, case and all, across the room; it struck the great mirror, shivered it just in the middle, and sent several loosened fragments crashing to the floor.

"Great heavens! Is the young lady mad?" exclaimed a voice behind us. Both turned and saw Dr. Karnac, a stealthy, sallow-faced Spaniard, for whom I had an invincible aversion. He was my uncle's physician, had been visiting a sick servant in the upper regions, and my adverse fate sent him to the door just at that moment with that unfortunate exclamation on his lips.

"What do you say?"

My uncle wheeled about and eyed the newcomer intently as he repeated his words. I have no doubt I looked like one demented, for I was desperately angry, pale and trembling with excitement, and as they fronted me with a curious expression of alarm on their faces, a sudden sense of the absurdity of the spectacle came over me; I laughed hysterically a moment, then broke into a passion of regretful tears, remembering that Guy was gone. As I sobbed behind my hands, I knew the gentlemen were whispering together and of me, but I never heeded them, for as I wept myself calmer a comforting thought occurred to me. Guy could not have gone far, for Sultan had been out all day, and though reckless of himself he was not of his horse, which he loved like a human being; therefore he was doubtless at the house of a humble friend nearby. If I could slip away unseen, I might undo my miserable work, or at least see him again before he went away into the world, perhaps never to return. This hope gave me courage for anything, and dashing away my tears, I took a covert survey. Dr. Karnac and my uncle still stood before the fire, deep in their low-toned conversation; their backs were toward me; and hushing the rustle of my dress, I stole away with noiseless steps into the hall, seized Guy's plaid, and, opening the great door unseen, darted down the avenue.

Not far, however; the wind buffeted me to and fro, the rain blinded me, the mud clogged my feet and soon robbed me of a slipper; groping for it in despair, I saw a light flash into the outer darkness; heard voices calling, and soon the swift tramp of steps behind me. Feeling like a hunted doe, I ran on, but before I had gained a dozen yards my shoeless foot struck a sharp stone, and I fell half stunned upon the wet grass of the wayside bank, Dr. Karnac reached me first, took me up as if I were a naughty child, and carried me back through a group of staring servants to the drawing room, my uncle following with breathless entreaties that I would be calm, and a most uncharacteristic display of bustle.

I was horribly ashamed; my head ached with the shock of the fall, my foot bled, my heart fluttered, and when the doctor put me down the crisis came, for as my uncle bent over me with the strange question "My poor girl, do you know me?" an irresistible impulse impelled me to push him from me, crying passionately, "Yes, I know and hate you; let me go! Let me go, or it will be too late!" Then, quite spent with the varying emotions of the last hour, for the first time in my life I swooned away.

Coming to myself, I found I was in my own room, with my uncle, the doctor, Janet, and Mrs. Best, the housekeeper, gathered about me, the latter saying, as she bathed my temples, "She's a sad sight, poor thing, so young, so bonny, and so unfortunate. Did you ever see her so before, Janet?"

"Bless you, no, ma'am; there was no signs of such a tantrum when I dressed her for dinner."

"What do they mean? Did they never see anyone angry before?" I dimly wondered, and presently, through the fast disappearing stupor that had held me, Dr. Karnac's deep voice came distinctly, saying, "If it continues, you are perfectly justified in doing so."

"Doing what?" I demanded sharply, for the sound both roused and irritated me, I disliked the man so intensely.

"Nothing, my dear, nothing," purred Mrs. Best, supporting me as I sat up, feeling weak and dazed, yet resolved to know what was going on. I was "a sad sight" indeed: my drenched hair hung about my shoulders, my dress was streaked with mud, one shoeless foot was red with blood, the other splashed and stained, and a white, wild-eyed face completed the ruinous image the opposite mirror showed me. Everything looked blurred and strange, and a feverish unrest possessed me, for I was not one to subside easily after such a mental storm. Leaning on my arm, I scanned the room and its occupants with all the composure I could collect. The two women eyed me curiously yet pitifully; Dr. Karnac stood glancing at me furtively as he listened to my uncle, who spoke rapidly in Spanish as he showed the little scar upon his hand.

That sight did more to restore me than the cordial just administered, and I rose erect, saying abruptly, "Please, everybody, go away; my head aches, and I want to be alone."

"Let Janet stay and help you, dear; you are not fit," began Mrs. Best; but I peremptorily stopped her.

"No, go yourself, and take her with you; I'm tired of so much stir about such foolish things as a broken glass and a girl in a pet."

"You will be good enough to take this quieting draft before I go, Miss Sybil."

"I shall do nothing of the sort, for I need only solitude and sleep to be perfectly well," and I emptied the glass the doctor offered into the fire.

He shrugged his shoulders with a disagreeable smile, and quietly began to prepare another draft, saying, "You are mistaken, my dear young lady; you need much care, and should obey, that your uncle may be spared further apprehension and anxiety."

My patience gave out at this assumption of authority; and I determined to carry matters with a high hand, for they all stood watching me in a way which seemed the height of impertinent curiosity.

"He is not my uncle! Never has been, and deserves neither respect nor obedience from me! I am the best judge of my own health, and you are not bettering it by contradiction and unnecessary fuss. This is my house, and you will oblige me by leaving it, Dr. Karnac; this is my room, and I insist on being left in peace immediately."

I pointed to the door as I spoke; the women hurried out with scared faces; the doctor bowed and followed, but paused on the threshold, while my uncle approached me, asking in a tone inaudible to those still hovering round the door, "Do you still persist in your refusal, Sybil?"

"How dare you ask me that again? I tell you I had rather die than marry you!"

"The Lord be merciful to us! Just hear how she's going on now about marrying Master. Ain't it awful, Jane?" ejaculated Mrs. Best, bobbing her head in for a last look.

"Hold your tongue, you impertinent creature!" I called out; and the fat old soul bundled away in such comical haste I laughed, in spite of languor and vexation.

My uncle left me, and I heard him say as he passed the doctor, "You see how it is."

"Nothing uncommon; but that virulence is a bad symptom," answered the Spaniard, and closing the door locked it, having dexterously removed the key from within.

I had never been subjected to restraint of any kind; it made me reckless at once, for this last indignity was not to be endured.

"Open this instantly!" I commanded, shaking the door. No one answered, and after a few ineffectual attempts to break the lock I left it, threw up the window and looked out; the ground was too far off for a leap, but the trellis where summer vines had clung was strong and high, a step would place me on it, a moment's agility bring me to the terrace below. I was now in just the state to attempt any rash exploit, for the cordial had both strengthened and excited me; my foot was bandaged, my clothes still wet; I could suffer no new damage, and have my own way at small cost. Out I crept, climbed safely down, and made my way to the lodge as I had at first intended. But Guy was not there; and returning, I boldly went in at the great door, straight to the room where my uncle and the doctor were still talking.

"I wish the key of my room" was my brief command.

Both started as if I had been a ghost, and my uncle exclaimed, "You here! How in heaven's name came you out?"

"By the window. I am no child to be confined for a fit of anger. I will not submit to it; tomorrow I shall go to Madame; till then I will be mistress in my own house. Give me the key, sir."

"Shall I?" asked the doctor of my uncle, who nodded with a whispered "Yes, yes; don't excite her again."

It was restored, and without another word I went loftily up to my room, locked myself in, and spent a restless, miserable night. When morning came, I breakfasted abovestairs, and then busied myself packing trunks, burning papers, and collecting every trifle Guy had ever given me. No one annoyed me, and I saw only Janet, who had evidently received some order that kept her silent and respectful, though her face still betrayed the same curiosity and pitiful interest as the night before. Lunch was brought up, but I could not eat, and began to feel that the exposure, the fall, and excitement of the evening had left me weak and nervous, so I gave up the idea of going to Madame till the morrow; and as the afternoon waned, tried to sleep, yet could not, for I had sent a note to several of Guy's haunts, imploring him to see me; but my messenger brought word that he was not to be found, and my heart was too heavy to rest.

When summoned to dinner, I still refused to go down; for I heard Dr. Karnac's voice, and would not meet him, so I sent word that I wished the carriage early the following morning, and to be left alone till then. In a few minutes, back came Janet, with a glass of wine set forth on a silver salver, and a card with these words: "Forgive, forget, for your father's sake, and drink with me, 'Oblivion to the past.' "

It touched and softened me. I knew my uncle's pride, and saw in this an entire relinquishment of the hopes I had so thoughtlessly fostered in his mind. I was passionate, but not vindictive. He had been kind, I very willful. His mistake was natural, my resentment ungenerous. Though my resolution to go remained unchanged, I was sorry for my part in the affair, and remembering that through me his son was lost to him, I accepted his apology, drank his toast, and sent him back a dutiful "Good night."

I was unused to wine. The draft I had taken was powerful with age, and, though warm and racy to the palate, proved too potent for me. Still sitting before my fire, I slowly fell into a restless drowse, haunted by a dim dream that I was seeking Guy in a ship, whose motion gradually lulled me into perfect unconsciousness.

Waking at length, I was surprised to find myself in bed, with a shimmer of daylight peeping through the curtains. Recollecting that I was to leave early, I sprang up, took one step, and remained transfixed with dismay, for the room was not my own! Utterly unfamiliar was every object on which my eyes fell. The place was small, plainly furnished, and close, as if long unused. My trunks stood against the wall, my clothes lay on a chair, and on the bed I had left trailed a fur-lined cloak I had often seen on my uncle's shoulders. A moment I stared about me bewildered, then hurried to the window. It was grated!

A lawn, sere and sodden, lay without, and a line of somber firs hid the landscape beyond the high wall which encompassed the dreary plot. More and more alarmed, I flew to the door and found it locked. No bell was visible, no sound audible, no human presence near me, and an ominous foreboding thrilled cold through nerves and blood, as, for the first time, I felt the paralyzing touch of fear. Not long, however. My native courage soon returned, indignation took the place of terror, and excitement gave me strength. My temples throbbed with a dull pain, my eyes were heavy, my limbs weighed down by an unwonted lassitude, and my memory seemed strangely confused; but one thing was clear to me: I must see somebody, ask questions, demand explanations, and get away to Madame without delay.

With trembling hands I dressed, stopping suddenly with a cry; for lifting my hands to my head, I discovered that my hair, my beautiful, abundant hair, was gone! There was no mirror in the room, but I could feel that it had been shorn away close about face and neck. This outrage was more than I could bear, and the first tears I shed fell for my lost charm. It was weak, perhaps, but I felt better for it, clearer in mind and readier to confront whatever lay before me. I knocked and called. Then, losing patience, shook and screamed; but no one came or answered me; and wearied out at last, I sat down and cried again in impotent despair.

An hour passed, then a step approached, the key turned, and a hard-faced woman entered with a tray in her hand. I had resolved to be patient, if possible, and controlled myself to ask quietly, though my eyes kindled, and my voice trembled with resentment, "Where am I, and why am I here against my will?"

"This is your breakfast, miss; you must be sadly hungry" was the only reply I got.

"I will never eat till you tell me what I ask."

"Will you be quiet, and mind me if I do, miss?"

"You have no right to exact obedience from me, but I'll try."

"That's right. Now all I know is that you are twenty miles from the Moors, and came because you are ill. Do you like sugar in your coffee?"

"When did I come? I don't remember it."

"Early this morning; you don't remember because you were put to sleep before being fetched, to save trouble."

"Ah, that wine! Who brought me here?"

"Dr. Karnac, miss."

"Alone?"

"Yes, miss; you were easier to manage asleep than awake, he said."

I shook with anger, yet still restrained myself, hoping to fathom the mystery of this nocturnal journey.

"What is your name, please?" I meekly asked.

"You can call me Hannah."

"Well, Hannah, there is a strange mistake somewhere. I am not ill—you see I am not—and I wish to go away at once to the friend I was to meet today. Get me a carriage and have my baggage taken out."

"It can't be done, miss. We are a mile from town, and have no carriages here; besides, you couldn't go if I had a dozen. I have my orders, and shall obey 'em."

"But Dr. Karnac has no right to bring or keep me here."

"Your uncle sent you. The doctor has the care of you, and that is all I know about it. Now I have kept my promise, do you keep yours, miss, and eat your breakfast, else I can't trust you again."

"But what is the matter with me? How can I be ill and not know or feel it?" I demanded, more and more bewildered.

"You look it, and that's enough for them as is wise in such matters. You'd have had a fever, if it hadn't been seen to in time."

"Who cut my hair off?"

"I did; the doctor ordered it."

"How dared he? I hate that man, and never will obey him."

"Hush, miss, don't clench your hands and look in that way, for I shall have to report everything you say and do to him, and it won't be pleasant to tell that sort of thing."

The woman was civil, but grim and cool. Her eye was unsympathetic, her manner businesslike, her tone such as one uses to a refractory child, half soothing, half commanding. I conceived a dislike to her at once, and resolved to escape at all hazards, for my uncle's inexplicable movements filled me with alarm. Hannah had left my door open, a quick glance showed me another door also ajar at the end of a wide hall, a glimpse of green, and a gate. My plan was desperately simple, and I executed it without delay. Affecting to eat, I presently asked the woman for my handkerchief from the bed. She crossed the room to get it. I darted out, down the passage, along the walk, and tugged vigorously at the great bolt of the gate, but it was also locked. In despair I flew into the garden, but a high wall enclosed it on every side; and as I ran round and round, vainly looking for some outlet, I saw Hannah, accompanied by a man as gray and grim as herself, coming leisurely toward me, with no appearance of excitement or displeasure. Back I would not go; and inspired with a sudden hope, swung myself into one of the firs that grew close against the wall. The branches snapped under me, the slender tree swayed perilously, but up I struggled, till the wide coping of the wall was gained. There I paused and looked back. The woman was hurrying through the gate to intercept my descent on the other side, and close behind me the man, sternly calling me to stop. I looked down; a stony ditch was below, but I would rather risk my life than tamely lose my liberty, and with a flying leap tried to reach the bank; failed, fell heavily among the stones, felt an awful crash, and then came an utter blank.

For many weeks I lay burning in a fever, fitfully conscious of Dr. Karnac and the woman's presence; once I fancied I saw my uncle, but was never sure, and rose at last a shadow of my former self, feeling pitifully broken, both mentally and physically. I was in a better room now, wintry winds howled without, but a generous fire glowed behind the high closed fender, and books lay on my table.

I saw no one but Hannah, yet could wring no intelligence from her beyond what she had already told, and no sign of interest reached me from the outer world. I seemed utterly deserted and forlorn, my spirit was crushed, my strength gone, my freedom lost, and for a time I succumbed to despair, letting one day follow another without energy or hope. It is hard to live with no object to give zest to life, especially for those still blessed with youth, and even in my prison house I soon found one quite in keeping with the mystery that surrounded me.

As I sat reading by day or lay awake at night, I became aware that the room above my own was occupied by some inmate whom I never saw. A peculiar person it seemed to be; for I heard steps going to and fro, hour after hour, in a tireless march that wore upon my nerves, as many a harsher sound would not have done. I could neither tease nor surprise Hannah into any explanation of the thing, and day after day I listened to it, till I longed to cover up my ears and implore the unknown walker to stop, for heaven's sake. Other sounds I heard and fretted over: a low monotonous murmur, as of someone singing a lullaby; a fitful tapping, like a cradle rocked on a carpetless floor; and at rare intervals cries of suffering, sharp but brief, as if forcibly suppressed. These sounds, combined with the solitude, the confinement, and the books I read, a collection of ghostly tales and weird fancies, soon wrought my nerves to a state of terrible irritability, and wore upon my health so visibly that I was allowed at last to leave my room.

The house was so well guarded that I soon relinquished all hope of escape, and listlessly amused myself by roaming through the unfurnished rooms and echoing halls, seldom venturing into Hannah's domain; for there her husband sat, surrounded by chemical apparatus, poring over crucibles and retorts. He never spoke to me, and I dreaded the glance of his cold eye, for it looked unsoftened by a ray of pity at the little figure that sometimes paused a moment on his threshold, wan and wasted as the ghost of departed hope.

The chief interest of these dreary walks centered in the door of the room above my own, for a great hound lay before it, eyeing me savagely as he rejected all advances, and uttering his deep bay if I approached too near. To me this room possessed an irresistible fascination. I could not keep away from it by day, I dreamed of it by night, it haunted me continually, and soon became a sort of monomania, which I condemned, yet could not control, till at length I found myself pacing to and fro as those invisible feet paced overhead. Hannah came and stopped me, and a few hours later Dr. Karnac appeared. I was so changed that I feared him with a deadly fear. He seemed to enjoy it; for in the pride of youth and beauty I had shown him contempt and defiance at my uncle's, and he took an ungenerous satisfaction in annoying me by a display of power. He never answered my questions or entreaties, regarded me as being without sense or will, insisted on my trying various mixtures and experiments in diet, gave me strange books to read, and weekly received Hannah's report of all that passed. That day he came, looked at me, said, "Let her walk," and went away, smiling that hateful smile of his.

Soon after this I took to walking in my sleep, and more than once woke to find myself roving lampless through that haunted house in the dead of night. I concealed these unconscious wanderings for a time, but an ominous event broke them up at last and betrayed them to Hannah.

I had followed the steps one day for several hours, walking below as they walked above; had peopled that mysterious room with every mournful shape my disordered fancy could conjure up; had woven tragical romances about it, and brooded over the one subject of interest my unnatural life possessed with the intensity of a mind upon which its uncanny influence was telling with perilous rapidity. At midnight I woke to find myself standing in a streak of moonlight, opposite the door whose threshold I had never crossed. The April night was warm, a single pane of glass high up in that closed door was drawn aside, as if for air; and as I stood dreamily collecting my sleep-drunken senses, I saw a ghostly hand emerge and beckon, as if to me. It startled me broad awake, with a faint exclamation and a shudder from head to foot. A cloud swept over the moon, and when it passed the hand was gone, but shrill through the keyhole came a whisper that chilled me to the marrow of my bones, so terribly distinct and imploring was it.

"Find it! For God's sake find it before it is too late!"

The hound sprang up with an angry growl; I heard Hannah leave her bed nearby; and with an inspiration strange as the moment, I paced slowly on with open eyes and lips apart, as I had seen *Amina* in the happy days when kind old Madame took me to the theater, whose mimic horrors I had never thought to equal with such veritable ones. Hannah appeared at her door with a light, but on I went in a trance of fear; for I was only kept from dropping in a swoon by the blind longing to fly from that spectral voice and hand. Past Hannah I went, she following; and as I slowly laid myself in bed, I heard her say to her husband, who just then came up, "Sleepwalking, John; it's getting worse and worse, as the doctor foretold; she'll settle down like the other presently, but she must be locked up at night, else the dog will do her a mischief."

The man yawned and grumbled; then they went, leaving me to spend hours of unspeakable suffering, which aged me more than years. What was I to find? Where was I to look? And when would it be too late? These questions tormented me; for I could find no answers to them, divine no meaning, see no course to pursue. Why was I here? What motive induced my uncle to commit such an act? And when should I be liberated? were equally unanswerable, equally tormenting, and they haunted me like ghosts. I had no power to exorcise or forget. After that I walked no more because I slept no more; sleep seemed scared away, and waking dreams harassed me with their terrors. Night after night I paced my room in utter darkness—for I was allowed no lamp—night after night I wept bitter tears wrung from me by anguish, for which I had no name; and night after night the steps kept time to mine, and the faint lullaby came down to me as if to soothe and comfort my distress. I felt that my health was going, my mind growing confused and weak; my thoughts wandered vaguely, memory began to fail, and idiocy or madness seemed my inevitable fate; but through it all my heart clung to Guy, yearning for him with a hunger that would not be appeased.

At rare intervals I was allowed to walk in the neglected garden, where no flowers bloomed, no birds sang, no companion came to me but surly John, who followed with his book or pipe, stopping when I stopped, walking when I walked, keeping a vigilant eye upon me, yet seldom speaking except to decline answering my questions. These walks did me no good, for the air was damp and heavy with vapors from the marsh; for the house stood near a half-dried lake, and hills shut it in on every side. No fresh winds from upland moor or distant ocean ever blew across the narrow valley; no human creature visited the place, and nothing but a vague hope that my birthday might bring some change, some help, sustained me. It did bring help, but of such an unexpected sort that its effects remained through all my afterlife. My birthday came, and with it my uncle. I was in my room, walking restlessly—for the habit was a confirmed one now—when the door opened, and Hannah, Dr. Karnac, my uncle, and a gentleman whom I knew to be his lawyer entered, and surveyed me as if I were a spectacle. I saw my uncle start and turn pale; I had never seen myself since I came, but if I had not suspected that I was a melancholy wreck of my former self, I should have known it then, such sudden pain and pity softened his ruthless countenance for a single instant. Dr. Karnac's eye had a magnetic power over me; I had always felt it, but in my present feeble state I dreaded, yet submitted to it with a helpless fear that should have touched his heart—it was on me then, I could not resist it, and paused fixed and fascinated by that repellent yet potent glance.

Hannah pointed to the carpet worn to shreds by my weary march, to the walls which I had covered with weird, grotesque, or tragic figures to while away the heavy hours, lastly to myself, mute, motionless, and scared, saying, as if in confirmation of some previous assertion, "You see, gentlemen, she is, as I said, quiet, but quite hopeless."

I thought she was interceding for me; and breaking from the bewilderment and fear that held me, I stretched my hands to them, crying with an imploring cry, "Yes, I *am* quiet! I *am* hopeless! Oh, have pity on me before this dreadful life kills me or drives me mad!"

Dr. Karnac came to me at once with a black frown, which I alone could see; I evaded him, and clung to Hannah, still crying frantically—for this seemed my last hope—"Uncle, let me go! I will give you all I have, will never ask for Guy, will be obedient and meek if I may only go to Madame and never hear the feet again, or see the sights that terrify me in this dreadful room. Take me out! For God's sake take me out!"

My uncle did not answer me, but covered up his face with a despairing gesture, and hurried from the room; the lawyer followed, muttering pitifully, "Poor thing! Poor thing!" and Dr. Karnac laughed the first laugh I had ever heard him utter as he wrenched Hannah from my grasp and locked me in alone. My one hope died then, and I resolved to kill myself rather than endure this life another month; for now it grew clear to me that they believed me mad, and death of the body was far more preferable than that of the mind. I think I *was* a little mad just then, but remember well the sense of peace that came to me as I tore strips from my clothing, braided them into a cord, hid it beneath my mattress, and serenely waited for the night. Sitting in the last twilight I thought to see in this unhappy world, I recollected that I had not heard the feet all day, and fell to pondering over the unusual omission. But if the steps had been silent in that room, voices had not, for I heard a continuous murmur at one time: the tones of one voice were abrupt and broken, the other low, yet resonant, and that, I felt assured, belonged to my uncle. Who was he speaking to? What were they saying? Should I ever know? And even then, with death before me, the intense desire to possess the secret filled me with its old unrest.

Night came at last; I heard the clock strike one, and listening to discover if John still lingered up, I heard through the deep hush a soft grating in the room above, a stealthy sound that would have escaped ears less preternaturally alert than mine. Like a flash came the thought, "Someone is filing bars or picking locks: will the unknown remember me and let me share her flight?" The fatal noose hung ready, but I no longer cared to use it, for hope had come to nerve me with the strength and courage I had lost. Breathlessly I listened; the sound went on, stopped; a dead silence reigned; then something brushed against my door, and with a suddenness that made me tingle from head to foot like an electric shock, through the keyhole came again that whisper, urgent, imploring, and mysterious, "Find it! For God's sake find it before it is too late!" Then fainter, as if breath failed, came the broken words, "The dog—a lock of hair—there is yet time."

Eagerness rendered me forgetful of the secrecy I should preserve, and I cried aloud, "What shall I find? Where shall I look?" My voice, sharpened by fear, rang shrilly through the house; Hannah's quick tread rushed down the hall; something fell; then loud and long rose a cry that made my heart stand still, so helpless, so hopeless was its wild lament. I had betrayed and I could not save or comfort the kind soul who had lost liberty through me. I was frantic to get out, and beat upon my door in a paroxysm of impatience, but no one came; and all night long those awful cries went on above, cries of mortal anguish, as if soul and body were being torn asunder. Till dawn I listened, pent in that room which now possessed an added terror; till dawn I called, wept, and prayed, with mingled pity, fear, and penitence; and till dawn the agony of that unknown sufferer continued unabated. I heard John hurry to and fro, heard Hannah issue orders with an accent of human sympathy in her hard voice; heard Dr. Karnac pass and repass my door; and all the sounds of confusion and alarm in that once quiet house. With daylight all was still, a stillness more terrible than the stir; for it fell so suddenly, remained so utterly unbroken, that there seemed no explanation of it but the dread word death.

At noon Hannah, a shade paler but grim as ever, brought me some food, saying she forgot my breakfast, and when I refused to eat, yet asked no questions, she bade me go into the garden and not fret myself over last night's flurry. I went, and passing down the corridor, glanced furtively at the door I never saw without a thrill; but I experienced a new sensation then, for the hound was gone, the door was open, and with an impulse past control, I crept in and looked about me. It was a room like mine, the carpet worn like mine, the windows barred like mine; there the resemblance ended, for an empty cradle stood beside the bed, and on that bed, below a sweeping cover, stark and still a lifeless body lay. I was inured to fear now, and an unwholesome craving for new terrors seemed to have grown by what it fed on: an irresistible desire led me close, nerved me to lift the cover and look below—a single glance—then with a cry as panic-stricken as that which rent the silence of the night, I fled away, for the face I saw was a pale image of my own. Sharpened by suffering, pallid with death, the features were familiar as those I used to see; the hair, beautiful and blond as mine had been, streamed long over the pulseless breast, and on the hand, still clenched in that last struggle, shone the likeness of a ring I wore, a ring bequeathed me by my father. An awesome fancy that it was myself assailed me; I had plotted death, and with the waywardness of a shattered mind, I recalled legends of spirits returning to behold the bodies they had left.

Glad now to seek the garden, I hurried down, but on the threshold of the great hall door was arrested by the sharp crack of a pistol; and as a little cloud of smoke dispersed, I saw John drop the weapon and approach the hound, who lay writhing on the bloody grass. Moved by compassion for the faithful brute whose long vigilance was so cruelly repaid, I went to him, and kneeling there, caressed the great head that never yielded to my touch before. John assumed his watch at once, and leaning against a tree, cleaned the pistol, content that I should amuse myself with the dying creature, who looked into my face with eyes of almost human pathos and reproach. The brass collar seemed to choke him as he gasped for breath, and leaning nearer to undo it, I saw, half hidden in his own black hair, a golden lock wound tightly round the collar, and so near its color as to be unobservable, except upon a close inspection. No accident could have placed it there; no head but mine in that house wore hair of that sunny hue—yes, one other, and my heart gave a sudden leap as I remembered the shining locks just seen on that still bosom.

"Find it—the dog—the lock of hair," rang in my ears, and swift as light came the conviction that the unknown help was found at last. The little band was woven close. I had no knife, delay was fatal. I bent my head as if lamenting over the poor beast and bit the knot apart, drew out a folded paper, hid it in my hand, and rising, strolled leisurely back to my own room, saying I did not care to walk till it was warmer. With eager eyes I examined my strange treasure trove. It consisted of two strips of thinnest paper, without address or signature, one almost illegible, worn at the edges and stained with the green rust of the collar; the other fresher, yet more feebly written, both abrupt and disjointed, but terribly significant to me. This was the first:

> *I have never seen you, never heard your name, yet I know that you are young, that you are suffering, and I try to help you in my poor way. I think you are not crazed yet, as I often am; for your voice is sane, your plaintive singing not like mine, your walking only caught from me, I hope. I sing to lull the baby whom I never saw; I walk to lessen the long journey that will bring me to the husband I have lost—stop! I*

must not think of those things or I shall forget. If you are not already mad, you will be; I suspect you were sent here to be made so; for the air is poison, the solitude is fatal, and Karnac remorseless in his mania for prying into the mysteries of human minds. What devil sent you I may never know, but I long to warn you. I can devise no way but this; the dog comes into my room sometimes, you sometimes pause at my door and talk to him; you may find the paper I shall hide about his collar. Read, destroy, but obey it. I implore you to leave this house before it is too late.

The other paper was as follows:

I have watched you, tried to tell you where to look, for you have not found my warning yet, though I often tie it there and hope. You fear the dog, perhaps, and my plot fails; yet I know by your altered step and voice that you are fast reaching my unhappy state; for I am fitfully mad, and shall be till I die. Today I have seen a familiar face; it seems to have calmed and strengthened me, and though he would not help you, I shall make one desperate attempt. I may not find you, so leave my warning to the hound, yet hope to breathe a word into your sleepless ear that shall send you back into the world the happy thing you should be. Child! Woman! Whatever you are, leave this accursed house while you have power to do it.

That was all. I did not destroy the papers, but I obeyed them, and for a week watched and waited till the propitious instant came. I saw my uncle, the doctor, and two others follow the poor body to its grave beside the lake, saw all depart but Dr. Karnac, and felt redoubled hatred and contempt for the men who could repay my girlish slights with such a horrible revenge. On the seventh day, as I went down for my daily walk, I saw John and Dr. Karnac so deep in some uncanny experiment that I passed out unguarded. Hoping to profit by this unexpected chance, I sprang down the steps, but the next moment dropped half stunned upon the grass; for behind me rose a crash, a shriek, a sudden blaze that flashed up and spread, sending a noisome vapor rolling out with clouds of smoke and flame.

Aghast, I was just gathering myself up when Hannah fled out of the house, dragging her husband senseless and bleeding, while her own face was ashy with affright. She dropped her burden beside me, saying, with white lips and and a vain look for help where help was not, "Something they were at has burst, killed the doctor, and fired the house! Watch John till I get help, and leave him at your peril." Then flinging open the gate she sped away.

"Now is my time," I thought, and only waiting till she vanished, I boldly followed her example, running rapidly along the road in an opposite direction, careless of bonnetless head and trembling limbs, intent only upon leaving that prison house far behind me. For several hours, I hurried along that solitary road; the spring sun shone, birds sang in the blooming hedges, green nooks invited me to pause and rest; but I heeded none of them, steadily continuing my flight, till spent and footsore I was forced to stop a moment by a wayside spring. As I stooped to drink, I saw my face for the first time in many months, and started to see how like that dead one it had grown, in all but the eternal peace which made that beautiful in spite of suffering and age. Standing thus and wondering if Guy would know me, should we ever meet, the sound of wheels disturbed me. Believing them to be coming from the place I had left, I ran desperately down the hill, turned a sharp corner, and before I could check myself passed a carriage slowly ascending. A face sprang to the window, a voice cried "Stop!" but on I flew, hoping the traveler would let me go unpursued. Not so, however; soon I heard fleet steps following, gaining rapidly, then a hand seized me, a voice rang in my ears, and with a vain struggle I lay panting in my captor's hold, fearing to look up and meet a brutal glance. But the hand that had seized me tenderly drew me close, the voice that had alarmed cried joyfully, "Sybil, it is Guy: Lie still, poor child, you are safe at last."

Then I knew that my surest refuge was gained, and too weak for words, clung to him in an agony of happiness, which brought to his kind eyes the tears I could not shed.

The carriage returned; Guy took me in, and for a time cared only to soothe and sustain my worn soul and body with the cordial of his presence, as we rolled homeward through a blooming world, whose beauty I had never truly felt before. When the first tumult of emotion had subsided, I told the story of my captivity and my escape, ending with a passionate entreaty not to be returned to my uncle's keeping, for henceforth there could be neither affection nor respect between us.

"Fear nothing, Sybil; Madame is waiting for you at the Moors, and my father's unfaithful guardianship has ended with his life."

Then with averted face and broken voice Guy went on to tell his father's purposes, and what had caused this unexpected meeting. The facts were briefly these: The knowledge that my father had come between him and a princely fortune had always rankled in my uncle's heart, chilling the ambitious hopes he cherished even in his boyhood, and making life an eager search for pleasure in which to drown his vain regrets. This secret was suspected by my father, and the household league was formed as some atonement for the innocent offense. It seemed to soothe my uncle's resentful nature, and as years went on he lived freely, assured that ample means would be his through his son. Luxurious, self-indulgent, fond of all excitements, and reckless in their pursuit, he took no thought for the morrow till a few months before his return. A gay winter in Paris reduced him to those straits of which women know so little; creditors were oppressive, summer friends failed him, gambling debts harassed him, his son reproached him, and but one resource remained—Guy's speedy marriage with the half-forgotten heiress. The boy had been educated to regard this fate as a fixed fact, and submitted, believing the time to be far distant; but the sudden summons came, and he rebelled against it, preferring liberty to love. My uncle pacified the claimants by promises to be fulfilled at my expense, and hurried home to press on the marriage, which now seemed imperative. I was taken to my future home, approved by my uncle, beloved by my cousin, and, but for my own folly, might have been a happy wife on that May morning when I listened to the unveiling of the past. My mother had been melancholy mad since that unhappy rumor of my father's death; this affliction had been well concealed from me, lest the knowledge should prey upon my excitable nature and perhaps induce a like misfortune. I believed her dead, yet I had seen her, knew where her solitary grave was made, and still carried in my bosom the warning she had sent me, prompted by the unerring instinct of a mother's heart. In my father's will a clause was added just below the one confirming my betrothal, a clause decreeing that, if it should appear that I inherited my mother's malady, the fortune should revert to my cousin, with myself a mournful legacy, to be cherished by him whether his wife or not. This passage, and that relating to my freedom of choice, had been omitted in the copy shown me on the night when my seeming refusal of Guy had induced his father to believe that I loved him, to make a last attempt to keep the prize by offering himself, and, when that failed, to harbor a design that changed my little comedy into the tragical experience I have told.

Dr. Karnac's exclamation had caused the recollection of that clause respecting my insanity to flash into my uncle's mind—a mind as quick to conceive as fearless to execute. I unconsciously abetted the stratagem, and Dr. Karnac was an unscrupulous ally, for love of gain was as strong as love of science; both were amply gratified, and I, poor victim, was given up to be experimented upon, till by subtle means I was driven to the insanity which would give my uncle full control of my fortune and my fate. How the black plot prospered has been told; but retribution speedily overtook them both, for Dr. Karnac paid his penalty by the sudden death that left his ashes among the blackened ruins of that house of horrors, and my uncle had preceded him. For before the change of heirs could be effected my mother died, and the hours spent in that unhealthful spot insinuated the subtle poison of the marsh into his blood; years of pleasure left little vigor to withstand the fever, and a week of suffering ended a life of generous impulses perverted, fine endowments wasted, and opportunities forever lost. When death drew near, he sent for Guy (who, through the hard discipline of poverty and honest labor, was becoming a manlier man), confessed all, and implored him to save me before it was too late. He did, and when all was told, when each saw the other by the light of this strange and sad experience—Guy poor again, I free, the old bond still existing, the barrier of misunderstanding gone—it was easy to see our way, easy to submit, to forgive, forget, and begin anew the life these clouds had darkened for a time.

Home received me, kind Madame welcomed me, Guy married me, and I was happy; but over all these years, serenely prosperous, still hangs for me the shadow of the past, still rises that dead image of my mother, still echoes that spectral whisper in the dark.

Thrice Tempted

SHE SAT ALONE in the dull, old-fashioned room, a slight, dark girl, with no beauty but much strength of character in her face, which, just then, wore an unwonted expression of happiness, for she was reading her first love-letter.

So absorbed was she that the entrance of another person was unobserved—a tall, brilliant girl, dressed with a taste and skill that enhanced her beauty, and bearing about her the indefinable air of one which instantly marks those who have been luxuriously nurtured from birth.

With noiseless steps and an arch smile on her lips she glided to the reader's side and glanced over her shoulder.

An expression of surprise rose to her face as she read the first words aloud:

"My own little Ruth!"

"Why, child, who writes to you in that style?" she added, hastily.

With a slight start Ruth turned the leaf, and at the bottom of the closely-written page pointed to a name, smiling a sudden smile, full of tender pride and happiness, as the other read the line:—"Yours always and entirely, Walter Strathsay."

"Upon my word, this is a revelation, and I must know all about it. Tell me the romance, Ruthie."

"I meant to have told you soon, but since you have forced my confidence, I need not wait. I am betrothed to Walter."

Slowly, quietly the girl spoke, and to many she would have seemed cold, but a nice observer would have seen her lips tremble, her eyes shine and in the low voice have detected an undertone of strong emotion.

Laura eyed her keenly, and laughed, with a touch of scorn in her laughter, as she answered:

"No need to tell me that, child; I want to know when and how it came about. You've never dropped a hint of it in your letters, and three months ago you solemnly assured me you should never marry."

"I thought I never should, but Walter came, and I changed my mind. I've nothing to tell except that his father was a friend of my father's and grandmamma asked him here when she heard of his return from the Crimea."

"He came, saw and conquered. It strikes me as very droll; but I wish you much joy, my dear."

"Why droll, Laura?"

"One never fancies you with a lover; you are so cool and quiet, so proud, so odd and unlike most girls."

"So plain and unattractive you mean," and Ruth's tone was sharp with pain, though she smiled as she finished the sentence.

"Well, if you don't mind, I agree to the addition. What sort of a man is this lover of yours? Show me his picture; I know you have one, for I never saw that charming chain on your neck before," and Laura put forth her hand to examine it.

"Guess before you look," cried Ruth, guarding her treasure, and speaking with unusual vivacity.

Lounging gracefully on the couch beside her, Laura answered with a sarcastic smile:

"I think he is much older than you, forty, perhaps; a rough, bronzed, gray-headed soldier, who has come home an invalid, and wants a kind, quiet little nurse to take care of him in his old age. He has money enough to be comfortable, and finding you alone, took pity on you, and when the old lady dies you will take her place. I am right, I fancy, by the odd look you wear. Now, let me see."

Drawing out a golden medallion, Ruth touched the spring, and in a pearl-set oval showed the portrait of a young and strikingly handsome man.

Laura uttered an exclamation, and then sat looking at it in silent admiration, while Ruth watched her with eyes full of triumph, and there was a touch of malice in her tone, as she asked:

"Does my lover suit your description?"

"He is my ideal of a lover and a hero! Tell me more; tell me everything. His age, his fortune, his family and all the story," answered Laura still holding the picture, and still gazing intently at the painted face, so full of manly beauty.

"He is five and twenty, has just come into the possession of a fine fortune, is the last of the ancient Scotch family of Strathsay, has fought gallantly, received many honors; and, he loves me tenderly."

As the last words were spoken and Ruth put out her hand to reclaim the likeness of her lover something in her voice made Laura look up and exclaim, in real astonishment:

"Bless the girl! how the 'grand passion' has improved her! Why, child, you look quite inspired with that color in your brown cheeks, and your black eyes all afire. It is a miracle; but such a man as this can work greater ones, I fancy."

Her eyes went back to the miniature, and a sigh rose to her lips, for among her many lovers she had not one like this.

Quickly repressing the involuntary betrayal of regret, she caught up the hand extended for the picture, and holding it fast, laughed mischievously as she examined the costly ring, turned inward for concealment.

"Diamonds, as I live! and such diamonds! seven beauties, and set in a style to win the heart of any woman! Upon my word, Ruthie, your Walter does things in a princely way. Why did you hide your splendor from me all day?"

"I didn't want to tell you just yet; neither did I want to take off my ring, because he put it on; so I hid it. But if it gives you pleasure to see pretty things, I can show you more, for Walter is indeed princely in his love."

With an air of pride, Ruth opened the old escritoir, and produced a quaint casket, steel-bound and clasped. Placing it on her lap she opened it, and let in the light upon a heap of glittering ornaments.

"They are the Strathsay jewels. Walter brought them all to me, and left them that I might decide upon new settings, for these are very antique, you see. But I like them as they are, for the stones are fine, and the curious setting pleases me."

"Ruth, they are magnificent! I never saw anything like them. Look how they become my arms. Happy girl to have won such a prize," and Laura sighed again as she clasped another bracelet on her round, white arm.

"I don't think this a prize, though I admire the jewels like a woman. Walter is better than a thousand diamond mines, and I care very little for these things, except as his gifts."

"So like you; but then they are not suited to your style, and that makes a difference, you know. I've always wanted to own real old lace and jewels, for money won't always buy them. I wish ours was an ancient family, and not a very new one. Papa left me a comfortable fortune, but neither rank nor position: and after all, money and beauty are not so valuable as an ancient name and heirlooms like these."

"Yes; I've nothing but my name, yet I find that has won me what richer, handsomer girls have failed to win; and I envy no one."

Ruth smiled down into her lover's face and for a moment forgot everything but the happy moment when a word made her lonely life supremely blest.

Laura, sitting with a strew of jewels about her, frowned and bit her lips as her eye went from the casket and the picture to the letter and the girl who had suddenly eclipsed her in everything but beauty. As the thought came, she suddenly glanced at Ruth's unconscious face, then at her own reflected in the mirror, and as she looked, the frown passed, for the strong contrast reassured her and she felt that one weapon still remained to her.

The letter lay open at their feet, and her keen eye ran down the page reading words that deepened her admiration, increased her envy, and confirmed the purpose already formed in her selfish heart.

"When are you to be married?" she asked abruptly.

"In autumn, if grandmamma is better."

"Where is Mr. Strathsay now?"

"My colonel is in London for a day or two, but will return soon and you can see him."

"Is the old lady pleased with the affair?"

"Delighted; she says she always wished it."

"Is he going to leave the army?"

"Yes; the fighting is over, and we want him at home."

"Shall you live in Scotland?"

"If I like, and I think I do. Walter leaves it all to me; but his old uncle wants him a little while before he dies, and it is right that we should do our best for the man who does so much for us."

"What will he do?"

"He leaves Walter his fortune and title, for he will soon be the last of the family. It makes no difference to me, but the people want another Sir Walter, so I consent for his sake."

"Lady Strathsay!" was all Laura said, as she flung the jewels into the casket, glanced again at the picture and restored the letter, with a curious expression. Her friend did not see it, and said softly:

"I like 'Little Ruth' better, and no title can be sweeter to me than what he bid me call him after the old Scottish fashion, 'my laddie.' "

"Very romantic. Long may it last. Marry soon, my dear, or the delightful glamour will pass away and the charm be broken for ever."

"How bitterly you speak, Laura! Has anything happened to grieve you since we parted? I've been so absorbed in my own happiness I forgot to ask how you had fared. Among so many lovers, have you not found one to reward?"

As she spoke with friendly warmth, Ruth put away her treasures and turned to the beauty who lay looking at her with an expression which troubled her, she knew not why.

"No, I've no tender secret to confide in return for yours, neither am I unhappy—why should I be? I'm only tired; so play to me and soothe my weariness like a good creature, as you are."

Ruth gladly complied, and filled the room with music, for this was her one gift, and she was justly proud of it. As she played, Laura lay looking dreamily out into the summer sunshine that shone warm over garden, grove and lawn. So lying, her eyes suddenly grew intent, her languid head rose erect, her cheek flushed, and her voice was unnaturally low, as she begged Ruth to play a stormy overture.

The girl's back was toward her, so her movements were unseen. Leaving the couch, she stole to the long window, and hidden in the folds of the curtain, peeped out to watch the approach of the man whom she had seen leave his horse at the foot of the lawn and come rapidly yet quietly toward the house, as if anxious to enter unseen. She knew him at a glance, for the picture had not lied, and the original was as comely as the miniature.

Noiselessly he reached the other open window and slipped in. Unconscious, Ruth played on, and pausing an instant to put down hat and gloves, her lover eyed her with a smile that made the watcher's heart beat with a strange mixture of emotions.

As the last chord died under her hand, Ruth said, without turning:

"Do you like it, Laura?"

"Not so well as the song, 'Oh, Welcome Hame, my Laddie,' " replied a man's voice, and with a cry that was full of gladder music than any air she played, Ruth ran to meet her lover.

"So soon—so soon! I thought it would be days before you came, Walter," she said, clinging to him in a quiet rapture of delight.

"I thought so too; but the time seemed so interminable I could not bear it, and came down almost as soon as my letter, for I cannot keep away from my little sweetheart a whole week."

"I'm glad, very glad, for if London is dull, what must this quiet place be? How long can you stay?"

"Two or three days, dear. Then I must run up again to get this tedious army business over. Now come and tell me everything you've done. Ah, ha! been playing my lady, have you, and trying on your trinkets. I'll take them back with me to have them reset, if you have decided."

"I've not changed my mind; I like them as they are. I did not take them out to play with, but to show to my friend. Laura has come, and wants so much to see you!"

"She does me honor; but I haven't the least desire to see her. I want you all to myself, little Ruth. Will she stay long?" asked Strathsay, leading the girl toward the door.

"Why, where is she? I forgot her entirely and she was here a minute before you came," cried Ruth, looking about her with sudden recollection.

"Gone like a shadow, it seems. So much the better. Come and see the dear old lady with me, and then let us go and be happy in rest."

They went away, arm-in-arm, leaving the room empty, for Laura had slipped out while the lovers were absorbed in each other.

Half an hour later, as they sat together in a flowery nook of the old garden, Ruth paused suddenly in something she was saying, for it was evident that Strathsay's attention wandered. Her eye followed his, and saw Laura in the grape walk, with her little Italian greyhound prancing beside her.

She looked very lovely, coming down the cool, green vista, her rosy muslins blowing in the balmy wind and her sunny-brown hair bound with a chaplet of young vine leaves. A book was in her hand, but she read little, and her fine eyes were fixed on the river that rolled below.

Grace is often more powerful than beauty, but when the two are united, few can resist the spell. Laura possessed both, and knew how to use them with the skill of an actress. Apparently unconscious, she went to and fro, artfully making every look, gesture, attitude and tone serve a purpose. Now, she walked with indolent ease, long lashes hiding the violet eyes, and lips smiling as at what she read. Then pausing, she displayed a fine arm by reaching to draw down a cluster of climbing roses, or drew attention to a slender waist by setting the flowers in her belt. The little greyhound frisked before her with a leaf from her book, and she pursued him with flying feet, chiding as she ran, and when the culprit crouched before her, she relented and petted the dainty creature with all manner of pretty words and caresses.

As if weary, she threw by her book, put down the dog, and dropping on a seat, half sat, half lay there in an attitude full of listless grace, and seemed to fall into a waking dream.

"Is that your friend?" asked Strathsay, forgetting to apologize for his absence.

"Yes, that is Laura."

"You never told me she was beautiful, Ruth."

"Indeed I did, and you said you hated beauties."

"So I do—mere dolls, such as one sees in society. That is no doll, but a very lovely girl. How long have you known her?"

"Only since last March. We met in town, and though she was a belle and I a nobody, she was kind to me, for my odd ways amused her. I asked her to come and see me in the summer, and here she is. Will you go and speak with her? I'll let you admire her, but no more. She has many lovers and does not need you, so beware."

As Ruth spoke, she rose and beckoned, but Strathsay drew her back, saying earnestly:

"Do you doubt me, dear?"

"No, but I know the power of beauty, and Laura has great skill in winning hearts. You are my all, and I cannot lose you, unworthy as I am to possess so much."

"Nay, I'll not go; if this girl is such a siren, I had better shun her for both our sakes, though upon my life, a touch of jealousy improves you, little Ruth."

He laughed as he spoke, and stroked the smooth cheek grown rosy with a sudden flush. The girl's dark eyes were full of tears, and a foreboding fear chilled her heart, as she answered with a troubled look:

"A strange feeling came over me just then, and all the sunshine seemed to vanish. You told me that you had known few women in your busy life, and that now every one you met seemed charming. I'm not even pretty, and though you love me now, I feel a sudden fear that I may lose you."

"Shall I swear and protest, or will you trust me entirely?" he asked, as if hurt by her doubt.

"I'll trust entirely. But Walter, a time may come when you will repent of your generosity to me; promise that if it should, you will frankly tell me. I can hear anything but deceit."

"I promise. Now forget this foolish fancy and take me to your friend; she sees us, and it is rude to leave her so long."

"Come then," and Ruth gave him her hand, trying to feel at ease; but a shadow had fallen on her sunshine, and her happy mood was gone.

Laura received Strathsay with a charming mixture of eagerness, timidity, and half-hidden admiration, which was very flattering. She had friends in the Crimea, and leading the conversation in that direction, irresistibly interested the young officer and brought out many exciting episodes and warlike reminiscences. She possessed the art of putting others at their ease, of making them do their best, and imparting to them a pleasurable consciousness that they charmed her as she did them. Ruth had none of this skill; cold and shy externally, few knew what a depth of passion and power lay below, for self-control had been early learned, and pride led her to conceal both pain and pleasure from all but a chosen few. As she watched her lover and her friend growing more and more absorbed in the conversation, Strathsay unconsciously betraying his admiration, and Laura freely expressing hers in praises of his bravery and interest in his fortunes, her heart grew heavier and heavier with the morning instinct, born of love. So strong grew this foreboding, that when she parted from Laura after a long evening of seeming harmony and gayety, she could not resist saying in a tone she tried to render playful:

"No poaching on my grounds; remember your power, and use it generously."

"What do you mean?" asked Laura, with well-feigned surprise.

"I mean that you must not take my one lover away, for the pleasure of adding another conquest to the many you have already won."

"Jealous creature, do you think he would be worth regretting if his love was so fickle that another could rob you of it? You insult him by the fear and me by the warning."

"Forgive me; I could not help it. I have been so poor, that my sudden riches make me suspicious and miserly. I will do better, and trust you both."

She did implicitly, for generous natures are easiest to deceive, and Laura's anger quieted Ruth's fears for a time. Strathsay's visit lengthened to a week, and so happily did the days pass, that Ruth scarcely heeded their flight, till some accidental trifle reminded her of the lapse of time. When she spoke of business to her lover, he told her it could be carried on by letter, and he should not leave her yet. At this she rejoiced and resigned herself to the new happiness, blindly trusting that all was well. Nothing could be more irreproachable than Laura's conduct, nothing more devoted than his to Ruth, and all three seemed frank and friendly in their daily intercourse. So another week went by, and then Ruth's trouble came again.

"Little girl, I must go to-morrow," abruptly began Strathsay as they sat alone one evening.

"Why so suddenly, Walter?"

"I've neglected my affairs too long, and must be off without delay."

"When will you return?"

"Can't say; you've had enough of me for a month at least, so I will leave you in peace."

"You know I have not. What is the matter? You look excited, yet sad; your voice is bitter and you turn your eyes away. Have I offended you, my laddie?" and the girl's tender face looked wistfully into his averted one, as her hand stole to his shoulder with an appealing touch.

An instant he sat silent, then turned to her, and with a deep flush on his bronzed cheek, but honest eyes fixed on her own, and steady voice full of humility, yet earnest with the truth, he said, rapidly:

"I promised not to deceive you, Ruth, and I will keep my word. With shame and contrition I confess that I go because I dare not stay."

"You love her, then?" faltered poor Ruth, pale and panic-stricken in a moment.

"No, I can truly say I do not yet, but I fear I may. She fascinates me by her beauty. Tell her to be less lovely and less kind; it will be better for us both. Indeed I do not love her, but her face haunts me, and makes me miserable because it is wrong. I have kept my word to you, and made you unhappy by the truth; but I am impetuous and weak, and fear that I may, in some unguarded moment, look or say more than I ought. Help me to be true to my real love and to cast off this unhappy delusion before it is too late."

"I will! Flee temptation, Walter. Leave me before a rash word mars our peace. Go away, and if it is a delusion you will forget it; if it is not, I can do my duty, and endure to see you happy even with Laura."

Both had spoken impulsively, and both were so absorbed that neither saw the shadow that flitted in and out behind them, or dreamed that Laura overheard their words.

Long they talked, each trying to be just and generous, and each conscious that the love they bore each other was true and deep, in spite of all delusions, doubts, or temptations.

On the morrow Strathsay went, and though Ruth watched eagerly, Laura betrayed no concern, but said good-by with her blithest smile, and gave him sundry trifling commissions, as if unconscious of his gravity, or the covert glances he gave at the beautiful face which haunted him against his will, and was to prove the phantom of his life.

Very dull and quiet were the days that followed Strathsay's departure, for he wrote but seldom, and the friends felt that they were friends no longer. Not a word was said, but the coldness increased, and neither made any effort to change it.

Fortunately for Ruth her invalid grandmother needed unusual care just then, and thus she was freed from the constraint of Laura's presence some hours of each day.

To her surprise Laura did not shorten her visit, but remained, and seemed happy in the quiet place, and the various amusements she devised for herself.

While Ruth sat with the old lady she walked, and always came home gay and rosy, with some little adventure to relate, or some report of the poor souls she had comforted, for she was charitable with that cheap charity which gives money, but neither sympathy nor care.

Ruth smiled at her caprices, especially the last one, till accident enlightened her.

Some three weeks after Strathsay's departure, old madam was one day possessed with a strong desire for a certain kind of jelly which no one could make but a former maid of her own, now married and living in the village.

Ruth was dispatched with the order, and as she approached the cottage, overtook a little lad carrying a letter with great care.

Being one of Martha's boys, she chatted with him as they walked, and in so doing her eye fell on the letter. There was nothing remarkable about it to other eyes, for it was simply directed to "Mrs. Martha Hale," in a plain, clear hand, and post-marked "London."

But Ruth looked long at it, and felt a curious interest in it, for the writing was wonderfully like Strathsay's, especially three letters in one corner, with a dash below.

The rest of the address was a little changed, but the letters were in his peculiar hand, "L.C.R.," and as she looked she involuntarily said to herself, "Laura Catharine Richmond."

Something in the child's manner struck her also, for as he saw her examining the letter, he dropped his hands beside him, saying, with a droll mixture of importance and anxiety:

"Mammy bids me always put 'em in my pocket, but it's all wet with berries, and I can't. Don't you tell you see it, else she'll scold."

"Why, Teddy?"

"Don't know, but she does if I ain't careful of her old letters, and she won't even give me the seals on 'em; they are pretty stags' heads, and I like 'em."

An intense desire to see the letter again seized Ruth on hearing that, and she managed to do so by interesting the child in a marvelous tale, till he forgot to hide his hand and the paper it held. No seal was visible, and she hoped her fear was groundless.

Coming to the cottage, Teddy hurried to find his mother, and Ruth gave her message. She was on her way home when a fine flower in a wayside field caused her to climb the bank to get it. As she sat in the long grass to rest, Laura passed in the path below.

Ruth was about to speak, when Laura took a letter from her pocket, tore off the cover, broke the seal of the enclosed envelope, and passed into the grove, reading eagerly as she went.

The instant she disappeared Ruth sprang down to the path, caught up the crumpled cover, and saw it was the same that Teddy had just taken to his mother.

There was no doubt now in her mind that Strathsay wrote to Laura, and a stern calmness came over Ruth as her quick wit cleared up the mystery of Laura's charitable freak of late. No tears, reproaches, or complaints; but an instant resolution to know all took possession of the girl, and that night she executed her purpose.

Laura was unusually gay and amiable, but went early to bed. Ruth watched till her light was out and she was unmistakably asleep, then, with soundless steps she entered the room, found the desk, possessed herself of the key, and returning to her own room, opened and searched the papers of this fair false friend. The letters were there, several from Strathsay, and two or three copies of those Laura had written, beginning with a brief note of thanks for the well-executed commissions, and a delicately expressed regret that Ruth's unhappy temper should disturb their pleasant friendship.

This had produced an explanation and defense from the lover, followed by further notes from Laura, hinting that Ruth loved to show her power and was proud of the prize she had won.

It was evident that she had told him Ruth was happy in his absence, contented with her narrow life, and in no haste to recall him.

Skillfully had she worked upon his pride and temper, overcoming honorable scruples, silencing self-reproachful condemnation, and mingling her falsehoods with such pity, sympathy, and half-confessed affection, that it was little wonder an ardent, impressionable man should be deceived and taught to think Ruth the cold, shallow-hearted, ambitious girl her false friend painted her.

His letters proved that he had not yielded without a struggle, and as she read, Ruth forgave him, for that last letter was full of remorse, doubts of the depth of the new passion, and regrets that he had ever seen the fair face which had robbed him of peace and self-respect. Ruth forgave and loved him still, believing him more sinned against than sinning; but such hatred and contempt for Laura sprang up within her, she trembled lest it should lead her to some rash act of retribution. When all was read, she safely restored the stolen desk and went back to a sleepless pillow, feeling as if a year had passed since that discovery was made.

Pale and quiet she rose next day, with a firm resolve to save Strathsay and unmask Laura.

Secretly they had wronged her, and as secretly would she revenge herself upon the chief sinner; the means she left to time and her own address.

"Jane tells me that fever has broken out in the village, so be careful how you and Laura go there, for it is a dangerous and malignant disease," said old madam next day, as her grandchild left her.

There was nothing in the words to startle Ruth, but she suddenly turned pale, for a black thought rose up in her mind, and like an evil spirit tempted her.

Laura would go to carry her reply; one of Martha's children lay sick; perhaps it was the fever; or if not already there, the air was full of it. She might take it, and then—

A host of conflicting emotions filled her mind, but out of the confusion rose the wish that Laura was dead and Strathsay all her own again. She sat and thought of this till her temples throbbed, and her heart beat quick with the guilty purpose stirring in it, for to that poor, passionate heart it seemed right to be revenged for the wrong so cruelly done it.

As Ruth's eyes roved restlessly to and fro they fell on Laura's figure going down the green lane to the town. She guessed her errand, and watched her tripping away, looking lovelier than ever as she glanced back with a smile, and then went on rejoicing in her treachery and conquest. Ruth set her teeth and clinched her hands, but never stirred till the girl was out of sight. Then, with a shiver, she dropped her head upon her arm, feeling the first bitterness of sin. In the act the miniature slid from her bosom and swung open before her, wearing to her eyes a reproachful look, that smote her heart. The memory of the past touched her better self, and, forgetting hatred in love, she put away the purpose that made her so unworthy of it.

Without pausing for a second thought, Ruth hurried after her friend, and reached her in time to tell her of the danger she incurred.

An expression of sudden shame passed over Laura's face as she turned back, warmly thanking the girl for the warning.

But it was given too late; she had been often among the cottages where the contagion had just broken out, and a week from that day Ruth watched beside her, listening to her incoherent ravings, thanking God that she had not yielded to the strong temptation, and that if Laura died it would not be through her. For many days the fever raged, then left her weak and wan as a shadow of her former self. Ruth nursed her faithfully, trying to stifle sinful regrets that she was spared for further harm. She could have forgiven her if any sign of penitence or sorrow had escaped her; but the utter falseness of her nature hardened Ruth's heart and left no room for any softer feeling than contempt.

Strathsay wrote seldom now, and knowing the cause, Ruth made no complaint. She could not deceive him, and so waited till she could put an end to his struggle and her own.

She watched if any note came from him to Laura; but her friend's maid was wrong, and Ruth discovered nothing till one night, as she lay apparently asleep on the couch in Laura's room, she saw her draw a paper from under her pillow, read it, kiss it, and then put it back, to drop asleep, little dreaming whose eyes were on her.

No need for Ruth to read the note; she knew whence it came; and sitting in the hush of midnight, she brooded over her misery till no sin, no sacrifice seemed too great, if it but won her back the heart she had lost.

As she sat thus gazing at the face whose beauty had been so fatal to her peace, a sudden gust of air from the half-opened window wafted the muslin drapery of the bed across the night-lamp burning near. Ruth would have risen to move the light, but the evil spell was on her, and she sat unmoved, watching with fascinated eyes the white curtains floating nearer and nearer the dangerous lamp.

Laura lay in a deep sleep, the house was lonely and the maids in distant rooms. She heard the rustle of the rising breeze, saw the quickened sweep of the bright drapery, but neither spoke nor stirred.

A dreadful calm possessed her, and when a sudden blaze lit the room, she only smiled—an awful smile—she saw it in the mirror and trembled at herself.

The flames shot up brighter and hotter as the woodwork caught; Laura woke suddenly, and stretching her arms through smoke and fire, cried feebly:

"Walter, save me! save me!"

He could not answer her, but he saved Ruth, for the sound of his name freed her from the evil spell that bound her. She tore Laura from the burning bed and fought the flames till they were conquered, finding a fierce delight in the excitement and danger. But when the peril was over and Laura soothed to sleep again, then Ruth felt weak and helpless as a child.

Burdened with the weight of the nearly-committed crime, and conscious of the power her unhappy love possessed to lead her into evil, she cried within herself:

"This must end; I can lead this life no longer for it will ruin me body and soul. Walter must decide between us, and the struggle cease."

In the gray dawn she wrote to her lover, bidding him come home, simply telling him she knew everything, and would forgive it if he would end both doubt and misery at once.

She sent the letter, told Laura what she had done, and besought her to make his happiness if she truly loved him, for there was no other claim upon him now.

Laura seemed annoyed at the act, but not humbled by the discovery of her own treason. She called Ruth "a romantic child," and promised to see what she could do for Walter. Her heartless words were daggers to Ruth, but she bore it patiently, longing to have all over and past doubt.

A line from Strathsay arrived, appointing a day for his return, but nothing more; and in this alacrity, this silence, Ruth read her fate.

As the time approached Laura grew restless and excited. She insisted on making a fine toilet though still too feeble to leave her room, and rouged her wan cheeks, that his eye should miss as little as possible of the beauty that won him.

"He is coming! I know his step along the garden path! Are you faint?" said Ruth, as Laura lay back in the deep chair with pale lips, and a look of pain in her face.

"I am only tired of waiting. Bring him to me quickly, Ruth," she answered, sitting erect, with the old smile, the old attitude and glance.

"Walter, let me say a few words first," said Ruth, as he came in, wearing an expression of mingled shame, sorrow, and relief, that wrung her heart. "I release you from the promise which has become a burden. I want a free heart or none. Choose for yourself beauty or love, and let the trial end at once. One word more—and believe me, I try to say it in a kind spirit. Let me warn you that a false friend may not make a true wife. Now go, and let it soon be over."

He faltered and looked at her with a searching glance; but she stood resolute and calm, as unable to express her sorrow as she had been to demonstrate her love, yet feeling both the deeper for that cause. He could not read the suffering heart. He thought her cold and careless, for with a few hurried words of gratitude and regret he left her.

A moment after a cry brought Ruth to his side. She found him distractedly chafing Laura's cold hand, and imploring her to speak to him. But no answer came, for there in the full glare of the sunshine, with the false bloom on her wasted cheeks, the set smile on her breathless lips, lay Laura, dead.

The physicians seemed little surprised, saying she was very frail, and the fever had left her too weak for any excitement. So when all restoratives failed, she was made ready for her last sleep, and her friends came to carry her to her last home.

Ruth had longed for this—had prayed that one of them might die; but now, when in a moment the wicked wish was granted, she repented and forgave her enemy.

"Rest in peace, Laura. I pardon you as I hope to be pardoned," she said, softly, as, standing alone beside the coffin, she looked down upon the quiet face, so powerless to harm her now. Uttering the words, she bent to put away a lock of hair fallen from its place. In doing so her hand touched

Laura's forehead, and a strange thrill shot through her, for it was *damp.* She put her hand on the heart, pulse and lips, but all were cold and still. She touched the brow again, but the first touch had wiped the slight dew from it, and it was now like ice. For several minutes Ruth stood white and motionless as the dead girl, while the old struggle, fiercer than ever, raged in her heart. Fear whispered that she was not dead. Pity pleaded for her, lying helplessly before her, and conscience sternly bade her do the right, forgetful of all else. But she would not listen, for Love cried out, passionately:

"Walter is my own again; she cannot separate us any more, or rob me of the one blessing of my life. Twice I have conquered temptation, and been generous only to be more wronged. Now, I will yield to it, and if a word could save this traitorous friend, I will not utter it."

Then, hardening her heart, Ruth shut out from her sight the face she hated, and left the doubt unsolved. She was the last who saw Laura; she never told the fear that haunted her; the girl was buried and the lovers took up their life again.

Strathsay seemed more bewildered than bereaved by the sudden check his infatuation had received. The charm was broken and when the first shock was over he never spoke of her, and seemed to wake from his short dream himself again.

Ruth uttered no reproach, but by every tender art showed how gladly she welcomed back the love, not lost but led astray. Strathsay soon seemed fonder than ever, trying eagerly to atone for the past. The future lay clear before her, and life would have been all sunshine but for the shadow of a single cloud. A vague sense of guilt weighed on her, growing heavier day by day, for the horrible fancy that Laura was not dead haunted her like a ghost. She had held her peace at first, fearing that the evil genius of her life should return to torment her again. She had kept her sinful vow till it was too late, and now the hidden memory became a spectre to mar her peace.

Months went on, the wedding-day was fixed, and in the excitement of that event, Ruth hoped she might forget. But it was in vain; the fear was always lying heavy at her heart, making her days wearisome with ceaseless anxiety, her nights terrible with dark dreams. She would not believe it anything but a wild fancy, yet felt that it was wearing upon her. She saw her cheeks grow thin, her eyes full of feverish unrest, her spirits failing, her life a daily struggle to cast off the gloom that poisoned her happiness. Her only comfort was in the hope that the approaching change might banish the hidden trouble.

Once Strathsay's wife, she believed that his love would banish every care and allay every haunting fear. She fancied that a time would come when she would dare to confide her foolish dread and see him smile at it. She clung to this hope, and often in those miserable nights, when the dead face confronted her in the darkness with a mute reproach in its dim eyes that scared sleep from her pillow, she would lie framing her confession into fitting words for his ear, mingling self-accusations with whispered prayers for pardon, and fond reminders that these trials and temptations were caused by her great love for him.

The night before her wedding day she lay down with the old fear stronger than ever, and fell into a deep sleep, filled with troubled dreams, which tormented her till dawn. Then she sprang up with a sense of unutterable relief, and for a while forgot herself in glad preparations for the approaching ceremony.

The day was fair and Ruth was happy, for the phantom fear was gone. A few friends came with good wishes, to celebrate the quiet nuptials; the hour arrived and all was ready, but Strathsay did not come.

They waited long, and still no bridegroom appeared. Messengers were sent to find him, but returned saying he had gone away at dawn and had not yet returned. Then Ruth's heart died within her, feeling that some affliction was in store for her, and she waited, racked with apprehensions that almost drove her wild. But still he did not come.

One by one the friends departed, wondering, and she was left alone with old madam and the clergyman. They tried to comfort her, but their words went by her like the wind.

Hour after hour she paced the room with eye, ear and mind strained to the utmost. Still Strathsay did not come.

Old madam slept at last, the good man went away, and friendly neighbors ceased to question and condole. She was utterly alone, and the red fire-light which she thought would have shone upon a happy wife now glimmered faintly on a pale, anxious woman with dead flowers on her breast and bridal garments mocking her desolation, as she sat waiting for the coming sorrow.

Suddenly Strathsay's step sounded in the hall, and, speechless with relief, she sprang to welcome him; but there was that in his face which drove her back. Haggard and wild it looked, as with white lips and eyes dilated with some secret horror, he stood gazing at her till she was cold with ominous dread.

She could not bear it long, and going to him, would have given him a tender greeting; but he shrank from her touch with averted head and hands outstretched to keep her off.

"Walter, what is it? Do not kill me with such looks—such dreadful silence! Tell me what has happened. I can bear anything but this!" she cried, clinging to him with a desperate hold.

A look of bitter pain swept over his face as his eyes met her imploring gaze. He held her close a moment, then put her from him with a shudder.

She sat where he placed her, without power to move or speak, while standing before her, with a countenance as hard and stern as rock, he said with an abrupt calmness, far more terrible than the wildest agitation:

"Ruth, last night I sat alone in this room after you left me; and while here a white figure with vacant eyes and pallid cheeks came gliding in and pausing there, it told a sad tale of deceit and wrong, of hidden sins and struggles, and confessed one crime which drove it like a restless ghost to betray its secrets when most fatal to its peace."

"It was Laura come back from her tomb to wrong and rob me again," cried Ruth, half unconscious of what she said as the old fear overwhelmed her anew.

"No, *it was you,* coming in your haunted sleep to tell the secret that is wearing your life away. It was awful to see you standing there with no light in your open eyes, no color in your expressionless face, and hear the tender words, meant to be spoken with repentant tears, uttered in unearthly tones by lips unconscious of their meaning, and then to see the self-accusing apparition glide away unmoved into the gloom, leaving such misery behind."

"Forgive me!—you will, you must, for it was you who drove me to this. I loved you better than my own soul, and she came between us. I have been sorely tempted, but for your sake I resisted more than once. Did I not set you free when my whole heart was bound up in you? Did I not relinquish everything for you and have I not proved how strong my love is by these sacrifices for your sake? Do not reproach me that I unconsciously betrayed the struggles I have endured, nor chide me that I rejoiced when Laura died. She is dead, and nothing, but my feverish fancy would ever have doubted it."

Strathsay's calmness vanished as she rapidly poured out this appeal.

The horror-stricken look returned to his eyes, and his voice sounded hoarsely through the silent room as he replied, with lips that whitened as he spoke:

"She *is* dead, thank God! but *was not when they buried her.* Ay, you may well fall on your knees and hide your guilty face, for you murdered her. Hear me, and cheat yourself with doubts no longer. Filled with alarm by your confession, and remembering the strange restlessness which has possessed you since her death, I went to-day to R——, where Laura lies. Alone I went into the tomb, but was brought out senseless; she had been buried alive! There was no doubt of it. She had turned in her coffin, and, too weak to break it, had perished miserably. May God forgive you, Ruth; I never can!"

"Oh! be merciful, Walter. I had suffered so much from her, I could not give you up. Be merciful, and do not cast me off when all the sin was for your dear sake," she cried, overcoming in her despair the horror and remorse that froze her blood.

But Strathsay never heeded her, and his stern purpose never wavered. He tore himself away with an aspect of deeper despair than her own, saying, solemnly, as he passed from her sight for ever:

"God pardon us both; our sins have wrought out their own punishment, and we must never meet again."

La Jeune; or, Actress and Woman

"JUST IN TIME for the theatre. You'll come, Ulster?"

"Decidedly not."

"And why?"

"Because I prefer a cigar, a novel, and my bottle of cliquot."

"But every one goes," began Brooke, in a dissatisfied tone.

"True, and for that reason, I keep away."

"You used to be as fond of it as I am."

"At your age I grant it; now, I'm ten years older and wiser. I'm tired of that as of most other pleasures, so go your way, my boy, and leave me in peace."

"Come, Ulster, don't play Timon yet. You are lazy, not used up nor misanthropic, so be obliging, and come like a good fellow."

Fanning away the cloud of smoke from before me, I took a look at my friend, for something in his manner convinced me that he had some particular reason for desiring my company. Arthur Brooke was a handsome young Briton, of four-and-twenty; blue-eyed, tawny-haired, ruddy and robust, with a frank face, cordial smile, and a heart both brave and tender. I loved him like a younger brother, and watched over him during his holiday in gay, delightful, wicked Paris. So far, he had taken his draught of pleasure with the relish of youth, but like a gentleman. Of late, he had turned moody, shunned me once or twice, and when I alluded to the change, affected surprise, assuring me that nothing was amiss. As I looked at him, I was surer than ever that all was not right. He was pale, and anxious lines had come on his smooth forehead; there was an excited glitter in his eyes, though he had scarcely touched wine at dinner; his smile seemed forced, his voice had lost its hearty ring, and his manner was half petulant, half pleading, as he stood undecidedly crushing up his gloves while he spoke.

"Why do you want me to go? Is it on your account, lad?" I asked, in an altered tone.

"Yes."

"Give me a reason, and I will."

He hesitated, colored all over his fair face, then looked me straight in the eyes, and answered steadily.

"I want you to see Mademoiselle Nairne."

"The deuce you do! Why, Brooke, you've not got into a scrape with La Jeune, I hope!" I exclaimed, sitting up, annoyed.

"Far from it, but I love, and mean to marry her if I can," he answered, in a resolute tone.

"Don't say that for heaven's sake. My dear boy, think of your father, your family, your prospects, and don't ruin yourself by such folly," I cried, in real anxiety.

"If you loved as I do, you wouldn't call it folly," he said, excitedly.

"Of course not, but it would be cursed folly nevertheless, and if some friend saved me from it, I should thank him for it when the delusion was over. Love her if you will, but don't marry her, I beg of you."

"That is impossible; she is as good as she is lovely, and will listen to none but honorable vows. Laugh, if you will, it's so, and actress as she is, there's not a purer woman than she in all Paris."

"Bless your innocence, that's not saying much for her. Why, my dear lad, she knows your fortune to a sou and makes her calculations accordingly. She sees that you are a simple, tender-hearted fellow, easy to catch, and not hard to manage when caught. She will marry you for your money, spend it like water, and when tired of the respectabilities, will elope with the first rich lover that comes along. Don't shoot me, I speak for your good; I know the world, and warn you of this woman."

"Do you know her?"

"No, but I know her class; they are all alike, mercenary, treacherous, and shallow."

"You are mistaken this time, Ulster. I know I'm young, easily gulled perhaps, and in no way your equal in such matters, but I'll stake my life that Natalie is not what you say."

"My poor boy, you are far gone, indeed! What can I do to save you?"

"Come and see her," he said, eagerly. "You don't know her, never saw her beauty or talent, yet you judge her, and would have me abide by your unjust decree."

"I'll go; the fever is on you, and you must be helped through the crisis, or you'll wreck your whole life. It always goes hard with your sort."

My indolence was quite conquered by anxiety, and away we went, Brooke armed with a great bouquet, and I mentally cursing his folly in wasting time, money, and the love of his honest heart, on a painted butterfly.

We took a box, and from the intense interest we showed in the piece, both of us might have been taken for ardent admirers of "La Jeune." I had never seen her, though all Paris had been running after her that season, as it was after any novelty from a learned pig to a hero. Having been bored by her praises, and annoyed by urgent entreaties to go, I perversely set my face against her, and affected even more indifference than I really felt. I was tired of such follies, fancied my day was over, and for a year or two had felt no interest in any actress less famous than Ristori or Rachel.

The play was one of those brilliant trifles possible only in Paris; for there, wit without vulgarity is appreciated, and art is so perfect, one forgets the absence of nature. The stage represented a charming boudoir, all mirrors, muslins, flowers and light. A coquettish soubrette was arranging the toilet as she delivered a few words that put the house in good humor, by whetting curiosity and raising a laugh, in the midst of which Madame la Marquise entered, not as most actresses take the stage, but as a pretty woman really would enter her room, going straight to the glass to see if the effect of her costume was quite destroyed by the vicissitudes of a bal-masque. She was beautiful—I could not deny that, but answered Brooke's eager inquiry with a shrug and the cruel words:

"Paint, dress, wine or opium."

He turned his back to me, and I devoted myself to the study of the woman he loved. She looked scarcely twenty, so fresh and brilliant was her face, so beautifully molded her figure, so youthful her charming voice, so elastic her graceful gestures. Petite and piquant, fair hair, dark eyes, a ravishing foot and hand, a dazzling neck and arm, made this rosy, dimpled little creature altogether captivating, even to one as *blasé* as myself. Gay, arch, and full of that indescribable coquetry which is as natural to a pretty woman as her beauty, La Jeune well deserved the sobriquet she had won.

Being a connoisseur in dress, I observed that hers was in perfect taste—a rare thing, for the costume of the Louis Quatorze era is usually overdone on the stage. But this woman had evidently copied some portrait, for everything was in keeping, coiffure, jewels, lace, brocade; and from the tiny patch on her white chin to the diamond buckles in her scarlet-heeled shoes, she was a true French marquise. Even in gesture, gait and accent, she kept up the illusion, causing modern France to be forgotten for the hour, and making that comedy a picture of the past, and winning applause from critics whose praise was tame.

Through the sparkling dialogue, the inimitable by-play, romantic incident and courtly intrigues of the piece, she played admirably, embodying not only the beauty and coquetry, but the wit, *finesse* and brilliancy of the part. I was interested in spite of myself; forgot my anxiety, and found myself applauding more than once. Brooke heard my hearty "Bravo!" and turned with an exultant smile.

"You are conquering your prejudices fast, *mon ami*. Is she not charming?"

"Very. I never questioned her skill as an actress, and readily accord my praise, for she plays capitally. But I'd rather not see her my friend's wife. Just fancy presenting her to your family."

He winced at that as his eye followed mine to the stage, which just then showed the marquise languishing in a great *fauteuil* before her mirror, surrounded by several fops, while her lover, disguised as a *coiffeur,* powdered her hair and dropped *billet doux* into her lap.

Fascinating, fair and frivolous as she was, how could he dream of transplanting her to a decorous English home, where her name alone would raise a storm, if coupled, even in jest, with his. He looked, sighed and sat silent till the curtain fell, then applauded till his gloves were in tatters, threw his bouquet at her feet as she reappeared, and turned to me, saying, with unabated eagerness:

"Now come and see her at home; the woman is more charming than the actress. I am asked to supper, and may bring a friend with me. Come, I beg of you."

To his surprise and satisfaction I consented at once, but did not tell him what had induced me to comply. It was a trifle, but it had weight with me, and hoping still to save my headstrong friend, I went away to sup with La Jeune.

The trifle was this: After one of her best scenes she left the stage, but did not go to her dressing room, as she must re-enter in a moment.

From our box we could command the opposite wings; a chair was placed there for her, and sinking into it, she waved away two or three devoted gentlemen who eagerly approached. They retired, and as if forgetting that she could be overlooked, La Jeune leaned back with a change of countenance that absolutely startled me. All the fire, the gayety, the youth, seemed to die out, leaving a weary, woeful face, the sadder for the contrast between its tragic pathos and the blithe comedy going on before us.

Brooke did not see her; he had seized the moment to sprinkle his flowers, already drooping in the hot air.

I said nothing, but watched that brief aside more eagerly than her best point. It was but an instant. Her cue came, and she swept on to the stage with a ringing laugh, looking the embodiment of joy.

This glimpse of the woman off the stage roused my curiosity, and made me anxious to see more of her.

As we drove away I asked Brooke if he had spoken yet, for I wished to know how to conduct myself in the affair.

"Not in words; my eyes and actions must have told her; but I delayed to speak till you had seen her, for willful as I seem, I value your advice, Ulster."

"Have you spoken of me?"

"Yes; once or twice. Some one asked why you never came with me, and I said you had forsworn theatres."

"How did she take that blunt reply?"

"Rather oddly, I thought, for, looking at me, she said, softly: 'It would be better for you if you followed the example of your mentor.' "

"Art, my child, all art; warn a man against anything, and he'll move heaven and earth to get it. How will you explain this visit of your mentor, who has forsworn theatres?" I said, nettled at having that sage and venerable name applied to me.

"It will be both gallant and truthful to say you came to see her. She bade me bring any friend I liked, and will be flattered at your coming, if you don't put on your haughty airs.

"I'll be amiable on your account. Here we are. Upon my word mademoiselle lodges sumptuously."

As we drove into a courtyard, lights shone in long windows of La Jeune's *appartement,* and the sound of music met us as we passed up the stairs.

Two large, luxurious rooms, brilliantly, yet tastefully decorated and furnished, received us as we stepped in unannounced. Half a dozen persons were scattered about, chatting, laughing and listening to a song from a member of the opera troupe then delighting Paris. Supper was laid in the further room, and while waiting till it was served, every one exerted themselves to amuse their hostess in return for the delight she had given them.

Mademoiselle seemed to have just arrived, for she was still *en costume,* and appeared to have thrown herself into a seat as if wearied with her labors.

The rich hue of the garnet velvet chair relieved her figure admirably, as she leaned back, with a white cloak half concealing her brilliant dress. The powder had shaken from her hair, leaving its gold undimmed as it hung slightly disheveled about her shoulders. She had wiped the rouge from her face, leaving it paler, but none the less lovely, for in resuming her own character, that face had changed entirely. No longer gay, arch, or coquetish, it was thoughtful, keen, and cold. She smiled graciously, received compliments tranquilly, and conversed wittily; but her heart evidently was not there, and she was still playing a part.

I made these observations and received these impressions during the brief pause at the door; then Brooke presented me with much *empressement,* plainly showing that he wished each to produce a favorable effect upon the other.

As my name was spoken a slight smile touched her lips, but her dark eyes scanned my face so gravely, that in spite of myself I paid my compliments with an ill grace.

"It is evident that this is not monsieur's first visit to Paris."

From another person, and in another mood, I should have accepted this speech as a compliment to my accent and manner, but from her I chose to see in it an ironical jest at my unwonted *maladresse,* a feminine return for my long negligence. Anxious to do myself justice, I gave a genuine French shrug and replied, with a satirical smile which belied my flattering words:

"I was about to say no, but I remember to whom I speak, and say yes, for by the magic of mademoiselle, modern Paris vanishes, and for the first time I visit Paris in the time of the Grand Monarque. The illusion was perfect, and like a hundred others, I am at a loss how to show my gratitude."

"That is easily done; madame is hungry; oblige her with a *morceau* of that *paté* and a glass of champagne."

Her mocking tone, the sparkle of her eye, and the wicked smile on her lips, annoyed me more than the unromantic request that made my speech absurd.

I obeyed with feigned devotion, telling Brooke to keep out of the way still longer, as I passed him on my way back. He had withdrawn a little, that I might see and judge for myself, and stood in an alcove near by, affecting to talk with a gentleman in the same sentimental plight as himself.

Mademoiselle ate and drank as if she was really hungry, inviting me to do the same with such hospitable grace that I drew up a little table and continued our *tête-a-tête,* while the others stood or sat about in groups in a pleasantly informal manner.

"My friend is much honored, I perceive. Mademoiselle shows both taste and judgment in her selection, for though young for his years, Brooke is a true gentleman," I said, observing that of all the many bouquets thrown at her feet his was the only one she kept.

"Do you know why I selected this?" she asked, with a quick glance after a slight pause.

"I can easily guess," I replied, with a significant smile.

She glanced over her shoulder, took up the great bouquet, and plunging her dimpled hand into the midst of the flowers, drew out a glittering bracelet, saying, as she offered it to me, with an air of pride that surprised me very much:

"I kept it that I might return this. It may annoy your friend less to take it from you, therefore restore it with my thanks, and tell him I can accept nothing but flowers."

"Nothing, mademoiselle?"

"Nothing, monsieur."

I put my question with emphasis, and as she answered she flashed a look at me that perplexed me, though I thought it a bit of clever acting.

Taking the bracelet, I said, in a tone of feigned regret: "Must I afflict the poor boy by returning his gift with such a cruel message?"

"If you would be a true friend to him do what I ask, and take him away from Paris."

Her urgent tone struck me even more than this unexpected frankness, and I involuntarily exclaimed:

"Does mademoiselle know what she banishes thus?"

"I know that Sir Richard Brooke would disinherit his only son if that son made a *mésalliance;* I know that I regard Arthur too much to mar his future, and—I banish him."

She spoke rapidly, and laid her hand upon her heart as if to hide its agitation, but her eyes were fixed steadily on mine with an expression which affected me with a curious sense of guilt for my hard judgment of her.

There was a pause, and in that pause I chid myself for letting a pair of lovely eyes ensnare my reason, or an enchanting smile bribe my judgment.

"Mademoiselle understands the perversity of mankind well. It will be impossible to get Arthur away after a command like yours," I said, coldly.

She deliberately examined my face, and a change passed over her own. The earnestness vanished, the soft trouble was replaced by an almost bitter smile, and her voice had a touch of scorn in it as she said, sharply:

"Then Telemachus had better find a truer Mentor."

A gentleman approached; she welcomed him with a genial look, and I retired, feeling more ruffled than I would confess.

As soon as I joined Brooke in the alcove he demanded in English, and with lover-like eagerness:

"What is your opinion of her?"

"Hush; she will overhear you!"

"She speaks no English—she is absorbed—answer freely."

"Well, then, I think her a charming, artful, dangerous woman, and the sooner you leave her the better," I answered, abruptly.

"But, Ulster, don't joke. How artful? Why dangerous? I'll *not* leave her till I've tried my fate," he cried, half angry, half hurt.

I told him our conversation, gave him the jewel, and advised him to disappoint her hopes by departing without another word.

"You think she means to win me by affecting to sacrifice her own heart to my welfare?" he said as I paused.

"Exactly; she did it capitally, but I am not to be duped; and I tell you she will never let so rich a prize escape her unless she has a richer in sight, which I doubt."

"I'll not believe it! You wrong us both; you distrust all women, and insult her by such bare suspicions. You are deceived."

"I *never* am deceived; I read men and women like books, and no character is too mysterious for me to decipher. I tell you, I am right, and I'll prove it if you will keep silent for a few weeks longer."

"How?" demanded Brooke, hotly.

"I'll study this woman, and report my discoveries to you; thus, step by step, I'll convince you that she is all I say, and save you from the folly you are about to commit. Will you agree to this?"

"Yes; but you'll take no unfair advantage, you'll deal justly by us both, and if you fail—".

"I *never fail*—but if such an unheard of thing occurs, I'll own I'm conquered, and pay any penalty you decree."

"Then, I say, done. Prove that I'm a blind fool, and I'll submit to your advice, will forget Natalie and leave Paris."

Grateful for any delay, and already interested in the test, I pledged my word to act fair throughout, and turned to begin my work. Mademoiselle was surrounded by several gentlemen, and seemed to have recovered from her fatigue. Her eyes shone, a brilliant color burned on her cheek, she talked gayly, and mingled her silvery laughter in the peals of merriment her witty sallies produced. As we joined the group, some one was speaking of tragedy, and assuring La Jeune that she would excel in that as in comedy.

"*Mon Dieu,* no; one has tragedy enough off the stage; let us feign gayety in public, and laugh on even though our hearts ache," she answered, with a charming smile.

"Yet I can testify that mademoiselle would act tragedy well if I may judge by the sample I have seen."

I spoke significantly and her eye was instantly upon me, as she exclaimed with visible surprise:

"Seen! where?"

"To-night, as mademoiselle reposed a moment in the wing between the fourth and fifth acts."

She knit her brows, thought an instant, then as if recalling the fact, clapped her hands and broke into that ringing laugh of hers, as she cried:

"Monsieur has penetration! It is true, I was in a tragic mood for the spur of one of my buckles wounded my foot cruelly, and I could not complain. Behold how I suffered," and she showed a spot of scarlet that had stained through silk stocking and satin shoe.

"Great heaven! and does mademoiselle still wear the cruel ornament. Permit me to relieve this charming foot," cried one of the Frenchmen, in a pathetic tone; and going down upon his knee undid the buckle.

I was leaning on the back of her chair just then, and during the little stir said quietly:

"I congratulate mademoiselle, for if the pin-prick can call up such a woeful expression, her rendering of a mighty sorrow would be wonderfully truthful."

"I believe it would."

She looked up at me as she spoke, and in those beautiful eyes I fancied I read something like reproach. For what? Had I touched some secret wound, and was her explanation a skillful feint, as I thought it? Or did she feel with a woman's quick instinct that I was an enemy and set herself to disarm me by her beauty? I inclined to the latter belief, and instantly saw that if I would execute my purpose, I must convince her that I was a friend, an admirer, a lover even. It was evident that simple Brooke had allowed her to perceive that I did not approve his suit; this hurt her pride, and she distrusted me. Deciding to warm gradually, I looked back at her, saying gently, as if replying to that reproachful glance alone:

"I sincerely hope mademoiselle may never be called upon to play a part in any tragedy off the stage, for smiles, not tears, should be the portion of La Jeune."

Her face softened beautifully, and the dark curled lashes fell as if to hide the sudden dew that dimmed her eyes.

"You are kind, I thank you," she murmured, in a tone that touched me, skeptic as I was. "I receive much flattery, and value it for what it is worth; but a friendly wish, simple and sincere, is very sweet to me, for even a path strewn with flowers has its thorns."

She spoke as if to herself more than to me, and fancying that sentiment might succeed better than sarcasm, I began one of those speeches that may mean much or little; but in the middle of it detected her in a yawn behind her little hand, and stopped abruptly. She laughed, and with the arch expression that made her face piquante she said with a shake of the head:

"Ah, monsieur, that's but a waste of eloquence. I detect false sympathy in an instant, and betray that I do. Pardon my rudeness, and turn me a charming compliment; that is more in your style."

"Mademoiselle is fatigued; we are unmerciful to leave her no time for rest. Brooke, we should go," I said, repentantly.

"I *am* tired," she answered, with the air of a sleepy child. "*Au revoir,* not adieu, for you will come again."

"If mademoiselle permits," and with that we bowed ourselves away.

★ ★ ★ ★ ★

For a month I studied La Jeune in ways as skillful as unobtrusive. I made four discoveries, reported them to Brooke, and flattered myself that I should be able to save him from this fascinating, yet dangerous woman.

My first discovery was this. Fearing to rouse suspicion by too suddenly feigning admiration and regard, I began with an occasional call, contenting myself meantime with cultivating the friendship of a gossipy old Frenchman, who lodged in the same house. From him I learned various hints of Natalie, for the old gentleman adored her, and was as garrulous as an old woman. He said there was one room in mademoiselle's suite that none of the servants of the house were allowed to enter.

Several times a week, early in the morning, when her mistress was invisible to every one else, Jocelynd, the maid, admitted a man, who came and went as if anxious to escape observation. He was young, handsome, an Italian, and evidently deeply interested in all concerning Mademoiselle Nairne.

"A lover, without doubt," the old man said. I agreed with him, and Brooke, on learning this, could be with difficulty restrained from demanding an explanation from La Jeune.

My second discovery was made unexpectedly. One night, when she did not play, I went to see her on pretense of finding Brooke, who, I knew, was not there.

Mademoiselle was out, but expected momently, so I went in to wait. I heard her arrive soon after and enter an adjoining room, followed by the maid, who cast a glance into the *salon* as she passed. I stood in the deep window idly looking into the street below, and Jocelynd did not see me, for I heard her say:

"There is no one here, mademoiselle. Pierre was mistaken, and Monsieur Ulster did not wait."

"Thank heaven! I am so fatigued I can see no one to-night. Count this for me. I have been playing for a high stake, but I have won, and Florimond shall profit by my success."

I heard the clink of money, and noiselessly stole away, saying to myself as I went to join Brooke: "She gambles—so much the better."

A week afterward I chanced to be in one of those dark little stores in the Rue Bonaparte, where cigars, cosmetics, perfumery, and drugs are sold. I was standing in the back part of the shop selecting a certain sort of toilet soap which I fancied, when a woman came in, and, beckoning the wife of the shopman aside, handed her a peculiar little flask saying in a low tone:

"The same quantity as usual, madame, but stronger."

The woman nodded, disappeared, and returned; but having left the stopper on the counter, she passed me with the flask uncorked, and I plainly perceived the acrid scent of laudanum. I knew it well, having used it during a nervous illness, and left the shop convinced that La Jeune was an opium-eater, like many of her class, for the woman I had seen was Jocelynd.

The fourth discovery was that some secret anxiety or grief preyed upon mademoiselle, for during that month she altered visibly. Her spirits were variable, her cheek lost its bloom, her form its roundness, and her eyes burned with feverish brilliancy, as if some devouring care preyed upon her life.

I could mark these changes carefully, for I was a frequent and a welcome guest now. By imperceptible degrees I had won my way, and making Brooke my pretext, often led her to speak of him, fancying that topic the one most likely to interest her. Soon I let her see that she had wakened my admiration as an actress, for I was as constant at the theatre as Brooke. Then I, with feigned reluctance, betrayed my susceptibility to her charms as a woman, and by look, sigh, act and word, permitted her to believe that I was one of her most devout adorers.

Upon my life, I sometimes felt as if in truth I was, and half longed to drop my mask and tell her that, with all her faults and follies, I found her more dangerous to my peace than any woman I had ever known. More than once I was tempted to believe that had I been a richer man she would have smiled upon me in spite of Brooke and the unknown Florimond.

As time passed this fancy of mine increased for I observed that with others she was as careless, gay and witty as ever, but with me, especially if we were alone, her manner was subdued, her glance restless, timid and troubled, her voice often agitated or constrained, her whole air that of a woman whose heart is full and pride alone keeps her from letting it overflow.

To Brooke she was uniformly kind, but cold, and often shunned him. At first I believed this only a ruse to lure him to the point, but soon my own penetration, vanity, if you will, led me to think that for a time at least she would hold mercenary motives in check and let the master-passion rule her in spite of interest.

This belief of mine added new excitement to my task, and my undisguisable absorption in it roused Brooke's jealousy, and nothing but a promise to hold his peace till the month was up restrained him from ruining everything, for he refused to accept my discoveries without further proof.

On the last day of the month I went to Natalie at noon, knowing that Arthur would speak that night. I had never been admitted so early before, but sending in an urgent request, it was granted.

I scarcely knew what I meant to say or do, for although my friend and I were freed by mutual consent from the pledge we had given one another, I was hardly ready to fetter myself with a lifelong tie, even to Natalie, whom I no longer disguised from myself that I loved.

I dared make no other offer, for in spite of the gossip and prejudice which always surrounds a young and beautiful actress, I felt that Natalie was innocent, from pride if not from principle, and would be to me a wife or nothing. I loved my freedom well, yet half resolved to lose it for her sake, for in spite of past experiences, I was conscious of a more ardent love at eight-and-thirty than any I had known in my youth.

Natalie came in, looking pale, yet very lovely, for her eyes possessed the soft lustre that follows tears, and on her face there was a look I had never seen before.

She wore a white cashmere *peignoir,* and was wrapt in a soft white mantle. Her hair hung in loose, glittering masses about her face, and her only ornament was a rosary of ebony and gold that hung from her neck.

The room was shaded by heavy curtains, which she did not draw aside, and as she seated herself in the deep velvet chair, her face was much in shadow. I regretted this, for never having seen her by day, except driving, I wished to see and study her when free from the illusion which dress and lamp-light can throw about the plainest woman.

Her hand trembled as I kissed it, her eyes avoided mine, and while I paid my compliments, she listened with drooping lids, a shy smile on her lips, and such a quickly beating heart that the rosary on her bosom stirred visibly. This agitation, coupled with her unusual welcome, banished my last doubt, and before I had decided to betray my passion, the words passed my lips.

As I paused, breathless with the impetuous petition I had made, she looked up with an unmistakable flash of triumph in her eye, an irrepressible accent of joy in her voice, as she answered, with a smile that thrilled my heart:

"Then you love me? You ask my hand? and give your happiness into my keeping?"

"I do."

"You forget what I am—forget that you know nothing of my past; that my heart is a sealed book to you, and that you have seen only the gay, frivolous side I show the world."

"I forget nothing, and glory in your talent as in the fame it wins you. I know you better than you think, for during a month I have studied you deeply, and I read you like an open book. I have discovered faults and follies, mysteries and entanglements, but I can forgive all, forget all, for the sake of this crowning discovery. You love me; I guess it; but I long to hear you confess it, and to know in words that I am blest."

She had questioned eagerly, with her keen eyes full on my face as I replied, but in the act of answering my last speech she rose suddenly as a swift change passed across her face, and in a tone of bitterest contempt, uttered these startling words:

"You say you know me well; you boast that you never are deceived; you believe that you have discovered the secret passions, vices and ambitions of my life; you affirm that I have had a lover, that I gamble, eat opium, and—love you. That last is the blindest blunder of the four, for of all men living, *you* are the one for whom I have the supremest contempt."

I had risen involuntarily when she did, but dropped into my seat as if flung back by the forceful utterance of that last word. I was so entirely taken by surprise that speech, self-possession, and courage deserted me for the moment, and I sat staring at her in dumb amazement. In a voice full of passionate pride, she rapidly continued, with her steady eyes holding me fast by their glittering spell:

"You were wise in your own conceit, and needed humbling. I heard your boast, your plot and pledge, made in this room a month ago, and resolved to teach you a lesson. You flatter yourself you know me thoroughly, yet you have not caught even a glimpse of my true nature, and Arthur's honest instinct has won the day against your worldly wisdom."

"Prove it!" I cried, angrily, for her words, her glance, roused me like insults.

"I will. First let us dispose of the discoveries so honorably made, and used to blast my reputation in a good man's eyes. My lover is an Italian physician, who comes to serve a suffering friend whom I shelter; the laudanum is for the same unhappy invalid. The money I won was honestly *played for*—on the stage, and the secret love you fancied I cherished was not for you—but Arthur."

"Hang the boy; it is a plot between you," I cried, forgetting self-command in my rising wrath.

"Wrong again; he knew nothing of my purpose, never guessed my love till to-day."

"To-day! he has been here already!" I exclaimed, "and you have snared him in spite of my sacrifice. Good! I am right in one thing, the richer prize tempts the mercenary enchantress."

"Still deceived; I have refused him, and no earthly power can change my purpose," she answered, almost solemnly.

"Refused him! and why?" I gasped, feeling more bewildered every moment.

"Because I am married, and—dying."

As the last dread word dropped from her lips, I felt my heart stand still, and I could only mutter hoarsely:

"No! no! it is impossible!"

"It is true; look here and believe it."

With a sudden gesture she swept aside the curtain, gathered back her clustered hair, dropped the shrouding mantle, and turned her face full to the glare of noonday light.

I did believe, for in the wasted figure, no longer disguised with a woman's skill, the pallid face, haggard eyes, and hollow temples, I saw that mysterious something which foreshadows death. It shocked me horribly, and I covered up my eyes without a word, suffering the sharpest pang I had ever known. Through the silence, clear and calm as an accusing angel's, came her voice, saying slowly:

"Judge not, lest ye be judged. Let me tell you the truth, that you may see how much you have wronged me. You think me a Frenchwoman, and you believe me to be under five-and-twenty. I am English, and thirty-seven tomorrow."

"English! thirty-seven!" I ejaculated in a tone of utter incredulity.

"I come of a race whom time touches lightly, and till the last five years of my life, sorrow, pain, and care have been strangers to me," she said, in pure English, and with a faint smile on her pale lips. "I am of good family, but misfortune overtook us, and at seventeen I was left an orphan, poor, and nearly friendless. Before trouble could touch me Florimond married and took me away to a luxurious home in Normandy. He was much older than myself, but he has been fond as a father, as faithful, tender and devoted as a lover all these years. I married him from gratitude, not love, yet I have been happy and heart-free till I met Arthur."

Her voice faltered there, and she pressed her hands against her bosom, as if to stifle the heavy sigh that broke from her.

"You love him; you will break the tie that binds you, and marry him?" I said, bitterly, forgetting in my jealous pain that she had refused him.

"Never! See how little you know my true character," she answered, with a touch of indignation in the voice that now was full of a pathetic weariness. "For years my husband cherished me as the apple of his eye; then, through the treachery of others, came ruin, sickness, and a fate worse than death. My poor Florimond is an imbecile, helpless as a child. All faces are strange to him but mine, all voices empty sounds but mine, and all the world a blank except when I am with him. Can I rob him of this one delight—he who left no wish of mine ungratified, who devoted his life to me, and even in this sad eclipse clings to the one love that has escaped the wreck? No, I cannot forget the debt I owe him. I am grateful, and in spite of all temptations, I remain his faithful wife till death."

How beautiful she was as she said that! Never in her most brilliant hour, on stage or in *salon,* had she shone so fair or impressed me with her power as she did now. That was art, this nature. I admired the actress, I adored the woman, and feeling all the wrong I had done her, felt my eyes dim with the first tears they had known for years. She did not see my honest grief; her gaze went beyond me, as if some invisible presence comforted and strengthened her. With every moment that went by I seemed passing further and further from her, as if she dropped me out of her world henceforth, and knew me no more.

"Now you divine why I became an actress, hid my name, my grief, and for his sake smiled, sung, and feigned both youth and gayety, that I might keep him from that. I had lived so long in France that I was half a Frenchwoman; I had played often, and with success, in my own pretty theatre at Villeroy. I was unknown in Paris, for we seldom came hither, and when left alone with Florimond to care for, I decided to try my fortune on the stage. Beginning humbly, I have worked my way up till I dared to play in Paris. Knowing that youth, beauty and talent attract most when surrounded by luxury, gayety and freedom, I hid my cares, my needs, and made my *debut* as one unfettered, rich and successful. The bait took; I am flattered, *fêted,* loaded with gifts, lavishly paid, and, for a time, the queen of my small realm. Few guess the heavy heart I bear, or dream that a mortal malady is eating my life away. But I am resigned; for if I live three months and am able to play on, I shall leave Florimond secure against want, and that is now my only desire."

"Is there no hope, no help for you?" I said, imploringly, finding it impossible to submit to the sad decree which she received so bravely.

"None. I have tried all that skill can do, and tried in vain. It is too late, and the end approaches fast. I do not suffer much, but daily feel less strength, less spirit, and less interest in the world about me. Do not look at me with such despair; it is not hard to die," she answered, softly.

"But for one so beautiful, so beloved, to die alone is terrible," I murmured, brokenly.

"Not alone, thank heaven; one friend remains, tender and true, faithful to the end."

A blissful smile broke over her face as she stretched her arms toward the place her eye had often sought during that interview. If any further punishment was needed, I received it when I saw Arthur gather the frail creature close to his honest heart, reading his reward in the tender, trusting face that turned so gladly from me to him.

It was no place for me, and murmuring some feeble farewell, I crept away, heart-struck and humbled, feeling like one banished from Paradise; for despite the shadow of sorrow, pain and death, love made a heaven for those I left behind.

* * * * *

I quitted Paris the next day, and four months later Brooke returned to England, bringing me the ebony rosary I knew so well, a parting gift from La Jeune, with her pardon and adieu, for Arthur left her and her poor Florimond quiet under the sod at Pere La Chaise.

Psyche's Art

"Handsome is that handsome does."

I

ONCE UPON A TIME there raged in a certain city one of those fashionable epidemics which occasionally attack our youthful population. It wasn't the music mania, nor gymnastic convulsions, nor that wide-spread malady, croquet. Neither was it one of the new dances which, like a tarantula-bite, set every one a-twirling, nor stage madness, nor yet that American lecturing influenza which yearly sweeps over the land. No, it was a new disease called the Art fever, and it attacked the young women of the community with great violence.

Nothing but time could cure it, and it ran its course to the dismay, amusement, or edification of the beholders, for its victims did all manner of queer things in their delirium. They besieged potteries for clay, drove Italian plaster-workers out of their wits with unexecutable orders, got neuralgia and rheumatism sketching perched on fences and trees like artistic hens, and caused a rise in the price of bread, paper, and charcoal, by their order in crayoning. They covered canvas with the expedition of scene-painters, had classes, lectures, receptions, and exhibitions, made models of each other, and rendered their walls hideous with bad likenesses of all their friends. Their conversation ceased to be intelligible to the uninitiated, and they prattled prettily of "chiaro-oscuro, French sauce, refraction of the angle of the eye, seventh spinus process, depth and juiciness of color, tender touch, and a good tone." Even in dress the artistic disorder was visible; some cast aside crinoline altogether, and stalked about with a severe simplicity of outline worthy of Flaxman. Others flushed themselves with scarlet, that no landscape which they adorned should be without some touch of Turner's favorite tint. Some were *blue* in every sense of the word, and the heads of all were adorned with classic braids, curls tied Hebe-wise, or hair dressed à la hurricane.

It was found impossible to keep them safe at home, and, as the fever grew, these harmless maniacs invaded the sacred retreats where artists of the other sex did congregate, startling those anchorites with visions of large-eyed damsels bearing portfolios in hands delicately begrimed with crayon, chalk, and clay, gliding through the corridors hitherto haunted only by shabby paletots, shadowy hats, and cigar smoke. This irruption was borne with manly fortitude, not to say cheerfulness, for studio doors stood hospitably open as the fair invaders passed, and studies from life were generously offered them in glimpses of picturesque gentlemen posed before easels, brooding over master-pieces in "a divine despair," or attitudinizing upon couches as if exhausted by the soarings of genius.

An atmosphere of romance began to pervade the old buildings when the girls came, and nature and art took turns. There were peepings and whisperings, much stifled laughter and whisking in and out; not to mention the accidental rencontres, small services, and eye telegrams, which somewhat lightened the severe studies of all parties.

Half-a-dozen young victims of this malady met daily in one of the cells of a great art-bee-hive called "Raphael's Rooms," and devoted their shining hours to modelling fancy heads, gossiping the while; for the poor things found the road to fame rather dull and dusty without such verbal sprinklings.

"Psyche Dean, you've had an adventure! I see it in your face; so tell it at once, for we are as stupid as owls here to-day," cried one of the sisterhood, as a bright-eyed girl entered with some precipitation.

"I dropped my portfolio, and a man picked it up, that's all," replied Psyche, hurrying on her gray linen pinafore.

"That won't do; I know something interesting happened, for you've been blushing, and you look brisker than usual this morning," said the first speaker, polishing off the massive nose of her Homer.

"It wasn't anything," began Psyche, a little reluctantly. "I was coming up in a hurry when I ran against a man coming down in a hurry. My portfolio slipped, and my papers went flying all about the landing. Of course we both laughed and begged pardon, and I began to pick them up, but he wouldn't let me; so I held the book while he collected the sketches. I saw him glance at them as he did so, and that made me blush, for they are wretched things, you know."

"Not a bit of it; they are capital, and you are a regular genius, as we all agree," cut in the Homeric Miss Cutter.

"Never tell people they are geniuses unless you wish to spoil them," returned Psyche, severely. "Well, when the portfolio was put to rights I was going on, but he fell to picking up a little bunch of violets I had dropped; you know I always wear a posy into town to give me inspiration. I didn't care for the dusty flowers, and told him so, and scrambled away before any one came. At the top of the stairs I peeped over the railing, and there he was, gathering up every one of those half-dead violets as carefully as if they had been tea-roses."

"Psyche Dean, you have met your fate this day!" exclaimed a third damsel, with straw-colored tresses, and a good deal of weedy shrubbery in her hat, which gave an Ophelia-like expression to her sentimental countenance.

Psyche frowned and shook her head as if half sorry she had told her little story.

"Was he handsome?" asked Miss Larkins, the believer in fate.

"I didn't particularly observe."

"It was the red-headed man, whom we call Titian; he's always on the stairs."

"No, it wasn't; his hair was brown and curly," cried Psyche, innocently falling into the trap.

"Like Peerybingle's baby when its cap was taken off," quoted Miss Dickenson, who pined to drop the last two letters of her name.

"Was it Murillo, the black-eyed one?" asked the fair Cutter, for the girls had a name for all the attitudinizers and promenaders whom they oftenest met.

"No, he had gray eyes, and very fine ones they were too," answered Psyche, adding, as if to herself, "he looked as I imagine Michael Angelo might have looked when young."

"Had he a broken nose like the great Mike?" asked an irreverent damsel.

"If he had, no one would mind it, for his head is splendid; he took his hat off, so I had a fine view. He isn't handsome, but he'll *do* something," said Psyche, prophetically, as she recalled the strong, ambitious face which she had often observed, but never mentioned before.

"Well, dear, considering that you didn't 'particularly look' at the man, you've given us a very good idea of his appearance. We'll call him Michael Angelo, and he shall be your idol. I prefer stout old Rembrandt myself, and Larkie adores that dandefied Raphael," said the lively Cutter, slapping away at Homer's bald pate energetically, as she spoke.

"Raphael is a dear, but Rubens is more to my taste now," returned Miss Larkins. "He was in the hall yesterday talking with Sir Joshua, who had his inevitable umbrella, like a true Englishman. Just as I came up, the umbrella fell right before me. I started back; Sir Joshua laughed but Rubens said, 'Deuce take it!' and caught up the umbrella, giving me a never-to-be-forgotten look. It was perfectly thrilling."

"Which,—the umbrella, the speech, or the look?" asked Psyche, who was not sentimental.

"Ah, you have no soul for art in nature, and nature in art," sighed the amber-tressed Larkins. "I have, for I feed upon a glance, a tint, a curve, with exquisite delight. Rubens is adorable (*as a study*); that lustrous eye, that night of hair, that sumptuous cheek, are perfect. He only needs a cloak, lace collar, and slouching hat to be the genuine thing."

"This isn't the genuine thing by any means. What *does* it need?" said Psyche, looking with a despondent air at the head on her stand.

Many would have pronounced it a clever thing; the nose was strictly Greek, the chin curved upward gracefully, the mouth was sweetly haughty, the brow classically smooth and low, and the breezy hair well done. But something was wanting; Psyche felt that, and could have taken her Venus by the dimpled shoulders, and given her a hearty shake, if that would have put strength and spirit into the lifeless face.

"Now *I* am perfectly satisfied with my Apollo, though you all insist that it is the image of Theodore Smythe. He says so himself, and assures me it will make a sensation when we exhibit," remarked Miss Larkins, complacently caressing the ambrosial locks of her Symthified Phebus.

"What shall you do if it don't?" asked Miss Cutter, with elegance.

"I shall feel that I have mistaken my sphere, shall drop my tools, veil my bust, and cast myself into the arms of Nature, since Art rejects me," replied Miss Larkins, with a tragic gesture and an expression which strongly suggested that in her eyes Nature meant Theodore.

"She must have capacious arms if she is to receive all Art's rejected admirers. Shall I be one of them?"

Psyche put the question to herself as she turned to work, but somehow ambitious aspirations were not in a flourishing condition that morning; her heart was not in tune, and head and hands sympathized. Nothing went well, for certain neglected home-duties had dogged her into town, and now worried her more than dust, or heat, or the ceaseless clatter of tongues. Tom, Dick, and Harry's unmended hose persisted in dancing a spectral jig before her mental eye, mother's querulous complaints spoilt the song she hummed to cheer herself, and little May's wistful face put the goddess of beauty entirely out of countenance.

"It's no use; I can't work till the clay is wet again. Where is Giovanni?" she asked, throwing down her tools with a petulant gesture and a dejected air.

"He is probably playing truant in the empty upper rooms as usual. I can't wait for him any longer, so I'm doing his work myself," answered Miss Dickenson, who was tenderly winding a wet bandage round her Juno's face, one side of which was so much plumper than the other that it looked as if the Queen of Olympus was being hydropathically treated for a severe fit of ague.

"I'll go and find the little scamp; a run will do me good; so will a breath of air and a view of the park from the upper windows."

Doffing her apron, Psyche strolled away up an unfrequented staircase to the empty apartments, which seemed to be too high even for the lovers of High Art. On the western side they were shady and cool, and, leaning from one of the windows, Psyche watched the feathery treetops ruffled by the balmy wind, that brought spring odors from the hills, lying green and sunny far away. Silence and solitude were such pleasant companions that the girl forgot herself, till a shrill whistle disturbed her day-dreams, and reminded her what she came for. Following the sound she found the little Italian errandboy busily uncovering a clay model which stood in the middle of a scantily furnished room near by.

"He is not here; come and look; it is greatly beautiful," cried Giovanni, beckoning with an air of importance.

Psyche did look and speedily forgot both her errand and herself. It was the figure of a man, standing erect, and looking straight before him with a wonderfully life-like expression. It was neither a mythological nor a historical character, Psyche thought, and was glad of it, being tired to death of gods and heroes. She soon ceased to wonder what it was, feeling only the indescribable charm of something higher than beauty. Small as her knowledge was, she could see and enjoy the power visible in every part of it; the accurate anatomy of the vigorous limbs, the grace of the pose, the strength and spirit in the countenance, clay though it was. A majestic figure, but the spell lay in the face, which, while it suggested the divine, was full of human truth and tenderness, for pain and passion seemed to have passed over it and a humility half-pathetic, a courage half-heroic, seemed to have been born from some great loss or woe.

How long she stood there Psyche did not know. Giovanni went away unseen, to fill his water-pail, and in the silence, she just stood and looked. Her eyes kindled, her color rose, despondency and discontent vanished, and her soul was in her face, for she loved beauty passionately, and all that was best and truest in her did honor to the genius of the unknown worker.

"If I could do a thing like that I'd die happy!" she exclaimed, impetuously, as a feeling of despair came over her at the thought of her own poor attempts.

"Who did it, Giovanni?" she asked, still looking up at the grand face with unsatisfied eyes.

"Paul Gage."

It was not the boy's voice, and, with a start, Psyche turned to see her Michael Angelo, standing in the door-way attentively observing her. Being too full of artless admiration to think of herself just yet, she neither blushed nor apologized, but looked straight at him, saying heartily:—

"You have done a wonderful piece of work, and I envy you more than I can tell."

The enthusiasm in her face, the frankness of her manner, seemed to please him, for there was no affectation about either. He gave her a keen, kind glance out of the "fine gray eyes," a little bow, and a grateful smile, saying quietly:—

"Then my Adam is not a failure in spite of his fall?"

Psyche turned from the sculptor to his model with increased admiration in her face, and earnestness in her voice, as she exclaimed, delighted:—

"Adam! I might have known it was he. O sir, you have indeed succeeded, for you have given that figure the power and pathos of the first man who sinned and suffered, and began again."

"Then I am satisfied." That was all he said, but the look he gave his work was a very eloquent one, for it betrayed that he had paid the price of success in patience and privation, labor and hope.

"What can one do to learn your secret?" asked the girl wistfully, for there was nothing in the man's manner to disturb her self-forgetful mood, but much to foster it, because to the solitary worker this confiding guest was as welcome as the doves who often hopped in at his window.

"Work and wait, and meantime feed heart, soul, and imagination with the best food one can get," he answered slowly, finding it impossible to give a receipt for genius.

"I can work and wait a long time to gain my end; but I don't know where to find the food you speak of," she answered, looking at him like a hungry child.

"I wish I could tell you, but each needs different fare, and each must look for it in different places."

The kindly tone and the sympathizing look, as well as the lines in his forehead, and a few gray hairs among the brown, gave Psyche courage to say more.

"I love beauty so much that I not only want to possess it myself, but to gain the power of seeing it in all things, and the art of reproducing it with truth. I have tried very hard to do it, but something is wanting; and in spite of my intense desire I never get on."

As she spoke the girl's eyes filled and fell in spite of herself, and turning a little with sudden shamefacedness she saw, lying on the table beside her among other scraps in manuscript and print, the well-known lines:—

"I slept, and dreamed that life was beauty;
I woke, and found that life was duty.
Was thy dream then a shadowy lie?
Toil on, sad heart, courageously,
And thou shalt find thy dream to be
A noonday light and truth to thee."

She knew them at a glance, had read them many times, but now they came home to her with sudden force, and, seeing that his eye had followed hers, she said in her impulsive fashion:—

"Is doing one's duty a good way to feed heart, soul, and imagination?"

As if he had caught a glimpse of what was going on in her mind, Paul answered emphatically:—

"Excellent; for if one is good, one is happy, and if happy, one can work well. Moulding character is the highest sort of sculpture, and all of us should learn that art before we touch clay or marble."

He spoke with the energy of a man who believed what he said, and did his best to be worthy of the rich gift bestowed upon him. The sight of her violets in a glass of water, and Giovanni staring at her with round eyes, suddenly recalled Psyche to a sense of the proprieties which she had been innocently outraging for the last ten minutes. A sort of panic seized her; she blushed deeply, retreated precipitately to the door, and vanished murmuring thanks and apologies as she went.

"Did you find him? I thought you had forgotten," said Miss Dickenson, now hard at work.

"Yes, I found him. No, I shall not forget," returned Psyche, thinking of Gage, not Giovanni.

She stood before her work, eying it intently for several minutes; then, with an expression of great contempt for the whole thing, she suddenly tilted her cherished Venus on to the floor, gave the classical face a finishing crunch, and put on her hat in a decisive manner, saying briefly to the dismayed damsels:—

"Good-by, girls; I shan't come any more, for I'm going to work at home hereafter."

II

The prospect of pursuing artistic studies at home was not brilliant, as one may imagine when I mention that Psyche's father was a painfully prosaic man, wrapt in flannel, so to speak; for his woollen mills left him no time for anything but sleep, food, and newspapers. Mrs. Dean was one of those exasperating women who pervade their mansions like a domestic steam-engine one week and take to their sofas the next, absorbed by fidgets and foot-stoves, shawls, and lamentations. There were three riotous and robust young brothers, whom it is unnecessary to describe except by stating that they were *boys* in the broadest sense of that delightful word. There was a feeble little sister, whose patient, suffering face demanded constant love and care to mitigate the weariness of a life of pain. And last, but not least by any means, there were two Irish ladies, who, with the best intentions imaginable, produced a universal state of topsy-turvyness when left to themselves for a moment.

But being very much in earnest about doing her duty, not because it *was* her duty, but as a means toward an end, Psyche fell to work with a will, hoping to serve both masters at once. So she might have done, perhaps, if flesh and blood had been as plastic as clay, but the live models were so exacting in their demands upon her time and strength, that the poor statues went to the wall. Sculpture and sewing, calls and crayons, Ruskin and receipt-books, didn't work well together, and poor Psyche found duties and desires desperately antagonistic. Take a day as a sample.

"The washing and ironing is well over, thank goodness, ma used up and quiet, the boys out of the way, and May comfortable, so I'll indulge myself in a blissful day after my own heart," Psyche said, as she shut herself into her little studio, and prepared to enjoy a few hours of hard study and happy day-dreams.

With a book on her lap, and her own round, white arm going through all manner of queer evolutions, she was placidly repeating, "Deltoids, Biceps, Triceps, Pronator, Supinator, Palmanis, Flexor carpi ulnaris—"

"Here's Flexis what-you-call-ums for you," interrupted a voice, which began in a shrill falsetto and ended in a gruff bass, as a flushed, dusty, long-legged boy burst in, with a bleeding hand obligingly extended for inspection.

"Mercy on us, Harry, what have you done to yourself now? Split your fingers with a cricket-ball again?" cried Psyche, as her arms went up and her book went down.

"No, sir. I just pitched into one of the fellows because he got mad and said pa was going to fail."

"O Harry, is he?"

"Course he isn't! It's hard times for every one, but pa will pull through like a brick. No use to try and explain it all; girls can't understand business; so you just tie me up, and don't bother," was the characteristic reply of the young man, who, being three years her junior, of course treated the weaker vessel with lordly condescension.

"What a dreadful wound! I hope nothing is broken, for I haven't studied the hand much yet, and may do mischief doing it up," said Psyche, examining the great grimy paw with tender solicitude.

"Much good your biceps, and deltoids, and things do you, if you can't right up a little cut like that," squeaked the ungrateful hero.

"I'm not going to be a surgeon, thank Heaven; I intend to make perfect hands and arms, not mend damaged ones," retorted Psyche, in a dignified tone, somewhat marred by a great piece of court-plaster on her tongue.

"I should say a surgeon could improve *that* perfect thing, if he didn't die a-laughing before he began," growled Harry, pointing with a scornful grin at a clay arm humpy with muscles all carefully developed in the wrong places.

"Don't hoot, Hal, for you don't know anything about it. Wait a few years and see if you're not proud of me."

"Sculp away then, do your prettiest, and I'll hurrah for your mud-pies like a good one;" with which cheering promise the youth departed, having effectually disturbed his sister's peaceful mood.

Anxious thoughts of her father rendered "biceps, deltoids, and things" uninteresting, and, hoping to compose her mind, she took up The Old Painters and went on with the story of Claude Lorraine. She had just reached the tender scene where:—

"Calista gazed with enthusiasm, while she looked like a being of heaven rather than earth. 'My friend,' she cried, 'I read in thy picture thy immortality!' As she spoke, her head sunk upon his bosom, and it was several moments before Claude perceived that he supported a lifeless form."

"How sweet!" said Psyche, with a romantic sigh.

"Faith, and swate it is thin!" echoed Katy, whose red head had just appeared round the half-opened door. "It's gingybread I'm making the day, miss, and will I be puttin' purlash or sallyrathis into it, if ye plase?"

"Purlash by all means," returned the girl, keeping her countenance, fearing to enrage Katy by a laugh; for the angry passions of the red-haired one rose more quickly than her bread. As she departed with alacrity to add a spoonful of starch and a pinch of whiting to her cake, Psyche, feeling better for her story and her smile, put on her bib and paper cap and fell to work on the deformed arm. An hour of bliss, then came a ring at the door-bell, followed by Biddy to announce callers, and add that as "the mistress was in her bed, miss must go and take care of 'em." Whereat "miss" cast down her tools in despair, threw her cap one way, her bib another, and went in to her guests with anything but a rapturous welcome.

Dinner being accomplished after much rushing up and down stairs with trays and messages for Mrs. Dean, Psyche fled again to her studio, ordering no one to approach under pain of a scolding. All went well till, going in search of something, she found her little sister sitting on the floor with her cheek against the studio door.

"I didn't mean to be naughty, Sy, but ma's asleep, and the boys all gone, so I just came to be near you; it's so lonely everywhere," she said, apologetically, as she lifted up the heavy head that always ached.

"The boys are very thoughtless. Come in and stay with me; you are such a mouse you won't disturb me. Wouldn't you like to play be a model, and let me draw your arm, and tell you all about the nice little bones and muscles?" asked Psyche, who had the fever very strong upon her just then.

May didn't look as if the proposed amusement overwhelmed her with delight, but meekly consented to be perched upon a high stool with one arm propped up by a dropsical plaster cherub, while Psyche drew busily, feeling that duty and pleasure were being delightfully combined.

"Can't you hold your arm still, child? It shakes so I can't get it right," she said, rather impatiently.

"No, it will tremble, 'cause it's weak. I try hard, Sy, but there don't seem to be any strongness in me lately."

"That's better; keep it so a few minutes and I'll be done," cried the artist, forgetting that a few minutes may seem ages.

"My arm is so thin you can see the bunches nicely,—can't you?"

"Yes, dear."

Psyche glanced up at the wasted limb and when she drew again there was a blur before her eyes for a minute.

"I wish I was as fat as this white boy; but I get thinner every day somehow, and pretty soon there won't be any of me left but my little bones," said the child, looking at the winged cherub with sorrowful envy.

"Don't, my darling; don't say that," cried Psyche, dropping her work with a sudden pang at her heart. "I'm a sinful, selfish girl to keep you here; you're weak for want of air; come out and see the chickens, and pick dandelions, and have a good romp with the boys."

The weak arms were strong enough to clasp Psyche's neck, and the tired face brightened beautifully as the child exclaimed, with grateful delight:—

"Oh, I'd like it very much! I wanted to go dreadfully; but everybody is so busy all the time. I don't want to play, Sy; but just to lie on the grass with my head in your lap while you tell stories and draw me pretty things as you used to."

The studio was deserted all that afternoon, for Psyche sat in the orchard drawing squirrels on the wall, pert robbins hopping by, buttercups and mosses, elves and angels; while May lay contentedly enjoying sun and air, sisterly care, and the "pretty things" she loved so well. Psyche did not find the task a hard one; for this time her heart was in it, and if she needed any reward she surely found it; for the little face on her knee lost its weary look, and the peace and beauty of nature soothed her own troubled spirit, cheered her heart, and did her more good than hours of solitary study.

Finding, much to her own surprise, that her fancy was teeming with lovely conceits, she did hope for a quiet evening. But ma wanted a dish of gossip, pa must have his papers read to him, the boys had lessons and rips and grievances to be attended to, May's lullaby could not be forgotten, and the maids had to be looked after, lest burly "cousins" should be hidden in the boiler, or lucifer matches among the shavings. So Psyche's day ended, leaving her very tired, rather discouraged, and almost heart-sick with the shadow of a coming sorrow.

All summer she did her best, but accomplished very little as she thought; yet this was the teaching she most needed, and in time she came to see it. In the autumn May died, whispering with her arms about her sister's neck:—

"You make me so happy, Sy, I wouldn't mind the pain if I could stay a little longer. But if I can't, good-by, dear, good-by."

Her last look and word and kiss were all for Psyche, who felt then with grateful tears that her summer had not been wasted; for the smile upon the little dead face was more to her than any marble perfection her hands could have carved.

In the solemn pause which death makes in every family, Psyche said, with the sweet self-forgetfulness of a strong yet tender nature:—

"I must not think of myself, but try to comfort them;" and with this resolution she gave herself heart and soul to duty, never thinking of reward.

A busy, anxious, humdrum winter, for, as Harry said, "it was hard times for every one." Mr. Dean grew gray with the weight of business cares about which he never spoke; Mrs. Dean, laboring under the delusion that an invalid was a necessary appendage to the family, installed herself in the place the child's death left vacant, and the boys needed much comforting, for the poor lads never knew how much they loved "the baby" till the little chair stood empty. All turned to Sy for help and consolation, and her strength seemed to increase with the demand upon it. Patience and cheerfulness, courage and skill, came at her call like good fairies who had bided their time. House-keeping ceased to be hateful, and peace reigned in parlor and kitchen, while Mrs. Dean, shrouded in shawls, read Hahnemann's Lesser Writings on her sofa. Mr. Dean sometimes forgot his mills when a bright face came to meet him, a gentle hand smoothed the wrinkles out of his anxious forehead, and a daughterly heart sympathized with all his cares. The boys found home very pleasant with Sy always there ready to "lend a hand," whether it was to make fancy ties, help conjugate "a confounded verb," pull candy, or sing sweetly in the twilight when all thought of little May and grew quiet.

The studio door remained locked till her brothers begged Psyche to open it and make a bust of the child. A flush of joy swept over her face at the request, and her patient eyes grew bright and eager, as a thirsty traveller's might at the sight or sound of water. Then it faded as she shook her head, saying, with a regretful sigh, "I'm afraid I've lost the little skill I ever had."

But she tried, and with great wonder and delight discovered that she could work as she had never done before. She thought the newly found power lay in her longing to see the little face again; for it grew like magic under her loving hands, while every tender memory, sweet thought, and devout hope she had ever cherished, seemed to lend their aid. But when it was done and welcomed with tears and smiles, and praise more precious than any the world could give, then Psyche said within herself like one who saw light at last:—

"He was right; doing one's duty *is* the way to feed heart, soul, and imagination; for if one is good, one is happy, and if happy, one can work well."

III

"She broke her head, and went home to come no more," was Giovanni's somewhat startling answer when Paul asked about Psyche, finding that he no longer met her on the stairs or in the halls. He understood what the boy meant, and with an approving nod turned to his work again, saying, "I like that! If there is any power in her, she has taken the right way to find it out, I suspect."

How she prospered he never asked; for, though he met her more than once that year, the interviews were brief ones in street, concert-room, or picture-gallery, and she carefully avoided speaking of herself. But, possessing the gifted eyes which can look below the surface of things, he detected in the girl's face something better than beauty, though each time he saw it, it looked older and more thoughtful, often anxious and sad.

"She is getting on," he said to himself with a cordial satisfaction which gave his manner a friendliness as grateful to Psyche as his wise reticence.

Adam was finished at last, proved a genuine success, and Paul heartily enjoyed the well-earned reward for years of honest work. One blithe May morning, he slipped early into the art-gallery, where the statue now stood, to look at his creation with paternal pride. He was quite alone with the stately figure that shone white against the purple draperies and seemed to offer him a voiceless welcome from its marble lips. He gave it one loving look, and then forgot it, for at the feet of his Adam lay a handful of wild violets, with the dew still on them. A sudden smile broke over his face as he took them up, with the thought, "She has been here and found my work good."

For several moments he stood thoughtfully turning the flowers to and fro in his hands; then, as if deciding some question within himself, he said, still smiling:—

"It is just a year since she went home; she must have accomplished something in that time; I'll take the violets as a sign that I may go and ask her what."

He knew she lived just out of the city, between the river and the mills, and as he left the streets behind him, he found more violets blooming all along the way like flowery guides to lead him right. Greener grew the road, balmier blew the wind, and blither sang the birds, as he went on enjoying his holiday with the zest of a boy, until he reached a most attractive little path winding away across the fields. The gate swung invitingly open, and all the ground before it was blue with violets. Still following their guidance he took the narrow path, till, coming to a mossy stone beside a brook, he sat down to listen to the blackbirds singing deliciously in the willows overhead. Close by the stone, half hidden in the grass lay a little book, and, taking it up, he found it was a pocket-diary. No name appeared on the fly-leaf, and, turning the pages to find some clue to its owner, he read here and there enough to give him glimpses into an innocent and earnest heart which seemed to be learning some hard lesson patiently. Only near the end did he find the clue in words of his own, spoken long ago, and a name. Then, though longing intensely to know more, he shut the little book and went on, showing by his altered face that the simple record of a girl's life had touched him deeply.

Soon an old house appeared nestling to the hillside with the river shining in the low green meadows just before it.

"She lives there," he said, with as much certainty as if the pansies by the door-stone spelt her name, and, knocking, he asked for Psyche.

"She's gone to town, but I expect her home every minute." "Ask the gentleman to walk in and wait, Katy," cried a voice from above, where the whisk of skirts was followed by the appearance of an inquiring eye over the banisters.

The gentleman did walk in, and while he waited looked about him. The room, though very simply furnished, had a good deal of beauty in it, for the pictures were few and well chosen, the books such as never grow old, the music lying on the well-worn piano of the sort which is never out of fashion, and standing somewhat apart was one small statue in a recess full of flowers. Lovely in its simple grace and truth was the figure of a child looking upward as if watching the airy flight of some butterfly which had evidently escaped from the chrysalis still lying in the little hand.

Paul was looking at it with approving eyes when Mrs. Dean appeared with his card in her hand, three shawls on her shoulders, and in her face a somewhat startled expression, as if she expected some novel demonstration from the man whose genius her daughter so much admired.

"I hope Miss Psyche is well," began Paul, with great discrimination if not originality.

The delightfully commonplace remark tranquillized Mrs. Dean at once, and, taking off the upper shawl with a fussy gesture, she settled herself for a chat.

"Yes, thank Heaven, Sy is well. I don't know what would become of us if she wasn't. It has been a hard and sorrowful year for us with Mr. Dean's business embarrassments, my feeble health, and May's death. I don't know that you were aware of our loss, sir;" and unaffected maternal grief gave sudden dignity to the faded, fretful face of the speaker.

Paul murmured his regrets, understanding better now the pathetic words on a certain tear-stained page of the little book still in his pocket.

"Poor dear, she suffered everything, and it came very hard upon Sy, for the child wasn't happy with any one else, and almost lived in her arms," continued Mrs. Dean, dropping the second shawl to get her handkerchief.

"Miss Psyche has not had much time for art-studies this year, I suppose?" said Paul, hoping to arrest the shower natural as it was.

"How could she, with two invalids, the housekeeping, pa and the boys to attend to? No, she gave that up last spring, and though it was a great disappointment to her at the time, she has got over it now, and is happier than she ever was before, I think," added her mother, remembering as she spoke that Psyche even now went about the house sometimes pale and silent, with a hungry look in her eyes.

"I am glad to hear it," though a little shadow passed over his face as Paul spoke, for he was too true an artist to believe that any work could be as happy as that which he loved and lived for. "I thought there was much promise in Miss Psyche, and I sincerely believe that time will prove me a true prophet," he said with mingled regret and hope in his voice as he glanced about the room, which betrayed the tastes still cherished by the girl.

"I'm afraid ambition isn't good for women; I mean the sort that makes 'em known by coming before the public in any way. But Sy deserves some reward, I'm sure, and I know she'll have it, for a better daughter never lived."

Here the third shawl was cast off, as if the thought of Psyche, or the presence of a genial guest, had touched Mrs. Dean's chilly nature with a comfortable warmth.

Further conversation was interrupted by the avalanche of boys, which came tumbling down the front stairs as Tom, Dick, and Harry shouted in a sort of chorus:—

"Sy, my balloon has got away; lend us a hand at catching him!"

"Sy, I want a lot of paste made, right off."

"Sy, I've split my jacket down the back; come sew me up, there's a dear!"

On beholding a stranger the young gentlemen suddenly lost their voices, found their manners, and with nods and grins took themselves away as quietly as could be expected of six clumping boots and an unlimited quantity of animal spirits in a high state of effervescence. As they trooped off an unmistakable odor of burnt milk pervaded the air, and the crash of china, followed by an Irish wail, caused Mrs. Dean to clap on her three shawls again and excuse herself in visible trepidation.

Paul laughed quietly to himself, then turned sober and said, "Poor Psyche!" with a sympathetic sigh. He roamed about the room impatiently till the sound of voices drew him to the window to behold the girl coming up the walk with her clumsy old father leaning on one arm, the other loaded with baskets and bundles, and her hands occupied by a remarkably ugly turtle.

"Here we are!" cried a cheery voice, as they entered without observing the new-comer. "I've done all my errands and had a lovely time. There is Tom's gunpowder, Dick's fishhooks, and one of Professor Gazzy's famous turtles for Harry. Here are your bundles, mother dear, and, best of all, here's pa, home in time for a good rest before dinner. I went to the mill and got him."

Psyche spoke as if she had brought a treasure; and so she had, for though Mr. Dean's face usually was about as expressive as the turtle's, it woke and warmed with the affection which his daughter had fostered till no amount of flannel could extinguish it. His big hand patted her cheek very gently as he said, in a tone of fatherly love and pride:—

"My little Sy never forgets old pa, does she?"

"Good gracious me, my dear, there's *such* a mess in the kitchen! Katy's burnt up the pudding, put castor-oil instead of olive in the salad, smashed the best meat-dish, and here's Mr. Gage come to dinner," cried Mrs. Dean in accents of despair as she tied up her head in a fourth shawl.

"Oh, I'm so glad; I'll go in and see him a few minutes, and then I'll come and attend to everything; so don't worry, mother."

"How did you find me out?" asked Psyche as she shook hands with her guest and stood looking up at him with all the old confiding frankness in her face and manner.

"The violets showed me the way."

She glanced at the posy in his button-hole and smiled.

"Yes, I gave them to Adam, but I didn't think you would guess. I enjoyed your work for an hour to-day, and I have no words strong enough to express my admiration."

"There is no need of any. Tell me about yourself; what have you been doing all this year?" he asked, watching with genuine satisfaction the serene and sunny face before him, for discontent, anxiety, and sadness were no longer visible there.

"I've been working and waiting," she began.

"And succeeding, if I may believe what I see and hear and read," he said with an expressive little wave of the book as he laid it down before her.

"My diary! I didn't know I had lost it. Where did you find it?"

"By the brook where I stopped to rest. The moment I saw your name I shut it up. Forgive me, but I can't ask pardon for reading a few pages of that little gospel of patience, love, and self-denial."

She gave him a reproachful look and hurried the telltale book out of sight as she said, with a momentary shadow on her face:—

"It has been a hard task; but I think I have learned it, and am just beginning to find that my dream *is* 'a noonday light and truth,' to me."

"Then you do not relinquish your hopes and lay down your tools?" he asked with some eagerness.

"Never! I thought at first that I could not serve two masters; but in trying to be faithful to one I find I am nearer and dearer to the other. My cares and duties are growing lighter every day (or I have learned to bear them better), and when my leisure does come I shall know how to use it, for my head is full of ambitious plans, and I feel that I can do something *now.*"

All the old enthusiasm shone in her eyes, and a sense of power betrayed itself in voice and gesture as she spoke.

"I believe it," he said heartily. "You have learned the secret, as that proves."

Psyche looked at the childish image as he pointed to it, and into her face there came a motherly expression that made it very sweet.

"That little sister was so dear to me I could not fail to make her lovely, for I put my heart into my work. The year has gone, but I don't regret it, though this is all I have done."

"You forgot your three wishes; I think the year has granted them."

"What were they?"

"To possess beauty in yourself, the power of seeing it in all things, and the art of reproducing it with truth."

She colored deeply under the glance which accompanied the threefold compliment, and answered with grateful humility,—

"You are very kind to say so; I wish I could believe it." Then, as if anxious to forget herself, she added rather abruptly,—

"I hear you think of giving your Adam a mate,—have you begun yet?"

"Yes, my design is finished, all but the face."

"I should think you could image Eve's beauty since you have succeeded so well with Adam's."

"The features perhaps, but not the expression. That is the charm of feminine faces, a charm so subtile that few can catch and keep it. I want a truly womanly face, one that shall be sweet and strong without being either weak or hard. A hopeful, loving, earnest face, with a tender touch of motherliness in it, and perhaps the shadow of a grief that has softened but not saddened it."

"It will be hard to find a face like that."

"I don't expect to find it in perfection; but one sometimes sees faces which suggest all this, and in rare moments give glimpses of a lovely possibility."

"I sincerely hope you will find one then," said Psyche, thinking of the dinner.

"Thank you; *I* think I have."

Now, in order that every one may be suited, we will stop here, and leave our readers to finish the story as they like. Those who prefer the good old fashion may believe that the hero and heroine fell in love, were married and lived happily ever afterward. But those who can conceive of a world outside of a wedding-ring may believe that the friends remained faithful friends all their lives, while Paul won fame and fortune, and Psyche grew beautiful with the beauty of a serene and sunny nature, happy in duties which became pleasures, rich in the art which made life lovely to herself and others.

My Mysterious Mademoiselle

At Lyons I engaged a coupé, laid in a substantial lunch, got out my novels and cigars, and prepared to make myself as comfortable as circumstances permitted; for we should not reach Nice till morning, and a night journey was my especial detestation. Nothing would have induced me to undertake it in mid-winter, but a pathetic letter from my sister, imploring me to come to her, as she was failing fast, and had a precious gift to bestow upon me before she died. This sister had mortally offended our father by marrying a Frenchman. The old man never forgave her, never would see her, and cut her off with a shilling in his will. I had been forbidden to have any communication with her on pain of disinheritance, and had obeyed, for I shared my father's prejudice, and made no attempt to befriend my sister, even when I learned that she was a widow, although my father's death freed me from my promise. For more than fifteen years we had been utterly estranged; but when her pleading letter came to me, my heart softened, and I longed to see her. My conscience reproached me, and, leaving my cozy bachelor establishment in London, I hurried away, hoping to repair the neglect of years by tardy tenderness and care.

My thoughts worried me that night, and the fear of being too late haunted me distressfully. I could neither read, sleep, nor smoke, and soon heartily wished I had taken a seat in a double carriage, where society of some sort would have made the long hours more endurable. As we stopped at a way-station, I was roused from a remorseful reverie by the guard, who put in his head to inquire, with an insinuating shrug and smile:

"Will monsieur permit a lady to enter? The train is very full, and no place remains for her in the first-class. It will be a great kindness if monsieur will take pity on the charming little mademoiselle."

He dropped his voice in uttering the last words, and gave a nod, which plainly expressed his opinion that monsieur would not regret the courtesy. Glad to be relieved from the solitude that oppressed me, I consented at once, and waited with some curiosity to see what sort of companion I was to have for the next few hours.

The first glance satisfied me; but, like a true Englishman, I made no demonstration of interest beyond a bow and a brief reply to the apologies and thanks uttered in a fresh young voice as the new-comer took her seat. A slender girl of sixteen or so, simply dressed in black, with a little hat tied down over golden curls, and a rosy face, lit up by lustrous hazel eyes, at once arch, modest and wistful. A cloak and a plump traveling bag were all her luggage, and quickly arranging them, she drew out a book, sank back in her corner, and appeared to read, as if anxious to render me forgetful of her presence as soon as possible.

I liked that, and resolved to convince her at the first opportunity that I was no English bear, but a gentleman who could be very agreeable when he chose.

The opportunity did not arrive as soon as I hoped, and I began to grow impatient to hear the fresh young voice again. I made a few attempts at conversation, but the little girl seemed timid, for she answered in the briefest words, and fell to reading again, forcing me to content myself with admiring the long curled lashes, the rosy mouth, and the golden hair of this demure demoiselle.

She was evidently afraid of the big, black-bearded gentleman, and would not be drawn out, so I solaced myself by watching her in the windows opposite, which reflected every movement like a mirror.

Presently the book slipped from her hand, the bright eyes grew heavy, the pretty head began to nod, and sleep grew more and more irresistible. Half closing my eyes, I feigned slumber, and was amused at the little girl's evident relief. She peeped at first, then took a good look, then smiled to herself as if well pleased, yawned, and rubbed her eyes like a sleepy child, took off her hat, tied a coquettish rose-colored rigolette over her soft hair, viewed herself in the glass, and laughed a low laugh, so full of merriment, that I found it difficult to keep my countenance. Then, with a roguish glance at me, she put out her hand toward the flask of wine lying on the leaf, with a half-open case of chocolate croquettes, which I had been munching, lifted the flask to her lips, put it hastily down again, took one bon-bon, and, curling herself up like a kitten, seemed to drop asleep at once.

"Poor little thing," I thought to myself, "she is hungry, cold, and tired; she longs for a warm sip, a sugar-plum, and a kind word, I dare say.

She is far too young and pretty to be traveling alone. I must take care of her."

In pursuance of which friendly resolve I laid my rug lightly over her, slipped a soft shawl under her head, drew the curtains for warmth, and then repaid myself for these attentions by looking long and freely at the face encircled by the rosy cloud. Prettier than ever when flushed with sleep did it look, and I quite lost myself in the pleasant reverie which came to me while leaning over the young girl, watching the silken lashes lying quietly on the blooming cheeks, listening to her soft breath, touching the yellow curls that strayed over the arm of the seat, and wondering who the charming little person might be. She reminded me of my first sweetheart—a pretty cousin, who had captivated my boyish heart at eighteen, and dealt it a wound it never could forget. At five-and-thirty these little romances sometimes return to one's memory fresher and dearer for the years that have taught us the sweetness of youth—the bitterness of regret. In a sort of waking dream I sat looking at the stranger, who seemed to wear the guise of my first love, till suddenly the great eyes flashed wide open, the girl sprung up, and, clasping her hands, cried, imploringly:

"Ah, monsieur, do not hurt me, for I am helpless. Take my little purse; take all I have, but spare my life for my poor mother's sake!"

"Good heavens, child, do you take me for a robber?" I exclaimed, startled out of my sentimental fancies by this unexpected performance.

"Pardon; I was dreaming; I woke to find you bending over me, and I was frightened," she murmured, eying me timidly.

"That was also a part of your dream. Do I look like a rascal, mademoiselle?" I demanded, anxious to reassure her.

"Indeed, no; you look truly kind, and I trust you. But I am not used to traveling alone; I am anxious and timid, yet now I do not fear. Pardon, monsieur; pray, pardon a poor child who has no friend to protect her."

She put out her hand with an impulsive gesture, as the soft eyes were lifted confidingly to mine, and what could I do but kiss the hand in true French style, and smile back into the eyes with involuntary tenderness, as I replied, with unusual gallantry:

"Not without a friend to protect her, if mademoiselle will permit me the happiness. Rest tranquil, no one shall harm you. Confide in me, and you shall find that we 'cold English' have hearts, and may be trusted."

"Ah, so kind, so pitiful! A thousand thanks; but do not let me disturb monsieur. I will have no more panics, and can only atone for my foolish fancy by remaining quiet, that monsieur may sleep."

"Sleep! Not I; and the best atonement you can make is to join me at supper, and wile away this tedious night with friendly confidences. Shall it be so, mademoiselle?" I asked, assuming a paternal air to reassure her.

"That would be pleasant; for I confess I am hungry, and have nothing with me. I left in such haste I forgot—" She paused suddenly, turned scarlet, and drooped her eyes, as if on the point of betraying some secret.

I took no notice, but began to fancy that my little friend was engaged in some romance which might prove interesting. Opening my traveling-case, I set forth cold chicken, *tartines,* wine, and sweetmeats, and served her as respectfully as if she had been a duchess, instead of what I suspected—a run-away school-girl. My manner put her at her ease, and she chatted away with charming frankness, though now and then she checked some word on her lips, blushed and laughed, and looked so merry and mysterious, that I began to find my school-girl a most captivating companion. The hours flew rapidly now; remorse and anxiety slept; I felt blithe and young again, for my lost love seemed to sit beside me; I forgot my years, and almost fancied myself an ardent lad again.

What mademoiselle thought of me I could only guess; but look, tone and manner betrayed the most flattering confidence. I enjoyed the little adventure without a thought of consequences.

At Toulon we changed cars, and I could not get a coupé, but fortunately found places in a carriage, whose only occupant was a sleepy old woman. As I was about taking my seat, after bringing my companion a cup of hot coffee, she uttered an exclamation, dragged her vail over her face, and shrunk into the corner of our compartment.

"What alarms you?" I asked, anxiously, for her mystery piqued my curiosity.

"Look out and see if a tall young man is not promenading the platform, and looking into every carriage," returned mademoiselle, in good English, for the first time.

I looked out, saw the person described, watched him approach, and observed that he glanced eagerly into each car as he passed.

"He is there, and is about to favor us with an inspection. What are your commands, mademoiselle?" I asked.

"Oh, sir, befriend me; cover me up; say that I am ill; call yourself my father for a moment—I will explain it all. Hush, he is here!" and the girl clung to my arm with a nervous gesture, an imploring look, which I could not resist.

The stranger appeared, entered with a grave bow, seated himself opposite, and glanced from me to the muffled figure at my side. We were off in a moment, and no one spoke, till a little cough behind the vail gave the new-comer a pretext for addressing me.

"Mademoiselle is annoyed by the air; permit me to close the window."

"Madame is an invalid, and will thank you to do so," I replied, taking a malicious satisfaction in disobeying the girl, for the idea of passing as her father disgusted me, and I preferred a more youthful title.

A sly pinch of the arm was all the revenge she could take; and, as I stooped to settle the cloaks about her, I got a glance from the hazel eyes, reproachful, defiant, and merry.

"Ah, she has spirit, this little wandering princess. Let us see what our friend opposite has to do with her," I said to myself, feeling almost jealous of the young man, who was a handsome, resolute-looking fellow, in a sort of uniform.

"Does he understand English, madame, my wife?" I whispered to the girl.

"Not a word," she whispered back, with another charming pinch.

"Good; then tell me all about him. I demand an explanation."

"Not now; not here, wait a little. Can you not trust me, when I confide so much to you?"

"No, I am burning with curiosity, and I deserve some reward for my good behavior. Shall I not have it, *ma amie?*"

"Truly, you do, and I will give you anything by-and-by," she began.

"*Anything?*" I asked, quickly.

"Yes; I give you my word."

"I shall hold you to your promise. Come, we will make a little bargain. I will blindly obey you till we reach Nice, if you will frankly tell me the cause of all this mystery before we part."

"Done!" cried the girl, with an odd laugh.

"Done!" said I, feeling that I was probably making a fool of myself.

The young man eyed us sharply as we spoke, but said nothing, and, wishing to make the most of my bargain, I pillowed my little wife's head on my shoulder, and talked in whispers, while she nestled in shelter of my arm, and seemed to enjoy the escapade with all the thoughtless *abandon* of a girl. Why she went off into frequent fits of quiet laughter I did not quite understand, for my whispers were decidedly more tender than witty; but I fancied it hysterical, and, having made up my mind that some touching romance was soon to be revealed to me, I prepared myself for it, by playing my part with spirit, finding something very agreeable in my new *rôle* of devoted husband.

The remarks of our neighbors amused us immensely; for, the old lady, on waking, evidently took us for an English couple on a honeymoon trip, and confided her opinion of the "mad English" to the young man, who knit his brows and mused moodily.

To our great satisfaction, both of our companions quitted us at midnight; and the moment the door closed behind them, the girl tore off her vail, threw herself on the seat opposite me, and laughed till the tears rolled down her cheeks.

"Now, mademoiselle, I demand an explanation," I said, seriously, when her merriment subsided.

"You shall have it; but first tell me what do I look like?" and she turned her face toward me with a wicked smile, that puzzled me more than her words.

"Like a very charming young lady who has run way from school or *pension,* either to escape from a lover or to meet one."

"My faith! but that is a compliment to my skill," muttered the girl, as if to herself; then aloud, and soberly, though her eyes still danced with irrepressible mirth: "Monsieur is right in one thing. I have run away from school, but not to meet or fly a lover. Ah, no; I go to find my mother. She is ill; they concealed it from me; I ran away, and would have walked from Lyons to Nice if old Justine had not helped me."

"And this young man—why did you dread him?" I asked, eagerly.

"He is one of the teachers. He goes to find and reclaim me; but, thanks to my disguise, and your kindness, he has not discovered me."

"But why should he reclaim you? Surely, if your mother is ill, you have a right to visit her, and she would desire it."

"Ah, it is a sad story! I can only tell you that we are poor. I am too young yet to help my mother. Two rich aunts placed me in a fine school, and support me till I am eighteen, on condition that my mother does not see me. They hate her, and I would have rejected their charity, but for the thought that soon I can earn my bread and support her. She wished me to go, and I obeyed, though it broke my heart. I study hard. I suffer many trials. I make no complaint; but I hope and wait, and when the time comes I fly to her, and never leave her any more."

What had come to the girl? The words poured from her lips with impetuous force; her eyes flashed; her face glowed; her voice was possessed with strange eloquence, by turns tender, defiant, proud, and pathetic. She clinched her hands, and dashed her little hat at her feet with a vehement gesture when speaking of her aunts. Her eyes shone through indignant tears when alluding to her trials; and, as she said, brokenly, "I fly to her, and never leave her any more," she opened her arms as if to embrace and hold her mother fast.

It moved me strangely; for, instead of a shallow, coquettish schoolgirl, I found a passionate, resolute creature, ready to do and dare anything for the mother she loved. I resolved to see the end of this adventure, and wished my sister had a child as fond and faithful to comfort and sustain her; but her only son had died a baby, and she was alone, for I had deserted her.

"Have you no friends but these cruel aunts?" I asked, compassionately.

"No, not one. My father is dead, my mother poor and ill, and I am powerless to help her," she answered, with a sob.

"Not quite; remember I am a friend."

As I spoke I offered my hand; but, to my intense surprise, the girl struck it away from her with a passionate motion, saying, almost fiercely:

"No; it is too late—too late! You should have come before."

"My poor child, calm yourself. I *am* indeed a friend; believe it, and let me help you. I can sympathize with your distress, for I, too, go to Nice to find one dear to me. My poor sister, whom I have neglected many years; but now I go to ask pardon, and to serve her with all my heart. Come, then, let us comfort one another, and go hopefully to meet those who love and long for us."

Still another surprise; for, with a face as sweetly penitent as it had been sternly proud before, this strange girl caught my hand in hers, kissed it warmly, and whispered, gratefully:

"I often dreamed of a friend like this, but never thought to find him so. God bless you, my——" She paused there, hid her face an instant, then looked up without a shadow in her eyes, saying more quietly, and with a smile I could not understand:

"What shall I give you to prove my thanks for your kindness to me?"

"When we part, you shall give me an English good-by."

"A kiss on the lips! Fie! monsieur will not demand that of me," cried the girl, whose changeful face was gay again.

"And, why not, since I am old enough to be called your father."

"Ah, that displeased you! Well, you had your revenge; rest content with that, *mon mari,*" laughed the girl, retreating to a corner with a rebellious air.

"I shall claim my reward when we part; so resign yourself, mademoiselle. By-the-way, what name has my little friend?"

"I will tell you when I pay my debt. Now let me sleep. I am tired, and so are you. Good-night, Monsieur George Vane," and, leaving me to wonder how she had learned my name, the tormenting creature barricaded herself with cloaks and bags, and seemed to sleep tranquilly.

Tired with the long night, I soon dropped off into a doze, which must have been a long one; for, when I woke, I found myself in the dark.

"Where the deuce are we?" I exclaimed; for the lamp was out, and no sign of dawn visible, though I had seen a ruddy streak when I last looked out.

"In the long tunnel near Nice," answered a voice from the gloom.

"Ah, mademoiselle is awake! Is she not afraid that I may demand payment now?"

"Wait till the light comes, and if you deserve it *then,* you shall have it," and I heard the little gipsy laughing in her corner. The next minute a spark glowed opposite me; the odor of my choice cigarettes filled the air, and the crackle of a bon-bon was heard.

Before I could make up my mind how to punish these freaks, we shot out of the tunnel, and I sat petrified with amazement, for there, opposite me, lounged, not my pretty blonde school-girl, but a handsome black-haired, mischievous lad, in the costume of a pupil of a French military academy; with his little cap rakishly askew, his blue coat buttoned smartly to the chin, his well-booted feet on the seat beside him, and his small hands daintily gloved, this young rascal lay staring at me with such a world of fun in his fine eyes, that I tingled all over with a shock of surprise which almost took my breath away.

"Have a light, uncle?" was the cool remark that broke the long silence.

"Where is the girl?" was all I could say, with a dazed expression.

"There, sir," pointing to the bag, with a smile that made me feel as if I was not yet awake, so like the girl's was it.

"And who the devil are you?" I cried, getting angry all at once.

Standing as straight as an arrow, the boy answered, with a military salute:

"George Vane Vandeleur, at your service, uncle."

"My sister has no children; her boy died years ago, you young villain."

"He tried to, but they wouldn't let him. I'm sorry to contradict you, sir; but I'm your sister's son, and that will prove it."

Much bewildered, I took the letter he handed me, and found it impossible to doubt the boy's word. It was from my sister to her son, telling him that she had written to me, that I had answered kindly, and promised to come to her. She bade the boy visit her if possible, that I might see him, for she could not doubt that I would receive him for her sake, and free him from dependence on the French aunts who made their favors burdensome by reproach and separation.

As I read, I forgave the boy his prank, and longed to give him a hearty welcome; but recollections of my own part in that night's masquerade annoyed me so much that to conceal my chagrin I assumed a stern air, and demanded, coldly:

"Was it necessary to make a girl of yourself in order to visit your mother?"

"Yes, sir," answered the boy, promptly, adding, with the most engaging frankness: "I'll tell you how it was, uncle, and I know you will pardon me, because mamma has often told me of your pranks when a boy, and I made you my hero. See, then, mamma sends me this letter, and I am wild to go, that I may embrace her and see my uncle. But my aunts say, 'No,' and tell them at school that I am to be kept close. Ah, they are strict there; the boys are left no freedom, and my only chance was the one holiday when I go to my aunts. I resolved to run away, and walk to mamma, for nothing shall part us but her will. I had a little money, and I confided my plan to Justine, my old nurse. She is a brave one! She said:

" 'You shall go, but not as a beggar. See, I have money. Take it, my son, and visit your mother like a gentleman.'

"That was grand; but I feared to be caught before I could leave Lyons, so I resolved to disguise myself, and then if they followed I should escape them. Often at school I have played girl-parts, because I am small, and have as yet no beard. So Justine dressed me in the skirt, cloak and hat of her granddaughter. I had the blonde wig I wore on the stage, a little rouge, a soft tone, a modest air, and—*voilà mademoiselle!*"

"Exactly; it was well done, though at times you forgot the 'modest air,' nephew," I said, with as much dignity as suppressed merriment permitted.

"It was impossible to remember it at all times; and you did not seem to like mademoiselle the less for a little coquetry," replied the rogue, with a sly glance out of the handsome eyes that had bewitched me.

"Continue your story, sir. Was the young man we met really a teacher?"

"Yes, uncle; but you so kindly protected me that he could not even suspect your delicate wife."

The boy choked over the last word, and burst into a laugh so irresistibly infectious that I joined him, and lost my dignity for ever.

"George, you are a scapegrace," was the only reproof I had breath enough to make.

"But uncle pardons me, since he gives me my name, and looks at me so kindly that I must embrace him."

And with a demonstrative affection which an English boy would have died rather than betray, my French nephew threw his arms about my neck, and kissed me heartily on both cheeks. I had often ridiculed the fashion, but now I rather liked it, and began to think my prejudice ill-founded, as I listened to the lad's account of the sorrows and hardships they had been called on to suffer since his father died.

"Why was I never told of your existence?" I asked, feeling how much I had lost in my long ignorance of this bright boy, who was already dear to me.

"When I was so ill while a baby, mamma wrote to my grandfather, hoping to touch his heart; but he never answered her, and she wrote no more. If uncle had cared to find his nephew, he might easily have done so; the channel is not very wide."

The reproach in the last words went straight to my heart; but I only said, stroking the curly head:

"Did you never mean to make yourself known to me? When your mother was suffering, could you not try me?"

"I never could beg, even for her, and trusted to the good God, and we were helped. I did mean to make myself known to you when I had done something to be proud of; not before."

I knew where that haughty spirit came from, and was as glad to see it as I was to see how much the boy resembled my once lovely sister.

"How did you know me, George?" I asked, finding pleasure in uttering the familiar name, unspoken since my father died.

"I saw your name on your luggage at Marseilles, and thought you looked like the picture mamma cherishes so tenderly, and I resolved to try and touch your heart before you knew who I was. The guard put me into your coupé, for I bribed him, and then I acted my best; but it was so droll I nearly spoiled it all by some boy's word, or a laugh. My faith, uncle, I did not know the English were so gallant."

"It did not occur to you that I might be acting also, perhaps? I own I was puzzled at first, but I soon made up my mind that you were some little adventuress out on a lark, as we say in England, and I behaved accordingly."

"If all little adventuresses got on as well as I did, I fancy many would go on this lark of yours. A talent for acting runs in the family, that is evident," said the boy.

"Hold your tongue, jackanapes!" sternly. "How old are you, my lad?" mildly.

"Fifteen, sir."

"That young to begin the world, with no friends but two cold-hearted old women!"

"Ah, no, I have the good God and my mother, and now—may I say an uncle who loves me a little, and permits me to love him with all my heart?"

Never mind what answer I made; I have recorded weaknesses enough already, so let that pass, as well as the conversation which left both pair of eyes a little wet, but both pair of hearts very happy.

As the train thundered into the station at Nice, just as the sun rose gloriously over the blue Mediterranean, George whispered to me, with the irrepressible impudence of a mischief-loving boy:

"Uncle, shall I give you 'the English good-by' now?"

"No, my lad; give me a hearty English welcome, and God bless you!" I answered, as we shook hands, manfully, and walked away together, laughing over the adventure with my mysterious mademoiselle.

Cupid and Chow-chow

MAMMA BEGAN IT by calling her rosy, dimpled, year-old baby Cupid, and as he grew up the name became more and more appropriate, for the pretty boy loved everyone, everyone loved him, and he made those about him fond of one another, like a regular little god of love.

Especially beautiful and attractive did he look as he pranced on the door-steps one afternoon while waiting the arrival of a little cousin. Our Cupid's costume was modernized out of regard to the prejudices of society, and instead of wings, bandage, bow and arrow, he was gorgeous to behold in small buckled shoes, purple silk hose, black velvet knickerbockers, and jacket with a lace collar, which, with his yellow hair cut straight across the forehead, and falling in long, curling love-locks behind, made him look like an old picture of a young cavalier.

It was impossible for the little sprig to help being a trifle vain when every one praised his comeliness, and every mirror showed him a rosy face, with big blue eyes, smiling lips, white teeth, a cunning nose, and a dimple in the chin, not to mention the golden mane that hung about his neck.

Yes, Cupid was vain; and as he waited, he pranced, arranged the dear buckled shoes in the first position, practised his best bow, felt of his dimple, and smiled affably as he pictured to himself the pleasure and surprise of the little cousin when he embraced her in the ardent yet gentle way which made his greetings particularly agreeable to those who liked such tender demonstrations.

Cupid had made up his mind to love Chow-chow very much, both because she was his cousin, and because she must be interesting if all papa's stories of her were true. Her very name was pleasing to him, for it suggested Indian sweetmeats, though papa said it was given to her because she was such a mixture of sweet and sour that one never knew whether he would get his tongue bitten by a hot bit of ginger, or find a candied plum melting in his mouth when he tried that little jar of Chow-chow.

"I know I shall like her, and of course she will like me lots, 'cause everybody does," thought Cupid, settling his love-locks and surveying his purple legs like a contented young peacock.

Just then a carriage drove up the avenue, stopped at the foot of the steps, and out skipped a tall, brown man, a small, pale lady, and a child, who whisked away to the pond so rapidly that no one could see what she was like.

A great kissing and hand-shaking went on between the papas and mammas, and Cupid came in for a large share, but did not enjoy it as much as usual, for the little girl had fled and he *must* get at her. So the instant Aunt Susan let him go he ran after the truant, quite panting with eagerness and all aglow with amiable intentions, for he was a hospitable little soul, and loved to do the honors of his pleasant home like a gentleman.

A little figure, dressed in a brown linen frock, with dusty boots below it, and above it a head of wild black hair, tied up with a large scarlet bow, stood by the pond throwing stones at the swans, who ruffled their feathers in stately anger at such treatment. Suddenly a pair of velvet arms embraced her, and half turning she looked up into a rosy, smiling face, with two red lips suggestively puckered for a hearty kiss.

Chow-chow's black eyes sparkled, and her little brown face flushed as red as her ribbon as she tried to push the boy away with a shrill scream.

"Don't be frightened. I'm Cupid. I must kiss you. I truly must. I always do when people come, and I like you very much."

With this soothing remark, the velvet arms pressed her firmly, and the lips gave her several soft kisses, which, owing to her struggles, lit upon her nose, chin, top-knot, and ear; for, having begun, Cupid did not know when to leave off.

But Chow-chow's wrath was great, her vengeance swift, and getting one hand free she flung the gravel it held full in the flushed and smiling face of this bold boy who had dared to kiss her without leave.

Poor Cupid fell back blinded and heart-broken at such a return for his warm welcome, and while he stood trying to clear his smarting eyes, a fierce little voice said close by,—

"Does it hurt?"

"Oh! Dreadfully!"

"I'm glad of it."

"Then you don't love me?"

"I hate you!"

"I don't see why."

"I don't like to be hugged and kissed. I don't let anybody but papa and mamma do it, ever,—so, now!"

"But I'm your cousin, and you *must* love me. Won't you, please?" besought Cupid, with one eye open and a great tear on his nose.

"I'll see about it. I don't like crying boys," returned the hard-hearted damsel.

"Well, you made me; but I forgive you," and Cupid magnanimously put out his hand for a friendly shake. But Chow-chow was off like a startled deer, and vanished into the house, singing at the top of her voice a nursery rhyme to this effect,—

"And she bids you to come in,
With a dimple in your chin,
Billy boy, Billy boy."

When Cupid, with red eyes and a sad countenance, made his appearance, he found Chow-chow on her father's knee eating cake, while the elders talked. She had told the story, and now from the safe stronghold of papa's arm condescended to smile upon the conquered youth.

Cupid went to mamma, and in one long whisper told his woes; then sat upon the cushion at her feet, and soon forgot them all in the mingled joys of eating macaroons and giving Chow-chow smile for smile across the hearth-rug.

"I predict that we shall be much amused and edified by the progress of the friendship just begun," said Cupid's papa, a quiet man, who loved children and observed them with affectionate interest.

"And I predict a hard time of it for your young man, if he attempts to tame my strong-minded little woman here. Her mother's ideas are peculiar, and she wants to bring Chow-chow up according to the new lights,—with contempt for dress and all frivolous pursuits; to make her hardy, independent, and quite above caring for such trifles as love, domestic life, or the feminine accomplishments we used to find so charming."

As Chow-chow's papa spoke, he looked from the child in her ugly gray frock, thick boots, and mop of hair tied up in a style neither pretty nor becoming, to his wife in *her* plain dress, with *her* knob of hair, decided mouth, sarcastic nose, and restless eyes that seemed always on the watch to find some new wrong and protest against it.

"Now, George, how can you misrepresent my views and principles so? But it's no use trying to convince or out-talk you. We never get a chance, and our only hope is to bring up our girls so that they may not be put down as we are," returned Mrs. Susan, with a decided air.

"Show us how you are going to defend your sex and conquer ours, Chow-chow; give us your views generally. Now, then, who is in favor of the Elective Franchise?" said Uncle George, with a twinkle of the eye.

Up went Aunt Susan's hand, and to the great amusement of all up went Chow-chow's also; and, scrambling to her feet on papa's knee, she burst into a harangue which convulsed her hearers, for in it the child's voice made queer work with the long words, and the red bow wagged belligerently as she laid down the law with energy, and defined her views, closing with a stamp of her foot.

"This is our platform: Free speech, free love, free soil, free every thing; and Woman's Puckerage for ever!"

Even Aunt Susan had to laugh at that burst, for it was delivered with such vigor that the speaker would have fallen on her nose if she had not been sustained by a strong arm.

Cupid laughed because the rest did, and then turned his big eyes full of wonder on his mother, asking what it all meant.

"Only fun, my dear."

"Now, Ellen, that's very wrong. Why don't you explain this great subject to him, and prepare him to take a nobler part in the coming struggle than those who have gone before him have done?" said Mrs. Susan, with a stern look at her husband, who was petting the little daughter, who evidently loved him best.

"I don't care to disturb his happy childhood with quarrels beyond his comprehension. I shall teach him to be as good and just a man as his father, and feel quite sure that no woman will suffer wrong at his hands," returned Mrs. Ellen, smiling at Cupid's papa, who nodded back as if they quite understood each other.

"We never did agree and we never shall, so I will say no more; but we shall see what a good effect my girl's strength of character will have upon your boy, who has been petted and spoiled by too much tenderness."

So Aunt Susan settled the matter; and as the days went on, the elder people fell into the way of observing how the little pair got on together, and were much amused by the vicissitudes of that nursery romance.

In the beginning Chow-chow rode over Cupid rough-shod, quite trampled upon him in fact; and he bore it, because he wanted her to like him, and had been taught that the utmost courtesy was due a guest. But when he got no reward for his long-suffering patience he was sometimes tempted to rebel, and probably would have done so if he had not had mamma to comfort and sustain him. Chow-chow was very quick at spying out the weaknesses of her friends and alarmingly frank in proclaiming her discoveries; so poor Cupid's little faults were seen and proclaimed very soon, and life made a burden to him, until he found out the best way of silencing his tormentor was by mending the faults.

"My papa says you are a dandy-prat, and you are," said Chow-chow, one day when the desire to improve her race was very strong upon her.

"What is a dandy-prat?" asked Cupid, looking troubled at the new accusation.

"I asked him, and he said a vain fellow, and you are vain,—so now!"

"Am I?" and Cupid stopped to think it over.

"Yes; you're horrid vain of your hair, and your velvet clothes, and the dimple in your chin. I know it, 'cause you always look in the glass when you are dressed up, and keep feeling of that ugly hole in your chin, and I see you brush your hair ever so much."

Poor Cupid colored up with shame, and turn his back to the mirror, as the sharp-tongued young monitor went on:—

"My mamma said if you were her boy she'd cut off your curls, put you in a plain suit, and stick some court-plaster over that place till you forgot all about it."

Chow-chow expected an explosion of grief or anger after that last slap; but to her amazement the boy walked out of the room without a word. Going up to his mother as she sat busy with a letter, he asked in a very earnest voice,—

"Mamma, am I vain?"

"I'm afraid you are a little, my dear," answered mamma, deep in her letter.

With a sad but resolute face Cupid went back to Chow-chow, bearing a pair of shears in one hand and a bit of court-plaster in the other.

"You may cut my hair off, if you want to. I ain't going to be a dandy-prat any more," he said, offering the fatal shears with the calmness of a hero.

Chow-chow was much surprised, but charmed with the idea of shearing this meek sheep, so she snipped and slashed until the golden locks lay shining on the floor, and Cupid's head looked as if rats had been gnawing his hair.

"Do you like me better now?" he asked, looking in her eyes as his only mirror, and seeing there the most approving glance they had ever vouchsafed him.

"Yes, I do; girl-boys are hateful."

He might have retorted, "So are boy-girls," but he was a gentleman, so he only smiled and held up his chin for her to cover the offending dimple, which she did with half a square of black plaster.

"I shall never wear my velvet clothes any more unless mamma makes me, and I don't think she will when I tell her about it, 'cause she likes to have me cure my faults," said Cupid when the sacrifice was complete, and even stern Chow-chow was touched by the sweetness with which he bore the rebuke, the courage with which he began the atonement for his little folly.

When he appeared at dinner, great was the outcry; and when the story was told, great was the effect produced. Aunt Susan said with satisfaction,—

"You see what an excellent effect my girl's Spartan training has on her, and how fine her influence is on your effeminate boy."

Uncle George laughed heartily, but whispered something to Chow-chow that made her look ashamed and cast repentant glances at her victim. Cupid's papa shook hands with the boy, and said, smiling, "I am rather proud of my 'dandy-prat,' after all."

But mamma grieved for the lost glory of her little Absalom, and found it hard to pardon naughty Chow-chow, until Cupid looked up at her with a grave, clear look which even the big patch could not spoil, and said manfully,—

"You know I *was* vain, mamma, but I won't be any more, and you'll be glad, because you love *me* better than my hair, don't you?"

Then she hugged the cropped head close, and kissed the hidden dimple without a word of reproach; but she laid the yellow locks away as if she *did* love them after all, and often followed the little lad in the rough gray suit, as if his sacrifice had only made him more beautiful in her eyes.

Chow-chow was quite affable for some days after this prank, and treated her slave with more gentleness, evidently feeling that, though belonging to an inferior race, he deserved a trifle of regard for his obedience to her teachings. But her love of power grew by what it fed on and soon brought fresh woe to faithful Cupid, who adored her, though she frowned upon his little passion and gave him no hope.

"You are a 'fraid-cat," asserted her majesty, one afternoon as they played in the stable, and Cupid declined to be kicked by the horse Chow-chow was teasing.

"No, I ain't; but I don't like to be hurt, and it's wrong to fret Charley, and I won't poke him with my hoe."

"Well, it isn't wrong to turn this thing, but you don't dare to put your finger on that wheel and let me pinch it a little bit," added Chow-chow, pointing to some sort of hay-cutting machine that stood near by.

"What for?" asked Cupid, who did object to being hurt in any way.

"To show you ain't a 'fraid-cat. I know you are. I'm not, see there," and Chow-chow gave her own finger a very gentle squeeze.

"I can bear it harder than that," and devoted Cupid laid his plump forefinger between two wheels, bent on proving his courage at all costs.

Chow-chow gave a brisk turn to the handle, slipped in doing so, and brought the whole weight of the cruel cogs on the tender little finger, crushing the top quite flat. Blood flowed, Chow-chow stopped aghast; and Cupid, with one cry of pain, caught and reversed the handle, drew out the poor finger, walked unsteadily in to mamma, saying, with dizzy eyes and white lips, "She didn't mean to do it," and then fainted quite away in a little heap at her feet.

The doctor came flying, shook his head over the wound, and drew out a case of dreadful instruments that made even strong-minded Aunt Susan turn away her head, and bound up the little hand that might never be whole and strong again. Chow-chow stood by quite white and still until it was all over and Cupid asleep in his mother's arms; then she dived under the sofa and sobbed there, refusing to be comforted until her father came home. What that misguided man said to her no one ever knew, but when Cupid was propped up on the couch at tea-time, Chow-chow begged piteously to be allowed to feed him.

The wounded hero, with his arm in a sling, permitted her to minister to him; and she did it so gently, so patiently, that her father said low to Mrs. Ellen,—

"I have hopes of her yet, for all the woman is not taken out of her, in spite of the new lights."

When they parted for the evening, Cupid, who had often sued for a good-night kiss and sued in vain, was charmed to see the red top-knot bending over him, and to hear Chow-chow whisper, with a penitent kiss, "I truly didn't mean to, Coopy."

The well arm held her fast as the martyr whispered back, "Just say I ain't a 'fraid-cat, and I don't mind smashing my finger."

Chow-chow said it that night and thought it next day and for many following days, for each morning, when the doctor came to dress the "smashed" finger, she insisted on being by as a sort of penance. She forced herself to watch the bright instruments without shivering, she ran for warm water, she begged to spread the salve on the bandage, to hold the smelling-bottle, and to pick all the lint that was used.

And while she performed these small labors of love, she learned a little lesson that did her more good than many of mamma's lectures. For Cupid showed her the difference between the rash daring that runs foolish risks, and the steady courage that bears pain without complaint. Every day the same scene took place; Chow-chow would watch for and announce the doctor; would bustle out the salve-box, bandage, and basin, set the chair, and call Cupid from his book with a new gentleness in her voice.

The boy would answer at once, take his place, and submit the poor swollen hand to the ten minutes' torture of little probes and scissors, caustic and bathing, without a word, a tear, or sound of suffering. He only turned his head away, grew white about the lips, damp on the forehead, and when it was all over would lean against his mother for a minute, faint and still.

Then Chow-chow would press her hands together with a sigh of mingled pity, admiration, and remorse, and when the boy looked up to say stoutly, "It didn't hurt very much," she would put his sling on for him, and run before to settle the pillows, carry him the little glass of wine and water he was to take, and hover round him until he was quite himself again, when she would subside close by, and pick lint or hem sails while he read aloud to her from one of his dear books.

"It is a good lesson in surgery and nursing for her. I intend to have her study medicine if she shows any fondness for it," said Aunt Susan.

"It is a good lesson in true courage, and I am glad to have her learn it early," added Uncle George, who now called Cupid a "trump" instead of a "dandy-prat."

"It is a good lesson in loving and serving others for love's sake, as all women must learn to do soon or late," said gentle Mrs. Ellen.

"It is teaching them both how to bear and forbear, to teach and help, and comfort one another, and take the pains and pleasures of life as they should do together," concluded Cupid's papa, watching the little couple with the wise kind eyes that saw a pretty story in their daily lives.

Slowly the finger healed, and to every one's surprise was not much disfigured, which Cupid insisted was entirely owing to Chow-chow's superior skill in spreading salve and picking lint. Before this time, however, Chow-chow, touched by his brave patience, his generous refusal to blame her for the mishap, and his faithful affection, had in a tender moment confessed to her little lover that she did "like him a great deal," and consented to go and live in the old swan-house on the island in the pond as soon as he was well enough.

But no sooner had she enraptured him by these promises than she dashed his joy by adding certain worldly conditions which she had heard discussed by her mamma and her friends.

"But we can't be married until we have a lot of money. Nobody does, and we *must* have ever so much to buy things with."

"Yes, but papa said he'd give us some little furniture to put in our house, and mamma will let us have as much cake and milk-tea as we want, and I shall be very fond of you, and what's the use of money?" asked the enamoured Cupid, who believed in love in a cottage, or swan-house rather.

"I shan't marry a poor boy, so now!" was the mercenary Chow-chow's decision.

"Well, I'll see how much I've got; but I should think you would like me just as well without," and Cupid went away to inspect his property with as much anxiety as any man preparing for matrimony.

But Cupid's finances were in a bad state, for he spent his pocket-money as fast as he got it, and had lavished gifts upon his sweetheart with princely prodigality. So he punched a hole in his savings-bank and counted his small hoard, much afflicted to find it only amounted to seventy-eight cents, and a button put in for fun. Bent on winning his mistress, no sacrifice seemed too great, so he sold his livestock, consisting of one lame hen, a rabbit, and a choice collection of caterpillars. But though he drove sharp bargains, these sales only brought him in a dollar or two. Then he went about among his friends, and begged and borrowed small sums, telling no one his secret lest they should laugh at him, but pleading for a temporary accommodation so earnestly and prettily that no one could refuse.

When he had strained every nerve and tried every wile, he counted up his gains and found that he had four dollars and a half. That seemed a fortune to the innocent; and, getting it all in bright pennies, he placed it in a new red purse, and with pardonable pride laid his offering at Chow-chow's feet.

But alas for love's labor lost! The cruel fair crushed all his hopes by saying coldly,—

"That isn't half enough. We ought to have ten dollars, and I won't like you until you get it."

"O Chow-chow! I tried so hard; do play it's enough," pleaded poor Cupid.

"No, I shan't. I don't care much for the old swan-house now, and you ain't half so pretty as you used to be."

"*You* made me cut my hair off, and now you don't love me 'cause I'm ugly," cried the afflicted little swain, indignant at such injustice.

But Chow-chow was in a naughty mood, so she swung on the gate, and would not relent in spite of prayers and blandishments.

"I'll get some more money somehow, if you will wait. Will you, please?"

"I'll see 'bout it."

And with that awful uncertainty weighing upon his soul, poor Cupid went away to wrestle with circumstances. Feeling that matters had now reached a serious point, he confided his anxieties to mamma; and she, finding that it was impossible to laugh or reason him out of his untimely passion, comforted him by promising to buy at high prices all the nosegays he could gather out of his own little garden.

"But it will take a long time to make ten dollars that way. Don't you think Chow-chow might come now, when it is all warm and pleasant, and not stop until summer is gone, and no birds and flowers and nice things to play with? It's so hard to wait," sighed Cupid, holding his cropped head in his hands, and looking the image of childish despair.

"So it is, and *I* think Chow is a little goose not to go at once and enjoy love's young dream without wasting precious time trying to make money. Tell her papa said so, and he ought to know," added Uncle George; under his breath, for he *had* tried it, and found that it did not work well.

Cupid did tell her, but little madam had got the whim into her perverse head; and the more she was urged to give in, the more decided she grew. So Cupid accepted his fate like a man, and delved away in his garden, watering his pinks, weeding his mignonette, and begging his roses to bloom as fast and fair as they could, so that he might be happy before the summer was gone. Rather a pathetic little lover, mamma thought, as she watched him tugging away with the lame hand, or saw him come beaming in with his posies to receive the precious money that was to buy a return for his loyal love.

Tender-hearted Mrs. Ellen tried to soften Chow-chow and teach her sundry feminine arts against the time she went to housekeeping on the island, for Mrs. Susan was so busy hearing lectures, reading reports, and attending to the education of other people's children that her own ran wild. In her good moods, Chow-chow took kindly to the new lessons, and began to hem a table-cloth for the domestic board at which she was to preside; also swept and dusted now and then, and once cooked a remarkable mess, which she called "Coopy's favorite pudding," and intended to surprise him with it soon after the wedding. But these virtuous efforts soon flagged, the table-cloth was not finished, the duster was converted into a fly-killer, and her dolls lay unheeded in corners after a few attempts at dressing and nursing had ended in *ennui*.

How long matters would have gone on in this unsatisfactory way no one knows; but a rainy day came, and the experiences it gave the little pair brought things to a crisis.

The morning was devoted to pasting pictures and playing horse all over the house, with frequent pauses for refreshment and an occasional squabble. After dinner, as the mammas sat sewing and the papas talking or reading in one room, the children played in the other, quite unconscious that they were affording both amusement and instruction to their elders.

"Let's play house," suggested Cupid, who was of a domestic turn, and thought a little rehearsal would not be amiss.

"Well, I will," consented Chow-chow, who was rather subdued by the violent exercises of the morning.

So a palatial mansion was made of chairs, the dolls' furniture arranged, the stores laid in, and housekeeping begun.

"Now, you must go off to your business while I 'tend to my work," said Chow-chow, after they had breakfasted off a seed-cake and sugar and water tea in the bosom of their family.

Cupid obediently put on papa's hat, took a large book under his arm, and went away to look at pictures behind the curtains, while Mrs. C. bestirred herself at home in a most energetic manner, spanking her nine dolls until their cries rent the air, rattling her dishes with perilous activity, and going to market with the coal-hod for her purchases.

Mr. Cupid returned to dinner rather early, and was scolded for so doing, but pacified his spouse by praising her dessert,—a sandwich of sliced apple, bread, and salt, which he ate like a martyr.

A ride on the rocking-horse with his entire family about him filled the soul of Mr. Cupid with joy, though the trip was rendered a little fatiguing by his having to dismount frequently to pick up the various darlings as they fell out of his pockets or their mother's arms as she sat behind him on a pillion.

"Isn't this beautiful?" he asked, as they swung to and fro,—Mrs. Cupid leaning her head on his shoulder, and dear little Claribel Maud peeping out of his breast-pocket, while Walter Hornblower and Rosie Ruth, the twins, sat up between the horse's ears, their china faces beaming in a way to fill a father's heart with pride.

"It will be much nicer if the horse runs away and we all go smash. I'll pull out his tail, then he'll rear, and we must tumble off," proposed the restless Mrs. C., whose dramatic soul delighted in tragic adventures.

So the little papa's happy moment was speedily banished as he dutifully precipitated himself and blooming family upon the floor, to be gathered up and doctored with chalk and ink, and plasters of paper stuck all over their faces.

When this excitement subsided, it was evening, and Mrs. Cupid bundled her children off to bed, saying,—

"Now, you must go to your club, and I am going to my lecture."

"But I thought you'd sew now and let me read to you, and have our little candles burn, and be all cosey, like papa and mamma," answered Cupid, who already felt the discomfort of a strong-minded wife.

"My papa and mamma don't do so. He always goes to the club, and smokes and reads papers and plays chess, and mamma goes to Woman's Puckerage meetings,—so I must."

"Let me go too; I never saw a Puckerage lecture, and I'd like to," said Cupid, who felt that a walk arm-in-arm with his idol would make any sort of meeting endurable.

"No, you can't! Papa *never* goes; he says they are all gabble and nonsense, and mamma says his club is all smoke and slang, and they *never* go together."

So Chow-chow locked the door, and the little pair went their separate ways; while the older pair in the other room laughed at the joke, yet felt that Cupid's plan was the best, and wondered how Ellen and her husband managed to get on so well.

Chow-chow's lecture did not seem to be very interesting, for she was soon at home again. But Mr. Cupid, after smoking a lamp-lighter with his feet up, fell to reading a story that interested him, and forgot to go home until he finished it. Then, to his great surprise, he was told that it was morning, that he had been out all night, and couldn't have any breakfast. This ruffled him, and he told madam she was a bad wife, and he wouldn't love her if she did not instantly give him his share of the little pie presented by cook, as a bribe to keep them out of the kitchen.

Mrs. C. sternly refused, and locked up the pie, declaring that she hated housekeeping and wouldn't live with him any more, which threat she made good by quitting the house, vowing not to speak to him again that day, but to play alone, free and happy.

The deserted husband sat down among his infants with despair in his soul, while the spirited wife, in an immense bonnet, pranced about the room, waving the key of the pie-closet and rejoicing in her freedom. Yes, it was truly pathetic to see poor Mr. Cupid's efforts at housekeeping and baby-tending; for, feeling that they had a double claim upon him now, he tried to do his duty by his children. But he soon gave it up, piled them all into one bed, and covered them with a black cloth, saying mournfully, "I'll play they all died of mumps, then I can sell the house and go away. I can't bear to stay here when *she* is gone."

The house was sold, the dead infants buried under the sofa, and then the forsaken man was a homeless wanderer. He tried in many ways to amuse himself. He travelled to China on the tailless horse, went to California in a balloon, and sailed around the world on a raft made of two chairs and the hearth-brush. But these wanderings always ended near the ruins of his home, and he always sat down for a moment to watch the erratic movements of his wife.

That sprightly lady fared better than he, for her inventive fancy kept her supplied with interesting plays, though a secret sense of remorse for her naughtiness weighed upon her spirits at times. She had a concert, and sang surprising medleys, with drum accompaniments. She rode five horses in a circus, and jumped over chairs and foot-stools in the most approved manner. She had a fair, a fire, and a shipwreck; hunted lions, fished for crocodiles, and played be a monkey in a style that would have charmed Darwin.

But somehow none of these festive games had their usual relish. There was no ardent admirer to applaud her music, no two-legged horse to help her circus with wild prancings and life-like neighs, no devoted friend and defender to save her from the perils of flood and fire, no comrade to hunt with her, no fellow-monkey to skip from perch to perch with social jabberings, as they cracked their cocoa-nuts among imaginary palms. All was dull and tiresome.

A strong sense of loneliness fell upon her, and for the first time she appreciated her faithful little friend. Then the pie weighed upon her conscience; there it was, wasting its sweetness in the closet, and no one ate it. She had not the face to devour it alone; she could not make up her mind to give it to Cupid; and after her fierce renunciation of him, how could she ask him to forgive her? Gradually her spirits declined, and about the time that the other wanderer got back from his last trip she sat down to consider her position.

Hearing no noise in the other room, Uncle George peeped in and saw the divided pair sitting in opposite corners, looking askance at each other, evidently feeling that a wide gulf lay between them, and longing to cross it, yet not quite knowing how. A solemn and yet a comical sight, so Uncle George beckoned the others to come and look.

"My boy will give in first. See how beseechingly he looks at the little witch!" whispered Mrs. Ellen, laughing softly.

"No, he won't; she hurt his feelings very much by leaving him, and he won't relent until she goes back; then he'll forgive and forget like a man," said Cupid's papa.

"I hope my girl will remain true to her principles," began Aunt Susan.

"She'll be a miserable baby if she does," muttered Uncle George.

"I was going on to say that, finding she has done wrong, I hope she will have the courage to say so, hard as it is, and so expiate her fault and try to do better," added Aunt Susan, fast and low, with a soft look in her eyes, as she watched the little girl sitting alone, while so much honest affection was waiting for her close by, if pride would let her take it.

Somehow Uncle George's arm went round her waist when she said that, and he gave a quick nod, as if something pleased him very much.

"Shall I speak, and help the dears bridge over their little trouble?" asked Mrs. Ellen, pretending not to see the older children making up their differences behind her.

"No; let them work it out for themselves. I'm curious to see how they will manage," said papa, hoping that his boy's first little love would prosper in spite of thorns among the roses.

So they waited, and presently the affair was settled in a way no one expected. As if she could not bear the silence any longer, Chow-chow suddenly bustled up, saying to herself,—

"I haven't played lecture. I always like that, and here's a nice place."

Pulling out the drawers of a secretary like steps, she slowly mounted to the wide ledge atop, and began the droll preachment her father had taught her in ridicule of mamma's hobby.

"Do stop her, George; it's so absurd," whispered Mrs. Susan.

"Glad you think so, my dear," laughed Uncle George.

"There is some sense in it, and I have no doubt the real and true will come to pass when we women learn how far to go, and how to fit ourselves for the new duties by doing the old ones well," said Mrs. Ellen, who found good in all things, and kept herself so womanly sweet and strong that no one could deny her any right she chose to claim.

"She is like so many of those who mount your hobby, Susan, and ride away into confusions of all sorts, leaving empty homes behind them. The happy, womanly women will have the most influence after all, and do the most to help the bitter, sour, discontented ones. They need help, God knows, and I shall be glad to lend a hand toward giving them their rights in all things."

As papa spoke, Chow-chow, who had caught sight of the peeping faces, and was excited thereby, burst into a tremendous harangue, waving her hands, stamping her feet, and dancing about on her perch as if her wrongs had upset her wits. All of a sudden the whole secretary lurched forward, out fell the drawers, open flew the doors, down went Chow-chow with a screech, and the marble slab came sliding after, as if to silence the irrepressible little orator forever. How he did it no one knew, but before the top fell Cupid was under it, received it on his shoulders, and held it up with all his might, while Chow-chow scrambled out from the ruins with no hurt but a bump on the forehead. Papa had his boy out in a twinkling, and both mammas fell upon their rescued darlings with equal alarm and tenderness; for Mrs. Susan got her little girl in her arms before Mr. George could reach her, and Chow-chow clung there, sobbing away her fright and pain as if the maternal purring was a new and pleasant solace.

"I'll never play that nasty old puckerage any more," she declared, feeling of the purple lump on her brow.

"Nor I either, in that way," whispered her mamma, with a look that made Chow-chow ask curiously,—

"Why, did you hurt yourself too?"

"I am afraid I did."

"Be sure that your platform is all right before you try again, Poppet, else it will let you down when you least expect it, and damage your best friends as well as yourself," said Mr. George, setting up the fallen rostrum.

"I'm not going to have any flatporm; I'm going to be good and play with Coopy, if he'll let me," added the penitent Chow-chow, glancing with shy, wet eyes at Cupid, who stood near with a torn jacket and a bruise on the already wounded hand.

His only answer was to draw her out of her mother's arms, embrace her warmly, and seat her beside him on the little bench he loved to share with her. This ready and eloquent forgiveness touched Chow-chow's heart, and the lofty top-knot went down upon Cupid's shoulder as if the little fortress lowered its colors in token of entire surrender. Cupid's only sign of triumph was a gentle pat on the wild, black head, and a nod towards the spectators, as he said, smiling all over his chubby face,—

"Every thing is nice and happy now, and we don't mind the bumps."

"Let us sheer off, we are only in the way," said Mr. George, and the elders retired, but found it impossible to resist occasional peeps at the little pair, as the reconciliation scene went on.

"O Coopy! I *was* so bad, I don't think you *can* love me any more," began the repentant one with a sob.

"Oh, yes I can; and just as soon as I get money enough, we'll go and live in the swan-house, won't we?" returned the faithful lover, making the most of this melting mood.

"I'll go right away tomorrow, I don't care about the money. I like the nice bright pennies, and we don't need much, and I've got my new saucepan to begin with," cried Chow-chow in a burst of generosity, for, like a true woman, though she demanded impossibilities at first, yet when her heart was won she asked nothing but love, and was content with a saucepan.

"O Goody! And I've got my drum," returned the enraptured Cupid, as ready as the immortal Traddles to go to housekeeping with a toasting fork and a bird-cage, or some such useful trifles.

"But I *was* bad about the pie," cried Chow-chow as her sins kept rising before her; and, burning to make atonement for this one, she ran to the closet, tore out the pie, and, thrusting it into Cupid's hands, said in a tone of heroic resolution, "There, you eat it *all,* and I won't taste a bit."

"No, *you* eat it all, I'd like to see you. I don't care for it, truly, 'cause I love you more than a million pies," protested Cupid, offering back the treasure in a somewhat ruinous state after its various vicissitudes.

"Then give me a tiny bit, and you have the rest," said Chow-chow, bent on self-chastisement.

"The fairest way is to cut it 'zactly in halves, and each have a piece. Mamma says that's the right thing to do always." And Cupid, producing a jack-knive, proceeded to settle the matter with masculine justice.

So side by side they devoured the little bone of contention, chattering amicably about their plans; and as the last crumb vanished, Cupid said persuasively, as if the league was not quite perfect without that childish ceremony,—

"Now let's kiss and be friends, and never quarrel any more."

As the rosy mouths met in a kiss of peace, the sound was echoed from the other room, for Mr. George's eyes made the same proposal, and his wife answered it as tenderly as Chow-chow did Cupid. Not a word was said, for grown people do not " 'fess" and forgive with the sweet frankness of children; but both felt that the future would be happier than the past, thanks to the lesson they had learned from the little romance of Cupid and Chow-chow.

Queen Aster

FOR MANY SEASONS the Golden-rods had reigned over the meadow, and no one thought of choosing a king from any other family, for they were strong and handsome, and loved to rule.

But one autumn something happened which caused great excitement among the flowers. It was proposed to have a queen, and such a thing had never been heard of before. It began among the Asters; for some of them grew outside the wall beside the road, and saw and heard what went on in the great world. These sturdy plants told the news to their relations inside; and so the Asters were unusually wise and energetic flowers, from the little white stars in the grass to the tall sprays tossing their purple plumes above the mossy wall.

"Things are moving in the great world, and it is time we made a change in our little one," said one of the roadside Asters, after a long talk with a wandering wind. "Matters are not going well in the meadow; for the Golden-rods rule, and they care only for money and power, as their name shows. Now, *we* are descended from the stars, and are both wise and good, and our tribe is even larger than the Golden-rod tribe; so it is but fair that we should take our turn at governing. It will soon be time to choose, and I propose our stately cousin, Violet Aster, for queen this year. Whoever agrees with me, say Aye."

Quite a shout went up from all the Asters; and the late Clovers and Buttercups joined in it, for they were honest, sensible flowers, and liked fair play. To their great delight the Pitcher-plant, or Forefathers' Cup, said "Aye" most decidedly, and that impressed all the other plants; for this fine family came over in the "Mayflower," and was much honored every where.

But the proud Cardinals by the brook blushed with shame at the idea of a queen; the Fringed Gentians shut their blue eyes that they might not see the bold Asters; and Clematis fainted away in the grass, she was so shocked. The Golden-rods laughed scornfully, and were much amused at the suggestion to put them off the throne where they had ruled so long.

"Let those discontented Asters try it," they said. "No one will vote for that foolish Violet, and things will go on as they always have done; so, dear friends, don't be troubled, but help us elect our handsome cousin who was born in the palace this year."

In the middle of the meadow stood a beautiful maple, and at its foot lay a large rock overgrown by a wild grape-vine. All kinds of flowers sprung up here; and this autumn a tall spray of Golden-rod and a lovely violet Aster grew almost side by side, with only a screen of ferns between them. This was called the palace; and seeing their cousin there made the Asters feel that their turn had come, and many of the other flowers agreed with them that a change of rulers ought to be made for the good of the kingdom.

So when the day came to choose, there was great excitement as the wind went about collecting the votes. The Golden-rods, Cardinals, Gentians, Clematis, and Bitter-sweet voted for the Prince, as they called the handsome fellow by the rock. All the Asters, Buttercups, Clovers, and Pitcher-plants voted for Violet; and to the surprise of the meadow the Maple dropped a leaf, and the Rock gave a bit of lichen for her also. They seldom took part in the affairs of the flower people,—the tree living so high above them, busy with its own music, and the rock being so old that it seemed lost in meditation most of the time; but they liked the idea of a queen (for one was a poet, the other a philosopher), and both believed in gentle Violet.

Their votes won the day, and with loud rejoicing by her friends she was proclaimed queen of the meadow and welcomed to her throne.

"We will never go to Court or notice her in any way," cried the haughty Cardinals, red with anger.

"Nor we! Dreadful, unfeminine creature! Let us turn our backs and be grateful that the brook flows between us," added the Gentians, shaking their fringes as if the mere idea soiled them.

Clematis hid her face among the vine leaves, feeling that the palace was no longer a fit home for a delicate, high-born flower like herself. All the Golden-rods raged at this dreadful disappointment, and said many untrue and disrespectful things of Violet. The Prince tossed his yellow head behind the screen, and laughed as if he did not mind, saying carelessly,—

"Let her try; she never can do it, and will soon be glad to give up and let me take my proper place."

So the meadow was divided: one half turned its back on the new queen; the other half loved, admired, and believed in her; and all waited to see how the experiment would succeed. The wise Asters helped her with advice; the Pitcher-plant refreshed her with the history of the brave Puritans who loved liberty and justice and suffered to win them; the honest Clovers sweetened life with their sincere friendship, and the cheerful Buttercups brightened her days with kindly words and deeds. But her best help came from the rock and the tree,—for when she needed strength she leaned her delicate head against the rough breast of the rock, and courage seemed to come to her from the wise old stone that had borne the storms of a hundred years; when her heart was heavy with care or wounded by unkindness, she looked up to the beautiful tree, always full of soft music, always pointing heavenward, and was comforted by these glimpses of a world above her.

The first thing she did was to banish the evil snakes from her kingdom; for they lured the innocent birds to death, and filled many a happy nest with grief. Then she stopped the bees from getting tipsy on the wild grapes and going about stupid, lazy, and cross, a disgrace to their family and a terror to the flowers. She ordered the field-mice to nibble all the stems of the clusters before they were ripe; so they fell and withered, and did no harm. The vine was very angry, and the bees and wasps scolded and stung; but the Queen was not afraid, and all her good subjects thanked her. The Pitcher-plant offered pure water from its green and russet cups to the busy workers, and the wise bees were heartily glad to see the Grape-vine saloon shut up.

The next task was to stop the red and black ants from constantly fighting; for they were always at war, to the great dismay of more peaceful insects. She bade each tribe keep in its own country, and if any dispute came up, to bring it to her, and she would decide it fairly. This was a hard task; for the ants loved to fight, and would go on struggling after their bodies were separated from their heads, so fierce were they. But she made them friends at last, and every one was glad.

Another reform was to purify the news that came to the meadow. The wind was telegraph-messenger; but the birds were reporters, and some of them very bad ones. The larks brought tidings from the clouds, and were always welcome; the thrushes from the wood, and all loved to hear their pretty romances; the robins had domestic news, and the lively wrens bits of gossip and witty jokes to relate. But the magpies made much mischief with their ill-natured tattle and evil tales, and the crows criticised and condemned every one who did not believe and do just as they did; so the magpies were forbidden to go gossiping about the meadow, and the gloomy black crows were ordered off the fence where they liked to sit cawing dismally for hours at a time.

Every one felt safe and comfortable when this was done, except the Cardinals, who liked to hear their splendid dresses and fine feasts talked about, and the Golden-rods, who were so used to living in public that they missed the excitement, as well as the scandal of the magpies and the political and religious arguments and quarrels of the crows.

A hospital for sick and homeless creatures was opened under the big burdock leaves; and there several belated butterflies were tucked up in their silken hammocks to sleep till spring, a sad lady-bug who had lost all her children found comfort in her loneliness, and many crippled ants sat talking over their battles, like old soldiers, in the sunshine.

It took a long time to do all this, and it was a hard task, for the rich and powerful flowers gave no help. But the Asters worked bravely, so did the Clovers and Buttercups; and the Pitcher-plant kept open house with the old-fashioned hospitality one so seldom sees now-a-days. Everything seemed to prosper, and the meadow grew more beautiful day by day. Safe from their enemies the snakes, birds came to build in all the trees and bushes, singing their gratitude so sweetly that there was always music in the air. Sunshine and shower seemed to love to freshen the thirsty flowers and keep the grass green, till every plant grew strong and fair, and passersby stopped to look, saying with a smile,—

"What a pretty little spot this is!"

The wind carried tidings of these things to other colonies, and brought back messages of praise and good-will from other rulers, glad to know that the experiment worked so well.

This made a deep impression on the Golden-rods and their friends, for they could not deny that Violet had succeeded better than any one dared to hope; and the proud flowers began to see that they would have to give in, own they were wrong, and become loyal subjects of this wise and gentle queen.

"We shall have to go to Court if ambassadors keep coming with such gifts and honors to her Majesty; for they wonder not to see us there, and will tell that we are sulking at home instead of shining as *we* only can," said the Cardinals, longing to display their red velvet robes at the feasts which Violet was obliged to give in the palace when kings came to visit her.

"Our time will soon be over, and I'm afraid we must humble ourselves or lose all the gayety of the season. It is hard to see the good old ways changed; but if they must be, we can only gracefully submit," answered the Gentians, smoothing their delicate blue fringes, eager to be again the belles of the ball.

Clematis astonished every one by suddenly beginning to climb the maple-tree and shake her silvery tassels like a canopy over the Queen's head.

"I cannot live so near her and not begin to grow. Since I must cling to something, I choose the noblest I can find, and look up, not down, forevermore," she said; for like many weak and timid creatures, she was easily guided, and it was well for her that Violet's example had been a brave one.

Prince Golden-rod had found it impossible to turn his back entirely upon her Majesty, for he was a gentleman with a really noble heart under his yellow cloak; so he was among the first to see, admire, and love the modest faithful flower who grew so near him. He could not help hearing her words of comfort or reproof to those who came to her for advice. He saw the daily acts of charity which no one else discovered; he knew how many trials came to her, and how bravely she bore them; how humbly she asked help, and how sweetly she confessed her shortcomings to the wise rock and the stately tree.

"She has done more than ever we did to make the kingdom beautiful and safe and happy, and I'll be the first to own it, to thank her and offer my allegiance," he said to himself, and waited for a chance.

One night when the September moon was shining over the meadow, and the air was balmy with the last breath of summer, the Prince ventured to serenade the Queen on his wind-harp. He knew she was awake; for he had peeped through the ferns and seen her looking at the stars with her violet eyes full of dew, as if something troubled her. So he sung his sweetest song, and her Majesty leaned nearer to hear it; for she much longed to be friends with the gallant Prince, and only waited for him to speak to own how dear he was to her, because both were born in the palace and grew up together very happily till coronation time came.

As he ended she sighed, wondering how long it would be before he told her what she knew was in his heart.

Golden-rod heard the soft sigh, and being in a tender mood, forgot his pride, pushed away the screen, and whispered, while his face shone and his voice showed how much he felt,—

"What troubles you, sweet neighbor? Forget and forgive my unkindness, and let me help you if I can,—I dare not say as Prince Consort, though I love you dearly; but as a friend and faithful subject, for I confess that you are fitter to rule than I."

As he spoke the leaves that hid Violet's golden heart opened wide and let him see how glad she was, as she bent her stately head and answered softly,—

"There is room upon the throne for two: share it with me as King, and let us rule together; for it is lonely without love, and each needs the other."

What the Prince answered only the moon knows; but when morning came all the meadow was surprised and rejoiced to see the gold and purple flowers standing side by side, while the maple showered its rosy leaves over them, and the old rock waved his crown of vine-leaves as he said,—

"This is as it should be; love and strength going hand in hand, and justice making the earth glad."

PART II

NOVELS AND NOVELLAS

Louisa May Alcott's adult novel Moods, *as her preface to the 1882 edition indicates, represents both her youth and her maturity. But the preface is a bit misleading: Alcott implies that thirty years passed between the inception of* Moods *and the revised edition, when in fact,* Moods *was a product of the early 1860s. Eighteen years separate the novel's first publication in 1864 from its reappearance in 1882. Perhaps Alcott exaggerated her immaturity on first writing* Moods *because of the adverse criticism it then received. In any event, the work is that of one who has already served her literary apprenticeship. Her editor at Roberts Brothers, Thomas Niles, admired the novel and repeatedly urged Alcott to write another in the same vein. When she seemed unable to produce one, he persuaded her to obtain the copyright from Loring, its original publisher, so that Roberts could publish a new edition. Both the early edition, from which she was forced to omit a number of chapters, and the revised edition, in which she apparently restored them, present the tragic disparity between a woman's expectations and opportunities and a man's. The problem that the heroine, Sylvia Yule, inherits from her parents is not so much a moody nature as a rigidly gendered world that allows no scope for her prodigious energy and talent. Counseled by the man she loves to forget herself and live for others, Sylvia resolves to live for the man who loves her, denying her own needs for both passion and achievement. Thus Alcott, in her first published novel, explores the issues raised by Margaret Fuller in her feminist tract* Woman in the Nineteenth Century, *including many of the dilemmas and double binds that continue to confront women today.*

In 1991, Sarah Elbert edited the 1864 edition of Moods *for Rutgers University Press and appended the chapters omitted from that edition. What follows is the first modern reprint of the 1882 edition, providing, arguably, a reading experience close to the one Alcott originally intended. The 1864* Moods, *however, contained a subplot in which Adam Warwick was romantically entangled with an unprincipled Cuban beauty, a complication dropped from the 1882 version. A second major difference, which Alcott alludes to in her preface, is the substitution of a happy ending for the original tragic one. A third, and perhaps the most important, difference between the two texts is the restoration of several original chapters, including "Moor," which illuminates his character; "Warwick," which depicts the initial meeting between him and Sylvia; and "Sermons," in which Warwick's advice leads Sylvia fatally astray. In addition, crucial scenes were restored to other chapters, including Sylvia's dramatic performances in "Afloat." The restored chapters and passages, most of which appear in the first half of the book, contain images and allusions that prepare the reader for what is to come. But they also point toward the original tragic conclusion. Thus, perhaps the ideal version of* Moods *would be one in which the omitted passages are restored and the original ending retained. One cannot help being impressed, however, by the myriad minute changes Alcott made in the second half of the 1882 edition to prepare for the reconciliation of Sylvia and her husband. And many of the earlier foreboding images still serve to foreshadow the death of Warwick as well as the harrowing of Sylvia's soul.*

MOODS

PREFACE

When "Moods" was first published, an interval of some years having then elapsed since it was written, it was so altered, to suit the taste and convenience of the publisher, that the original purpose of the story was lost sight of, and marriage appeared to be the theme instead of an attempt to show the mistakes of a moody nature, guided by impulse, not principle. Of the former subject a girl of eighteen could know but little, of the latter most girls know a good deal; and they alone among my readers have divined the real purpose of the book in spite of its many faults, and have thanked me for it.

As the observation and experience of the woman have confirmed much that the instinct and imagination of the girl felt and tried to describe, I wish to give my first novel, with all its imperfections on its head, a place among its more successful sisters; for into it went the love, labor, and enthusiasm that no later book can possess.

Several chapters have been omitted, several of the original ones restored; and those that remain have been pruned of as much fine writing as could be done without destroying the youthful spirit of the little romance. At eighteen death seemed the only solution for Sylvia's perplexities; but thirty years later, having learned the possibility of finding happiness after disappointment, and making love and duty go hand in hand, my heroine meets a wiser if less romantic fate than in the former edition.

Hoping that the young people will accept the amendment, and the elders will sympathize with the maternal instinct which makes unfortunate children the dearest, I reintroduce my first-born to the public which has so kindly welcomed my later offspring.

L. M. ALCOTT.

CONCORD, January, 1882.

CONTENTS

CHAPTER I

Sylvia

"Come, Sylvia, it is nine o'clock! Little slug-a-bed, don't you mean to get up to-day?" said Miss Yule, bustling into her sister's room with the wide-awake appearance of one to whom sleep was a necessary evil, to be endured and gotten over as soon as possible.

"No; why should I?" And Sylvia turned her face away from the flood of light that poured into the room as Prue put aside the curtains and flung up the window.

"Why should you? What a question, unless you are ill; I was afraid you would suffer for that long row yesterday, and my predictions seldom fail."

"I am not suffering from any cause whatever, and your prediction does fail this time. I am only tired of everybody and everything, and see nothing worth getting up for; so I shall just stay here till I do. Please put the curtain down and leave me in peace."

Prue had dropped her voice to the foreboding tone so irritating to nervous persons whether sick or well, and Sylvia laid her arm across her eyes with an impatient gesture as she spoke sharply.

"Nothing worth getting up for," cried Prue, like an aggravating echo. "Why, child, there are a hundred pleasant things to do if you would only think so. Now don't be dismal and mope away this lovely day. Get up and try my plan; have a good breakfast, read the papers, and then work in your garden before it grows too warm; that is wholesome exercise, and you've neglected it sadly of late."

"I don't wish any breakfast; I hate newspapers, they are so full of lies; I'm tired of the garden, for nothing goes right this year; and I detest taking exercise merely because it's wholesome. No, I'll not get up for that."

"Then stay in the house and draw, read, or practise. Sit with Max in the studio; give Miss Hemming directions about your summer things, or go into town about your bonnet. There is a matinée, try that; or make calls, for you owe fifty at least. Now I'm sure there's employment enough and amusement enough for any reasonable person."

Prue looked triumphant, but Sylvia was not a "reasonable person," and went on in her former despondingly petulant strain.

"I'm tired of drawing; my head is a jumble of other people's ideas already, and Herr Pedalsturm has put the piano out of tune. Max always makes a model of me if I go to him, and I don't like to see my eyes, arms, or hair in all his pictures. Miss Hemming's gossip is worse than fussing over new things that I don't need. Bonnets are my torment, and matinées are wearisome, for people whisper and flirt till the music is spoiled. Making calls is the worst of all; for what pleasure or profit is there in running from place to place to tell the same polite fibs over and over again, and listen to scandal that makes you pity or despise your neighbors? I shall not get up for any of these things."

Prue leaned on the bedpost meditating with an anxious face till a forlorn hope appeared which caused her to exclaim,—

"Max and I are going to see Geoffrey Moor this morning, just home from Switzerland, where his poor sister died, you know. You really ought to come with us and welcome him, for though you can hardly remember him, he's been so long away, still, as one of the family, it is a proper compliment on your part. The drive will do you good, Geoffrey will be glad to see you, it is a lovely old place, and as it is years since you saw the inside of the house you cannot complain that you are tired of that yet."

"Yes, I can, for it will never seem as it has done, and I can no longer go where I please now that a master's presence spoils its freedom and solitude for me. I don't know him, and don't care to, though his name is so familiar. New people always disappoint me, especially if I've heard them praised ever since I was born. I shall not get up for any Geoffrey Moor, so that bait fails."

Sylvia smiled involuntarily at her sister's defeat, but Prue fell back upon her last resource in times like this. With a determined gesture she plunged her hand into an abysmal pocket, and from a miscellaneous collection of treasures selected a tiny vial, presenting it to Sylvia with a half-pleading, half-authoritative look and tone.

"I'll leave you in peace if you'll only take a dose of chamomilla. It is so soothing, that instead of tiring yourself with all manner of fancies, you'll drop into a quiet sleep, and by noon be ready to get up like a civilized being. Do take it, dear; just four sugarplums, and I'm satisfied."

Sylvia received the bottle with a docile expression; but the next minute it flew out of the window, to be shivered on the walk below, while she said, laughing like a wilful creature as she was,—

"I have taken it in the only way I ever shall, and the sparrows can try its soothing effects with me; so be satisfied."

"Very well. I shall send for Dr. Baum, for I'm convinced that you are going to be ill. I shall say no more, but act as I think proper, because it's like talking to the wind to reason with you in one of these perverse fits."

As Prue turned away, Sylvia frowned and called after her,—

"Spare yourself the trouble, for Dr. Baum will follow the chamomilla, if you bring him here. What does he know about health,—a fat German, looking lager-beer and talking sauer-kraut? Bring me *bona fide* sugarplums and I'll take them; but arsenic, mercury, and nightshade are not to my taste."

"Would you feel insulted if I ask whether your breakfast is to be sent up, or kept waiting till you choose to come down?"

Prue looked rigidly calm, but Sylvia knew that she felt hurt, and with one of the sudden impulses which ruled her the frown melted to a smile, as drawing her sister down she kissed her in her most loving manner.

"Dear old soul, I'll be good by and by, but now I'm tired and cross, so let me keep out of every one's way and drowse myself into a cheerier frame of mind. I want nothing but solitude, a draught of water, and a kiss."

Prue was mollified at once, and after stirring fussily about for several minutes gave her sister all she asked, and departed to the myriad small cares that made her happiness. As the door closed, Sylvia sighed a long sigh of relief, and, folding her arms under her head, drifted away into the land of dreams, where ennui is unknown.

All the long summer morning she lay wrapped in sleeping and waking dreams, forgetful of the world about her, till her brother played the Wedding March upon her door on his way to lunch. The desire to avenge the sudden downfall of a lovely castle in the air roused Sylvia, and sent her down to skirmish with Max. Before she could say a word, however, Prue began to talk in a steady stream, for the good soul had a habit of jumbling news, gossip, private opinions, and public affairs into a colloquial hodge-podge, that was often as trying to the intellects as the risibles of her hearers.

"Sylvia, we had a charming call, and Geoffrey sent his love to you. I asked him over to dinner, and we shall dine at six, because then my father can be with us. I shall have to go to town first, for there are a dozen things suffering for attention. You can't wear a round hat and lawn jackets without a particle of set all summer. I want some things for dinner,—and the carpet must be got. What a lovely one Geoffrey had in the library!

Then I must see if poor Mrs. Beck has had her leg comfortably off, find out if Freddy Lennox is dead, and order home the mosquito nettings. Now don't read all the afternoon, and be ready to receive any one who may come if I should get belated."

The necessity of disposing of a suspended mouthful produced a lull, and Sylvia seized the moment to ask in a careless way, intended to bring her brother out upon his favorite topic,—

"How did you find your saint, Max?"

"The same sunshiny soul as ever, though he has had enough to make him old and grave before his time. He is just what we need in our neighborhood, and particularly in our house, for we are a dismal set at times, and he will do us all a world of good."

"What will become of me, with a pious, prosy, perfect creature eternally haunting the house and exhorting me on the error of my ways!" cried Sylvia.

"Don't disturb yourself; he is not likely to take much notice of you; and it is not for an indolent, freakish midge to scoff at a man whom she does not know, and couldn't appreciate if she did," was Max's lofty reply.

"I rather liked the appearance of the saint, however," said Sylvia, with an expression of naughty malice, as she began her lunch.

"Why, where did you see him?" exclaimed her brother.

"I went over there yesterday to take a farewell run in the neglected garden before he came. I knew he was expected, but not that he was here; and when I saw the house open, I slipped in and peeped wherever I liked. You are right, Prue; it is a lovely old place."

"Now I know you did something dreadfully unladylike and improper. Put me out of suspense, I beg of you."

Prue's distressful face and Max's surprise produced an inspiring affect upon Sylvia, who continued, with an air of demure satisfaction,—

"I strolled about, enjoying myself, till I got into the library, and there I rummaged, for it was a charming place, and I was happy as only those are who love books, and feel their influence in a room whose finest ornaments they are."

"I hope Moor came in and found you trespassing."

"No, I went out and caught him playing. When I'd stayed as long as I dared, and borrowed a very interesting book—"

"Sylvia! did you really take one without asking?" cried Prue, looking almost as much alarmed as if she had stolen the spoons.

"Yes; why not? I can apologize prettily, and it will open the way for more. I intend to browse over that library for the next six months."

"But it was such a liberty,—so rude, so—dear, dear; and he as fond and careful of his books as if they were his children! Well, I wash my hands of it, and am prepared for anything now!"

Max enjoyed Sylvia's pranks too much to reprove, so he only laughed while one sister lamented and the other placidly went on,—

"When I had put the book nicely in my pocket, Prue, I walked into the garden. But before I'd picked a single flower, I heard little Tilly laugh behind the hedge and some strange voice talking to her. So I hopped upon a roller to see, and nearly tumbled off again; for there was a man lying on the grass, with the gardener's children rioting over him. Will was picking his pockets, and Tilly eating strawberries out of his hat, often thrusting one into the mouth of her long neighbor, who always smiled when the little hand came fumbling at his lips. You ought to have seen the pretty picture, Max."

"Did he see the interesting picture on your side of the wall?"

"No; I was just thinking what friendly eyes he had, listening to his pleasant talk with the little folks, and watching how they nestled to him as if he were a girl, when Tilly looked up and cried, 'I see Silver!' So I ran away, expecting to have them all come racing after. But no one appeared, and I only heard a laugh instead of the 'stop thief' that I deserved."

"If I had time, I should convince you of the impropriety of such wild actions; as I haven't, I can only implore you never to do so again on Geoffrey's premises," said Prue, rising as the carriage drove round.

"I can safely promise that," answered Sylvia, with a dismal shake of the head, as she leaned listlessly from the window till her brother and sister were gone.

At the appointed time Moor entered Mr. Yule's hospitably open door; but no one came to meet him, and the house was as silent as if nothing human inhabited it. He divined the cause of this, having met Prue and Max going townward some hours before, and saying to himself, "The boat is late," he disturbed no one, but strolled into the drawing-rooms and looked about him. Being one of those who seldom find time heavy on their hands, he amused himself with observing what changes had been made during his absence. His journey round the apartments was not a long one, for, coming to an open window, he paused with an expression of mingled wonder and amusement.

A pile of cushions, pulled from chair and sofa, lay before the long window, looking very like a newly deserted nest. A warm-hued picture lifted from the wall stood in a streak of sunshine; a half-cleared leaf of fruit lay on a taboret, and beside it, with a red stain on its titlepage, appeared the stolen book. At sight of this, Moor frowned, caught up his desecrated darling, and put it in his pocket. But as he took another glance at the various indications of what had evidently been a solitary revel very much after his own heart, he relented, laid back the book, and, putting aside the curtain floating in the wind, looked out into the garden, attracted thither by the sound of a spade.

A girl was at work near by; a slender creature in a short linen frock, stout boots, and a wide-brimmed hat, drawn low over the forehead. Whistling softly, she dug with active gestures; and, having made the necessary cavity, set a shrub, filled up the hole, trod it down scientifically, and then fell back to survey the success of her labors. But something was amiss, something had been forgotten, for suddenly up came the shrub, and seizing a wheelbarrow that stood near by, away rattled the girl round the corner out of sight. Moor smiled at this impetuosity, and awaited her return with interest, suspecting who it was.

Presently up the path she came, with head down and steady pace, trundling a barrow full of richer earth, surmounted by a watering-pot. Never stopping for breath, she fell to work again, enlarged the hole, flung in the loam, poured in the water, reset the shrub, and, when the last stamp and pat were given, performed a little dance of triumph about it, at the close of which she pulled off her hat and began to fan her heated face. The action caused the observer to lean and look again, thinking, as he recognized the energetic worker with a smile, "What a changeful thing it is! haunting one's premises unseen, and stealing one's books unsuspected; dreaming one half the day and working hard the other half. What will happen next?"

Holding the curtain between the window and himself, Moor peeped through the semi-transparent screen, enjoying the little episode immensely. Sylvia fanned and rested a few minutes then went up and down among the flowers, often pausing to break a dead leaf, to brush away some harmful insect, or lift some struggling plant into the light; moving among them as if akin to them, and cognizant of their sweet wants. If she had seemed strong-armed and sturdy as a boy before, now she was tender-fingered as a woman, and went humming here and there like any happy-hearted bee.

"Curious child!" thought Moor, watching the sunshine glitter on her uncovered head, and listening to the air she left half sung. "I've a great desire to step out and see how she will receive me. Not like any other girl, I fancy."

But, before he could execute his design, the roll of a carriage was heard in the avenue, and pausing an instant, with head erect like a startled doe, Sylvia turned and vanished, dropping flowers as she ran. Mr. Yule, accompanied by his son and daughter, came hurrying in with greetings, explanations, and apologies, and in a moment the house was full of a pleasant stir. Steps went up and down, voices echoed through the rooms, savory odors burst forth from below, and doors swung in the wind, as if the spell was broken and the sleeping palace had wakened with a word.

Prue made a hasty toilet and harassed the cook to the verge of spontaneous combustion, while Max and his father devoted themselves to their guest. Just as dinner was announced Sylvia came in, as calm and cool as if wheelbarrows were myths and short gowns unknown. She welcomed the new-comer with a quiet hand-shake, a shy greeting, and a look that seemed to say, "Wait a little; I take no friends on trust."

Moor watched her with unusual interest, for he remembered the freakish child he left five years ago better than she remembered him. She was a little creature still, looking hardly fifteen though two years older. A delicate yet beautifully moulded figure, as the fine hands showed, and the curve of the shoulder under the pale violet dress that was both exquisitely simple and becoming. The face was full of contradictions; youthful, maidenly, and intelligent, yet touched with the melancholy of a temperament too mixed to make life happy. The mouth was sweet and tender, the brow touched with that indescribable something which suggests genius, and there was much pride in the spirited carriage of the small head with its hair of wavy gold gathered into a violet snood whence little tendrils kept breaking loose to dance about her forehead or hang upon her neck. But the eyes were by turns eager, absent, or sad, with now and then an upward look that showed how dark and lustrous they were. A most significant but not a beautiful face, because of its want of harmony, for the deep eyes among their fair surroundings disturbed the sight as a discord jars upon the ear; even when they smiled the shadow of black lashes seemed to fill them with a gloom never quite lost. The voice too, which should have been a girlish treble, was full and low as a matured woman's, with a silvery ring to it occasionally, as if another and a blither creature spoke.

All through dinner, though she sat as silent as a well-bred child, she looked and listened with an expression of keen intelligence that children do not wear, and sometimes smiled to herself, as if she saw or heard something that pleased and interested her. When they rose from table she followed Prue upstairs, quite forgetting the disarray in which the drawing-room was left. The gentlemen took possession before either sister returned, and Max's annoyance found vent in a philippic against oddities in general and Sylvia in particular; but his father and friend sat in the cushionless chairs, and pronounced the scene amusingly novel. Prue appeared in the midst of the laugh, and, having discovered other delinquencies above, her patience was exhausted, and her regrets found no check in the presence of so old a friend as Moor.

"Something must be done about that child, father, for she is getting entirely beyond my control. If I attempt to make her study, she writes poetry instead of her exercises, draws caricatures instead of sketching properly, and bewilders her music-teacher by asking questions about Beethoven and Mendelssohn, as if they were personal friends of his. If I beg her to take exercise, she rides like an Amazon all over the Island, grubs in the garden as if for her living, or goes paddling about the bay till I'm distracted lest the tide should carry her out to sea. She is so wanting in moderation she gets ill, and when I give her proper medicines she flings them out of the window, and threatens to send that worthy, Dr. Baum, after them. Yet she must need something to set her right, for she is either overflowing with unnatural spirits or melancholy enough to break one's heart."

"What have you done with the little black sheep of my flock,—not banished her, I hope?" said Mr. Yule placidly, ignoring all complaints.

"She is in the garden, attending to some of her disagreeable pets, I fancy. If you are going out there to smoke, please send her in, Max; I want her."

As Mr. Yule was evidently yearning for his after-dinner nap, and Max for his cigar, Moor followed his friend, and they stepped through the window into the garden, now lovely with the fading glow of a soft spring sunset.

"You must know that this peculiar little sister of mine clings to some of her childish beliefs and pleasures in spite of Prue's preaching and my raillery," began Max, after a refreshing whiff or two. "She is overflowing with love and good-will, but being too shy or too proud to offer it to her fellow-creatures, she expends it upon the necessitous inhabitants of earth, air, and water with the most charming philanthropy. Her dependants are neither beautiful nor very interesting, nor is she sentimentally enamored of them, but the more ugly and desolate the creature, the more devoted is she. Look at her now; most young ladies would have hysterics over any one of those pets of hers."

Moor looked and thought the group a very pretty one, though a plump toad sat at Sylvia's feet, a roly-poly caterpillar was walking up her sleeve, a blind bird chirped on her shoulder, bees buzzed harmlessly about her head, as if they mistook her for a flower, and in her hand a little field mouse was breathing its short life away. Any tender-hearted girl might have stood thus surrounded by helpless things that pity had endeared, but few would have regarded them with an expression like that which Sylvia wore. Figure, posture, and employment were so childlike in their innocent unconsciousness, that the contrast was all the more strongly marked between them and the tender thoughtfulness that made her face singularly attractive with the charm of dawning womanhood. Moor spoke before Max could dispose of his smoke.

"This is a great improvement upon the boudoir full of lapdogs, worsted-work, and novels, Miss Sylvia. May I ask if you feel no repugnance to some of your patients; or is your charity strong enough to beautify them all?"

"I dislike many people, but few animals, because however ugly I pity them, and whatever I pity I am sure to love. It may be silly, but I think it does me good; and till I am wise enough to help my fellow-beings, I try to do my duty to these humbler sufferers, and find them both grateful and affectionate."

There was something very winning in the girl's manner as she spoke, touching the little creature in her hand almost as tenderly as if it had been a child. It showed the new-comer another phase of this many-sided character; and while Sylvia related the histories of her pets at his request, he was enjoying that finer history which every ingenuous soul writes on its owner's countenance for gifted eyes to read and love. As she paused, the little mouse lay stark and still in her gentle hand; and though they smiled at themselves, both young men felt like boys again as they helped her scoop a grave among the pansies, owning the beauty of compassion, though she showed it to them in such a simple shape.

Then Max delivered his message, and Sylvia went away to receive Prue's lecture, with outward meekness, but such an absent mind that the words of wisdom went by her like the wind.

"Now come and take our twilight stroll, while Max keeps Mr. Moor in the studio and Prue prepares another exhortation," said Sylvia, as her father woke; and, taking his arm, they paced along the wide piazza that encircled the whole house.

"Will father do me a little favor?"

"That is all he lives for, dear."

"Then his life is a very successful one." And the girl folded her other hand over that already on his arm. Mr. Yule shook his head with a regretful sigh, but asked benignly,—

"What shall I do for my little daughter?"

"Forbid Max to execute a plot with which he threatens me. He says he will bring every gentleman he knows (and that is a great many) to the house, and make it so agreeable that they will keep coming; for he insists that I need amusement, and nothing will be so entertaining as a lover or two. Please tell him not to, for I don't want any lovers yet."

"Why not?" asked her father, much amused at her twilight confidences.

"I'm afraid. Love is so cruel to some people, I feel as if it would be to me, for I am always in extremes, and continually going wrong while trying to go right. Love bewilders the wisest, and it would make me quite blind or mad, I know; therefore I'd rather have nothing to do with it for a long, long while."

"Then Max shall be forbidden to bring a single specimen. I very much prefer to keep you as you are. And yet you may be happier to do as others do; try it, if you like, my dear."

"But I can't do as others do; I've tried and failed. Last winter, when Prue made me go about, though people probably thought me a stupid little thing, moping in corners, I was enjoying myself in my own way, and making discoveries that have been very useful ever since. I know I'm whimsical, and hard to please, and have no doubt the fault was in myself, but I was disappointed in nearly every one I met, though I went into what Prue calls 'our best society.' The girls seemed all made on the same pattern; they all said, did, thought, and wore about the same things, and knowing one was as good as knowing a dozen. Jessie Hope was the only one I cared much for, and she is so pretty, she seems made to be looked at and loved."

"How did you find the young gentlemen, Sylvia?"

"Still worse; for, though lively enough among themselves, they never found it worth their while to offer us any conversation but such as was very like the champagne and ice-cream they brought us,—sparkling, sweet, and unsubstantial. Almost all of them wore the superior air they put on before women, an air that says as plainly as words, 'I may ask you and I may not.' Now that is very exasperating to those who care no more for them than so many grasshoppers, and I often longed to take the conceit out of them by telling some of the criticisms passed upon them by the amiable young ladies who looked as if waiting to say meekly, 'Yes, thank you.' "

"Don't excite yourself, my dear; it is all very lamentable and laughable, but we must submit till the world learns better. There are often excellent young persons among the 'grasshoppers,' and if you cared to look you might find a pleasant friend here and there," said Mr. Yule, leaning a little toward his son's view of the matter.

"No, I cannot even do that without being laughed at; for no sooner do I mention the word friendship than people nod wisely and look as if they said, 'Oh, yes, every one knows what that sort of thing amounts to.' I *should* like a friend, father; some one beyond home, because he would he newer; a man (old or young, I don't care which), because men go where they like, see things with their own eyes, and have more to tell if they choose. I want a person simple, wise, and entertaining; and I think I should make a very grateful friend if such an one was kind enough to like me."

"I think you would, and perhaps if you try to be more like others you will find friends as they do, and so be happy, Sylvia."

"I cannot be like others, and their friendships would not satisfy me. I don't try to be odd; I long to be quiet and satisfied, but I cannot; and when I do what Prue calls wild things, it is not because I am thoughtless or idle, but because I am trying to be good and happy. The old ways fail, so I attempt new ones, hoping they will succeed; but they don't, and I still go looking and longing for happiness, yet always failing to find it, till sometimes I think I am a born disappointment."

"Perhaps love would bring the happiness, my dear?"

"I'm afraid not; but, however that may be, I shall never go running about for a lover as half my mates do. When the true one comes I shall know him, love him at once, and cling to him forever, no matter what may happen. Till then I want a friend, and I will find one if I can. Don't you believe there may be real and simple friendships between men and women without falling into this everlasting sea of love?"

Mr. Yule was laughing quietly under cover of the darkness, but composed himself to answer gravely,—

"Yes, for some of the most beautiful and famous friendships have been such, and I see no reason why there may not be again. Look about, Sylvia, make yourself happy; and, whether you find friend or lover, remember there is always the old Papa, glad to do his best for you in both capacities."

Sylvia's hand crept to her father's shoulder, and her voice was full of daughterly affection, as she said,—

"I'll have no lover but 'the old Papa' for a long while yet. But I will look about, and if I am fortunate enough to find and good enough to keep the person I want, I shall be very happy; for, father, I really think I need a friend."

Here Max called his sister in to sing to them, a demand that would have been refused but for a promise to Prue to behave her best as an atonement for past pranks. Stepping in, she sat down and gave Moor another surprise, as from her slender throat there came a voice whose power and pathos made a tragedy of the simple ballad she was singing.

"Why did you choose that plaintive thing, all about love, despair, and death? It quite breaks one's heart to hear it," said Prue, pausing in a mental estimate of her morning's shopping.

"It came into my head, and so I sung it. Now I'll try another, for I am bound to please you—if I can." And she broke out again with an airy melody as jubilant as if a lark had mistaken moonlight for the dawn and soared skyward, singing as it went. So blithe and beautiful were both voice and song, they caused a sigh of pleasure, a sensation of keen delight in the listener, and seemed to gift the singer with an unsuspected charm. As she ended Sylvia turned about, and, seeing the satisfaction of their guest in his face, prevented him from expressing it in words by saying, in her frank way,—

"Never mind the compliments. I know my voice is good, for that you may thank nature; that it is well trained, for that praise Herr Pedalsturm; and that you have heard it at all, you owe to my desire to atone for certain trespasses of yesterday and to-day, because I seldom sing before strangers."

"Allow me to offer my hearty thanks to Nature, Pedalsturm, and Penitence, and also to hope that in time I may be regarded, not as a stranger, but a neighbor and a friend."

Something in the gentle emphasis of the last word struck pleasantly on the girl's ear, and seemed to answer an unspoken longing. She looked up at him with a searching glance, appeared to find some 'assurance given by looks,' and as a smile broke over her face, she offered her hand, as if obeying a sudden impulse, and said, half to him, half to herself,—

"I think I have found the friend already."

CHAPTER II

Moor

Moor was pacing to and fro along the avenue of overarching elms that led to the old Manse. The May sunshine flickered on his uncovered head, a soft wind sighed among the leaves, and earth and sky were full of the vernal loveliness of spring. But he was very lonely, and this home-coming full of pain, for he had left a grave behind him, and the old house was peopled only with tender memories of parents and sister, whose loss left him a solitary man. The pleasant rooms were so silent, the dear pictured faces so eloquent, the former duties and delights so irksome with none to share them, that he was often drawn to seek forgetfulness in the sympathy and society without which his heart was hungry and life barren.

Nature always comforted him, and to her he turned, sure of welcome, strength, and solace. He was enjoying this wordless, yet grateful communion as he walked along the grass-grown path where he had played as a boy, dreamed as a youth, and now trod as a man, wondering who would come to share and love it with him, since he was free now to live for himself.

For an hour he had lingered there, letting thought, memory, and fancy weave themselves into a little song called "Waiting," and was about to go in and put it upon paper, when, as he paused on the wide doorstone for a last look down the green vista, a figure appeared coming from the sunshine into the shadows that made the leafy arches cool and calm as a cathedral aisle.

He knew it at once, and went to meet it so gladly that his face gave a welcome before he spoke. It was Sylvia with a book in her hand, the end of her mantle full of fresh green things, and her eyes both shy and merry as she said when they met,—

"Prue stopped at the Lodge to see Mrs. Dodd, and I ran on to beg pardon for stealing this, as she bade me; also to ask if I could have the other volumes, which I am longing to read."

"With pleasure, and anything else in my library. What made you choose this?" asked Moor, turning the pages of "Wilhelm Meister" with an inquiring smile as they went on together.

"I heard some people talking about 'Mignon,' and I wanted to know who she was; but when I asked for the book Papa said, 'Tut, child, you are too young for that yet.' It always vexes me to be called young, because I feel very old; I was seventeen in April, though no one will believe it."

Sylvia pushed back her hat as she spoke, and lifted her head with a disdainful little air at the stupidity of her elders, looking very young indeed with her lap full of the pretty weeds and mosses children love.

"I was just wishing for a playfellow, for Tilly is rather too young. If your mature age does not prevent your enjoying what I can offer, we may amuse ourselves till Miss Prue arrives. Will you go in and rummage the library, or shall we roam about and enjoy the fine weather?" asked Moor, finding his guest much to his liking, she was in such harmony with time and place.

"Let us go into the garden; I used to walk there very often, and like it very much, it is so old-fashioned and well kept," answered Sylvia, leading the way to a gate in the hawthorn hedge, beginning to redden in the late May sunshine.

Just beyond lay trim beds of herbs; in a warm corner stood a row of beehives, and before them, watching to see the busy people go in and out, sat a little child, humming in pretty mimicry of the bees, who seemed to take her for a flower, so harmlessly did they buzz about her.

Hearing steps, she turned, and at sight of Sylvia uttered a cry of joy, scrambled up, and came running with outstretched arms, for "Silver" was her dearest playmate.

The girl caught her up to kiss the red cheeks, fondle the curly head, and let the chubby hands pat her face and pull her ribbons.

"Tilly has missed you. Do not let her wait so long again, but feel that the garden is as much yours now as ever," said Moor, enjoying the pretty picture they made together.

"I thought I should be in the way, but I did long to come. I hate calls generally, and Prue was charmed when I proposed to make this one. How nice it looks here now!" And Sylvia glanced about her as if glad to be again in the quiet place which still seemed haunted by the presence of the happy family who had lived and loved there.

"This is the old herb-garden put to rights. My father planted it, my mother kept her bees here, and both used to sit upon this rustic seat, he reading Evelyn, Cowley, or Tusser, while she watched her boy and girl playing here and there. A very dear old place to me, though so solitary now."

The voice was cheerful still, but something in the look that wandered to and fro as if searching for familiar forms touched Sylvia, and with the quick instinct of a sympathetic nature she tried to comfort him by showing interest in the spot he loved.

"Let me sit here and play with Tilly while you tell me something about herbs, if you will. I've read of herb-gardens, but never saw one before, and find it quaint and pleasant."

She had evidently proposed a congenial pastime, for Moor looked gratified, and while she settled Tilly in her lap with a watch and chatelaine to absorb her little wits and fingers, he went to and fro, gathering a leaf here, a twig there, till he had a small but odorous nosegay to offer her. Then he came and sat beside her, glad to tell her something of the origin, fine associations, and grateful properties which should give these comfortable plants a place in every garden.

"Here is basil, an old-fashioned herb no longer cultivated in this country," he began. "I see you have read Keats's poem; that gives it a romantic interest, but it has a useful side also. Zelty tells us that 'the smell thereof is good for the head and heart; its seed cureth infirmities of the brain, taketh away melancholy, and maketh one merrie and glad. Its leaves yield a savory smell, and it is said the touch of a fair lady causeth it to thrive.' The farmers in Elizabeth's time used to keep it to offer their guests, as I do mine." And Moor laughingly laid the green sprig in Sylvia's hand.

She liked the fancy, and stroked the leaves with as sincere wish that they might thrive as any ancient lady who had a firmer faith in the power of her touch. Seeing her interest, Moor selected another specimen and went on with his herbaceous entertainment.

"Here is fennel. The physicians in Pliny's time discovered that, having wounded a fennel stalk, serpents bathed their eyes in the juice; thus they learned that this herb had a beneficial effect upon the sight. This perhaps is the reason why old ladies take it to church, that neither sleep nor dimness of vision may prevent their criticising each other's Sunday best."

Sylvia laughed now, and asked, touching another sprig,—

"Is this lavender?"

"Yes. It takes its name 'à lavendo' from bathing, being much used in baths for its fragrance in old times. In England I saw great fields of it, and when in blossom it was very lovely. It was said that the precious balm called nard was drawn from shrubs which grew only in two places in Judæa, and these spots were kept sacred to the kings."

"I can give you a feminine bit of information in return for your wise one. The blossom gives its name to a pretty color, which with a dash of pink makes violet,—my favorite tint, it is so delicate and expressive."

Moor glanced at her hair for the snood he liked to see her wear; but it was gone, and Tilly's great blue eyes were the only reminder of what Sylvia's should have been to make her face as harmonious as it was attractive. With an imperceptible shake of the head he hastened to finish his list, studying his listener meantime as carefully as she did the herbs which he laid one by one upon her knee.

"Here are several sorts of mint, and rosemary once used at weddings and funerals; sweet marjoram and sage, so full of virtues that the ancients had a saying, 'Why need a man die while sage grows in his garden?' 'There's rue for you, and here's some for me; we may call it herb of grace o' Sundays.' And this is thyme."

"I know a bank whereon the wild thyme grows," hummed Sylvia, as if his lines reminded her of one of her favorite songs.

Tilly looked up and began to hum also; then, being tired of the trinkets, ran away to catch a white miller that flew by. "Do the bees never sting her?" asked Sylvia, as she thanked her host and put the little posy in her belt.

"No; she has been taught not to touch them, and they never hurt her. I suspect they understand one another, for there is a sort of freemasonry among children, birds, bees, and butterflies, you know. Some grown people possess it. I have a friend who can charm the wildest creatures, and attract the shyest people, though he is rather an imposing personage himself. You have the same gift, I think, if I may judge by the pets I saw about you once."

"Perhaps I have, for I can always get on with dumb animals, they are so honest and simple. People tire me, so I fly to the woods when books give out," answered the girl, with a sigh, remembering how many hours these friends had brightened when Prue scolded and Max tormented her.

Thinking she was weary of the herb-garden, Moor was about to propose going on, when Prue's voice was heard, and they went to meet her. Leading them in, their host entertained one sister in the drawing-room, leaving the other to enjoy herself at her own sweet will in the library.

It was a pleasant place, lofty, cool, and quiet. Pines sighed before two deep windows, green draperies and a mossy carpet of the same hue softened the sunshine that came in at a third window, before which stood the writing-table. The ancient furniture seemed at home there, the book-lined walls invited one to sit and read, and a few fine pictures refreshed the eye as it wandered from Correggio's Fates, above the old-fashioned fireplace, to portraits of poets, or the busts of philosophers sitting up aloft, serenely presiding over the wit and wisdom of ages stored on the shelves below.

Sylvia enjoyed herself immensely as she roved to and fro, full of girlish curiosity and more than girlish interest in this studious place. She peeped into the portfolios, tried the ancient chairs, pondered over the faces on the walls, and scrutinized the table where a little vase of early wild-flowers stood among wise books in unknown tongues, and many papers suggested brainwork of some sort. Coming at last to a certain cabinet where favorite authors seemed to be enshrined, she possessed herself of the much-desired volumes, and sat down in a great velvet chair to read on. But the murmur of voices disturbed her, and she fell to musing with her eyes on the weird Sisters hanging just above her.

She was wondering how it would have fared with her if this quiet homelike place had been her home, that sweet-faced woman her mother, the benign old man her father, and she the sister to whom Geoffrey had devoted so many years. Would she have been better, happier than now, if she had grown up in the atmosphere of domestic peace, affection, and refinement that still seemed to pervade the place and make its indefinable but potent charm? Her own home was not harmonious, and she felt the need of cherishing as much as a motherless bird in a chilly nest. She had neither the skill nor power to change anything, she could only suffer and submit, wondering as she did so why fate was not kinder.

The old place had always been wonderfully attractive to her, and now, as she sat in the heart of it, she felt a curious sort of content, and wished to stay, sure that it would be long before she tired of this restful and congenial spot. The soft arms of the old chair embraced her as if she sat in a grandmother's capacious lap; the pines whispered a soothing lullaby, the perfume of herbs recalled that pleasant half-hour in the garden;

and the little picture of happy parents and children rose before her again, making the silence and solitude doubly pathetic.

Moor found her sitting so, and thought the musing little figure far more agreeable than prim Prue in her rustling plum-colored silk and best bonnet.

"Your sister has kindly gone to give my housekeeper some directions for my comfort. What can I do for you meantime, Miss Sylvia?" he said, with such a friendly air that she felt no hesitation in freely asking anything caprice suggested.

"I was wondering if there was any way of making those old women spin our threads as we want them. They look very stern and pitiless," she said, pointing to the picture.

"If I believed in fate, I should say No; but as I do not, I think we *can* twist our own threads very much as we will, if we only have the patience and courage to try."

"Don't you think there are some persons born to be dissatisfied, defeated in all ways, and dreadfully unhappy?"

"Many people are born with troubles of mind or body that try them very much, but they can be outlived, subdued, or submitted to so sweetly that the affliction is a blessing in disguise. 'Man is his own star,' you know, and a belief in God is far better than any superstition about fate."

Remembering what his own life had been, Sylvia felt that he practised what he preached, and was ashamed to say more about the moods that tormented her and made a blind belief in fate so easy to her. She was strongly tempted to speak, for confidence seemed natural with Moor, and the few times they had met had already made them friends. She wished she was little Sylvia again, to sit upon his knee and tell her perplexities as she once told her childish troubles, sure of help and sympathy. But young as she was in years, the girl was fast changing to the woman, and learning to hide what lay nearest her heart. So now she smiled and turned to another picture, saying with a cheerier ring in her voice, as if caught from his,—

"I'll try for the patience and the courage then, and let the old sisters spin as they will. Please tell me who that is? It looks like Jove, but has no eagle nor thunderbolts."

Moor laughed as he pushed away the curtain that she might see the fine engraving better as it hung in the recess above the cabinet.

"That is a modern Jove, the writer of the book you like so well, Goethe."

"What a splendid head! I wish he lived now, I would so love to see and know him. I always envied Bettina and longed to be in her place. People nowadays are so unheroic and disappointing, even the famous ones."

"I can show you a man who resembles this magnificent old fellow very much. He is not so great a genius, but sufficiently 'many-sided' to astonish and perplex his friends as much as young Wolfgang did his during the 'storm and stress period.' I hope to see him here before long, and I am sure you will not find him unheroic, though he may be disappointing."

"If he looks like that, and is honest and wise, I don't care how odd he may be. I like original people who speak their minds out and don't worry about trifles," said Sylvia, looking upon the picture with great favor.

"Then he will suit you. I will say no more, but leave you to find him out alone; that always adds to the interest of a new acquaintance." And Moor smiled to himself at the prospect of a meeting between his tempestuous friend and this precocious little girl whom he had already named Ariel in his fancy.

"May I dare to ask about this picture too? It is so beautiful I feel as if I ought to pay my respects to the sweet lady of the house."

Sylvia stood up as she spoke, and made a little gesture of salutation, with her eyes on the face of the portrait in the place of honor above the writing-table.

The color came into Moor's cheek, and he thanked her with a look she long remembered; for this mother had been very dear to him and made him what he was. Gladly he told her many things that made the hour sweet and memorable to both listener and narrator; for the son was eloquent, and Sylvia found the woman he described her ideal of that dearest, loveliest of human creatures, a good mother. Tears were in both their eyes when he paused, but the girl begged him to go on, and he told the pathetic little story of his patient sister, making Sylvia ashamed of her visionary trials, and deepening her newly awakened interest in this man to admiration and respect, though he said nothing of himself.

Prue came bustling in as he ended, and there was no chance for poetry or pathos where she was. Their host went with them to the great gate, and they left him standing bareheaded in the rosy sunset that wrapped Sylvia in a soft haze as she went musing home, while Moor lingered back along the path that was no longer solitary, for a slender figure seemed to walk beside him, with tender, innocent eyes looking into his.

CHAPTER III

Dull, But Necessary

Whoever cares only for incident and action in a book had better skip this chapter and read on; but those who take an interest in the delineation of character will find the key to Sylvia's here.

John Yule might have been a poet, painter, or philanthropist, for Heaven had endowed him with fine gifts; he was a prosperous merchant, with no ambition but to leave a fortune to his children and live down the memory of a bitter past. On the threshold of his life he stumbled and fell; for as he paused there, Providence tested and found him wanting. On one side Poverty offered the aspiring youth her meagre hand; but he was not wise enough to see the virtues hidden under her hard aspect, nor brave enough to learn the stern yet salutary lessons which labor, necessity, and patience teach, giving to those who serve and suffer the true success. On the other hand Opulence allured him with her many baits, and, silencing the voice of conscience, he yielded to temptation and wrecked his nobler self.

A loveless marriage was the price he paid for his ambition; not a costly one, he thought, till time taught him that whosoever mars the integrity of his own soul by transgressing the great laws of life, even by so much as a hair's breadth, entails upon himself and heirs the inevitable retribution which proves their worth and keeps them sacred. The tie that bound and burdened the unhappy twain, worn thin by constant friction, snapped at last, and in the solemn pause death made in his busy life, there rose before him those two ghosts who sooner or later haunt us all, saying with reproachful voices, "This I might have been" and "This I am." Then he saw the failure of his life. At fifty he found himself poorer than when he made his momentous choice; for the years that had given him wealth, position, children, had also taken from him youth, self-respect, and many a gift whose worth was magnified by loss. He endeavored to repair the fault so tardily acknowledged, but found it impossible to cancel it when remorse, imbittered effort, and age left him powerless to redeem the rich inheritance squandered in his prime.

If ever man received punishment for a self-inflicted wrong, it was John Yule,—a punishment as subtle as the sin; for in the children growing up about him every relinquished hope, neglected gift, lost aspiration, seemed to live again; yet on each and all was set the direful stamp of imperfection, which made them visible illustrations of the great law broken in his youth.

In Prudence, as she grew to womanhood, he saw his own practical tact and talent, nothing more. She seemed the living representative of the years spent in strife for profit, power, and place; the petty cares that fret the soul, the mercenary schemes that waste a life, the worldly formalities, frivolities, and fears, that so belittle character. All these he saw in this daughter's shape; and with pathetic patience bore the daily trial of an over-active, over-anxious, affectionate, but most prosaic child.

In Max he saw his ardor for the beautiful, his love of the poetic, his reverence for genius, virtue, heroism. But here too the subtle blight had fallen. This son, though strong in purpose, was feeble in performance; for some hidden spring of power was wanting, and the shadow of that earlier defeat chilled in his nature the energy which is the first attribute of all success. Max loved art, and gave himself to it; but, though studying all forms of beauty, he never reached its soul, and every effort tantalized him with fresh glimpses of the fair ideal which he could not reach. He loved the true, but high thoughts seldom blossomed into noble deeds; for when the hour came the man was never ready, and disappointment was his daily portion. A sad fate for the son, a far sadder one for the father who had bequeathed it to him from the irrecoverable past.

In Sylvia he saw, mysteriously blended, the two natures that had given her life, although she was born when the gulf between regretful husband and sad wife was widest. As if indignant Nature rebelled against the outrage done her holiest ties, adverse temperaments gifted the child with the good and ill of each. From her father she received pride, intellect, and will; from her mother passion, imagination, and the fateful melancholy of a woman defrauded of her dearest hope. These conflicting temperaments, with all their aspirations, attributes, and inconsistencies, were woven into a nature fair and faulty; ambitious, yet not self-reliant; sensitive, yet not keen-sighted. These two masters ruled soul and body, warring against each other, making Sylvia an enigma to herself and her life a train of moods.

A wise and tender mother would have divined her nameless needs, answered her vague desires, and through the medium of the most omnipotent affection given to humanity, have made her what she might have been. But Sylvia had never known mother-love, for her life came through death; and the only legacy bequeathed her was a ceaseless craving for affection, and the shadow of a tragedy that wrung from the pale lips, that grew cold against her baby cheek, the cry, "Free at last, thank God!"

Prudence could not fill the empty place, though the good-hearted housewife did her best. Neither sister understood the other, and each tormented the other through her very love. Prue unconsciously exasperated Sylvia, Sylvia unconsciously shocked Prue, and they hitched along together, each trying to do well, and each taking diametrically opposite measures to effect her purpose. Max briefly but truly described them when he said, "Sylvia trims the house with flowers, Prudence dogs her with a dust-pan."

Mr. Yule was now a busy, silent man, who, having said one fatal "No" to himself, made it the satisfaction of his life to say a never varying "Yes" to his children. But though he left no wish of theirs ungratified, he seemed to have forfeited his power to draw and hold them to himself. He was more like an unobtrusive guest than a master in his house. His children loved, but never clung to him, because unseen, yet impassable, rose the barrier of an instinctive protest against the wrong done their dead mother, unconscious on their part but terribly significant to him.

Max had been years away, studying abroad; and though the brother and sister were tenderly attached, sex, tastes, and pursuits kept them too far apart, and Sylvia was solitary even in this social-seeming home. Dissatisfied with herself, she endeavored to make her life what it should be with the energy of an ardent, aspiring nature; and through all experiences, sweet or bitter, all varying moods, successes, and defeats, a sincere desire for happiness the best and highest was the little rushlight of her soul that never wavered or went out.

She had never known friendship in its truest sense, for next to love it is the most abused of words. She had called many "friend," but was still ignorant of that sentiment, cooler than passion, warmer than respect, more just and generous than either, which recognizes a kindred spirit in another, and, claiming its right, keeps it sacred by the wise reserve that is to friendship what the purple bloom is to the grape, a charm which once destroyed can never be restored. Love she dreaded, feeling that when it came its power would possess her wholly, and she had no wish to lose her freedom yet. Therefore she rejoiced over a more tranquil pleasure, and believed that she had found a friend in the neighbor who after long absence had returned to his old place.

Nature had done much for Geoffrey Moor, but the wise mother also gave him those teachers to whose hard lessons she often leaves her dearest children. Five years spent in the service of a sister, who through the sharp discipline of pain was fitting her meek soul for heaven, had given him an experience such as few young men receive. This fraternal devotion proved a blessing in disguise; it preserved him from any profanation of his youth, and the companionship of the helpless creature whom he loved had proved an ever present stimulant to all that was best and sweetest in the man. A single duty, faithfully performed, had set the seal of integrity upon his character, and given him grace to see at thirty the rich compensation he had received for the ambitions silently sacrificed at twenty-five. When his long vigil was over, he looked into the world to find his place again. But the old desires were dead, the old allurements had lost their charm, and while he waited for time to show him what good work he should espouse, no longing was so strong as that for a home, where he might bless and be blessed in writing that immortal poem, a virtuous and happy life.

Sylvia soon felt the power and beauty of this nature, and, remembering how well he had ministered to a physical affliction, often looked into the face whose serenity was a perpetual rebuke, longing to ask him to help and heal the mental ills that perplexed and burdened her. Moor soon divined the real isolation of the girl, read the language of her wistful eyes, felt that he could serve her, and invited confidence by the cordial alacrity with which he met her least advance.

But while he served, he learned to love her; for Sylvia, humble in her own conceit, and guarded by the innocence of an unspoiled youth, freely showed the regard she felt, with no thought of misapprehension, no fear of consequences,—unconscious that such impulsive demonstration made her only more attractive, that every manifestation of her frank esteem was cherished in her friend's heart of hearts, and that through her he was enjoying the blossom time of life. So, peacefully and pleasantly, the spring ripened into summer, and Sylvia's interest into an enduring friendship, full of satisfaction till a stronger influence came to waken and disturb her.

CHAPTER IV

Warwick

A wild storm had raged all night, and now, though the rain had ceased, the wind still blew furiously and the sea thundered on the coast. It had been a dull day for Sylvia, and she had wandered about the house like an unquiet spirit in captivity. She had sewed a little while with Prue, stood an hour to Max as Clytemnestra with a dagger in her hand, read till her eyes ached, played till her fingers were weary, and at last fallen asleep in the sofa corner when even day-dreams failed to lighten her ennui.

She was wakened by a watery gleam of sunshine, and, welcoming the good omen, she sprung up, eager as a caged bird for air and liberty.

"The sea will be magnificent after this gale, and I must see it. Prue will say no if I ask her, so I will run away, and beg pardon when I come back," thought Sylvia, as she clasped her blue cloak and caught up the hat she never wore when she could help it.

Off she went, through byways, over walls, under dripping trees, and among tall grass bowed by the rain, straight toward the sea, whose distant music sounded like a voice calling her to come and share its tempestuous mood. The keen wind buffeted her as she ran, but its breath kissed fresh roses into her pale cheeks, filled her lungs with new life, and seemed to sweep her along like a creature born to love and live in such wild hours as this. The lonely cliffs looked like old friends to her, though wearing their grimmest aspect, with torn seaweed clinging to them below and foam flying high up their rough fronts. The tide was coming in, but a strip of sand still lay bare, and, climbing down, sure-footed as a goat, Sylvia reached the rock which usually rose tall and dry from the waves that rolled in and out of the little bay. It was wet now, and the path that led to it rapidly narrowing as the tide rose higher with each billow that hurried to dash and break upon the shore.

"Ah, this is glorious!" sighed the girl, with a long breath of the sweet cold air that came winging its way across the wide Atlantic to refresh her. "Now I shall be happy, and can sing my heart out without disturbing any one."

Wrapping her cloak about her, she leaned in the recess that made her favorite seat, and let her voice rise and ring above the turmoil of the waves, as if she too felt the need of pouring out the restless spirit pent up in that young breast of hers. Sweet and shrill sounded the mingled music, and the wind caught it up to carry it with flecks of foam, sea scents, and flying leaves to the cliffs above, where a solitary figure stood to watch the storm.

A strange medley, for the girl set her songs to the fitful music of wind and wave, finding a sort of ecstasy in the mood that now possessed her, born of the hour and the place. Ariel's dirge mingled with the Lorelei's song, and the moaning of the Harbor Bar died away into a wail for Mary on the sands of Dee.

The narrow strip of beach was dwindling to a thread, and on that thread a life depended; but Sylvia did not see it, and the treacherous tide crept on.

The first exultation over, she let her thoughts voyage away as if carried by the ships whose white wings shone against the dark horizon like sea-birds flying to distant homes. She longed to follow with the vague desire that tempts young hearts to sigh for the unknown, unconscious that the sweetest mysteries of life lie folded up in their own bosoms. She pictured in the fairest colors the new world that lay beyond the dim line where sky and ocean met and melted. What friends should she find, what happiness, what answer to the questions that no one could solve here? Would she ever sail away across this wide sea to reach and rest in that fair country, peopled with all the beautiful, heroic shapes her hungry heart and eager fancy conjured up? She hoped so, and, dreaming of the future, utterly forgot the peril of the present.

An ominous sound was in the air, and each billow broke higher on the rock where she lay wrapped in her own thoughts; but Sylvia never heeded, and the treacherous tide crept on.

From wondering and longing for the unknown of this world she passed to marvelling what the change would be when she landed on the shore of that other world, where every wave that breaks carries a human soul. She longed to know, and felt a strange yearning to find again the mother whose very name was but a memory. The tender tie broken so soon still seemed to thrill with a warmth death could not chill, and the girl often felt irresistibly drawn to seek some clearer knowledge, some nearer hold of this lost love, without which life was lonely and the world never could be home to her.

Tears dropped fast, and, hiding her head, she sobbed like a broken-hearted child grieving for its mother. She never let Prue know the want she felt, never told her father how powerless his indulgent affection was to feed this natural craving, nor found elsewhere the fostering care she pined for. Only in hours like these the longing vented itself in bitter tears, that left the eyes dim, the heart heavy for days afterward.

A voice called her from the cliff above, a step sounded on the rocky path behind, but Sylvia did not hear them, nor see a figure hurrying through the deepening water toward her, till a great wave rolled up and broke over her feet, startling her with its chill.

Then she sprung up and looked about her with a sudden thrill of fear, for the green billows tumbled everywhere, the path was gone, and the treacherous tide was in.

A moment she stood dismayed, then flung away her cloak, and was about to plunge into the sea when a commanding voice called, "Stop, I am coming!" And before she could turn a strong arm caught her up, flung the cloak round her, and she felt herself carried high above the hungry waves that leaped up as if disappointed of their prey.

On the first dry slope of the path she was set down, unmuffled by a quick hand, and found herself face to face with a strange man, who said with a smile that made her forget fear in shame,—

"Next time you play Undine have a boat near, for there may be no Kuhlborn at hand to save you."

"I never was caught before, and could easily have saved myself by swimming. Nevertheless I thank you, sir, though I am hardly worth a wetting."

Sylvia began petulantly, being nettled by the satiric glimmer in the keen eyes fixed upon her; but she ended courteously, though her own eyes were still wet with sadder tears than any from the sea.

"Shall I drop you back again? Nothing easier, if you prefer to weep your life away down there to making it useful and pleasant up here," said the man, still smiling, but with a sudden softening of the face as he read sorrow, not sentimentality, in the young countenance before him.

It touched Sylvia with its quick sympathy, and simply as a child she said, lifting those lovely eyes of hers full of gratitude and grief,—

"I was crying for my mother, and I think if you had not come I should have been glad to go to her."

"Make her glad and proud to welcome you, and never think yourself ready for death till you have learned to live. Shall we go up higher?"

As he spoke the man led the way, and the girl followed, feeling rebuked and comforted at the same time. Half-way up he paused on a little green plateau that nestled in a sunny crevice of the cliff. A hardy flower or two grew there, a slender birch and a young pine stood side by side, and birds were chirping in the branches as they brooded on their nests. It was a pretty place midway between sea and sky, sheltered and safe yet not solitary, for the ocean sang below, the sun shone warmly above, and every air that blew brought some hint of land or sea.

"Rest a moment here; the path above is a steep one and you are breathless," said the man, looking down at Sylvia much as the tall cliffs looked at the little pimpernel close shut in its pink curtains among the stones at their feet.

"It is the wind that takes my breath away. I like to climb, and can show you an easier path than that," said the girl, gathering up the hair that blew about her face in a golden cloud.

"I always take the shortest way, no matter how rough it is. Never fear, I'll pull you up if you will trust me."

"I will, because I know you now." And Sylvia smiled as she looked at the vigorous frame and fine face before her.

"Who am I?" asked the stranger, amused at her answer.

"Adam Warwick."

"Right. How did you guess?"

"Mr. Moor said you were like a picture in his study, and you are. I thought it was meant for Jupiter, but it was Goethe."

Sylvia got no further, for, Warwick laughed out so heartily she could not resist joining him, as she leaned against the little birch-tree, glad to get rid of her sadness and embarrassment so easily.

"He glorifies his friends like a woman, and I thank him for saying a good word in behalf of such a vagabond as I. You are Max Yule's sister? I was sure of it when I saw you singing like a mermaid down there. He used to tell of your pranks. I see he did not exaggerate."

Sylvia was annoyed at the idea of her brother's tales, and wished Moor had told her something of this person, that she might know what manner of man he was and treat him accordingly. She was not afraid of him, though he looked very tall and powerful, standing straight and strong against the cliff, with the dark shadow of the pine upon him. A masterful man, she thought, but a kindly one, and original in speech and manner at least, for the first was very blunt and the latter decided, yet genial at moments.

"Shall we go on?" said the girl, anxious to escape all discussion of herself.

"Yes; it is getting late and we are wet. Now then!" And, taking her hand, Warwick literally did pull her up the face of the cliff in a half a dozen vigorous strides and swings, planting her on the top and still holding her, for the wind blew a gale above there.

She liked it, however, and stood a moment laughing and panting, while the blue cloak flapped and the long hair fluttered in spite of her efforts to confine it under her hat. Something fresh and strong seemed to have taken possession of her, and a pleasant excitement made her eyes shine, her cheeks glow, her lips smile, and life look happy in spite of the trials that she had just been bemoaning.

Agreeable as it was to watch that buoyant little figure, and listen to its frank conversation, Warwick, more mindful of her damp feet than his own dripping ones, said presently,—

"This is a fine sight, but we must leave it. I shall come again, and hope to find you here rather than down below."

"I shall not try that again, nor this either," answered Sylvia. "It is sad and dangerous in that cave of mine, it is too rough and high and gusty up here for me, but in Mr. Moor's little nook half-way between it is safe and sunny, and there one gets the best of both sea and sky, with green grass and birds and flowers."

Warwick looked at her keenly as she spoke, reading in her face, her tone, her gesture, a double significance to her simple words.

"You are right; keep to the happy, wholesome places in life, and leave the melancholy sea, the wandering winds, and craggy peaks to those who are made for them."

Sylvia glanced up as if surprised at being so well understood, but before she could speak Warwick moved on, saying in a different tone,—

"Will you come to the Manse and be made comfortable? I arrived unexpectedly and Geoffrey is away, but I shall be glad to play host in his absence."

"Thanks, I will run home at once. No one knows where I am, and Prue will begin to worry if I don't appear. Come and let my father thank you better than I can."

"I will. Good-night." And with a nod and a smile they parted, Warwick to tramp down the avenue without looking back, and Sylvia to hasten home, feeling that if she went out seeking for adventures, she certainly had been gratified.

She said nothing to Prue, and when, later in the evening, Moor brought his friend to see Max and inquire for the half-drowned damsel, she emerged from behind the curtains looking as brilliant and serene as if salt water and gales of wind agreed with her admirably.

As Warwick was formally presented to the sisters, Sylvia put her finger on her lips and with a look besought silence regarding her last prank. Warwick answered with a quick glance, a courteous greeting, and turned away as if they had never met before. Moor smiled, but said nothing, and soon the gentlemen were deep in conversation, while Prue dozed behind a fire-screen and Sylvia sat in the sofa corner studying the faces before her.

Presently her brother caught her eye, and as art was not the topic under discussion just at that moment, he strolled over to ask the cause of her unusual condescension, for she generally vanished when strangers came.

"What are you doing here all by yourself, young person?"

"I am watching your two friends, and thinking what a fine study they make with the red firelight on their faces."

They did make a fine study, for both were goodly men, yet utterly unlike; one being of the heroic, the other of the poetic type. Warwick was a head taller than his tall friend, broad-shouldered, strong-limbed, and bronzed by wind and weather. A massive head, covered with waves of ruddy brown hair, gray eyes that seemed to pierce through all disguises, an eminent nose, and a beard like one of Max's stout saints. Power, intellect, and courage were stamped on face and figure, making him the manliest man Sylvia had ever seen. He sat in an easy-chair, yet nothing could have been less reposeful than his attitude, for the native energy of the man asserted itself in spite of the soothing influences of time and place; while his conversation was so vigorous that Mr. Yule looked both startled and fascinated by its unusual charm.

Moor was much slighter, and betrayed in every gesture the unconscious grace and ease of the gentleman born. A most attractive face, with its broad brow, serene eyes, and the cordial smile about the mouth. A sweet, strong nature, one would say, which, having used life well, had learned the secret of content. Inward tranquillity seemed his, and as he listened to his friend, it was plain to see that no touch of light or color in the pleasant room, no word or look or laugh, was without its charm and its significance for him.

"Tell me about Mr. Warwick, Max. I have heard you speak of him since you came home, but, supposing he was some blowzy artist, I never cared to ask, and Mr. Moor would not say much. Now I have seen him, I want to know more," said Sylvia, as her brother sat down beside her with an approving glance at the group opposite.

"I met him in Germany when I first went over, and since then we have often met in our wanderings. He never writes, but goes and comes intent upon his own affairs; yet one never can forget him, and is always glad to feel the grip of his hand again, it seems to put such life and courage into one."

"So it does," said Sylvia, remembering the grasp that swept her out of danger and led her up the cliff. "Is he good?" she added, woman-like, beginning with the morals.

"Violently virtuous. He is a masterful soul, bent on living out his aspirations and beliefs at any cost; much given to denunciation of wrongdoing everywhere, and eager to execute justice upon all offenders high or low. Yet he possesses great nobility of character, great audacity of mind, and leads a life of the sternest integrity."

"Is he rich?"

"In his own eyes, because he makes his wants so few."

"Is he married?"

"No; he has no family and not many friends, for he says what he means in the bluntest English, and few stand the test his sincerity applies."

"What does he do in the world?"

"Studies it, as we do books; dives into everything, analyzes character, and builds up his own with materials which will last. If that's not genius, it is something better."

"Then he will do much good and be famous, won't he?"

"Great good to many, but never will be famous, I fear. He is too fierce an iconoclast to suit the old party, too individual a reformer to join the new; so he must bide his time, and do what he can."

"Is he learned?"

"Very, in uncommon sorts of wisdom. He left college after a year of it, because it could not give him what he wanted, and, taking the world for his book, life for his tutor, says he shall not graduate till his term ends with his days."

"I like that, and I think I shall like him very much."

"I hope so. He is a grand man in the rough, and an excellent tonic for those who have the courage to try him. He did me much good, and I admire him heartily."

Sylvia was silent, thinking over what she had just heard, and finding much to interest her in it, because to her imaginative and enthusiastic nature there was something irresistibly attractive in the strong, free, self-reliant man.

Max watched her for a moment, then asked with lazy curiosity,—

"How do you like this other friend of mine whom you know better?"

"He went away when I was such a child that since he came back I have had to begin again, but so far he is all you said, and I feel that I should like to make him my friend too, he is so gentle, wise, and patient with me."

Max laughed at the innocent frankness of his sister's speech, and answered warningly, "Better leave Platonics alone till you are forty. Though Moor is years older than you, he is a young man still, and you are getting to be a very captivating little woman."

Sylvia looked both scornful and indignant.

"You need have no fears. There *is* such a thing as honest friendship between men and women, and if I can find no one of my own sex to suit me, why may I not look for help and happiness elsewhere, and accept them in whatever shape they come?"

"You may, my dear, and I'll lend a hand with all my heart, only you must be ready to take the consequences in whatever shape *they* come," said Max, well pleased with the prospect his fancy conjured up, stimulated by certain signs which he saw more clearly than his sister did.

"I will," replied Sylvia loftily, and fate took her at her word.

Here several neighbors came in, and when the little stir was over the girl found Warwick on the sofa, to which she had retired again as the guests were absorbed by other members of the family. She thought he would allude to their first meeting, but he sat silently scrutinizing the faces before him as if quite unconscious of his little neighbor.

"I must say something," thought Sylvia, when the pause had lasted several minutes, and, turning toward him, she asked rather timidly,—

"Don't you care for conversation, Mr. Warwick?"

"I seldom get any."

"Why, what is that going on all about us?"

"Listen a moment and you will hear."

She obeyed, and began to laugh, for her ear received a medley of sounds and subjects so oddly blended and so flippantly discussed that the effect was very ludicrous. On one side she heard, "Mr. Moor, it was the divinest polka I ever danced;" on the other Prue was declaring, "My dear, nothing is so good for an inflamed eye as a delicate alum curd;" behind her Max was tenderly explaining, "You see, Miss Jessie, it is the effect of this shadow which gives the picture its depth and juiciness of tone;" and above all rose Mr. Yule's decided opinion that "We must protect our own interests, sir, or the country is in danger."

"Do you like pictures?" asked Sylvia, changing the subject, as her first venture proved a failure.

"That sort very much," answered Warwick, with a glance at the various faces he had been studying so intently.

"So do I!" cried the girl, feeling that they should get on now, for she loved to study character in that way, and was quick to read it. "I fancy faces are the illustrations to the books which people are. Some titlepages are very plain to read, some very difficult, a few most attractive; but as a general thing I don't care to go farther. Do you?"

"Yes; I find them all interesting and instructive, and am never tired of turning the pages and reading between the lines. Let us see how skilful you are. What do you call Max?" asked Warwick, looking as if he found the small volume just opened to him rather attractive.

"He is a portfolio of good, bad, and indifferent pictures. I hope he will fall to work and finish one at least; the portrait of a happy man and a successful artist." And Sylvia's eyes were full of wistful affection as they rested on her handsome, indolent brother, who never gave her an opportunity to be proud of him.

"I think he will if he does not waste his time studying fashion-plates," said Warwick, regarding the young lady whom Max was evidently wooing, very much as a lion might regard a butterfly.

"There is a heart under the ruffles, and we are all fond of Jessie. Don't you think her pretty, sir?"

"No."

"That's frank," thought the girl, adding aloud, "Why not?"

"Because she has no more character in her face than the white rose in her hair."

"But the rose has a very sweet odor, and no thorns for those who handle it gently, as flowers should be handled," said Sylvia, with a reproachful look from her brother's happy face to the rather grim one beside her.

"I am apt to forget that, so I get pricked, and deserve it. Will Max's sister forgive Max's friend, who sincerely wishes him well?"

"With all my heart, and thank you for the wish," cried the girl readily, adding in a moment with womanly tact, "But I did not finish my catalogue. Do you want to hear the rest and tell me if I am right?"

"Yes; who comes next?"

"Prue is a receipt book, Mr. Moor a volume of fine poems, and Papa a ledger with dead flowers and old love-letters hidden away in its dull-looking leaves."

"Very good; and what am I? Come, you have made up your mind, I think, and I shall like to see how correct you are."

Sylvia hesitated an instant, but something in the commanding voice and the challenge of the eye gave her courage to answer with a smile and a blush,—

"You remind me of Sartor Resartus, which I once heard called a fine mixture of truth, satire, wisdom, and oddity."

Warwick looked as if he had got another prick, but laughed his deep laugh, exclaiming in surprise,—

"Bless the child! how came she to read that book?"

"Oh, I found it and liked it, for, though I could not understand all of it, I felt stirred and strengthened by the strong words and large thoughts. Don't you like it?" asked Sylvia, taking a girlish pleasure in his astonishment.

"It is one of my favorite books, and the man who wrote it one of my most honored masters."

"Did you ever see him?" asked the girl eagerly.

He had, and went on to tell her in brief, expressive phrases much that delighted and comforted her, for she was a hero-worshipper and loved to find new gods to look up to and love.

It was a delicious half-hour to Sylvia, for the talk wandered far and wide, led by intelligent questions, eloquent answers, and mutual enthusiasm; though almost a monologue, she felt that this was conversation in the true sense of the word. Moor stole up behind them and listened silently, enjoying both speaker and listener, who welcomed him with a look and felt the charm of his genial presence.

The end came all too soon, and Sylvia was forced to leave the fine society of poets and philosophers and bid her neighbors good-night. She felt as if she had fallen from the clouds, and with a vague hope of continuing the pleasant talk she said to Warwick, as they stood together while Moor made his adieux with the old-fashioned courtesy Mr. Yule liked,—

"Tell me what sort of book I am; and tell me truly as I did you."

" 'The Story without an End.' Did you ever read it?" he asked with the look of benignity that sometimes made his face beautiful.

"Yes; I wish I might be as lovely, innocent, and true as that is. Thank you very much." And Sylvia put her small hand into the large one as confidingly as the child in the pretty allegory might have done, feeling better for the cordial grasp that accompanied his good-night.

"How do you like Adam, sir?" asked Max of his father when the family were alone.

"A fine man, but he needs polishing," answered Mr. Yule, who had found his guest interesting, but far too radical for his taste.

"What is your opinion, Prue?"

"He rather affects me like a gale of wind, refreshing, but one never knows where one may be carried; and when he looks about with those searching eyes of his, I am painfully conscious of every speck of lint on the carpet, for nothing seems to escape him," answered Prue, setting the disordered furniture to rights, lest the thought of it should keep her from sleeping.

"Well, Sylvia, is he odd enough to suit your taste?"

"I like him very, very much, only I feel unusually young and small and silly beside him, and he makes me dreadfully tired, much as I enjoy him."

She looked so, as she pressed her hands against her flushed cheeks, for her eyes were bright and eager, her whole air unquiet yet weary, and she wore the look of inward excitement which henceforth was to mark her intercourse with Adam Warwick.

CHAPTER V

Afloat

A week later Sylvia sat sewing in the sunshine one lovely morning, longing to roam away as she used to do, but restrained by a hope stronger than obedience to Prue's commands. She had been left much to herself of late, for Max had been away with Moor and Warwick, enjoying themselves in their own fashion, and the girl had only had brief glimpses of the three friends. Max brought home such tantalizing accounts of their sayings and doings that she felt an ever increasing desire to share the good things which were more to her taste than girlish trifles or the solitary revels she used to like.

"I don't see why I must sit here and hem night-cap strings when the world is full of pleasant places and delightful people, if I could only be allowed to go and find them. Prue is much too particular, and thinks all men alike. I know they would like to have me over there if Max would only take me. I've stood hours for him and he forgets it. Brothers are all selfish, I'm afraid. I wish I were a boy, or could be contented with what other girls like."

Here voices roused her from her reverie, and looking up she saw Max and his friends approaching. Her first impulse was to throw down her work and run to meet them, her second to remember her dignity and sit still, awaiting them with well-bred composure, quite unconscious that the white figure among the vines added a picturesque finish to the scene.

They came up warm and merry from a brisk row across the bay, and Sylvia greeted them with a face that gave a heartier welcome than her words, as she began to gather up her work when they seated themselves in the bamboo chairs scattered along the wide piazza.

"You need not disturb yourself," said Max; "we are only making this a way station *en route* for the studio. Can you tell me where my knapsack is to be found? After one of Prue's stowages, nothing short of a divining rod will find it, I'm afraid."

"I know where it is. Are you going away again so soon, Max?"

"Only a two or three days' trip up the river with these mates of mine. No, Sylvia, it can't be done."

"I did not say anything."

"Not in words, but you looked a whole volley of 'Can't I goes?' and I answered it. No girl but you would dream of such a thing; you hate picnics, and as this will be a long and rough one, don't you see how absurd it would be for you to try it?"

"I don't quite see it, Max, for this would not be an ordinary picnic; it would be like a little romance to me, and I had rather have it than any present you could give me. We used to have such happy times together before we were grown up, I don't like to be so separated now. But if it is not best, I'm sorry that I even looked a wish."

Sylvia tried to keep both disappointment and desire out of her voice as she spoke, though a most intense longing had taken possession of her when she heard of a projected pleasure so entirely after her own heart.

But there was an unconscious reproach in her last words, a mute appeal in the wistful eyes that looked across the glittering bay to the green hills beyond. Now Max was both fond and proud of the young sister, who, while he was studying art abroad, had studied nature at home, till the wayward but winning child had bloomed into a most attractive girl. He remembered her devotion to him, his late neglect of her, and longed to make atonement. With elevated eyebrows and inquiring glances he turned from one friend to another.

"Why not?" asked Moor, with a smile of pleasure.

"By all means," said Warwick, with a decided nod.

Being satisfied on that point, though still very doubtful of the propriety of the step, Max relented, saying suddenly,—

"You can go, Sylvia."

"What!" cried his sister, starting up with a characteristic impetuosity that sent her basket tumbling down the steps, and crowned her dozing cat with Prue's nightcap frills. "Do you mean it, Max? Wouldn't it spoil your pleasure, Mr. Moor? Shouldn't I be a trouble, Mr. Warwick? Tell me frankly, for if I can go I shall be happier than I can express."

The gentlemen smiled at her eagerness, but as they saw the altered face she turned toward them, each felt already repaid for any loss of freedom they might experience hereafter, and gave unanimous consent. Upon receipt of which Sylvia felt inclined to dance about the three and bless them audibly, but restrained herself, and beamed upon them in a state of wordless gratitude pleasant to behold. Having given a rash consent, Max now thought best to offer a few obstacles to enhance its value and try his sister's mettle.

"Don't ascend into the air like a young balloon, child, but hear the conditions upon which you go, for if you fail to work three miracles it is all over with you. Firstly, the consent of the higher powers, for father will dread all sorts of dangers, you are such a freakish creature, and Prue will be scandalized because trips like this are not the fashion for young ladies."

"I beg your pardon, but they are. I went with a party of young people last year and camped out for a week. All were brothers and sisters or cousins, and we had a lovely time. Papa likes me to be happy, and Prue won't mind, as you are all so much older than I am, and two of you like brothers to me. Consider that point settled, and go on to the next," said Sylvia, who, having ruled the house ever since she was born, had no fears of success with either father or sister.

"Secondly, you must do yourself up in as compact a parcel as possible, for though you little women are very ornamental on land you are not very convenient for transportation by water. Cambric gowns and French slippers are highly appropriate and agreeable at the present moment, but must be sacrificed to the stern necessities of the case. You must make a dowdy of yourself in some usefully short, scant, dingy costume, which will try the nerves of all beholders, and triumphantly prove that women were never meant for such excursions."

"Wait five minutes and I'll triumphantly prove to the contrary," answered Sylvia, as she ran into the house.

Her five minutes were sufficiently elastic to cover fifteen, for she was ravaging her wardrobe to effect her purpose and convince her brother, whose artistic tastes she consulted with a skill that did her good service in the end. Rapidly assuming a gray gown, with a jaunty jacket of the same, she kilted the skirt over one of green, the pedestrian length of which displayed boots of uncompromising thickness. Over her shoulder, by a broad ribbon, she slung a prettily wrought pouch, and ornamented her hat pilgrimwise with a cockle shell. Then, taking her brother's alpenstock, she crept down, and, standing in the doorway, presented a little figure all in gray and green, like the earth she was going to wander over, and a face that blushed and smiled and shone as she asked demurely,—

"Please, Max, am I picturesque and convenient enough to go?"

He wheeled about and stared approvingly, forgetting cause in effect till Warwick began to laugh like a merry bass-viol, and Moor joined him, saying,—

"Come, Max, own that you are conquered, and let us turn our commonplace voyage into a pleasure pilgrimage, with a lively lady to keep us knights and gentlemen wherever we are."

"I say no more; only remember, Sylvia, if you get burnt, drowned, or blown away, I'm not responsible for the damage, and shall have the satisfaction of saying, 'There, I told you so.' "

"That satisfaction may be mine when I come home quite safe and well," replied Sylvia serenely. "Now for the last condition."

Warwick looked with interest from the sister to the brother; for, being a solitary man, domestic scenes and relations possessed the charm of novelty to him.

"Thirdly, you are not to carry a boat-load of luggage, cloaks, pillows, silver forks, or a dozen napkins, but are to fare as we fare, sleeping in hammocks, barns, or on the bare ground, without shrieking at bats or bewailing the want of mosquito netting; eating when, where, and what is most convenient, and facing all kinds of weather, regardless of complexion, dishevelment, and fatigue. If you can promise all this, be here loaded and ready to go off at six o'clock to-morrow morning."

After which cheerful picture of the joys to come, Max marched away to his studio, taking his friends with him.

Sylvia worked the three miracles, and at half-past five A. M. was discovered sitting on the piazza, with her hammock rolled into a twine sausage at her feet, her hat firmly tied on, her scrip packed, and her staff in her hand. "Waiting till called for," she said, as her brother passed her, late and yawning as usual. As the clock struck six the carriage drove round, and Moor and Warwick came up the avenue in nautical array. Then arose a delightful clamor of voices, slamming of doors, hurrying of feet, and frequent peals of laughter; for every one was in holiday spirits, and the morning seemed made for pleasuring.

Mr. Yule regarded the voyagers with an aspect as benign as the summer sky overhead; Prue ran to and fro pouring forth a stream of counsels, warnings, and predictions; men and maids gathered on the lawn or hung out of upper windows; and even old Hecate, the cat, was seen chasing imaginary rats and mice in the grass till her yellow eyes glared with excitement. "All in," was announced at last, and as the carriage rolled away its occupants looked at one another with faces of blithe satisfaction that their pilgrimage was so auspiciously begun.

A mile or more up the river the large, newly painted boat awaited them. The embarkation was a speedy one, for the cargo was soon stowed in lockers and under seats; Sylvia forwarded to her place in the bow; Max, as commander of the craft, took the helm; Moor and Warwick, as crew, sat waiting orders; and Hugh, the coachman, stood ready to push off at the word of command. Presently it came, a strong hand sent them rustling through the flags, down dropped the uplifted oars, and with a farewell cheer from a group upon the shore the Kelpie glided out into the stream.

Sylvia, too full of genuine content to talk, sat listening to the musical dip of well-pulled oars, watching the green banks on either side, dabbling her hands in the eddies as they rippled by, and singing to the wind, as cheerful and serene as the river that gave her back a smiling image of herself. What her companions talked of she neither heard nor cared to know, for she was looking at the great picture-book that always lies ready for the turning of the youngest or the oldest hands, was receiving the welcome of the playmates she best loved, and was silently yielding herself to the power which works all wonders with its benignant magic. Hour after hour she journeyed along that fluent road. Under bridges where early fishers lifted up their lines to let them through; past gardens tilled by unskilful townsmen, who harvested an hour of strength to pay the daily tax the city levied on them; past honeymoon cottages where young wives walked with young husbands in the dew, or great houses shut against the morning. Lovers came floating down the stream with masterless rudder and trailing oars. College race-boats shot by with modern Greek choruses in full blast and the frankest criticisms from their scientific crews. Fathers went rowing to and fro with argosies of pretty children, who gave them gay good-morrows. Sometimes they met fanciful nutshells manned by merry girls, who made for shore at sight of them with most erratic movements and novel commands included in their Art of Navigation. Now and then some poet or philosopher went musing by, fishing for facts or fictions where other men catch pickerel or perch.

All manner of sights and sounds greeted Sylvia, and she felt as if she were watching a panorama painted in water-colors by an artist who had breathed into his work the breath of life and given each figure power to play its part. Never had human faces looked so lovely to her eye, for morning beautified the plainest with its ruddy kiss; never had human voices sounded so musical to her ear, for daily cares had not yet brought discord to the instruments tuned by sleep and touched by sunshine into pleasant sound; never had the whole race seemed so near and dear to her, for she was unconsciously pledging all she met in that genuine Elixir Vitæ which sets the coldest blood aglow and makes the whole world kin; never had she felt so truly her happiest self, for, of all the costlier pleasures she had known, not one had been so congenial as this, as she rippled farther and farther up the stream and seemed to float into a world whose airs brought only health and peace. Her comrades wisely left her to her thoughts, a smiling Silence for their figure-head, and none among them but found the day fairer and felt himself fitter to enjoy it for the innocent companionship of maidenhood and a happy heart.

At noon they dropped anchor under a group of wide-spreading hemlocks that stood on the river's edge, a green tent for wanderers like themselves; there they ate their first meal spread among white clovers, with a pair of squirrels staring at them as curiously as human spectators ever watched royalty at dinner, while several meek cows courteously left their guests the shade and went away to dine at a side-table spread in the sun. They spent an hour or two talking or drowsing luxuriously on the grass; then the springing up of a fresh breeze roused them all, and weighing anchor they set sail for another port.

Now Sylvia saw new pictures, for, leaving all traces of the city behind them, they went swiftly countryward. Sometimes by hayfields, each an idyl in itself, with white-sleeved mowers all arow; the pleasant sound of whetted scythes; great loads rumbling up lanes, with brown-faced children shouting atop; rosy girls raising fragrant windrows or bringing water for thirsty sweethearts leaning on their rakes. Often they saw ancient farm-houses with mossy roofs, and long well-sweeps suggestive of fresh draughts and the drip of brimming pitchers; orchards and cornfields rustling on either hand, and grandmotherly caps at the narrow windows, or stout matrons tending babies in the doorway as they watched smaller selves playing keep house under the "laylocks" by the wall. Villages, like white flocks, slept on the hillsides; martinbox schoolhouses appeared here and there, astir with busy voices, alive with wistful eyes; and more than once they came upon little mermen bathing, who dived with sudden splashes, like a squad of turtles tumbling off a sunny rock.

Then they went floating under vernal arches, where a murmurous rustle seemed to whisper, "Stay!" along shadowless sweeps, where the blue turned to gold and dazzled with its unsteady shimmer; passed islands so full of birds they seemed green cages floating in the sun, or doubled capes that opened long vistas of light and shade, through which they sailed into the pleasant land where summer reigned supreme. To Sylvia it seemed as if the inhabitants of these solitudes had flocked down to the shore to greet her as she came. Fleets of lilies unfurled their sails on either hand, and early cardinal flowers waved their scarlet flags among the green. The pontederia lifted its blue spears from arrowy leaves; wild roses smiled at her with blooming faces; meadow lilies rang their flame-colored bells; and clematis and ivy hung garlands everywhere, as if hers were a floral progress, and each came to do her honor.

Her neighbors kept up a flow of conversation as steady as the river's, and Sylvia listened now. Insensibly the changeful scenes before them recalled others, and in the friendly atmosphere that surrounded them these reminiscences found free expression. Each of the three had been fortunate in seeing much of foreign life; each had seen a different phase of it, and all were young enough to be still enthusiastic, accomplished enough to serve up their recollections with taste and skill, and give Sylvia glimpses of the world through spectacles sufficiently rose-colored to lend it the warmth which even Truth allows to her sister Romance.

The wind served them till sunset; then the sail was lowered, and the rowers took to their oars. Sylvia demanded her turn, and wrestled with one big oar while Warwick sat behind and did the work. Having blistered her hands and given herself as fine a color as any on her brother's palette, she professed herself satisfied, and went back to her seat to watch the evening red transfigure earth and sky, making the river and its banks a more royal pageant than splendor-loving Elizabeth ever saw along the Thames.

Anxious to reach a certain point, they rowed on into the twilight, growing stiller and stiller as the deepening hush seemed to hint that Nature was at her prayers. Slowly the Kelpie floated along the shadowy way, and as the shores grew dim, the river dark with leaning hemlocks or an overhanging cliff, Sylvia felt as if she were making the last voyage across that fathomless stream where a pale boatman plies and many go lamenting.

The long silence was broken first by Moor's voice, saying,—

"Adam, sing."

If the influences of the hour had calmed Max, touched Sylvia, and made Moor long for music, they had also softened Warwick. Leaning on his oar, he lent the music of a mellow voice to the words of a German Volkslied, and launched a fleet of echoes such as any tuneful vintager might have sent floating down the Rhine. Sylvia was no weeper, but, as she listened, all the day's happiness which had been pent up in her heart found vent in sudden tears, that streamed down noiseless and refreshing as a warm south rain. Why they came she could not tell, for neither song nor singer possessed the power to win so rare a tribute, and at another time she would have restrained all visible expression of this indefinable, yet sweet emotion. Max and Moor had joined in the burden of the song, and when that was done, took up another; but Sylvia only sat, and let her tears flow while they would, singing at heart, though her eyes were full and her cheeks wet faster than the wind could kiss them dry.

After frequent peerings and tackings here and there, Max at last discovered the haven he desired, and with much rattling of oars, clanking of chains, and splashing of impetuous boots, a landing was effected, and Sylvia found herself standing on a green bank with her hammock in her arms and much wonderment in her mind whether the nocturnal experiences in store for her would prove as agreeable as the daylight ones had been. Max and Moor unloaded the boat and prospected for an eligible sleeping-place. Warwick, being an old campaigner, set about building a fire, and the girl began her sylvan housekeeping. The scene rapidly brightened into light and color as the blaze sprang up, showing the little kettle slung gypsy-wise on forked sticks, and the supper prettily set forth in a leafy table-service on a smooth, flat stone. Soon four pairs of wet feet surrounded the fire; an agreeable oblivion of *meum* and *tuum* concerning plates, knives, and cups did away with etiquette; and every one was in a comfortable state of weariness, which rendered the thought of bed so pleasant that they deferred their enjoyment of the reality, as children keep the best bite till the last.

Stories were told, comic, weird, and stirring, and when it came to Sylvia's turn Max said,—

"We have worked and you have played; now while we rest amuse us with some of your dramatic pictures and pieces, as you do me when you are tired of posing. Make that rock your dressing-room and come out into the firelight when you are ready. She really has a very pretty talent for that sort of thing, and I've taught her to drape and pose well."

Excited by the day's pleasure and emboldened by the shadows, Sylvia needed little urging, for she was very grateful and ardently desired to make herself agreeable in return for the willing service of her "knights and gentlemen." She vanished, taking with her a red rug, a white shawl, and her blue cloak as wardrobe. The friends sat talking of the great actors they had known, and forgot her for the moment. A sudden start from Moor, who faced the rock, made the others turn to see Ophelia standing on the smooth plat of grass that lay between the fire and the sombre pines that made a most effective background for the white figure with its crown of ferns, wild weeds, and falling hair. One hand held the folds of the shawl that draped her, the other slowly drew from it the flowers Sylvia had gathered that day, to offer them now to imaginary spectators with vacant smiles, wandering eyes, and broken snatches of song the more pathetic for their gayety.

Even Max was surprised by the grace and skill with which she played her part; the others looked in silence too charmed to break the spell, and when the poor girl dropped her last garland on the mimic grave with plaintive music, and then went smiling and courtesying away to her sad end, they sat a moment silent with sympathy, before their applause assured the young actress that her effort was successful.

Quicker than they thought possible she was there again, still wrapped in the same shawl, a white scarf about the head, and a pine cone in her hand to represent a candle, for this was Lady Macbeth walking in her haunted sleep. The sightless eyes were fixed, the brow knit with remorseful pain, the hands wrung together as the light fell, and the lips apart to vent the heavy breathing of a sleeper. She spoke the words in a muffled tone that gave an awful meaning to her ominous confessions, and when she vanished, beckoning her accomplice away, the watchers seemed to see the guilty pair going to their doom.

"That is wonderful! The child has more than talent, Max, or has been trained by a better master than yourself," said Moor, looking charmed yet troubled by this display of unsuspected power.

"She has it in her, and needs no master. It is a perilous gift, but has its uses, for the pent-up emotions can find a safer vent in this way than in melancholy dreams or daring action," answered Warwick, remembering the tragic face he had caught a glimpse of when he saved Sylvia from the sea.

"She is a wonderful little thing in many ways, and I often puzzle my head thinking what will become of her, for I am convinced she will never settle down like other girls without some sort of tribulation or adventure," said Max, much flattered by the commendation of his friends.

"It will be interesting to watch the unfolding of this modern Mignon; I hope I shall be here to see it," answered Moor, little dreaming how hard a part he was to play in the drama of Love's Labor Lost.

"Let her alone, give her plenty of liberty, and I think time and experience will make a noble woman of her," added Warwick, feeling a strong sympathy for this ardent girl, who with all the luxury about her still hungered for a food she could not find.

A blithe laugh recalled them, and Rosalind sauntered from behind the rock wrapped in the cloak, with a little cap improvised from a blue silk handkerchief upon her tucked-up curls, and a switch in her hand, saying aside as she feigned to meet Orlando,—

"I'll speak to him like a saucy lacquey, and under that habit play the knave with him. I pray you, what is't o'clock?"

Then with quick changes of voice and manner from the half-indifferent man to the audacious maid, she gave the scene between the two with a spirit and grace which kept her listeners laughing till she disappeared looking over her shoulder with a face full of merry malice as she led the invisible Orlando away.

"Capital! Bravo! Encore!" cried the audience, eager for more; and inspired by their hearty pleasure, Sylvia gave them the balcony scene from Romeo and Juliet leaning over the rock with all her bright hair unbound, white arms bare, and shawl and scarf disposed as effectively as circumstances would permit against the scarlet rug.

This was the best of all, and a revelation even to her brother; for the excitement of former efforts, the desire to do her best, and the indescribable charm the part always had for her, made her act the impassioned Juliet to the life. Place and hour aided her, for the moon had risen and shone into the little glade, lending to the romantic figure an enchantment no stage moon ever gave it. Max also helped her, for he had played the part, and, burning to distinguish himself, sprang forward to make a comely Romeo, in spite of the high boots, blue flannel shirt, and waterproof mantle. He put Jessie Hope in Sylvia's place, and wooed her so ardently that she was able to act with all her heart, rendering the tender speeches with looks and gestures full of an innocent abandon both delightful and dangerous to the beholders.

"What a lover she will make when the time comes," thought Moor, with a thrill, as she leaned to Romeo full of a love and longing which made the girlish face wonderfully eloquent.

"What power and passion the little creature has! and a voice to lure a man's heart out of his breast," said Warwick, as Juliet cried, with her arms about her lover's neck,—

"Sweet, so would I;
Yet I should kill thee with much cherishing.
Good-night! good-night! parting is such sweet sorrow,
That I shall say good-night till it be to-morrow!"

Then, as if abashed at her forgetfulness of self, Sylvia slipped behind the rock, leaving her Romeo to resume his place, exclaiming complacently,—

"That was not bad, I fancy. Shakespeare forgive me for the liberties I took with him! I haven't acted since I played this part with Fräulein Hoffmann in Munich last year. She had no more idea of the part than that cow looking over the wall at us, but Sylvia really did very well."

"Too well for one of her age, I am afraid. Yet it was very lovely," said Moor, looking as if he still saw the white arms outstretched, and heard the tender words.

"Sentiment is perilous stuff; better let her get rid of her romance in mimic love scenes than in real ones, or leave it fermenting in that precocious head and heart of hers."

Yet Warwick had enjoyed it most of all, and was the first to rise and thank her when she came demurely back to her seat, with no sign of the actress about her but a deeper color in the usually pale cheeks, and eyes that seemed to have lost their shadows and grown young.

She took their praises modestly, rejoicing inwardly over the new sense of power that came to her as she saw not only admiration but wonder and respect in the faces of those she most desired to please. Generally she cared nothing for the regard of men, but these two were different from any she had known, and she felt that whatever they gave her was worth the having.

They sat late, for sleep had been banished by pleasure, and they lingered talking over the immortal characters which will always be full of intense interest to those who love to study human nature as painted by the Master who seemed to have found the key to all the passions, and set them to a music of which we never tire.

A distant clock struck eleven; Max suggested bed, and the proposition was unanimously accepted.

"Where are you going to hang me?" asked Sylvia, as she laid hold of her hammock and looked about her with nearly as much interest as if her suspension was to be of the perpendicular order.

"You are not to be swung up in a tree to-night, but laid like a ghost, and requested not to walk till morning. There is an unused barn close by, so we shall have a roof over us for one night longer," answered Max, playing chamberlain while the others remained to quench the fire and secure the larder.

The moon lighted Sylvia to bed, and when shown her half the barn—which, as she was a Marine, was very properly the bay, Max explained—she scouted the idea of being nervous or timid in such rude quarters, made herself a cosey nest, and bade her brother a merry good-night.

More weary than she would confess, Sylvia fell asleep at once, despite the novelty of her situation and the noises that fill a summer night with fitful rustlings and tones. How long she slept she did not know, but woke suddenly and sat erect with that curious thrill which sometimes startles one out of deepest slumber, and is often the forerunner of some dread or danger. She felt this hot tingle through blood and nerves, and stared about her, thinking of fire. But everything was dark and still, and after waiting a few moments she decided that her nest had been too warm, for her temples throbbed and her cheeks were feverish with the close air of the barn half filled with new-made hay.

Creeping up a fragrant slope, she spread her cloak again and lay down where a cool breath flowed through wide chinks in the wall. Sleep was slowly returning when the rustle of footsteps scared it quite away and set her heart beating fast, for they came toward the new couch she had chosen. Holding her breath, she listened. The quiet tread drew nearer and nearer till it paused within a yard of her, then some one seemed to throw himself down, sigh heavily a few times, and grow still as if falling asleep.

"It is Max," thought Sylvia, and whispered his name; but no one answered, and from the far corner of the barn she heard her brother muttering in his sleep. Who was it, then? Max had said there were no cattle near. She was sure neither of her comrades had left their bivouac, for there was her brother talking as usual in his dreams; some one seemed restless and turned often with decided motion; that was Warwick, she thought; while the quietest sleeper of the three betrayed his presence by laughing once with the low-toned merriment she recognized as Moor's. These discoveries left her a prey to visions of grimy strollers, maudlin farm-servants, and infectious emigrants in dismal array. A strong desire to cry out possessed her for a moment, but was checked; for with all her sensitiveness Sylvia had much common sense, and that spirit which hates to be conquered even by a natural fear. She remembered her scornful repudiation of the charge of timidity, and the endless jokes she would have to undergo if her mysterious neighbor should prove some harmless wanderer or an imaginary terror of her own, so she held her peace, thinking valiantly as the drops gathered on her forehead, and every sense grew painfully alert,—

"I'll not call if my hair turns gray with fright, and I find myself an idiot to-morrow. I told them to try me, and I won't be found wanting at the first alarm. I'll be still, if the thing does not touch me, till dawn, when I shall know how to act at once, and so save myself from ridicule at the cost of a wakeful night."

Holding fast to this resolve, Sylvia lay motionless, listening to the cricket's chirp without, and taking uncomfortable notes of the state of things within, for the new-comer stirred heavily, sighed long and deeply, and seemed to wake often, like one too sad or weary to rest. It would have been wiser to scream her scream and have the rout over, for she tormented herself with the ingenuity of a lively fancy, and suffered more from her own terrors than at the discovery of a dozen vampires. Every tale of *diablerie* she had ever heard came most inopportunely to haunt her now, and though she felt their folly, she could not free herself from their dominion. She wondered till she could wonder no longer what the morning would show her. She tried to calculate in how many springs she could reach and fly over the low partition which separated her from her sleeping body-guard. She wished with all her heart that she had stayed in her nest which was nearer the door, and watched for dawn with eyes that ached to see the light.

In the midst of these distressful sensations the far-off crow of some vigilant chanticleer assured her that the short summer night was wearing away and relief was at hand. This comfortable conviction had so good an effect that she lapsed into what seemed a moment's oblivion, but was in fact an hour's restless sleep, for when her eyes unclosed again the first red streaks were visible in the east, and a dim light found its way into the barn through the great door which had been left ajar for air. An instant Sylvia lay collecting herself, then rose on her arm, looked resolutely behind her, stared with round eyes a moment, and dropped down again, laughing with a merriment which, coming on the heels of her long alarm, was rather hysterical. All she saw was a little soft-eyed Alderney calf, which lifted its stag-like head, and regarded her with a confiding aspect that won her pardon for its innocent offence.

Through the relief of both mind and body which she experienced in no small degree, the first thought that came was a thankful "What a mercy I didn't call Max, for I should never have heard the last of this!" And, having fought her fears alone, she enjoyed her success alone, and, girl-like, resolved to say nothing of her first night's adventures. Gathering herself up, she crept nearer, and caressed her late terror, which stretched its neck toward her with a comfortable sound, and munched her shawl like a cosset lamb. But before this new friendship was many minutes old, Sylvia's heavy lids fell together, her head dropped lower and lower, her hand lay still on the dappled neck, and with a long sigh of weariness she dropped back upon the hay, leaving little Alderney to watch over her much more tranquilly than she had watched over it.

CHAPTER VI

Through Flood and Field and Fire

Very early were they afloat again, and as they glided up the stream Sylvia watched the earth's awakening, seeing in it, what her own should be. The sun was not yet visible above the hills, but the sky was ready for his coming, with the soft flush of color dawn gives only to her royal lover. Birds were chanting matins as if all the jubilance of their short lives must be poured out at once. Flowers stirred and brightened like children after sleep. A balmy wind came whispering from the wood, bringing the aroma of pines, the cool breath of damp nooks, the healthful kiss that leaves a glow behind. Light mists floated down the river like departing visions that had haunted it by night, and every ripple breaking on the shore seemed to sing a musical good-morrow.

Sylvia could not conceal the weariness her long vigil left behind; and after betraying herself by a drowsy lurch that nearly took her overboard, she made herself comfortable, and slept till the grating of the keel on a pebbly shore woke her to find a new harbor reached under the lee of a cliff, whose deep shadow was very grateful after the glare of noon upon the water.

"How do you intend to dispose of yourself this afternoon, Adam?" asked Max, when dinner was over and his sister busy feeding the birds.

"In this way," answered Warwick, producing a book and settling himself in a commodious cranny of the rock.

"Moor and I want to climb the cliff and sketch the view; but it is too rough a road for Sylvia. Would you mind mounting guard for an hour or two? Read away, and leave her to amuse herself; only don't let her get into mischief by way of enjoying her liberty, for she fears nothing and is fond of experiments."

"I'll do my best," replied Warwick, with an air of resignation.

Having slung the hammock and seen Sylvia safely into it, the climbers departed, leaving her to enjoy the luxury of motion. For half an hour she swung idly, looking up into the green pavilion overhead, where many insect families were busy with their small joys and cares, or out over the still landscape basking in the warmth of a cloudless afternoon. Then she opened a book Max had brought for his own amusement, and began to read as intently as her companion, who leaned against the bowlder slowly turning his pages, with leafy shadows flickering over his uncovered head and touching it with alternate sun and shade. The book proved interesting, and Sylvia was rapidly skimming into the heart of the story, when an unguarded motion caused her swing to slope perilously to one side, and in saving herself she lost her book. This produced a predicament, for being helped into a hammock and getting out alone are two very different things. She eyed the distance from her nest to the ground, and fancied it had been made unusually great to keep her stationary. She held fast with one hand and stretched downward with the other, but the book insolently flirted its leaves just out of reach. She took a survey of Warwick; he had not perceived her plight, and she felt an unwonted reluctance to call for help, because he did not look like one used to come and go at a woman's bidding. After several fruitless essays she decided to hazard an ungraceful descent; and, gathering herself up, was about to launch boldly out, when Warwick cried, "Stop!" in a tone that nearly produced the catastrophe he wished to avert. Sylvia subsided, and coming up he lifted the book, glanced at the title, then keenly at the reader.

"Do you like this?"

"So far very much."

"Are you allowed to read what you choose?"

"Yes, sir. That is Max's choice, however; I brought no book."

"I advise you to skim it into the river; it is not a book for you."

Sylvia caught a glimpse of the one he had been reading himself, and, impelled by a sudden impulse to see what would come of it, she answered with a look as keen as his own,—

"You disapprove of my book; would you recommend yours?"

"In this case yes; for in one you will find much falsehood in purple and fine linen, in the other some truth in fig-leaves. Take your choice."

He offered both; but Sylvia took refuge in civility.

"Thank you, I'll have neither; but if you will please steady the hammock, I will try to find some more harmless amusement for myself."

He obeyed with one of the humorous expressions which often passed over his face. Sylvia descended as gracefully as circumstances permitted, and went roving up and down the cliffs. Warwick resumed his seat and the "barbaric yawp," but seemed to find Truth in demi-toilet less interesting than Youth in a gray gown and round hat, for which his taste is to be commended. The girl had small scope for amusement, and when she had gathered moss for pillows, laid out a white fungus to dry for a future pin-cushion, harvested pennyroyal in little sheaves tied with grass-blades, watched a battle between black ants and red, and learned the landscape by heart, she was at the end of her resources, and leaning on a stone surveyed earth and sky with a somewhat despondent air.

"You would like something to do, I think."

"Yes, sir; for, being rather new to this sort of life, I have not yet learned how to dispose of my time."

"I see that, and, having deprived you of one employment, will try to replace it by another."

Warwick rose, and, going to the single birch that glimmered among the pines like a delicate spirit of the wood, he presently returned with strips of silvery bark.

"You were wishing for baskets to hold your spoils, yesterday; shall we make some now?" he asked.

"How stupid in me not to think of that! Yes, thank you, I should like it very much." And, producing her house-wife, Sylvia fell to work with a brightening face.

Warwick sat a little below her on the rock, shaping his basket in perfect silence. This did not suit Sylvia; for, feeling lively and loquacious, she wanted conversation to occupy her thoughts as pleasantly as the birch rolls were occupying her hands, and there sat a person who could do it perfectly if he chose. She reconnoitred with covert glances, made sundry overtures, and sent out envoys in the shape of scissors, needles, and thread. But no answering glance met hers; her remarks received the briefest replies, and her offers of assistance were declined with an absent "No, thank you." Then she grew indignant at this seeming neglect, and thought, as she sat frowning over her work, behind his back,—

"He treats me like a child,—very well then, I'll behave like one, and beset him with questions till he is driven to speak; for he can talk, he ought to talk, he shall talk."

"Mr. Warwick, do you like children?" she began, with a determined aspect.

"Better than men or women."

"Do you enjoy amusing them?"

"Exceedingly, when in the humor."

"Are you in the humor now?"

"Yes, I think so."

"Then why don't you amuse me?"

"Because you are not a child."

"I fancied you thought me one."

"If I had, I probably should have put you on my knee, and told you fairy tales, or cut dolls for you out of this bark, instead of sitting respectfully silent and making a basket for your stores."

There was a curious smile about Warwick's mouth as he spoke, and Sylvia was rather abashed by her first exploit. But there was a pleasure in the daring, and choosing another topic she tried again.

"Max was telling me last night about the great college you had chosen; I thought it must be a very original and interesting way to educate one's self, and wanted very much to know what you had been studying lately. May I ask you now?"

"Men and women," was the brief answer.

"Have you got your lesson, sir?"

"Not yet."

"May I ask which part you are studying now?"

"The latter."

"Do you find it interesting?"

"Very."

Sylvia paused to wonder what sort of woman he would care to study, and sat silent till she had completed a canoe-shaped basket, the useful size of which produced a sudden desire to fill it. Her eye had already spied a knoll across the river covered with vines, and so suggestive of berries that she now found it impossible to resist the desire for an exploring trip in that direction. The boat was too large for her to manage alone, but an enterprising spirit had taken possession of her, and, having made one voyage of discovery with small success, she resolved to try again, hoping a second in another direction might prove more fruitful.

"Is your basket done?" she asked.

"Yes; will you have it?"

"Why, you have made it as an Indian would, using grass instead of thread. It is much more complete than mine, for the green stitches ornament the white bark, but the black ones disfigure it. I should know a man made your basket and a woman mine."

"Because one is ugly and strong, the other graceful but unable to stand alone?" asked Warwick, rising, with a gesture that sent the silvery shreds flying away on the wind.

"One holds as much as the other, however; and I fancy the woman would fill hers soonest if she had the wherewithal to do it. Do you know there are berries on that hillside opposite?"

"I see vines, but consider fruit doubtful, for boys and birds are thicker than blackberries."

"I've a firm conviction that they have left some for us; and as Max says you like frankness, I think I shall venture to ask you to row me over and help me fill the baskets on the other side."

Sylvia looked up at him with a merry mixture of doubt and daring in her face, and offered him his hat.

"Very good, I will," said Warwick, leading the way to the boat with an alacrity which proved how much pleasanter to him was action than repose.

There was no dry landing-place just opposite, and as he rowed higher, Adam fixed his eyes on Sylvia with a look peculiar to himself, a gaze more keen than soft, which seemed to search one through and through with its rapid discernment. He was studying her, and finding his book grow more and more interesting every hour; for Sylvia, unvexed by home restraints and happy in congenial society, was now her best and sweetest self.

She could not be offended by the grave penetration of this glance, though an uncomfortable consciousness that she was being analyzed and tested made her meet it with a look intended to be dignified, but which was also somewhat defiant, and more than one smile passed over Warwick's countenance as he watched her. The moment the boat glided with a soft swish among the rushes that fringed the shore, she sprung up the bank, and, leaving a basket behind her by way of hint, hurried to the sandy knoll, where, to her great satisfaction, she found the vines heavy with berries. As Warwick joined her she held up a shining cluster, saying with a touch of exultation in her voice,—

"My faith is rewarded; taste and believe."

He accepted them with a nod, and said pleasantly,—

"As my prophecy has failed, let us see if yours will be fulfilled."

"I accept the challenge." And down upon her knees went Sylvia among the vines, regardless of stains, rents, or wounded hands.

Warwick strolled away to leave her "claim" free, and silence fell between them; for one was too busy with thorns, the other with thoughts, to break the summer stillness. Sylvia worked with as much energy as if a silver cup was to be the reward of success. The sun shone fervently and the wind was cut off by the hill, drops gathered on her forehead, and her cheeks glowed; but she only pushed off her hat, thrust back her hair, and moved on to a richer spot. Vines caught at her by sleeve and skirt as if to dishearten the determined plunderer, but on she went with a wrench and a rip, an impatient "Ah!" and a hasty glance at damaged fabrics and fingers. Lively crickets flew up in swarms about her, surly wasps disputed her right to the fruit, and drunken bees blundered against her as they met, zigzagging homeward much the worse for blackberry wine. She never heeded any of them, though at another time she would gladly have made friends with all, but found compensation for her discomforts in the busy twitter of sand-swallows perched on the mullein-tops, the soft flight of yellow butterflies, and the rapidity with which the little canoe received its freight of "Ethiop sweets." As the last handful went in she sprung up, crying "Done!" with a suddenness that broke up the Long Parliament and sent its members skimming away as if a second "Noll" had appeared among them. "Done!" came back Warwick's answer like a deep echo from below, and hurrying down to meet him she displayed her success, saying archly,—

"I am glad we both won, though to be perfectly candid I think mine is decidedly the fullest." But as she swung up her birch pannier the handle broke, and down went basket, berries and all, into the long grass rustling at her feet.

Warwick could not restrain a laugh at the blank dismay that fell upon the exultation of Sylvia's face, and for a moment she was both piqued and petulant. Hot, tired, disappointed, and, hardest of all, laughed at, it was one of those times that try girls' souls. But she was too old to cry, too proud to complain, too well-bred to resent, so the little gust passed over unseen, she thought, and joining in the merriment she said, as she knelt down beside the wreck,—

"This is a practical illustration of the old proverb, and I deserve it for my boasting. Next time I'll try to combine strength and beauty in my work."

To wise people character is betrayed by trifles. Warwick stopped laughing, and something about the girlish figure in the grass, regathering with wounded hands the little harvest lately lost, seemed to touch him. His face softened suddenly as he collected several broad leaves, spread them on the grass, and, sitting down by Sylvia, looked under her hat-brim with a glance of mingled penitence and friendliness.

"Now, young philosopher, pile up your berries in that green platter while I repair the basket. Bear this in mind when you work in bark: make your handle the way of the grain, and choose a strip both smooth and broad."

Then drawing out his knife he fell to work, and while he tied green withes, as if the task were father to the thought, he told her something of a sojourn among the Indians, of whom he had learned much concerning their woodcraft, arts, and superstitions; lengthening the legend till the little canoe was ready for another launch. With her fancy full of war-trails and wampum, Sylvia followed to the river-side, and as they floated back dabbled her stained fingers in the water, comforting their smart with its cool flow till they swept by the landing-place, when she asked wonderingly,—

"Where are we going now? Have I been so troublesome that I must be taken home?"

"We are going to get a third course to follow the berries, unless you are afraid to trust yourself to me."

"Indeed, I'm not; take me where you like, sir."

Something in her frank tone, her confiding glance, seemed to please Warwick; he sat a moment looking into the brown depths of the water, and let the boat drift, with no sound but the musical drip of drops from the oars.

"We are going upon a rock."

"Not if I can help it." And a swift stroke averted the shock, to send them flying down the river till they reached the shore of a floating lily island. Here Warwick shipped his oars, saying,—

"You were asleep when we passed this morning; but I know you like lilies, so let us go a fishing."

"That I do!" cried Sylvia, capturing a great white flower with a clutch that nearly took her overboard. Warwick drew her back and did the gathering himself.

"Enough, quite enough! Here are plenty to trim our table and ourselves with; leave the rest for other voyagers who may come this way."

As Warwick offered her the dripping nosegay he looked at the white hand scored with scarlet lines.

"Poor hand! let the lilies comfort it. You are a true woman, Miss Sylvia, for though your palm is purple there's not a stain upon your lips, and you have neither worked nor suffered for yourself, it seems."

"I don't deserve that compliment, because I was only intent on outdoing you if possible; so you are mistaken again, you see."

"Not entirely, I think. Some faces are so true an index of character that one cannot be mistaken. If you doubt this, look down into the river, and such an one will inevitably smile back at you."

Pleased, yet somewhat abashed, Sylvia busied herself in knotting up the long brown stems and tingeing her nose with yellow pollen as she inhaled the bitter-sweet breath of the lilies. But when Warwick turned to resume the oars, she said,—

"Let us float out as we floated in. It is so still and lovely here I like to stay and enjoy it, for we may never see just such a scene again."

He obeyed, and both sat silent, watching the meadows that lay green and low along the shore, feeding their eyes with the beauty of the landscape, till its peaceful spirit seemed to pass into their own, and lend a subtle charm to that hour, which henceforth was to stand apart, serene and happy, in their memories forever. A still August day, with a shimmer in the air that veiled the distant hills with the mellow haze no artist ever truly caught. Midsummer warmth and ripeness brooded in the verdure of field and forest. Wafts of fragrance went wandering by from new-mown meadows and gardens full of bloom. All the sky wore its serenest blue, and up the river came frolic winds, ruffling the lily leaves until they showed their purple linings, sweeping shadowy ripples through the long grass, and lifting the locks from Sylvia's forehead with a grateful touch, as she sat softly swaying with the swaying of the boat. Slowly they drifted out into the current, slowly Warwick cleft the water with reluctant stroke, and slowly Sylvia's mind woke from its trance of dreamy delight, as with a gesture of assent she said,—

"Yes, I am ready now. That was a happy little moment, and I am glad to have lived it, for such times return to refresh me when many a more stirring one is quite forgotten." A moment after she added, eagerly, as a new object of interest appeared: "Mr. Warwick, I see smoke. I know there is a wood on fire; I want to see it; please land again."

He glanced over his shoulder at the black cloud trailing away before the wind, saw Sylvia's desire in her face, and silently complied; for being a keen student of character, he was willing to prolong an interview that gave him glimpses of a nature in which the woman and the child were curiously blended.

"I love fire, and that must be a grand one, if we could only see it well. This bank is not high enough; let us go nearer and enjoy it," said Sylvia, finding that an orchard and a knoll or two intercepted the view of the burning wood.

"It is too far."

"Not at all. I am no helpless, fine lady. I can walk, run, and climb like any boy; so you need have no fears for me. I may never see such a sight again, and you know you'd go if you were alone. Please come, Mr. Warwick."

"I promised Max to take care of you, and for the very reason that you love fire, I'd rather not take you into that furnace, lest you never come out again. Let us go back immediately."

The decision of his tone ruffled Sylvia, and she turned wilful at once, saying in a tone as decided as his own,—

"No; I wish to see it. I am always allowed to do what I wish, so I shall go;" with which mutinous remark she walked straight away towards the burning wood.

Warwick looked after her, indulging a momentary desire to carry her back to the boat, like a naughty child. But the resolute aspect of the figure going on before him convinced him that the attempt would be a failure, and with an amused expression he leisurely followed her.

Sylvia had not walked five minutes before she was satisfied that it *was* too far; but, having rebelled, she would not own herself in the wrong, and, being perverse, insisted upon carrying her point, though she walked all night. On she went over walls, under rails, across brooks, along the furrows of more than one ploughed field and in among the rustling corn, that turned its broad leaves to the sun, always in advance of her companion, who followed with exemplary submission, but also with a satirical smile, that spurred her on as no other demonstration could have done. Six o'clock sounded from the church behind the hill; still the wood seemed to recede as she pursued, still close behind her came the steady footfalls, with no sound of weariness in them, and still Sylvia kept on, till, breathless, but successful, she reached the object of her search.

Keeping to the windward of the smoke, she gained a rocky spot still warm and blackened by the late passage of the flames, and, pausing there, forgot her own pranks in watching those which the fire played before her eyes. Many acres were burning, the air was full of the rush and roar of the victorious element, the crash of trees that fell before it, and the shouts of men who fought it unavailingly.

"Ah, this is grand! I wish Max and Mr. Moor were here. Aren't you glad you came?"

Sylvia glanced up at her companion, as he stood regarding the scene with the intent, alert expression one often sees in a hound when he scents danger in the air. But Warwick did not answer, for as she spoke a long, sharp cry of human suffering rose above the tumult, terribly distinct and full of ominous suggestion.

"Some one was killed when that tree fell! Stay here till I come back." And Adam strode away into the wood as if his place were where the peril lay.

For ten minutes Sylvia waited, pale and anxious; then her patience gave out, and, saying to herself, "I can go where he does, and women are always more helpful than men at such times," she followed in the direction whence came the fitful sound of voices. The ground was hot underneath her feet, red eyes winked at her from the blackened sod, and fiery tongues darted up here and there, as if the flames were lurking still, ready for another outbreak. Intent upon her charitable errand, and excited by the novel scene, she pushed recklessly on, leaping charred logs, skirting still burning stumps, and peering eagerly into the dun veil that wavered to and fro. The appearance of an impassable ditch obliged her to halt, and, pausing to take breath, she became aware that she had lost her way. The echo of voices had ceased, a red glare was deepening in front, and clouds of smoke enveloped her in a stifling atmosphere. A sense of bewilderment crept over her; she knew not where she was; and after a rapid flight in what she believed a safe direction had been cut short by the fall of a blazing tree before her, she stood still, taking counsel with herself. Darkness and danger seemed to encompass her, fire flickered on every side, and suffocating vapors shrouded earth and sky. A bare rock suggested one hope of safety, and, muffling her head in her skirt, she lay down faint and blind, with a dull pain in her temples, and a fear at her heart fast deepening into terror as her breath grew painful and her head began to swim.

"This is the last of the pleasant voyage! Oh, why does no one think of me?"

As the regret rose, a cry of suffering and entreaty broke from her. She had not called for help till now, thinking herself too remote, her voice too feeble to overpower the din about her. But some one had thought of her, for as the cry left her lips, steps came crashing through the wood, a pair of strong arms caught her up, and before she could collect her scattered senses she was set down beyond all danger on the green bank of a little pool.

"Well, salamander, have you had fire enough?" asked Warwick, as he dashed a handful of water in her face with such energetic good-will that it took her breath away.

"Yes, oh yes,—and of water, too! Please stop, and let me get my breath!" gasped Sylvia, warding off a second baptism and staring dizzily about her.

"Why did you quit the place where I left you?" was the next question, somewhat sternly put.

"I wanted to know what had happened."

"So you walked into a bonfire to satisfy your curiosity, though you had been told to keep out of it? You'd never make a Casabianca."

"I hope not, for of all silly children that boy was the silliest, and he deserved to be blown up for his want of common sense," cried the girl petulantly.

"Obedience is an old-fashioned virtue, which you would do well to cultivate along with your common sense, young lady."

Sylvia changed the subject, for Warwick stood regarding her with an irate expression that was somewhat alarming. Fanning herself with the wet hat, she asked abruptly,—

"Was the man hurt, sir?"

"Yes."

"Very much?"

"Yes."

"Can I not do something for him? He is very far from any house, and I have some experience in wounds."

"He is past all help now."

"Dead, Mr. Warwick?"

"Quite dead."

Sylvia sat down as suddenly as she had risen, and covered her face, with a shiver, remembering that her own wilfulness had tempted a like fate, and she too might now have been "past help." Warwick went down to the pool to batbe his hot face and blackened hands; as he returned, Sylvia met him with a submissive—

"I will go back now if you are ready, sir."

If the way had seemed long in coming, it was doubly so in returning, for neither pride nor perversity sustained her now, and every step cost an effort. "I can rest in the boat," was her sustaining thought; great therefore was her dismay when, on reaching the river, no boat was to be seen.

"Why, Mr. Warwick, where is it?"

"A long way down the river by this time, probably. Believing that we landed only for a moment, I did not fasten it, and the tide has carried it away."

"But what shall we do?"

"One of two things,—spend the night here, or go round by the bridge."

"Is it far?"

"Some three or four miles, I think."

"Is there no shorter way? no boat or carriage to be had?"

"If you care to wait, I can look for our runaway, or get a wagon from the town."

"It is growing late, and you would be gone a long time, I suppose?"

"Probably."

"Which had we better do?"

"I should not venture to advise. Suit yourself, I will obey orders."

"If you were alone, what would you do?"

"Swim across."

Sylvia looked disturbed, Warwick impenetrable, the river wide, the road long, and the cliffs the most inaccessible of places. An impressive pause ensued, then she said frankly,—

"It is my own fault, and I'll take the consequences. I choose the bridge, and leave you the river. If I don't appear till dawn, tell Max I sent him a good night." And girding up her energies she walked bravely off, with much external composure and internal chagrin.

As before, Warwick followed in silence. For a time she kept in advance, then allowed him to gain upon her, and presently fell behind, plodding doggedly on through thick and thin, vainly trying to conceal the hunger and fatigue that were fast robbing her of both strength and spirits. Adam watched her with a masculine sense of the justice of the retribution which his wilful comrade had brought upon herself. But as he saw the elasticity leave her steps, the color fade from her cheeks, the resolute mouth relax, and the wistful eyes dim once or twice with tears of weariness and vexation, pity got the better of pique, and he relented. His steady tramp came to a halt, and, stopping by a wayside spring, he pointed to a mossy stone, saying, with no hint of superior powers,—

"We are tired, let us rest."

Sylvia dropped down at once, and for a few minutes neither spoke, for the air was full of sounds more pertinent to the summer night than human voices. From the copse behind them came the coo of wood-pigeons, from the grass at their feet the plaintive chirp of crickets; a busy breeze whispered through the willow, the little spring dripped musically from the rock, and across the meadows came the sweet chime of a bell. Twilight was creeping over forest, hill, and stream, and seemed to drop refreshment and repose upon all weariness of soul and body, more grateful to Sylvia than the welcome seat and leafy cup of water Warwick brought her from the spring.

The appearance of a thirsty sparrow gave her thoughts a pleasant turn, for, sitting motionless, she watched the little creature trip down to the pool, drink and bathe, then, flying to a willow spray, dress its feathers, dry its wings, and sit chirping softly as if it sang its evening hymn. Warwick saw her interest, and searching in his pocket, found the relics of a biscuit, strewed a few bits upon the ground before him, and began a low, sweet whistle, which rose gradually to a varied strain, alluring, spirited, and clear as any bird-voice of the wood. Little sparrow ceased his twitter, listened with outstretched neck and eager eye, hopping restlessly from twig to twig, until he hung just over the musician's head, agitated with a small flutter of surprise, delight, and doubt. Gathering a crumb or two into his hand, Warwick held it toward the bird, while softer, sweeter, and more urgent rose the invitation, and nearer and nearer drew the winged guest, fascinated by the spell.

Suddenly a belated blackbird lit upon the wall, surveyed the group, and burst into a jubilant song, that for a moment drowned his rival's notes. Then, as if claiming the reward, he fluttered to the grass, ate his fill, took a sip from the mossy basin by the way, and flew singing over the river, leaving a trail of music behind him. There was a dash and daring about this which fired little sparrow with emulation. His last fear seemed conquered, and he flew confidingly to Warwick's palm, pecking the crumbs with grateful chirps and friendly glances from its quick, bright eye. It was a pretty picture for the girl to see; the man an image of power, in his hand the feathered atom, that, with unerring instinct, divined and trusted the superior nature which had not yet lost its passport to the world of innocent delights that Nature gives to those who love her best. Involuntarily Sylvia clapped her hands, and, startled by the sudden sound, little sparrow skimmed away.

"Thank you for the pleasantest sight I've seen for many a day. How did you learn this gentle art, Mr. Warwick?"

"I was a solitary boy, and found my only playmates in the woods and fields. I learned their worth, they saw my need, and when I asked their friendship, gave it freely. Now we should go; you are very tired, let me help you."

He held his hand to her, and she put her own into it with a confidence as instinctive as the bird's. Then, hand in hand, they crossed the bridge and struck into the wilderness again; climbing slopes still warm and odorous, passing through dells full of chilly damps, along meadows spangled with fireflies and haunted by sonorous frogs, over rocks crisp with pale mosses, and between dark firs, where shadows brooded and melancholy breezes rocked themselves to sleep; speaking seldom, yet feeling no consciousness of silence, no sense of restraint, for they no longer seemed like strangers to each other, and this spontaneous friendliness lent an indefinable charm to the dusky walk. Warwick found satisfaction in the knowledge of her innocent faith in him, the touch of the little hand he held, the sight of the quiet figure at his side. Sylvia felt that it was pleasant to be the object of his care, fancied that they would learn to know each other better in three days of this free life than in as many months at home, and rejoiced over the discovery of unsuspected traits in him, like the soft lining of the chestnut burr, to which she had compared him more than once that afternoon. So, mutually and unconsciously yielding to the influence of the hour and the mood it brought them, they walked through the twilight in that eloquent silence which often proves more persuasive than the most fluent speech.

The welcome blaze of their own fire gladdened them at length, and when the last step was taken, Sylvia sat down with an inward conviction she never could get up again. Warwick told their mishap in the fewest possible words, while Max, in a spasm of brotherly solicitude, goaded the fire to a roar that his sister's feet might be dried, administered a cordial as a preventive against cold, and prescribed her hammock the instant supper was done. She went away with him, but a moment after she came to Warwick with a box of Prue's ointment and a soft handkerchief stripped into bandages.

"What now?" he asked.

"I wish to dress your burns, sir."

"They will do well enough with a little water; go you and rest."

"Mr. Warwick, you know you ate your supper with your left hand, and put both behind you when you saw me looking at them. Please let me make them easier; they were burnt for me, and I shall get no sleep till I have had my way."

There was a curious mixture of command and entreaty in her manner, and before their owner had time to refuse or comply, the scorched hands were taken possession of, the red blisters covered with a cool bandage, and the frown of pain smoothed out of Warwick's forehead by the prospect of relief. As she tied the last knot, Sylvia glanced up with a look that mutely asked pardon for past waywardness, and expressed gratitude for past help; then, as if her heart were set at rest, she was gone before her patient could return his thanks.

She did not reappear, Max went to send a lad after the lost boat, and the two friends were left alone; Warwick watching the blaze, Moor watching him, till, with a nod toward a pair of diminutive boots that stood turning out their toes before the fire, Adam said,—

"The wearer of those defiant-looking articles is the most capricious piece of humanity it was every my fortune to see. You have no idea of the life she has led me since you left."

"I can imagine it."

"She is as freakish and wears as many shapes as Puck,—a will-o-the wisp, a Sister of Charity, an imperious woman, a meek-faced child,—and one does not know in which part she pleases most. Hard the task of him who wins and tries to hold her."

"Hard, yet happy; for a word will tame the high spirit, a look touch the tender heart, a kind act be repaid with one still kinder. She is a creature to be tenderly taught, and cherished with the wisest love."

Moor spoke low, and on his face the firelight seemed to shed a ruddier glow than it had a moment before. Warwick eyed him an instant, then said, with his usual abruptness,—

"Geoffrey, you should marry."

"I hope to in good time. Will you follow my example?"

"When some woman is dearer to me than my liberty. It will be hard to find a mate, and I am in no haste. God bless your wooing, Geoffrey."

"And yours, Adam."

Then with a hearty hand-shake more expressive of affection than many a tenderer demonstration the friends parted, Warwick to watch the stars for hours, and Moor to muse beside the fire till the little boots were dry.

CHAPTER VII

A Golden Wedding

Hitherto they had been a most decorous crew, but the next morning something in the air seemed to cause a general overflow of spirits, and they went up the river like a party of children on a merry-making. Sylvia decorated herself with vines and flowers till she looked like a woodnymph; Max, as skipper, issued his orders with the true nautical twang; Moor kept up a fire of fun-provoking raillery; Warwick sang like a jovial giant; the Kelpie danced over the water as if inspired by the universal gayety, and the very ripples seemed to laugh as they hurried by.

"This is just the day for adventures; I hope we shall have some," said Sylvia, waving her bulrush wand as if to conjure up fresh delights of some sort.

"I should think you had enough yesterday to satisfy even your adventurous soul," answered Max, remembering her forlorn plight the night before.

"I never have enough! Life was made to enjoy, and each day ought to be different from the last; then one wouldn't get so tired of everything. See how easy it is. Just leave the old behind and find so much that is new and lovely within a few miles of home. I believe in adventures, and mean to go and seek them if they don't come to me," cried Sylvia, looking about her as if her new kingdom had inspired her with new ambitions.

"I think an adventure is about to arrive, and a very stirring one, if I may believe those black clouds piling up yonder." And Warwick pointed to the sky where the frolicsome west-wind seemed to have prepared a surprise for them in the shape of a thunder-shower.

"I shall like that. I'm fond of storms, and have no fear of lightning, though it always dances round me as if it had designs upon me. Let it come; the heavier the storm the better. We can sit in a barn and watch it rave itself quiet," said Sylvia, looking up with such an air of satisfaction the young men felt reassured, and rowed on, hoping to find shelter before the rain.

It was after lunch, and, refreshed by the cooler wind, the deepening shadows, the rowers pulled lustily, sending the boat through the water with the smooth speed given by strength and skill. Sylvia steered, but often forgot her work to watch the faces rising and falling before her, full of increasing resolution and vigor, for soon the race between the storm and the men grew exciting. No hospitable house or barn appeared, and Max, who knew the river best, thought that this was one of its wildest parts, for marshes lay on one hand, and craggy banks on the other, with here and there a stretch of hemlocks leaning to their fall as the current slowly washed away the soil that held their roots. A curtain of black cloud edged with sullen red swept rapidly across the sky, giving an unearthly look to both land and water. Utter silence reigned as birds flew to covert, and cattle herded together in the fields. Only now and then a long, low sigh went through the air like the pant of the rising storm, or a flash of lightning without thunder seemed like the glare of angry eyes.

"We are in for a drenching, if that suits you," said Max, turning from the bow where he sat, ready to leap out and pull the boat ashore the instant shelter of any sort appeared.

"I shall just wrap my old cloak about me and not mind it. Don't think of me, and if anything does happen, Mr. Warwick is used to saving me, you know."

Sylvia laughed and colored as she spoke, but her eyes shone and a daring spirit looked out at them as if it loved danger as well as his own.

"Hold fast then, for here it comes," answered Adam, dropping his oar to throw the rug about her feet, his own hat into the bottom of the boat, and then to look beyond her at the lurid sky with the air of one who welcomed the approaching strife of elements.

"Lie down and let me cover you with the sail!" cried Moor anxiously, as the first puff of the rising gale swept by.

"No, no; I want to see it all. Row on, or land, I don't care which. It is splendid, and I must have my share of it," answered Sylvia, sending her hat after Warwick's, and sitting erect, eager to prove her courage.

"We are safer here than in those woods, or soaking in that muddy marsh, so pull away, mates, and we shall reach a house before long, I am sure. This girl has had the romance of roughing it, now let us see how the reality suits her." And Max folded his arms to enjoy his sister's dismay, for just then, as if the heavens were suddenly opened, down came a rush of rain that soon drenched them to the skin.

Sylvia laughed, and shook her wet hair out of her eyes, drank the great drops as they fell, and still declared that she liked it. Moor looked anxious, Warwick interested, and Max predicted further ills like a bird of evil omen.

They came, whirlwind and rain; thunder that deafened, lightning that dazzled, and a general turmoil that for a time might have daunted a braver heart than the girl's. It is one thing to watch a storm, safely housed, with feather-beds, non-conductors, and friends to cling to; but quite another thing to be out in the tempest, exposed to all its perils, tossing in a boat on an angry river, far from shelter, with novelty, discomfort, and real danger to contend with.

But Sylvia stood the test well, seeming to find courage from the face nearest her; for that never blenched when the sharpest bolt fell, the most vivid flash blinded, or the gale drove them through hissing water, and air too full of rain to show what rock or quicksand might lie before them. She did enjoy it in spite of her pale cheeks, dilated eyes, and clutching hands; and sat in her place silent and steady, with the pale glimmer of electricity about her head, while the thunder crashed and tongues of fire tore the black clouds, swept to and fro by blasts that bowed her like a reed.

One bolt struck a tree, but it fell behind them, and just as Moor was saying, "We must land; it is no longer safe here," Max cried out,—

"A house! a house! Pull for your lives, and we will be under cover in ten minutes."

Sylvia never forgot that brief dash round the bend, for the men bent to their oars with a will, and the Kelpie flew like a bird, while with streaming hair and smiling lips the girl held fast, enjoying the rapture of swift motion; for the friends had rowed in many waters and were masters of their craft.

Landing in hot haste, they bade Sylvia run on, while they paused to tie the boat and throw the sail over their load, lest it should be blown away as well as drenched.

When they turned to follow, they saw the girl running down the long slope of meadow as if excitement gave her wings. Max raced after her, but the others tramped on together, enjoying the spectacle; for few girls know how to run or dare to try; so this new Atalanta was the more charming for the spirit and speed with which she skimmed along, dropping her cloak and looking back as she ran, bent on outstripping her brother.

"A pretty piece of energy. I didn't know the creature had so much life in her," said Warwick, laughing as Sylvia leaped a brook at a bound and pressed up the slope beyond, like a hunted doe.

"Plenty of it; that is why she likes this wild frolic so heartily. She should have more of such wholesome excitement and less fashionable dissipation. I spoke to her father about it, and persuaded Prue to let her come," answered Moor, eagerly watching the race.

"I thought you had been at work, or that excellent piece of propriety never would have consented. You can persuade the hardest-hearted, Geoffrey. I wish I had your talent."

"That remains to be seen," began Moor; then both forgot what they were saying to give a cheer as Sylvia reached the road and stood leaning on a gate-post panting, flushed, and proud, for Max had pressed her hard in spite of the advantage she had at the start.

They found themselves, a moist and mirthful company, before a red farm-house standing under venerable elms, with a patriarchal air which promised hospitable treatment and good cheer,—a promise speedily fulfilled by the lively old woman, who appeared with an energetic "Shoo!" for the speckled hens congregated in the porch, and a hearty welcome for the weather-beaten strangers.

"Sakes alive!" she exclaimed; "you be in a mess, ain't you? Come right in and make yourselves to home. Abel, take the men-folks up chamber, and fit 'em out with anything dry you kin lay hands on. Phebe, see to this poor little creeter, and bring her down lookin' less like a drownded kitten. Nat, clear up your wittlin's, so 's 't they kin toast their feet when they come down; and, Cinthy, don't dish up dinner jest yet."

These directions were given with such vigorous illustration, and the old face shone with such friendly zeal, that the four submitted at once, sure that the kind soul was pleasing herself in serving them, and finding something very attractive in the place, the people, and their own position. Abel, a staid farmer of forty, obeyed his mother's order regarding the "men-folks;" and Phebe, a buxom girl of sixteen, led Sylvia to her own room, eagerly offering her best.

As she dried and redressed herself, Sylvia made sundry discoveries, which added to the romance and the enjoyment of the adventure. A smart gown lay on the bed in the low chamber, also various decorations upon chair and table, suggesting that some festival was afoot; and a few questions elicited the facts. Grandpa had seven sons and three daughters, all living, all married, and all blessed with flocks of children. Grandpa's birthday was always celebrated by a family gathering; but to-day, being the fiftieth anniversary of his wedding, the various households had resolved to keep it with unusual pomp; and all were coming for a supper, a dance, and a "sing" at the end. Upon receipt of which intelligence Sylvia proposed an immediate departure; but the grandmother and daughter cried out at this, pointed to the still falling rain, the lowering sky, the wet heap on the floor, and insisted on the strangers all remaining to enjoy the festival, and give an added interest by their presence.

Half promising what she wholly desired, Sylvia put on Phebe's best blue gingham gown, for the preservation of which she added a white apron, and, completing the whole with a pair of capacious shoes, went down to find her party, and reveal the state of affairs. They were bestowed in the prim best parlor, and greeted her with a peal of laughter, for all were *en costume*. Abel was a stout man, and his garments hung upon Moor with a melancholy air; Max had disdained them, and with an eye to effect, laid hands on an old uniform, in which he looked like a volunteer of

1812; while Warwick's superior height placed Abel's wardrobe out of the question; and grandpa, taller than any of his seven goodly sons, supplied him with a sober suit,—roomy, square-flapped and venerable,—which became him, and with his beard, produced the curious effect of a youthful patriarch. To Sylvia's relief, it was unanimously decided to remain, trusting to their own penetration to discover the most agreeable method of returning the favor; and, regarding the adventure as a welcome change, after two days' solitude, all went out to dinner prepared to enact their parts with spirit.

The meal being despatched, Max and Warwick went to help Abel with some out-door arrangements; and, begging grandma to consider him one of her own boys, Moor tied on an apron and fell to work with Sylvia, laying the long table which was to receive the coming stores. True breeding is often as soon felt by the uncultivated as by the cultivated; and the zeal with which the strangers threw themselves into the business of the hour won the family, and placed them all in friendly relations at once. The old lady let them do what they would, admiring everything, and declaring over and over again that her new assistants "beat her boys and girls to nothin' with their tastiness and smartness." Sylvia trimmed the table with common flowers till it was an inviting sight before a viand appeared upon it, and hung green boughs about the room, with candles here and there to lend a festal light. Moor trundled a great cheese in from the dairy, brought milk-pans without mishap, disposed dishes, and caused Nat to cleave to him by the administration of surreptitious titbits and jocular suggestions; while Phebe tumbled about in every one's way, quite wild with excitement; and grandma stood in her pantry like a culinary general, swaying a big knife for a bâton, as she issued orders and marshalled her forces, the busiest and merriest of them all.

When the last touch was given, Moor discarded his apron and went to join Max. Sylvia presided over Phebe's toilet, and then sat herself down to support Nat through the trying half-hour before the party arrived. The twelve years' boy was a cripple, one of those household blessings which, in the guise of an affliction, keep many hearts tenderly united by a common love and pity. A cheerful creature, always chirping like a cricket on the hearth, as he sat carving or turning bits of wood into useful or ornamental shapes for such as cared to buy them of him, and hoarding up the proceeds like a little miser for one more helpless than himself.

"What are these, Nat?" asked Sylvia, with the interest that always won small people, because their quick instincts felt that it was sincere.

"Them are spoons—'postle spoons, they call 'em. You see I've got a cousin what reads a sight, and one day he says to me, 'Nat, in a book I see somethin' about a set of spoons with a 'postle's head on each of 'em; you make some and they'll sell, I bet.' So I got gramper's Bible, found the picters of the 'postles, and worked and worked till I got the faces good; and now it's fun, for they do sell, and I'm savin' up a lot. It ain't for me, you know, but mother, 'cause she's wuss'n I be."

"Is she sick, Nat?"

"Oh, ain't she! Why she hasn't stood up this nine year. We was smashed in a wagon that tipped over when I was three years old. It done somethin' to my legs, but it broke her back, and made her no use, only jest to pet me, and keep us all kind of stiddy, you know. Ain't you seen her? Don't you want to?"

"Would she like it?"

"She admires to see folks, and asked about you at dinner; so I guess you'd better go see her. Look ahere, you like them spoons, and I'm agoin' to give you one; I'd give you all on 'em if they wasn't promised. I can make one more in time, so you jest take your pick, 'cause I like you, and want you not to forgit me."

Sylvia chose Saint John, because it resembled Moor, she thought; bespoke and paid for a whole set, and privately resolved to send tools and rare woods to the little artist that he might serve his mother in his own pretty way. Then Nat took up his crutches and hopped nimbly before her to the room, where a plain, serene-faced woman lay knitting, with her best cap on, her clean handkerchief and large green fan laid out upon the coverlet. This was evidently the best room of the house; and as Sylvia sat talking to the invalid her eye discovered many traces of that refinement which comes through the affections. Nothing seemed too good for "daughter Patience;" birds, books, flowers, and pictures were plentiful here though visible nowhere else. Two easy-chairs beside the bed showed where the old folks oftenest sat; Abel's home corner was there by the antique desk covered with farmers' literature and samples of seeds; Phebe's work-basket stood in the window; Nat's lathe in the sunniest corner; and from the speckless carpet to the canary's clear water-glass all was exquisitely neat, for love and labor were the handmaids who served the helpless woman and asked no wages but her comfort.

Sylvia amused her new friends mightily; for, finding that neither mother nor son had any complaints to make, any sympathy to ask, she exerted herself to give them what both needed, and kept them laughing by a lively recital of her voyage and its mishaps.

"Ain't she prime, mother?" was Nat's candid commentary when the story ended, and he emerged red and shiny from the pillows where he had burrowed with boyish explosions of delight.

"She's very kind, dear, to amuse two stay-at-home folks like you and me, who seldom see what's going on outside four walls. You have a merry heart, miss, and I hope will keep it all your days, for it's a blessed thing to own."

"I think you have something better, a contented one," said Sylvia, as the woman regarded her with no sign of envy or regret.

"I ought to have; nine years on a body's back can teach a sight of things that are wuth knowin'. I've learnt patience pretty well, I guess, and contentedness ain't fur away; for though it sometimes seems ruther long to look forward to, perhaps nine more years layin' here, I jest remember it might have been wuss, and if I don't do much now there's all eternity to come."

Something in the woman's manner struck Sylvia as she watched her softly beating some tune on the sheet with her quiet eyes turned toward the light. Many sermons had been less eloquent to the girl than the look, the tone, the cheerful resignation of that plain face. She stooped and kissed it, saying gently,—

"I shall remember this."

"Hooray! there they be; I hear Ben!"

And away clattered Nat to be immediately absorbed into the embraces of a swarm of relatives who now began to arrive in a steady stream. Old and young, large and small, rich and poor, with overflowing hands or trifles humbly given, all were received alike, all hugged by grandpa, kissed by grandma, shaken half breathless by Uncle Abel, welcomed by Aunt Patience, and danced round by Phebe and Nat till the house seemed a great hive of hilarious and affectionate bees. At first the strangers stood apart, but Phebe spread their story with such complimentary additions of her own that the family circle opened wide and took them in at once.

Sylvia was enraptured with the wilderness of babies, and, leaving the others to their own devices, followed the matrons to "Patience's room," and gave herself up to the pleasant tyranny of the small potentates, who swarmed over her as she sat on the floor, tugging at her hair, exploring her eyes, covering her with moist kisses, and keeping up a babble of little voices more delightful to her than the discourse of the flattered mammas who benignly surveyed her admiration and their offspring's prowess.

The young people went to romp in the barn; the men, armed with umbrellas, turned out *en masse* to inspect the farm and stock, and compare notes over pig-pens and garden gates. But Sylvia lingered where she was, enjoying a scene which filled her with a tender pain and pleasure; for each baby was laid on grandma's knee, its small virtues, vices, ailments, and accomplishments rehearsed, its beauties examined, its strength tested, and the verdict of the family oracle pronounced upon it as it was cradled, kissed, and blessed on the kind old heart which had room for every care and joy of those who called her mother. It was a sight the girl never forgot, because just then she was ready to receive it. Her best lessons did not come from books, and she learned one then as she saw the fairest success of a woman's life while watching this happy grandmother with fresh faces framing her withered one, daughterly voices chorusing good wishes, and the harvest of half a century of wedded life beautifully garnered in her arms.

The fragrance of coffee and recollections of Cynthia's joyful aberrations at such periods caused a breaking up of the maternal conclave. The babies were borne away to simmer between blankets until called for. The women unpacked baskets, brooded over teapots, and kept up an harmonious clack as the table was spread with pyramids of cake, regiments of pies, quagmires of jelly, snow-banks of bread, and gold mines of butter; every possible article of food, from baked beans to wedding cake, finding a place on that sacrificial altar.

Fearing to be in the way, Sylvia departed to the barn, where she found her party in a chaotic Babel; for the offshoots had been as fruitful as the parent tree, and some four dozen young immortals were in full riot. The bashful roosting with the hens on remote lofts and beams; the bold flirting or playing in the full light of day; the boys whooping, the girls screaming, all effervescing as if their spirits had reached the explosive point and must find vent in noise. Max was in his element, introducing all manner of new games, the liveliest of the old, and keeping the revel at its height; for rosy, bright-eyed girls were plenty, and the ancient uniform universally approved. Warwick had a flock of lads about him absorbed in the marvels he was producing with knife, stick, and string; and Moor, a rival flock of little lasses breathless with interest in the tales he told. One on each knee, two at each side, four in a row on the hay at his feet, and the boldest of all with an arm about his neck and a curly head upon his shoulder, for Uncle Abel's clothes seemed to invest the wearer with a passport to their confidence at once. Sylvia joined this group, and partook of a quiet entertainment with as childlike a relish as any of them, while the merry tumult went on about her.

The toot of the horn sent the whole barnful streaming into the house like a flock of hungry chickens, where, by some process known only to the mothers of large families, every one was wedged close about the table, and the feast began. This was none of your stand-up, wafery, bread-and-butter teas, but a thorough-going, sit-down supper, and all settled themselves with a smiling satisfaction, prophetic of great powers and an equal willingness to employ them. A detachment of half-grown girls was drawn up behind grandma, as waiters; Sylvia insisted on being one of them, and proved herself a neat-handed Phillis, though for a time slightly bewildered by the gastronomic performances she beheld. Babies ate pickles, small boys sequestered pie with a velocity that made her wink, women swam in the tea, and the men, metaphorically speaking, swept over the table like a swarm of locusts, while the host and hostess beamed upon one another and their robust descendants with an honest pride, which was beautiful to see.

"That Mr. Wackett ain't eat scursely nothin', he jest sets lookin' round kinder 'mazed like. Do go and make him fall to on somethin', or I sha'n't take a mite of comfort in my vittles," said grandma, as the girl came with an empty cup.

"He is enjoying it with all his heart and eyes, ma'am, for we don't see such fine spectacles every day. I'll take him something that he likes and make him eat it."

"Sakes alive! be you to be Mis' Wackett? I'd no idee of it, you look so young."

"Nor I; we are only friends, ma'am."

"Oh!" and the monosyllable was immensely expressive, as the old lady confided a knowing nod to the teapot, into whose depths she was just then peering. Sylvia walked away wondering why persons were always thinking and saying such things.

As she paused behind Warwick's chair with a glass of new milk and a round of brown bread, he looked up at her with his blandest expression, though a touch of something like regret was in his voice.

"This is a sight worth living eighty hard years to see, and I envy that old couple as I never envied any one before. To rear ten virtuous children, put ten useful men and women into the world, and give them health and courage to work out their own salvation as these honest souls will do, is a better job done for the Lord, than winning a battle or ruling a State. Here is all honor to them. Drink it with me."

He put the glass to her lips, drank what she left, and, rising, placed her in his seat with the decisive air which few resisted.

"You take no thought for yourself and are doing too much; sit here a little, and let me take a few steps where you have taken many."

He served her, and, standing at her back, bent now and then to speak, still with that softened look upon the face so seldom stirred by the gentler emotions that lay far down in that deep heart of his.

All things must have an end, even a family feast, and by the time the last boy's buttons peremptorily announced, "Thus far shalt thou go and no farther," all professed themselves satisfied, and a general uprising took place. The surplus population were herded in parlor and chambers, while a few energetic hands cleared away, and with much clattering of dishes and wafting of towels, left grandma's clean premises as immaculate as ever. It was dark when all was done, so the kitchen was cleared, the candles lighted, Patience's door set open, and little Nat established in an impromptu orchestra, composed of a table and a chair, whence the first squeak of his fiddle proclaimed that the ball had begun.

Everybody danced; the babies, stacked on Patience's bed or penned behind chairs, sprawled and pranced in unsteady mimicry of their elders. Ungainly farmers, stiff with labor, recalled their early days, and tramped briskly as they swung their wives about with a kindly pressure of the hard hands that had worked so long together. Little pairs toddled gravely through the figures, or frisked promiscuously in a grand conglomeration of arms and legs. Gallant cousins kissed pretty cousins at exciting periods, and were not rebuked. Max wrought several of these incipient lovers to a pitch of despair, by his devotion to the comeliest damsels, and the skill with which he executed unheard-of evolutions before their admiring eyes. Moor led out the poorest and the plainest with a respect that caused their homely faces to shine, and their scant skirts to be forgotten. Warwick skimmed his five years' partner through the air in a way that rendered her speechless with delight; and Sylvia danced as she never danced before. With sticky-fingered boys, sleepy with repletion, but bound to last it out; with rough-faced men who paid her paternal compliments; with smart youths who turned sheepish with that white lady's hand in their big brown ones, and one ambitious lad who confided to her his burning desire to work a sawmill, and marry a girl with black eyes and yellow hair. While, perched aloft, Nat bowed away till his pale face glowed, till all hearts warmed, all feet beat responsive to the good old tunes which have put so much health into human bodies, and so much happiness into human souls.

At the stroke of nine the last dance came. All down the long kitchen stretched two breathless rows; grandpa and grandma at the top, the youngest pair of grandchildren at the bottom, and all between fathers, mothers, uncles, aunts, and cousins, while such of the babies as were still extant bobbed with unabated vigor, as Nat struck up the Virginia Reel, and the sturdy old couple led off as gallantly as the young one who came tearing up to meet them. Away they went, grandpa's white hair flying in the wind, grandma's impressive cap awry with excitement, as they ambled down the middle, and finished with a kiss when their tuneful journey was done, amid immense applause from those who regarded this as the crowning event of the day.

When all had had their turn, and twirled till they were dizzy, a short lull took place, with refreshments for such as still possessed the power of enjoying them. Then Phebe appeared with an armful of books, and all settled themselves for the family "sing."

Sylvia had heard much fine music, but never any that touched her like this, for, though often discordant, it was hearty, with that undercurrent of feeling which adds sweetness to the rudest lay, and is often more attractive than the most florid ornament or faultless execution. Every one sang as every one had danced, with all their might; shrill children, soft-voiced girls, lullaby-singing mothers, gruff boys, and strong-lunged men; the old pair quavered, and still a few indefatigable babies crowed behind their little coops. Songs, ballads, comic airs, popular melodies, and hymns came in rapid succession. And when they ended with that song which should be classed with sacred music for association's sake, and, standing hand in hand about the room with the golden bride and bride-groom in their midst, sang "Home," Sylvia leaned against her brother with dim eyes and a heart too full to sing.

Still standing thus when the last note had soared up and died, the old man folded his hands and began to pray. It was an old-fashioned prayer, such as the girl had never heard from the Bishop's lips; ungrammatical, inelegant, and long. A quiet talk with God, manly in its straightforward confession of short-comings, childlike in its appeal for guidance, fervent in its gratitude for all good gifts, and the crowning one of loving children. As if close intercourse had made the two familiar, this human father turned to the Divine, as these sons and daughters turned to him, as free to ask, as confident of a reply, as all afflictions, blessings, cares, and crosses were laid down before him, and the work of eighty years submitted to his hand. There were no sounds in the room but the one voice often tremulous with emotion and with age, the coo of some dreaming baby, or the low sob of some mother whose arms were empty, as the old man stood there, rugged and white atop as the granite hills, with the old wife at his side, a circle of sons and daughters girdling them round, and in all hearts the thought that as the former wedding had been made for time, this golden one at eighty must be for eternity.

While Sylvia looked and listened, a sense of genuine devotion stole over her; the beauty and the worth of prayer grew clear to her through the earnest speech of that unlettered man, and for the first time she fully felt the nearness and the dearness of the Universal Father, whom she had been taught to fear, yet longed to love.

"Now, my children, you must go before the little folks are tuckered out," said Grandpa heartily. "Mother and me can't say enough to thank you for the presents you have fetched us, the dutiful wishes you have give us, the pride and comfort you have alers ben toe us. I ain't no hand at speeches, so I sha'n't make none, but jest say ef any 'fliction falls on any on you, remember mother's here toe help you bear it; ef any worldly loss comes toe you, remember father's house is yourn while it stans, and so the Lord bless and keep us all."

"Three cheers for gramper and grammer!" roared a six-foot scion as a safety-valve for sundry unmasculine emotions, and three rousing hurras made the rafters ring, struck terror to the heart of the oldest inhabitant of the rat-haunted garret, and summarily woke all the babies.

Then the good-byes began; the flurry of wrong baskets, pails and bundles in wrong places; the sorting out of small folk too sleepy to know or care what became of them; the maternal cluckings and paternal shouts for Kitty, Cy, Ben, Bill, or Mary Ann; the piling into vehicles with much ramping of indignant horses unused to such late hours; the last farewells, the roll of wheels, as one by one the happy loads departed, and peace fell upon the household for another year.

"I declare for't, I never had sech an out an' out good time sense I was born into the world. A'bram, you are fit to drop, and so be I; now let's set and talk it over along of Patience 'fore we go to bed."

The old couple got into their chairs, and as they sat there side by side, remembering that she had given no gift, Sylvia crept behind them, and, lending the magic of her voice to the simple air, sang the fittest song for time and place,—"John Anderson, my Jo." It was too much for grandma, the old heart overflowed, and reckless of the cherished cap she laid her head on her "John's" shoulder, exclaiming through her tears,—

"That's the cap sheaf of the hull, and I can't bear no more to-night. A'bram, lend me your hankchif, for I dunno where mine is, and my face is all of a drip."

Before the red bandanna in grandpa's hand had gently performed its work, Sylvia slipped away to share Phebe's bed in the old garret; lying long awake, full of new and happy thoughts, and lulled to sleep at last by the pleasant patter of the rain upon the roof.

CHAPTER VIII

Sermons

The summer shower was over long before dawn, and the sun rose, giving promise of a sultry day. It was difficult to get away, for the good people found their humdrum life much enlivened by these pleasant guests. The old lady consoled herself by putting up a sumptuous lunch from the relics of the feast; the grateful wanderers left their more solid thanks in Nat's pocket, and departed with friendliest farewells.

It was Sunday, and the chime of distant church bells tolled them sweetly down the river, till the heat drove them to the refreshing shade of three great oaks in a meadow where a spring bubbled up among the gnarled roots of one tree to overflow its mossy basin, and steal into the brook babbling through the grass.

Here they lunched, and rested, the young men going off to bathe, and Sylvia falling asleep among the ferns that fringed the old oak like elves dancing round a giant. A delicious hour for her, so still, so green, so grateful was all about her, so peaceful her own spirit, so dreamless her tranquil slumber. Nature seemed to have taken her restless little child to her beneficent bosom, and blessed her with the sleep which comforts mind and body.

So Warwick thought, coming upon her unaware as he paused to drink, and a soft gust parted the tall ferns that waved above her. She looked so young, so peaceful, and so happy on her green couch, with the light shadows flickering on her face, her head pillowed on her arms, ease, grace, and the loveliness of youth in every limb and outline, that Warwick could not resist the desire to linger for a moment.

Max would have seen a pretty picture; Moor, the creature whom he loved; Adam seemed to see not only what she was, but what she might be. Some faces are blank masks when asleep, some betray the lower nature painfully, others seem to grow almost transparent and let the soul shine through. This comes oftenest when suffering has refined the flesh, or death touched it with the brief beauty that writes the story of a lifetime on perishable clay before it crumbles into dust. In certain high and happy moods unconsciousness brings out harmonious lines, soft tints, and ennobles a familiar face till we feel that we see the true self, and recognize the soul we love.

It seemed so then; and as he leaned against the oak, listening to the music of the brook and looking down at the winsome figure at his feet, Warwick found himself shaping the life and character of the woman still folded up in the girl, and shaping it to fit an ideal he had made and cherished, yet never met. An heroic creature, strong and sweet, aspiring as a flame, and true as steel. Not an impossible woman, but a rare one; and the charm Sylvia had for him was a suggestion of this possibility when time had taught and discipline tamed the wildness that was akin to his own.

He let his daring fancy paint her as she would be ten years hence, himself her lover, and the life they might lead together, as free as his was now, but happier for the inspiration of such sweet and helpful comradeship.

He had forgotten Sylvia, and was just entering a new world with the noble mate he had evoked from his own ardent and powerful imagination, when Moor's distant voice startled him, and, as if unready to be seen in that soft mood, he swung himself up into the tree, rapidly disappearing in the green wilderness above.

The same sound roused Sylvia, and made her hasten to bathe her face with cool drops caught in her hands, to rebraid her long hair, and retrim her dress with knots of wild-flowers at throat and belt; then, her rustic toilet made, she stepped out of her nest, rosy, fresh, and sunny as a little child just waking from its nap.

Fancying a green band for her head, she strolled away to the riverside where the rushes grew, and took her little Bible with her, remembering the commands pious Prue laid upon her "not to be quite a heathen while she was gone."

She lingered for half an hour, feeling unusually devout in that tranquil spot, with no best clothes to disturb her thoughts, no over-fussy sister to vex her spirit, no neglected duties or broken resolutions to make church-going a penitential period of remorse. When she returned to the oaks she found the three friends discussing religion as young men seldom fail to do in these days of speculation and spiritual discontent. She modestly hovered at a distance till a pause came, then approached, asking meekly,—

"Please, could I come to church if I sit very still?"

"Come on," said Max, from the grass where he was lying.

Moor sprang up to offer her the rug with an air of welcome which she could not doubt, and Warwick nodded with a somewhat belligerent expression, as if suddenly checked in some verbal tournament.

"Prue said if we stayed over Sunday I must go to church, and I have done my best," said Sylvia, glancing at the little book in her hand. "Now, if Mr. Moor or Mr. Warwick would give us a sermon, Max and I can say we obeyed her."

"Come, Geoffrey, your memory is full of good and pious poetry; give us something new and true. We need n't sing it, but it may suggest a sermon, and that is more in Adam's line than yours," added Max, ready to while away another hour till the afternoon grew cooler.

Moor thought a moment, and then, as if their conversation suggested it, repeated one of Herbert's quaint old hymns.

"Lord, with what care hast thou begirt us round!
Parents first season us: then schoolmasters
Deliver us to laws; they send us bound
To rules of reason, holy messengers,

"Pulpits and Sundayes, sorrow dogging sinne,
Afflictions sorted, anguish of all sizes,
Fine nets and stratagems to catch us in;
Bibles laid open, millions of surprises;

"Blessings beforehand, tyes of gratefulnesse;
The sound of glorie ringing in our eares;
Without, our shame; within, our consciences;
Angels and grace, eternall hopes and feares.

"Yet all these fences and their whole array,
One cunning bosome-sin blows quite away."

"There is your text, Adam, take it and hold forth; you were born for a field preacher and have missed your vocation. I wish you would turn minister and beat the dust out of some of the old pulpit cushions, for we need a livelier theology than most of us get nowadays," said Max, as Moor paused and Sylvia looked as if the hymn pleased her much.

"If I did stray into a pulpit you would get the gospel undiluted, and sins of all sorts would fare hardly, for I would cry aloud and spare not."

"Try it now; it will be immensely amusing to be raked fore and aft while lounging here as if we were getting to heaven 'on flowery beds of ease.' Begin with me. I'm fair game, and furnish material for a dozen sermons on a dozen sins," laughed Max, hoping to draw his friend out and astonish his sister.

"Good! I will." And Warwick looked as if belaboring frail humanity was a task he relished.

"Your bosom sin is indolence of soul and body, heart and mind. Fortune has been your bane, liberty ill used, life your plaything, not your lesson; for you have not learned how to use either fortune, liberty, or life. Pride is your only energy; patience simple endurance of whatever you have not courage to overcome; ambition a vacillating desire for success which every failure lessens, and the aim of existence is to be carried painlessly through a world waiting for every man to help on its salvation by making his own life a victory, not a defeat. Shall I go on?"

"Fire away; every shot tells. It is rather sharp rifle-practice while it lasts, but the target is the better for it, I dare say."

Max spoke gayly and still lounged on the grass; but Sylvia knew, by the gesture that half averted his face, and the interest with which he punched holes in the turf, that it *was* rather hard upon one more used to praise than blame. Warwick knew it also, and there was a perceptible softening of the ruthless voice as he went on.

"You need a purpose, Max, an object beyond your own satisfaction or success. This would show you what good gifts you now neglect, teach you their uses, and prove to you that the best culture lies in perfecting these tools for the education of yourself and others. Adversity may spur you into action, love may supply a noble motive, or experience make you what you should be,—a man with a work and a will to do it. You owe this to your father, and I believe the debt will be honestly paid."

"It shall be!" And Max sat up with a sudden energy pleasant to behold. Resolution, regret, and affection made his usually listless face manly and serious as well as tender, for that allusion to his father touched him, and the thought of Jessie lightened a task he knew would be a very hard one.

Always quick to spare others embarrassment or pain, Moor said pleasantly, "Now take the next member of your flock, and do not spare him, Adam."

Warwick looked as if he would rather let this sheep go, but, loving justice as well as truth, he hardened his heart and spoke out.

"You are enamored of self-sacrifice, Geoffrey, and if you lived in monkish times would wear a spiked girdle or haircloth shirt, lest you should be too comfortable. Unlike Max, you polish your tools carefully and are skilful in handling them, but you use them entirely for others, forgetting that we owe a good deal to ourselves. You have made a small circle your world, and lived in the affections too much. You need a larger life and more brain-work to keep you from growing narrow or weak. One sacrifice beautifully and faithfully made must have its reward. For years you have lived for others, now learn to live a little for yourself, heartily and happily, else the feminine in you will get the uppermost."

"Thank you, I will as soon as possible." And Moor gave Warwick a look which was both grateful and glad, since the friendly advice confirmed a cherished purpose of his own.

"Lost lamb, come into the fold and be shorn!" called Max, enjoying Sylvia's face, which wore an expression of mingled interest, amusement, and trepidation. With a start she gathered herself up, and went to sit on a little stone before the censor, folding her hands and meekly asking,—

"What must *I* do?"

"Forget yourself."

Sylvia colored to her brow, but answered bravely,—

"Show me how."

"My panacea for most troubles is work. Try it, and I think you will find that it will promote that healthfulness of spirit which is the life of life. Don't let fogs hide your sunshine; don't worry your young wits with metaphysics, or let romantic dreams take the charm from the wholesome, homely realities, without which we cannot live sanely and safely. Get out of yourself awhile, and when you go back you will find, I hope, a happy soul in a healthy body, and be what God intended you to be, a brave and noble woman."

Warwick saw the girl's color rise, her eyes fall, and in her face a full acknowledgment of the veracity of both censure and commendation. That satisfied him, and before she could speak he turned on Max, saying with a sudden change from gentle gravity to the satirical tone more habitual to him,—

"Now you will say, 'Physician, heal thyself,' and ask for my chief sin. I'll give you a sample of it."

Then, looking very much like a war-horse when trumpets blow, he launched into a half-earnest, half-humorous philippic against falsehood everywhere, giving to his vigorous speech the aids of satire, sense, and an unusually varied experience for one of his age. Max sat up and applauded, Moor listened with delight, and Sylvia felt as if the end of all things was at hand. Such an audacious onslaught upon established customs, creeds, and constitutions, she had never heard before; for, as Warwick charged, down went the stern religion that preaches heaven for the saint and hell for the sinner, the base legislation which decrees liberty to the white and slavery to the black, the false public opinion that grants all suffrages to man and none to woman yet judges both alike,—all knavery in high places, all gilded shams, all dead beliefs,—and up went the white banner of infinite justice, truth, and love. It was a fight well fought but not wholly won; for in spite of sagacity, eloquence, and zeal, Warwick's besetting sin was indomitable, and those who listened, while they owned the sincerity, felt the power, admired the enthusiasm, saw that this valiant St. George rode without a Una, and in executing justice forgot mercy, like many another young crusader who, in his ardor to set up the New Jerusalem, breaks the commandments of the Divine Reformer who immortalized the old.

When at last he reined himself in, looking ready for another breakage of idols at the slightest provocation, Max said with a waggish glance at his sister,—

"You seem to be holding on to that stone as if you thought the foundations of the earth were giving way. How do you like your sermon, Sylvia?"

"Very much, what I understand of it; but I do feel as if there had been an earthquake, and it will take me some time to get settled again. It is a little startling to have all the props one has been taught to lean upon knocked away at once, and be left to walk alone without quite knowing where the road ends."

Max laughed; Moor looked as if she had exactly expressed the feeling most persons felt after one of Adam's "upheavals," as his friend called them; but Warwick said, with his decided nod, as if well pleased,—

"That is just as it should be. I'm a pioneer, and love to plough in any soil, no matter how sandy or rough it may be. The sower comes after me, and if the harvest is a good one, I am satisfied to do the hard work without wages."

He certainly received them this time, for Sylvia looked up at him as he rose, evidently tired of longer repose, and said, with the sweetest confidence and gratitude in her face,—

"Let me thank you for this and many other lessons which will set me thinking, and help me to be what you so kindly hope. I shall not forget them, and trust they have not fallen on a barren soil."

It was not a child's face that Warwick saw then, but a woman's, earnest, humble, and lovely with the awakening of an innocent, aspiring soul. Involuntarily he took his hat off, with a look both reverent and soft.

"A virgin soil is always the richest, and I have no fear that the harvest will fail. Heaven send you sun and rain, and a wise husbandman to help you gather it in."

Then he went away to get the boat ready for the evening sail. Max went off to a farm-house for milk, and Moor and Sylvia were left alone.

Touched to the heart by the blessing that came with redoubled power from lips so lately full of denunciation, the girl still sat upon her little stone, seemingly wrapped in thoughts that both excited and troubled her, for presently she sighed.

Moor, who lay reading in the grass, stealing a glance at his companion now and then, was glad of an opportunity to speak, and, sitting up, asked in his friendly voice,—

"Has all this talk tired you?"

"No, it has stirred me up and made me feel as if I must lay hold of something at once, or drift away I don't know where. Mr. Warwick has pulled my world to pieces, but has given me no other, and I don't know where to look. His philosophy is too large for me, I get lost in it, and though I admire I cannot manage it yet, and so feel bewildered." Sylvia spoke out as if the thoughts in her mind must find a vent at any cost, and to no one could she so freely utter them as to this friend who was always kind and patient with her moods.

"You must not let Adam's thunder and lightning disturb you. We have seen the world through his glass, which, though a powerful one, is not always well regulated, so we get a magnified view of things. He is a self-reliant genius, intent on his own aims, which, fortunately, are high ones, for he would go vigorously wrong if it were not for the native integrity which keeps him vigorously right. He has his work to do, and will do it manfully when he gets through the 'storm and stress period' of which I told you."

"I like it because I think I am in a little period of my own. If I dared, I should like to ask you how best to get out of it."

"You may ask anything of me!"

Sylvia spoke hesitatingly, but Moor's eager answer made it easy to go on, it was so clear that these confidences were acceptable; she little knew how much so.

"Do you believe in sudden conversions?" she asked presently.

"Yes; for often what seems sudden is only the flowering of some secret growth, unsuspected till the heat of pain or passion calls it out. We feel the need of help that nothing human can give us, instinctively ask it of a higher power, and, receiving it in marvelous ways, gratefully and devoutly say, 'I believe.' "

"That time has not come to me." Then, as if a wave of feeling too strong to be repressed rolled up and broke into words, Sylvia rapidly went on: "I know that I need something to lean upon, believe in, and love; for I am not steadfast, and every wind blows me about. I try to find the help I want. I look into people's faces, watch their lives, and endeavor to imitate all that I admire and respect. I read the best and wisest books I can find, and tire my weak wits trying to understand them. I pray prayers, sing hymns, and go to church, hoping to find the piety which makes life good and happy. I ask all whom I dare to help me, yet I am not helped. My father says, 'Keep happy, dear, and no fear but you will get to heaven.' Prue says, 'Read your Bible and talk to the Bishop.' Max laughs, and tells me to fall in love if I desire beatitude. Every one assures me that religion is a blessed thing and salvation impossible without it, yet no one gives me a simple sustaining faith to love, to lean on, and live by. So I stumble to and fro, longing, hoping, looking for the way to go, yet never finding it, for I have no mother to take me in her arms and show me God."

With the last words Sylvia's voice broke, and she spread her hands before her face; not weeping, but overcome by an emotion too deep for tears.

Moor had seen many forms of sorrow, but never one that touched him more than this motherless girl hiding a spiritual sorrow on the bosom of a rock. Sylvia had ceased to seem a child, and this was no childish grief to be comforted with a kind word. She was a woman to him, dearer and deeper-hearted than she knew, yet he would not take advantage of this tender moment and offer her a human love when she asked for the divine. His own religion was that simplest, perhaps truest type, which is lived, not spoken; an inborn love of godliness, a natural faith, unquestioning, unshakable by the trials and temptations of life. But this piety, though all pervading and all sustaining as the air, was as hard to grasp and give to another. It was no easy task for one humble in his own conceit, a young man and a lover, to answer such an appeal, the harder for the unspoken confidence in him which it confessed. A wise book lay upon his knee, a good book had slipped to Sylvia's feet, and, glancing about him for inspiration in that eloquent pause, he found it there. Never had his voice sounded so sweet and comfortable as now.

"Dear Sylvia, I understand your trouble and long to cure it as wisely and tenderly as I ought. I can only tell you where I have found a cure for doubt, despondency, and grief. God and Nature are the true helper and comforter for all of us. Do not tire yourself with books, creeds, and speculations; let them wait, and believe that simply wishing and trying to be good is piety, for faith and endeavor are the wings that carry souls to heaven. Take Nature for your friend and teacher. You love and feel near to her already; you will find her always just and genial, patient and wise. Watch the harmonious laws that rule her, imitate her industry, her sweet sanity; and soon I think you will find that this benignant mother will take you in her arms and show you God."

Without another word Moor rose, laid his hand an instant on the girl's bent head in the first caress he had ever dared to give her, and went away leaving her to the soothing ministrations of the comforter he had suggested.

When they all met at supper Sylvia's face was as serene and lovely as the sky "clear shining after rain," though she said little and seemed shy of her older comrades; both of whom were unusually thoughtful of her, as if they felt some fear that in handling this young soul they might have harmed it, as even the most careful touch destroys the delicate down on the wing of the butterfly, that is its symbol.

They embarked at sunset, as the tide against which they had pulled in coming up would soon sweep them rapidly along and make it easy to retrace in a few hours the way they had loitered over for days.

All night Sylvia lay under the canopy of boughs Moor made to shield her from the dew, listening to the soft sounds about her; the twitter of a restless bird, the bleat of some belated lamb, the ripple of a brook babbling like a baby in its sleep, the fitful murmur of voices mingling with the plash of water as sail or oar drove them on. All night she watched the changing shores, silvery green or dark with slumberous shadow, and followed the moon in its tranquil journey through the sky. When it set, she drew her cloak about her, and, pillowing her head upon the sweet fern Warwick piled for her, exchanged the waking for a sleeping dream as beautiful and happy.

A thick mist encompassed her when she awoke. Above the sun shone dimly, below rose and fell the unquiet tide, before her sounded the city's hum, and far behind lay the green wilderness where she had lived and learned so much. Slowly the fog lifted, the sun came dazzling down upon the sea, and out into the open bay they sailed with the blue pennon streaming in the morning wind. But still with backward gaze the girl watched the misty wall that lay between her and that charmed river, and still with wondering heart confessed how sweet that brief experience had been; for, though she had not yet discovered it, like the fairy Lady of Shalott,

> *"She had left the web and left the loom,*
> *Had seen the water-lilies bloom,*
> *Had seen the helmet and the plume,*
> *And had looked down to Camelot."*

CHAPTER IX

Why Sylvia Was Happy

"I never did understand you, Sylvia; and this last mouth you have been a perfect enigma to me."

With rocking-chair in full action, suspended needle, and thoughtful expression, Miss Yule had watched her sister for ten minutes as she sat with her work at her feet, her hands folded on her lap, and her eyes dreamily fixed on vacancy.

"I always was to myself, Prue, and am more so than ever now," answered Sylvia, waking out of her reverie with a smile that proved it had been a pleasant one.

"There must be some reason for this great change in you. Come, tell me, dear."

With a motherly gesture Miss Yule drew the girl to her knee, brushed back the bright hair, and looked into the face so freely turned to hers. Through all the years they had been together, the elder sister had never seen before the expression which the younger's face now wore. A vague expectancy sat in her eyes, some nameless content sweetened her smile, a beautiful repose replaced the varying enthusiasm, listlessness, and melancholy that used to haunt her countenance and make it such a study. Miss Yule could not read the secret of the change, yet felt its novel charm; Sylvia could not explain it, though penetrated by its power: and for a moment the sisters looked into each other's faces, wondering why each seemed altered. Then Prue, who never wasted much time in speculations of any kind, shook her head, and repeated,—

"I don't understand it, but it must be right, because you are so improved in every way. Ever since that wild trip up the river you have been growing quiet, lovable, and cheerful, and I really begin to hope that you will become like other people."

"I only know that I am happy, Prue. Why it is so I cannot tell; but now I seldom have the old dissatisfied and restless feeling. Everything looks pleasant to me, every one seems kind, and life begins to be both sweet and earnest. It is only one of my moods, I suppose; but I am grateful for it, and pray that it may last."

So earnestly she spoke, so cheerfully she smiled, that Miss Yule blessed the mood and echoed Sylvia's wish, exclaiming in the next breath, with a sudden inspiration,—

"My dear, I've got it! You are growing up."

"I think I am. You tried to make a woman of me at sixteen, but it was impossible until the right time came. That wild trip up the river, as you call it, did more for me than I can ever tell, and when I seemed most like a child I was learning to be a woman."

"Well, my dear, go on as you've begun, and I shall be more than satisfied. What merry-making is on foot to-night? Max and these friends of his keep you in constant motion with their riding, rowing, and rambling excursions, and if it did not agree with you so excellently, I really should like a little quiet after a month of bustle."

"They are only coming up as usual, and that reminds me that I must go and dress."

"There is another new change, Sylvia. You never used to care what you wore or how you looked, no matter how much time and trouble I expended on you and your wardrobe. Now you do care, and it does my heart good to see you always charmingly dressed, and looking your prettiest," said Miss Yule, with the satisfaction of a woman who heartily believed in costume as well as all the other elegances and proprieties of fashionable life.

"Am I ever that, Prue?" asked Sylvia, pausing on the threshold with a shy yet wistful glance.

"Ever what, dear?"

"Pretty?"

"Always so to me; and now I think every one finds you very attractive because you try to please, and seem to succeed delightfully."

Sylvia had never asked that question before, had never seemed to know or care, and could not have chosen a more auspicious moment for her frank inquiry than the present. The answer seemed to satisfy her, and, smiling at some blithe anticipation of her own, she went away to make a lampless toilet in the dusk, which proved how slight a hold the feminine passion for making one's self pretty had yet taken upon her.

The September moon was up and shining clearly over garden, lawn, and sea, when the sound of voices called her down. At the stair-foot she paused with a disappointed air, for only one hat lay on the hall table, and a glance showed her only one guest with Max and Prue. She strolled irresolutely through the breezy hall, looked out at either open door, sung a little to herself, but broke off in the middle of a line, and, as if following a sudden impulse, went out into the mellow moonlight, forgetful of uncovered head or dewy damage to the white hem of her gown. Halfway down the avenue she paused before a shady nook, and looked in. The evergreens that enclosed it made the seat doubly dark to eyes inured to the outer light, and, seeing a familiar seeming figure sitting with its head upon its hand, Sylvia leaned in, saying, with a daughterly caress,—

"Why, what is my romantic father doing here?"

The sense of touch was quicker than that of sight, and with an exclamation of surprise she had drawn back before Warwick replied,—

"It is not the old man, but the young one, who is romancing here."

"I beg your pardon! We have been waiting for you; what were you thinking of that you forgot us all?"

Sylvia was a little startled, else she would scarcely have asked so plain a question. But Warwick often asked much blunter ones, always told the naked truth without prevarication or delay, and straightway answered,—

"The sweetest woman I ever met," then checked himself and said more quietly, as if to turn the conversation, "This moonlight recalls our voyage up the river and our various adventures."

"Ah, that happy voyage! I wish it had been longer," answered Sylvia in a tone of such intense regret it was plain she had forgotten nothing. "It is too lovely to go in just yet; come and walk, and talk a little of that pleasant time."

She beckoned as she spoke, and he came out of the shadow wearing a look she had never seen before. His face was flushed, his eye unquiet, his manner eager yet restrained. She had seen him intellectually excited, but never emotionally till now. Something wayward yet warm in this new mood attracted her because so like her own. But with a tact as native as her sympathy, she showed no sign of observing this change, and, fancying some memory or care oppressed him, tried to cheer him by speaking of the holiday he had recalled.

"What did you enjoy most in those four days?" she asked, as they paced slowly up the avenue side by side.

He longed to answer "Our walk together," for that little journey hand in hand seemed very precious to him now, and it was with difficulty he refrained from telling her how beautiful it would be to have that slender figure always walking with him on the longer pilgrimage which of late looked lonely and uninviting. But he folded his arms, averted his eyes, and said briefly,—

"All was pleasant; perhaps the Golden Wedding most so."

"Yes, that did me so much good. I never shall forget it. I think that voyage was the happiest time I ever knew. I seemed to learn more in those few days than in years at home, and all my lessons were helpful ones, for which I shall be better and happier, I am sure."

She spoke earnestly, still looking up, and the moonlight showed how grateful, how perilously sweet and candid, the young face was. Warwick saw it with a quick glance, and said within himself, "I too learned a lesson; better I may be, but not happier." Then aloud, and with a laugh that did not ring quite true,—

"I see my sermon was laid to heart, harsh as it seemed when preached. Some of the melancholy moods were left behind, I think, and brighter ones brought home, if we may judge from the metamorphosis of the dripping Undine I first met to the happy girl who now makes sunshine for us all."

"Yes; I feel as if I found my soul there in the woods, and learned how to keep it in better order than when I half longed to have the sea rid me of the care of such a restless, troublesome guest."

"You found a soul, and I lost a heart," thought Warwick, still carrying on that double conversation; for even love could not subdue the sense of humor which made much sentiment impossible. Aloud he added, more genially,—

"I often make these excursions into the wilderness when civilization tires or troubles me, and always find medicine for my impatient spirit in the quiet, freedom, and good company waiting for me there. Try it again when other things fail, and so keep serene and happy as now."

"I will. Mr. Moor told me the same, and I like the prescription, for the desire of my life is to be as sunshiny, wise, and excellent as he is."

"You could not have a better model or set your life to finer music than he does. Have you ever read his poetry?"

Warwick spoke heartily now, and seemed glad to slip away from a subject too interesting to be quite safe for him.

"No. Max said he wrote, and I hope I shall see it some time when he thinks I am worthy of the honor. Do you make poems also?" asked Sylvia, as if any feat were possible to this new friend of hers.

"Never! An essay now and then, but pen work is not in my line. First live, then write. I have not time to let fancy play, when hard facts keep me busy."

"When you do write, I think it will be very interesting to read what you have lived. Max says you have been visiting prisons all over the world, and trying to make them better. That is a brave, good thing to do. I wish I were old and wise enough to help," said Sylvia, with such respect and admiration in face and voice that Warwick found it impossible to restrain a fervent—

"I wish you were!" adding more calmly, "I love liberty so much myself, that my sympathy naturally turns to those deprived of it. Yet the saddest prisoners I find are not in cells, and they are the hardest to help."

"You mean those bound by sins and sorrows, temperaments and temptations?"

"Yes, and another class tied by prejudices, creeds, and customs. Even duties and principles make slaves of us sometimes, and we find the captivity very hard to bear."

"I cannot imagine you bound by anything. I often envy you your splendid freedom."

"I am bound this moment by honor, and I long to break loose!"

The words broke from Adam against his will, and startled Sylvia by their passionate energy.

"Can I help you? The mouse helped the lion, you remember?"

She spoke without fear, for with Warwick she always felt the sort of freedom one feels with those who are entirely sincere and natural, sure of being understood, and one's sympathy received as frankly as it is offered.

"Dear mouse, you cannot! This net is too strong, and the lion must stay bound till time or a happy fortune sets him free. Let us go in."

The sudden change from the almost tender gratitude of the first words to the stern brevity of the last ones perplexed Sylvia more than any of the varying moods she had seen that night, and with a sudden sense of some dangerous electricity in the mental atmosphere, she hastened up the steps before which Warwick had abruptly halted.

Pausing on the upper stair to gather a day-lily from the urn that stood there, she looked back an instant before she vanished, and he seemed to see again the Juliet he so well remembered leaning to her lover bathed in the magic moonlight of the wood.

"That did the mischief; till then I thought her a child. The romance of that scene took me unawares, and all that followed helped the sweet poison work. A midsummer night's dream which I shall not soon forget."

With a long breath of the cool air, an impatient sigh at his own weakness, and a half-angry tug at his brown beard, Warwick went to the drawing-room looking very like the captive lion Sylvia had spoken of.

She was not there, and he fell upon the first trifling task he found, as if "in work was salvation, in idleness alone perpetual despair."

Sylvia soon appeared with the basket of Berlin wools she had promised to wind for her sister.

"What have you been doing to give yourself such an uplifted expression?" said Max, as she came in.

"Feasting my eyes on lovely colors. Does not that look like a folded rainbow?" she answered, laying her brilliant burden on the table where Warwick sat examining a broken reel, and Prue was absorbed in getting a carriage blanket under way.

"Come, Sylvia, I shall soon be ready for the first shade," she said, clashing her formidable needles. "Is that past mending, Mr. Warwick?"

"Yes, without better tools than a knife, two pins, and a bodkin."

"Then you must put the skeins on a chair, Sylvia. Try not to tangle them, and spread your handkerchief in your lap, for that maroon shade will stain sadly. Now don't speak to me, for I must count my stitches."

Sylvia began to wind the wools with a swift dexterity as natural to her hands as certain little graces of gesture which made their motions pleasant to watch. Warwick never rummaged work-baskets, gossiped, or paid compliments for want of something to do. If no little task appeared for them, he kept his hands out of mischief, and if nothing occurred to make words agreeable or necessary, he proved that he understood the art of silence, and sat with those vigilant eyes of his fixed upon whatever object attracted them. Just then the object was a bright band slipping round the chair-back, with a rapidity that soon produced a snarl, but no help till patient fingers had smoothed and wound it up. Then, with the look of one who says to himself, "I will!" he turned, planted himself squarely before Sylvia, and held out his hands.

"Here is a reel that will neither tangle nor break your skeins; will you use it?"

"Yes, thank you, and in return I'll wind your color first."

"Which is my color?"

"This fine scarlet, strong, enduring, and martial, like yourself."

"You are right."

"I thought so; Mr. Moor prefers blue, and I violet."

"Blue and red make violet," called Max from his corner, catching the word "color," though busy with a sketch for Jessie Hope.

Moor was with Mr. Yule in his study, Prue mentally wrapped in her blanket, and when Sylvia was drawn into an artistic controversy with her brother, Warwick fell into deep thought.

He had learned many lessons in his adventurous life, and learned them well, but never the one that now had in truth taken him unaware, roused a passion stronger than his own strong will, and in a month taught him the mystery and the might of love.

He tried to disbelieve and silence it; attacked it with reason, starved it with neglect, and chilled it with contempt. But when he fancied it was dead, the longing rose again, and, with a clamorous cry, undid his work. For the first time this free spirit felt the master's hand, confessed a need its own power could not supply, and saw that no man can live alone, on even the highest aspirations, without suffering for the vital warmth of the affections. A month ago he would have disdained the sentiment that now was so dear to him. But imperceptibly the influences of domestic life had tamed and won him. Solitude looked barren, vagrancy had lost its charm; his life seemed cold and bare, for, though devoted to noble aims, it was wanting in the social sacrifices, cares, and joys that foster charity and sweeten character. An impetuous desire to enjoy the rich experience which did so much for others came over him to-night as it had often done while sharing the delights of this home, where he had made so long a pause. But with the desire came a memory that restrained him better than his promise. He saw what others had not yet discovered, and, obeying the code of honor which governs the true gentleman, loved his friend better than himself, and held his peace.

The last skein came, and as she wound it, Sylvia's glance involuntarily rose from the strong hands to the face above them, and lingered there, for the penetrating gaze was averted, and an unwonted mildness inspired confidence as its usual expression of power commanded respect. His silence troubled her, and with curious yet respectful scrutiny, she studied his face as she had never done before. She found it full of a noble gravity and kindliness; candor and courage spoke in the lines of the mouth, benevolence and intellect in the broad arch of the forehead, ardor and energy in the fire of the eye, and on every lineament the stamp of that genuine manhood which no art can counterfeit. Intent upon discovering the secret of the mastery he exerted over all who approached him, Sylvia had quite forgotten herself, when suddenly Warwick's eyes were fixed full upon her own. What spell lay in them she could not tell, for human eye had never shed such sudden summer over her. Admiration was not in it, for it did not agitate; nor audacity, for it did not abash; but something that thrilled warm through blood and nerves, that filled her with a glad submission to some power, absolute yet tender, and caused her to turn her innocent face freely to his gaze, letting him read therein a sentiment for which she had not yet found a name.

It lasted but a moment; yet in that moment each saw the other's heart, and each turned a new page in the romance of their lives. Sylvia's eyes fell first, but no blush followed, no sign of anger or perplexity, only a thoughtful silence which continued till the last violet thread dropped from his hands, and she said almost regretfully,—

"This is the end."

"Yes, this is the end."

As he echoed the words Warwick rose suddenly and went to talk with Max, whose sketch was done. Sylvia sat a moment as if quite forgetful where she was, so absorbing was some thought or emotion. Presently she seemed to glow and kindle with an inward fire; over face and forehead rushed an impetuous color, her eyes shone, and her lips trembled with the fluttering of her breath. Then a panic appeared to seize her, for, stealing noiselessly away, she hurried to her room, and covering up her face as if to hide it even from herself, whispered to that full heart of hers,—

"Now I know why I am happy!"

How long she lay there musing in the moonlight she never knew. Her sister's call broke in upon the first love dream she had ever woven for herself, and she went down to bid the friends good-night. The hall was only lighted by the moon, and in the dimness no one saw traces of that midsummer shower on her cheeks, nor detected the soft trouble in her eyes, but for the first time Moor felt her hand tremble in his own, and welcomed the good omen joyfully.

Hating all forms, Warwick seldom shook hands, but that night he gave a hand to all with his most cordial expression, and Sylvia felt both her own taken in a warm lingering grasp, although he only said, "Good-by!" Then they went; but while the others paused on the steps, held by the beauty of the night, back on the wings of the wind came Warwick's sonorous voice singing the song that Sylvia best loved. All down the avenue and far along the winding road they traced his progress, till the music died in the distance, leaving only the echo of the song to link them to the singer.

When evening came again the girl waited on the lawn to greet the friends, for love made her very shy. But Moor came alone, and his first words were,—

"Console me, Sylvia, Adam is gone. He went as unexpectedly as he came, and when I woke this morning a note was all the farewell I found."

Pride kept her from betraying the sharp pang this disappointment cost her, and all that evening she seemed her gayest self, supported by an unnatural excitement till alone.

Then the reaction came, and Sylvia spent the night struggling with doubt, despair, shame, and bewilderment. She had deceived herself. It was not love she saw in Adam's eyes last night, but pity. He read her secret before that compassionate glance revealed it to herself, and had gone away to spare her further folly. She was not the woman of whom he thought, forgetful of time and place, of whom he spoke with such a kindling face, to whom he had gone so eagerly when absence grew unbearable.

All night she tortured herself with this idea, but in the morning hope came, always the first consoler of the young, whispering that she *had* read that look aright, that some promise bound him which he had gone to be released from, and when free he would write or come to her. To this hope she clung, saying to herself,—

"He is so true, I will trust and wait."

But days grew to weeks, and Warwick neither wrote nor came.

CHAPTER X

No

November, the dreariest month of all the year, had come; leaves lay sear and sodden on the frosty ground, and a chill rain dripped without as if joining in the lamentation of the melancholy wind.

Winter fires were kindled, and basking in the full glow of one of these lay Sylvia, coiled up in a deep chair, solacing her weariness with recollections of the happiest summer of her life.

As books open at pages oftenest read, she had been reliving that memorable voyage, the brightest hours of which were those spent with Warwick, guarding these as tenderly as patient Elaine guarded the shield, waiting for Launcelot to come again.

So vividly did those days return to her, that Sylvia forgot the pain of suspense, the thorn of regret, and was far away; so strong was the power of Adam's influence upon her even in absence, that he seemed to be before her; so intense was her longing to feel again the touch of his hand, that like one in a dream she stretched her own toward the vision, whispering, half aloud,—

"Come!"

"I am here."

A voice answered, a hand took hers, and starting up she saw Moor looking down at her. Hastening to compose herself, she smiled and leaned back in her chair, saying quietly,—

"I am glad you came, for I have built castles in the air long enough, and you will give me more substantial entertainment, as you always do."

The broken dream had left tokens of its presence in the unwonted warmth of Sylvia's manner; Moor felt it, and for a moment did not answer. Much of her former shyness had crept over her of late; she sometimes shunned him, was less free in conversation, less frank in demonstration, and once or twice had colored deeply as she caught his eye upon her. These betrayals of Warwick's image in her thoughts seemed to Moor the happy omens he had waited eagerly to see, and each day his hope grew more assured. He had watched her unseen while she was busied with her mental pastime, and as he looked, his heart had grown unspeakably tender, for never had her power over him been so fully felt, and never had he so longed to claim her in the name of his exceeding love. A pleasant peace reigned through the house, the girl sat waiting at his side, the moment looked auspicious, the desire grew irresistible, and he yielded to it.

"You are thinking of something new and pleasant to tell me, I hope,—something in keeping with this quiet place and hour?" said Sylvia, glancing up at him with the traitorous softness still in her eyes.

"Yes, and hoping you would like it."

"Then I have never heard it before?"

"Never from me."

"Go on, please; I am ready."

She folded her hands together on her knee, turned her face attentively to his, and unwittingly composed herself to listen to the sweet story so often told, and yet so hard to tell. Moor meant to woo her very gently, for he believed that love was new to her. He had planned many graceful illustrations for his tale, and rounded many smoothly flowing sentences in which to unfold it. But the emotions are not well bred, and when the moment came, nature conquered art. No demonstration seemed beautiful enough to grace the betrayal of his passion, no language eloquent enough to tell it, no power strong enough to hold in check the impulse that mastered him. He went to her, knelt down upon the cushion at her feet, and, lifting to her a face flushed and fervent with the ardor of a man's first love, said impetuously,—

"Sylvia, read it here!"

There was no need for her to look; act, touch, and tone told the story better than the most impassioned speech. The supplication of his attitude, the eager beating of his heart, the tender pressure of his hand, dispelled her blindness in the drawing of a breath, and showed her what she had done. Now neglected warnings, selfish forgetfulness, and the knowledge of an unconscious, but irremediable wrong frightened and bewildered her; she hid her face, and shrunk back trembling with remorse and shame. Moor, seeing in her agitation only maiden happiness or hesitancy, accepted and enjoyed a blissful moment while he waited her reply. It was so long in coming that he gently tried to draw her hands away and look into her face, whispering like one scarcely doubtful of assent,—

"You love me, Sylvia?"

"No."

Only half audible was the reluctant answer, yet he heard it, smiled at what he fancied a shy falsehood, and said tenderly,—

"Will you let me love you, dear?"

"No."

Fainter than before was the one word, but it reached and startled him. Hurriedly he asked,—

"Am I nothing to you but a friend?"

"No."

With a quick gesture he put down her hands and looked at her. Grief, regret, and pity filled her face with trouble, but no love was there. He saw, yet would not believe the truth,—felt that the sweet certainty of love had gone, yet could not relinquish the fond hope.

"Sylvia, do you understand me?"

"I do, I do! but I cannot say what you would have me, and I must tell the truth, although it breaks my heart. Geoffrey, I do not love you."

"Can I not teach you?" he pleaded eagerly.

"I have no desire to learn."

Softly she spoke, remorseful she looked, but the words wounded like a blow. All the glad assurance died, the passionate glow faded, the caress, half tender, half timid, fell away, and nothing of the happy lover remained in face or figure. He rose slowly as if the heavy disappointment oppressed both soul and body. He fixed on her a glance of mingled incredulity, reproach, and pain, and said, like one bent on ending suspense at once,—

"Did you not see that I loved you? Can you have been trifling with me? Sylvia, I thought you too simple and sincere for heartless coquetry."

"I am! You shall not suspect me of that, though I deserve all other reproaches. I have been very selfish, very blind. I should have remembered that in your great kindness you might like me too well for your own peace. I should have believed Max, and been less candid in my expressions of esteem. But I wanted a friend so much; I found all I could ask in you; I thought my youth, my faults, my follies, would make it impossible for you to see in me anything but a wayward girl, who frankly showed her regard, and was proud of yours. It was one of my sad mistakes; I see it now; and now it is too late for anything but penitence. Forgive me if you can; I've taken all the pleasure, and left you all the pain."

Sylvia spoke in a paroxysm of remorseful sorrow. Moor listened with a sinking heart, and when she dropped her face into her hands again, unable to endure the pale expectancy of his, he turned away, saying with an accent of quiet despair,—

"Then I have worked and waited all this summer to see my harvest fail at last. Oh, Sylvia, I so loved, so trusted you!"

He leaned his arm on the low chimney-piece, laid down his head upon it and stood silent, trying to forgive.

It is always a hard moment for any woman, when it demands her bravest sincerity to look into a countenance of eager love, and change it to one of bitter disappointment by the utterance of a monosyllable. To Sylvia it was doubly hard; for now her blindness seemed as incredible as cruel, her past frankness unjustifiable, her pleasure selfish, her refusal the blackest ingratitude, and her dream of friendship forever marred. In the brief pause that fell, every little service he had rendered her rose freshly in her memory; every hour of real content and genuine worth that he had given her seemed to come back and reproach her; every look, accent, action, of both happy past and sad present seemed to plead for him. Her conscience cried out against her, her heart overflowed with penitence and pity. She looked at him, longing to say something, do something that should prove her repentance, and assure him of the affection which she felt. As she looked, two great tears fell glittering to the hearth, and lay there such eloquent reproaches, that, had Sylvia's heart been hard and cold as the marble where they shone, it would have melted then. She could not bear it; she went to him, took in both her own the rejected hand that hung at his side, and, feeling that no act could too tenderly express her sorrow, lifted it to her lips and kissed it.

An instant she was permitted to lay her cheek against it as a penitent child mutely imploring pardon might have done. Then it broke from her hold, and, gathering her to himself, Moor looked up, exclaiming with renewed hope, unaltered longing,—

"You do care for me, then? You give yourself to me in spite of that hard No? Ah, Sylvia, you are capricious even in your love."

She could not answer, for if that first No had been hard to utter, this was impossible. It seemed like turning the knife in the wound, to disappoint the hope that had gathered strength from despair, and she could only lay her head down on his breast, weeping the saddest tears she had ever shed. Still happy in his new delusion, Moor softly stroked the shining hair, smiling so tenderly, so delightedly, that it was well for her she did not see the smile, the words were enough.

"Dear Sylvia, I have tried so hard to make you love me, how could you help it?"

The reason sprung to her lips, but maiden pride and shame withheld it. What could she tell except that she had cherished a passion, based only on a look? She had deceived herself in her belief that Moor was but a friend; she had deceived herself in believing Warwick was a lover. She could not own this secret, its betrayal could not alter her reply nor heal

Moor's wound, but the thought of Warwick strengthened her. It always did, as surely as the influence of his friend always soothed her, for one was an embodiment of power, the other of tenderness.

"Geoffrey, let me be true to you and to myself," she said, so earnestly that it gave weight to her broken words. "I cannot be your wife, but I can be your friend forever. Try to believe this,—make my task easier by giving up your hope,—and oh, be sure that while I live I cannot do enough to show my sorrow for the great wrong I have done you."

"Must it be so? I find it very hard to accept the truth and give up the hope that has made my happiness so long. Let me keep it, Sylvia; let me wait and work again. I have a firm belief that you *will* love me yet, because I cleave to you with heart and soul, long for you continually, and think you the one woman of the world."

"Ah, if it were only possible!" she sighed.

"Let me make it so! In truth, I think I should not labor long. You are so young, dear, you have not learned to know your own heart yet. It was not pity nor penitence alone that brought you here to comfort me. Was it, Sylvia?"

"Yes. Had it been love, could I stand as I am now and not show it?"

She looked up at him, showed him that though her cheeks were wet there was no rosy dawn of passion there; though her eyes were as full of affection as of grief, there was no shy avoidance of his own, no dropping of the lids, lest they should tell too much; and though his arm encircled her, she did not cling to him as loving women cling when they lean on the strength which, touched by love, can both cherish and sustain. That look convinced him better than a flood of words. A long sigh broke from his lips, and, turning from her the eyes that had so wistfully searched and found not, they went wandering drearily hither and thither as if seeking the hope whose loss made life seem desolate. Sylvia saw it, groaned within herself, but still held fast to the hard truth, and tried to make it kinder.

"Geoffrey, I once heard you say to Max, 'Friendship is the best college character can graduate from. Believe in it, seek for it, and when it comes keep it as sacredly as love.' All my life I have wanted a friend, have looked for one, and when he came I welcomed him. May I not keep him, and preserve the friendship dear and sacred still, although I cannot offer love?"

Softly, seriously, she spoke, but the words sounded cold to him; friendship seemed so poor now, love so rich, he could not leave the blessed sunshine which transfigured the whole earth and sit down in the little circle of a kindly fire without keen regret.

"I ought to say yes, I will try to do it if nothing easier remains to me. Sylvia, for five years I have longed and waited for a home. Duty forbade it then, because poor Marion had only me to make her sad life happy, and my mother left her to my charge. Now the duty is ended, the old house very empty, my heart very hungry for affection. You are all in all to me, and I find it so difficult to relinquish my dream that I must be importunate. I have spoken too soon; you have had no time to think, to look into yourself and question your own heart. Go, now, recall what I have said, remember that I will wait for you patiently, and when I leave, an hour hence, come down and give me my last answer."

Sylvia was about to speak, but the sound of an approaching step brought over her the shyness she had not felt before, and without a word she darted from the room. Then romance also fled, for Prue came bustling in, and Moor was called to talk of influenzas, while his thoughts were full of love.

Alone in her chamber Sylvia searched herself. She pictured the life that would be hers with Moor. The old house so full of something better than its opulence, an atmosphere of genial tranquillity which made it home-like to whoever crossed its threshold. Herself the daily companion and dear wife of the master who diffused such sunshine there, whose serenity soothed her restlessness, whose affection would be as enduring as his patience, whose character she so truly honored. She felt that no woman need ask a happier home, a truer or more tender lover. But when she looked into herself she found the cordial, unimpassioned sentiment he first inspired still unchanged, and her heart answered,—

"This is friendship."

She thought of Warwick, and the other home that might be hers. Fancy painted in glowing colors the stirring life, the novelty, excitement, and ever new delight such wanderings would have for her. The joy of being always with him; the proud consciousness that she was nearest and dearest to such a man; the certainty that she might share the knowledge of his past, might enjoy his present, help to shape his future. There was no time to look into her heart, for up sprang its warm blood to her cheek, its hope to her eye, its longing to her lips, its answer glad and ready,—

"Ah, this is love!" She could not wait to prove the wisdom of either sentiment; impulse ruled her, and the mood of the moment blinded her now as often before.

The clock struck ten, and after lingering a little Sylvia went down. Slowly, because her errand was a hard one; thoughtfully, because she knew not where nor how she could best deliver it. No need to look for him or linger for his coming; he was already there. Alone in the hall, absently smoothing a little silken shawl she often wore, and waiting with a melancholy patience that smote her to the heart. He went to meet her, took both her hands in his, and looked into her face so tenderly, so wistfully!—

"Sylvia, is it good-night or good-by?"

Her eyes filled, her hands trembled, her color paled, but she answered steadily,—

"Forgive me! it is good-by."

CHAPTER XI

Yes

Moor went away to live down his disappointment. The houses by the sea were shut, and the Yules went to town for the winter. No word came from Warwick, and Sylvia ceased to hope.

It is easy to say, "I will forget," but perhaps the hardest task given us is to lock up a natural yearning of the heart, and turn a deaf ear to its plaint, for captive and jailer must inhabit the same small cell. Sylvia was proud, with that pride which is both sensitive and courageous, which can not only suffer, but wring strength from suffering. While she struggled with a grief that aged her with its pain, she asked no help, made no complaint; but when the forbidden passion stretched its arms to her, she thrust it back, and turned to pleasure for oblivion.

Those who knew her best were troubled and surprised by the craving for excitement which now took possession of her, the avidity with which she gratified it, regardless of time, health, or money. All day she hurried here and there, driving, shopping, sightseeing, or entertaining guests at home. Night brought no cessation of her dissipation, for when balls, masquerades, and concerts failed, there still remained the theatre. This soon became both a refuge and a solace, for, believing it to be less harmful than other excitements, her father indulged her new whim. But, had he known it, this was the most dangerous pastime she could have chosen. Calling for no exertion of her own, it left her free to passively receive a stimulant to her unhappy love in watching its mimic semblance through all phases of tragic suffering and sorrow, for she would see no comedies, and Shakespeare's tragedies became her study.

This lasted for a time, then the reaction came. A black melancholy fell upon her, and energy deserted soul and body. She found it a weariness to get up in the morning, and weariness to lie down at night. She no longer cared even to seem cheerful, owned that she was spiritless, hoped she should be ill, and did not care if she died to-morrow. When this dark mood seemed about to become chronic, she began to mend, for youth is wonderfully recuperative, and the deepest wounds soon heal even against the sufferer's will. A quiet apathy replaced the gloom, and she let the tide drift her where it would, hoping nothing, expecting nothing, asking nothing but that she need not suffer any more.

She lived fast; all processes with her were rapid; and the secret experience of that winter taught her many things. She believed it had only taught her to forget, for now the outcast love lay very still, and no longer beat despairingly against the door of her heart, demanding to be taken in from the cold. She fancied that neglect had killed it, and that its grave was green with many tears. Alas for Sylvia! how could she know that it had only sobbed itself to sleep, and would wake beautiful and strong at the first sound of its master's voice.

Max became eventful. In his fitful fashion he had painted a picture of the Golden Wedding, from sketches taken at the time. Moor had suggested and bespoken it, that the young artist might have a motive for finishing it, because, though he excelled in scenes of that description, he thought them beneath him, and, tempted by more ambitious designs, neglected his true branch of the art. In April it was finished, and at his father's request Max reluctantly sent it with his Clytemnestra to the annual Exhibition. One morning at breakfast, Mr. Yule suddenly laughed out behind his paper, and with a face of unmixed satisfaction passed it to his son, pointing to a long critique upon the picture. Max prepared himself to receive with becoming modesty the praises lavished upon his great work, but was stricken with amazement to find Clytemnestra disposed of in a single sentence, and the Golden Wedding lauded in a long enthusiastic paragraph.

"What the deuce does the man mean!" he ejaculated, staring at his father.

"He means that the work which warms the heart is greater than that which freezes the blood, I suspect. Moor knew what you could do, and has made you do it, sure that if you worked for fame unconsciously, you would win it. This is a success that I can appreciate, and I congratulate you heartily, my son."

"Thank you, sir. But upon my word I don't understand it, and if this wasn't written by the best Art critic in the country I should feel inclined to say the writer was a fool. Why, that little thing was a daub compared to the other."

He got no farther in his protest against this unexpected freak of fortune, for Sylvia seized the paper and read the paragraph aloud with such happy emphasis amid Prue's outcries and his father's applause, that Max began to feel that he really had done something praiseworthy, and that the "daub" was not so despicable after all.

"I'm going to look at it from this new point of sight," was his sole comment as he went away.

Several hours afterward he appeared to Sylvia as she sat sewing alone, and startled her with the mysterious announcement,—

"I've done it!"

"Done what? Have you burnt poor Clytemnestra?"

"Hang Clytemnestra! I'll begin at the beginning and prepare you for the grand finale. I went to the Exhibition, and stared at Father Blake and his family for an hour. Decided that wasn't bad, though I still admire the other more. Then people began to come and crowd up, so that I slipped away, for I couldn't stand the compliments. Dahlmann, Scott, and all the rest of my tribe were there, and, as true as my name is Max Yule, every man of them ignored the Greek party and congratulated me upon the success of that confounded Golden Wedding."

"My dearest boy, I am so proud! so glad! What is the matter? Have you been bitten by a tarantula?"

She might well ask, for Max was dancing all over the carpet in a most extraordinary style, and only stopped long enough to throw a little case into Sylvia's lap, asking as a whole faceful of smiles broke loose,—

"What does that mean?"

She opened it, and a suspicious circle of diamonds appeared, at sight of which she clapped her hands, and cried out,—

"You're going to ask Jessie to wear it!"

"I have! I have!" sang Max, dancing more wildly than ever. Sylvia chased him into a corner and held him there, almost as much excited as he, while she demanded a full explanation, which he gave her, laughing like a boy and blushing like a girl.

"You have no business to ask, but of course I'm dying to tell you. I went from that Painter's Purgatory, as we call it, to Mr. Hope's, and asked for Miss Jessie. My angel came down; I told her of my success, and she smiled as never a woman did before; I added that I'd only waited to make myself more worthy of her, by showing that I had talent, as well as love and money to offer her, and she began to cry; whereat I took her in my arms and ascended straight into heaven."

"Please be sober, Max, and tell me all about it. Was she glad? Did she say she would? And is everything as we would have it?"

"It is all perfect, divine, and rapturous, to the last degree. Jessie has liked me ever since she was born, she thinks; adores you and Prue for sisters; yearns to call my parent father; allowed me to say and do whatever I liked; and gave me a ravishing kiss just there. Sacred spot! I shall get a mate to it when I put this on her blessed little finger. Try it for me; I want it to be right, and your hands are of a size. That fits grandly. When shall I see a joyful sweetheart doing this on his own behalf, Sylvia?"

"Never!"

She shook off the ring as if it burned her, watching it roll glittering away with a somewhat tragical expression. Then she calmed herself, and, sitting down to her work, enjoyed Max's raptures for an hour.

The happiness this new element brought into the family worked a change in all of them. Mr. Yule was proud of his son, Prue in a flutter of importance and pleasure at the prospect of a wedding, and Sylvia found it very interesting to watch the lovers, to enjoy a little of the sunshine that surrounded them, and to envy the tender regard all felt for them. Romance was not dead in her, nor the desire to be loved, by those at home at least, since fate denied the heart she coveted.

Having known Warwick, it was easy to admire courage, strength, and heroism; having known Moor, it was impossible not to see and feel the beauty of self-sacrifice; and, being in a mood both humble and remorseful, Sylvia longed to combine in herself some touch of the virtues she so respected in the man she loved and the man who loved her. She knew it would fill her family with comfort and gladness if she could love Moor; it seemed as if entire self-renunciation would be following Adam's counsel, and in trying to make the real lover happy she might forget the imaginary one.

All through the winter there had come at intervals letters from Moor to Max, and gifts to herself, as if their friend desired to show them that he still thought of them and was glad to show that though his loss was great it had not imbittered the old affection.

This touched Sylvia, and during the holidays, when all the world feels kindly and akin, she wrote to thank him for the holly that made her Christmas gay, the lovely picture that came at New Year, and the good wishes which she heartily returned.

It was April now, and on Sylvia's birthday arrived a basket full of moss in which snowdrops were set as if growing, with a card bearing only, "From your friend G. M." The word "friend" was lightly underscored, as if to assure her that he still cherished the one tie permitted him, and sent the pretty token to lighten his regret that she could give him no tenderer one.

As she read, warm over Sylvia's sore heart rushed the grateful thought, "He cares for me! he remembers me! If he would come back I would try to love him now."

Did he hear the wordless cry, divine the loneliness that made the young heart ache for love, and come to profit by this propitious mood?

As the city clocks struck nine that night, a man paused before the house and scrutinized each window. Many were alight, but on the drawn curtain of one a woman's shadow came and went. He watched it for a moment, then noiselessly went in. The hall was bright and solitary; from above came the sound of voices; from a room on the right the stir of papers and the scratch of a pen; from one on the left a rustle as of silk swept slowly to and fro. To the threshold of this door he stepped and looked in.

Sylvia was just turning in her walk, and as she came musing down the room, Moor saw her well. With some women dress has no relation to states of mind; with Sylvia it was often an indication of the mental garb she wore. Moor remembered this trait, and saw in both countenance and costume the change which had befallen her during his long absence. Her face was neither gay nor melancholy, but serious and coldly quiet, as if some inward twilight reigned. Her dress, a soft, sad gray with no decoration but a knot of snowdrops in the bosom. On these pale flowers her eyes were fixed, and as she walked with folded arms and drooping head, she sang low to herself St. Agnes' song,—

"Upon the convent roof the snows
Lie sparkling to the moon;
My breath to heaven like incense goes,
May my soul follow soon.

"Lord, make my spirit pure and clear
As are the frosty skies,
Or this first snowdrop of the year,
That in my bosom lies."

"Sylvia!"

Very gentle was the call, but she started as if it were an answer to a wish, looked an instant while light and color flashed into her face, then ran to him, exclaiming joyfully,—

"Oh, Geoffrey! I am glad! I am glad!"

There could be but one reply to such a welcome, and Sylvia received it as she stood there, not weeping now, but smiling with the sincerest satisfaction, the happiest surprise. Moor shared both emotions, feeling as a man might feel when, parched with thirst, he stretches out his hand for a drop of rain, and receives a brimming cup of water. He drank a deep draught gratefully, then, fearing that it might be as suddenly withdrawn, asked anxiously,—

"Sylvia, are we friends or lovers?"

"Anything, if you will only stay."

She looked up as she spoke, and her face betrayed that a conflict between desire and doubt was going on within her. Impulse had sent her there, and now it was so sweet to know herself beloved, she found it hard to go away. Her brother's happiness had touched her heart, roused the old craving for affection, and brought a strong desire to fill the aching void her lost love had left with this recovered one. She had not learned to reason yet, she could only feel, because, owing to the unequal development of her divided nature, the heart grew faster than the intellect. Instinct was her surest guide, and when she followed it, unblinded by a passion, unthwarted by a mood, she prospered. But now she was so blinded and so thwarted, and now her great temptation came. Ambition, man's idol, had tempted the father; love, woman's god, tempted the daughter; and, as if the father's atonement was to be wrought out through his dearest child, the daughter also made the false step that might be as fatal as his own.

"Then you *have* learned to love me, Sylvia?"

"No; the old feeling has not changed except to grow more remorseful, more eager to prove its truth. Once you asked me if I did not wish to love you; then I did not, now I sincerely do. If you still want me with my many faults, and will teach me in your gentle way to be all I should to you, I will gladly learn, because I never needed love as I do now. Geoffrey, shall I stay or go?"

"Stay, Sylvia. Thank God for this!"

If she had ever hoped that Moor would forget her for his own sake, she now saw how vain such hope would have been, and was both touched and troubled by the knowledge of her supremacy which that hour gave her. She was as much the calmer as friendship is than love, and was the first to speak again, still standing there content although her words expressed a doubt.

"Are you very sure you want me? Are you not tired of the thorn that has fretted you so long? Remember, I am so young, so ignorant, and unfitted for a wife. Can I give you real happiness? make home what you would have it? and never see in your face regret that some wiser, better woman was not in my place?"

"I am sure of myself, and satisfied with you, as you are, no wiser, no better, nothing but my Sylvia."

"It is very sweet to hear you say that with such a look. I do not deserve it, but I will. Is the pain I once gave you gone now, Geoffrey?"

"Gone forever."

"Then I am satisfied, and will begin my life anew by trying to learn well the lesson my kind master is to teach me."

When Moor went that night Sylvia followed him, and as they stood together, this happy moment seemed to recall that other bitter one, for, taking her hands again, he asked, smiling now,—

"Dear, is it good-night or good-by?"

"It is good-night, and come to-morrow."

CHAPTER XII

Wooing

Nothing could have been more unlike than the two pairs of lovers who from April to August haunted Mr. Yule's house. One pair was of the popular order, for Max was tenderly tyrannical, Jessie adoringly submissive, and at all hours of the day they were to be seen making tableaux of themselves. The other pair were of the peculiar order, undemonstrative and unsentimental, but quite as happy. Moor knew his power, but used it generously, asking little while giving much. Sylvia as yet found nothing to regret, for so gently was she taught, the lesson could not seem hard, and when her affection remained unchanged in kind, although it deepened in degree, she said within herself,—

"That strong and sudden passion was not true love, but an unwise, unhappy delusion of my own. I should be glad that it is gone, because I know I am not fit to be Warwick's wife. This quiet feeling which Geoffrey inspires must be a safer love for me, and I should be grateful that in making his happiness I may yet find my own."

She tried heartily to forget herself in others, unconscious that there are times when the duty we owe ourselves is greater than that we owe to them. In the atmosphere of cheerfulness that now surrounded her she could not but be cheerful, and soon it would have been difficult to find a more harmonious household than this. One little cloud alone remained to mar the general sunshine. Max was in a frenzy to be married and had set his heart on a double wedding, but Sylvia would not fix a time, always pleading,—

"Let me be quite sure of myself before I take this step, and do not wait."

Matters stood thus till Max, having prepared his honeymoon cottage between his father's house and the Manse, as a relief to his impatience, found it so irresistible that he announced his marriage for the first of August, and declared no human power should change his purpose. Sylvia promised to think of it, but would give no decided answer, because, though she hardly owned it to herself, she longed to hear some news of Warwick before it was too late.

Max and Jessie came in from the city one warm morning and found Sylvia sitting idly in the breezy hall. She left all her preparations to Prue, who revelled in such affairs, and applied herself diligently to her new lesson as if afraid she might not learn it as well as she ought. Half-way up stairs Max paused to say,—

"You remember Warwick, Sylvia."

"Yes." And if the hall had not been so dark, her brother might have seen the flush of mingled pain and joy that came to Sylvia's listless face.

"Well, I met a friend from England to-day who told me he came across old Adam, who was preparing to join one of the Polar expeditions. Isn't that just like him?" And Max went on with a laugh.

As if chilled by a breath from that icy region, Sylvia's last half-unconscious hope died then, and she gave herself with entire abandon to the happiness of others.

Moor had written to his friend when his suit failed, but the letter was still following Warwick in his wanderings, and, receiving no reply, Moor waited to hear some tidings of him before he wrote again to tell his happy news; while Adam, finding time and absence fail to lessen his love, seemed to have decided to go to the ends of the earth and cool his passion among the icebergs.

Max went on to consult Prue about his wedding gloves, and Jessie began to display her purchases before eyes that only saw a blur of shapes and colors.

"I should enjoy my pretty things a thousand times more if you would only please us all by being married when we are," sighed Jessie, looking at her veil.

"I will."

"What, really? Sylvia, you are a perfect darling! Max! Prue! she says she will!"

Away flew Jessie to proclaim the glad news, and Sylvia, with a curious expression of relief and resolve, repeated to herself that decided "I will."

All took care that Miss Caprice should not have time to change her mind. The whole house was soon in a bustle, for Prue ruled supreme. Mr. Yule fled from the din of women's tongues; the bridegrooms elect were kept on a very short allowance of bride, and Sylvia and Jessie were almost invisible, for milliners and mantua-makers swarmed about them till they felt like animated pin-cushions.

The last evening came at length, and weary Sylvia was just planning to escape into the garden, when Prue, whose tongue wagged as rapidly as her hands worked, exclaimed incoherently as usual,—

"How can you stand staring out of window when there is so much to do? Here are all these trunks to pack, Maria in bed with a frightful toothache, and that capable Jane What's-her-name gone off while I was putting a chamomile poultice on her face. If you are tired sit down and try on all your shoes, for though Mr. Peggit has your measure, those absurd clerks seem to think it a compliment to send children's sizes to grown women. I'm sure my rubbers were a perfect insult."

Sylvia sat down, tugged on one boot and fell into a reverie with the other in her hand, while Prue clacked on like a wordmill in full operation.

"How I'm ever to get all these gowns into that trunk passes my comprehension. There's a tray for each, of course; but a ball dress is such a fractious thing. I could shake that Antoinette Roche for disappointing you at the last minute; and what you are to do for a maid, I don't know. You'll have so much dressing to do you will be quite worn out; and I want you to look your best on all occasions, for you will meet everybody. This collar won't wear well; Clara hasn't a particle of judgment, though her taste is sweet. These hose, now, are a good, firm article; I chose them myself. Do be sure you get all your things from the wash. At those great hotels there's a deal of pilfering, and you are so careless."

Here Sylvia came out of her reverie with a sigh that was almost a groan.

"Don't they fit? I knew they wouldn't!" said Prue, with an air of triumph.

"The boots suit me, but the hotels do not; and if it was not ungrateful, after all your trouble, I should like to make a bonfire of this roomful of haberdashery, and walk quietly away to my new home by the light of it."

As if the bare idea of such an awful proceeding robbed her of all strength, Miss Yule sat suddenly down in the trunk by which she was standing. Fortunately it was nearly full, but her appearance was decidedly ludicrous as she sat with the collar in one uplifted hand, the hose in the other, and the ball dress laid over her lap like a fainting lady; while she said, with imploring solemnity, which changed abruptly from the pathetic to the comic at the end of her speech,—

"Sylvia, if I ever cherished a wish in this world of disappointment, it is that your wedding shall have nothing peculiar about it, because every friend and relation you've got expects it. Do let me have the comfort of knowing that every one was surprised and pleased; for if the expression was elegant (which it isn't, and only suggested by my trials with those dressmakers), I should say I was on pins and needles till it's all over. Bless me! and so I am, for here are three on the floor and one in my shoe." Prue paused to extract the appropriate figure of speech which she had chosen, and Sylvia said,—

"If we have everything else as you wish it, would you mind if we didn't go the journey?"

"Of course I should. Every one goes a wedding trip, it's part of the ceremony; and if two carriages and two bridal pairs don't leave here tomorrow, I shall feel as if all my trouble had been thrown away."

"I'll go, Prue, I'll go; and you shall be satisfied. But I thought we might go from here in style, and then slip off on some quieter trip. I am so tired I dread the idea of frolicking for a whole month, as Max and Jessie mean to do."

It was Prue's turn to groan now, and she did so dismally. But Sylvia had never asked a favor in vain, and this was not the moment to refuse to her anything, so worldly pride yielded to sisterly affection, and Prue said with resignation, as she fell to work more vigorously than ever, because she had wasted five good minutes,—

"Do as you like, dear, you shall not be crossed on your last day at home. Ask Geoffrey, and if you are happy I'm satisfied."

Before Sylvia could thank her sister there came a tap and a voice asking,—

"Might I come in?"

"If you can get in," answered Prue, as, reversing her plan in her hurry, she whisked the collar into a bag and the hose into a bandbox.

Moor paused on the threshold in a masculine maze, that one small person could need so much drapery.

"May I borrow Sylvia for a little while? A breath of air will do her good, and I want her bright and blooming for to-morrow, else young Mrs. Yule will outshine young Mrs. Moor."

"What a thoughtful creature you are, Geoffrey! Take her and welcome, only pray put on a shawl, Sylvia, and don't stay out late, for a bride with a cold in her head is the saddest of spectacles."

Glad to be released, Sylvia went away, and, dropping the shawl as soon as she was out of Prue's sight, paced up and down the garden walks upon her lover's arm. Having heard her wish and given a hearty assent, Moor asked,—

"Where shall we go? Tell me what you would like best and you shall have it. You will not let me give you many gifts, but this pleasure you will accept from me, I know."

"You give me yourself; that is more than I deserve. But I should like to have you take me to the place you like best. Don't tell me beforehand, let it be a surprise."

"I will; it is already settled, and I know you will like it. Is there no other wish to be granted, no doubt to be set at rest, or regret withheld that I should know? Tell me, Sylvia, for if ever there should be confidence between us it is now."

As he spoke the desire to tell him of her love for Adam rose within her, but with the desire came a thought that modified the form in which impulse prompted her to make confession. Moor was both sensitive and proud; would not the knowledge of the fact mar for him the friendship that was so much to both? From Warwick he would never learn it, from her he should have only a half confidence, and so love both friend and wife with an untroubled heart. Few of us can always control the rebellious nature that so often betrays and then reproaches, few always weigh the moment and the act that bans or blesses it, and where is the life that has not known some turning-point when a fugitive emotion has decided great issues for good or ill? Such an emotion came to Sylvia then, and another temptation, wearing the guise of generosity, urged her to another false step, for when the first is taken a second inevitably follows.

"I have no wish, no regret, nothing but the old doubt of my unstable self, and the fear that I may fail to make you happy. But I should like to tell you something. I don't know that you will care for it, or that there is any need to tell it, but when you said there should be confidence between us, I felt that I wanted you to know that I had loved some one before I loved you."

He did not see her face, he only heard her quiet voice. He had no thought of Adam, whom she had known so short a time, who was so indifferent to women, and who always spoke of and treated Sylvia as a child. He fancied that she thought of some young lover who had touched her heart, and while he smiled at the nice sense of honor that prompted the innocent confession, he said, with no coldness, no curiosity in voice or face,—

"No need to tell it, dear. I have no jealousy of any one who has gone before me. Rest assured of this, for if I could not share so large a heart with one who will never claim my share I should not deserve it."

"That is so like you! Now I am quite at ease."

He looked down at her as she went beside him, thinking that of all the brides he had ever seen his own looked least like one.

"I always thought that you would make a very ardent lover, Sylvia; that you would be excited, gay, and brilliant at a time like this. But you are so quiet, so absorbed, and so unlike your former self that I begin to think I do not know you yet."

"You will in time. I am passionate and restless by nature, but I am also very sensitive to all influences, personal or otherwise, and were you different from your tranquil, sunshiny self, I too should change. I am quiet because I seem in a pleasant state, half waking, half dreaming, from which

I never wish to wake. I am tired of the past, contented with the present, and to you I leave the future."

"It shall be a happy one if I can make it so, and to-morrow you will give me the dear right to try."

"Yes," she said; and, thinking of the solemn promises to be then made, she added thoughtfully, "I think I love, I know I honor, I will try to obey. Can I do more?"

Well for them both if they could have known that friendship is love's twin, and the gentle sisters are too often mistaken for each other; that Sylvia was innocently deceiving both her lover and herself, by wrapping her friendship in the garb her lost love had worn, forgetting that the wanderer might return and claim its own, leaving the other to suffer for the borrowed warmth. They did not know it, and walked tranquilly together in the summer night, planning the new life as they went, and when they parted Moor pointed to a young moon hanging in the sky.

"See, Sylvia, our honeymoon has risen."

"May it be a happy one!"

"It will be, and when the anniversary of this glad night comes round it shall be shining still. God bless my little wife!"

CHAPTER XIII

Wedding

Sylvia was awakened on her wedding morning by a curious choking sound, and starting up found Prue crying over her as if her heart were broken.

"What has happened? Is Geoffrey ill? Is all the silver stolen? Can't the Bishop come?" she asked, wondering what calamity could move her sister to tears at such a busy time.

Prue took Sylvia in her arms, and, rocking to and fro as if she was still a baby, poured forth a stream of words and tears together.

"Nothing has happened; I came to call you, and broke down because it was the last time I should do it. I've been awake all night, thinking of you and all you've been to me since I took you in my arms eighteen years ago, and said you should be mine. My little Sylvia, I've been neglectful of so many things, and now I see them all; I've fretted you with my ways, and haven't been patient enough with yours; I've been selfish even about your wedding, and it won't be as you like it; you'll reproach me in your heart, and I shall hate myself for it when you are gone never to be my care and comfort any more. And—oh, my dear, my dear, what shall I do without you!"

This unexpected demonstration from her prosaic sister touched Sylvia more than the most sentimental lamentations from another. It brought to mind all the past devotion, the future solitude of Prue's life, and she clung about her neck tearless but very tender.

"I never shall reproach you, never cease to love and thank you for all you've been to me, my dear old Prue. You mustn't grieve over me, or think I shall forget you, for you never shall be forsaken; and very soon I shall be back, almost as much your Sylvia as ever. Max will live on one side, I shall live on the other, and we'll be merry and cosey together. And who knows but when we are both out of your way you will learn to think of yourself and marry also."

At this Prue began to laugh hysterically, and exclaimed, with more than her usual incoherency,—

"I *must* tell you, it was so very odd! I didn't mean to do so, because you children would tease me; but now I wish to laugh, for it's a bad omen to cry over a bride, they say. My dear, that gouty Mr. MacGregor, when I went in with some of my nice broth last week (Hugh slops so, and he's such a fidget, I took it myself), after he had eaten every drop before my eyes, wiped his mouth and asked me to marry him."

"And you would not, Prue?"

"Bless me, child, how could I? I must take care of my poor dear father, and he isn't pleasant in the least, you know, but would wear my life out in a week. I really pitied him, however, when I refused him, with a napkin round his neck, and he tapped his waistcoat with a spoon so comically, when he offered me his heart, as if it were something good to eat."

"How very funny! What made him do it, Prue?"

"He said he'd watched the preparations from his window, and got so interested in weddings that he wanted one himself, and felt drawn to me, I was so sympathetic. That means a good nurse and cook, my dear. I understand these invalid gentlemen, and will be a slave to no man so fat and fussy as Mr. Mac, as my brother calls him. It's not respectful, but I like to refresh myself by saying it just now."

"Never mind the old soul, Prue, but go and have your breakfast comfortably; for there is much to be done, and no one is to dress me but your own dear self."

At this Prue relapsed into the pathetic again, and cried over her sister as if, despite the omen, brides were plants that needed much watering.

The appearance of the afflicted Maria, with her face still partially eclipsed by the chamomile comforter, and an announcement that the waiters had come and were "ordering round dreadful," caused Prue to pocket her handkerchief and descend to turn the tables in every sense of the word.

The prospect of the wedding breakfast made the usual meal a mere mockery. Every one was in a driving hurry, every one was very much excited, and nobody but Prue and the colored gentlemen brought anything to pass. Sylvia went from room to room bidding them good-by as the child who had played there so long. But each looked unfamiliar in its state and festival array, and the old house seemed to have forgotten her already. She spent an hour with her father, paid Max a little call in the empty studio where he was bidding adieu to the joys of bachelorhood, and preparing himself for the jars of matrimony by a composing smoke, and then Prue claimed her.

The agonies she suffered during that long toilet are beyond the powers of language to portray, for Prue surpassed herself and was the very essence of fussiness. But Sylvia bore it patiently as a last sacrifice, because her sister was very tender-hearted still, and laughed and cried over her work till all was done, when she surveyed the effect with pensive satisfaction.

"You are very sweet, my dear, and so delightfully calm, you really do surprise me. I always thought you'd have hysterics on your wedding-day, and got my *vinaigrette* all ready. Keep your hands just as they are, with the handkerchief and bouquet; it looks very easy and rich. Dear me, what a spectacle I've made of myself! But I shall cry no more, not even during the ceremony, as many do. Such displays of feeling are in very bad taste, and I shall be firm, perfectly firm; so if you hear any one sniff, you'll know it isn't me. Now I must go and scramble on my dress; first, let me arrange you smoothly in a chair. There, my precious, now think of soothing things, and don't stir till Geoffrey comes for you."

Too tired to care what happened just then, Sylvia sat as she was placed, feeling like a fashion-plate of a bride, and wishing she could go to sleep. Presently the sound of steps as fleet as Max's, but lighter, waked her up, and, forgetting orders, she rustled to the door with an expression which fashion-plates have not yet attained.

"Good-morning, little bride."

"Good-morning, bonny bridegroom."

Then they looked at one another, and both smiled. But they seemed to have changed characters; for Moor's usually tranquil face was full of pale excitement, Sylvia's usually vivacious one full of quietude, and her eyes wore the unquestioning content of a child who accepts some friendly hand, sure that it will lead it right.

"Prue desires me to take you out into the upper hall, and when Mr. Deane beckons, we are to go down at once. The rooms are full, and Jessie is ready. Shall we go?"

"One moment: Geoffrey, are you quite happy now?"

"Supremely happy!"

"Then it shall be the first duty of my life to keep you so." And with a gesture soft yet solemn, Sylvia laid her hand in his, as if endowing him with both gift and giver. He held it fast, and never let it go until it was his own.

In the upper hall they found Max hovering about Jessie like an agitated bee about a very full-blown flower, and Clara Deane flapping him away, lest he should damage the effect of this beautiful white rose. For ten minutes, ages they seemed, the five stood together listening to the stir below, looking at one another till they were tired of the sight and scent of orange blossoms, and wishing that the whole affair was safely over. But the instant a portentous "Hem!" was heard, and a white glove seen to beckon from the stair-foot, every one fell into a flutter. Moor turned paler still, and Sylvia felt his heart beat hard against her hand. She herself was seized with a momentary desire to run away and say "No" again. Max looked as if nerving himself for immediate execution, and Jessie feebly whispered,—

"O Clara, I'm going to faint!"

"Good heavens, what shall I do with her? Max, support her! My darling girl, smell this and bear up. For mercy sake, do something, Sylvia, and don't stand there looking as if you'd been married every day for a year."

In his excitement, Max gave his bride a little shake. Its effect was marvellous. She rallied instantly, with a reproachful glance at her crumpled veil and a decided—

"Come quick, I can go now."

Down they went, through a wilderness of summer silks, black coats, and bridal gloves. How they reached their places none of them ever knew; Max said afterward, that the instinct of self-preservation led him to the only means of extrication that circumstances allowed. The moment the Bishop opened his book, Prue took out her handkerchief and cried steadily through the entire ceremony; for, dear as were the proprieties, the "children" were dearer still.

At Sylvia's desire, Max was married first, and as she stood listening to the sonorous roll of the service falling from the Bishop's lips, she tried to feel devout and solemn, but failed to do so. She tried to keep her thoughts from wandering, but continually found herself wondering if that sob came from Prue, if her father felt it very much, and when it would be done. She tried to keep her eyes fixed timidly upon the carpet as she had been told to do, but they would rise and glance about against her will.

One of these derelictions from the path of duty nearly produced a catastrophe. Little Tilly, the gardener's pretty child, had strayed in from among the servants peeping at a long window in the rear, and established herself near the wedding group, looking like a small ballet girl in her full white frock and wreath pushed rakishly askew on her curly pate. As she stood regarding the scene with dignified amazement, her eye met Sylvia's. In spite of the unusual costume, the baby knew her playmate, and, running to her, thrust her head under the veil with a delighted "Peep a bo!" Horror seized Jessie, Max was on the brink of a laugh, and Moor looked like one fallen from the clouds. But Sylvia drew the little marplot close to her with a warning word, and there she stayed, quietly amusing herself with "pooring" the silvery dress, smelling the flowers, and staring at the Bishop.

After this, all prospered. The gloves came smoothly off, the rings went smoothly on; no one cried but Prue, no one laughed but Tilly; the brides were admired, the grooms envied; the service pronounced impressive, and when it ended, a tumult of congratulations arose.

Sylvia always had a very confused idea of what happened during the next hour. She remembered being kissed till her cheeks burned, and shaken hands with till her fingers tingled; bowing in answer to toasts, and forgetting to reply when addressed by the new name; trying to eat and drink, and discovering that everything tasted of wedding cake; finding herself up stairs hurrying on her travelling dress, then down stairs saying good-by; and when her father embraced her last of all, suddenly realizing, with a pang, that she was married and going away, never to be little Sylvia any more.

Prue *was* gratified to her heart's content, for, when the two bridal carriages had vanished with handkerchiefs flying from their windows, in answer to the white whirlwind on the lawn, Mrs. Grundy, with an approving smile on her aristocratic countenance, pronounced this the most charming affair of the season.

CHAPTER XIV

Sylvia's Honeymoon

It began with a pleasant journey. Day after day they loitered along country roads that led them through many scenes of summer beauty; pausing at old-fashioned inns and wayside farmhouses, or gypsying at noon in some green nook where their four-footed comrades dined off their tablecloth while they made merry over the less simple fare their last hostess had provided for them. When the scenery was uninteresting, as was sometimes the case,—for Nature will not disturb her domestic arrangements for any bridal pair,—one or the other read aloud, or both sang, while conversation was a never-failing pastime and silence had charms which they could enjoy. Sometimes they walked a mile or two, ran down a hillside, rustled through a grain-field, strolled into an orchard, or feasted from fruitful hedges by the way, as care-free as the squirrels on the wall, or the jolly brown bees lunching at the sign of "The Clover-top." They made friends with sheep in meadows, cows at the brook, travellers morose or bland, farmers full of a sturdy sense that made their chat as wholesome as the mould they delved in; school-children barefooted and blithe, and specimens of womankind, from the buxom housewife, who took them under her motherly wing at once, to the sour, snuffy, shoe-binding spinster with "No Admittance" written all over her face.

To Moor the world was glorified with the purple light which seldom touches it but once for any of us; the journey was a wedding march, made beautiful by summer, victorious by joy; his young wife the queen of women, and himself an equal of the gods, because no longer conscious of a want. Sylvia could not be otherwise than happy; for, finding unbounded liberty and love her portion, she had nothing to regret, and regarded marriage as an agreeable process which had simply changed her name and given her protector, friend, and lover all in one. She was therefore her sweetest and sincerest self, miraculously docile and charmingly gay; interested in all she saw, and quite overflowing with delight when the last days of the week betrayed the secret that her destination was the mountains.

Loving the sea so well, her few flights from home had given her only marine experiences, and the flavor of entire novelty was added to the feast her husband had provided for her. It came to her not only when she could enjoy it most, but when she needed it most, soothing the unquiet, stimulating the nobler, elements which ruled her life by turns, and fitting her for what lay before her. Choosing the quietest roads, Moor showed her the wonders of a region whose wild grandeur and beauty make its memory a lifelong satisfaction. Day after day they followed mountain paths, studying the changes of an ever-varying landscape, watching the flush of dawn redden the granite fronts of these Titans scarred with centuries of storm, the lustre of noon brood over them until they smiled, the evening purple wrap them in its splendor, or moonlight touch them with its magic; till Sylvia, always looking up at that which filled her heart with reverence and awe, was led to look beyond, and through the medium of the friend beside her, learned that human love brings us nearer to the Divine, and is the surest means to that great end.

The last week of the honeymoon came all too soon, for then they had promised to return. The crowning glory of the range was left until the last, and after a day of memorable delights Sylvia sat in the sunset feasting her eyes upon the wonders of a scene which is indescribable, for words have limits and that is apparently illimitable. Presently Moor came to her, asking,—

"Will you join a party to the great ice palace, and see three acres of snow in August, worn by a waterfall into a cathedral, as white if not as durable as any marble?"

"I sit so comfortably here I think I had rather not. But you must go, because you like such wonders, and I shall rest till you come back."

"Then I shall take myself off and leave you to muse over the pleasures of the day, which for a few hours has made you one of the most eminent women this side the Rocky Mountains. There is a bugle at the house here with which to make the echoes. I shall take it with me, and from time to time send up a sweet reminder that you are not to stray away and lose yourself."

Sylvia sat for half an hour, then, wearied by the immensity of the wide landscape, she tried to rest her mind by examining the beauties close at hand. Strolling down the path the sightseers had taken, she found herself in a rocky basin, scooped in the mountain side like a cup for a little pool, so clear and bright it looked a diamond set in jet. A fringe of scanty herbage had collected about its brim, russet mosses, purple heath, and delicate white flowers, like a band of tiny hill-people keeping their revels by some fairy well. The spot attracted her, and, remembering that she was not to stray away, she sat down beside the path to wait for her husband's return.

In the act of bending over the pool to sprinkle the thirsty little company about it, her hand was arrested by the tramp of approaching feet, and, looking up to discover who was the disturber of her retreat, she saw a man pausing at the top of the path opposite to that by which she had come. He seemed scrutinizing the solitary occupant of the dell before descending; but as she turned her face to him he flung away knapsack, hat, and staff, and then with a great start she saw no stranger, but Adam Warwick. Coming down to her so joyfully, so impetuously, she had only time to recognize him, and cry out, when she was swept up in an embrace as tender as irresistible, and lay there conscious of nothing, but that happiness, like some strong swift angel, had wrapt her away into the promised land so long believed in, hungered for, and despaired of, as forever lost. Soon she heard his voice, breathless, eager, but so fond it seemed another voice than his.

"My darling! did you think I should never come?"

"I thought you had forgotten me. Adam, put me down."

But he only held her closer, and laughed such a happy laugh that Sylvia felt the truth before he uttered it.

"How could I forget you even if I had never come to tell you this? Sylvia, I know much that has passed. Geoffrey's failure gave me courage to hope for success, and that the mute betrothal made with a look so long ago had been to you all it has been to me."

"Adam, you are both right and wrong,—you do not know all,—let me tell you," began Sylvia, as these proofs of ignorance brought her to herself with a shock of recollection and dismay. But Warwick was as absolute in his happiness as he had been in his self-denial, and took possession of her mentally as well as physically with a despotism too welcome and entire to be at once resisted.

"You shall tell me nothing till I have shown the cause of my hard-seeming silence. I must throw off that burden first, then I will listen to you until morning if you will. I have earned this moment by a year of patience; let me keep you here and enjoy it without alloy."

The old charm had lost none of its power, for absence seemed to have gifted it with redoubled potency, the confirmation of that early hope to grace it with redoubled warmth. Sylvia let him keep her close beside him, feeling that he had earned that small reward for a year's endeavor, resolving to grant all now left her to bestow, a few moments more of blissful ignorance, then to show him his loss and comfort him, sure that her husband would find no disloyalty in a compassion scarcely less deep and self-forgetful than his own would have been had he shared their secret. Only pausing to put off her hat and turn her face to his, regarding it with such unfeigned and entire content that she forgot everything but the rapid words she listened to, the countenance she watched, so beautifully changed and softened that it seemed as if she had never seen or known the man before.

"The night we walked together by the river—such a wilful yet winning comrade as I had that day, and how I enjoyed it all!—that night I suspected that Geoffrey loved you, Sylvia, and was glad to think it. A month later I was sure of it, and found in that knowledge the great hardship of my life, because I loved you myself. Audacious thing! how dared you steal into my heart and take possession when I had barred the door to love? You never seemed a child to me, Sylvia, because you have an old soul in a young body, and your father's trials and temptations live again in you. This first attracted me. I liked to watch, to question, to study the human enigma to which I had found a clew from its maker's lips. I liked your candor and simplicity, your courage and caprice. Even your faults found favor in my eyes; for pride, will, impetuosity, were old friends of mine, and I liked to see them working in another shape. At first you were a curiosity, then an amusement, then a necessity. I wanted you, not occasionally, but constantly. You put salt and savor into life for me; for whether you spoke or were silent, were sweet or sour, friendly or cold, I was satisfied to feel your nearness, and always took away an inward content which nothing else could give me. This affection was so unlike what I had fancied love to be that I deceived myself for a time—not long. I soon knew what had befallen me, soon felt that this sentiment was good to feel, because I forgot my turbulent and worser self and felt the nobler regenerated by the innocent companionship you gave me. I wanted you, but it was not the touch of hands or lips, the soft encounter of eyes, the tones of tenderness, I wanted most. It was that something beyond my reach, vital and vestal, invisible, yet irresistible; that something, be it heart, soul, or mind, which drew me to you by an attraction genial and genuine as itself. My Sylvia, that was love, and when it came to me I took it in, sure that whether its fruition was granted or denied I should be a manlier man for having harbored it even for an hour. Why turn your face away? Well, hide it if you will, but listen, for I have much to say."

Still silent, Sylvia listened, as she would have done to one about to die.

"On that September evening, as I sat alone, I had been thinking of what might be and what must be. Had decided that I would go away for Geoffrey's sake. He was fitter than I to have you, being so gentle, and in all ways ready to possess a wife. I was so rough, such a vagrant, so full of my own purposes and plans, how could I dare to take into my keeping such a tender little creature as yourself? I thought you did not care for me; I knew any knowledge of my love would only mar his own; so it was best to go at once and leave him to the happiness he so well deserved. Just then you came to me, as if the wind had blown my desire to my arms. Such a loving touch that was! it nearly melted my resolve, and made it very hard not to take the one thing I wanted when it came to me so opportunely. You could not understand my trouble, and when I sat before you so still, perhaps looking grim and cold, you did not know how I was wrestling with my unruly self. I am not truly generous, for the relinquishment of any cherished object always costs a battle, and I too often find I am worsted. For the first time I dared not meet your eyes till you dived into mine with that expression wistful and guileless, which has often made me feel as if we stood divested of our bodies, soul to soul.

"Tongue I could control, heart I could not. Up it sprung, stronger than will, swifter than thought, and answered you. Sylvia, had there been one ray of self-consciousness in those steady eyes of yours, one atom of maiden shame, or fear, or trouble, I should have claimed you as my own. There was not; and though you let me read your face like an open book, you never dreamed what eloquence was in it. Innocent heart, that loved and had not learned to know it! I saw this instantly, saw that a few more such encounters would show it to you likewise, and felt more strongly than before that if ever the just deed to you, the generous one to Geoffrey, were done, it should be then. For that was the one moment when your half-awakened heart could fall painlessly asleep again, if I did not disturb it, and dream on till Geoffrey woke it, to find a gentler master than I could be to it."

"It could not, Adam; you had wholly roused it, and it cried for you so long, so bitterly, oh, why did you not come to answer it before?"

"How could I till I heard that Geoffrey had failed? He told me he should labor long and wait patiently till he won you, and I could not doubt that he would succeed. I went away singing the farewell I dared not speak, and for a year have kept myself hard at work. If ever labor of mine is blessed it will be that, for into it I put the heartiest endeavor of my life.

"So strong was my impulse to return to you that I put the sea between us, for I could not trust myself, and knew that Geoffrey would write me if he failed. He did; but, as if Providence meant to teach me patience, that one letter went astray and never reached me till two weeks ago."

"My fate!" sighed Sylvia bitterly.

"No, my fault. I should have written, but I feared to betray myself to Geoffrey. It is hard to hide my thoughts behind words. I knew he would discover me, and sacrifice himself. I meant he should be happy at all costs. I did write him before I was to leave on my long voyage; but the lost letter arrived, and, never waiting for his reply to mine, I came as fast as steam could bring me to find you and tell you this."

He bent to give her a tender welcome to eager heart and arms, but Sylvia arrested him.

"Not yet, Adam. Tell me all, and then I will answer you."

He thought it was some maidenly scruple, and though he smiled at it he respected it; for this coyness in the midst of all her whims had always been one of her charms to him.

"Shy thing! I shall tame you yet, and draw you to me as confidingly as I drew the little bird to hop into my hand and eat. You must not fear me, or I shall grow tyrannical; for I hate fear, and love to see people freely and bravely accept what belongs to them, as I do now to you."

"It is not you I fear, it is myself," murmured Sylvia, adding aloud, anxious yet dreading to have the story done. "What led you here, Adam, hoping so much, knowing so little?"

Warwick laughed as he shook the hair off his broad forehead, and looked down at her, with a look she dared not meet.

"Do I not always aim straight at the end I have in view and pursue it by the shortest roads, heedless of obstacles? I often fail and go back to the slower, surer way; but my own is always the one tried first as impetuously as I hurled myself down that path, more as if storming a battery than going to meet my sweetheart. Among the persons I met on landing was a friend of your father's: he was driving away in hot haste with his son; but, catching a glimpse of the familiar face, I bethought me that as it was the season for summer travel, you might be away, he would know, and time be saved. I asked one question, 'Where are the Yules?' He answered, as he vanished, 'The young people are all at the mountains.' That was enough, and, congratulating myself on the forethought which would save me some hundred miles of needless delay, away I went, and for days have been searching for you everywhere on that side of these hills which I know so well. But no Yules had passed, and, feeling sure you were on this side, I came, not around, but straight over, for this seemed a royal road to my love, and here I found her waiting for me by the way. Now, Sylvia, are your doubts all answered, your fears all laid, your heart at rest on mine?"

As the time drew nearer, Sylvia's task daunted her. Warwick was so confident, so glad and tender over her, it seemed like pronouncing the death doom to say those hard words, "It is too late." While she struggled to find some expression that should tell all kindly yet entirely, Adam, seeming to read some hint of her trouble, asked, with that new gentleness which now overlaid his former abruptness, and was the more alluring for the contrast,—

"Have I been too arrogant a lover? too sure of happiness, too blind to my small deserts? Sylvia, have I misunderstood the greeting you have given me?"

"Yes, Adam."

He knit his brows, his eyes grew anxious, his content seemed rudely broken, but still hopefully he said,—

"You mean that absence has changed you, that you do not love me as you did, and pity made you kind? Well, I receive the disappointment, but I do not relinquish my hope. What has been may be; let me try again to earn you; teach me to be humble, patient, all that I should be to make myself more dear to you. Something disturbs you; be frank with me. I have shown you all my heart; what have you to show me in return?"

"Only this."

She freed herself entirely from his hold and held up her hand before him. He did not see the ring; he thought she gave him all he asked, and with a glow of gratitude extended both his own to take it. Then she saw that delay was worse than weak, and though she trembled she spoke out bravely, ending his suspense at once,—

"Adam, I do *not* love you as I did, nor can I wish or try to bring it back, because—I am married."

He sprang up as if shot through the heart, nor could a veritable bullet from her hand have daunted him with a more intense dismay than those three words. An instant's incredulity, then conviction came to him, and he met it like a man; for though his face whitened and his eye burned with an expression that wrung her heart, he demanded steadily,—

"To whom, if not to Geoffrey?"

This was the hardest question of all, for well she knew the name would wound the deeper for its dearness, since he believed his friend had failed; and while it lingered pitifully upon her lips its owner answered for himself. Clear and sweet came up the music of the horn, bringing them a familiar air they all loved, and had often sung together. Warwick knew it instantly, felt the hard truth but rebelled against it, and put out his arm as if to ward it off as he exclaimed, with real anguish in countenance and voice,—

"Sylvia, it *is* he?"

"Yes!"

Then, as if all strength had gone out of her, she dropped down upon the mossy stone and covered up her face, feeling that the first sharpness of a pain like this was not for human eyes to witness. How many minutes passed she could not tell, the stillness of the spot remained unbroken by any sound but the whisper of the wind, and in this silence Sylvia found time to marvel at the calmness which came to her. Self had been forgotten in surprise and sympathy, and still her one thought was how to comfort Warwick. She had expected some outburst of feeling, some gust of anger or despair, but neither sigh nor sob, reproach nor regret, reached her, and soon she stole an anxious glance to see how it went with him. He was standing where she left him, both hands locked together till they were white with the passionate pressure. His eyes fixed on some distant object with a regard as imploring as unseeing, and through those windows of the soul he looked out darkly, not despairingly; but as if sure that somewhere there was help for him, and he waited for it with a stern patience more terrible to watch than the most tempestuous grief. Sylvia could not bear it, and, remembering that her confession had not yet been made, seized that instant for the purpose, prompted by an instinct which assured her that the knowledge of her pain would help him to bear his own.

She told him all, and ended, saying imploringly,—

"Adam, how can I comfort you?"

Sylvia was right; for through the sorrowful bewilderment that brought a brief eclipse of hope and courage, sympathy reached him like a friendly hand to uphold him till he found the light again. While speaking, she had seen the immobility that frightened her break up, and Warwick's whole face flush and quiver with the rush of emotions controllable no longer. But the demonstration which followed was one she had never thought to see from him, for when she stretched her hands to him with that remorseful cry, she saw the deep eyes fill, and overflow. Then he threw himself down before her, and for the first time in her short life showed her that sad type of human suffering, a man weeping like a woman.

Warwick was one of those whose passions, as his virtues, were in unison with the powerful body they inhabited, and in such a crisis as the present but one of two reliefs was possible to him,—either wrathful denunciation, expostulation, and despair, or the abandon of a child. Against the former he had been struggling dumbly till Sylvia's words had turned the tide; and, too entirely natural to feel a touch of shame at that which is not a weakness but a strength, too wise to reject so safe an outlet for so dangerous a grief, he yielded to it, letting the merciful magic of tears quench the fire, wash the first bitterness away, and leave reproaches only writ in water. It was better so, and Sylvia acknowledged it within herself as she sat mute and motionless, softly touching the brown head lying on the moss, her poor consolation silenced by the pathos of the sight, while through it all rose and fell the fitful echo of the horn, in very truth "a sweet reminder not to stray away and lose herself." An hour ago it would have been a welcome sound, for peak after peak gave back the strain, and airy voices whispered it until the faintest murmur died. But now she let it soar and sigh half heard, for audible to her alone still came its sad accompaniment of bitter human tears. To Warwick it was far more; for Music, the comforter, laid her balm on his sore heart as no mortal pity could have done, and wrought the miracle which changed the friend who seemed to have robbed him of his love to an unconscious Orpheus, who subdued the savage and harmonized the man. Soon he was himself again; for to those who harbor the strong virtues with patient zeal, no lasting ill can come, no affliction can wholly crush, no temptation wholly vanquish. He rose with eyes the clearer for their stormy rain, twice a man for having dared to be a child again; humbler and happier for the knowledge that neither vain resentment nor unjust accusation had defrauded of its dignity the heavy hour that left him desolate but not degraded.

"I *am* comforted, Sylvia, rest assured of that. And now there is little more to say, but one thing to do. I shall not see your husband yet, and leave you to tell him what seems best; for with the instinct of an animal, I always go away to outlive my hurts alone. But remember that I acquit you of blame, and believe that I can yet be happy in your happiness. I know if Geoffrey were here, he would let me do this, because he has suffered as I suffer now."

Bending, he gathered her to an embrace as different from that other as despair is from delight, and while he held her there, crowding into one short minute all the pain and passion of a year, she heard a low, but exceeding bitter cry,—"Oh, my Sylvia! it is hard to give you up." Then, with a solemn satisfaction, which assured her as it did himself, he spoke out clear and loud,—

"Thank God for the merciful Hereafter, in which we may retrieve the blunders we make here."

With that he left her, never turning till the burden so joyfully cast down had been resumed. Then, staff and hat in hand, he paused on the margin of that granite cup, to him a cup of sorrow, and looked into its depths again. Clouds were trooping eastward, but in that pause the sun glanced full on Warwick's figure, lifting his powerful head into a flood of light, as he waved his hand to Sylvia with a gesture of courage and good cheer. The look, the act, the memories they brought her, made her heart ache with a sharper pang than pity, and filled her eyes with tears of impotent regret, as she turned her head as if to chide the blithe clamor of the horn. When she looked again, the figure and the sunshine were both gone, leaving her alone and in the shadow.

Her husband found her sitting where he left her, but so pale it filled him with anxiety and self-reproach.

"My poor child, you are tired out, and this rarefied air is too much for you. We will go down at once and you shall rest."

"Yes, mountain-tops are too high for me; I am safer in the valley with you, Geoffrey," she answered, clinging to his arm as if quite spent with the fateful hour that waked her from a dream of forgetfulness.

CHAPTER XV

A Fireside Fête

"Welcome to your new home. May it be a happy one to you, little dearest!" said Moor, some days later, as he led her into the old Manse, now wearing its holiday air in honor of the coming of a mistress.

"It does not seem new but very dear and lovely, Geoffrey. I was always happy here, and hope to be so now, if you are," answered Sylvia, with a wistful look in the eyes that wandered to and fro as if seeking the peace she used to find in this tranquil place.

"No fear for me since you are here. Now will you rest a little or run about and view your new kingdom before you take possession?" asked Moor, eager to see her in the place he had so often pictured her as filling.

"Come and show me everything yourself. But, Geoffrey, please let all go on as before while I learn to be a housekeeper. Mrs. Best will like that, and Prue won't worry over my failures as she did at home when she tried to teach me her own thrifty ways. I had rather be with you, if I may, and not let the prose of married life disturb the poetry too soon. Do you mind?"

Charmed with the suggestion and glad to keep her to himself, Moor readily consented, and Sylvia began her new life so quietly that little seemed changed from the old, except the constant presence of the friend who still was more like a lover than a husband, and lived for her alone, knowing nothing of the inner world his young wife hid from him.

Of Warwick's confession she had never spoken, for it came too late to bring happiness to her, too soon to make it possible for her to cloud Moor's joy by telling it. She would be as brave as Adam, and silently live down importunate memories, dangerous thoughts, vain regrets; folding the leaf over the bitter past, trying to make the present what it should be, leaving the future to Heaven's will submissively.

The knowledge that she had not given that first love of hers unsought soothed her pride, comforted her heart, and made compassion for Adam seem a safe sentiment to cherish, since any softer one was now forbidden. She had suffered so much before that now regret had lost its sharpest sting, renunciation grown easier, and a sincere desire to be worthy the regard of both the men who loved her gave her a strength that for a time at least wore the semblance of content, if not happiness.

Max wondered at the quiet life she preferred, Prue thought her wise to leave the reins in Mrs. Best's accomplished hands, and her father hoped she was safely anchored in a peaceful harbor with a very tender pilot to guard her if storms came. It seemed a lovely home, and those who saw its proud master, its little mistress, fancied that their future was without a cloud, blessed as they were with all that makes this world a foretaste of Heaven.

But the high mood which sustained Sylvia's soul at first, as the pure mountain air braced her body, slowly lost its efficacy when the strain of daily life began to wear upon her nerves, and duty passed from willing effort to a constant struggle to forget. It was possible for days, and she would think she had won an enduring calm, when some trifle would bring the old pang, some truant thought would stray from her control, some involuntary wish startle her with a fear of disloyalty, and the battle was all to be fought over again.

Moor felt a subtle change in her, indescribable, yet visible, for she seemed to have left girlhood behind her with her honeymoon, and to be pausing on the threshold of womanhood, half fearing to cross it and assume the weightier duties, more sacred joys, and tenderer hopes that lay waiting for her beyond. He had been a faithful friend and a patient lover, now he was a generous and devoted husband, leaving time and tenderness to make her wholly his. He asked no questions, made no comments, demanded no sacrifices, but bore her moods as if he loved her in any guise she chose to wear, and never doubted that he should one day understand all that perplexed or troubled him now. So three months passed, and then Moor unconsciously marred his own peace by a vain effort to please Sylvia, whose growing ennui could not escape his anxious eyes.

"Just a year to-night since a hard-hearted little girl said she would not even try to love me. I thought she would change her mind, and this proves that I was right. Were you thinking of it also?" he asked, coming into the study one dull November evening to find Sylvia in the great chair gazing at the fire that glowed on the wide hearth.

She looked up and smiled, as she always did when he joined her.

"No; this splendid fire reminded me of another before which I once sat roasting corn and apples, and telling stories."

"Ah, that was our voyage up the river. You enjoyed that very much, I remember."

"Yes, I was a little girl then, and felt so free, so happy, it is impossible to forget it."

Sylvia spoke honestly, for she was always true when it was possible, as if the memory of one secret made her anxious to have no more.

"Dear child, you speak as if you had left youth far behind you and 'age had clawed you in its clutch,' " said Moor, leaning over the high chair-back to smooth the wavy gold of the beloved head that leaned there.

"I do feel very old sometimes. My responsibilities rather weigh upon me, and I want to drop them for an hour and be a little girl again. Just one of my moods; don't mind it, Geoffrey."

"Nothing shall burden you if I can help it. Drop these troublesome responsibilities now, and be a little girl again. I'll show you how."

Moor spoke so cheerfully, looked so well pleased at something, and seemed so ready to grant her wish that Sylvia sat up with an inquiring face, a lighter tone in her quiet voice.

"You are always ready to please me and I'm very grateful, dear. What shall we do? You look as if you had some nice little plan or surprise waiting to be told."

"I have; but my surprise comes to-morrow, and you can amuse yourself with guessing what it is till then. My plan now is to sit upon the rug and roast apples, pop corn, tell stories, and be young again. It is so rainy no one will come, unless Max happens in, and he will give us another comrade. I wish Adam were here, then we should have all the actors in that pretty little play of ours."

Sylvia did not echo the wish aloud, but as if to escape from thought by action, she sprang up eagerly, and Moor, fancying the plan pleased her well, threw himself heartily into it for her sake.

"That sweeping dress of yours and the crown of hair with which you try to make yourself look matronly will never do for the little girl. Run away and change yourself into the Sylvia you were that summer, then nothing will break the illusion. I'll put on my garden-jacket and look as much like the old Geoffrey as possible."

"Yes, do; I always like you so because you look like Shelley, with the round jacket, the fine forehead, and poetic eyes," said Sylvia, with the affectionate pride which pleased him, though he vaguely felt its lack of wifely warmth.

"I'll write you a poem in return for that compliment. Now I must set the stage and prepare for a fireside fête which shall prove that all the poetry is not gone from married life."

No lad could have spoken with a blither face, for Moor had preserved much of the boy in spite of his thirty years. His cheerfulness was so infectious, that Sylvia already began to forget her ennui, and hurried away to do her part. Putting on a short, girlish gown, kept for scrambles among the rocks, she braided her long hair, with butterfly bows at the ends, and improvised a pinafore. When she went down she found her husband in the garden-jacket, collar turned over a ribbon, hair in a curly tumble, and jackknife in hand, seated on the rug before a roaring fire and a semicircle of apples, whittling and whistling like a very boy. They examined one another with mirthful commendations, and Moor began his part by saying,—

"Isn't this jolly? Now come and sit beside me, and see which will keep it up the longest."

"What would Prue say? and who would recognize the elegant Mr. Moor in this big boy? Putting dignity and broadcloth aside makes you look about eighteen, and very charming I find you," said Sylvia, looking about twelve herself, and also very charming.

"Here is a wooden fork for you to tend the roast with, while I prepare a vegetable snowstorm. What will you have, little girl? You look as if you wanted something?"

"I was only thinking that I should have a doll to match your knife. I feel as if I should enjoy trotting a staring fright on my knee, and singing Hush-a-by. But I fancy even your magic cannot produce such a thing,—can it, my lad?"

"In exactly five minutes a lovely doll will appear, though such a thing has not been seen in my bachelor establishment for years."

With which mysterious announcement Moor ran off, blundering over the ottomans and slamming the doors as a true boy should. Sylvia pricked chestnuts, and began to forget her bosom trouble as she wondered what would come with the impatient curiosity appropriate to the character she had assumed. Presently her husband reappeared with a squirming bundle in his arms. Triumphantly unfolding a shawl, he displayed little Tilly in her nightgown.

"There is sorcery for you, and a doll worth having. Being one of the sort that can shut its eyes, it was going to bed, but its mamma relented and lends it to us for an hour. She is spending the night here, as her husband is away, so your wish could easily be granted. Here are some clothes, so you can dress your dolly to suit yourself or leave her as she is."

Sylvia received her pretty plaything with enthusiasm, and Tilly felt herself suddenly transported to a baby's Paradise, where beds were unknown and fruit and freedom were her welcome portion. Merrily popped the corn, nimbly danced the nuts upon the shovel, lustily remonstrated the rosy martyrs on the hearth, and cheerfully the minutes slipped away. Sylvia sang every jubilant air she knew, Moor whistled astonishing accompaniments, and Tilly danced over the carpet with nutshells on her toes, and tried to fill her little gown with "pitty flowers" from its garlands and bouquets. Without the wind lamented, the sky wept, and the sea thundered on the shore; but within, youth, innocence, and love held their blithe revel undisturbed.

"How are the spirits now?" asked one playmate of the other.

"Quite merry, thank you; and I should think I was little Sylvia again but for the sight of this."

She held up the hand that wore a single ornament; but the hand had grown so slender since it was first put on, that the ring would have fallen had she not caught it at her finger-tip. There was nothing of the boy in her companion's face, as he said, with an anxious look,—

"If you go on thinning so fast I shall begin to fear that the little wife is not happy with her old husband. Is she, dear?"

"She would be a most ungrateful woman if she were not. I always get thin as winter comes on; but I'm so careless I'll find a guard for my ring to-morrow."

"No need to wait till then; wear this to please me, and let Marion's cipher signify that you are *mine*."

With a gravity that touched her more than the bestowal of so dear a relic, Moor unslung a signet ring from his watchguard, and with some difficulty pressed it to its place on Sylvia's finger, a most effectual keeper for that other ring whose tenure seemed so slight. She shrunk a little and glanced up at him, because his touch was more firm than tender, and his face wore a masterful expression seldom seen there; for instinct, subtler than perception, prompted both act and aspect. Then her eye fell and fixed upon the dark stone with the single letter engraved upon its tiny oval, and to her it took a double significance as her husband held it there, claiming her again, with that emphatic "Mine." She did not speak, but something in her manner caused the fold between his brows to smooth itself away as he regarded the small hand lying passively in his, and said, half playfully, half earnestly,—

"Forgive me if I hurt you, but you know my wooing is not over yet; and till you love me with real love I cannot feel that my wife is wholly mine."

"Wait for me, Geoffrey, a little longer, for indeed I do my best to be all you would have me."

Something brought tears into her eyes and made her lips tremble, but in a breath the smile came back, and she added gayly,—

"How can I help being grave sometimes, and getting thin, with so many housekeeping cares upon my shoulders, and such an exacting, tyrannical husband to wear upon my nerves. Don't I look like the most miserable of wives?"

She certainly did not as she shook the popper laughingly, and looked over her shoulder at him, with the bloom of firelight on her cheeks, its cheerfulness in her eyes.

"Keep that expression for every-day wear, and I am satisfied. I want no tame Griselda, but the young girl who once said she was always happy with me. Assure me of that, and, having won my Leah, I can work and wait still longer for my Rachel. Bless the baby! what has she done to herself now?"

Tilly had retired behind the sofa, after she had swarmed over every chair and couch, examined everything within her reach, on *étagère* and table, embraced the Hebe in the corner, played a fantasia on the piano, and choked herself with the stopper of the odor bottle. A doleful wail betrayed her hiding-place, and she now emerged with a pair of nutcrackers, ditto of pinched fingers, and an expression of great mental and bodily distress. Her woes vanished instantaneously, however, when the feast was announced, and she performed an unsteady *pas seul* about the banquet, varied by darts at any unguarded viand that tempted her.

No ordinary table service would suit the holders of this fireside *fête.* The corn was heaped in a bronze urn, the nuts in a graceful basket, the apples lay on a plate of curiously ancient china, and the water turned to wine through the medium of a purple flagon of Bohemian glass. The refection was spread upon the rug as on a flowery table, and all the lustres were lighted, filling the room with a festal glow. Prue would have held up her hands in dismay, like the benighted piece of excellence she was, but Max would have enjoyed the picturesque group and sketched a mate to the Golden Wedding. For Moor, armed with the wooden fork, did the honors; Sylvia, leaning on her arm, dropped corn after corn into a baby mouth that birdlike always gaped for more; and Tilly lay luxuriously between them, warming her little feet as she ate and babbled to the flames.

The clock was on the stroke of eight, the revel at its height, when the door opened and a servant announced,—

"Miss Dane and Mr. Warwick."

An impressive pause followed, broken by a crow from Tilly, who seized this propitious moment to bury one hand in the nuts and with the other capture the big red apple which had been denied her. The sound seemed to dissipate the blank surprise that had fallen on all parties, and brought both host and hostess to their feet, the former exclaiming heartily,—

"Welcome, friends, to a modern saturnalia and the bosom of the Happy Family!"

"I know you did not expect us till to-morrow, but Mr. Warwick was impatient, I was a little anxious, and so we came on at once," said Miss Dane, looking about her as if the cheerful scene and faces were the reverse of what she expected to find.

Warwick also looked rather bewildered and very anxious. But Moor seemed quite satisfied with the effect of his surprise, for he had written to both simply saying that he wanted them at once.

"We are playing children to-night, so just put yourselves back a dozen years, and let us all be merry together. Sylvia, this is the cousin of whom I have told you so much. Faith, here is your new kinswoman, not as imposing as she would have been if you had not taken a base advantage of us. Little dearest, I invited these friends because I thought they would do us good. I wanted you to know Faith, and could not resist the desire to catch Adam before he set off to the North Pole, if he ever does."

A short stir ensued while hands were shaken, wraps put away, and some degree of order restored to the room, then they all sat down and began to talk. With well-bred oblivion of the short gown and long braids of her bashful-looking hostess, Miss Dane suggested and discussed various subjects of mutual interest, while Sylvia tried to keep her eyes from wandering to the mirror opposite, which reflected the figures of her husband and his friend.

Warwick sat erect in the easy-chair, for he never lounged; and Moor, still supporting his character, was perched upon the arm, talking with boyish vivacity. Every sense being unwontedly alert, Sylvia found herself listening to both guests at once, and bearing her own part in one conversation so well that occasional lapses were only attributed to natural embarrassment. What she and Miss Dane said she never remembered; what the other pair talked of she never forgot. The first words she caught were her husband's.

"You see I have begun to live for myself, Adam."

"I also see that it agrees with you excellently."

"Better than so much solitude does with you. What have you been at to get this gaunt, uncanny look, Adam?"

"Carrying on the old fight with the world, the flesh, and the devil, and getting the worst of it sometimes."

"Then it will be good for you to rest a little in a friend's house. You should not have waited to be asked. Remember that whatever changes come to me, my home is always yours."

"I know it, but I feared to disturb your happiness. Your brief note alarmed me, for I thought something must be amiss, and hurried to you at once."

"I thought that mysterious message would bring you. Peace reigns here, as you see, but I fancied Sylvia needed more society; she is hard to please, and I knew you and Faith would suit her. No need to tell how glad I am to see my two best friends under my roof."

"Was it wise to surprise her? Are you sure she will like it?" asked Warwick, with such unaccustomed doubt and hesitation that Moor laughed, and pulled a lock of the brown mane as if to tease the lion into a display of the self-confidence and composure he seemed to have lost.

"How shy you are of speaking the new name! 'She' will like it, I assure you, for she makes my friends hers. Sylvia, come here, and tell Adam he is welcome; he dares to doubt it. Come and talk over old times while I do the same with Faith."

She went, trembling inwardly, but outwardly composed, for she took refuge in one of those commonplace acts which in such moments we gladly perform, and bless in our secret souls. She had often wondered where they would next meet, and how she should comport herself at such a trying time. She had never imagined that he would come in this way, or that a hearth-brush would save her from the betrayal of emotion. So it was, however, and an involuntary smile passed over her face as she managed to say quite naturally, while brushing the nutshells tidily out of sight,—

"You know you are always welcome, Mr. Warwick. 'Adam's Room,' as we call it, is always ready, and Geoffrey was wishing for you only yesterday."

"I am sure of his satisfaction at my coming, can I be equally sure of yours? May I, ought I to stay?"

He leaned forward as he spoke, with an eager, yet submissive look, that Sylvia dared not meet, and in her anxiety to preserve her self-possession, she forgot that to this listener every uttered word became a truth, because his own were always so.

"Why not, if you can bear our quiet life, for we are a Darby and Joan already, though we do not look so to-night, I acknowledge."

Men seldom understand the subterfuges women instinctively use to conceal many a natural emotion which they are not strong enough to control, not brave enough to confess. To Warwick, Sylvia seemed almost careless, her words a light answer to the real meaning of his question, her smile one of tranquil welcome. Her manner wrought an instant change in him, and when he spoke again he was the Warwick of a year ago.

"I hesitated, Mrs. Moor, because I have sometimes heard young wives complain that their husbands' friends were marplots, and I have no desire to be one."

This speech, delivered with frosty gravity, made Sylvia as cool and quiet as itself. She put her ally down, looked full at Warwick, and said with a blending of dignity and cordiality which even the pinafore could not destroy,—

"Whatever pleases Geoffrey pleases me. Do not let my presence here make him inhospitable to old friends."

"Thanks; and now that the hearth is scrupulously clean may I offer you a chair?"

The old keenness was in his eye, the old firmness about the mouth, as Warwick presented the seat, with an inclination that to her seemed ironical. She sat down, but when she cast about her mind for some safe and easy topic to introduce, every idea had fled; even memory and fancy turned traitors; not a lively sally could be found, not a pleasant remembrance returned to help her, and she sat dumb. Before the dreadful pause grew awkward, however, rescue came in the form of Tilly. Nothing daunted by the severe simplicity of her little wrapper, she planted herself before Warwick, and, shaking her hair out of her eyes, stared at him with an inquiring glance and cheeks as red as her apple. She seemed satisfied in a moment, and climbing to his knee established herself there, coolly taking possession of his watch, and examining the brown beard curiously as it parted with the white flash of teeth, when Warwick smiled his warmest smile.

"This recalls the night you fed the sparrow in your hand. Do you remember, Adam?" and Sylvia looked and spoke like her old self again.

"I seldom forget anything. But pleasant as that hour was this is more to me, for the bird flew away, the baby stays and gives me what I need."

He wrapped the child closer in his arms, leaned his dark head on the bright one, and took the little feet into his hand with a fatherly look that caused Tilly to pat his cheek and begin an animated recital of some nursery legend, which ended in a sudden gape, reminding Sylvia that one of her guests was keeping late hours.

"What comes next?" asked Warwick.

"Now I lay me, and byelow in the trib," answered Tilly, stretching herself over his arm with a great yawn.

Warwick kissed the rosy half-open mouth, and seemed loath to part with the pious baby, for he took the shawl Sylvia brought and did up the drowsy bundle himself. While so busied she stole a furtive glance at him, having looked without seeing before. Thinner and browner, but as strong as ever was the familiar face she saw, yet neither sad nor stern, for the grave gentleness which had been a fugitive expression before now seemed habitual. This, with a slow dropping of the eyes, as if an inward life absorbed him more, were the only tokens of the sharp experience he had been passing through. Born for conflict and endurance, he seemed to have manfully accepted the sweet uses of adversity and grown the richer for his loss.

Those who themselves are quick to suffer are also quick to see the marks of suffering in others; that hasty scrutiny assured Sylvia of all she had yearned to know, yet wrung her heart with a pity the deeper for its impotence. Tilly's heavy head drooped between her bearer and the light as they left the room, but in the dusky hall a few hot tears fell on the baby's hair, and her new nurse lingered long after the lullaby was done. When she reappeared the girlish dress was gone, and she was Madam Moor again, as her husband called her when she assumed the stately air and trailing silks that failed to make a matron of her. All smiled at the change, but he alone spoke of it.

"I win the applause, Sylvia; for I sustain my character to the end, while you give up before the curtain falls. You are not so good an actress as I thought you."

Sylvia's smile was sadder than her tears as she briefly answered,—

"No; I find I cannot be a child again."

CHAPTER XVI

Early and Late

One of Sylvia's first acts when she rose was most significant. She shook down her abundant hair, carefully arranged a part in thick curls over cheeks and forehead, gathered the rest into its usual coil, and said to herself, as she surveyed her face half hidden in the shining cloud,—

"It looks very sentimental, and I hate the weakness that drives me to it, but it must be done, because my face is such a traitor. Poor Geoffrey! he said I was no actress; I am learning fast."

Why every faculty seemed sharpened, every object assumed an unwonted interest, and that quiet hour possessed an excitement that made her own room and countenance look strange to her, she would not ask herself, as she paused on the threshold of the door to ascertain if her guests were stirring. Nothing was heard but the sound of regular footfalls on the walk before the door, and with an expression of relief, she slowly went down. Moor was taking his morning walk bareheaded in the sun. Usually Sylvia ran to join him, but now she stood musing on the steps, until he saw and came to her. As he offered the flower always ready for her, he said smiling,—

"Did the play last night so captivate you that you go back to the curls because you cannot keep the braids?"

"A sillier whim than that, even. I am afraid of those two people; and as I am so quick to show my feelings in my face, I intend to hide behind this veil if I get shy or troubled. Did you think I could be so artful?"

"Your craft amazes me. But, dearest child, you need not be afraid of Faith and Adam. Both already love you for my sake, and soon will for your own. Both are so much older that they can easily overlook any little shortcoming, in consideration of your youth. Sylvia, I want to tell you something which will both amuse and interest you, I hope. Faith wrote me some time ago that she had met Adam, and found him all I had told her. He also sent me a message once, that he had discovered a superior woman, who sympathized in his ideas and purposes. I mentioned it at the time to you, I think? We so seldom hear from this nomadic fellow that news is an event."

"Yes, I remember."

Sylvia's head was bent as if to enjoy the sweetness of the flower she held, and all her husband saw was the bright hair blowing in the wind.

"Now you will laugh, for I confess that, being very happy myself, I took it into my head that these two fine creatures belonged to one another, and only needed a little gentle management to find it out. I wanted to see them together, so invited them here, knowing you would enjoy them, and hoping they would take a hint from us and go and do likewise."

"God forbid!" thought Sylvia. The pathetic unconsciousness of her husband filled her with new remorse, and made it impossible for her to wish Warwick the shadow of happiness which she vainly tried to change into its substance.

"I never thought you would turn match-maker, Geoffrey. Isn't it a dangerous part to play?" she asked, half wishing some insurmountable barrier might rise between her and the man whose presence always dominated her will and excited her heart.

"Not as I shall play it, and you can help. I fancy Adam already feels the hand of the great tamer, and that explains the new gentleness I see in him. I intend to study him and satisfy myself of this. You must say a good word for him to Faith, as you women so well know how to do. You like and believe in him; paint him in your vivid, happy way, and help her to know him. A mate like Faith is what he needs to perfect him, and we can show him this unless I am greatly mistaken."

"Perhaps for all his blindness Geoffrey is right; perhaps in this way I may atone for the pain I have given Adam. Heaven help me to do my duty and forget myself," thought Sylvia, feeling as if a new page in the tragic romance of her life was turned for her by the hand that tried to make it a tender, happy story for them all.

"I had best not meddle, Geoffrey, I am so ignorant, so unlucky. Let me see you play the good genius and not risk spoiling your work."

"I think you will soon be glad to lend a hand; most women find it impossible to abstain. I mean to make the week very pleasant to them both. Adam shall revisit his old haunts, and we will show Faith ours. In the evening we will have Prue, Max, and Jessie over here, or all go and entertain your father; so the days shall be busy and the nights cheerful with the sort of pleasure we all like best. Faith longs to know you, and I am sure she is the friend you need to fill a place I cannot fill."

A touch of regret made the last word a little sad, and Sylvia felt it like a keen reproach; but less now than ever could she tell the secret that would destroy her husband's peace and mar all his happy hopes for others. With an earnest longing to find Faith all he suggested, she answered with a look of satisfaction that gratified Moor more than her words,—

"I know that I shall love her; and if I need any one beside you, dear, she shall help me to be what I ought, to make you as happy as I wish you. Now let us speak of something else, or my telltale face will betray that we have been talking of our guests, when we meet them."

They did so, and as Warwick parted his curtains, the first sight he saw was his friend walking in the sunshine with the young wife who hung upon his arm as if she loved to lean there listening to his voice.

For a moment Adam's face was darkened by a shadow, then it passed, as he bravely accepted the seeming truth, and turned to join them, saying to himself,—

"Geoffrey is happy and she is learning to forget. I may venture to stay since I am here. I can trust myself, and perhaps give them some pleasure."

In pursuance of his plan Moor took Adam out for a long tramp soon after breakfast, and Sylvia devoted herself to Miss Dane. In the absence of the greater interest she enjoyed the lesser, soon felt at ease, and began to study her new relative.

Faith was thirty, shapely and tall, with much native dignity of carriage, and a face singularly attractive from its mild and earnest beauty. Looking at her one felt assured that here was a right womanly woman, gentle, just, and true; possessed of a well-balanced mind, a self-reliant soul, and that fine gift which is so rare, the power of a noble character to act as a touchstone to all who approached, forcing them to rise or fall to their true level, unconscious of the test applied. Her presence was comfortable, her voice had motherly tones in it, her eyes a helpful look. Even the soft hue of her dress, the brown gloss of her hair, the graceful industry of her hands, had their attractive influence. Sylvia saw and felt these things with the quickness of her susceptible temperament, and found herself so warmed and won, that soon it cost her an effort to withhold anything that tried or troubled her, for Faith was a born consoler, and Sylvia's heart was full.

However gloomy her day might have been, she always brightened in the evening as naturally as moths begin to flutter when candles come. On the evening of this day, the friendly atmosphere about her and the excitement of Warwick's presence so affected her, that though the gayety of girlhood was quite gone she looked as softly brilliant as some late flower that has gathered the summer to itself and gives it out again in the bloom and beauty of a single hour.

When tea was over (for heroes and heroines must eat if they are to do anything worth the paper on which their triumphs and tribulations are recorded), the women gathered about the library table, work in hand, as female tongues go easier when their fingers are occupied. Sylvia left Prue and Jessie to enjoy Faith, and while she fabricated some trifle with scarlet silk and an ivory shuttle, she listened to the conversation of the gentlemen who roved about the room till a remark of Prue's brought the party together.

"Helen Chesterfield has run away from her husband in the most disgraceful manner."

Max and Moor drew near, Adam leaned on the chimney-piece, the workers paused, and, having produced her sensation, Prue proceeded to gratify their curiosity as briefly as possible; for all knew the parties in question, and all waited anxiously to hear particulars.

"She married a Frenchman old enough to be her father, but very rich. She thought she loved him, but when she got tired of her fine establishment, and the novelties of Paris, she found she did not, and was miserable. Many of her new friends had lovers, so why should not she; and presently she began to amuse herself with this Louis Gustave Isadore Theodule de Trouville—there's a name for a Christian man! Well, she began in play, grew in earnest, and when she could bear her domestic trouble no longer she just ran away, ruining herself for this life, and really I don't know but for the next also."

"Poor soul! I always thought she was a fool, but upon my word I pity her," said Max.

"Remember she was very young, so far away from her mother, with no real friend to warn and help her, and love is so sweet. No wonder she went."

"Sylvia, how can you excuse her in that way? She should have done her duty whether she loved the old gentleman or not, and kept her troubles to herself in a proper manner. You young girls think so much of love, so little of moral obligations, decorum, and the opinions of the world, you are not fit judges of the case. Mr. Warwick agrees with me, I am sure."

"Not in the least."

"Do you mean to say that Helen should have left her husband?"

"Certainly, if she could not love him."

"Do you also mean to say that she did right to run off with that Gustave Isadore Theodule creature?"

"By no means. It is worse than folly to attempt the righting of one wrong by the commission of another."

"Then what in the world should she have done?"

"She should have honestly decided which she loved, have frankly told the husband the mistake both had made, and demanded her liberty. If the lover was worthy, have openly married him and borne the world's censures. If not worthy, have stood alone, an honest woman in God's eyes, whatever the blind world might have thought."

Prue was scandalized to the last degree; for with her marriage was more a law than a gospel,—a law which ordained that a pair once yoked should abide by their bargain, be it good or ill, and preserve the proprieties in public no matter how hot a hell their home might be for them and for their children.

"What a dreadful state society would be in if your ideas were adopted! People would constantly be finding out that they were mismatched, and go running about as if playing that game where every one changes places. I'd rather die at once than live to see such a state of things as that," said the worthy spinster.

"So would I, and recommend prevention rather than a dangerous cure."

"I really should like to hear your views, Mr. Warwick, for you quite take my breath away."

Much to Sylvia's surprise Adam appeared to like the subject, and placed his views at Prue's disposal with alacrity.

"I would begin at the beginning, and teach young people that marriage is not the only aim and end of life, yet would fit them for it as for a sacrament too high and holy to be profaned by a light word or thought. Show them how to be worthy of it and how to wait for it. Give them a law of life both cheerful and sustaining; a law that shall keep them hopeful if single, sure that here or hereafter they will find that other self and be accepted by it; happy if wedded, for their own integrity of heart will teach them to know the true god when he comes, and keep them loyal to the last."

"That is all very excellent and charming, but what are the poor souls to do who haven't been educated in this fine way?" asked Prue.

"Unhappy marriages are the tragedies of our day, and will be, till we learn that there are truer laws to be obeyed than those custom sanctions, other obstacles than inequalities of fortune, rank, and age. Because two persons love, it is not always safe or wise for them to marry, nor need it necessarily wreck their peace to live apart. Often what seems the best affection of our hearts does more for us by being thwarted than if granted its fulfilment and proved a failure which imbitters two lives instead of sweetening one."

He paused there; but Prue wanted a clearer answer, and turned to Faith, sure that the woman would take her own view of the matter.

"Which of us is right, Miss Dane, in Helen's case?"

"I cannot venture to judge the young lady, knowing so little of her character or the influences that have surrounded her, and believing that a certain divine example is best for us to follow at such times. I agree with Mr. Warwick, but not wholly, for his summary mode of adjustment would not be quite just nor right in all cases. If both find that they do not love, the sooner they part the wiser; if one alone makes the discovery, the case is sadder still, and harder for either to decide. But as I speak from observation only, my opinions are of little worth."

"Of great worth, Miss Dane; for to women like yourself observation often does the work of experience, and despite your modesty I wait to hear the opinions."

Warwick spoke, and spoke urgently, for the effect of all this upon Sylvia was too absorbing a study to be relinquished yet. As he turned to her, Faith gave him an intelligent glance, and answered like one speaking with intention and to some secret but serious issue,—

"You shall have them. Let us suppose that Helen was a woman possessed of a stronger character, a deeper nature; the husband a younger, nobler man; the lover truly excellent, and above even counselling the step this pair have taken. In a case like that the wife, having promised to guard another's happiness, should sincerely endeavor to do so, remembering that in making the joy of others we often find our own, and that having made so great a mistake the other should not bear all the loss. If there be a strong attachment on the husband's part, and he a man worthy of affection and respect, who has given himself confidingly, believing himself beloved by the woman he so loves, she should leave no effort unmade, no self-denial unexacted, till she has proved beyond all doubt that it is impossible to be a true wife. Then, and not till then, has she the right to dissolve the tie that has become a sin, because where no love lives inevitable suffering and sorrow enter in, falling not only upon guilty parents, but the innocent children who may be given them."

"And the lover, what of him?" asked Adam, still intent upon his purpose; for though he looked steadily at Faith, he knew that Sylvia drove the shuttle in and out with a desperate industry that made her silence significant to him.

"I would have the lover suffer and wait; sure that, however it may fare with him, he will be the richer and the better for having known the joy and pain of love."

"Thank you." And to Max's surprise Warwick bowed gravely, and Miss Dane resumed her work with a preoccupied air.

"Well, for a confirmed celibate, it strikes me you take a remarkable interest in matrimony," said Max. "Or is it merely a base desire to speculate upon the tribulations of your fellow-beings, and congratulate yourself upon your escape from them?"

"Neither; I not only pity and long to alleviate them, but have a strong desire to share them, for the wish of my life for the last year has been to marry."

Outspoken as Warwick was at all times and on all subjects, there was something in this avowal that touched those present, for with the words a quick rising light and warmth illuminated his whole countenance, and the energy of his desire tuned his voice to a key which caused one heart to beat fast, one pair of eyes to fill with sudden tears. Moor could not see his friend's face, but he saw Max's, divined the indiscreet inquiry hovering on his lips, and arrested it with a warning gesture.

Prue spoke first, very much disturbed by having her prejudices and opinions opposed, and very anxious to prove herself in the right.

"Max and Geoffrey look as if they agreed with Mr. Warwick in his—excuse me if I say, dangerous ideas; but I fancy the personal application of them would change their minds. Now, Max, just look at it; suppose some one of Jessie's lovers should discover an affinity for her, and she for him, what would you do?"

"Shoot him or myself, or all three, and make a neat little tragedy of it."

"There is no getting a serious answer from you, and I wonder I ever try. Geoffrey, I put the case to you; if Sylvia should find she adored Julian Haize, who fell ill when she was married, you know, and should inform you of that agreeable fact some fine day, should you think it quite reasonable and right to say, "Go, my dear; I'm very sorry, but it can't be helped."

The way in which Prue put the case made it impossible for her hearers not to laugh. But Sylvia held her breath while waiting for her husband's answer. He was standing behind her chair, and spoke with the smile still on his lips, too confident to harbor even a passing fancy.

"Perhaps I ought to be generous enough to do so, but not being a Jaques, with a convenient glacier to help me out of the predicament, I am afraid I should be hard to manage. I love but few, and those few are my world; so do not try me too hardly, Sylvia."

"I shall do my best, Geoffrey."

She dropped her shuttle as she spoke, and, stooping to pick it up, down swept the long curls over either cheek; thus, when she fell to work again, nothing of her face was visible but a glimpse of forehead, dark lashes, and faintly smiling mouth. Moor led the conversation to other topics, and was soon deep in an art discussion with Max and Miss Dane, while Prue and Jessie chatted away on that safe subject, dress. But Sylvia worked silently, and Warwick still leaned there, watching the busy hand as if he saw something more than a pretty contrast between the white fingers and the scarlet silk.

When the other guests had left, and Faith and himself had gone to their rooms, Warwick, bent on not passing another sleepless night, went down again to get a book. The library was still lighted, and standing there alone he saw Sylvia, wearing an expression that startled him. Both hands pushed back and held her hair away as if she scorned concealment from herself. Her eyes seemed fixed with a despairing glance on some invisible disturber of her peace. All the light and color that made her beautiful were gone, leaving her face worn and old, and the language of both countenance and attitude was that of one suddenly confronted with some hard fact, some heavy duty, that must be accepted and performed.

This revelation lasted but a moment. Moor's step came down the hall, the hair fell, the anguish passed, and nothing but a wan and weary face remained. But Warwick had seen it, and as he stole away unperceived he pressed his hands together, saying mournfully within himself, "I was mistaken. God help us all!"

CHAPTER XVII

In the Twilight

If Sylvia needed another trial, to make that hard week harder, it soon came to her in the knowledge that Warwick watched her. She well knew why, and vainly endeavored to conceal from him that which she had succeeded in concealing entirely from others. But he possessed the key to her variable moods; he alone knew that now painful forethought, not caprice, dictated many of her seeming whims, and ruled her simplest action. To others she appeared busy, gay, and full of interest in all about her; to him, the industry was a preventive of forbidden thoughts; the gayety, a daily endeavor to forget; the interest, an anxiety concerning the looks and words of her companions, because she must guard her own.

Sylvia felt something like terror in the presence of this penetrating eye, this daring will; for the vigilance was unflagging and unobtrusive, and with all her efforts she could not read his heart as she felt her own was being read. Adam could act no part, but, bent on learning the truth for the sake of all, he surmounted the dangers of the situation by no artifice, no rash indulgence, but by simply shunning solitary interviews with Sylvia as carefully as the courtesy due his hostess would allow. In walks and drives and general conversation, he bore his part, surprising and delighting those who knew him best by the genial change which seemed to have softened his rugged nature. But the instant the family group fell apart, and Moor's devotion to his cousin left Sylvia alone, Warwick was away into the wood or out upon the sea, lingering there till some meal, some appointed pleasure, or the evening lamp brought all together. Sylvia understood this, and loved him for it even while she longed to have it otherwise. But Moor reproached him for his desertion, doubly felt since the gentler acquirements made him dearer to his friend. Hating all disguises, Warwick found it hard to withhold the fact which was not his own to give, and, sparing no blame to himself, answered Moor's playful complaint with a sad sincerity that freed him from all further pleadings,—

"Geoffrey, I have a question to settle and you cannot help me. Leave it to time, and let me come and go as of old, enjoying the social hour when I can, flying to solitude when I must."

Much as Sylvia had longed to see these friends, she counted the hours of their stay; for the presence of one was a daily disquieting, because spirits would often flag, conversation fail, and an utter weariness creep over her when she could least account for or yield to it. More than once during that week she longed to lay her head on Faith's kind bosom and ask help. Deep as was her husband's love, it did not possess the soothing power of a woman's sympathy, and though is cradled her as tenderly as if she had been a child, Faith's compassion would have been like motherly arms to fold and foster. But friendly as they soon became, frank as was Faith's regard for Sylvia, earnest as was Sylvia's affection for Faith, she never seemed to reach that deeper place where she desired to be. Always when she thought she had found the innermost that each of us seek for in our friend, she felt that Faith drew back, and a reserve as delicate as inflexible barred her approach with chilly gentleness. This seemed so foreign to Faith's nature that Sylvia pondered and grieved over it till the belief came to her that this woman, so truly excellent and loveworthy, did not desire to receive her confidence, and sometimes a bitter fear assailed her that Warwick was not the only reader of her secret trouble.

All things have an end, and the last day came none too soon for one dweller under that hospitable roof. Faith refused all entreaties to stay, and looked somewhat anxiously at Warwick as Moor turned from herself to him with the same urgency.

"Adam, you will stay? Promise me another week?"

"I never promise, Geoffrey."

Believing that, as no denial came, his request was granted, Moor gave his whole attention to Faith, who was to leave them in an hour.

"Sylvia, while I help our cousin to select and fasten up the books she likes to take with her, will you fill your prettiest basket with flowers? Servants should not perform these pleasant services for one's best friends."

Glad to be away, Sylvia went into the conservatory, and was standing in a corner trimming her basket with ferns when Warwick's step approached. He did not see her, nor seem intent on following her; he walked slowly, hat in hand, so slowly that he was midway down the leafy lane when Faith's voice arrested him. She was in haste, as her hurried step and almost breathless words betrayed; and, losing not an instant, she said before they met,—

"Adam, you will come with me? I cannot leave you here."

"Do you doubt me, Faith?"

"No; but loving women are so weak."

"So strong, you mean; men are weakest when they love."

"Adam, *will* you come?"

"I will follow you; I shall speak with Geoffrey first."

"Must you tell him so soon?"

"I must."

Faith's hand had been on Warwick's arm; as he spoke the last words she looked up at him for an instant, then without another word turned and hurried back as rapidly as she had come, while Warwick stood where she left him, motionless as if buried in some absorbing thought.

All had passed in a moment, a moment too short, too full of intense surprise, to leave Sylvia time for recollection and betrayal of her presence. Half hidden and wholly unobserved, she had seen the unwonted agitation of Faith's countenance and manner, had heard Warwick's softly spoken answers to those eager appeals, and with a great pang had discovered that some tender confidence existed between these two of which she had never dreamed. Sudden as the discovery was its acceptance and belief; for, knowing her own weakness, Sylvia found something like relief in the hope that a new happiness for Warwick had ended all temptation, and in time all pain for herself. Impulsive as ever, she leaned upon the seeming truth, and, making of the fancy a fact, passed into a perfect passion of self-abnegation, thinking, in the brief pause that followed Faith's departure,—

"This is the change we see in him; this made him watch me, hoping I had forgotten, as I once said and believed. I should be glad, I will be glad, and let him see that even while I suffer I can rejoice in that which helps us both."

Full of her generous purpose, yet half doubtful how to execute it, Sylvia stepped from the recess where she had stood, and slowly passed toward Warwick, apparently intent on settling her flowery burden as she went. At the first sound of her light step on the walk he turned, feeling at once that she must have heard, and eager to learn what significance that short dialogue possessed for her. Only a hasty glance did she give him as she came, but it showed him flushed cheeks, excited eyes, and lips a little tremulous as they said,—

"These are for Faith; will you hold the basket while I cover it with leaves?"

He took it and as the first green covering was deftly laid, he asked, below his breath,

"Sylvia, did you hear us?"

To his unutterable amazement she looked up clearly, and all her heart was in her voice, as she answered with a fervency he could not doubt,—

"Yes; and I was glad to hear, to know that a nobler woman filled the place I cannot fill. Oh, believe it Adam! and be sure that the knowledge of your happiness will lighten the terrible regret which you have seen as nothing else ever could have done."

Down fell the basket at their feet, and, taking her face between his hands, Warwick bent and searched with a glance that seemed to penetrate to her heart's core. For a moment she struggled to escape, but the grasp that held her was immovable. She tried to oppose a steadfast front and baffle that perilous inspection, but quick and deep rushed the traitorous color over cheek and forehead with its mute betrayal. She tried to turn her eyes away, but those other eyes, dark and dilated with intensity of purpose, fixed her own, and the confronting countenance wore an expression which made its familiar features look awfully large and grand to her panic-stricken sight. A sense of utter helplessness fell on her, courage deserted her, pride changed to fear, defiance to despair; as the flush faded, the fugitive glance was arrested and the upturned face became a pale blank, ready to receive the answer that strong scrutiny was slowly bringing to the light, as invisible characters start out upon a page when fire passes over them. Neither spoke, but soon through all opposing barriers the magnetism of an indomitable will drew forth the truth, set free the captive passion pent so long, and wrung from those reluctant lineaments a full confession of his power and her weakness.

The instant this assurance was his own beyond a doubt, Warwick released her, snatched up his hat, and, hurrying down the path, vanished in the wood. Spent as with an hour's excitement, and bewildered by emotions which she could no longer master, Sylvia lingered in the fern-walk till her husband called her. Then, hastily refilling her basket, she shook her hair about her face and went to bid Faith good-by. Moor was to accompany her to the city, and they left early, that Faith might pause for adieux to Max and Prudence.

"Where is Adam? Has he gone before, or been inveigled into staying?"

Moor spoke to Sylvia; but, busied in fastening the basket-lid, she seemed not to hear, and Faith replied for her,—

"He will take a later boat, we need not wait for him."

When Faith embraced Sylvia, all the coldness had melted from her manner, and her voice was tender as a mother's as she whispered low in her ear,—

"Dear child, if ever you need any help that Geoffrey cannot give, remember Cousin Faith."

For two hours Sylvia sat alone, not idle, for in the first real solitude she had enjoyed for seven days, she looked deeply into herself, and putting by all disguises owned the truth, and resolved to repair the past if possible, as Faith had counselled in the case which she had now made her own. Like so many of us, Sylvia often saw her errors too late to avoid committing them, and, failing to do the right thing at the right moment, kept herself forever in arrears with that creditor who must inevitably be satisfied. She had been coming to this decision all that weary week, and these quiet hours left her both resolute and resigned.

As she sat there while the early twilight began to gather, her eye often turned to Warwick's travelling-bag, which Faith, having espied it ready in his chamber, had brought down and laid in the library, as a reminder of her wish. As she looked at it, Sylvia's heart yearned toward it in the fond, foolish way which women have of endowing the possessions of those they love with the attractions of sentient things, and a portion of their owner's character or claim upon themselves. It was like Warwick, simple and strong, no key, and every mark of the long use which had tested its capabilities and proved them durable. A pair of gloves lay beside it on the chair, and though she longed to touch anything of his, she resisted the temptation till, pausing near them in one of her journeys to the window, she saw a rent in the glove that lay uppermost,—that appeal was irresistible,—"Poor Adam! there has been no one to care for him so long, and Faith does not yet know how; surely I may perform so small a service for him if he never knows how tenderly I do it?"

Standing ready to drop her work at a sound, Sylvia snatched a brief satisfaction which solaced her more than an hour of idle lamentation, and as she put down the glove with eyes that dimly saw where it should be, perhaps there went as much real love and sorrow into that little act as ever glorified some greater deed. Then she went to lie in the "Refuge," as she had named the ancient chair, with her head on its embracing arm. Not weeping, but quietly watching the flicker of the fire, which filled the room with warm duskiness, making the twilight doubly pleasant, till a sudden blaze leaped up, showing her that her watch was over, and Warwick come. She had not heard him enter, but there he was, close before her, his face glowing with the frosty air, his eye clear and kind, and in his aspect that nameless charm which won for him the confidence of whosoever read his countenance. Scarce knowing why, Sylvia felt reassured that all was well, and looked up with more welcome in her heart than she dared betray in words.

"Come at last! where have you been so long, Adam?"

"Round the Island, I suspect, for I lost my way, and had no guide but instinct to lead me home again. I like to say that word, for though it is not home it seems so to me now. May I sit here before I go, and warm myself at your fire, Sylvia?"

Sure of his answer he established himself in the low lounging-chair beside her, stretched his hands to the grateful blaze, and went on with some inward resolution lending its power and depth to his voice.

"I had a question to settle with myself and went to find my best counsellors in the wood. Often when I am harassed by some perplexity or doubt to which I can find no wise or welcome answer, I walk myself into a belief that it will come; then it appears. I stoop to break a handsome flower, to pick up a cone, or watch some little creature happier than I, and there lies my answer, like a good luck penny, ready to my hand."

"Faith has gone, but Geoffrey hopes to keep you for another week," said Sylvia, ignoring one unsafe topic for another.

"Shall he have his wish?"

"Faith expects you to follow her."

"And you think I ought?"

"I think you will."

"When does the next boat leave?"

"An hour hence."

"I'll wait for it here. Did I wake you coming in?"

"I was not asleep; only lazy, warm, and quiet."

"And deadly tired;—dear soul, how can it be otherwise, leading the life you lead!"

There was such compassion in his voice, such affection in his eye, such fostering kindliness in the touch of the hand he aid upon her own, that Sylvia cried within herself, "Oh, if Geoffrey would only come!" and, hoping for that help to save her from herself, she hastily replied,—

"You are mistaken, Adam,—my life is easier than I deserve,—I am very—"

"Miserable,—the truth to me, Sylvia."

Warwick rose as he spoke, closed the door, and came back wearing an expression which caused her to start up with a gesture of entreaty,—

"No, no, I will not hear you! Adam, you must not speak!"

He paused opposite her, leaving a little space between them, which he did not cross through all that followed, and with that look, inflexible yet pitiful, he answered steadily,—

"I *must* speak and you *will* hear me. But understand me, Sylvia, I desire and design no French sentiment nor sin like that we heard of, and what I say now I would say if Geoffrey stood between us. I ask nothing for myself. I have settled this point after long thought and the heartiest prayers I ever prayed; but you have much at stake and I speak for your sake, not my own. Therefore do not entreat nor delay, but listen and let me show you the wrong you are doing yourself, your husband, and your friend."

"Does Faith know all the past? does she desire you to do this that her happiness may be secure?" demanded Sylvia.

"Faith is no more to me, nor I to Faith, than the friendliest regard can make us. She suspected that I loved you long ago; she now believes that you love me; she pities her cousin tenderly, but will not meddle with the tangle we have made of our three lives. But I believe that secrets kill, the truth alone can save and heal; so let me speak. When we parted I thought that you loved Geoffrey; so did you. When I came here I was sure of it for a day; but on that second night I saw your face as you stood here alone, and then I knew what I have since assured myself of. God knows, I think my gain dearly purchased by his loss. I see your double trial; I know the tribulations in store for all of us; yet as an honest man, I must speak out, because you ought not to delude yourself or Geoffrey another day."

"What right have you to come between us and decide my duty, Adam?" Sylvia spoke passionately, roused to resistance by his manner and the turmoil of emotions warring within her.

"The right of a sane man to save the woman he loves from destroying her own peace forever, and undermining the confidence of the friend dearest to them both. I know this is not the world's way in such matters; but I care not; because I believe one human creature has a right to speak to another in times like these, as if they two stood alone. I will not command, I will appeal to you, and if you are the candid soul I think you, your own words shall prove the truth of what I say. Sylvia, do you love your husband?"

"Yes, Adam, dearly."

"More than you love me?"

"I wish I did! I wish I did!"

"Are you happy with him?"

"I was till you came; I shall be when you are gone."

"It is impossible to go back to the blind tranquillity you once enjoyed. Now a single duty lies before you; delay is weak, deceit is wicked; utter sincerity alone can help us. Tell Geoffrey all; then whether you live your life alone, or stay with him, there is no false dealing to repent of, and looking the hard fact in the face robs it of one half its terrors. Will you do this, Sylvia?"

"No, Adam. Remember what he said that night: 'I love but few, and those few are my world,'—I am chief in that world; shall I destroy it, for my selfish pleasure? He waited for me very long, is waiting still; can I for a second time disappoint the patient heart that would find it easier to give up life than the poor possession which I am? No, I ought not, dare not do it yet."

"If you dare not speak the truth to your friend, you do not deserve him, and the name is a lie. You ask me to remember what he said that night,—I ask you to recall the look with which he begged you not to try him too hardly. Put it to yourself,—which is the kinder justice, a full confession now, or a late one hereafter, when longer subterfuge has made it harder for you to offer, bitterer for him to receive? I tell you, Sylvia, it were more merciful to murder him outright than to slowly wear away his faith, his peace, and love by a vain endeavor to perform as a duty what should be your sweetest pleasure, and what will soon become a burden heavier than you can bear."

"You do not see as I see; you cannot understand what I am to him, nor can I tell you what he is to me. It is not as if I could dislike or despise him for any unworthiness of his own; nor as if he were a lover only. Then I could do much which now is worse than impossible, for I have married him, and it is too late."

"O Sylvia! why could you not have waited?"

"Why? Because I am what I am, too easily led by circumstances, too entirely possessed by whatever hope, belief, or fear rules me for the hour. Give me a steadfast nature like your own and I will be as strong. I know I am weak, but I am not wilfully wicked; and when I ask you to be silent, it is because I want to save him from the pain of doubt, and try to teach myself to love him as I should. I must have time, but I can bear much and endeavor more persistently than you believe. If I forgot you once, can I not again? and should I not? I am all in all to him, while you, so strong, so self-reliant, can do without my love as you have done till now, and will soon outlive your sorrow for the loss of that which might have made us happy had I been more patient."

"Yes, I shall outlive it, else I should have little faith in myself. But I shall not forget; and if you would remain forever what you now are to me, you will so act that nothing may mar this memory, since it can be no more. I doubt your power to forget an affection which has survived so many changes and withstood assaults such as Geoffrey must unconsciously have made upon it. But I have no right to condemn your beliefs, to order your actions, or force you to accept my code of morals if you are not ready for it. You must decide, but do not again deceive yourself, and through whatever comes, hold fast to that which is better worth preserving than husband, happiness, or friend,—truth."

His words fell cold on Sylvia's ear, for with the inconsistency of a woman's heart she thought he gave her up too readily, yet honored him more truly for sacrificing both himself and her to the principle that ruled his life and made him what he was. His seeming resignation steadied her, for now he waited her decision, while before he was only bent on executing the purpose wherein he believed salvation lay. She girded up her strength, collected her thoughts, and tried to show him what she believed to be her duty.

"Let me tell you how it is with me, Adam, and be patient if I am not wise and brave like you, but far too young, too ignorant, to bear such troubles well. I am not leaning on my own judgment now, but on Faith's, and though you do not love her as I hoped, you feel she is one to trust. She said the wife, in that fictitious case which was so real to us,—the wife should leave no effort unmade, no self-denial unexacted, till she had fairly proved that she could not be what she had promised. Then, and then only, had she a right to undo the tie that had bound her. I must do this before I think of your love or my own, for on my marriage morning I made a vow within myself that Geoffrey's happiness should be the first duty of my life. I shall keep that vow as sacredly as I will those I made before the world, until I find that it is utterly beyond my power, then I will break all together."

"You have tried that once, and failed."

"No, I have never tried it as I shall now. At first, I did not know the truth, then I was afraid to believe, and struggled blindly to forget. Now I see clearly, I confess it, I resolve to conquer it, and I will not yield until I have done my best. You say you must respect me. Could you do so if I no longer respected myself? I should not, if I forgot all Geoffrey had borne and done for me, and could not bear and do this thing for him. I must make the effort, and make it silently; for he is very proud with all his gentleness, and would reject the seeming sacrifice though he would make one doubly hard for love of me. If I am to stay with him, it spares him the bitterest pain he could suffer; if I am to go, it gives him a few more months of happiness, and I may so prepare him that the parting will be less hard. How others would act I cannot tell, I only know that this seems right to me; and I must fight my fight alone, even if I die in doing it."

She was so earnest, yet so humble; so weak in all but the desire to do well; so young to be tormented with such fateful issues, and withal so steadfast in the grateful yet remorseful tenderness she bore her husband, that though sorely disappointed and not one whit convinced, Warwick could only submit to this woman-hearted child, and love her with redoubled love, both for what she was and what she aspired to be.

"Sylvia, what can I do to help you?"

"You must go away, Adam; because when you are near me my will is swayed by yours, and what you desire I long to do. Go quite away, and through Faith you may learn whether I succeed or fail. It is hard to say this, yet you know it is a truer hospitality in me to send you from my door than to detain and offer you temptation for your daily bread."

It was hard to submit; for though he asked nothing for himself, he longed intensely to share in some way the burden that he could not lighten.

"Ah, Sylvia! I thought that parting on the mountain was the hardest I could ever know, but this is harder; for now I know I have but to say Come to me! and you would come."

But the bitter moment had its drop of honey, whose sweetness nourished him when all else failed. Sylvia answered with a perfect confidence in that integrity which even her own longing could not bribe,—

"Yes, Adam, but you will *not* say it, because, feeling as I feel, you know I must not come to you."

He did know it, and confessed his submission by folding fast the arms half opened for her, and standing dumb with the words trembling on his lips. It was the bravest action of a life full of real valor, for the sacrifice was not made with more than human fortitude. The man's heart clamored for its right, patience was weary, hope despaired, and all natural instincts mutinied against the command that bound them. But no grain of virtue ever falls wasted to the ground; it drops back upon its giver a regathered strength, and cannot fail of its reward in some kindred soul's approval, imitation, or delight. It was so then, as Sylvia went to him; for though she did not touch nor smile upon him, he felt her nearness; and the parting assured him that its power bound them closer than the happiest union. In her face there shone a look half fervent, half devout, and her voice had no falter in it now.

"You show me what I should be. All my life I have desired strength of heart and stability of soul; may I not hope to earn for myself a little of the integrity I love in you? If courage, self-denial, and self-help make you what you are, can I have a more effectual guide? You say you shall outlive this passion; why should not I imitate your brave example, and find the consolations you shall find? O Adam, let me try."

"You shall."

"Then go; go now, while I can say it as I should."

"The good Lord bless and help you, Sylvia."

She gave him both her hands, but though he only pressed them silently, that pressure nearly destroyed the victory she had won; for the strong grasp snapped the slender guard-ring Moor had given her a week ago. She heard it drop with a golden tinkle on the hearth, saw the dark oval, with its doubly significant character, roll into the ashes, and felt Warwick's hold tighten as if he echoed the emphatic word uttered when the ineffectual gift was first bestowed. Superstition flowed in Sylvia's blood, and was as unconquerable as the imagination which supplied its food. This omen startled her. It seemed a forewarning that endeavor would be vain, that submission was wisdom, and that the husband's charm had lost its virtue when the stronger power claimed her. The desire to resist began to waver as the old passionate longing sprang up more eloquent than ever; she felt the rush of a coming impulse, knew that it would sweep her into Warwick's arms, there to forget her duty, to forfeit his respect. With the last effort of a sorely tried spirit she tore her hands away, fled up to the room which had never needed lock or key till now, and stifling the sound of those departing steps among the cushions of the couch where she had already hidden many tears, she struggled with the great sorrow of her too early womanhood, uttering with broken voice that petition oftenest quoted from the one prayer which expresses all our needs,—

"Lead me not into temptation, but deliver me from evil."

CHAPTER XVIII

Asleep and Awake

March winds were howling round the house, the clock was striking two, the library lamp still burned, and Moor sat writing with an anxious face. Occasionally he paused to look backward through the leaves of the book in which he wrote; sometimes he sat with suspended pen, thinking deeply; and once or twice he laid it down, to press his hand over eyes more weary than the mind that compelled them to this late service.

Returning to his work after one of these pauses, he was a little startled to see Sylvia standing on the threshold of the door. Rising hastily to ask if she were ill, he stopped half-way across the room, for, with a thrill of apprehension and surprise, he saw that she was asleep. Her eyes were open, fixed, and vacant, her face reposeful, her breathing regular, and every sense apparently wrapped in the profoundest unconsciousness. Fearful of awakening her too suddenly, Moor stood motionless, yet full of interest, for this was his first experience of somnambulism, and it was a strange, almost an awful sight, to witness the blind obedience of the body to the soul that ruled it.

For several minutes she remained where she first appeared. Then, as if the dream demanded action, she stooped, and seemed to take some object from a chair beside the door, held it an instant, kissed it softly and laid it down. Slowly and steadily she went across the room, avoiding all obstacles with the unerring instinct that often leads the sleep-walker through dangers that appall his waking eyes, and sat down in the great chair he had left, leaned her cheek upon its arm, and rested tranquilly for several minutes. Soon the dream disturbed her, and, lifting her head, she bent forward, as if addressing or caressing some one seated at her feet. Involuntarily her husband smiled; for often when they were alone he sat there reading or talking to her, while she played with his hair, likening its brown abundance to young Shelley's curling locks in the picture overhead. The smile had hardly risen when it was scared away; for Sylvia suddenly sprang up with both hands out, crying in a voice that rent the silence with its imploring energy,—

"No, no, you must not speak! I will not hear you!"

Her own cry woke her. Consciousness and memory returned together, and her face whitened with a look of terror, as her bewildered eyes showed her not Warwick, but her husband. This look, so full of fear, yet so intelligent, startled Moor more than the apparition or the cry had done, for a conviction flashed into his mind that some unsuspected trouble had been burdening Sylvia, and was now finding vent against her will. Anxious to possess himself of the truth, and bent on doing so, he veiled his purpose for a time, letting his unchanged manner reassure and compose her.

"Dear child, don't look so lost and wild. You are quite safe, and have only been wandering in your sleep. Why, Lady Macbeth, have you murdered some one, that you go crying out in this uncanny way, frightening me as much as I seem to have frightened you?"

"I have murdered sleep. What did I do? what did I say?" she asked, trembling and shrinking as she dropped into her chair.

Hoping to quiet her, he took his place on the low seat, and told her what had passed. At first, she listened with a divided mind, for so strongly was she still impressed with the vividness of the dream, she half expected Warwick to rise like Banquo, and claim the seat that a single occupancy seemed to have made his own. An expression of intense relief replaced that of fear, when she had heard all, and she composed herself with the knowledge that her secret was still hers. For, dreary bosom-guest as it was, she had not yet resolved to end her trial.

"What set you walking, Sylvia?"

"I recollect hearing the clock strike one, and thinking I would come down to see what you were doing so late, but must have dropped off and carried out my design asleep. You see I put on wrapper and slippers as I always do when I take nocturnal rambles awake. How pleasant the fire feels, and how cosey you look here; no wonder you like to stay and enjoy it."

She leaned forward, warming her hands in unconscious imitation of Adam, on the night which she had been recalling before she slept. Moor watched her with increasing disquiet; for never had he seen her in a mood like this. She evaded his question, she averted her eyes, she half hid her face, and with a gesture that of late had grown habitual, seemed to try to hide her heart. Often had she baffled him, sometimes grieved him, but never before showed that she feared him. This wounded both his love and pride, and this fixed his resolution to wring from her an explanation of the changes which had passed over her during those winter months, for they had been many and mysterious. As if she feared silence, Sylvia soon spoke again.

"Why are you up so late? This is not the first time I have seen your lamp burning when I woke. What are you studying so deeply?"

"My wife."

Leaning on the arm of her chair, he looked up wistfully, tenderly, as if inviting confidence, suing for affection. The words, the look, smote Sylvia to the heart, and but for the thought, "I have not tried long enough," she would have uttered the confession that leaped to her lips. Once spoken, it would be too late for secret effort or success, and this man's happiest hopes would vanish in a breath. Knowing that his nature was almost as sensitively fastidious as a woman's, she also knew that the discovery of her love for Adam, innocent as it had been, self-denying as it tried to be, would mar the beauty of his wedded life for Moor. No hour of it would seem sacred, no act, look, or word of hers entirely his own, nor any of the dear delights of home remain undarkened by the shadow of his friend. She could not speak yet, and, turning her eyes to the fire, she asked,—

"Why study me? Have you no better book?"

"None that I love to read so well or have such need to understand; because, though nearest and dearest as you are to me, I seem to know you less than any friend I have. I do not wish to wound you, dear, nor be exacting; but since we were married you have grown more shy than ever, and the act which should have drawn us tenderly together seems to have estranged us. You never talk now of yourself, or ask me to explain the working of that busy mind of yours; and lately you have sometimes shunned me, as if solitude were pleasanter than my society. Is it, Sylvia?"

"Sometimes; I always liked to be alone, you know."

She answered as truly as she could, feeling that his love demanded every confidence but the one cruel one which would destroy its peace past help.

"I knew I had a most tenacious heart, but I hoped it was not a selfish one," he sorrowfully said. "Now I see that it is, and deeply regret that my hopeful spirit, my impatient love, has brought disappointment to us both. I should have waited longer, should have been less confident of my own power to win you, and never let you waste your life in vain endeavors to be happy when I was not all to you that you expected. I should not have consented to your wish to spend the winter here so much alone with me. I should have known that such a quiet home and studious companion could not have many charms for a young girl like you. Forgive me, I will do better, and this one-sided life of ours shall be changed; for while I have been happy you have been miserable."

It was impossible to deny it, and with a tearless sob she laid her arm about his neck, her head on his shoulder, and mutely confessed the truth of what he said. The trouble deepened in his face, but he spoke out more cheerfully, believing that he had found the secret sorrow.

"Thank heaven, nothing is past mending; and we will yet be happy. An entire change shall be made; you shall no longer devote yourself to me, but I to you. Will you go abroad, and forget this dismal home until its rest grows inviting, Sylvia?"

"No, Geoffrey, not yet. I will learn to make the home pleasant, I will work harder, and leave no time for ennui and discontent. I promised to make your happiness, and I can do it better here than anywhere. Let me try again."

"No, Sylvia, you work too hard already; you do everything with such vehemence you wear out your body before your will is weary, and that brings melancholy. I am very credulous, but when I see that acts belie words I cease to believe. These months assure me that you are not happy; have I found the secret thorn that frets you?"

She did not answer, for truth she could not, and falsehood she would not, give him. He rose, went walking to and fro, searching memory, heart, and conscience for any other cause, but found none, and saw only one way out of his bewilderment. He drew a chair before her, sat down, and, looking at her with the masterful expression dominant in his face, asked briefly,—

"Sylvia, have I been tyrannical, unjust, unkind, since you came to me?"

"O Geoffrey, too generous, too just, too tender!"

"Have I claimed any rights but those you gave me? entreated or demanded any sacrifices knowingly and wilfully?"

"Never."

"Now I do claim my right to know your heart; I do entreat and demand one thing, your confidence."

Then she felt that the hour had come, and tried to prepare to meet it as she should by remembering that she had endeavored prayerfully, desperately, despairingly, to do her duty, and had failed. Warwick was right, she could not forget him. There was such vitality in the man and in the sentiment he inspired, that it endowed his memory with a power more potent than the visible presence of her husband. The knowledge of his love now undid the work that ignorance had helped patience and pride to achieve before. Once she had held the secret, now it held her; the hidden wound was poisoning her life, and tempting her to escape by thoughts of death. Now she saw the wisdom of Adam's warning, and felt that he knew both his friend's heart and her own better than herself. Now she bitterly regretted that she had not spoken out when he was there to help her, and before the least deceit had taken the dignity from sorrow. Nevertheless, though she trembled she resolved; and while Moor spoke on, she made ready to atone for past silence by a perfect loyalty to truth.

"My wife, concealment is not generosity, for the heaviest trouble shared together could not so take the sweetness from my life, the charm from home, or make me more miserable than this want of confidence. It is a double wrong, because you not only mar my peace but destroy your own by wasting health and happiness in vain endeavors to bear some grief alone. Your eye seldom meets mine now, your words are measured, your actions cautious, your innocent gayety all gone. You hide your heart from me, you hide your face; I seem to have lost the frank girl whom I loved, and found a melancholy woman, who suffers silently till her honest nature rebels, and brings her to confession in her sleep. There is no page of my life which I have not freely shown you; do I not deserve an equal candor? Shall I not receive it?"

"Yes!"

"Sylvia, what stands between us?"

"Adam Warwick."

Earnest as a prayer, brief as a command, had been the question; instantaneous was the reply, as Sylvia knelt down before him, put back the veil that should never hide her from him any more, looked up into her husband's face without one shadow in her own, and steadily told all.

The revelation was too utterly unexpected, too difficult of belief, to be at once accepted or understood. Moor started at the name, then leaned forward, breathless and intent, as if to seize the words before they left her lips; words that recalled incidents and acts dark and unmeaning till the spark of intelligence fired a long train of memories and enlightened him with terrible rapidity. Blinded by his own devotion and the knowledge of Adam's character, the thought that he loved Sylvia never had occurred to him, and seemed incredible even when her own lips told it. She had been right in fearing the effect this knowledge would have upon him. It stung his pride, wounded his heart, and for a time at least marred his faith in love and friendship. As the truth broke over him, cold and bitter as a billow of the sea, she saw gathering in his face the still white grief and indignation of an outraged spirit, suffering with all a woman's pain, with all a man's intensity of passion. His eye grew fiery and stern, the veins rose dark upon his forehead, the lines about the mouth showed hard and grim, the whole face altered terribly. As she looked, Sylvia thanked heaven that Warwick was not there to feel the sudden atonement for an innocent offence which his friend might have exacted before this natural temptation had passed by.

"Now I have given all my confidence, though I may have broken both our hearts in doing it. I do not hope for pardon yet, but I am sure of pity, and I leave my fate in your hands. Geoffrey, what shall I do?"

"Wait for me." And, putting her away, Moor left the room.

Suffering too much in mind to remember that she had a body, Sylvia remained where she was, and leaning her head upon her hands tried to recall what had passed, to nerve herself for what was to come. Her first sensation was one of unutterable relief. The long struggle was over; the haunting care was gone; there was nothing now to conceal; she might be herself again, and her spirit rose with something of its old elasticity as the heavy burden was removed. A moment she enjoyed this hard-won freedom; then the memory that the burden was not lost, but laid on other shoulders, filled her with an anguish too sharp to find vent in tears, too deep to leave any hope of cure except in action. But how act? She had performed the duty so long, so vainly delayed, and when the first glow of satisfaction passed, found redoubled anxiety, regret, and pain before her. Clear and hard the truth stood there, and no power of hers could recall the words that showed it to her husband, could give them back the early blindness, or the later vicissitudes of hope and fear. In the long silence that filled the room she had time to calm her perturbation and comfort her remorse by the vague but helpful belief which seldom deserts sanguine spirits, that something, as yet unseen and unsuspected, would appear to heal the breach, to show what was to be done, and to make all happy in the end.

Where Moor went or how long he stayed Sylvia never knew, but when at length he came, her first glance showed her that pride is as much to be dreaded as passion. No gold is without alloy, and now she saw the shadow of a nature which had seemed all sunshine. She knew he was very proud, but never thought to be the cause of its saddest manifestation: one which showed her that its presence could make the silent sorrow of a just and gentle man a harder trial to sustain than the hottest anger, the bitterest reproach. Scarcely paler than when he went, there was no sign of violent emotion in his countenance. His eye shone keen and dark, an anxious fold crossed his forehead, and a melancholy gravity replaced the cheerful serenity his face once wore. Wherein the alteration lay Sylvia could not tell, but over the whole man some subtle change had passed. The sudden frost which had blighted the tenderest affection of his life seemed to have left its chill behind, robbing his manner of its cordial charm, his voice of its heartsome ring, and giving him the look of one who sternly said, "I must suffer, but it shall be alone."

Cold and quiet, he stood regarding her with a strange expression, as if endeavoring to realize the truth, and see in her not his wife but Warwick's lover. Oppressed by the old fear, now augmented by a measureless regret, she could only look up at him, feeling that her husband had become her judge. Yet as she looked she was conscious of a momentary wonder at the seeming transposition of character in the two so near and dear to her. Strong-hearted Warwick wept like any child, but accepted his disappointment without complaint and bore it manfully. Moor, from whom she would sooner have expected such demonstration, grew stormy first, then stern, as she once believed his friend would have done. She forgot that Moor's pain was the sharper, his wound the deeper, for the patient hope cherished so long; the knowledge that he never had been loved as he loved; the sense of wrong that could not but burn even in the meekest heart at such a late discovery, such an entire loss.

Sylvia spoke first, not audibly, but with a little gesture of supplication, a glance of sorrowful submission. He answered both, not by lamentation or reproach, but by just enough of his accustomed tenderness in touch and tone to make her tears break forth, as he placed her in the ancient chair so often occupied together, took the one opposite, and, sweeping a clear space on the table between them, looked across it with the air of a man bent on seeing his way and following it at any cost.

"Now, Sylvia, I can listen as I should."

"O Geoffrey, what can I say?"

"Repeat all you have already told me. I only gathered one fact then, now I want the circumstances, for I find this confession difficult of belief."

Perhaps no sterner expiation could have been required of her than to sit there, face to face, eye to eye, and tell again that little history of thwarted love and fruitless endeavor. Excitement had given her courage for the first confession, now it was torture to carefully repeat what had poured freely from her lips before. But she did it, glad to prove her penitence by any test he might apply. Tears often blinded her, uncontrollable emotion often arrested her; and more than once she turned on him a beseeching look, which asked as plainly as words, "Must I go on?"

Intent on learning all, Moor was unconscious of the trial he imposed, unaware that the change in himself was the keenest reproach he could have made, and still, with a persistency as gentle as inflexible, he pursued his purpose to the end. When great drops rolled down her cheeks he dried them silently; when she paused, he waited till she calmed herself; and when she spoke, he listened with few interruptions but a question now and then. Occasionally a sudden flush of passionate pain swept across his face, as some phrase, implying rather than expressing Warwick's love or Sylvia's longing, escaped the narrator's lips; and when she described their parting on that very spot, his eye went from her to the hearth her words seemed to make desolate, with a glance she never could forget. But when the last question was answered, the last appeal for pardon brokenly uttered, nothing but the pale pride remained; and his voice was cold and quiet as his mien.

"Yes, it is this which has baffled and kept me groping in the dark so long, for I wholly trusted what I wholly loved."

"Alas, it was that very confidence that made my task seem so necessary and so hard. How often I longed to go to you with my great trouble as I used to do with lesser ones! But here you would suffer more than I; and, having done the wrong, it was for me to pay the penalty. So, like many another weak yet willing soul, I tried to keep you happy at all costs."

"One frank word before I married you would have spared us this. Could you not foresee the end and dare to speak it, Sylvia?"

"I see it now, I did not then, else I would have spoken as freely as I speak to-night. I thought I had outlived my love for Adam; it seemed kind to spare you a knowledge that would disturb your friendship, so, though I told the truth, I did not tell it all. I thought temptations came from without; I could withstand such, and I did, even when it wore Adam's shape. This temptation came so suddenly, seemed so harmless, generous, and just, that I yielded to it, unconscious that it was one. Surely I deceived myself as cruelly as I did you, and God knows I have tried to atone for it when time taught me the fatal error of yielding to a mood."

"Poor child, it was too soon for you to play the perilous game of hearts. I should have known it, and left you to the safe and simple joys of girlhood. Forgive me that I have kept you a prisoner so long; take off the fetter I put on, and go, Sylvia."

"No, do not put me from you yet; do not think that I can hurt you so, and then be glad to leave you suffering alone. Look like your kind self if you can; talk to me as you used to; let me show you my heart and you will see how large a place you fill in it. Let me begin again, for now the secret is told, there is no fear to keep out love; and I can give my whole strength to learning the lesson you have tried so patiently to teach."

"You cannot, Sylvia. We are as much divorced as if judge and jury had decided the righteous but hard separation for us. You can never be a wife to me with an unconquerable affection in your heart; I can never be your husband while the shadow of a fear remains. I will have all or nothing."

"Adam foretold this. He knew you best, and I should have followed the brave counsel he gave me long ago. Oh, if he were only here to help us now!"

The desire broke from Sylvia's lips involuntarily as she turned for strength to the strong soul that loved her. But it was like wind to smouldering fire; a pang of jealousy wrung Moor's heart, and he spoke out with a flash of the eye that startled Sylvia more than the rapid change of voice and manner.

"Hush! Say anything of yourself or me, and I can bear it, but spare me the sound of Adam's name to-night. A man's nature is not forgiving like a woman's, and the best of us harbor impulses you know nothing of. If I am to lose wife, friend, and home, for God's sake leave me my self-respect."

All the coldness and pride passed from Moor's face as the climax of his sorrow came; with an impetuous gesture he threw his arms across the table, and laid down his head in a paroxysm of tearless suffering such as men only know.

How Sylvia longed to speak! But what consolation could the tenderest words supply? She searched for some alleviating suggestion, some happier hope; none came. Her eye turned to the pictured Fates above her as if imploring them to aid her. But they looked back at her inexorably dumb, and instinctively her thought passed beyond them to the Ruler of all fates, asking the help which never is refused. No words embodied her appeal, no sound expressed it, only a voiceless cry from the depths of a contrite spirit, owning its weakness, making known its want. She prayed for submission, but her deeper need was seen, and when she asked for patience to endure, Heaven sent her power to act, and out of this sharp trial brought her a better strength and clearer knowledge of herself than years of smoother experience could have bestowed. A sense of security, of stability, came to her as that entire reliance assured her by its all-sustaining power that she had found what she most needed to make life clear to her and duty sweet. With her face in her hands, she sat, forgetful that she was not alone, as in that brief but precious moment she felt the exceeding comfort of a childlike faith in the one Friend who, when we are deserted by all, even by ourselves, puts forth His hand and gathers us tenderly to Himself.

Her husband's voice recalled her, and looking up she showed him such an earnest, patient countenance, it touched him like an unconscious rebuke. The first tears she had seen rose to his eyes, and all the old tenderness came back into his voice, softening the dismissal which had been more coldly begun.

"Dear, silence and rest are best for both of us to-night. We cannot treat this trouble as we should till we are calmer; then we will take counsel how soonest to end what never should have been begun. Forgive me, pray for me, and in sleep forget me for a little while."

He held the door for her, but as she passed Sylvia lifted her face for the good-night caress without which she had never left him since she became his wife. She did not speak, but her eye humbly besought this token of forgiveness; nor was it denied. Moor laid his hand upon her lips, and kissed her on the forehead.

Such a little thing: but it overcame Sylvia with the sorrowful certainty of the loss which had befallen both, and she crept away, feeling herself an exile from the heart and home whose happy mistress she might have been.

Moor watched the little figure going upward, and weeping softly as it went, as if he echoed the sad "never any more," which those tears expressed, and when it vanished with a backward look, shut himself in alone with his great sorrow.

CHAPTER XIX

What Next?

Sylvia laid her head down on her pillow, believing that this night would be the longest, saddest she had ever known. But before she had time to sigh for sleep it wrapped her in its comfortable arms, and held her till day broke. Sunshine streamed across the room, and early birds piped on the budding boughs that swayed before the window. But no morning smile saluted her, no morning flower awaited her, and nothing but a little note lay on the unpressed pillow at her side.

"Sylvia, I have gone away to Faith, because this proud, resentful spirit of mine must be subdued before I meet you. I leave that behind me which will speak to you more kindly, calmly, than I can now, and show you that my effort has been equal to my failure. There is nothing for me to do but submit; manfully if I must, meekly if I can; and this short exile will prepare me for the longer one to come. Take counsel with those nearer and dearer to you than myself, and secure the happiness which I have so ignorantly delayed, but cannot wilfully destroy. God be with you, and through all that is and is to come, remember that you remain beloved forever in the heart of Geoffrey Moor."

Sylvia had known many sad uprisings, but never a sadder one than this, and the hours that followed aged her more than any year had done. All day she wandered aimlessly to and fro, for the inward conflict would not let her rest. The house seemed home no longer when its presiding genius was gone, and everywhere some token of his former presence touched her with its mute reproach.

She asked no counsel of her family, for well she knew the outburst of condemnation, incredulity, and grief that would assail her there. They could not help her yet; they would only augment perplexities, weaken convictions, and distract her mind. When she was sure of herself she would tell them, endure their indignation and regret, and steadily execute the new purpose, whatever it should be.

To many it might seem an easy task to break the bond that burdened and assume the tie that blessed. But Sylvia had grown wise in self-knowledge, timorous through self-delusion; therefore the greater the freedom given her, the more she hesitated to avail herself of it. The nobler each friend grew as she turned from one to the other, the more impossible seemed the decision; for generous spirit and loving heart contended for the mastery, yet neither won. She knew that Moor had put her from him never to be recalled till some miracle was wrought that should make her truly his. This renunciation showed her how much he had become to her, how entirely she had learned to lean upon him, and how great a boon such perfect love was in itself. Even the prospect of a life with Warwick brought forebodings with its hope. Reason made her listen to many doubts which hitherto passion had suppressed. Would she never tire of his unrest? Could she fill so large a heart and give it power as well as warmth? Might not the two wills clash, the ardent natures inflame one another, the stronger intellect exhaust the weaker, and disappointment come again? And as she asked these questions, conscience, the monitor whom no bribe can tempt, no threat silence, invariably answered "Yes."

But chief among the cares that beset her was one that grew more burdensome with thought. By her own will she had put her liberty into another's keeping; law confirmed the act, gospel sanctioned the vow, and it could only be redeemed by paying the costly price demanded of those who own that they have drawn a blank in the lottery of marriage. Public opinion is a grim ghost that daunts the bravest, and Sylvia knew that trials lay before her from which she would shrink and suffer, as only a woman sensitive and proud as she could shrink and suffer. Once apply this remedy, and any tongue would have the power to wound, any eye to insult with pity or contempt, any stranger to criticise or condemn, and she would have no means of redress, no place of refuge, even in that stronghold, Adam's heart.

All that dreary day she wrestled with these stubborn facts, but could neither mould nor modify them as she would, and evening found her spent, but not decided. Too excited for sleep, yet too weary for exertion, she turned bedward, hoping that the darkness and the silence of night would bring good counsel, if not rest.

Till now she had shunned the library as one shuns the spot where one has suffered most. But as she passed the open door, the gloom that reigned within seemed typical of that which had fallen on its absent master, and, following the impulse of the moment, Sylvia went in to light it with the little glimmer of her lamp. Nothing had been touched; for no hand but her own preserved the order of this room, and all household duties had been neglected on that day. The old chair stood where she had left it, and over its arm was thrown the velvet coat Moor liked to wear at this household trysting-place. Sylvia bent to fold it smoothly as it hung, and, feeling that she must solace herself with some touch of tenderness, laid her cheek against the soft garment, whispering "Good-night." Something glittered on the cushion of the chair, and looking nearer she found a steel-clasped book, upon the cover of which lay a dead heliotrope, a little key.

It was Moor's Diary, and now she understood that passage of the note which had been obscure before. "I leave that behind me which will speak to you more kindly, calmly, than I can now, and show you that my effort has been equal to my failure." She had often begged to read it, threatened to pick the lock, and felt the strongest curiosity to learn what was contained in the long entries that he daily made. Her requests had always been answered with the promise of entire possession of the book when the year was out. Now he gave it, though the year was not gone, and many leaves were yet unfilled. He thought she would come to this room first, would see her morning flower laid ready for her, and, sitting in what they called their Refuge, would draw some comfort for herself, some palliation for his innocent offence, from the record so abruptly ended.

She took it, went away to her own room, unlocked the short romance of his wedded life, and found her husband's heart laid bare before her.

It was a strange and solemn thing to look so deeply into the private experience of a fellow-being; to trace the birth and progress of purposes and passions, the motives of action, the secret aspirations, the besetting sins that made up the inner life he had been leading beside her. Moor wrote with an eloquent sincerity, because he had put himself into his book, as if, feeling the need of some *confidante,* he had chosen the only one that pardons egotism. Here, too, Sylvia saw her chameleon self, etched with loving care, endowed with all gifts and graces, studied with unflagging zeal, and made the idol of a life.

Often a tuneful spirit seemed to assert itself, and, passing from smooth prose to smoother poetry, sonnet, song, or psalm, flowed down the page in cadences stately, sweet, or solemn, filling the reader with delight at the discovery of a gift so genuine, yet so shyly folded up within itself, unconscious that its modesty was the surest token of its worth. More than once Sylvia laid her face into the book, and added her involuntary comment on some poem or passage made pathetic by the present; more than once paused to wonder, with exceeding wonder, why she could not give such genius and affection its reward; and more than once asked the Maker of these mysterious hearts of ours to work the miracle which should change a tender friendship to an undying love.

All night she lay there like some pictured Magdalene, purer but as penitent as Correggio's Mary, with the book, the lamp, the melancholy eyes, the golden hair that painters love. All night she read, gathering courage and consolation from those pages; for seeing what she was not showed her what she might become, and when she turned the little key upon that story without an end, Sylvia the girl was dead, but Sylvia the woman had begun to live.

Lying in the rosy hush of dawn, there came to her a sudden memory,—

"If ever you need help that Geoffrey cannot give, remember Cousin Faith."

This was the hour Faith foresaw. Moor had gone to her with his trouble; why not follow, and let this woman, wise, discreet, and gentle, show her what should come next?

The newly risen sun saw Sylvia away upon her journey to Faith's home among the hills. She lived alone, a cheerful, busy, solitary soul, demanding little of others, yet giving freely to whomsoever asked an alms of her.

Sylvia found the gray cottage nestled in a hollow of the mountain side; a pleasant hermitage, secure and still. Mistress and maid composed the household, but none of the gloom of isolation darkened the sunshine that pervaded it; peace seemed to sit upon its threshold, content to brood under its eaves, and the atmosphere of home to make it beautiful.

When some momentous purpose or event absorbs us, we break through fears and formalities, act out ourselves, forgetful of reserve, and use the plainest phrases to express emotions which need no ornament and little aid from language. Sylvia illustrated this fact then; for, without hesitation or embarrassment, she entered Miss Dane's door, called no servant to announce her, but went, as if by instinct, straight to the room where Faith sat alone, and with the simplest greeting asked,—

"Is Geoffrey here?"

"He was an hour ago, and will be an hour hence. I sent him out to rest, for he cannot sleep. I am glad you came to him; he has not learned to do without you yet."

With no bustle of surprise or sympathy Faith put away her work, took off the hat and cloak, drew her guest beside her on the couch before the one deep window looking down the valley, and gently chafing the chilly hands in warm ones, said nothing more till Sylvia spoke.

"He has told you all the wrong I have done him?"

"Yes, and found a little comfort here. Do you need consolation also?"

"Can you ask? But I need something more, and no one can give it to me so well as you. I want to be set right, to hear things called by their true names, to be taken out of myself and made to see why I am always doing wrong while trying to do well."

"Your father, sister, or brother, is fitter for that task than I. Have you tried them?"

"No, and I will not. They love me, but they could not help me; for they would beg me to conceal if I cannot forget, to endure if I cannot conquer, and abide by my mistake at all costs. That is not the help I want. I desire to know the one just thing to be done, and to be made brave enough to do it, though friends lament, gossips clamor, and the heavens fall. I am in earnest now. Rate me sharply, drag out my weaknesses, shame my follies, show no mercy to my selfish hopes; and when I can no longer hide from myself put me in the way I should go, and I will follow it though my feet bleed at every step."

She was in earnest now, terribly so, but still Faith drew back, though her compassionate face belied her hesitating words.

"Adam is wise and just, but he, as well as Geoffrey, loves me too well to decide for me." Sylvia went on: "You stand between them, wise as the one, gentle as the other, and you do not care for me enough to let affection hoodwink reason. Faith, you bade me come; do not cast me off, for if you shut your heart against me I know not where to go."

Despairingly she spoke, disconsolate she looked, and Faith's reluctance vanished. The maternal aspect returned, her voice resumed its warmth, her eye its benignity, and Sylvia was reassured before a word was spoken.

"I do not cast you off, nor shut my heart against you. I only hesitated to assume such responsibility, and shrank from the task because of compassion, not coldness. Sit here, and tell me all your trouble, Sylvia."

"That is so kind! It seems quite natural to turn to you as if I had a claim upon you. Let me have; and if you can, love me a little, because I have no mother, and need one very much."

"My child, you shall not need one any more."

"I feel that, and am comforted already. Tell me first which of the two who love me I should have married had fate given me a choice in time."

"Neither."

Sylvia paled and trembled, as if the oracle she had invoked was an unanswerable voice pronouncing the truth she must abide by.

"Why, Faith?"

"Because you were too young, too unstable, and guided by impulse, not by principle. You, of all women, should have waited long, chosen carefully, and guarded yourself from every shadow of doubt before it was too late."

"Had I done so, would it have been safe and happy to have loved Adam?"

"No, Sylvia, never."

"Why, Faith?"

"If you were blind, a cripple, or cursed with some incurable infirmity of body, would you not hesitate to bind yourself and your affliction to another?"

"You know I should not only hesitate, but utterly refuse."

"I do know it, therefore I venture to tell you why, according to my belief, you should not marry Adam. There are diseases more subtle and dangerous than any that vex our flesh,—diseases that should be as carefully cured, if curable, as inexorably prevented from increasing, as any malady we dread. A feeble will, a morbid mind, a mad temper, an evil heart, a blind soul, are afflictions to be as much regarded as bodily infirmities; nay, more, inasmuch as souls are of greater value than perishable flesh. Where this is religiously taught, believed, and practised, marriage becomes, in truth, a sacrament blessed of God; children thank parents for the gift of life; parents see in children living satisfactions and rewards, not reproaches or retributions doubly heavy to be borne, for the knowledge that where two sinned, many must inevitably suffer."

"You try to tell me gently, Faith, but I see that you consider me one of the innocent unfortunates, who have no right to marry till they be healed, perhaps never. I have dimly felt this during the past year, now I know it, and thank God that I have no child to reproach me hereafter for bequeathing it the mental ills I have not yet outlived."

"Dear Sylvia, you are an exceptional case in all respects, because an extreme one. The ancient theology of two contending spirits in one body is strangely exemplified in you, for each rules by turn, and each helps or hinders as moods and circumstances lead. Even in the great event of a woman's life you were thwarted by conflicting powers,—impulse and ignorance, passion and pride, hope and despair. Now you stand at the parting of the ways, looking wistfully along the pleasant one where love seems to beckon, while I point down the rugged one that leads to duty, and, though my heart aches as I do it, counsel you as I would a daughter of my own."

"I thank you; I will follow you, but life looks very barren."

"Not as barren as if you possessed your desire, and found in it another misery and mistake. Could you love Geoffrey, it would be safe and well with you; loving Adam, it would be neither. Let me show you why. He is an exception like yourself; perhaps that explains your attraction for each other. In him the head rules, in Geoffrey the heart. The one criticises, the other loves, mankind. Geoffrey is proud and private in all that lies nearest him, clings to persons, and is faithful as a woman. Adam has only the pride of an intellect which tests all things and abides by its own insight. He clings to principles; persons are but animated facts or ideas; he seizes, searches, uses them, and when they have no more for him, drops them like the husk, whose kernel he has secured; passing on to find and study other samples without regret, but with unabated zeal. For life to him is perpetual progress, and he obeys the law of his nature as steadily as sun or sea. Is not this so?"

"All true; what more, Faith?"

"Few women, if wise, would dare to marry this man, noble as he is, till time has tamed and experience developed him. Even then the risk is great, for he demands and unconsciously absorbs into himself the personality of others, making large returns, but of a kind which only those as strong, sagacious, and steadfast as himself can receive and adapt to their individual uses, without being overcome and possessed. That none of us should be, except by the Spirit stronger than man, purer than woman. You feel, though you do not understand this power. You know that his presence excites, yet wearies you; that, while you love, you fear him, and even when you long to be all in all to him, you doubt your ability to make his happiness. Am I not right?"

"I must say yes."

"Then it is scarcely necessary for me to tell you that I think this unequal marriage would be but a brief one for you; bright at the beginning, dark at its end. With him you would exhaust yourself in passionate endeavors to follow where he led. He would not see this; you would not confess it, but too late you would both learn that you were too young, too frail in all but the strength of love, to be his wife. It is like a wood bird mating with an eagle; straining its little wings to scale the sky with him, blinding itself with gazing at the sun, vainly striving to fill and warm the wild eyrie, and perishing in the stern solitude the other loves."

"Faith, you frighten me! You seem to see and show me all the dim forebodings I have hidden away from myself because I could not understand or dared not face them. How have you learned so much? How can you read me so well?"

"I had an unhappy girlhood in a discordant home, and there was no escape except by a marriage that would be slavery to me. Many cares and losses made me early old, and taught me to observe the failures, mistakes, and burdens of others. Since then solitude has led me to study and reflect upon the question toward which my thoughts inevitably turned."

"But, Faith, why have you never found a home and partner for yourself, as other women do?—you who are so nobly fitted for all the duties, joys, and sorrows of married life?"

"Because I never met the man who could satisfy me. My ideal is a high one, and I believe that whatever we are worthy of we shall find and enjoy hereafter if not here."

"Not even Adam? Surely he is heroic enough for any woman's ideal."

"Not even Adam, for the reasons I have told you. I know his value, and feel the charm of his strength, truth, and courage, but I should not dare to marry him. Sylvia, unhappy marriages are the tragedies of the world, and will be till men and women are taught to make principle not pleasure, love not passion, mutual fitness not reckless impulse, the guides and guards to the most beautiful and sacred relation God gives us for our best training and highest happiness."

"Ah, if some one had told me these things a year ago, how much pain I might have spared myself and others! Prue thinks whatever is is right, and poor Papa cares only to see me happy. All this will break his heart."

Sylvia paused to sigh over his great disappointment; then returned with a still heavier sigh to her own.

"Who told you so much about us? You cannot have divined it all?"

"Concerning yourself Geoffrey told me much, but Adam more."

"Have you seen him? Has he been here? When, Faith, when?"

Light and color flashed back into Sylvia's face, and the eagerness of her voice was a pleasant sound after the despair which had saddened it before. Faith answered fully and with care, while the compassion of her look deepened as she spoke,—

"I saw him but a week ago; vehement and vigorous as ever. He has come hither often during the winter. He said you bade him hear of you through me; that he preferred to come, not write, for letters were often false interpreters, but face to face one gets the real thought of one's friend by look as well as word, and the result is satisfactory."

"That is Adam! But what more did he say? How did you advise him? I know he asked counsel of you, as we all have done."

"He did, and I gave it as frankly as to you and Geoffrey. He made me understand you, judge you leniently, see in you the virtues you have cherished despite drawbacks such as few have to struggle with. Your father made Adam his confessor during the happy month when you first knew him. I need not tell you how he received and preserved such a trust. He betrayed no confidence, but in speaking of you I saw that his knowledge of the father taught him to understand the daughter. It was well and beautifully done, and did we need anything to endear him to us this trait of character would do it; for it is a rare endowment,—the power of overcoming all obstacles of pride, age, and the sad reserve self-condemnation brings us, and making confession a grateful healing."

"I know it; we tell our sorrows to such as Geoffrey, our sins to such as Adam. But, Faith, when you spoke of me, did you say to him what you have been saying to me about my unfitness to be his wife because of inequality and my unhappy inheritance?"

"Could I do otherwise when he fixed that commanding eye of his upon me, asking, 'Is my love as wise as it is warm?' He is one of those who force the hardest truths from us by the simple fact that they can bear it, and would do the same for us. He needed it then; for though instinct was right,—hence his anxious question,—his heart, never so entirely roused as now, made it difficult for him to judge of your relations to each other, and there my woman's insight helped him."

"What did he do when you told him? I see that you hesitate to tell me. I think you have been preparing me to hear it. Speak out. Though my cheeks whiten and my hands tremble, I can bear it, for you shall be the law by which I will abide."

"You shall be a law to yourself, my brave Sylvia. Put your hands in mine, and hold fast to the friend who loves and honors you for this. I will tell you what Adam did and said. He sat in deep thought many minutes; but with him to see is to do, and soon he turned to me with the courageous expression which in him signifies that the fight is fought, the victory won. 'It is necessary to be true, it is not necessary to be happy. I would never marry Sylvia, even if I might,'—and with that paraphrase of words, whose meaning seemed to fit his need, he went away. I think he will not come again either to me—or you."

How still the room grew as Faith's reluctant lips uttered the last words! Sylvia sat motionless, looking out into the sunny valley with eyes that saw nothing but the image of that beloved friend leaving her perhaps forever. Well she knew that with this man to see *was* to do, and with a woful sense of desolation falling cold upon her heart, she felt that there was nothing more to hope for but a brave submission like his own. Yet in that pause there came a feeling of relief after the first despair. The power of choice was no longer left her, and the help she needed was bestowed by one who could decide against himself, inspired by a sentiment which curbed a strong man's love of self, and made it subject to a just man's love of right. Great examples never lose their virtue; what Pompey was to Warwick that Warwick became to Sylvia, and in the moment of supremest sorrow she felt the fire of a noble emulation kindled in her from the spark he left behind.

"Faith, what must I do?"

"Your duty."

"And that is?"

"To love and live for Geoffrey."

"Can I ever forget? Will he ever forgive? Is there anything before me but one long repentance for the suffering I have given?"

"The young always think that life is ruined by one misfortune, one mistake; but they learn that it is possible to forget, forgive, and live on till they have wrung both strength and happiness out of the hard experience that seemed to crush them. Wait a year, do nothing hastily, lest, when the excitement of this hour is past, you find you have renounced or promised more than you can give up or perform. Geoffrey will pardon freely, wait patiently, and if I know you both, will welcome back in time a wife who will be worthy of his love and confidence."

"Can time work that miracle?" asked Sylvia, ready to learn more, yet incredulous of the possibility of such an utter change in herself.

"You have been the victim of moods, now live by principle, and hold fast by the duty you see and acknowledge. Let nothing turn you from it; shut your ears to the whispers of temptation, keep your thoughts from straying, your heart full of hope, your soul of faith, humility, submission, and leave the rest to God."

"I will! Faith, what comes next?"

"This." And she was gathered close while Faith confessed how hard her task had been by letting tears fall fast upon the head which seemed to have found its proper resting-place, as if, despite her courage and her wisdom, her woman's heart was half broken with its pity. Better than any words was the motherly embrace, the tender tears, the balm of sympathy which soothed the wounds it could not heal.

Leaning on each other, the two hearts talked together in the silence, feeling the beauty of the tie kind Nature weaves between consoler and consoled. Faith often turned her lips to Sylvia's forehead, brushed back her hair with a lingering touch, and drew her closer, as if it was very sweet to see and feel the young creature in her arms. Sylvia lay there, tearless and tranquil, thinking thoughts for which she had no words, trying to prepare herself for the life before her, and to pierce the veil that hid the future. Her eyes rested on the valley where the river flowed, the elms waved their budding boughs in the bland air, and the meadows wore their earliest tinge of green. But she was not conscious of these things till the sight of a solitary figure coming slowly up the hill recalled her to the present and the duties it still held for her.

"Here is Geoffrey! How wearily he walks, how changed and old he looks,—oh, why was I born to be a curse to all who love me!"

"Hush, Sylvia, say anything but that, because it casts reproach upon your father. Your life is but just begun; make it a blessing, not a curse, as all of us have power to do; and remember that for every affliction there are two helpers, who can heal or end the heaviest we know,—Time and Death. The first we may invoke and wait for; the last God alone can send when it is better not to live."

"I will try to be patient. Will you meet and tell Geoffrey what has passed? I have no strength left but for passive endurance."

Faith went; Sylvia heard the murmur of earnest conversation; then steps came rapidly along the hall, and Moor was in the room. She rose involuntarily, but for a moment neither spoke, for never had they met as now. Each regarded the other as if a year had rolled between them since they parted, and each saw in the other the changes that one day had wrought. Neither the fire of resentment nor the frost of pride now rendered Moor's face stormy or stern. Anxious and worn it was, with newly graven lines upon the forehead, and melancholy curves about the mouth, but the peace of a conquered spirit touched it with a pale serenity, and some perennial hope shone in the glance he bent upon his wife. For the first time in her life Sylvia was truly beautiful,—not physically, for never had she looked more weak and wan, but spiritually, as the inward change made itself manifest in an indescribable expression of meekness and of strength. With suffering came submission, with repentance came regeneration, and the power of the woman yet to be, touched with beauty the pathos of the woman now passing through the fire.

"Faith has told you what has passed between us, and the advice she gives us in our present strait?"

"I submit, Sylvia; I can still hope and wait."

So humbly he said it, so heartily he meant it, she felt that his love was as indomitable as Warwick's will, and the wish to be worthy of it woke with all its old intensity, since no other was possible to her.

"It is not for one so unstable as I to say, 'I shall not change.' I leave all to time and my earnest longing to do right. Go, and leave me to grow worthy of you; and if death parts us, remember that however I may thwart your life here, there is a beautiful eternity where you may forget me and be happy."

"I will go, I will stay till you recall me, but death will not change me. Love is immortal, dear, and even in the 'beautiful eternity' I shall still hope and wait."

This invincible fidelity, so patient, so persistent, impressed Sylvia like a prophecy, and remained to comfort her in the hard year to come.

How soon it was all over,—the return to separate homes, the disclosures, and the storms; the preparations for the solitary voyage, for Moor decided to go abroad, the last charges and farewells!

Max would not, and Prue could not, go to see the traveller off,—the former too angry to lend his countenance to what he termed a barbarous banishment; the latter, being half blind with crying, stayed to nurse Jessie, whose soft heart was nearly broken at what seemed to her the most direful affliction under heaven.

But Sylvia and her father followed Moor till his foot left the soil, and still lingered on the wharf to watch the steamer out of port. An uncongenial place in which to part; carriages rolled up and down, a clamor of voices filled the air, the little steam-tug snorted with impatience, and the waves flowed seaward with the ebbing of the tide. But father and daughter saw only one object, heard only one sound,—Moor's face as it looked down upon them from the deck, Moor's voice as he sent cheery messages to those left behind. Mr. Yule was endeavoring to reply as cheerily, and Sylvia was gazing with eyes that saw very dimly through their tears, when both were aware of an instantaneous change in the countenance they watched. Something beyond themselves seemed to arrest Moor's eye; a moment he stood intent and motionless, then flushed to the forehead with the dark glow Sylvia remembered well, waved his hand to them, and vanished down the cabin stairs.

"Papa, what did he see?"

There was no need of any answer, for Warwick came striding through the crowd, saw them, paused with both hands out, and a questioning glance as if uncertain of his greeting. With one impulse the hands were taken; Sylvia could not speak, her father could, and did approvingly,—

"Welcome, Adam; you are come to say good-by to Geoffrey?"

"Rather to you, sir; he needs none, I go with him."

"With him!" echoed both hearers.

"Ay, that I will! Did you think I would let him go away alone, feeling bereaved of wife and home and friend?"

"We should have known you better. But, Warwick, he will shun you; he hid himself just now as you approached; he has tried to forgive, but he cannot so soon forget."

"All the more need of my helping him to do both. He cannot shun me long with no hiding-place to fly to but the sea, and I will so gently constrain him by the old-time love we bore each other, that he must relent and take me back into his heart again."

"O Adam! go with him, stay with him, and bring him safely back to me when time has helped us all."

"I shall do it, God willing."

Unmindful of all else, Warwick bent and took her to him as he gave the promise, seemed to put his whole heart into a single kiss, and left her trembling with the stress of his farewell. She saw him cleave his way through the throng, leap the space left by the gangway just withdrawn, and vanish in search of that lost friend. Then she turned her face to her father's shoulder, conscious of nothing but the fact that Warwick had come and gone.

A cannon boomed, the crowd cheered, the last cable was flung off, and the steamer glided from her moorings with the surge of water and the waft of wind, like some sea-monster eager to be out upon the ocean free again.

"Look up, Sylvia; she will soon pass from sight."

"Are they there?"

"No."

"Then I do not care to see. Look for me, father, and tell me when they come."

"They will not come, dear; both have said good-by, and we have seen the last of them for many a long day."

"They will come! Adam will bring Geoffrey to show me they are friends again. I know it; you shall see it. Lift me to that block, and watch the deck with me that we may see them the instant they appear."

Up she sprang, eyes clear now, nerves steady, faith strong. Leaning forward so utterly forgetful of herself, she would have fallen into the green water tumbling there below, had not her father held her fast. How slowly the minutes seemed to pass, how rapidly the steamer seemed to glide away, how heavily the sense of loss weighed on her heart as wave after wave rolled between her and her heart's desire!

"Come down, Sylvia, it is giving yourself useless pain to watch and wait. Come home, my child, and let us comfort each other."

She did not hear him; for as he spoke, the steamer swung slowly round to launch itself into the open bay, and with a cry that drew many eyes upon the young figure with its face of pale expectancy, Sylvia saw her hope fulfilled.

"I knew they would come! See, father, see! Geoffrey is smiling as he waves his handkerchief, and Adam's hand is on his shoulder. Answer them! oh, answer them! I can only look."

The old man did answer them enthusiastically, and Sylvia stretched her arms across the widening space as if to bring them back again. Side by side the friends stood now; Moor's eye upon his wife, while from his hand the little flag of peace streamed in the wind. But Warwick's glance was turned upon his friend, and Warwick's hand already seemed to claim the charge he had accepted.

Standing thus they passed from sight, never to come sailing home together as the woman on the shore was praying God to let her see them come.

CHAPTER XX

A Year

Sylvia was spared all effort but passive endurance during the first month of trial, for she fell ill. The overwrought mind preyed upon the body, and exhaustion forced both to rest. For a few days there was danger, and she knew it, yet was not glad as she once would have been. Lying in the shadow of death, her life looked such a sorrowful failure she longed for a chance to retrieve it. What had she done worth the doing? Whom had she made happy? Where was the humble satisfaction that should come hand in hand with death? There was a time when she would have answered these self-accusations by saying, "It is my fate," and so drifted on to life or death, ready for neither. Now conscience as well as heart suffered, and a nobler courage than resignation was growing in her. An earnest desire to atone, to rise above all obstacles and turn the seeming defeat into a sweet success, so possessed her that it seemed cowardly to die, and she asked for life, feeling that she had learned to use if not to enjoy it more truly than before. In those quiet weeks of enforced seclusion she grew fast, and when she rose a stronger and more patient soul shone through the frail body like the flame that makes the lamp transparent.

The ensuing year seemed fuller of events than any Sylvia had ever known. At first she found it very hard to live her life alone; for inward cares oppressed her, and external trials were not wanting. Only to the few who had a right to know, had the whole trouble been confided. They were discreet from family pride, if from no tenderer feeling; but the curious world outside of that small circle was full of shrewd surmises, of keen eyes for discovering domestic breaches, and shrill tongues for proclaiming them. Warwick escaped suspicion, being so little known, so seldom seen; but for the usual nine days matrons and venerable maids wagged their caps, lifted their hands, and sighed as they sipped their dish of scandal and of tea,—

"Poor young man! I always said how it would be, she was so peculiar. My dear creature, haven't you heard that Mrs. Moor isn't happy with her husband, and that he has gone abroad quite broken-hearted?"

Sylvia felt this deeply, but received it as her just punishment, and bore herself so meekly that public opinion soon turned a somersault, and the murmur changed to,—

"Poor young thing! what could she expect? My dear, I have it from the best authority, that Mr. Moor has made her miserable for a year, and now left her broken-hearted." After that the gossips took up some newer tragedy, and left Mrs. Moor to mend her heart as best she could, a favor very gratefully received.

As Hester Prynne seemed to see some trace of her own sin in every bosom, by the glare of the Scarlet Letter burning on her own, so Sylvia, living in the shadow of a household grief, found herself detecting various phases of her own experience in others. She had joined that sad sisterhood called disappointed women; a larger class than many deem it to be, though there are few of us who have not seen members of it. Unhappy wives; mistaken or forsaken lovers; meek souls, who make life a long penance for the sins of others; gifted creatures kindled into fitful brilliancy by some inward fire that consumes but cannot warm. These are the women who fly to convents, write bitter books, sing songs full of heartbreak, act splendidly the passion they have lost or never won; who smile, and try to lead brave uncomplaining lives, but whose tragic eyes betray them, whose voices, however sweet or gay, contain an undertone of hopelessness, whose faces sometimes startle one with an expression which haunts the observer long after it is gone.

Undoubtedly Sylvia would have joined the melancholy chorus, and fallen to lamenting that ever she was born, had she not possessed a purpose that took her out of herself and proved her salvation. Faith's words took root and blossomed. Intent on making her life a blessing, not a reproach to her father, she lived for him entirely. He had taken her back to him, as if the burden of her unhappy past should be upon his shoulders, the expiation of her faults come from him alone. Sylvia understood this now, and nestled to him so gladly, so confidingly, he seemed to have found again the daughter he had lost and be almost content to have her all his own.

How many roofs cover families or friends who live years together, yet never truly know each other; who love, and long, and try to meet, yet fail to do so till some unexpected emotion or event performs the work. In the year that followed the departure of the friends, Sylvia discovered this and learned to know her father. No one was so much to her as he; no one so fully entered into her thoughts and feelings; for sympathy drew them tenderly together, and sorrow made them equals. As man and woman they talked, as father and daughter they loved; and the beautiful relation became their truest solace and support.

Miss Yule both rejoiced at and rebelled against this; was generous, yet mortally jealous; made no complaint, but grieved in private, and one fine day amazed her sister by announcing that, being of no farther use at home, she had decided to be married. Both Mr. Yule and Sylvia had desired this event, but hardly dared to expect it in spite of sundry propitious signs and circumstances.

A certain worthy widower had haunted the house of late, evidently on matrimonial thoughts intent. A solid gentleman, both physically and financially speaking; possessed of an ill-kept house, bad servants, and nine neglected children. This prospect, however alarming to others, had great charms for Prue; nor was the Reverend Gamaliel Bliss repugnant to her, being a rubicund, bland personage, much given to fine linen, long dinners, and short sermons. His third spouse had been suddenly translated, and though the year of mourning had not yet expired, things went so hardly with Gamaliel, that he could no longer delay casting his pastoral eyes over the flock which had already given three lambs to his fold, in search of a fourth. None appeared whose meek graces were sufficiently attractive, or whose dowries were sufficiently large. Meantime the nine olive-branches grew wild, the servants revelled, the ministerial digestion suffered, the sacred shirts went buttonless, and their wearer was wellnigh distraught. At this crisis he saw Prudence, and fell into a way of seating himself before the well-endowed spinster, with a large cambric pocket-handkerchief upon his knee, a frequent tear meandering down his florid countenance, and volcanic sighs agitating his capacious waistcoat as he poured his woes into her ear. Prue had been deeply touched by these moist appeals, and was not much surprised when the reverend gentleman went ponderously down upon his knee before her in the good old-fashioned style which frequent use had endeared to him, murmuring with an appropriate quotation and a subterranean sob,—

"Miss Yule, 'a good wife is a crown to her husband;' be such an one to me, unworthy as I am, and a mother to my bereaved babes, who suffer for a tender woman's care."

She nearly upset her sewing-table with an appropriate start, but speedily recovered, and with a maidenly blush murmured in return,—

"Dear me, how very unexpected! pray speak to papa,—oh, rise, I beg."

"Call me Gamaliel, and I obey!" gasped the stout lover, divided between rapture and doubts of his ability to perform the feat alone.

"Gam-aliel," sighed Prue, surrendering her hand.

"My Prudence, blessed among women!" responded the blissful Bliss. And having saluted the fair member, allowed it to help him rise; when, after a few decorous endearments, he departed to papa, and the bride elect rushed up to Sylvia with the incoherent announcement,—

"My dearest child, I have accepted him! It was such a surprise, though so touchingly done. I was positively mortified; Maria had swept the room so ill, his knees were white with lint, and I'm a very happy woman, bless you, love!"

"Sit down, and tell me all about it," cried her sister. "Don't try to sew, but cry if you like, and let me pet you, for indeed I am rejoiced."

But Prue preferred to rock violently, and boggle down a seam as the best quietus for her fluttered nerves, while she told her romance, received congratulations, and settled a few objections made by Sylvia, who tried to play the prudent matron.

"I am afraid he is too old for you, my dear."

"Just the age; a man should always be ten years older than his wife. A woman of thirty-five is in the prime of life, and if she hasn't arrived at years of discretion then, she never will. Shall I wear pearl-colored silk and a white bonnet, or just a very handsome travelling dress?"

"Whichever you like. But, Prue, isn't he rather stout, I won't say corpulent?"

"Sylvia, how can you! Because papa is a shadow, you call a fine, manly person like Gam—Mr. Bliss, corpulent. I always said I would *not* marry an invalid (Macgregor died of apoplexy last week, I heard, at a small dinner-party; fell forward with his head upon the cheese, and expired without a groan), and where can you find a more robust and healthy man than Mr. Bliss? Not a gray hair, and gout his only complaint. So aristocratic. You know I've loads of fine old flannel, just the thing for him."

Sylvia commanded her countenance with difficulty, and went on with her maternal inquiries.

"He is a personable man, and an excellent one I believe, yet I should rather dread the responsibility of nine small children, if I were you."

"They are my chief inducement to the match. Just think of the state those dears must be in, with only a young governess, and half a dozen giddy maids to see to them. I long to be among them, and named an early day, because measles and scarlatina are coming round again, and only Fanny, and the twins, Gus and Gam, have had either. I know all their names and ages, dispositions and characters, and love them like a mother already. He perfectly adores them, and that is very charming in a learned man like Mr. Bliss."

"If that is your feeling it will all go well, I have no doubt. But, Prue,—I don't wish to be unkind, dear,—do you quite like the idea of being the fourth Mrs. Bliss?"

"Bless me, I never thought of that! Poor man, it only shows how much he must need consolation, and proves how good a husband he must have been. No, Sylvia, I don't care a particle. I never knew those estimable ladies, and the memory of them shall not keep me from making Gamaliel happy if I can. What he goes through now is almost beyond belief. My child, just think!—the coachman drinks; the cook has tea-parties whenever she likes, and supports her brother's family out of her perquisites, as she calls her barefaced thefts; the house-maids romp with the indoor man, and have endless followers; three old maids set their caps at him, and that hussy,—I must use a strong expression,—that hussy of a governess makes love to him before the children. It is my duty to marry him; I shall do it, and put an end to this fearful state of things."

Sylvia asked but one more question,—

"Now, seriously, do you love him very much? Will he make you as happy as my dear girl should be?"

Prue dropped her work, and, hiding her face on Sylvia's shoulder, answered with a plaintive sniff or two, and much real feeling,—

"Yes, my dear, I do. I tried to love him, and I did not fail. I shall be happy, for I shall be busy. I am not needed here any more, and so I am glad to go away into a home of my own, feeling sure that you can fill my place; and Maria knows my ways too well to let things go amiss. Now, kiss me, and smooth my collar, for papa may call me down."

The sisters embraced and cried a little, as women usually find it necessary to do at such interesting times; then fell to planning the wedding outfit, and deciding between the "light silk and white bonnet," or the "handsome travelling suit."

Miss Yule made a great sacrifice to the proprieties by relinquishing her desire for a stately wedding, and, much to Sylvia's surprise and relief, insisted that, as the family was then situated, it was best to have no stir or parade, but to be married quietly at church and slip unostentatiously out of the old life into the new. Her will was law, and as the elderly bridegroom felt that there was no time to spare, and the measles continued to go about seeking whom they might devour, Prue did not keep him waiting long. "Three weeks is very little time, and nothing will be properly done, for one must have everything new when one is married, of course, and mantua-makers are but mortal women (exorbitant in their charges this season, I assure you), so be patient, Gamaliel, and spend the time in teaching my little ones to love me before I come."

"My dearest creature, I will." And well did the enamored gentleman perform his promise.

Prue kept hers so punctually that she was married with the bastings in her wedding gown and two dozen pocket-handkerchiefs still unhemmed,—facts which disturbed her even during the ceremony. A quiet time throughout; and after a sober feast, a tearful farewell, Mrs. Gamaliel Bliss departed, leaving a great void behind and carrying joy to the heart of her spouse, comfort to the souls of the excited nine, destruction to the "High Life Below Stairs," and order, peace, and plenty to the realm over which she was to know a long and prosperous reign.

Hardly had the excitement of this event subsided when another occurred to keep Sylvia from melancholy and bring an added satisfaction to her lonely days. Across the sea there came to her a little book, bearing her name upon its titlepage. Quaintly printed, and bound in some foreign style, plain and unassuming without, but very rich within, for there she found Warwick's Essays, and between each of these one of the poems from Moor's Diary. Far away there in Switzerland they had devised this pleasure for her, and done honor to the woman whom they both loved, by dedicating to her the first fruits of their lives. "Alpen Rosen" was its title, and none could have better suited it in Sylvia's eyes, for to her

Warwick was the Alps and Moor the roses. Each had helped the other; Warwick's rugged prose gathered grace from Moor's poetry, and Moor's smoothly flowing lines acquired power from Warwick's prose. Each had given her his best, and very proud was Sylvia of the little book, over which she pored day after day, living on and in it, eagerly collecting all praises, resenting all censures, and thinking it the one perfect volume in the world.

Others felt and acknowledged its worth as well; for though fashionable libraries were not besieged by inquiries for it, and no short-lived enthusiasm welcomed it, a place was found for it on many study-tables, where real work was done. Innocent girls sang the songs and loved the poet, while thoughtful women, looking deeper, honored the man. Young men received the Essays as brave protests against the evils of the times, and old men felt their faith in honor and honesty revive. The wise saw great promise in it, and the most critical could not deny its beauty and its power.

Early in autumn arrived a fresh delight; and Jessie's little daughter became peacemaker as well as idol. Max forgave his enemies, and swore eternal friendship with all mankind the first day of his baby's life; and when his sister brought it to him he took both in his arms, making atonement for many hasty words and hard thoughts by the broken whisper,—

"I have two little Sylvias now."

This wonderful being absorbed both households, from grandpapa to the deposed sovereign Tilly, whom Sylvia called her own, and kept much with her; while Prue threatened to cause a rise in the price of stationery by the daily and copious letters full of warning and advice which she sent, feeling herself a mother in Israel among her tribe of nine, now safely carried through the Red Sea of scarlatina. Happy faces made perpetual sunshine round the little Sylvia, but to none was she so dear a boon as to her young godmother. Jessie became a trifle jealous of "old Sylvia," as she now called herself, for she almost lived in baby's nursery; hurrying over in time to assist at its morning ablutions, hovering about its crib when it slept, daily discovering beauties invisible even to its mother's eyes, and working early and late on dainty garments, rich in the embroidery which she now thanked Prue for teaching her against her will. The touch of the baby hands seemed to heal her sore heart; the sound of the baby voice, even when most unmusical, had a soothing effect upon her nerves; the tender cares its helplessness demanded absorbed her thoughts, and kept her happy in a new world whose delights she had never known till now.

From this time a restful expression replaced the patient hopelessness her face had worn before, and in the lullabies she sang the listeners caught echoes of the cheerful voice they had never thought to hear again. Gay she was not, but serene. Quiet was all she asked; and shunning society seemed happiest to sit at home with baby and its gentle mother, with Max, now painting as if inspired, or with her father, who relinquished business and devoted himself to her. A pleasant pause seemed to have come after troublous days; a tranquil hush in which she sat waiting for what time should bring her. But as she waited the woman seemed to bloom more beautifully than the girl had done. Light and color revisited her countenance, clearer and deeper than of old; fine lines ennobled features faulty in themselves; and the indescribable refinement of a deep inward life made itself manifest in look, speech, and gesture, giving promise of a gracious womanhood.

As if to sever the last tie that bound her to the old home and make the new one her most natural refuge, Mr. Yule died suddenly. So painlessly and peacefully that no memory of suffering, no sad decay of mind, added to the sorrow of those who loved him most. His last words had been for Sylvia, "Goodnight, my daughter, and God bless you." His last kiss was given to her, and she was the first to find him in the morning wrapped in the sleep from which there is no awakening here.

Then the tender satisfaction of knowing that her dutiful affection had been all in all to him was a cordial that sustained her, lightened her grief, and for a time made the new loneliness unfelt.

Max was master now, and Jessie took the seat Prue had filled so long. Sylvia wished it so, and thought to slip into her old place again as if nothing had been changed. But it was impossible; the wayward girl was gone, and in her place a thoughtful woman who could not be satisfied with what had fed her once. Youthful pleasures, hopes, and fancies were replaced by earnest aspirations, faithful labor, and quiet joys. She dreamed no more but lived, and in holy living and high thinking found the secret of self-knowledge and self-help.

As spring came on a great longing for a home of her own grew up in her, and where should she so naturally go as to the Manse, still waiting for its mistress? When she spoke of this Max inwardly exulted and Jessie openly rejoiced; both feeling that she would not long remain content there without recalling its master. They were right; for Sylvia's resolve had been strengthening slowly ever since her father died, and to test it she went back to the home she had made so desolate. April saw her there, busy, quiet, but happy, if one might trust the serene face that seemed to brighten the closed rooms even more than the sunshine she let in. Before she left everything to others, now she set her house in order herself with a loving care which plainly betrayed it was for the coming of some dear and welcome guest.

But for the sincerity of her purpose, the warmth of her desire, the fidelity that never wavered from its duty, the memories that haunted the old house would have made it terrible to live there alone. It was sad, and with each day Sylvia longed more ardently for the return of the one companion who had the right to share it with her, the power to make it happy,—not with the former show of peace, but with a sober happiness too genuine to be wrecked again.

Hope painted a future full of content; for the suffering of the past, the hard-won repose of the present, proved that there was compensation for every loss, and that out of bitter sorrow strength and sweetness might be distilled by the Worker of all miracles.

Faith came to help her, as she had come many times that year, confirming each step she made, and cheering her to climb on with a brave heart and eyes fixed on heaven.

When all was ready Sylvia made a little pilgrimage through her Paradise Regained, lingering in many places to relive the sad or happy hours spent there; and when she came again to the study, she stood a moment, looking up at the Fates with something softer than a smile upon her face, as she said aloud,—

"I no longer fear you, pagan sisters. I am learning to spin my own life, trusting to a kinder hand than yours to weave some gold among the gray, and cut the thread when I am ready for a higher lesson."

Faith entered as she spoke, heard what she said, saw the uplifted look, felt that the time she had hoped for and believed in had come, and longed to share it with the other patient waiter.

"Sylvia, I am writing to Geoffrey. Have you any message for him, dear?"

"Yes, this."

Slowly Sylvia drew from her bosom a little note, opened it and held it before Faith, asking as a child might of its mother, "Shall I send it?"

Only three words, but Faith's heart sang for joy as she answered, "Yes!" for the words were,—

"Husband, come home."

CHAPTER XXI

Adam Keeps His Promise

In a small Italian town not far from Rome, a traveller stood listening to an account of a battle lately fought near by, in which the place had suffered much, yet been forever honored in the eyes of its inhabitants by having been the headquarters of the Hero of Italy. An inquiry of the traveller's concerning a countryman of whom he was in search created a sensation at the little inn, and elicited the story of the battle, one incident of which was still the all-absorbing topic with the excited villagers. This was the incident which one of the group related with the dramatic effects of a language composed almost as much of gesture as of words, and an audience as picturesque as could well be conceived.

While the fight was raging on the distant plain, a troop of marauding Croats dashed into the town, whose defenders, although outnumbered, contested every inch of ground, while slowly driven back toward the convent, the despoiling of which was the object of the attack. This convent was both hospital and refuge; for there were gathered women and children, the sick, the wounded, and the old. To secure the safety of these rather than of the sacred relics, the Italians were bent on holding the town till the reinforcement for which they had sent could come up. It was a question of time, and every moment brought nearer the destruction of the helpless garrison, trembling behind the convent walls. A brutal massacre was in store for them if no help came; and remembering this the red-shirted Garibaldians fought as if they well deserved their sobriquet of "Scarlet Demons."

Help did come, not from below, but from above. Suddenly a cannon thundered royally, and down the narrow street rushed a deathful defiance, carrying disorder and dismay to the assailants, joy and wonder to the nearly exhausted defenders,—wonder, for well they knew the gun had stood silent and unmanned since the retreat of the enemy two days before, and this unexpected answer to their prayers seemed Heaven-sent. Those below looked up as they fought, those above looked down as they feared, and midway between all saw that a single man held the gun. A stalwart figure, bareheaded, stern-faced, sinewy-armed, fitfully seen through clouds of smoke and flashes of fire, working with a silent energy that seemed almost superhuman to the eyes of the superstitious souls, who believed they saw and heard the convent's patron saint proclaiming their salvation with a mighty voice.

This belief inspired the Italians, caused a panic among the Croats, and saved the town. A few rounds turned the scale, the pursued became the pursuers, and when the reinforcement arrived, there was little for it to do but join in the rejoicing and salute the brave cannoneer, who proved to be no saint, but a stranger come to watch the battle, and thus opportunely lend his aid.

Enthusiastic were the demonstrations; vivas, blessings, tears, hand-kissing, and invocation of all the saints in the calendar, till it was discovered that the unknown gentleman had a bullet in his breast, and was in need of instant help. Whereupon the women, clustering about him like bees, bore him away to the hospital ward, where the inmates rose up in their beds to welcome him, and the clamorous crowd were with difficulty persuaded to relinquish him to the priest, the surgeon, and the rest he needed. Nor was this all; the crowning glory of the event to the villagers was the coming of the Chief at nightfall, and the scene about the stranger's bed. Here the narrator glowed with pride, the women in the group began to sob, and the men took off their caps, with black eyes glittering through their tears.

"Excellenza, he who had fought for us like a tempest, an angel of doom, lay there beside my cousin Beppo, who was past help, and is now in holy Paradise. Speranza was washing the smoke and powder from him, the wound was easy. Death of my soul! may he who gave it die unconfessed! See you, I am there, I watch him, the friend of Excellenza, the great still man who smiled but said no word to us. Then comes the Chief,—silenzio, till I finish!—he comes, they have told him, he stays at the bed, he looks down, the fine eye shines, he takes the hand, he says low—'I thank you,'—he lays his cloak—the gray cloak we know and love so well—over the wounded breast, and so goes on. We cry out, but what does the friend? Behold! he lifts himself, he lays the cloak upon my Beppo, he says in that so broken way of his—'Comrade, the honor is for you who gave your life for him, I give but a single hour.' Beppo saw, heard, comprehended; thanked him with a glance, and rose up to die crying, 'Viva Italia! Viva Garibaldi!' "

The cry was caught up by all the listeners in a whirlwind of enthusiastic loyalty, and the stranger joined in it, thrilled with an equal love and honor for the Patriot Soldier, whose name upon Italian lips means liberty.

"Where is he now, this friend of mine, so nearly lost, so happily found?"

A dozen hands pointed to the convent, a dozen brown faces lighted up, and a dozen eager voices poured out directions, messages, and benedictions in a breath. Ordering his carriage to follow presently, the traveller rapidly climbed the steep road, guided by signs he could not well mistake. The convent gate stood open, and he paused for no permission to enter; for looking through it, down the green vista of an orchard path, he saw his friend and sprang to meet him.

"Adam!"

"Geoffrey!"

"Truant that you are, to desert me for ten days, and only let me find you when you have no need of me."

"I always need you, but am not always needed. I went away because the old restlessness came upon me in that dead city, Rome. You were happy there, but I scented war, followed and found it by instinct, and have had enough of it. Look at my hands."

He laughed as he showed them, still bruised and blackened with the hard usage they had received; nothing else but a paler shade of color from loss of blood showed that he had passed through any suffering or danger.

"Brave hands, I honor them for all their grime. Tell me about it, Adam; show me the wound; describe the scene, I want to hear it in calm English."

But Warwick was slow to do so, being the hero of the tale, and very brief was the reply Moor got.

"I came to watch, but found work ready for me. It is not clear to me even now what I did, nor how I did it. One of my Berserker rages possessed me, I fancy; my nerves and muscles seemed made of steel and gutta-percha; the smell of powder intoxicated, and the sense of power was grand. The fire, the smoke, the din were all delicious, and I felt like a giant, as I wielded that great weapon, dealing many deaths with a single pair of hands."

"The savage in you got the mastery just then; I've seen it, and have often wondered how you managed to control it so well. Now it has had a holiday and made a hero of you."

"The savage is better out than in, and any man may be a hero if he will. What have you been doing since I left you poring over pictures in a mouldy palace?"

"You think to slip away from the subject, and after facing death at a cannon's breach expect me to be satisfied with an ordinary greeting? I won't have it; I insist upon asking as many questions as I like, hearing about the wound and seeing if it is doing well. Where is it?"

Warwick showed it, a little purple spot above his heart. Moor's face grew anxious as he looked, but cleared again as he examined it, for the ball had glanced off and the wholesome flesh was already healing fast.

"Too near, Adam, but thank God it was no nearer. A little lower and I might have looked for you in vain."

"This heart of mine is a tough organ, bullet-proof, I dare say, though I wear no breastplate."

"But this!" Involuntarily Moor's eye asked the question his lips did not utter as he touched a worn and faded case hanging on the broad breast before him. Silently Warwick opened it, showing not Sylvia's face but that of an old woman, rudely drawn in sepia; the brown tints bringing out the marked features as no softer hue could have done, and giving to each line a depth of expression that made the serious countenance singularly lifelike and attractive.

Now Moor saw where Warwick got both keen eyes and firm mouth, as well as the gentler traits that softened his strong face; and felt that no other woman ever had or ever would hold so dear a place as the old mother whose likeness he had drawn and hung where other men wear images of mistress or of wife. With a glance as full of penitence as the other had been of disquiet, Moor laid back the little case, drew bandage and blouse over both wound and picture, and linked his arm in Warwick's as he asked,—

"Who shot you?"

"How can I tell? I knew nothing of it till that flock of women fell to kissing these dirty hands of mine; then I was conscious of a stinging pain in my shoulder, and a warm stream trickling down my side. I looked to see what was amiss, whereat the good souls set up a shriek, took possession of me, and for half an hour wept and wailed over me in a frenzy of emotion and good-will that kept me merry in spite of the surgeon's probes and the priest's prayers. The appellations showered upon me would have startled even your ears, accustomed to soft words. Were you ever called 'core of my heart,' 'sun of my soul,' or 'cup of gold'?"

"Cannonading suits your spirits excellently; I remember your telling me that you had tried and liked it. But there is to be no more of it, I have other plans for you. Before I mention them, tell me of the interview with Garibaldi."

"That now is a thing to ask one about; a thing to talk of and take pride in all one's days. I was half asleep and thought myself dreaming till he spoke. A right noble face, Geoffrey; full of thought and power; the look of one born to command others because master of himself. A square strong frame; no decorations, no parade; dressed like his men, yet as much the chief as if he wore a dozen orders on his scarlet shirt."

"Where is the cloak? I want to see and touch it; surely you kept it as a relic?"

"Not I. Having seen the man, what do I care for the garment that covered him? I keep the handshake, the 'Grazia,' for my share. Poor Beppo lies buried in the hero's cloak."

"I grudge it to him, every inch of it; for, not having seen the man, *I* do desire the garment. Who but you would have done it?"

Warwick smiled, knowing that his friend was well pleased with him for all his murmuring. They walked in silence till Moor abruptly asked,—

"When can you travel, Adam?"

"I was coming back to you to-morrow."

"Are you sure it is safe?"

"Quite sure; ten days is enough to waste upon a scratch like this."

"Come now, I cannot wait till to-morrow."

"Very good. Can you stop till I get my hat?"

"You don't ask me why I am in such haste."

Moor's tone caused Warwick to pause and look at him. Joy, impatience, anxiety, contended with each other in his countenance; and as if unable to tell the cause himself he put a little paper into the other's hand. Only three words were contained in it, but they caused Warwick's face to kindle with all the joy betrayed in that of his friend, none of the impatience nor anxiety.

"What can I say to show you my pleasure? The months have seemed very long, but now comes the reward. The blessed little letter! so like herself; the slender slip, the delicate handwriting, the three happy words, each saying volumes."

Moor did not speak, but still looked up anxiously, inquiringly; and Warwick answered with a glance he could not doubt,—

"Have no fears for me. I share the joy as heartily as I shared the sorrow; neither can separate us any more."

"Thank Heaven for that! But, Adam, as I accept this good gift, am I not robbing you again? You never speak of the past, how is it with you now?"

"Quite well and happy; the pain is gone, the peace remains. I would not have it otherwise. Time and suffering have cured the selfishness of love, and left the satisfaction which nothing can change or take away.

Believe that I say this without regret, and freely enjoy the happiness that comes to you."

"I will, but not as I once should; for though I feel that you need neither sympathy nor pity, still I seem to take so much and leave you nothing."

"You leave me myself, better and humbler than before. In the fierce half-hour I lived not long ago, I think a great and needful change was wrought in me. All lives are full of such, coming when least looked for, working out the end through unexpected means. The restless, domineering devil that haunted me was cast out then; and during the quiet time that followed a new spirit entered in and took possession."

"What is it, Adam?"

"I cannot tell, yet I welcome it. This peaceful mood may not last perhaps, but it brings me that rare moment—pity that it is so rare, and but a moment—when we seem to see temptation at our feet; when we are conscious of a willingness to leave all in God's hand, ready for whatever he may send; feeling that whether it be suffering or joy we shall see the Giver in the gift, and when He calls can answer cheerfully, 'Lord, here am I.' "

It *was* a rare moment, and in it Moor for the first time clearly saw the desire and design of his friend's life; saw it because it was accomplished, and for the instant Adam Warwick was what he aspired to be. A goodly man, whose stalwart body seemed a fit home for a strong soul, wise with the wisdom of a deep experience, genial with the virtues of an upright life, devout with that humble yet valiant piety which comes through hard-won victories over "the world, the flesh, and the devil." Despite the hope that warmed his heart, Moor felt poor beside him, as a new reverence warmed the old affection. His face showed it, though he did not speak and Warwick laid an arm about his shoulders as he had often done of late when they were alone, drawing him gently on again, as he said, with a touch of playfulness to set both at ease,—

"Tell me your plans, 'my cup of gold,' and let me lend a hand toward filling you brimful of happiness. You are going home?"

"At once; you also."

"Is it best?"

"Yes; you came for me, I stay for you, and Sylvia waits for both."

"She says nothing of me in this short, sweet note of hers," and Warwick smoothed it carefully in his large hand, eying it as if he wished there were some little word for him.

"True, but in the few letters she has written there always comes a message to you, though you never write a line; nor would you go to her now had she sent for you alone; she knew that, and sends for me, sure that you will follow."

"Being a woman she cannot quite forgive me for loving her too well to make her miserable. Dear soul, she will never know how much it cost me, but I knew that my only safety lay in flight. Tell her so a long while hence."

"You shall do it yourself, for you are coming to America with me."

"What to do there?"

"All you ever did; walk up and down the face of the earth, waxing in power and virtue, and coming often to us when we get fairly back into our former ways, for you are still the house friend."

"I shall not disturb you yet. I'll see you safe across, and then vanish for another year. I was wondering, as I walked here, what my next summons would be, when lo, you came. Go on, I'll follow you; one could hardly have a better guide."

"You are sure you are able, Adam?"

"Shall I uproot a tree or fling you over the wall to convince you, you motherly body? I am nearly whole again, and a breath of sea air will complete the cure. Let me cover my head, say farewell to the good Sisters, and I shall be glad to slip away without further demonstrations from the volcanoes below there."

Laying one hand on the low wall, Warwick vaulted over with a backward glance at Moor, who followed to the gateway, there to wait till the adieux were over. Very brief they were, and presently Warwick reappeared, evidently touched yet ill-pleased at something, for he both smiled and frowned as he paused on the threshold as if loath to go. A little white goat came skipping from the orchard, and, seeing the stranger, took refuge at Warwick's knee. The act of the creature seemed to suggest a thought to the man. Pulling off the gay handkerchief some grateful woman had knotted round his neck, he fastened it about the goat's, having secured something in one end, then rose as if content.

"What are you doing?" called Moor, wondering at this arrangement.

"Widening the narrow entrance into heaven set apart for rich men unless they leave their substance behind, as I am trying to do. The kind creatures cannot refuse it now; so trot away to your mistress, little Nanna, and tell no tales as you go."

As the goat went tapping up the steps a stir within announced the dreaded demonstration. Warwick did not seem to hear it; he stood looking far across the trampled plain and ruined town toward the mountains shining white against the deep Italian sky. A rapt, far-reaching look, as if he saw beyond the purple wall, and seeing forgot the present in some vision of the future.

"Come, Adam! I am waiting."

His eye came back, the rapt look passed, and cheerily he answered,—

"I am ready."

A fortnight later in the dark hour before the dawn, with a murky sky above them, a hungry sea below them, the two stood together, the last to leave a sinking ship.

"Room for one more, choose quick!" shouted a hoarse voice from the boat tossing underneath, freighted to the water's edge with trembling lives.

"Go, Geoffrey, Sylvia is waiting."

"Not without you, Adam."

"But you are exhausted; I can bear a rough hour better than yourself, and morning will bring help."

"It may not. Go, I am the lesser loss."

"What folly! I will force you to it; steady there, he is coming."

"Push off, I am *not* coming."

In times like that, few pause for pity or persuasion; the instinct of self-preservation rules supreme, and each is for himself, except those in whom love of another is stronger than love of life. Even while the friends generously contended the boat was swept away, and they were left alone in the deserted ship, swiftly making its last voyage downward. Spent with a day of intense excitement, and sick with hope deferred, Moor leaned on Warwick, feeling that it was adding bitterness to death to die in sight of shore. But Warwick never knew despair; passive submission was not in his power while anything remained to do or dare, and even then he did not cease to hope. It was certain death to linger there; other boats less heavily laden had put off before, and might drift across their track; wreckers waiting on the shore might hear and help; at least it were better to die bravely and not "strike sail to a fear." About his waist still hung a fragment of the rope which had lowered more than one baby to its mother's arms; before them the shattered taffrail rose and fell as the waves beat over it. Wrenching a spar away he lashed Moor to it, explaining his purpose as he worked. There was only rope enough for one, and in the darkness Moor believed that Warwick had taken equal precautions for himself.

"Now, Geoffrey, your hand, and when the next wave ebbs let us follow it. If we are parted and you see her first, tell her I remembered, and give her this."

In the black night with only Heaven to see them the men kissed tenderly as women, then hand in hand sprang out into the sea. Drenched and blinded they struggled up after the first plunge, and struck out for the shore, guided by the thunder of the surf they had listened to for twelve long hours, as it broke against the beach, and brought no help on its receding billows. Soon Warwick was the only one who struggled, for Moor's strength was gone, and he clung half conscious to the spar, tossing from wave to wave, a piteous plaything for the sea.

"I see a light!—they must take you in—hold fast—I'll save you for the little wife at home."

Moor heard but two words, "wife" and "home;" strained his dim eyes to see the light, spent his last grain of strength to reach it, and in the act lost consciousness, whispering, "She will thank you," as his head fell against Warwick's breast and lay there, heavy and still. Lifting himself above the spar, Adam lent the magnificent power of his voice to the shout he sent ringing through the storm. He did not call in vain, a friendly wind took the cry to human ears, a relenting wave swept them within the reach of human aid, and the boat's crew, pausing involuntarily, saw a hand clutch the suspended oar, a face flash up from the black water, and heard a breathless voice issue the command,—

"Take in this man! he saved you for your wives, save him for his."

One resolute will can sway a panic-stricken multitude; it did so then. The boat was rocking in the long swell of the sea; a moment and the coming wave would sweep them far apart. A woman sobbed, and as if moved by one impulse four sturdy arms clutched and drew Moor in. While loosening his friend Warwick had forgotten himself, and the spar was gone. He knew it, but the rest believed that they left the strong man a chance of life equal to their own in that overladen boat. Yet in the memories of all who caught that last glimpse of him there long remained the recollection of a dauntless face floating out into the night, a steady voice calling through the gale, "A good voyage, comrades!" as he turned away to enter port before them.

Wide was the sea and pitiless the storm, but neither could dismay the unconquerable spirit of the man who fought against the elements as bravely as if they were adversaries of mortal mould, and might be vanquished in the end. But it was not to be; soon he felt it, accepted it, turned his face upward toward the sky, where one star shone, and when Death whispered "Come!" answered as cheerily as to that other friend, "I am ready." Then with a parting thought for the man he had saved, the woman he had loved, the promise he had kept, a great and tender heart went down into the sea.

Sometimes the Sculptor, whose workshop is the world, fuses many metals and casts a noble statue; leaves it for humanity to criticise, and when time has mellowed both beauties and blemishes, removes it to that inner studio, there to be carved in enduring marble.

Adam Warwick was such an one, with much alloy and many flaws; but beneath all defects the Master's eye saw the grand lines that were to serve as models for the perfect man, and when the design had passed through all necessary processes,—the mould of clay, the furnace fire, the test of time,—He washed the dust away, and pronounced it ready for the marble.

CHAPTER XXII

At Last

News of the wreck reached the Yules some days before Moor could let them know of his safety and Adam's loss. The belief that both were gone was almost too much for Sylvia, and for a week she sat in the shadow of a great despair, feeling that her mistakes and weaknesses had sent them to their death.

"I was not worthy of either, and God denies me the reward I have worked so hard to earn. I could have spared Adam. I had given him up and learned to see that it was best. But Geoffrey, my husband, who had waited so long, who hoped so much, whom I was going to make so happy, never to know how well I loved him after all this pain and separation—oh, it is too hard, too bitter to lose him now!"

This was all her thought, her lamentation; Warwick seemed forgotten, the lesser loss was swallowed up in the greater, and Sylvia mourned for her husband like a woman and a wife, feeling at last the nearness and dearness of the sacred tie that bound them together. Death taught her in the anguish of that hour how impossible it was to love any other with the passion born of that pain, touched with the tender memory of his past loyalty, the fervent desire to atone by future devotion and the sincerest fidelity.

In the midst of this despair came the glad tidings that Moor was safe and on his way to her from the distant port whither the survivors had been carried by the ship that saved them.

Then Sylvia fell on her knees and made a thank-offering of her life, dedicating it with tears and prayers and voiceless hymns of gratitude to this man saved for her by the friend who loved them both better than his own life, and died so gladly for their sake.

Max thought the joy would kill her, but she came out of the room where she had lain in darkness, looking like one risen from the tomb. A peace beyond words to describe transfigured her face, "clear shining after rain," making her silence more eloquent than speech, and every hour seemed to bring new strength, beauty, and serenity to make the wan and weary body a fitter home for a soul just entering into the world of higher thought and feeling to which it had attained after much pain and struggle.

"Go and meet him, Max. I will wait for him at home, and give my welcome there. Come soon, and tell him I have no room for sorrow, my heart is so full of gratitude and joy."

May had come again and the Manse wore its loveliest aspect to greet its master, who came at last and alone. But not to an empty home, for on the threshold stood his wife, not the wayward child he wooed, the melancholy girl he married, but a woman with her soul in her face, her heart upon her lips, and outstretched arms that seemed to hold all that was dearest in the world when they clasped him with the tender cry,—

"Thank God! I have my husband safe."

They had been together for an hour. The first excitement was over, and Sylvia stood beside him pale but calm with intensity of joy, while Moor leaned his weary head against her, trying to forget his great sorrow, and realize the greater happiness that had befallen him. Hitherto all their talk had been of Adam, and as Moor concluded the history of the year so tragically ended, for the first time he ventured to express surprise at the calmness with which his bearer received the sad story.

"How quietly you listen to words it wrings my heart to utter. Have you wept your tears dry, or do you still hope?"

"No, I feel that we shall never see him again; but I have no desire to weep, for tears and lamentations do not belong to him. He died a noble death; the sea is a fitting grave for him, and it is pleasant to think of him quiet at last," answered Sylvia, still tearless and tranquil.

"I cannot feel so; I find it hard to think of him as dead; he was so full of life, so fit to live."

"And therefore fit to die. Imagine him as I do, enjoying the larger life he longed for, and growing to be the nobler man whose foreshadowing we saw and loved so here."

"Sylvia, I have told you of the beautiful change which came over him in those last weeks, and now I see something of the same change in you, as if the weaker part had slipped away and left the spirit visible. Are you, too, about to leave me, just as I have recovered you?"

Moor held her close and searched her face, feeling that he hardly dared believe the beautiful miracle time had wrought.

"I shall stay with you all my life, please God. There will be no shadow of turning now. Let me tell you why I do not mourn for Adam, and why you may trust the love that has cost us all so much."

Drawing his head to its former resting-place, she touched it very tenderly, seeing with a pang how many silver threads had come among the brown; and as her hand went to and fro with an inexpressibly soothing gesture she went on in a tone whose quietude controlled his agitation like a spell.

"Long ago in my great trouble, Faith told me that for every human effort or affliction there were two great helpers, Time and Death. After you left me I fell ill, more ill than you ever knew, dear, and for days believed that death was to end all perplexity and pain for me. I thought I should be glad that the struggle was over, but I was not, and longed to live that I might atone. While lying thus I had a dream which seemed to foreshadow what has come to pass. I did not understand it then, now I do. You have no faith in dreams, I have, and to this one I owe much of the faith that kept me up in those first hard days."

"God bless the dream then, and send another as helpful. Tell it to me, love."

"It was a strange and solemn vision; one to remember for its curious mingling of the familiar and the sublime, one to love for the message it seemed to bring me from lips that will never speak to me again. I dreamed that the last day of the world had come. I stood on the cliffs we know so well, you were beside me, and Adam apart and above us. All around as far as eye could reach thronged myriads of people, till the earth seemed white with human faces. All were mute and motionless, as if fixed in a trance of expectation, for none knew how the end would come. Utter silence filled the world, and across the sky a vast curtain of the blackest cloud was falling, blotting out face after face and leaving the world a blank. In that universal gloom and stillness, high above me in the heavens I saw the pale outlines of a word stretching from horizon to horizon. Letter after letter came out full and clear, till all across the sky, burning with a ruddy glory stronger than the sun, shone the great word Amen. As the last letter reached its bright perfection, a long waft of wind broke over me like a universal sigh of hope from human hearts. For far away on the horizon's edge all saw a line of light that widened as they looked, and through that rift, between the dark earth and the darker sky, rolled in a softly flowing sea. Wave after wave came on, so wide, so cool, so still. None trembled at their approach, none shrunk from their embrace, but all turned toward that ocean with a mighty rush, all faces glowed in its splendor, and million after million vanished with longing eyes fixed on the arch of light through which the ebbing sea would float them when its work was done. I felt no fear, only the deepest awe, for I seemed such an infinitesimal atom of the countless host that I forgot myself. Nearer and nearer came the flood, till its breath blew on my cheeks, and I, too, leaned to meet it, longing to be taken. It broke over us, but you held me fast, and when the bitter waters ebbed away we stood alone, stranded on the green nook where the pine and birch trees grow. I caught my breath and was so glad to live, that when the next billow came in, I clung to you longing to be kept. The great wave rolled up before me, and through its soft glimmer I saw a beautiful, benignant face, regarding us with something brighter than a smile, as the wave broke at our feet and receded carrying the face away to be lost in the sunshine that suddenly turned the sea to gold. Adam was gone, but I knew that I had seen him as he will look in Heaven, and woke wondering what the vision meant. Now I know."

For a moment neither spoke, for Sylvia was pale with the mere memory of that prophetic dream, and Moor absorbed in reading the interpretation of it in her altered face. She helped him by telling what God and Faith had done for her during that long year of probation, effort, and hard-won success. She laid her heart bare, and when the sad story reached its happy end Moor stood up to receive the reward she so gladly yet so meekly gave him, as she laid both hands in his saying with tears now,—

"I love you! Trust me, and let me try again."

No need to record his answer, nor the welcome she received as she was gathered to the home where she no longer felt an alien nor a prisoner.

Standing together in the hush of the pleasant room they both loved best, Sylvia pointed up to the picture which now replaced the weird Sisters, as if she hoped to banish the faces that had looked down relentless on that bitter night a year ago.

It was a lovely painting of the moonlight voyage down the river; Max's last gift and peace-offering to Sylvia. He had effaced himself behind the sail, a shadow in the light that silvered its white wing. But the moon shone full on Warwick at the helm, looking out straight and strong before him, with the vigilant expression native to him touched by the tender magic of the new sentiment for which he had found no name as yet. Moor leaned to look at Sylvia, a quiet figure full of grace and color, couched under the green arch; not asleep, but just waking, as if conscious of the eyes that watched and waited for an answering look. On either hand the summer woods made vernal gloom, behind the hills rose sharply up against the blue, and all before wound a shining road, along which the boat seemed floating like a white-winged bird between two skies.

"See, Geoffrey, how beautiful it is, not only as a souvenir of that happy time, but a symbol of the happier one to come. I am awake now, you see, and you are smiling as you used to smile. He is in the light, parted from us only by the silvery mist that rises from the stream. Could we have a better guide as we set sail again to voyage down the river that ends in the ocean he has already crossed?"

"No. Death makes a saint of him, may life make a hero of me," answered Moor, with no bitter drop to mar the sweetness of that memory now.

"Love and God's help can work all miracles since it has worked this one so well," answered Sylvia, with a look Adam might have owned, so full of courage, hope, and ardor was it as she turned from the painted romance to the more beautiful reality, to live, not dream, a long and happy life, unmarred by the moods that nearly wrecked her youth; for now she had learned to live by principle, not impulse, and this made it both sweet and possible for love and duty to go hand in hand.

THE END.

Behind a Mask: or, A Woman's Power *is probably Alcott's best-known and most highly regarded work of sensation fiction. It appeared as the title story in Madeleine B. Stern's first collection of Alcott's thrillers,* Behind a Mask: The Unknown Thrillers of Louisa May Alcott, *published by Avenel Books in 1975, and has since been reprinted several times. The novella was first published in James R. Elliott's* The Flag of Our Union *under the pseudonym A. M. Barnard two years after the publication of* Moods *and two years before* Little Women, *part 1. Stern's selection of* Behind a Mask *as the title for her volume suggests a major source of the story's appeal, for it implies that Alcott herself was writing from behind a mask of pseudonymity and thus insinuating herself into the literary marketplace much as her heroine, Jean Muir, was infiltrating the patriarchal home. Critics have gone on to speculate that Alcott's later portrayal of little women and her seeming advocacy of little women values constituted her real mask or disguise just as Jean's impersonation of an ingenue governess—both a little woman herself and a guide to one—enabled her to exploit and subvert Victorian notions of a woman's role. Surely, to read* Moods, Behind a Mask, *and* Little Women *in rapid succession is to gain a strong sense of the disjunctions and the continuities in Alcott's remarkably various career.*

Behind a Mask: or, A Woman's Power

I

Jean Muir

"Has she come?"

"No, Mamma, not yet."

"I wish it were well over. The thought of it worries and excites me. A cushion for my back, Bella."

And poor, peevish Mrs. Coventry sank into an easy chair with a nervous sigh and the air of a martyr, while her pretty daughter hovered about her with affectionate solicitude.

"Who are they talking of, Lucia?" asked the languid young man lounging on a couch near his cousin, who bent over her tapestry work with a happy smile on her usually haughty face.

"The new governess, Miss Muir. Shall I tell you about her?"

"No, thank you. I have an inveterate aversion to the whole tribe. I've often thanked heaven that I had but one sister, and she a spoiled child, so that I have escaped the infliction of a governess so long."

"How will you bear it now?" asked Lucia.

"Leave the house while she is in it."

"No, you won't. You're too lazy, Gerald," called out a younger and more energetic man, from the recess where he stood teasing his dogs.

"I'll give her a three days' trial; if she proves endurable I shall not disturb myself; if, as I am sure, she is a bore, I'm off anywhere, anywhere out of her way."

"I beg you won't talk in that depressing manner, boys. I dread the coming of a stranger more than you possibly can, but Bella *must* not be neglected; so I have nerved myself to endure this woman, and Lucia is good enough to say she will attend to her after tonight."

"Don't be troubled, Mamma. She is a nice person, I dare say, and when once we are used to her, I've no doubt we shall be glad to have her, it's so dull here just now. Lady Sydney said she was a quiet, accomplished, amiable girl, who needed a home, and would be a help to poor stupid me, so try to like her for my sake."

"I will, dear, but isn't it getting late? I do hope nothing has happened. Did you tell them to send a carriage to the station for her, Gerald?"

"I forgot it. But it's not far, it won't hurt her to walk" was the languid reply.

"It was indolence, not forgetfulness, I know. I'm very sorry; she will think it so rude to leave her to find her way so late. Do go and see to it, Ned."

"Too late, Bella, the train was in some time ago. Give your orders to me next time, Mother, and I'll see that they are obeyed," said Edward.

"Ned is just at an age to make a fool of himself for any girl who comes in his way. Have a care of the governess, Lucia, or she will bewitch him."

Gerald spoke in a satirical whisper, but his brother heard him and answered with a good-humored laugh.

"I wish there was any hope of your making a fool of yourself in that way, old fellow. Set me a good example, and I promise to follow it. As for the governess, she is a woman, and should be treated with common civility. I should say a little extra kindness wouldn't be amiss, either, because she is poor, and a stranger."

"That is my dear, good-hearted Ned! We'll stand by poor little Muir, won't we?" And running to her brother, Bella stood on tiptoe to offer him a kiss which he could not refuse, for the rosy lips were pursed up invitingly, and the bright eyes full of sisterly affection.

"I do hope she has come, for, when I make an effort to see anyone, I hate to make it in vain. Punctuality is *such* a virtue, and I know this woman hasn't got it, for she promised to be here at seven, and now it is long after," began Mrs. Coventry, in an injured tone.

Before she could get breath for another complaint, the clock struck seven and the doorbell rang.

"There she is!" cried Bella, and turned toward the door as if to go and meet the newcomer.

But Lucia arrested her, saying authoritatively, "Stay here, child. It is her place to come to you, not yours to go to her."

"Miss Muir," announced a servant, and a little black-robed figure stood in the doorway. For an instant no one stirred, and the governess had time to see and be seen before a word was uttered. All looked at her, and she cast on the household group a keen glance that impressed them curiously; then her eyes fell, and bowing slightly she walked in. Edward came forward and received her with the frank cordiality which nothing could daunt or chill.

"Mother, this is the lady whom you expected. Miss Muir, allow me to apologize for our apparent neglect in not sending for you. There was a mistake about the carriage, or, rather, the lazy fellow to whom the order was given forgot it. Bella, come here."

"Thank you, no apology is needed. I did not expect to be sent for." And the governess meekly sat down without lifting her eyes.

"I am glad to see you. Let me take your things," said Bella, rather shyly, for Gerald, still lounging, watched the fireside group with languid interest, and Lucia never stirred. Mrs. Coventry took a second survey and began:

"You were punctual, Miss Muir, which pleases me. I'm a sad invalid, as Lady Sydney told you, I hope; so that Miss Coventry's lessons will be directed by my niece, and you will go to her for directions, as she knows what I wish. You will excuse me if I ask you a few questions, for Lady Sydney's note was very brief, and I left everything to her judgment."

"Ask anything you like, madam," answered the soft, sad voice.

"You are Scotch, I believe."

"Yes, madam."

"Are your parents living?"

"I have not a relation in the world."

"Dear me, how sad! Do you mind telling me your age?"

"Nineteen." And a smile passed over Miss Muir's lips, as she folded her hands with an air of resignation, for the catechism was evidently to be a long one.

"So young! Lady Sydney mentioned five-and-twenty, I think, didn't she, Bella?

"No, Mamma, she only said she thought so. Don't ask such questions. It's not pleasant before us all," whispered Bella.

A quick, grateful glance shone on her from the suddenly lifted eyes of Miss Muir, as she said quietly, "I wish I was thirty, but, as I am not, I do my best to look and seem old."

Of course, every one looked at her then, and all felt a touch of pity at the sight of the pale-faced girl in her plain black dress, with no ornament but a little silver cross at her throat. Small, thin, and colorless she was, with yellow hair, gray eyes, and sharply cut, irregular, but very expressive features. Poverty seemed to have set its bond stamp upon her, and life to have had for her more frost than sunshine. But something in the lines of the mouth betrayed strength, and the clear, low voice had a curious mixture of command and entreaty in its varying tones. Not an attractive woman, yet not an ordinary one; and, as she sat there with her delicate hands lying in her lap, her head bent, and a bitter look on her thin face, she was more interesting than many a blithe and blooming girl. Bella's heart warmed to her at once, and she drew her seat nearer, while Edward went back to his dogs that his presence might not embarrass her.

"You have been ill, I think," continued Mrs. Coventry, who considered this fact the most interesting of all she had heard concerning the governess.

"Yes, madam, I left the hospital only a week ago."

"Are you quite sure it is safe to begin teaching so soon?"

"I have no time to lose, and shall soon gain strength here in the country, if you care to keep me."

"And you are fitted to teach music, French, and drawing?"

"I shall endeavor to prove that I am."

"Be kind enough to go and play an air or two. I can judge by your touch; I used to play finely when a girl."

Miss Muir rose, looked about her for the instrument, and seeing it at the other end of the room went toward it, passing Gerald and Lucia as if she did not see them. Bella followed, and in a moment forgot everything in admiration. Miss Muir played like one who loved music and was perfect mistress of her art. She charmed them all by the magic of this spell; even indolent Gerald sat up to listen, and Lucia put down her needle, while Ned watched the slender white fingers as they flew, and wondered at the strength and skill which they possessed.

"Please sing," pleaded Bella, as a brilliant overture ended.

With the same meek obedience Miss Muir complied, and began a little Scotch melody, so sweet, so sad, that the girl's eyes filled, and Mrs. Coventry looked for one of her many pocket-handkerchiefs. But suddenly the music ceased, for, with a vain attempt to support herself, the singer slid from her seat and lay before the startled listeners, as white and rigid as if struck with death. Edward caught her up, and, ordering his brother off the couch, laid her there, while Bella chafted her hands, and her mother rang for her maid. Lucia bathed the poor girl's temples, and

Gerald, with unwonted energy, brought a glass of wine. Soon Miss Muir's lips trembled, she sighed, then murmured, tenderly, with a pretty Scotch accent, as if wandering in the past, "Bide wi' me, Mither, I'm sae sick an sad here all alone."

"Take a sip of this, and it will do you good, my dear," said Mrs. Coventry, quite touched by the plaintive words.

The strange voice seemed to recall her. She sat up, looked about her, a little wildly, for a moment, then collected herself and said, with a pathetic look and tone, "Pardon me. I have been on my feet all day, and, in my eagerness to keep my appointment, I forgot to eat since morning. I'm better now; shall I finish the song?"

"By no means. Come and have some tea," said Bella, full of pity and remorse.

"Scene first, very well done," whispered Gerald to his cousin.

Miss Muir was just before them, apparently listening to Mrs. Coventry's remarks upon fainting fits; but she heard, and looked over her shoulders with a gesture like Rachel. Her eyes were gray, but at that instant they seemed black with some strong emotion of anger, pride, or defiance. A curious smile passed over her face as she bowed, and said in her penetrating voice, "Thanks. The last scene shall be still better."

Young Coventry was a cool, indolent man, seldom conscious of any emotion, any passion, pleasurable or otherwise; but at the look, the tone of the governess, he experienced a new sensation, indefinable, yet strong. He colored and, for the first time in his life, looked abashed. Lucia saw it, and hated Miss Muir with a sudden hatred; for, in all the years she had passed with her cousin, no look or word of hers had possessed such power. Coventry was himself again in an instant, with no trace of that passing change, but a look of interest in his usually dreamy eyes, and a touch of anger in his sarcastic voice.

"What a melodramatic young lady! I shall go tomorrow."

Lucia laughed, and was well pleased when he sauntered away to bring her a cup of tea from the table where a little scene was just taking place. Mrs. Coventry had sunk into her chair again, exhausted by the flurry of the fainting fit. Bella was busied about her; and Edward, eager to feed the pale governess, was awkwardly trying to make the tea, after a beseeching glance at his cousin which she did not choose to answer. As he upset the caddy and uttered a despairing exclamation, Miss Muir quietly took her place behind the urn, saying with a smile, and a shy glance at the young man, "Allow me to assume my duty at once, and serve you all. I understand the art of making people comfortable in this way. The scoop, please. I can gather this up quite well alone, if you will tell me how your mother likes her tea."

Edward pulled a chair to the table and made merry over his mishaps, while Miss Muir performed her little task with a skill and grace that made it pleasant to watch her. Coventry lingered a moment after she had given him a steaming cup, to observe her more nearly, while he asked a question or two of his brother. She took no more notice of him than if he had been a statue, and in the middle of the one remark he addressed to her, she rose to take the sugar basin to Mrs. Coventry, who was quite won by the modest, domestic graces of the new governess.

"Really, my dear, you are a treasure; I haven't tasted such tea since my poor maid Ellis died. Bella never makes it good, and Miss Lucia always forgets the cream. Whatever you do you seem to do well, and that is *such* a comfort."

"Let me always do this for you, then. It will be a pleasure, madam." And Miss Muir came back to her seat with a faint color in her cheek which improved her much.

"My brother asked if young Sydney was at home when you left," said Edward, for Gerald would not take the trouble to repeat the question.

Miss Muir fixed her eyes on Coventry, and answered with a slight tremor of the lips, "No, he left home some weeks ago."

The young man went back to his cousin, saying, as he threw himself down beside her, "I shall not go tomorrow, but wait till the three days are out."

"Why?" demanded Lucia.

Lowering his voice he said, with a significant nod toward the governess, "Because I have a fancy that she is at the bottom of Sydney's mystery. He's not been himself lately, and now he is gone without a word. I rather like romances in real life, if they are not too long, or difficult to read."

"Do you think her pretty?"

"Far from it, a most uncanny little specimen."

"Then why fancy Sydney loves her?"

"He is an oddity, and likes sensations and things of that sort."

"What do you mean, Gerald?"

"Get the Muir to look at you, as she did at me, and you will understand. Will you have another cup, Juno?"

"Yes, please." She liked to have him wait upon her, for he did it to no other woman except his mother.

Before he could slowly rise, Miss Muir glided to them with another cup on the salver; and, as Lucia took it with a cold nod, the girl said under her breath, "I think it honest to tell you that I possess a quick ear, and cannot help hearing what is said anywhere in the room. What you say of me is of no consequence, but you may speak of things which you prefer I should not hear; therefore, allow me to warn you." And she was gone again as noiselessly as she came.

"How do you like that?" whispered Coventry, as his cousin sat looking after the girl, with a disturbed expression.

"What an uncomfortable creature to have in the house! I am very sorry I urged her coming, for your mother has taken a fancy to her, and it will be hard to get rid of her," said Lucia, half angry, half amused.

"Hush, she hears every word you say. I know it by the expression of her face, for Ned is talking about horses, and she looks as haughty as ever you did, and that is saying much. Faith, this is getting interesting."

"Hark, she is speaking; I want to hear," and Lucia laid her hand on her cousin's lips. He kissed it, and then idly amused himself with turning the rings to and fro on the slender fingers.

"I have been in France several years, madam, but my friend died and I came back to be with Lady Sydney, till—" Muir paused an instant, then added, slowly, "till I fell ill. It was a contagious fever, so I went of my own accord to the hospital, not wishing to endanger her."

"Very right, but are you sure there is no danger of infection now?" asked Mrs. Coventry anxiously.

"None, I assure you. I have been well for some time, but did not leave because I preferred to stay there, than to return to Lady Sydney."

"No quarrel, I hope? No trouble of any kind?"

"No quarrel, but—well, why not? You have a right to know, and I will not make a foolish mystery out of a very simple thing. As your family, only, is present, I may tell the truth. I did not go back on the young gentleman's account. Please ask no more."

"Ah, I see. Quite prudent and proper, Miss Muir. I shall never allude to it again. Thank you for your frankness. Bella, you will be careful not to mention this to your young friends; girls gossip sadly, and it would annoy Lady Sydney beyond everything to have this talked of."

"Very neighborly of Lady S. to send the dangerous young lady here;

where there are *two* young gentlemen to be captivated. I wonder why she didn't keep Sydney after she had caught him," murmured Coventry to his cousin.

"Because she had the utmost contempt for a titled fool." Miss Muir dropped the words almost into his ear, as she bent to take her shawl from the sofa corner.

"How the deuce did she get there?" ejaculated Coventry, looking as if he had received another sensation. "She has spirit, though, and upon my word I pity Sydney, if he did try to dazzle her, for he must have got a splendid dismissal."

"Come and play billiards. You promised, and I hold you to your word," said Lucia, rising with decision, for Gerald was showing too much interest in another to suit Miss Beaufort.

"I am, as ever, your most devoted. My mother is a charming woman, but I find our evening parties slightly dull, when only my own family are present. Good night, Mamma." He shook hands with his mother, whose pride and idol he was, and, with a comprehensive nod to the others, strolled after his cousin.

"Now they are gone we can be quite cozy, and talk over things, for I don't mind Ned any more than I do his dogs," said Bella, settling herself on her mother's footstool.

"I merely wish to say, Miss Muir, that my daughter has never had a governess and is sadly backward for a girl of sixteen. I want you to pass the mornings with her, and get her on as rapidly as possible. In the afternoon you will walk or drive with her, and in the evening sit with us here, if you like, or amuse yourself as you please. While in the country we are very quiet, for I cannot bear much company, and when my sons want gaiety, they go away for it. Miss Beaufort oversees the servants, and takes my place as far as possible. I am very delicate and keep my room till evening, except for an airing at noon. We will try each other for a month, and I hope we shall get on quite comfortably together."

"I shall do my best, madam."

One would not have believed that the meek spiritless voice which uttered these words was the same that had startled Coventry a few minutes before, nor that the pale, patient face could ever have kindled with such sudden fire as that which looked over Miss Muir's shoulder when she answered her young host's speech.

Edward thought within himself, Poor little woman! She has had a hard life. We will try and make it easier while she is here; and began his charitable work by suggesting that she might be tired. She acknowledged she was, and Bella led her away to a bright, cozy room, where with a pretty little speech and a good-night kiss she left her.

When alone Miss Muir's conduct was decidedly peculiar. Her first act was to clench her hands and mutter between her teeth, with passionate force, "I'll not fail again if there is power in a woman's wit and will!" She stood a moment motionless, with an expression of almost fierce disdain on her face, then shook her clenched hand as if menacing some unseen enemy. Next she laughed, and shrugged her shoulders with a true French shrug, saying low to herself, "Yes, the last scene *shall* be better than the first. *Mon dieu,* how tired and hungry I am!"

Kneeling before the one small trunk which held her worldly possessions, she opened it, drew out a flask, and mixed a glass of some ardent cordial, which she seemed to enjoy extremely as she sat on the carpet, musing, while her quick eyes examined every corner of the room.

"Not bad! It will be a good field for me to work in, and the harder the task the better I shall like it. *Merci,* old friend. You put heart and courage into me when nothing else will. Come, the curtain is down, so I may be myself for a few hours, if actresses ever are themselves."

Still sitting on the floor she unbound and removed the long abundant braids from her head, wiped the pink from her face, took out several pearly teeth, and slipping off her dress appeared herself indeed, a haggard, worn, and moody woman of thirty at least. The metamorphosis was wonderful, but the disguise was more in the expression she assumed than in any art of costume or false adornment. Now she was alone, and her mobile features settled into their natural expression, weary, hard, bitter. She had been lovely once, happy, innocent, and tender; but nothing of all this remained to the gloomy woman who leaned there brooding over some wrong, or loss, or disappointment which had darkened all her life. For an hour she sat so, sometimes playing absently with the scanty locks that hung about her face, sometimes lifting the glass to her lips as if the fiery draught warmed her cold blood; and once she half uncovered her breast to eye with a terrible glance the scar of a newly healed wound. At last she rose and crept to bed, like one worn out with weariness and mental pain.

II

A Good Beginning

Only the housemaids were astir when Miss Muir left her room next morning and quietly found her way into the garden. As she walked, apparently intent upon the flowers, her quick eye scrutinized the fine old house and its picturesque surroundings.

"Not bad," she said to herself, adding, as she passed into the adjoining park, "but the other may be better, and I will have the best."

Walking rapidly, she came out at length upon the wide green lawn which lay before the ancient hall where Sir John Coventry lived in solitary splendor. A stately old place, rich in oaks, well-kept shrubberies, gay gardens, sunny terraces, carved gables, spacious rooms, liveried servants, and every luxury befitting the ancestral home of a rich and honorable race. Miss Muir's eyes brightened as she looked, her step grew firmer, her carriage prouder, and a smile broke over her face; the smile of one well pleased at the prospect of the success of some cherished hope. Suddenly her whole air changed, she pushed back her hat, clasped her hands loosely before her, and seemed absorbed in girlish admiration of the fair scene that could not fail to charm any beauty-loving eye. The cause of this rapid change soon appeared. A hale, handsome man, between fifty and sixty, came through the little gate leading to the park, and, seeing the young stranger, paused to examine her. He had only time for a glance, however; she seemed conscious of his presence in a moment, turned with a startled look, uttered an exclamation of surprise, and looked as if hesitating whether to speak or run away. Gallant Sir John took off his hat and said, with an old-fashioned courtesy which became him well, "I beg your pardon for disturbing you, young lady. Allow me to atone for it by inviting you to walk where you will, and gather what flowers you like. I see you love them, so pray make free with those about you."

With a charming air of maidenly timidity and artlessness, Miss Muir replied, "Oh, thank you, sir! But it is I who should ask pardon for trespassing. I never should have dared if I had not known that Sir John was absent. I always wanted to see this fine old place, and ran over the first thing, to satisfy myself."

"And *are* you satisfied?" he asked, with a smile.

"More than satisfied—I'm charmed; for it is the most beautiful spot I ever saw, and I've seen many famous seats, both at home and abroad," she answered enthusiastically.

"The Hall is much flattered, and so would its master be if he heard you," began the gentleman, with an odd expression.

"I should not praise it to him—at least, not as freely as I have to you, sir," said the girl, with eyes still turned away.

"Why not?" asked her companion, looking much amused.

"I should be afraid. Not that I dread Sir John; but I've heard so many beautiful and noble things about him, and respect him so highly, that I should not dare to say much, lest he should see how I admire and—"

"And what, young lady? Finish, if you please."

"I was going to say, love him. I will say it, for he is an old man, and one cannot help loving virtue and bravery."

Miss Muir looked very earnest and pretty as she spoke, standing there with the sunshine glinting on her yellow hair, delicate face, and downcast eyes. Sir John was not a vain man, but he found it pleasant to hear himself commended by this unknown girl, and felt redoubled curiosity to learn who she was. Too well bred to ask, or to abash her by avowing what she seemed unconscious of, he left both discoveries to chance; and when she turned, as if to retrace her steps, he offered her the handful of hothouse flowers which he held, saying, with a gallant bow, "In Sir John's name let me give you my little nosegay, with thanks for your good opinion, which, I assure you, is not entirely deserved, for I know him well."

Miss Muir looked up quickly, eyed him an instant, then dropped her eyes, and, coloring deeply, stammered out, "I did not know—I beg your pardon—you are too kind, Sir John."

He laughed like a boy, asking, mischievously, "Why call me Sir John? How do you know that I am not the gardener or the butler?"

"I did not see your face before, and no one but yourself would say that any praise was undeserved," murmured Miss Muir, still overcome with girlish confusion.

"Well, well, we will let that pass, and the next time you come we will be properly introduced. Bella always brings her friends to the Hall, for I am fond of young people."

"I am not a friend. I am only Miss Coventry's governess." And Miss Muir dropped a meek curtsy. A slight change passed over Sir John's manner. Few would have perceived it, but Miss Muir felt it at once, and bit her lips with an angry feeling at her heart. With a curious air of pride, mingled with respect, she accepted the still offered bouquet, returned Sir John's parting bow, and tripped away, leaving the old gentleman to wonder where Mrs. Coventry found such a piquant little governess.

"That is done, and very well for a beginning," she said to herself as she approached the house.

In a green paddock close by fed a fine horse, who lifted up his head and eyed her inquiringly, like one who expected a greeting. Following a sudden impulse, she entered the paddock and, pulling a handful of clover, invited the creature to come and eat. This was evidently a new proceeding on the part of a lady, and the horse careered about as if bent on frightening the newcomer away.

"I see," she said aloud, laughing to herself. "I am not your master, and you rebel. Nevertheless, I'll conquer you, my fine brute."

Seating herself in the grass, she began to pull daisies, singing idly the while, as if unconscious of the spirited prancings of the horse. Presently he drew nearer, sniffing curiously and eyeing her with surprise. She took no notice, but plaited the daisies and sang on as if he was not there. This seemed to pique the petted creature, for, slowly approaching, he came at length so close that he could smell her little foot and nibble at her dress. Then she offered the clover, uttering caressing words and making soothing sounds, till by degrees and with much coquetting, the horse permitted her to stroke his glossy neck and smooth his mane.

It was a pretty sight—the slender figure in the grass, the high-spirited horse bending his proud head to her hand. Edward Coventry, who had watched the scene, found it impossible to restrain himself any longer and, leaping the wall, came to join the group, saying, with mingled admiration and wonder in countenance and voice, "Good morning, Miss Muir. If I had not seen your skill and courage proved before my eyes, I should be alarmed for your safety. Hector is a wild, wayward beast, and has damaged more than one groom who tried to conquer him."

"Good morning, Mr. Coventry. Don't tell tales of this noble creature, who has not deceived my faith in him. Your grooms did not know how to win his heart, and so subdue his spirit without breaking it."

Miss Muir rose as she spoke, and stood with her hand on Hector's neck while he ate the grass which she had gathered in the skirt of her dress.

"You have the secret, and Hector is your subject now, though heretofore he has rejected all friends but his master. Will you give him his morning feast? I always bring him bread and play with him before breakfast."

"Then you are not jealous?" And she looked up at him with eyes so bright and beautiful in expression that the young man wondered he had not observed them before.

"Not I. Pet him as much as you will; it will do him good. He is a solitary fellow, for he scorns his own kind and lives alone, like his master," he added, half to himself.

"Alone, with such a happy home, Mr. Coventry?" And a softly compassionate glance stole from the bright eyes.

"That was an ungrateful speech, and I retract it for Bella's sake. Younger sons have no position but such as they can make for themselves, you know, and I've had no chance yet."

"Younger sons! I thought—I beg pardon." And Miss Muir paused, as if remembering that she had no right to question.

Edward smiled and answered frankly, "Nay, don't mind me. You thought I was the heir, perhaps. Whom did you take my brother for last night?"

"For some guest who admired Miss Beaufort. I did not hear his name, nor observe him enough to discover who he was. I saw only your kind mother, your charming little sister, and—"

She stopped there, with a half-shy, half-grateful look at the young man which finished the sentence better than any words. He was still a boy, in spite of his one-and-twenty years, and a little color came into his brown check as the eloquent eyes met his and fell before them.

"Yes, Bella is a capital girl, and one can't help loving her. I know you'll get her on, for, really, she is the most delightful little dunce. My mother's ill health and Bella's devotion to her have prevented our attending to her education before. Next winter, when we go to town, she is to come out, and must be prepared for that great event, you know," he said, choosing a safe subject.

"I shall do my best. And that reminds me that I should report myself to her, instead of enjoying myself here. When one has been ill and shut up a long time, the country is so lovely one is apt to forget duty for pleasure. Please remind me if I am negligent, Mr. Coventry."

"That name belongs to Gerald. I'm only Mr. Ned here," he said as they walked toward the house, while Hector followed to the wall and sent a sonorous farewell after them.

Bella came running to meet them, and greeted Miss Muir as if she had made up her mind to like her heartily. "What a lovely bouquet you have got! I never can arrange flowers prettily, which vexes me, for Mamma is so fond of them and cannot go out herself. You have charming taste," she said, examining the graceful posy which Miss Muir had much improved by adding feathery grasses, delicate ferns, and fragrant wild flowers to Sir John's exotics.

Putting them into Bella's hand, she said, in a winning way, "Take them to your mother, then, and ask her if I may have the pleasure of making her a daily nosegay; for I should find real delight in doing it, if it would please her."

"How kind you are! Of course it would please her. I'll take them to her while the dew is still on them." And away flew Bella, eager to give both the flowers and the pretty message to the poor invalid.

Edward stopped to speak to the gardener, and Miss Muir went up the steps alone. The long hall was lined with portraits, and pacing slowly down it she examined them with interest. One caught her eye, and, pausing before it, she scrutinized it carefully. A young, beautiful, but very haughty female face. Miss Muir suspected at once who it was, and gave a decided nod, as if she saw and caught at some unexpected chance. A soft rustle behind her made her look around, and, seeing Lucia, she bowed, half turned, as if for another glance at the picture, and said, as if involuntarily, "How beautiful it is! May I ask if it is an ancestor, Miss Beaufort?"

"It is the likeness of my mother" was the reply, given with a softened voice and eyes that looked up tenderly.

"Ah, I might have known, from the resemblance, but I scarcely saw you last night. Excuse my freedom, but Lady Sydney treated me as a friend, and I forget my position. Allow me."

As she spoke, Miss Muir stooped to return the handkerchief which had fallen from Lucia's hand, and did so with a humble mien which touched the other's heart; for, though a proud, it was also a very generous one.

"Thank you. Are you better, this morning?" she said, graciously. And having received an affirmative reply, she added, as she walked on, "I will show you to the breakfast room, as Bella is not here. It is a very informal meal with us, for my aunt is never down and my cousins are very irregular in their hours. You can always have yours when you like, without waiting for us, if you are an early riser."

Bella and Edward appeared before the others were seated, and Miss Muir quietly ate her breakfast, feeling well satisfied with her hour's work. Ned recounted her exploit with Hector, Bella delivered her mother's thanks for the flowers, and Lucia more than once recalled, with pardonable vanity, that the governess had compared her to her lovely mother, expressing by a look as much admiration for the living likeness as for the painted one. All kindly did their best to make the pale girl feel at home, and their cordial manner seemed to warm and draw her out; for soon she put off her sad, meek air and entertained them with gay anecdotes of her life in Paris, her travels in Russia when governess in Prince Jermadoff's family, and all manner of witty stories that kept them interested and merry long after the meal was over. In the middle of an absorbing adventure, Coventry came in, nodded lazily, lifted his brows, as if surprised at seeing the governess there, and began his breakfast as if the ennul of another day had already taken possession of him. Miss Muir stopped short, and no entreaties could induce her to go on.

"Another time I will finish it, if you like. Now Miss Bella and I should be at our books." And she left the room, followed by her pupil, taking no notice of the young master of the house, beyond a graceful bow in answer to his careless nod.

"Merciful creature! she goes when I come, and does not make life unendurable by moping about before my eyes. Does she belong to the moral, the melancholy, the romantic, or the dashing class, Ned?" said Gerald, lounging over his coffee as he did over everything he attempted.

"To none of them; she is a capital little woman. I wish you had seen her tame Hector this morning." And Edward repeated his story.

"Not a bad move on her part," said Coventry in reply. "She must be an observing as well as an energetic young person, to discover your chief weakness and attack it so soon. First tame the horse, and then the master. It will be amusing to watch the game, only I shall be under the painful necessity of checkmating you both, if it gets serious."

"You needn't exert yourself, old fellow, on my account. If I was not above thinking ill of an inoffensive girl, I should say you were the prize best worth winning, and advise you to take care of your own heart, if you've got one, which I rather doubt."

"I often doubt it, myself; but I fancy the little Scotchwoman will not be able to satisfy either of us upon that point. How does your highness like her?" asked Coventry of his cousin, who sat near him.

"Better than I thought I should. She is well bred, unassuming, and very entertaining when she likes. She has told us some of the wittiest stories I've heard for a long time. Didn't our laughter wake you?" replied Lucia.

"Yes. Now atone for it by amusing me with a repetition of these witty tales."

"That is impossible; her accent and manner are half the charm," said Ned. "I wish you had kept away ten minutes longer, for your appearance spoilt the best story of all."

"Why didn't she go on?" asked Coventry, with a ray of curiosity.

"You forgot that she overheard us last night, and must feel that you consider her a bore. She has pride, and no woman forgets speeches like those you made," answered Lucia.

"Or forgives them, either, I believe. Well, I must be resigned to languish under her displeasure then. On Sydney's account I take a slight interest in her; not that I expect to learn anything from her, for a woman with a mouth like that never confides or confesses anything. But I have a fancy to see what captivated him; for captivated he was, beyond a doubt, and by no lady whom he met in society. Did you ever hear anything of it, Ned?" asked Gerald.

"I'm not fond of scandal or gossip, and never listen to either." With which remark Edward left the room.

Lucia was called out by the housekeeper a moment after, and Coventry left to the society most wearisome to him, namely his own. As he entered, he had caught a part of the story which Miss Muir had been telling, and it had excited his curiosity so much that he found himself wondering what the end could be and wishing that he might hear it.

What the deuce did she run away for, when I came in? he thought. If she *is* amusing, she must make herself useful; for it's intensely dull, I own, here, in spite of Lucia. Hey, what's that?

It was a rich, sweet voice, singing a brilliant Italian air, and singing it with an expression that made the music doubly delicious. Stepping out of the French window, Coventry strolled along the sunny terrace, enjoying the song with the relish of a connoisseur. Others followed, and still he walked and listened, forgetful of weariness or time. As one exquisite air ended, he involuntarily applauded. Miss Muir's face appeared for an instant, then vanished, and no more music followed, though Coventry lingered, hoping to hear the voice again. For music was the one thing of which he never wearied, and neither Lucia nor Bella possessed skill enough to charm him. For an hour he loitered on the terrace or the lawn, basking in the sunshine, too indolent to seek occupation or society. At length Bella came out, hat in hand, and nearly stumbled over her brother, who lay on the grass.

"You lazy man, have you been dawdling here all this time?" she said, looking down at him.

"No, I've been very busy. Come and tell me how you've got on with the little dragon."

"Can't stop. She bade me take a run after my French, so that I might be ready for my drawing, and so I must."

"It's too warm to run. Sit down and amuse your deserted brother, who has had no society but bees and lizards for an hour."

He drew her down as he spoke, and Bella obeyed; for, in spite of his indolence, he was one to whom all submitted without dreaming of refusal.

"What have you been doing? Muddling your poor little brains with all manner of elegant rubbish?"

"No, I've been enjoying myself immensely. Jean is *so* interesting, so kind and clever. She didn't bore me with stupid grammar, but just talked to me in such pretty French that I got on capitally, and like it as I never expected to, after Lucia's dull way of teaching it."

"What did you talk about?"

"Oh, all manner of things. She asked questions, and I answered, and she corrected me."

"Questions about our affairs, I suppose?"

"Not one. She don't care two sous for us or our affairs. I thought she might like to know what sort of people we were, so I told her about Papa's sudden death, Uncle John, and you, and Ned; but in the midst of it she said, in her quiet way, 'You are getting too confidential, my dear. It is not best to talk too freely of one's affairs to strangers. Let us speak of something else.' "

"What were you talking of when she said that, Bell?"

"You."

"Ah, then no wonder she was bored."

"She was tired of my chatter, and didn't hear half I said; for she was busy sketching something for me to copy, and thinking of something more interesting than the Coventrys."

"How do you know?"

"By the expression of her face. Did you like her music, Gerald?"

"Yes. Was she angry when I clapped?"

"She looked surprised, then rather proud, and shut the piano at once, though I begged her to go on. Isn't Jean a pretty name?"

"Not bad; but why don't you call her Miss Muir?"

"She begged me not. She hates it, and loves to be called Jean, alone.

I've imagined such a nice little romance about her, and someday I shall tell her, for I'm sure she has had a love trouble."

"Don't get such nonsense into your head, but follow Miss Muir's well-bred example and don't be curious about other people's affairs. Ask her to sing tonight; it amuses me."

"She won't come down, I think. We've planned to read and work in my boudoir, which is to be our study now. Mamma will stay in her room, so you and Lucia can have the drawing room all to yourselves."

"Thank you. What will Ned do?"

"He will amuse Mamma, he says. Dear old Ned! I wish you'd stir about and get him his commission. He is so impatient to be doing something and yet so proud he won't ask again, after you have neglected it so many times and refused Uncle's help."

"I'll attend to it very soon; don't worry me, child. He will do very well for a time, quietly here with us."

"You always say that, yet you know he chafes and is unhappy at being dependent on you. Mamma and I don't mind; but he is a man, and it frets him. He said he'd take matters into his own hands soon, and then you may be sorry you were so slow in helping him."

"Miss Muir is looking out of the window. You'd better go and take your run, else she will scold."

"Not she. I'm not a bit afraid of her, she's so gentle and sweet. I'm fond of her already. You'll get as brown as Ned, lying here in the sun. By the way, Miss Muir agrees with me in thinking him handsomer than you."

"I admire her taste and quite agree with her."

"She said he was manly, and that was more attractive than beauty in a man. She does express things so nicely. Now I'm off." And away danced Bella, humming the burden of Miss Muir's sweetest song.

" 'Energy is more attractive than beauty in a man.' She is right, but how the deuce *can* a man be energetic, with nothing to expend his energies upon?" mused Coventry, with his hat over his eyes.

A few moments later, the sweep of a dress caught his ear. Without stirring, a sidelong glance showed him Miss Muir coming across the terrace, as if to join Bella. Two stone steps led down to the lawn. He lay near them, and Miss Muir did not see him till close upon him. She started and slipped on the last step, recovered herself, and glided on, with a glance of unmistakable contempt as she passed the recumbent figure of the apparent sleeper. Several things in Bella's report had nettled him, but this look made him angry, though he would not own it, even to himself.

"Gerald, come here, quick!" presently called Bella, from the rustic seat where she stood beside her governess, who sat with her hand over her face as if in pain.

Gathering himself up, Coventry slowly obeyed, but involuntarily quickened his pace as he heard Miss Muir say, "Don't call him; *he* can do nothing" for the emphasis on the word "he" was very significant.

"What is it, Bella?" he asked, looking rather wider awake than usual.

"You startled Miss Muir and made her turn her ankle. Now help her to the house, for she is in great pain; and don't lie there anymore to frighten people like a snake in the grass," said his sister petulantly.

"I beg your pardon. Will you allow me?" And Coventry offered his arm.

Miss Muir looked up with the expression which annoyed him and answered coldly, "Thank you, Miss Bella will do as well."

"Permit me to doubt that." And with a gesture too decided to be resisted, Coventry drew her arm through his and led her into the house. She submitted quietly, said the pain would soon be over, and when settled on the couch in Bella's room dismissed him with the briefest thanks. Considering the unwonted exertion he had made, he thought she might have been a little more grateful, and went away to Lucia, who always brightened when he came.

No more was seen of Miss Muir till teatime; for now, while the family were in retirement, they dined early and saw no company. The governess had excused herself at dinner, but came down in the evening a little paler than usual and with a slight limp in her gait. Sir John was there, talking with his nephew, and they merely acknowledged her presence by the sort of bow which gentlemen bestow on governesses. As she slowly made her way to her place behind the urn, Coventry said to his brother, "Take her a footstool, and ask her how she is, Ned." Then, as if necessary to account for his politeness to his uncle, he explained how he was the cause of the accident.

"Yes, yes. I understand. Rather a nice little person, I fancy. Not exactly a beauty, but accomplished and well bred, which is better for one of her class."

"Some tea, Sir John?" said a soft voice at his elbow, and there was Miss Muir, offering cups to the gentlemen.

"Thank you, thank you," said Sir John, sincerely hoping she had overheard him.

As Coventry took his, he said graciously, "You are very forgiving, Miss Muir, to wait upon me, after I have caused you so much pain."

"It is my duty, sir" was her reply, in a tone which plainly said, "but not my pleasure." And she returned to her place, to smile, and chat, and be charming, with Bella and her brother.

Lucia, hovering near her uncle and Gerald, kept them to herself, but was disturbed to find that their eyes often wandered to the cheerful group about the table, and that their attention seemed distracted by the frequent bursts of laughter and fragments of animated conversation which reached them. In the midst of an account of a tragic affair which she endeavored to make as interesting and pathetic as possible, Sir John burst into a hearty laugh, which betrayed that he had been listening to a livelier story than her own. Much annoyed, she said hastily, "I knew it would be so! Bella has no idea of the proper manner in which to treat a governess. She and Ned will forget the difference of rank and spoil that person for her work. She is inclined to be presumptuous already, and if my aunt won't trouble herself to give Miss Muir a hint in time, I shall."

"Wait till she has finished that story, I beg of you," said Coventry, for Sir John was already off.

"If you find that nonsense so entertaining, why don't you follow Uncle's example? I don't need you."

"Thank you. I will." And Lucia was deserted.

But Miss Muir had ended and, beckoning to Bella, left the room, as if quite unconscious of the honor conferred upon her or the dullness she left behind her. Ned went up to his mother, Gerald returned to make his peace with Lucia, and, bidding them good-night, Sir John turned homeward. Strolling along the terrace, he came to the lighted window of Bella's study, and wishing to say a word to her, he half pushed aside the curtain and looked in. A pleasant little scene. Bella working busily, and near her in a low chair, with the light falling on her fair hair and delicate profile, sat Miss Muir, reading aloud. "Novels!" thought Sir John, and smiled at them for a pair of romantic girls. But pausing to listen a moment before he spoke, he found it was no novel, but history, read with a fluency which made every fact interesting, every sketch of character memorable, by the dramatic effect given to it. Sir John was fond of history, and failing eyesight often curtailed his favorite amusement. He had tried readers, but none suited him, and he had given up the plan. Now as he listened, he thought how pleasantly the smoothly flowing voice would wile away his evenings, and he envied Bella her new acquisition.

A bell rang, and Bella sprang up, saying, "Wait for me a minute. I must run to Mamma, and then we will go on with this charming prince."

Away she went, and Sir John was about to retire as quietly as he came, when Miss Muir's peculiar behavior arrested him for an instant. Dropping the book, she threw her arms across the table, laid her head down upon them, and broke into a passion of tears, like one who could bear restraint no longer. Shocked and amazed, Sir John stole away; but all that night the kindhearted gentleman puzzled his brains with conjectures about his niece's interesting young governess, quite unconscious that she intended he should do so.

III

Passion and Pique

For several weeks the most monotonous tranquillity seemed to reign at Coventry House, and yet, unseen, unsuspected, a storm was gathering. The arrival of Miss Muir seemed to produce a change in everyone, though no one could have explained how or why. Nothing could be more unobtrusive and retiring than her manners. She was devoted to Bella, who soon adored her, and was only happy when in her society. She ministered in many ways to Mrs. Coventry's comfort, and that lady declared there never was such a nurse. She amused, interested and won Edward with her wit and womanly sympathy. She made Lucia respect and envy her for her accomplishments, and piqued indolent Gerald by her persistent avoidance of him, while Sir John was charmed with her respectful deference and the graceful little attentions she paid him in a frank and artless way, very winning to the lonely old man. The very servants liked her; and instead of being, what most governesses are, a forlorn creature hovering between superiors and inferiors, Jean Muir was the life of the house, and the friend of all but two.

Lucia disliked her, and Coventry distrusted her; neither could exactly say why, and neither owned the feeling, even to themselves. Both watched her covertly yet found no shortcoming anywhere. Meek, modest, faithful, and invariably sweet-tempered—they could complain of nothing and wondered at their own doubts, though they could not banish them.

It soon came to pass that the family was divided, or rather that two members were left very much to themselves. Pleading timidity, Jean Muir kept much in Bella's study and soon made it such a pleasant little nook that Ned and his mother, and often Sir John, came in to enjoy the music, reading, or cheerful chat which made the evening so gay. Lucia at first was only too glad to have her cousin to herself, and he too lazy to care what went on about him. But presently he wearied of her society, for she was not a brilliant girl, and possessed few of those winning arts which charm a man and steal into his heart. Rumors of the merrymakings that went on reached him and made him curious to share them; echoes of fine music went sounding through the house, as he lounged about the empty drawing room; and peals of laughter reached him while listening to Lucia's grave discourse.

She soon discovered that her society had lost its charm, and the more eagerly she tried to please him, the more signally she failed. Before long Coventry fell into a habit of strolling out upon the terrace of an evening, and amusing himself by passing and repassing the window of Bella's room, catching glimpses of what was going on and reporting the result of his observations to Lucia, who was too proud to ask admission to the happy circle or to seem to desire it.

"I shall go to London tomorrow, Lucia," Gerald said one evening, as he came back from what he called "a survey," looking very much annoyed.

"To London?" exclaimed his cousin, surprised.

"Yes, I must bestir myself and get Ned his commission, or it will be all over with him."

"How do you mean?"

"He is falling in love as fast as it is possible for a boy to do it. That girl has bewitched him, and he will make a fool of himself very soon, unless I put a stop to it."

"I was afraid she would attempt a flirtation. These persons always do, they are such a mischief-making race."

"Ah, but there you are wrong, as far as little Muir is concerned. She does not flirt, and Ned has too much sense and spirit to be caught by a silly coquette. She treats him like an elder sister, and mingles the most attractive friendliness with a quiet dignity that captivates the boy. I've been watching them, and there he is, devouring her with his eyes, while she reads a fascinating novel in the most fascinating style. Bella and Mamma are absorbed in the tale, and see nothing; but Ned makes himself the hero, Miss Muir the heroine, and lives the love scene with all the ardor of a man whose heart has just waked up. Poor lad! Poor lad!"

Lucia looked at her cousin, amazed by the energy with which he spoke, the anxiety in his usually listless face. The change became him, for it showed what he might be, making one regret still more what he was. Before she could speak, he was gone again, to return presently, laughing, yet looking a little angry.

"What now?" she asked.

" 'Listeners never hear any good of themselves' is the truest of proverbs. I stopped a moment to look at Ned, and heard the following flattering remarks. Mamma is gone, and Ned was asking little Muir to sing that delicious barcarole she gave us the other evening.

" 'Not now, not here,' she said.

" 'Why not? You sang it in the drawing room readily enough,' said Ned, imploringly.

" 'That is a very different thing,' and she looked at him with a little shake of the head, for he was folding his hands and doing the passionate pathetic.

" 'Come and sing it there then,' said innocent Bella. 'Gerald likes your voice so much, and complains that you will never sing to him.'

" 'He never asks me,' said Muir, with an odd smile.

" 'He is too lazy, but he wants to hear you.'

" 'When he asks me, I will sing—if I feel like it.' And she shrugged her shoulders with a provoking gesture of indifference.

" 'But it amuses him, and he gets so bored down here,' began stupid little Bella. 'Don't be shy or proud, Jean, but come and entertain the poor old fellow.'

" 'No, thank you. I engaged to teach Miss Coventry, not to amuse Mr. Coventry' was all the answer she got.

" 'You amuse Ned, why not Gerald? Are you afraid of him?' asked Bella.

"Miss Muir laughed, such a scornful laugh, and said, in that peculiar tone of hers, 'I cannot fancy anyone being *afraid* of your elder brother.'

" 'I am, very often, and so would you be, if you ever saw him angry.' And Bella looked as if I'd beaten her.

" 'Does he ever wake up enough to be angry?' asked that girl, with an air of surprise. Here Ned broke into a fit of laughter, and they are at it now, I fancy, by the sound."

"Their foolish gossip is not worth getting excited about, but I certainly would send Ned away. It's no use trying to get rid of 'that girl,' as you say, for my aunt is as deluded about her as Ned and Bella, and she really does get the child along splendidly. Dispatch Ned, and then she can do no harm," said Lucia, watching Coventry's altered face as he stood in the moonlight, just outside the window where she sat.

"Have you no fears for me?" he asked smiling, as if ashamed of his momentary petulance.

"No, have you for yourself?" And a shade of anxiety passed over her face.

"I defy the Scotch witch to enchant me, except with her music," he added, moving down the terrace again, for Jean was singing like a nightingale.

As the song ended, he put aside the curtain, and said, abruptly, "Has anyone any commands for London? I am going there tomorrow."

"A pleasant trip to you," said Ned carelessly, though usually his brother's movements interested him extremely.

"I want quantities of things, but I must ask Mamma first." And Bella began to make a list.

"May I trouble you with a letter, Mr. Coventry?"

Jean Muir turned around on the music stool and looked at him with the cold keen glance which always puzzled him.

He bowed, saying, as if to them all, "I shall be off by the early train, so you must give me your orders tonight."

"Then come away, Ned, and leave Jean to write her letter."

And Bella took her reluctant brother from the room.

"I will give you the letter in the morning," said Miss Muir, with a curious quiver in her voice, and the look of one who forcibly suppressed some strong emotion.

"As you please." And Coventry went back to Lucia, wondering who Miss Muir was going to write to. He said nothing to his brother of the purpose which took him to town, lest a word should produce the catastrophe which he hoped to prevent; and Ned, who now lived in a sort of dream, seemed to forget Gerald's existence altogether.

With unwonted energy Coventry was astir at seven next morning. Lucia gave him his breakfast, and as he left the room to order the carriage, Miss Muir came gliding downstairs, very pale and heavy-eyed (with a sleepless, tearful night, he thought) and, putting a delicate little letter into his hand, said hurriedly, "Please leave this at Lady Sydney's, and if you see her, say 'I have remembered.' "

Her peculiar manner and peculiar message struck him. His eye involuntarily glanced at the address of the letter and read young Sydney's name. Then, conscious of his mistake, he thrust it into his pocket with a hasty "Good morning," and left Miss Muir standing with one hand pressed on her heart, the other half extended as if to recall the letter.

All the way to London, Coventry found it impossible to forget the almost tragical expression of the girl's face, and it haunted him through the bustle of two busy days. Ned's affair was put in the way of being speedily accomplished, Bella's commissions were executed, his mother's pet delicacies provided for her, and a gift for Lucia, whom the family had given him for his future mate, as he was too lazy to choose for himself.

Jean Muir's letter he had not delivered, for Lady Sydney was in the country and her townhouse closed. Curious to see how she would receive his tidings, he went quietly in on his arrival at home. Everyone had dispersed to dress for dinner except Miss Muir, who was in the garden, the servant said.

"Very well; I have a message for her"; and, turning, the "young master," as they called him, went to seek her. In a remote corner he saw her sitting alone, buried in thought. As his step roused her, a look of surprise, followed by one of satisfaction, passed over her face, and, rising, she beckoned to him with an almost eager gesture. Much amazed, he went to her and offered the letter, saying kindly, "I regret that I could not deliver it. Lady Sydney is in the country, and I did not like to post it without your leave. Did I do right?"

"Quite right, thank you very much—it is better so." And with an air of relief, she tore the letter to atoms, and scattered them to the wind.

More amazed than ever, the young man was about to leave her when she said, with a mixture of entreaty and command, "Please stay a moment. I want to speak to you."

He paused, eyeing her with visible surprise, for a sudden color dyed her cheeks, and her lips trembled. Only for a moment, then she was quite self-possessed again. Motioning him to the seat she had left, she remained standing while she said, in a low, rapid tone full of pain and of decision:

"Mr. Coventry, as the head of the house I want to speak to you, rather than to your mother, of a most unhappy affair which has occurred during your absence. My month of probation ends today; your mother wishes me to remain; I, too, wish it sincerely, for I am happy here, but I ought not. Read this, and you will see why."

She put a hastily written note into his hand and watched him intently while he read it. She saw him flush with anger, bite his lips, and knit his brows, then assume his haughtiest look, as he lifted his eyes and said in his most sarcastic tone, "Very well for a beginning. The boy has eloquence. Pity that it should be wasted. May I ask if you have replied to this rhapsody?"

"I have."

"And what follows? He begs you 'to fly with him, to share his fortunes, and be the good angel of his life.' Of course you consent?"

There was no answer, for, standing erect before him, Miss Muir regarded him with an expression of proud patience, like one who expected reproaches, yet was too generous to resent them. Her manner had its effect. Dropping his bitter tone, Coventry asked briefly, "Why do you show me this? What can I do?"

"I show it that you may see how much in earnest 'the boy' is, and how open I desire to be. You can control, advise, and comfort your brother, and help me to see what is my duty."

"You love him?" demanded Coventry bluntly.

"No!" was the quick, decided answer.

"Then why make him love you?"

"I never tried to do it. Your sister will testify that I have endeavored to avoid him as I—" And he finished the sentence with an unconscious tone of pique, "As you have avoided me."

She bowed silently, and he went on:

"I will do you the justice to say that nothing can be more blameless than your conduct toward myself; but why allow Ned to haunt you evening after evening? What could you expect of a romantic boy who had nothing to do but lose his heart to the first attractive woman he met?"

A momentary glisten shone in Jean Muir's steel-blue eyes as the last words left the young man's lips; but it was gone instantly, and her voice was full of reproach, as she said, steadily, impulsively, "If the 'romantic boy' had been allowed to lead the life of a man, as he longed to do, he would have had no time to lose his heart to the first sorrowful girl whom he pitied. Mr. Coventry, the fault is yours. Do not blame your brother, but generously own your mistake and retrieve it in the speediest, kindest manner."

For an instant Gerald sat dumb. Never since his father died had anyone reproved him; seldom in his life had he been blamed. It was a new experience, and the very novelty added to the effect. He saw his fault, regretted it, and admired the brave sincerity of the girl in telling him of it. But he did not know how to deal with the case, and was forced to confess not only past negligence but present incapacity. He was as honorable as he was proud, and with an effort he said frankly, "You are right, Miss Muir. I *am* to blame, yet as soon as I saw the danger, I tried to avert it. My visit to town was on Ned's account; he will have his commission very soon, and then he will be sent out of harm's way. Can I do more?"

"No, it is too late to send him away with a free and happy heart. He must bear his pain as he can, and it may help to make a man of him," she said sadly.

"He'll soon forget," began Coventry, who found the thought of gay Ned suffering an uncomfortable one.

"Yes, thank heaven, that is possible, for men."

Miss Muir pressed her hands together, with a dark expression on her half-averted face. Something in her tone, her manner, touched Coventry; he fancied that some old wound bled, some bitter memory awoke at the approach of a new lover. He was young, heart-whole, and romantic, under all his cool nonchalance of manner. This girl, who he fancied loved his friend and who was beloved by his brother, became an object of interest to him. He pitied her, desired to help her, and regretted his past distrust, as a chivalrous man always regrets injustice to a woman. She was happy here, poor, homeless soul, and she should stay. Bella loved her, his mother took comfort in her, and when Ned was gone, no one's peace would be endangered by her winning ways, her rich accomplishments. These thoughts swept through his mind during a brief pause, and when he spoke, it was to say gently:

"Miss Muir, I thank you for the frankness which must have been painful to you, and I will do my best to be worthy of the confidence which you repose in me. You were both discreet and kind to speak only to me. This thing would have troubled my mother extremely, and have done no good. I shall see Ned, and try and repair my long neglect as promptly as possible. I know you will help me, and in return let me beg of you to remain, for he will soon be gone."

She looked at him with eyes full of tears, and there was no coolness in the voice that answered softly, "You are too kind, but I had better go; it is not wise to stay."

"Why not?"

She colored beautifully, hesitated, then spoke out in the clear, steady voice which was her greatest charm, "If I had known there were sons in this family, I never should have come. Lady Sydney spoke only of your sister, and when I found two gentlemen, I was troubled, because—I am so unfortunate—or rather, people are so kind as to like me more than I deserve. I thought I could stay a month, at least, as your brother spoke of going away, and you were already affianced, but—"

"I am not affianced."

Why he said that, Coventry could not tell, but the words passed his lips hastily and could not be recalled. Jean Muir took the announcement oddly enough. She shrugged her shoulders with an air of extreme annoyance, and said almost rudely, "Then you should be; you will be soon. But that is nothing to me. Miss Beaufort wishes me gone, and I am too proud to remain and become the cause of disunion in a happy family. No, I will go, and go at once."

She turned away impetuously, but Edward's arm detained her, and Edward's voice demanded, tenderly, "Where will you go, my Jean?"

The tender touch and name seemed to rob her of her courage and calmness, for, leaning on her lover, she hid her face and sobbed audibly.

"Now don't make a scene, for heaven's sake," began Coventry impatiently, as his brother eyed him fiercely, divining at once what had passed, for his letter was still in Gerald's hand and Jean's last words had reached her lover's ear.

"Who gave you the right to read that, and to interfere in my affairs?" demanded Edward hotly.

"Miss Muir" was the reply, as Coventry threw away the paper.

"And you add to the insult by ordering her out of the house," cried Ned with increasing wrath.

"On the contrary, I beg her to remain."

"The deuce you do! And why?"

"Because she is useful and happy here, and I am unwilling that your folly should rob her of a home which she likes."

"You are very thoughtful and devoted all at once, but I beg you will not trouble yourself. Jean's happiness and home will be my care now."

"My dear boy, do be reasonable. The thing is impossible. Miss Muir sees it herself; she came to tell me, to ask how best to arrange matters without troubling my mother. I've been to town to attend to your affairs, and you may be off now very soon."

"I have no desire to go. Last month it was the wish of my heart. Now I'll accept nothing from you." And Edward turned moodily away from his brother.

"What folly! Ned, you *must* leave home. It is all arranged and cannot be given up now. A change is what you need, and it will make a man of you. We shall miss you, of course, but you will be where you'll see something of life, and that is better for you than getting into mischief here."

"Are you going away, Jean?" asked Edward, ignoring his brother entirely and bending over the girl, who still hid her face and wept. She did not speak, and Gerald answered for her.

"No, why should she if you are gone?"

"Do you mean to stay?" asked the lover eagerly of Jean.

"I wish to remain, but—" She paused and looked up. Her eyes went from one face to the other, and she added decidedly, "Yes, I must go, it is not wise to stay even when you are gone."

Neither of the young men could have explained why that hurried glance affected them as it did, but each felt conscious of a willful desire to oppose the other. Edward suddenly felt that his brother loved Miss Muir, and was bent on removing her from his way. Gerald had a vague idea that Miss Muir feared to remain on his account, and he longed to show her that he was quite safe. Each felt angry, and each showed it in a different way, one being violent, the other satirical.

"You are right, Jean, this is not the place for you; and you must let me see you in a safer home before I go," said Ned, significantly.

"It strikes me that this will be a particularly safe home when your dangerous self is removed," began Coventry, with an aggravating smile of calm superiority.

"And *I* think that I leave a more dangerous person than myself behind me, as poor Lucia can testify."

"Be careful what you say, Ned, or I shall be forced to remind you that I am master here. Leave Lucia's name out of this disagreeable affair, if you please."

"You *are* master here, but not of me, or my actions, and you have no right to expect obedience or respect, for you inspire neither. Jean, I asked you to go with me secretly; now I ask you openly to share my fortune. In my brother's presence I ask, and *will* have an answer."

He caught her hand impetuously, with a defiant look at Coventry, who still smiled, as if at boy's play, though his eyes were kindling and his face changing with the still, white wrath which is more terrible than any sudden outburst. Miss Muir looked frightened; she shrank away from her passionate young lover, cast an appealing glance at Gerald, and seemed as if she longed to claim his protection yet dared not.

"Speak!" cried Edward, desperately. "Don't look to him, tell me truly, with your own lips, do you, can you love me, Jean?"

"I have told you once. Why pain me by forcing another hard reply," she said pitifully, still shrinking from his grasp and seeming to appeal to his brother.

"You wrote a few lines, but I'll not be satisfied with that. You shall answer; I've seen love in your eyes, heard it in your voice, and I know it is hidden in your heart. You fear to own it; do not hesitate, no one can part us—speak, Jean, and satisfy me."

Drawing her hand decidedly away, she went a step nearer Coventry, and answered, slowly, distinctly, though her lips trembled, and she evidently dreaded the effect of her words, "I will speak, and speak truly. You have seen love in my face; it is in my heart, and I do not hesitate to own it, cruel as it is to force the truth from me, but this love is not for you. Are you satisfied?"

He looked at her with a despairing glance and stretched his hand toward her beseechingly. She seemed to fear a blow, for suddenly she clung to Gerald with a faint cry. The act, the look of fear, the protecting gesture Coventry involuntarily made were too much for Edward, already excited by conflicting passions. In a paroxysm of blind wrath, he caught up a large pruning knife left there by the gardener, and would have dealt his brother a fatal blow had he not warded it off with his arm. The stroke fell, and another might have followed had not Miss Muir with unexpected courage and strength wrested the knife from Edward and flung it into the little pond near by. Coventry dropped down upon the seat, for the blood poured from a deep wound in his arm, showing by its rapid flow that an artery had been severed. Edward stood aghast, for with the blow his fury passed, leaving him overwhelmed with remorse and shame.

Gerald looked up at him, smiled faintly, and said, with no sign of reproach or anger, "Never mind, Ned. Forgive and forget. Lend me a hand to the house, and don't disturb anyone. It's not much, I dare say." But his lips whitened as he spoke, and his strength failed him. Edward sprang to support him, and Miss Muir, forgetting her terrors, proved herself a girl of uncommon skill and courage.

"Quick! Lay him down. Give me your handkerchief, and bring some water," she said, in a tone of quiet command. Poor Ned obeyed and watched her with breathless suspense while she tied the handkerchief tightly around the arm, thrust the handle of his riding whip underneath, and pressed it firmly above the severed artery to stop the dangerous flow of blood.

"Dr. Scott is with your mother, I think. Go and bring him here" was the next order; and Edward darted away, thankful to do anything to ease the terror which possessed him. He was gone some minutes, and while they waited Coventry watched the girl as she knelt beside him, bathing his face with one hand while with the other she held the bandage firmly in its place. She was pale, but quite steady and self-possessed, and her eyes shone with a strange brilliancy as she looked down at him. Once, meeting his look of grateful wonder, she smiled a reassuring smile that made her lovely, and said, in a soft, sweet tone never used to him before, "Be quiet. There is no danger. I will stay by you till help comes."

Help did come speedily, and the doctor's first words were "Who improvised that tourniquet?"

"She did," murmured Coventry.

"Then you may thank her for saving your life. By Jove! It was capitally done"; and the old doctor looked at the girl with as much admiration as curiosity in his face.

"Never mind that. See to the wound, please, while I run for bandages, and salts, and wine."

Miss Muir was gone as she spoke, so fleetly that it was in vain to call her back or catch her. During her brief absence, the story was told by repentant Ned and the wound examined.

"Fortunately I have my case of instruments with me," said the doctor, spreading on the bench a long array of tiny, glittering implements of torture. "Now, Mr. Ned, come here, and hold the arm in that way, while I tie the artery. Hey! That will never do. Don't tremble so, man, look away and hold it steadily."

"I can't!" And poor Ned turned faint and white, not at the sight but with the bitter thought that he had longed to kill his brother.

"I will hold it," and a slender white hand lifted the bare and bloody arm so firmly, steadily, that Coventry sighed a sigh of relief, and Dr. Scott fell to work with an emphatic nod of approval.

It was soon over, and while Edward ran in to bid the servants beware of alarming their mistress, Dr. Scott put up his instruments and Miss Muir used salts, water, and wine so skillfully that Gerald was able to walk to his room, leaning on the old man, while the girl supported the wounded arm, as no sling could be made on the spot. As he entered the chamber, Coventry turned, put out his left hand, and with much feeling in his fine eyes said simply, "Miss Muir, I thank you."

The color came up beautifully in her pale cheeks as she pressed the hand and without a word vanished from the room. Lucia and the housekeeper came bustling in, and there was no lack of attendance on the invalid. He soon wearied of it, and sent them all away but Ned, who remorsefully haunted the chamber, looking like a comely young Cain and feeling like an outcast.

"Come here, lad, and tell me all about it. I was wrong to be domineering. Forgive me, and believe that I care for your happiness more sincerely than for my own."

These frank and friendly words healed the breach between the two brothers and completely conquered Ned. Gladly did he relate his love passages, for no young lover ever tires of that amusement if he has a sympathizing auditor, and Gerald *was* sympathetic now. For an hour did he lie listening patiently to the history of the growth of his brother's passion. Emotion gave the narrator eloquence, and Jean Muir's character was painted in glowing colors. All her unsuspected kindness to those about her was dwelt upon; all her faithful care, her sisterly interest in Bella, her gentle attentions to their mother, her sweet forbearance with Lucia, who plainly showed her dislike, and most of all, her friendly counsel, sympathy, and regard for Ned himself.

"She would make a man of me. She puts strength and courage into me as no one else can. She is unlike any girl I ever saw; there's no sentimentality about her; she is wise, and kind, and sweet. She says what she means, looks you straight in the eye, and is as true as steel. I've tried her, I know her, and—ah, Gerald, I love her so!"

Here the poor lad leaned his face into his hands and sighed a sigh that made his brother's heart ache.

"Upon my soul, Ned, I feel for you; and if there was no obstacle on her part, I'd do my best for you. She loves Sydney, and so there is nothing for it but to bear your fate like a man."

"Are you sure about Sydney? May it not be some one else?" and Ned eyed his brother with a suspicious look.

Coventry told him all he knew and surmised concerning his friend, not forgetting the letter. Edward mused a moment, then seemed relieved, and said frankly, "I'm glad it's Sydney and not you. I can bear it better."

"Me!" ejaculated Gerald, with a laugh.

"Yes, you; I've been tormented lately with a fear that you cared for her, or rather, she for you."

"You jealous young fool! We never see or speak to one another scarcely, so how could we get up a tender interest?"

"What do you lounge about on that terrace for every evening? And why does she get fluttered when your shadow begins to come and go?" demanded Edward.

"I like the music and don't care for the society of the singer, that's why I walk there. The fluttering is all your imagination; Miss Muir isn't a woman to be fluttered by a man's shadow." And Coventry glanced at his useless arm.

"Thank you for that, and for not saying 'little Muir,' as you generally do. Perhaps it was my imagination. But she never makes fun of you now, and so I fancied she might have lost her heart to the 'young master.' Women often do, you know."

"She used to ridicule me, did she?" asked Coventry, taking no notice of the latter part of his brother's speech, which was quite true nevertheless.

"Not exactly, she was too well bred for that. But sometimes when Bella and I joked about you, she'd say something so odd or witty that it was irresistible. You're used to being laughed at, so you don't mind, I know, just among ourselves."

"Not I. Laugh away as much as you like," said Gerald. But he did mind, and wanted to know what Miss Muir had said, yet was too proud to ask. He turned restlessly and uttered a sigh of pain.

"I'm talking too much; it's bad for you. Dr. Scott said you must be quiet. Now go to sleep, if you can."

Edward left the bedside but not the room, for he would let no one take his place. Coventry tried to sleep, found it impossible, and after a restless hour called his brother back.

"If the bandage was loosened a bit, it would ease my arm and then I could sleep. Can you do it, Ned?"

"I dare not touch it. The doctor gave orders to leave it till he came in the morning, and I shall only do harm if I try."

"But I tell you it's too tight. My arm is swelling and the pain is intense. It can't be right to leave it so. Dr. Scott dressed it in a hurry and did it too tight. Common sense will tell you that," said Coventry impatiently.

"I'll call Mrs. Morris; she will understand what's best to be done." And Edward moved toward the door, looking anxious.

"Not she, she'll only make a stir and torment me with her chatter. I'll bear it as long as I can, and perhaps Dr. Scott will come tonight. He said he would if possible. Go to your dinner, Ned. I can ring for Neal if I need anything. I shall sleep if I'm alone, perhaps."

Edward reluctantly obeyed, and his brother was left to himself. Little rest did he find, however, for the pain of the wounded arm grew unbearable, and, taking a sudden resolution, he rang for his servant.

"Neal, go to Miss Coventry's study, and if Miss Muir is there, ask her to be kind enough to come to me. I'm in great pain, and she understands wounds better than anyone else in the house."

With much surprise in his face, the man departed and a few moments after the door noiselessly opened and Miss Muir came in. It had been a very warm day, and for the first time she had left off her plain black dress. All in white, with no ornament but her fair hair, and a fragrant posy of violets in her belt, she looked a different woman from the meek, nunlike creature one usually saw about the house. Her face was as altered as her dress, for now a soft color glowed in her cheeks, her eyes smiled shyly, and her lips no longer wore the firm look of one who forcibly repressed every emotion. A fresh, gentle, and charming woman she seemed, and Coventry found the dull room suddenly brightened by her presence. Going straight to him, she said simply, and with a happy, helpful look very comforting to see, "I'm glad you sent for me. What can I do for you?"

He told her, and before the complaint was ended, she began loosening the bandages with the decision of one who understood what was to be done and had faith in herself.

"Ah, that's relief, that's comfort?" ejaculated Coventry, as the last tight fold fell away. "Ned was afraid I should bleed to death if he touched me. What will the doctor say to us?"

"I neither know nor care. I shall say to him that he is a bad surgeon to bind it so closely, and not leave orders to have it untied if necessary. Now I shall make it easy and put you to sleep, for that is what you need. Shall I? May I?"

"I wish you would, if you can."

And while she deftly rearranged the bandages, the young man watched her curiously. Presently he asked, "How came you to know so much about these things?"

"In the hospital where I was ill, I saw much that interested me, and when I got better, I used to sing to the patients sometimes."

"Do you mean to sing to me?" he asked, in the submissive tone men unconsciously adopt when ill and in a woman's care.

"If you like it better than reading aloud in a dreamy tone," she answered, as she tied the last knot.

"I do, much better," he said decidedly.

"You are feverish. I shall wet your forehead, and then you will be quite comfortable." She moved about the room in the quiet way which made it a pleasure to watch her, and, having mingled a little cologne with water, bathed his face as unconcernedly as if he had been a child. Her proceedings not only comforted but amused Coventry, who mentally contrasted her with the stout, beer-drinking matron who had ruled over him in his last illness.

"A clever, kindly little woman," he thought, and felt quite at his ease, she was so perfectly easy herself.

"There, now you look more like yourself," she said with an approving nod as she finished, and smoothed the dark locks off his forehead with a cool, soft hand. Then seating herself in a large chair near by, she began to sing, while tidily rolling up the fresh bandages which had been left for the morning. Coventry lay watching her by the dim light that burned in the room, and she sang on as easily as a bird, a dreamy, low-toned lullaby, which soothed the listener like a spell. Presently, looking up to see the effect of her song, she found the young man wide awake, and regarding her with a curious mixture of pleasure, interest, and admiration.

"Shut your eyes, Mr. Coventry," she said, with a reproving shake of the head, and an odd little smile.

He laughed and obeyed, but could not resist an occasional covert glance from under his lashes at the slender white figure in the great velvet chair. She saw him and frowned.

"You are very disobedient; why won't you sleep?"

"I can't, I want to listen. I'm fond of nightingales."

"Then I shall sing no more, but try something that has never failed yet. Give me your hand, please."

Much amazed, he gave it, and, taking it in both her small ones, she sat down behind the curtain and remained as mute and motionless as a statute. Coventry smiled to himself at first, and wondered which would tire first. But soon a subtle warmth seemed to steal from the soft palms that enclosed his own, his heart beat quicker, his breath grew unequal, and a thousand fancies danced through his brain. He sighed, and said dreamily, as he turned his face toward her, "I like this." And in the act of speaking, seemed to sink into a soft cloud which encompassed him about with an atmosphere of perfect repose. More than this he could not remember, for sleep, deep and dreamless, fell upon him, and when he woke, daylight was shining in between the curtains, his hand lay alone on the coverlet, and his fair-haired enchantress was gone.

IV

A Discovery

For several days Coventry was confined to his room, much against his will, though everyone did their best to lighten his irksome captivity. His mother petted him, Bella sang, Lucia read, Edward was devoted, and all the household, with one exception, were eager to serve the young master. Jean Muir never came near him, and Jean Muir alone seemed to possess the power of amusing him. He soon tired of the others, wanted something new; recalled the piquant character of the girl and took a fancy into his head that she would lighten his ennui. After some hesitation, he carelessly spoke of her to Bella, but nothing came of it, for Bella only said Jean was well, and very busy doing something lovely to surprise Mamma with. Edward complained that he never saw her, and Lucia ignored her existence altogether. The only intelligence the invalid received was from the gossip of two housemaids over their work in the next room. From them he learned that the governess had been "scolded" by Miss Beaufort for going to Mr. Coventry's room; that she had taken it very sweetly and kept herself carefully out of the way of both young gentlemen, though it was plain to see that Mr. Ned was dying for her.

Mr. Gerald amused himself by thinking over this gossip, and quite annoyed his sister by his absence of mind.

"Gerald, do you know Ned's comission has come?"

"Very interesting. Read on, Bella."

"You stupid boy! You don't know a word I say," and she put down the book to repeat her news.

"I'm glad of it; now we must get him off as soon as possible—that is, I suppose he will want to be off as soon as possible." And Coventry woke up from his reverie.

"You needn't check yourself, I know all about it. I think Ned was very foolish, and that Miss Muir has behaved beautifully. It's quite impossible, of course, but I wish it wasn't, I do so like to watch lovers. You and Lucia are so cold you are not a bit interesting."

"You'll do me a favor if you'll stop all that nonsense about Lucia and me. We are not lovers, and never shall be, I fancy. At all events, I'm tired of the thing, and wish you and Mamma would let it drop, for the present at least."

"Oh Gerald, you know Mamma has set her heart upon it, that Papa desired it, and poor Lucia loves you so much. How can you speak of dropping what will make us all so happy?"

"It won't make me happy, and I take the liberty of thinking that this is of some importance. I'm not bound in any way, and don't intend to be till I am ready. Now we'll talk about Ned."

Much grieved and surprised, Bella obeyed, and devoted herself to Edward, who very wisely submitted to his fate and prepared to leave home for some months. For a week the house was in a state of excitement about his departure, and everyone but Jean was busied for him. She was scarcely seen; every morning she gave Bella her lessons, every afternoon drove out with Mrs. Coventry, and nearly every evening went up to the Hall to read to Sir John, who found his wish granted without exactly knowing how it had been done.

The day Edward left, he came down from bidding his mother good-bye, looking very pale, for he had lingered in his sister's little room with Miss Muir as long as he dared.

"Good-bye, dear. Be kind to Jean," he whispered as he kissed his sister.

"I will, I will," returned Bella, with tearful eyes.

"Take care of Mamma, and remember Lucia," he said again, as he touched his cousin's beautiful cheek.

"Fear nothing. I will keep them apart," she whispered back, and Coventry heard it.

Edward offered his hand to his brother, saying, significantly, as he looked him in the eye, "I trust you, Gerald."

"You may, Ned."

Then he went, and Coventry tired himself with wondering what Lucia meant. A few days later he understood.

Now Ned is gone, little Muir will appear, I fancy, he said to himself; but "little Muir" did not appear, and seemed to shun him more carefully than she had done her lover. If he went to the drawing room in the evening hoping for music, Lucia alone was there. If he tapped at Bella's door, there was always a pause before she opened it, and no sign of Jean appeared though her voice had been audible when he knocked. If he went to the library, a hasty rustle and the sound of flying feet betrayed that the room was deserted at his approach. In the garden Miss Muir never failed to avoid him, and if by chance they met in hall or breakfast room, she passed him with downcast eyes and the briefest, coldest greeting. All this annoyed him intensely, and the more she eluded him, the more he desired to see her—from a spirit of opposition, he said, nothing more. It fretted and yet it entertained him, and he found a lazy sort of pleasure in thwarting the girl's little maneuvers. His patience gave out at last, and he resolved to know what was the meaning of this peculiar conduct. Having locked and taken away the key of one door in the library, he waited till Miss Muir went in to get a book for his uncle. He had heard her speak to Bella of it, knew that she believed him with his mother, and smiled to himself as he stole after her. She was standing in a chair, reaching up, and he had time to see a slender waist, a pretty foot, before he spoke.

"Can I help you, Miss Muir?".

She started, dropped several books, and turned scarlet, as she said hurriedly, "Thank you, no; I can get the steps."

"My long arm will be less trouble. I've got but one, and that is tired of being idle, so it is very much at your service. What will you have?"

"I—I—you startled me so I've forgotten." And Jean laughed, nervously, as she looked about her as if planning to escape.

"I beg your pardon, wait till you remember, and let me thank you for the enchanted sleep you gave me ten days ago. I've had no chance yet, you've shunned me so pertinaciously."

"Indeed I try not to be rude, but—" She checked herself, and turned her face away, adding, with an accent of pain in her voice, "It is not my fault, Mr. Coventry. I only obey orders."

"Whose orders?" he demanded, still standing so that she could not escape.

"Don't ask; it is one who has a right to command where you are concerned. Be sure that it is kindly meant, though it may seem folly to us. Nay, don't be angry, laugh at it, as I do, and let me run away, please."

She turned, and looked down at him with tears in her eyes, a smile on her lips, and an expression half sad, half arch, which was altogether charming. The frown passed from his face, but he still looked grave and said decidedly, "No one has a right to command in this house but my mother or myself. Was it she who bade you avoid me as if I was a madman or a pest?"

"Ah, don't ask. I promised not to tell, and you would not have me break my word, I know." And still smiling, she regarded him with a look of merry malice which made any other reply unnecessary. It was Lucia, he thought, and disliked his cousin intensely just then. Miss Muir moved as if to step down; he detained her, saying earnestly, yet with a smile, "Do you consider me the master here?"

"Yes," and to the word she gave a sweet, submissive intonation which made it expressive of the respect, regard, and confidence which men find pleasantest when women feel and show it. Unconsciously his face softened, and he looked up at her with a different glance from any he had ever given her before.

"Well, then, will you consent to obey me if I am not tyrannical or unreasonable in my demands?"

"I'll try."

"Good! Now frankly, I want to say that all this sort of thing is very disagreeable to me. It annoys me to be a restraint upon anyone's liberty or comfort, and I beg you will go and come as freely as you like, and not mind Lucia's absurdities. She means well, but hasn't a particle of penetration or tact. Will you promise this?"

"No."

"Why not?"

"It is better as it is, perhaps."

"But you called it folly just now."

"Yes, it seems so, and yet—" She paused, looking both confused and distressed.

Coventry lost patience, and said hastily, "You women are such enigmas I never expect to understand you! Well, I've done my best to make you comfortable, but if you prefer to lead this sort of life, I beg you will do so."

"I *don't* prefer it; it is hateful to me. I like to be myself, to have my liberty, and the confidence of those about me. But I cannot think it kind to disturb the peace of anyone, and so I try to obey. I've promised Bella to remain, but I will go rather than have another scene with Miss Beaufort or with you."

Miss Muir had burst out impetuously, and stood there with a sudden fire in her eyes, sudden warmth and spirit in her face and voice that amazed Coventry. She was angry, hurt, and haughty, and the change only made her more attractive, for not a trace of her former meek self remained. Coventry was electrified, and still more surprised when she added, imperiously, with a gesture as if to put him aside, "Hand me that book and move away. I wish to go."

He obeyed, even offered his hand, but she refused it, stepped lightly down, and went to the door. There she turned, and with the same indignant voice, the same kindling eyes and glowing cheeks, she said rapidly, "I know I have no right to speak in this way. I restrain myself as long as I can, but when I can bear no more, my true self breaks loose, and I defy everything. I am tired of being a cold, calm machine; it is impossible with an ardent nature like mine, and I shall try no longer. I cannot help it if people love me. I don't want their love. I only ask to be left in peace, and why I am tormented so I cannot see. I've neither beauty, money, nor rank, yet every foolish boy mistakes my frank interest for something warmer, and makes me miserable. It is my misfortune. Think of me what you will, but beware of me in time, for against my will I may do you harm."

Almost fiercely she had spoken, and with a warning gesture she hurried from the room, leaving the young man feeling as if a sudden thunder-gust had swept through the house. For several minutes he sat in the chair she left, thinking deeply. Suddenly he rose, went to his sister, and said, in his usual tone of indolent good nature, "Bella, didn't I hear Ned ask you to be kind to Miss Muir?"

"Yes, and I try to be, but she is so odd lately."

"Odd! How do you mean?"

"Why, she is either as calm and cold as a statue, or restless and queer; she cries at night, I know, and sighs sadly when she thinks I don't hear. Something is the matter."

"She frets for Ned perhaps," began Coventry.

"Oh dear, no; it's a great relief to her that he is gone. I'm afraid that she likes someone very much, and someone don't like her. Can it be Mr. Sydney?"

"She called him a 'titled fool' once, but perhaps that didn't mean anything. Did you ever ask her about him?" said Coventry, feeling rather ashamed of his curiosity, yet unable to resist the temptation of questioning unsuspecting Bella.

"Yes, but she only looked at me in her tragical way, and said, so pitifully, 'My little friend, I hope you will never have to pass through the scenes I've passed through, but keep your peace unbroken all your life.' After that I dared say no more. I'm very fond of her, I want to make her happy, but I don't know how. Can you propose anything?"

"I was going to propose that you make her come among us more, now Ned is gone. It must be dull for her, moping about alone. I'm sure it is for me. She is an entertaining little person, and I enjoy her music very much. It's good for Mamma to have gay evenings; so you bestir yourself, and see what you can do for the general good of the family."

"That's all very charming, and I've proposed it more than once, but Lucia spoils all my plans. She is afraid you'll follow Ned's example, and that is so silly."

"Lucia is a—no, I won't say fool, because she has sense enough when she chooses; but I wish you'd just settle things with Mamma, and then Lucia can do nothing but submit," said Gerald angrily.

"I'll try, but she goes up to read to Uncle, you know, and since he has had the gout, she stays later, so I see little of her in the evening. There she goes now. I think she will captivate the old one as well as the young one, she is so devoted."

Coventry looked after her slender black figure, just vanishing through the great gate, and an uncomfortable fancy took possession of him, born of Bella's careless words. He sauntered away, and after eluding his cousin, who seemed looking for him, he turned toward the Hall, saying to himself, I will see what is going on up here. Such things have happened. Uncle is the simplest soul alive, and if the girl is ambitious, she can do what she will with him.

Here a servant came running after him and gave him a letter, which he thrust into his pocket without examining it. When he reached the Hall, he went quietly to his uncle's study. The door was ajar, and looking in, he saw a scene of tranquil comfort, very pleasant to watch. Sir John leaned in his easy chair with one foot on a cushion. He was dressed with his usual care and, in spite of the gout, looked like a handsome, well-preserved old gentleman. He was smiling as he listened, and his eyes rested complacently on Jean Muir, who sat near him reading in her musical voice, while the sunshine glittered on her hair and the soft rose of her cheek. She read well, yet Coventry thought her heart was not in her task, for once when she paused, while Sir John spoke, her eyes had an absent expression, and she leaned her head upon her hand, with an air of patient weariness.

Poor girl! I did her great injustice; she has no thought of captivating the old man, but amuses him from simple kindness. She is tired. I'll put an end to her task; and Coventry entered without knocking.

Sir John received him with an air of polite resignation, Miss Muir with a perfectly expressionless face.

"Mother's love, and how are you today, sir?"

"Comfortable, but dull, so I want you to bring the girls over this evening, to amuse the old gentleman. Mrs. King has got out the antique costumes and trumpery, as I promised Bella she should have them, and tonight we are to have a merrymaking, as we used to do when Ned was here."

"Very well, sir, I'll bring them. We've all been out of sorts since the lad left, and a little jollity will do us good. Are you going back, Miss Muir?" asked Coventry.

"No, I shall keep her to give me my tea and get things ready. Don't read anymore, my dear, but go and amuse yourself with the pictures, or whatever you like," said Sir John; and like a dutiful daughter she obeyed, as if glad to get away.

"That's a very charming girl, Gerald," began Sir John as she left the room. "I'm much interested in her, both on her own account and on her mother's."

"Her mother's! What do you know of her mother?" asked Coventry, much surprised.

"Her mother was Lady Grace Howard, who ran away with a poor Scotch minister twenty years ago. The family cast her off, and she lived and died so obscurely that very little is known of her except that she left an orphan girl at some small French pension. This is the girl, and a fine girl, too. I'm surprised that you did not know this."

"So am I, but it is like her not to tell. She is a strange, proud creature. Lady Howard's daughter! Upon my word, that is a discovery," and Coventry felt his interest in his sister's governess much increased by this fact; for, like all wellborn Englishmen, he valued rank and gentle blood even more than he cared to own.

"She has had a hard life of it, this poor little girl, but she has a brave spirit, and will make her way anywhere," said Sir John admiringly.

"Did Ned know this?" asked Gerald suddenly.

"No, she only told me yesterday. I was looking in the *Peerage* and chanced to speak of the Howards. She forgot herself and called Lady Grace her mother. Then I got the whole story, for the lonely little thing was glad to make a confidant of someone."

"That accounts for her rejection of Sydney and Ned: she knows she is their equal and will not snatch at the rank which is hers by right. No, she's not mercenary or ambitious."

"What do you say?" asked Sir John, for Coventry had spoken more to himself than to his uncle.

"I wonder if Lady Sydney was aware of this?" was all Gerald's answer.

"No, Jean said she did not wish to be pitied, and so told nothing to the mother. I think the son knew, but that was a delicate point, and I asked no questions."

"I shall write to him as soon as I discover his address. We have been so intimate I can venture to make a few inquiries about Miss Muir, and prove the truth of her story."

"Do you mean to say that you doubt it?" demanded Sir John angrily.

"I beg your pardon, Uncle, but I must confess I have an instinctive distrust of that young person. It is unjust, I dare say, yet I cannot banish it."

"Don't annoy me by expressing it, if you please. I have some penetration and experience, and I respect and pity Miss Muir heartily. This dislike of yours may be the cause of her late melancholy, hey, Gerald?" And Sir John looked suspiciously at his nephew.

Anxious to avert the rising storm, Coventry said hastily as he turned away, "I've neither time nor inclination to discuss the matter now, sir, but will be careful not to offend again. I'll take your message to Bella, so good-bye for an hour, Uncle."

And Coventry went his way through the park, thinking within himself, The dear old gentleman is getting fascinated, like poor Ned. How the deuce does the girl do it? Lady Howard's daughter, yet never told us; I don't understand that.

V

How the Girl Did It

At home he found a party of young friends, who hailed with delight the prospect of a revel at the Hall. An hour later, the blithe company trooped into the great saloon, where preparations had already been made for a dramatic evening.

Good Sir John was in his element, for he was never so happy as when his house was full of young people. Several persons were chosen, and in a few moments the curtains were withdrawn from the first of these impromptu tableaux. A swarthy, darkly bearded man lay asleep on a tiger skin, in the shadow of a tent. Oriental arms and drapery surrounded him; an antique silver lamp burned dimly on a table where fruit lay heaped in costly dishes, and wine shone redly in half-emptied goblets. Bending over the sleeper was a woman robed with barbaric splendor. One hand turned back the embroidered sleeve from the arm which held a scimitar; one slender foot in a scarlet sandal was visible under the white tunic; her purple mantle swept down from snowy shoulders; fillets of gold bound her hair, and jewels shone on neck and arms. She was looking over her shoulder toward the entrance of the tent, with a steady yet stealthy look, so effective that for a moment the spectators held their breath, as if they also heard a passing footstep.

"Who is it?" whispered Lucia, for the face was new to her.

"Jean Muir," answered Coventry, with an absorbed look.

"Impossible! She is small and fair," began Lucia, but a hasty "Hush, let me look!" from her cousin silenced her.

Impossible as it seemed, he was right nevertheless; for Jean Muir it was. She had darkened her skin, painted her eyebrows, disposed some wild black locks over her fair hair, and thrown such an intensity of expression into her eyes that they darkened and dilated till they were as fierce as any southern eyes that ever flashed. Hatred, the deepest and bitterest, was written on her sternly beautiful face, courage glowed in her glance, power spoke in the nervous grip of the slender hand that held the weapon, and the indomitable will of the woman was expressed—even the firm pressure of the little foot half hidden in the tiger skin.

"Oh, isn't she splendid?" cried Bella under her breath.

"She looks as if she'd use her sword well when the time comes," said someone admiringly.

"Good night to Holofernes; his fate is certain," added another.

"He is the image of Sydney, with that beard on."

"Doesn't she look as if she really hated him?"

"Perhaps she does."

Coventry uttered the last exclamation, for the two which preceded it suggested an explanation of the marvelous change in Jean. It was not all art: the intense detestation mingled with a savage joy that the object of her hatred was in her power was too perfect to be feigned; and having the key to a part of her story, Coventry felt as if he caught a glimpse of the truth. It was but a glimpse, however, for the curtain dropped before he had half analyzed the significance of that strange face.

"Horrible! I'm glad it's over," said Lucia coldly.

"Magnificent! Encore! Encore!" cried Gerald enthusiastically.

But the scene was over, and no applause could recall the actress. Two or three graceful or gay pictures followed, but Jean was in none, and each lacked the charm which real talent lends to the simplest part.

"Coventry, you are wanted," called a voice. And to everyone's surprise, Coventry went, though heretofore he had always refused to exert himself when handsome actors were in demand.

"What part am I to spoil?" he asked, as he entered the green room, where several excited young gentlemen were costuming and attitudinizing.

"A fugitive cavalier. Put yourself into this suit, and lose no time asking questions. Miss Muir will tell you what to do. She is in the tableau, so no one will mind you," said the manager pro tem, throwing a rich old suit toward Coventry and resuming the painting of a moustache on his own boyish face.

A gallant cavalier was the result of Gerald's hasty toilet, and when he appeared before the ladies a general glance of admiration was bestowed upon him.

"Come along and be placed; Jean is ready on the stage." And Bella ran before him, exclaiming to her governess, "Here he is, quite splendid. Wasn't he good to do it?"

Miss Muir, in the charming prim and puritanical dress of a Roundhead damsel, was arranging some shrubs, but turned suddenly and dropped the green branch she held, as her eye met the glittering figure advancing toward her.

"You!" she said with a troubled look, adding low to Bella, "Why did you ask *him?* I begged you not."

"He is the only handsome man here, and the best actor if he likes. He won't play usually, so make the most of him." And Bella was off to finish powdering her hair for "The Marriage à la Mode."

"I was sent for and I came. Do you prefer some other person?" asked Coventry, at a loss to understand the half-anxious, half-eager expression of the face under the little cap.

It changed to one of mingled annoyance and resignation as she said,

"It is too late. Please kneel here, half behind the shrubs; put down your hat, and—allow me—you are too elegant for a fugitive."

As he knelt before her, she disheveled his hair, pulled his lace collar awry, threw away his gloves and sword, and half untied the cloak that hung about his shoulders.

"That is better; your paleness is excellent—nay, don't spoil it. We are to represent the picture which hangs in the Hall. I need tell you no more. Now, Roundheads, place yourselves, and then ring up the curtain."

With a smile, Coventry obeyed her; for the picture was of two lovers, the young cavalier kneeling, with his arm around the waist of the girl, who tries to hide him with her little mantle, and presses his head to her bosom in an ecstasy of fear, as she glances back at the approaching pursuers. Jean hesitated an instant and shrank a little as his hand touched her; she blushed deeply, and her eyes fell before his. Then, as the bell rang, she threw herself into her part with sudden spirit. One arm half covered him with her cloak, the other pillowed his head on the muslin kerchief folded over her bosom, and she looked backward with such terror in her eyes that more than one chivalrous young spectator longed to hurry to the rescue. It lasted but a moment; yet in that moment Coventry experienced another new sensation. Many women had smiled on him, but he had remained heart-whole, cool, and careless, quite unconscious of the power which a woman possesses and knows how to use, for the weal or woe of man. Now, as he knelt there with a soft arm about him, a slender waist yielding to his touch, and a maiden heart throbbing against his cheek, for the first time in his life he felt the indescribable spell of womanhood, and looked the ardent lover to perfection. Just as his face assumed this new and most becoming aspect, the curtain dropped, and clamorous encores recalled him to the fact that Miss Muir was trying to escape from his hold, which had grown painful in its unconscious pressure. He sprang up, half bewildered, and looking as he had never looked before.

"Again! Again!" called Sir John. And the young men who played the Roundheads, eager to share in the applause, begged for a repetition in new attitudes.

"A rustle has betrayed you, we have fired and shot the brave girl, and she lies dying, you know. That will be effective; try it, Miss Muir," said one. And with a long breath, Jean complied.

The curtain went up, showing the lover still on his knees, unmindful of the captors who clutched him by the shoulder, for at his feet the girl lay dying. Her head was on his breast, now, her eyes looked full into his, no longer wild with fear, but eloquent with the love which even death could not conquer. The power of those tender eyes thrilled Coventry with a strange delight, and set his heart beating as rapidly as hers had done. She felt his hands tremble, saw the color flash into his cheek, knew that she had touched him at last, and when she rose it was with a sense of triumph which she found it hard to conceal. Others thought it fine acting; Coventry tried to believe so; but Lucia set her teeth, and, as the curtain fell on that second picture, she left her place to hurry behind the scenes, bent on putting an end to such dangerous play. Several actors were complimenting the mimic lovers. Jean took it merrily, but Coventry, in spite of himself, betrayed that he was excited by something deeper than mere gratified vanity.

As Lucia appeared, his manner changed to its usual indifference; but he could not quench the unwonted fire of his eyes, or keep all trace of emotion out of his face, and she saw this with a sharp pang.

"I have come to offer my help. You must be tired, Miss Muir. Can I relieve you?" said Lucia hastily.

"Yes, thank you. I shall be very glad to leave the rest to you, and enjoy them from the front."

So with a sweet smile Jean tripped away, and to Lucia's dismay Coventry followed.

"I want you, Gerald; please stay," she cried.

"I've done my part—no more tragedy for me tonight." And he was gone before she could entreat or command.

There was no help for it; she must stay and do her duty, or expose her jealousy to the quick eyes about her. For a time she bore it; but the sight of her cousin leaning over the chair she had left and chatting with the governess, who now filled it, grew unbearable, and she dispatched a little girl with a message to Miss Muir.

"Please, Miss Beaufort wants you for Queen Bess, as you are the only lady with red hair. Will you come?" whispered the child, quite unconscious of any hidden sting in her words.

"Yes, dear, willingly though I'm not stately enough for Her Majesty, nor handsome enough," said Jean, rising with an untroubled face, though she resented the feminine insult.

"Do you want an Essex? I'm all dressed for it," said Coventry, following to the door with a wistful look.

"No, Miss Beaufort said *you* were not to come. She doesn't want you both together," said the child decidedly.

Jean gave him a significant look, shrugged her shoulders, and went away smiling her odd smile, while Coventry paced up and down the hall in a curious state of unrest, which made him forgetful of everything till the young people came gaily out to supper.

"Come, bonny Prince Charlie, take me down, and play the lover as charmingly as you did an hour ago. I never thought you had so much warmth in you," said Bella, taking his arm and drawing him on against his will.

"Don't be foolish, child. Where is—Lucia?"

Why he checked Jean's name on his lips and substituted another's, he could not tell; but a sudden shyness in speaking of her possessed him, and though he saw her nowhere, he would not ask for her. His cousin came down looking lovely in a classical costume; but Gerald scarcely saw her, and, when the merriment was at its height, he slipped away to discover what had become of Miss Muir.

Alone in the deserted drawing room he found her, and paused to watch her a moment before he spoke; for something in her attitude and face struck him. She was leaning wearily back in the great chair which had served for a throne. Her royal robes were still unchanged, though the crown was off and all her fair hair hung about her shoulders. Excitement and exertion made her brilliant, the rich dress became her wonderfully, and an air of luxurious indolence changed the meek governess into a charming woman. She leaned on the velvet cushions as if she were used to such support; she played with the jewels which had crowned her as carelessly as if she were born to wear them; her attitude was full of negligent grace, and the expression of her face half proud, half pensive, as if her thoughts were bitter-sweet.

One would know she was wellborn to see her now. Poor girl, what a burden a life of dependence must be to a spirit like hers! I wonder what she is thinking of so intently. And Coventry indulged in another look before he spoke.

"Shall I bring you some supper, Miss Muir?"

"Supper!" she ejaculated, with a start. "Who thinks of one's body when one's soul is—" She stopped there, knit her brows, and laughed faintly as she added, "No, thank you. I want nothing but advice, and that I dare not ask of anyone."

"Why not?"

"Because I have no right."

"Everyone has a right to ask help, especially the weak of the strong. Can I help you? Believe me, I most heartily offer my poor services."

"Ah, you forget! This dress, the borrowed splendor of these jewels, the freedom of this gay evening, the romance of the part you played, all blind you to the reality. For a moment I cease to be a servant, and for a moment you treat me as an equal."

It was true; he *had* forgotten. That soft, reproachful glance touched him, his distrust melted under the new charm, and he answered with real feeling in voice and face, "I treat you as an equal because you *are* one; and when I offer help, it is not to my sister's governess alone, but to Lady Howard's daughter."

"Who told you that?" she demanded, sitting erect.

"My uncle. Do not reproach him. It shall go no further, if you forbid it. Are you sorry that I know it?"

"Yes."

"Why?"

"Because I will not be pitied!" And her eyes flashed as she made a half-defiant gesture.

"Then, if I may not pity the hard fate which has befallen an innocent life, may I admire the courage which meets adverse fortune so bravely, and conquers the world by winning the respect and regard of all who see and honor it?"

Miss Muir averted her face, put up her hand, and answered hastily, "No, no, not that! Do not be kind; it destroys the only barrier now left between us. Be cold to me as before, forget what I am, and let me go on my way, unknown, unpitied, and unloved!"

Her voice faltered and failed as the last word was uttered, and she bent her face upon her hand. Something jarred upon Coventry in this speech, and moved him to say, almost rudely, "You need have no fears for me. Lucia will tell you what an iceberg I am."

"Then Lucia would tell me wrong. I have the fatal power of reading character; I know you better than she does, and I see—" There she stopped abruptly.

"What? Tell me and prove your skill," he said eagerly.

Turning, she fixed her eyes on him with a penetrating power that made him shrink as she said slowly, "Under the ice I see fire, and warn you to beware lest it prove a volcano."

For a moment he sat dumb, wondering at the insight of the girl; for she was the first to discover the hidden warmth of a nature too proud to confess its tender impulses, or the ambitions that slept till some potent voice awoke them. The blunt, almost stern manner in which she warned him away from her only made her more attractive; for there was no conceit or arrogance in it, only a foreboding fear emboldened by past suffering to be frank. Suddenly he spoke impetuously:

"You are right! I am not what I seem, and my indolent indifference is but the mask under which I conceal my real self. I could be as passionate, as energetic and aspiring as Ned, if I had any aim in life. I have none, and so I am what you once called me, a thing to pity and despise."

"I never said that!" cried Jean indignantly.

"Not in those words, perhaps; but you looked it and thought it, though you phrased it more mildly. I deserved it, but I shall deserve it no longer. I am beginning to wake from my disgraceful idleness, and long for some work that shall make a man of me. Why do you go? I annoy you with my confessions. Pardon me. They are the first I ever made; they shall be the last."

"No, oh no! I am too much honored by your confidence; but is it wise, is it loyal to tell *me* your hopes and aims? Has not Miss Beaufort the first right to be your confidante?"

Coventry drew back, looking intensely annoyed, for the name recalled much that he would gladly have forgotten in the novel excitement of the hour. Lucia's love, Edward's parting words, his own reserve so strangely thrown aside, so difficult to resume. What he would have said was checked by the sight of a half-open letter which fell from Jean's dress as she moved away. Mechanically he took it up to return it, and, as he did so, he recognized Sydney's handwriting. Jean snatched it from him, turning pale to the lips as she cried, "Did you read it? What did you see? Tell me, tell me, on your honor!"

"On my honor, I saw nothing but this single sentence, 'By the love I bear you, believe what I say.' No more, as I am a gentleman. I know the hand, I guess the purport of the letter, and as a friend of Sydney, I earnestly desire to help you, if I can. Is this the matter upon which you want advice?"

"Yes."

"Then let me give it?"

"You cannot, without knowing all, and it is so hard to tell!"

"Let me guess it, and spare you the pain of telling. May I?" And Coventry waited eagerly for her reply, for the spell was still upon him.

Holding the letter fast, she beckoned him to follow, and glided before him to a secluded little nook, half boudoir, half conservatory. There she paused, stood an instant as if in doubt, then looked up at him with confiding eyes and said decidedly, "I will do it; for, strange as it may seem, you are the only person to whom I *can* speak. You know Sydney, you have discovered that I am an equal, you have offered your help. I accept it; but oh, do not think me unwomanly! Remember how alone I am, how young, and how much I rely upon your sincerity, your sympathy!"

"Speak freely. I am indeed your friend." And Coventry sat down beside her, forgetful of everything but the soft-eyed girl who confided in him so entirely.

Speaking rapidly, Jean went on, "You know that Sydney loved me, that I refused him and went away. But you do not know that his importunities nearly drove me wild, that he threatened to rob me of my only treasure, my good name, and that, in desperation, I tried to kill myself. Yes, mad, wicked as it was, I did long to end the life which was, at best, a burden, and under his persecution had become a torment. You are shocked, yet what I say is the living truth. Lady Sydney will confirm it, the nurses at the hospital will confess that it was not a fever which brought me there; and here, though the external wound is healed, my heart still aches and burns with the shame and indignation which only a proud woman can feel."

She paused and sat with kindling eyes, glowing cheeks, and both hands pressed to her heaving bosom, as if the old insult roused her spirit anew. Coventry said not a word, for surprise, anger, incredulity, and admiration mingled so confusedly in his mind that he forgot to speak, and Jean went on, "That wild act of mine convinced him of my indomitable dislike. He went away, and I believed that this stormy love of his would be cured by absence. It is not, and I live in daily fear of fresh entreaties, renewed persecution. His mother promised not to betray where I had gone, but he found me out and wrote to me. The letter I asked you to take to Lady Sydney was a reply to his, imploring him to leave me in peace. You failed to deliver it, and I was glad, for I thought silence might quench hope. All in vain; this is a more passionate appeal than ever, and he vows he will never desist from his endeavors till I give another man the right to protect me. I *can* do this—I am sorely tempted to do it, but I rebel against the cruelty. I love my freedom, I have no wish to marry at this man's bidding. What can I do? How can I free myself? Be my friend, and help me!"

Tears streamed down her cheeks, sobs choked her words, and she clasped her hands imploringly as she turned toward the young man in all the abandonment of sorrow, fear, and supplication. Conventry found it hard to meet those eloquent eyes and answer calmly, for he had no experience in such scenes and knew not how to play his part. It is this absurd dress and that romantic nonsense which makes me feel so unlike myself, he thought, quite unconscious of the dangerous power which the dusky room, the midsummer warmth and fragrance, the memory of the "romantic nonsense," and, most of all, the presence of a beautiful, afflicted woman had over him. His usual self-possession deserted him, and he could only echo the words which had made the strongest impression upon him:

"You *can* do this, you are tempted to do it. Is Ned the man who can protect you?"

"No" was the soft reply.

"Who then?"

"Do not ask me. A good and honorable man; one who loves me well, and would devote his life to me; one whom once it would have been happiness to marry, but now—"

There her voice ended in a sigh, and all her fair hair fell down about her face, hiding it in a shining veil.

"Why not now? This is a sure and speedy way of ending your distress. Is it impossible?"

In spite of himself, Gerald leaned nearer, took one of the little hands in his, and pressed it as he spoke, urgently, compassionately, nay, almost tenderly. From behind the veil came a heavy sigh, and the brief answer, "It is impossible."

"Why, Jean?"

She flung her hair back with a sudden gesture, drew away her hand, and answered, almost fiercely, "Because I do not love him! Why do you torment me with such questions? I tell you I am in a sore strait and cannot see my way. Shall I deceive the good man, and secure peace at the price of liberty and truth? Or shall I defy Sydney and lead a life of dread? If he menaced my life, I should not fear; but he menaces that which is dearer than life—my good name. A look, a word can tarnish it; a scornful smile, a significant shrug can do me more harm than any blow; for I am a woman—friendless, poor, and at the mercy of his tongue. Ah, better to have died, and so have been saved the bitter pain that has come now!"

She sprang up, clasped her hands over her head, and paced

despairingly through the little room, not weeping, but wearing an expression more tragical than tears. Still feeling as if he had suddenly stepped into a romance, yet finding a keen pleasure in the part assigned him, Coventry threw himself into it with spirit, and heartily did his best to console the poor girl who needed help so much. Going to her, he said as impetuously as Ned ever did, "Miss Muir—nay, I will say Jean, if that will comfort you—listen, and rest assured that no harm shall touch you if I can ward it off. You are needlessly alarmed. Indignant you may well be, but, upon my life, I think you wrong Sydney. He is violent, I know, but he is too honorable a man to injure you by a light word, an unjust act. He did but threaten, hoping to soften you. Let me see him, or write to him. He is my friend; he will listen to me. Of that I am sure."

"Be sure of nothing. When a man like Sydney loves and is thwarted in his love, nothing can control his headstrong will. Promise me you will not see or write to him. Much as I fear and despise him, I will submit, rather than any harm should befall you—or your brother. You promise me, Mr. Coventry?"

He hesitated. She clung to his arm with unfeigned solicitude in her eager, pleading face, and he could not resist it.

"I promise; but in return you must promise to let me give what help I can; and, Jean, never say again that you are friendless."

"You are so kind! God bless you for it. But I dare not accept your friendship; *she* will not permit it, and I have no right to mar her peace."

"Who will not permit it?" he demanded hotly.

"Miss Beaufort."

"Hang Miss Beaufort!" exclaimed Coventry, with such energy that Jean broke into a musical laugh, despite her trouble. He joined in it, and, for an instant they stood looking at one another as if the last barrier were down, and they were friends indeed. Jean paused suddenly, with the smile on her lips, the tears still on her cheek, and made a warning gesture. He listened: the sound of feet mingled with calls and laughter proved that they were missed and sought.

"That laugh betrayed us. Stay and meet them. I cannot." And Jean darted out upon the lawn. Coventry followed; for the thought of confronting so many eyes, so many questions, daunted him, and he fled like a coward. The sound of Jean's flying footsteps guided him, and he overtook her just as she paused behind a rose thicket to take breath.

"Fainthearted knight! You should have stayed and covered my retreat. Hark! they are coming! Hide! Hide!" she panted, half in fear, half in merriment, as the gay pursuers rapidly drew nearer.

"Kneel down; the moon is coming out and the glitter of your embroidery will betray you," whispered Jean, as they cowered behind the roses.

"Your arms and hair will betray you. 'Come under my plaiddie,' as the song says." And Coventry tried to make his velvet cloak cover the white shoulders and fair locks.

"We are acting our parts in reality now. How Bella will enjoy the thing when I tell her!" said Jean as the noises died away.

"Do not tell her," whispered Coventry.

"And why not?" she asked, looking up into the face so near her own, with an artless glance.

"Can you not guess why?"

"Ah, you are so proud you cannot bear to be laughed at."

"It is not that. It is because I do not want you to be annoyed by silly tongues; you have enough to pain you without that. I am your friend, now, and I do my best to prove it."

"So kind, so kind! How can I thank you?" murmured Jean. And she involuntarily nestled closer under the cloak that sheltered both.

Neither spoke for a moment, and in the silence the rapid beating of two hearts was heard. To drown the sound, Coventry said softly, "Are you frightened?"

"No, I like it," she answered, as softly, then added abruptly, "But why do we hide? There is nothing to fear. It is late. I must go. You are kneeling on my train. Please rise."

"Why in such haste? This flight and search only adds to the charm of the evening. I'll not get up yet. Will you have a rose, Jean?"

"No, I will not. Let me go, Mr. Coventry, I insist. There has been enough of this folly. You forget yourself."

She spoke imperiously, flung off the cloak, and put him from her. He rose at once, saying, like one waking suddenly from a pleasant dream, "I do indeed forget myself."

Here the sound of voices broke on them, nearer than before. Pointing to a covered walk that led to the house, he said, in his usually cool, calm tone, "Go in that way; I will cover your retreat." And turning, he went to meet the merry hunters.

Half an hour later, when the party broke up, Miss Muir joined them in her usual quiet dress, looking paler, meeker, and sadder than usual. Coventry saw this, though he neither looked at her nor addressed her. Lucia saw it also, and was glad that the dangerous girl had fallen back into her proper place again, for she had suffered much that night. She appropriated her cousin's arm as they went through the park, but he was in one of his taciturn moods, and all her attempts at conversation were in vain. Miss Muir walked alone, singing softly to herself as she followed in the dusk. Was Gerald so silent because he listened to that fitful song? Lucia thought so, and felt her dislike rapidly deepening to hatred.

When the young friends were gone, and the family were exchanging good-nights among themselves, Jean was surprised by Coventry's offering his hand, for he had never done it before, and whispering, as he held it, though Lucia watched him all the while, "I have not given my advice, yet."

"Thanks, I no longer need it. I have decided for myself."

"May I ask how?"

"To brave my enemy."

"Good! But what decided you so suddenly?"

"The finding of a friend." And with a grateful glance she was gone.

VI

On the Watch

"If you please, Mr. Coventry, did you get the letter last night?" were the first words that greeted the "young master" as he left his room next morning.

"What letter, Dean? I don't remember any," he answered, pausing, for something in the maid's manner struck him as peculiar.

"It came just as you left for the Hall, sir. Benson ran after you with it, as it was marked 'Haste.' Didn't you get it, sir?" asked the woman, anxiously.

"Yes, but upon my life, I forgot all about it till this minute. It's in my other coat, I suppose, if I've not lost it. That absurd masquerading put everything else out of my head." And speaking more to himself than to the maid, Coventry turned back to look for the missing letter.

Dean remained where she was, apparently busy about the arrangement of the curtains at the hall window, but furtively watching meanwhile with a most unwonted air of curiosity.

"Not there, I thought so!" she muttered, as Coventry impatiently thrust his hand into one pocket after another. But as she spoke, an expression of amazement appeared in her face, for suddenly the letter was discovered.

"I'd have sworn it wasn't there! I don't understand it, but she's a deep one, or I'm much deceived." And Dean shook her head like one perplexed, but not convinced.

Coventry uttered an exclamation of satisfaction on glancing at the address and, standing where he was, tore open the letter.

> Dear C:
>
> I'm off to Baden. Come and join me, then you'll be out of harm's way; for if you fall in love with J. M. (and you can't escape if you stay where she is), you will incur the trifling inconvenience of having your brains blown out by
>
> Yours truly, F. R. Sydney

"The man is mad!" ejaculated Coventry, staring at the letter while an angry flush rose to his face. "What the deuce does he mean by writing to me in that style? Join him—not I! And as for the threat, I laugh at it. Poor Jean! This headstrong fool seems bent on tormenting her. Well, Dean, what are you waiting for?" he demanded, as if suddenly conscious of her presence.

"Nothing, sir; I only stopped to see if you found the letter. Beg pardon, sir."

And she was moving on when Coventry asked, with a suspicious look, "What made you think it was lost? You seem to take an uncommon interest in my affairs today."

"Oh dear, no, sir. I felt a bit anxious, Benson is so forgetful, and it was me who sent him after you, for I happened to see you go out, so I felt responsible. Being marked that way, I thought it might be important so I asked about it."

"Very well, you can go, Dean. It's all right, you see."

"I'm not so sure of that," muttered the woman, as she curtsied respectfully and went away, looking as if the letter had *not* been found.

Dean was Miss Beaufort's maid, a grave, middle-aged woman with keen eyes and a somewhat grim air. Having been long in the family, she enjoyed all the privileges of a faithful and favorite servant. She loved her young mistress with an almost jealous affection. She watched over her with the vigilant care of a mother and resented any attempt at interference on the part of others. At first she had pitied and liked Jean Muir, then distrusted her, and now heartily hated her, as the cause of the increased indifference of Coventry toward his cousin. Dean knew the depth of Lucia's love, and though no man, in her eyes, was worthy of her mistress, still, having honored him with her regard, Dean felt bound to like him, and the late change in his manner disturbed the maid almost as much as it did the mistress. She watched Jean narrowly, causing that amiable creature much amusement but little annoyance, as yet, for Dean's slow English wit was no match for the subtle mind of the governess. On the preceding night, Dean had been sent up to the Hall with costumes and had there seen something which much disturbed her. She began to speak of it while undressing her mistress, but Lucia, being in an unhappy mood, had so sternly ordered her not to gossip that the tale remained untold, and she was forced to bide her time.

Now I'll see how *she* looks after it; though there's not much to be got out of *her* face, the deceitful hussy, thought Dean, marching down the corridor and knitting her black brows as she went.

"Good morning, Mrs. Dean. I hope you are none the worse for last night's frolic. You had the work and we the play," said a blithe voice behind her; and turning sharply, she confronted Miss Muir. Fresh and smiling, the governess nodded with an air of cordiality which would have been irresistible with anyone but Dean.

"I'm quite well, thank you, miss," she returned coldly, as her keen eye fastened on the girl as if to watch the effect of her words. "I had a good rest when the young ladies and gentlemen were at supper, for while the maids cleaned up, I sat in the 'little anteroom.' "

"Yes, I saw you, and feared you'd take cold. Very glad you didn't. How is Miss Beaufort? She seemed rather poorly last night" was the tranquil reply, as Jean settled the little frills about her delicate wrists. The cool question was a return shot for Dean's hint that she had been where she could oversee the interview between Coventry and Miss Muir.

"She is a bit tired, as any *lady* would be after such an evening. People who are *used* to *play-acting* wouldn't mind it, perhaps, but Miss Beaufort don't enjoy *romps* as much as *some* do."

The emphasis upon certain words made Dean's speech as impertinent as she desired. But Jean only laughed, and as Coventry's step was heard behind them, she ran downstairs, saying blandly, but with a wicked look, "I won't stop to thank you now, lest Mr. Coventry should bid me good-morning, and so increase Miss Beaufort's indisposition."

Dean's eyes flashed as she looked after the girl with a wrathful face, and went her way, saying grimly, "I'll bide my time, but I'll get the better of her yet."

Fancying himself quite removed from "last night's absurdity," yet curious to see how Jean would meet him, Coventry lounged into the breakfast room with his usual air of listless indifference. A languid nod and murmur was all the reply he vouchsafed to the greetings of cousin, sister, and governess as he sat down and took up his paper.

"Have you had a letter from Ned?" asked Bella, looking at the note which her brother still held.

"No" was the brief answer.

"Who then? You look as if you had received bad news."

There was no reply, and, peeping over his arm, Bella caught sight of the seal and exclaimed, in a disappointed tone, "It is the Sydney crest. I don't care about the note now. Men's letters to each other are not interesting."

Miss Muir had been quietly feeding one of Edward's dogs, but at the name she looked up and met Coventry's eyes, coloring so distressfully that he pitied her. Why he should take the trouble to cover her confusion, he did not stop to ask himself, but seeing the curl of Lucia's lip, he suddenly addressed her with an air of displeasure, "Do you know that Dean is getting impertinent? She presumes too much on her age and your indulgence, and forgets her place."

"What has she done?" asked Lucia coldly.

"She troubles herself about my affairs and takes it upon herself to keep Benson in order."

Here Coventry told about the letter and the woman's evident curiosity.

"Poor Dean, she gets no thanks for reminding you of what you had forgotten. Next time she will leave your letters to their fate, and perhaps it will be as well, if they have such a bad effect upon your temper, Gerald."

Lucia spoke calmly, but there was an angry color in her cheek as she rose and left the room. Coventry looked much annoyed, for on Jean's face he detected a faint smile, half pitiful, half satirical, which disturbed him more than his cousin's insinuation. Bella broke the awkward silence by saying, with a sigh, "Poor Ned! I do so long to hear again from him. I thought a letter had come for some of us. Dean said she saw one bearing his writing on the hall table yesterday."

"She seems to have a mania for inspecting letters. I won't allow it. Who was the letter for, Bella?" said Coventry, putting down his paper.

"She wouldn't or couldn't tell, but looked very cross and told me to ask you."

"Very odd! I've had none," began Coventry.

"But I had one several days ago. Will you please read it, and my reply?" And as she spoke, Jean laid two letters before him.

"Certainly not. It would be dishonorable to read what Ned intended for no eyes but your own. You are too scrupulous in one way, and not enough so in another, Miss Muir." And Coventry offered both the letters with an air of grave decision, which could not conceal the interest and surprise he felt.

"You are right. Mr. Edward's note *should* be kept sacred, for in it the poor boy has laid bare his heart to me. But mine I beg you will read, that you may see how well I try to keep my word to you. Oblige me in this, Mr. Coventry; I have a right to ask it of you."

So urgently she spoke, so wistfully she looked, that he could not refuse and, going to the window, read the letter. It was evidently an answer to a passionate appeal from the young lover, and was written with consummate skill. As he read, Gerald could not help thinking, If this girl writes in this way to a man whom she does *not* love, with what a world of power and passion would she write to one whom she *did* love. And this thought kept returning to him as his eye went over line after line of wise argument, gentle reproof, good counsel, and friendly regard. Here and there a word, a phrase, betrayed what she had already confessed, and Coventry forgot to return the letter, as he stood wondering who was the man whom Jean loved.

The sound of Bella's voice recalled him, for she was saying, half kindly, half petulantly, "Don't look so sad, Jean. Ned will outlive it, I dare say. You remember you said once men never died of love, though women might. In his one note to me, he spoke so beautifully of you, and begged me to be kind to you for his sake, that I try to be with all my heart, though if it was anyone but you, I really think I should hate them for making my dear boy so unhappy."

"You are too kind, Bella, and I often think I'll go away to relieve you of my presence; but unwise and dangerous as it is to stay, I haven't the courage to go. I've been so happy here." And as she spoke, Jean's head dropped lower over the dog as it nestled to her affectionately.

Before Bella could utter half the loving words that sprang to her lips, Coventry came to them with all languor gone from face and mien, and laying Jean's letter before her, he said, with an undertone of deep feeling in his usually emotionless voice, "A right womanly and eloquent letter, but I fear it will only increase the fire it was meant to quench. I pity my brother more than ever now."

"Shall I send it?" asked Jean, looking straight up at him, like one who had entire reliance on his judgment.

"Yes, I have not the heart to rob him of such a sweet sermon upon self-sacrifice. Shall I post it for you?"

"Thank you; in a moment." And with a grateful look, Jean dropped her eyes. Producing her little purse, she selected a penny, folded it in a bit of paper, and then offered both letter and coin to Coventry, with such a pretty air of business, that he could not control a laugh.

"So you won't be indebted to me for a penny? What a proud woman you are, Miss Muir."

"I am; it's a family failing." And she gave him a significant glance, which recalled to him the memory of who she was. He understood her feeling, and liked her the better for it, knowing that he would have done the same had he been in her place. It was a little thing, but if done for effect, it answered admirably, for it showed a quick insight into his character on her part, and betrayed to him the existence of a pride in which he sympathized heartily. He stood by Jean a moment, watching her as she burnt Edward's letter in the blaze of the spirit lamp under the urn.

"Why do you do that?" he asked involuntarily.

"Because it is my duty to forget" was all her answer.

"Can you always forget when it becomes a duty?"

"I wish I could! I wish I could!"

She spoke passionately, as if the words broke from her against her will, and, rising hastily, she went into the garden, as if afraid to stay.

"Poor, dear Jean is very unhappy about something, but I can't discover what it is. Last night I found her crying over a rose, and now she runs away, looking as if her heart was broken. I'm glad I've got no lessons."

"What kind of a rose?" asked Coventry from behind his paper as Bella paused.

"A lovely white one. It must have come from the Hall; we have none like it. I wonder if Jean was ever going to be married, and lost her lover, and felt sad because the flower reminded her of bridal roses."

Coventry made no reply, but felt himself change countenance as he recalled the little scene behind the rose hedge, where he gave Jean the flower which she had refused yet taken. Presently, to Bella's surprise, he flung down the paper, tore Sydney's note to atoms, and rang for his horse with an energy which amazed her.

"Why, Gerald, what has come over you? One would think Ned's restless spirit had suddenly taken possession of you. What are you going to do?"

"I'm going to work" was the unexpected answer, as Coventry turned toward her with an expression so rarely seen on his fine face.

"What has waked you up all at once?" asked Bella, looking more and more amazed.

"You did," he said, drawing her toward him.

"I! When? How?"

"Do you remember saying once that energy was better than beauty in a man, and that no one could respect an idler?"

"I never said anything half so sensible as that. Jean said something like it once, I believe, but I forgot. Are you tired of doing nothing, at last, Gerald?"

"Yes, I neglected my duty to Ned, till he got into trouble, and now I reproach myself for it. It's not too late to do other neglected tasks, so I'm going at them with a will. Don't say anything about it to anyone, and don't laugh at me, for I'm in earnest, Bell."

"I know you are, and I admire and love you for it, my dear old boy," cried Bella enthusiastically, as she threw her arms about his neck and kissed him heartily. "What will you do first?" she asked, as he stood thoughtfully smoothing the bright head that leaned upon his shoulder, with that new expression still clear and steady in his face.

"I'm going to ride over the whole estate, and attend to things as a master should; not leave it all to Bent, of whom I've heard many complaints, but have been too idle to inquire about them. I shall consult Uncle, and endeavor to be all that my father was in his time. Is that a worthy ambition, dear?"

"Oh, Gerald, let me tell Mamma. It will make her so happy. You are her idol, and to hear you say these things, to see you look so like dear Papa, would do more for her spirits than all the doctors in England."

"Wait till I prove what my resolution is worth. When I have really done something, then I'll surprise Mamma with a sample of my work."

"Of course you'll tell Lucia?"

"Not on any account. It is a little secret between us, so keep it till I give you leave to tell it."

"But Jean will see it at once; she knows everything that happens, she is so quick and wise. Do you mind her knowing?"

"I don't see that I can help it if she is so wonderfully gifted. Let her see what she can, I don't mind her. Now I'm off." And with a kiss to his sister, a sudden smile on his face, Coventry sprang upon his horse and rode away at a pace which caused the groom to stare after him in blank amazement.

Nothing more was seen of him till dinnertime, when he came in so exhilarated by his brisk ride and busy morning that he found some difficulty in assuming his customary manner, and more than once astonished the family by talking animatedly on various subjects which till now had always seemed utterly uninteresting to him. Lucia was amazed, his mother delighted, and Bella could hardly control her desire to explain the mystery; but Jean took it very calmly and regarded him with the air of one who said, "I understand, but you will soon tire of it." This nettled him more than he would confess, and he exerted himself to silently contradict that prophecy.

"Have you answered Mr. Sydney's letter?" asked Bella, when they were all scattered about the drawing room after dinner.

"No," answered her brother, who was pacing up and down with restless steps, instead of lounging near his beautiful cousin.

"I ask because I remembered that Ned sent a message for him in my last note, as he thought you would know Sydney's address. Here it is, something about a horse. Please put it in when you write," and Bella laid the note on the writing table nearby.

"I'll send it at once and have done with it," muttered Coventry and, seating himself, he dashed off a few lines, sealed and sent the letter, and then resumed his march, eyeing the three young ladies with three different expressions, as he passed and repassed. Lucia sat apart, feigning to be intent upon a book, and her handsome face looked almost stern in its haughty composure, for though her heart ached, she was too proud to own it. Bella now lay on the sofa, half asleep, a rosy little creature, as unconsciously pretty as a child. Miss Muir sat in the recess of a deep window, in a low lounging chair, working at an embroidery frame with a graceful industry pleasant to see. Of late she had worn colors, for Bella had been generous in gifts, and the pale blue muslin which flowed in soft waves about her was very becoming to her fair skin and golden hair. The close braids were gone, and loose curls dropped here and there from the heavy coil wound around her well-shaped head. The tip of one dainty foot was visible, and a petulant little gesture which now and then shook back the falling sleeve gave glimpses of a round white arm. Ned's great hound lay nearby, the sunshine flickered on her through the leaves, and as she sat smiling to herself, while the dexterous hands shaped leaf and flower, she made a charming picture of all that is most womanly and winning; a picture which few men's eyes would not have liked to rest upon.

Another chair stood near her, and as Coventry went up and down, a strong desire to take it possessed him. He was tired of his thoughts and wished to be amused by watching the changes of the girl's expressive face, listening to the varying tones of her voice, and trying to discover the spell which so strongly attracted him in spite of himself. More than once he swerved from his course to gratify his whim, but Lucia's presence always restrained him, and with a word to the dog, or a glance from the window, as pretext for a pause, he resumed his walk again. Something in his cousin's face reproached him, but her manner of late was so repellent that he felt no desire to resume their former familiarity, and, wishing to show that he did not consider himself bound, he kept aloof. It was a quiet test of the power of each woman over this man; they instinctively felt it, and both tried to conquer. Lucia spoke several times, and tried to speak frankly and affably; but her manner was constrained, and Coventry, having answered politely, relapsed into silence. Jean said nothing, but silently appealed to eye and ear by the pretty picture she made of herself, the snatches of song she softly sang, as if forgetting that she was not alone, and a shy glance now and then, half wistful, half merry, which was more alluring than graceful figure or sweet voice. When she had tormented Lucia and tempted Coventry long enough, she quietly asserted her supremacy in a way which astonished her rival, who knew nothing of the secret of her birth, which knowledge did much to attract and charm the young man. Letting a ball of silk escape from her lap, she watched it roll toward the promenader, who caught and returned it with an alacrity which added grace to the trifling service. As she took it, she said, in the frank way that never failed to win him, "I think you must be tired; but if exercise is necessary, employ your energies to some purpose and put your mother's basket of silks in order. They are in a tangle, and it will please her to know that you did it, as your brother used to do."

"Hercules at the distaff," said Coventry gaily, and down he sat in the long-desired seat. Jean put the basket on his knee, and as he surveyed it, as if daunted at his task, she leaned back, and indulged in a musical little peal of laughter charming to hear. Lucia sat dumb with surprise, to see her proud, indolent cousin obeying the commands of a governess, and looking as if he heartily enjoyed it. In ten minutes she was as entirely forgotten as if she had been miles away; for Jean seemed in her wittiest, gayest mood, and as she now treated the "young master" like an equal, there was none of the former meek timidity. Yet often her eyes fell, her color changed, and the piquant sallies faltered on her tongue, as Coventry involuntarily looked deep into the fine eyes which had once shone on him so tenderly in that mimic tragedy. He could not forget it, and though neither alluded to it, the memory of the previous evening seemed to haunt both and lend a secret charm to the present moment. Lucia bore this as long as she could, and then left the room with an air of an insulted princess; but Coventry did not, and Jean feigned not to see her go. Bella was fast asleep, and before he knew how it came to pass, the young man was listening to the story of his companion's life. A sad tale, told with wonderful skill, for soon he was absorbed in it. The basket slid unobserved from his knee, the dog was pushed away, and, leaning forward, he listened eagerly as the girl's low voice recounted all the hardships, loneliness, and grief of her short life. In the midst of a touching episode she started, stopped, and looked straight before her, with an intent expression which changed to one of intense contempt, and her eye turned to Coventry's, as she said, pointing to the window behind him, "We are watched."

"By whom?" he demanded, starting up angrily.

"Hush, say nothing, let it pass. I am used to it."

"But *I* am not, and I'll not submit to it. Who was it, Jean?" he answered hotly.

She smiled significantly at a knot of rose-colored ribbon, which a little gust was blowing toward them along the terrace. A black frown darkened the young man's face as he sprang out of the long window and went rapidly out of sight, scrutinizing each green nook as he passed. Jean laughed quietly as she watched him, and said softly to herself, with her eyes on the fluttering ribbon, "That was a fortunate accident, and a happy inspiration. Yes, my dear Mrs. Dean, you will find that playing the spy will only get your mistress as well as yourself into trouble. You would not be warned, and you must take the consequences, reluctant as I am to injure a worthy creature like yourself."

Soon Coventry was heard returning. Jean listened with suspended breath to catch his first words, for he was not alone.

"Since you insist that it was you and not your mistress, I let it pass, although I still have my suspicions. Tell Miss Beaufort I desire to see her for a few moments in the library. Now go, Dean, and be careful for the future, if you wish to stay in my house."

The maid retired, and the young man came in looking both ireful and stern.

"I wish I had said nothing, but I was startled, and spoke involuntarily. Now you are angry, and I have made fresh trouble for poor Miss Lucia. Forgive me as I forgive her, and let it pass. I have learned to bear this surveillance, and pity her causeless jealousy," said Jean, with a self-reproachful air.

"I will forgive the dishonorable act, but I cannot forget it, and I intend to put a stop to it. I am not betrothed to my cousin, as I told you once, but you, like all the rest, seem bent on believing that I am. Hitherto I have cared too little about the matter to settle it, but now I shall prove beyond all doubt that I am free."

As he uttered the last word, Coventry cast on Jean a look that affected her strangely. She grew pale, her work dropped on her lap, and her eyes rose to his, with an eager, questioning expression, which slowly changed to one of mingled pain and pity, as she turned her face away, murmuring in a tone of tender sorrow, "Poor Lucia, who will comfort her?"

For a moment Coventry stood silent, as if weighing some fateful purpose in his mind. As Jean's rapt sigh of compassion reached his ear, he had echoed it within himself, and half repented of his resolution; then his eye rested on the girl before him looking so lonely in her sweet sympathy for another that his heart yearned toward her. Sudden fire shot into his eye, sudden warmth replaced the cold sternness of his face, and his steady voice faltered suddenly, as he said, very low, yet very earnestly, "Jean, I have tried to love her, but I cannot. Ought I to deceive her, and make myself miserable to please my family?"

"She is beautiful and good, and loves you tenderly; is there no hope for her?" asked Jean, still pale, but very quiet, though she held one hand against her heart, as if to still or hide its rapid beating.

"None," answered Coventry.

"But can you not learn to love her? Your will is strong, and most men would not find it a hard task."

"I cannot, for something stronger than my own will controls me."

"What is that?" And Jean's dark eyes were fixed upon him, full of innocent wonder.

His fell, and he said hastily, "I dare not tell you yet."

"Pardon! I should not have asked. Do not consult me in this matter; I am not the person to advise you. I can only say that it seems to me as if any man with an empty heart would be glad to have so beautiful a woman as your cousin."

"My heart is not empty," began Coventry, drawing a step nearer, and speaking in a passionate voice. "Jean, I *must* speak; hear me. I cannot love my cousin, because I love you."

"Stop!" And Jean sprang up with a commanding gesture. "I will not hear you while any promise binds you to another. Remember your mother's wishes, Lucia's hopes, Edward's last words, your own pride, my humble lot. You forget yourself, Mr. Coventry. Think well before you speak, weigh the cost of this act, and recollect who I am before you insult me by any transient passion, any false vows."

"I have thought, I do weigh the cost, and I swear that I desire to woo you as humbly, honestly as I would any lady in the land. You speak of my pride. Do I stoop in loving my equal in rank? You speak of your lowly lot, but poverty is no disgrace, and the courage with which you bear it makes it beautiful. I should have broken with Lucia before I spoke, but I could not control myself. My mother loves you, and will be happy in my happiness. Edward must forgive me, for I have tried to do my best, but love is irresistible. Tell me, Jean, is there any hope for me?"

He had seized her hand and was speaking impetuously, with ardent face and tender tone, but no answer came, for as Jean turned her eloquent countenance toward him, full of maiden shame and timid love, Dean's prim figure appeared at the door, and her harsh voice broke the momentary silence, saying, sternly, "Miss Beaufort is waiting for you, sir."

"Go, go at once, and be kind, for my sake, Gerald," whispered Jean, for he stood as if deaf and blind to everything but her voice, her face.

As she drew his head down to whisper, her cheek touched his, and regardless of Dean, he kissed it, passionately, whispering back, "My little Jean! For your sake I can be anything."

"Miss Beaufort is waiting. Shall I say you will come, sir?" demanded Dean, pale and grim with indignation.

"Yes, yes, I'll come. Wait for me in the garden, Jean." And Coventry hurried away, in no mood for the interview but anxious to have it over.

As the door closed behind him, Dean walked up to Miss Muir, trembling with anger, and laying a heavy hand on her arm, she said below her breath, "I've been expecting this, you artful creature. I saw your game and did my best to spoil it, but you are too quick for me. You think you've got him. There you are mistaken; for as sure as my name is Hester Dean, I'll prevent it, or Sir John shall."

"Take your hand away and treat me with proper respect, or you will be dismissed from this house. Do you know who I am?" And Jean drew herself up with a haughty air, which impressed the woman more deeply than her words. "I am the daughter of Lady Howard and, if I choose it, can be the wife of Mr. Coventry."

Dean drew back amazed, yet not convinced. Being a well-trained servant, as well as a prudent woman, she feared to overstep the bounds of respect, to go too far, and get her mistress as well as herself into trouble. So, though she still doubted Jean, and hated her more than ever, she controlled herself. Dropping a curtsy, she assumed her usual air of deference, and said, meekly, "I beg pardon, miss. If I'd known, I should have conducted myself differently, of course, but ordinary governesses make so much mischief in a house, one can't help mistrusting them. I don't wish to meddle or be overbold, but being fond of my dear young lady, I naturally take her part, and must say that Mr. Coventry has not acted like a gentleman."

"Think what you please, Dean, but I advise you to say as little as possible if you wish to remain. I have not accepted Mr. Coventry yet, and if he chooses to set aside the engagement his family made for him, I think he has a right to do so. Miss Beaufort would hardly care to marry him against his will, because he pities her for her unhappy love," and with a tranquil smile, Miss Muir walked away.

VII

The Last Chance

"*S*he will tell Sir John, will she? Then I must be before her, and hasten events. It will be as well to have all sure before there can be any danger. My poor Dean, you are no match for me, but you may prove annoying, nevertheless."

These thoughts passed through Miss Muir's mind as she went down the hall, pausing an instant at the library door, for the murmur of voices was heard. She caught no word, and had only time for an instant's pause as Dean's heavy step followed her. Turning, Jean drew a chair before the door, and, beckoning to the woman, she said, smiling still, "Sit here and play watchdog. I am going to Miss Bella, so you can nod if you will."

"Thank you, miss. I will wait for my young lady. She may need me when this hard time is over." And Dean seated herself with a resolute face.

Jean laughed and went on; but her eyes gleamed with sudden malice, and she glanced over her shoulder with an expression which boded ill for the faithful old servant.

"I've got a letter from Ned, and here is a tiny note for you," cried Bella as Jean entered the boudoir. "Mine is a very odd, hasty letter, with no news in it, but his meeting with Sydney. I hope yours is better, or it won't be very satisfactory."

As Sydney's name passed Bella's lips, all the color died out of Miss Muir's face, and the note shook with the tremor of her hand. Her very lips were white, but she said calmly, "Thank you. As you are busy, I'll go and read my letter on the lawn." And before Bella could speak, she was gone.

Hurrying to a quiet nook, Jean tore open the note and read the few blotted lines it contained.

> I have seen Sydney; he has told me all; and, hard as I found it to believe, it was impossible to doubt, for he has discovered proofs which cannot be denied. I make no reproaches, shall demand no confession or atonement, for I cannot forget that I once loved you. I give you three days to find another home, before I return to tell the family who you are. Go at once, I beseech you, and spare me the pain of seeing your disgrace.

Slowly, steadily she read it twice over, then sat motionless, knitting her brows in deep thought. Presently she drew a long breath, tore up the note, and rising, went slowly toward the Hall, saying to herself, "Three days, only three days! Can it be accomplished in so short a time? It shall be, if wit and will can do it, for it is my last chance. If this fails, I'll not go back to my old life, but end all at once."

Setting her teeth and clenching her hands, as if some memory stung her, she went on through the twilight, to find Sir John waiting to give her a hearty welcome.

"You look tired, my dear. Never mind the reading tonight; rest yourself, and let the book go," he said kindly, observing her worn look.

"Thank you, sir. I am tired, but I'd rather read, else the book will not be finished before I go."

"Go, child! Where are you going?" demanded Sir John, looking anxiously at her as she sat down.

"I will tell you by-and-by, sir." And opening the book, Jean read for a little while.

But the usual charm was gone; there was no spirit in the voice of the reader, no interest in the face of the listener, and soon he said, abruptly, "My dear, pray stop! I cannot listen with a divided mind. What troubles you? Tell your friend, and let him comfort you."

As if the kind words overcame her, Jean dropped the book, covered up her face, and wept so bitterly that Sir John was much alarmed; for such a demonstration was doubly touching in one who usually was all gaiety and smiles. As he tried to soothe her, his words grew tender, his solicitude full of a more than paternal anxiety, and his kind heart overflowed with pity and affection for the weeping girl. As she grew calmer, he urged her to be frank, promising to help and counsel her, whatever the affliction or fault might be.

"Ah, you are too kind, too generous! How can I go away and leave my one friend?" sighed Jean, wiping the tears away and looking up at him with grateful eyes.

"Then you do care a little for the old man?" said Sir John with an eager look, an involuntary pressure of the hand he held.

Jean turned her face away, and answered, very low, "No one ever was so kind to me as you have been. Can I help caring for you more than I can express?"

Sir John was a little deaf at times, but he heard that, and looked well pleased. He had been rather thoughtful of late, had dressed with unusual care, been particularly gallant and gay when the young ladies visited him, and more than once, when Jean paused in the reading to ask a question, he had been forced to confess that he had not been listening; though, as she well knew, his eyes had been fixed upon her. Since the discovery of her birth, his manner had been peculiarly benignant, and many little acts had proved his interest and goodwill. Now, when Jean spoke of going, a panic seized him, and desolation seemed about to fall upon the old Hall. Something in her unusual agitation struck him as peculiar and excited his curiosity. Never had she seemed so interesting as now, when she sat beside him with tearful eyes, and some soft trouble in her heart which she dared not confess.

"Tell me everything, child, and let your friend help you if he can." Formerly he said "father" or "the old man," but lately he always spoke of himself as her "friend."

"I will tell you, for I have no one else to turn to. I must go away because Mr. Coventry has been weak enough to love me."

"What, Gerald?" cried Sir John, amazed.

"Yes; today he told me this, and left me to break with Lucia; so I ran to you to help me prevent him from disappointing his mother's hopes and plans."

Sir John had started up and paced down the room, but as Jean paused he turned toward her, saying, with an altered face. "Then you do not love him? Is it possible?"

"No, I do not love him," she answered promptly.

"Yet he is all that women usually find attractive. How is it that you have escaped, Jean?"

"I love someone else" was the scarcely audible reply.

Sir John resumed his seat with the air of a man bent on getting at a mystery, if possible.

"It will be unjust to let you suffer for the folly of these boys, my little girl. Ned is gone, and I was sure that Gerald was safe; but now that his turn has come, I am perplexed, for he cannot be sent away."

"No, it is I who must go; but it seems so hard to leave this safe and happy home, and wander away into the wide, cold world again. You have all been too kind to me, and now separation breaks my heart."

A sob ended the speech, and Jean's head went down upon her hands again. Sir John looked at her a moment, and his fine old face was full of genuine emotion, as he said slowly, "Jean, will you stay and be a daughter to the solitary old man?"

"No, sir" was the unexpected answer.

"And why not?" asked Sir John, looking surprised, but rather pleased than angry.

"Because I could not be a daughter to you; and even if I could, it would not be wise, for the gossips would say you were not old enough to be the adopted father of a girl like me. Sir John, young as I am, I know much of the world, and am sure that this kind plan is impractical; but I thank you from the bottom of my heart."

"Where will you go, Jean?" asked Sir John, after a pause.

"To London, and try to find another situation where I can do no harm."

"Will it be difficult to find another home?"

"Yes. I cannot ask Mrs. Coventry to recommend me, when I have innocently brought so much trouble into her family; and Lady Sydney is gone, so I have no friend."

"Except John Coventry. I will arrange all that. When will you go, Jean?"

"Tomorrow."

"So soon!" And the old man's voice betrayed the trouble he was trying to conceal.

Jean had grown very calm, but it was the calmness of desperation. She had hoped that the first tears would produce the avowal for which she waited. It had not, and she began to fear that her last chance was slipping from her. Did the old man love her? If so, why did he not speak? Eager to profit by each moment, she was on the alert for any hopeful hint, any propitious word, look, or act, and every nerve was strung to the utmost.

"Jean, may I ask one question?" said Sir John.

"Anything of me, sir."

"This man whom you love—can he not help you?"

"He could if he knew, but he must not."

"If he knew what? Your present trouble?"

"No. My love."

"He does know this, then?"

"No, thank heaven! And he never will."

"Why not?"

"Because I am too proud to own it."

"He loves you, my child?"

"I do not know—I dare not hope it," murmured Jean.

"Can I not help you here? Believe me, I desire to see you safe and happy. Is there nothing I can do?"

"Nothing, nothing."

"May I know the name?"

"No! No! Let me go; I cannot bear this questioning!" And Jean's distressful face warned him to ask no more.

"Forgive me, and let me do what I may. Rest here quietly. I'll write a letter to a good friend of mine, who will find you a home, if you leave us."

As Sir John passed into his inner study, Jean watched him with despairing eyes and wrung her hands, saying to herself, Has all my skill deserted me when I need it most? How can I make him understand, yet not overstep the bounds of maiden modesty? He is so blind, so timid, or so dull he will not see, and time is going fast. What shall I do to open his eyes?

Her own eyes roved about the room, seeking for some aid from inanimate things, and soon she found it. Close behind the couch where she sat hung a fine miniature of Sir John. At first her eye rested on it as she contrasted its placid comeliness with the unusual pallor and disquiet of the living face seen through the open door, as the old man sat at his desk trying to write and casting covert glances at the girlish figure he had left behind him. Affecting unconsciousness of this, Jean gazed on as if forgetful of everything but the picture, and suddenly, as if obeying an irresistible impulse, she took it down, looked long and fondly at it, then, shaking her curls about her face, as if to hide the act, pressed it to her lips and seemed to weep over it in an uncontrollable paroxysm of tender grief. A sound startled her, and like a guilty thing, she turned to replace the picture; but it dropped from her hand as she uttered a faint cry and hid her face, for Sir John stood before her, with an expression which she could not mistake.

"Jean, why did you do that?" he asked, in an eager, agitated voice.

No answer, as the girl sank lower, like one overwhelmed with shame. Laying his hand on the bent head, and bending his own, he whispered, "Tell me, is the name John Coventry?"

Still no answer, but a stifled sound betrayed that his words had gone home.

"Jean, shall I go back and write the letter, or may I stay and tell you that the old man loves you better than a daughter?"

She did not speak, but a little hand stole out from under the falling hair, as if to keep him. With a broken exclamation he seized it, drew her up into his arms, and laid his gray head on her fair one, too happy for words. For a moment Jean Muir enjoyed her success; then, fearing lest some sudden mishap should destroy it, she hastened to make all secure. Looking up with well-feigned timidity and half-confessed affection, she said softly, "Forgive me that I could not hide this better. I meant to go away and never tell it, but you were so kind it made the parting doubly hard. Why did you ask such dangerous questions? Why did you look, when you should have been writing my dismissal?"

"How could I dream that you loved me, Jean, when you refused the only offer I dared make? Could I be presumptuous enough to fancy you would reject young lovers for an old man like me?" asked Sir John caressing her.

"You are not old, to me, but everything I love and honor!" interrupted Jean, with a touch of genuine remorse, as this generous, honorable gentleman gave her both heart and home, unconscious of deceit. "It is I who am presumptuous, to dare to love one so far above me. But I did not know how dear you were to me till I felt that I must go. I ought not to accept this happiness. I am not worthy of it; and you will regret your kindness when the world blames you for giving a home to one so poor, and plain, and humble as I."

"Hush, my darling. I care nothing for the idle gossip of the world. If you are happy here, let tongues wag as they will. I shall be too busy enjoying the sunshine of your presence to heed anything that goes on about me. But, Jean, you are sure you love me? It seems incredible that I should win the heart that has been so cold to younger, better men than I."

"Dear Sir John, be sure of this, I love you truly. I will do my best to be a good wife to you, and prove that, in spite of my many faults, I possess the virtue of gratitude."

If he had known the strait she was in, he would have understood the cause of the sudden fervor of her words, the intense thankfulness that shone in her face, the real humility that made her stoop and kiss the generous hand that gave so much. For a few moments she enjoyed and let him enjoy the happy present, undisturbed. But the anxiety which devoured her, the danger which menaced her, soon recalled her, and forced her to wring yet more from the unsuspicious heart she had conquered.

"No need of letters now," said Sir John, as they sat side by side, with the summer moonlight glorifying all the room. "You have found a home for life; may it prove a happy one."

"It is not mine yet, and I have a strange foreboding that it never will be," she answered sadly.

"Why, my child?"

"Because I have an enemy who will try to destroy my peace, to poison your mind against me, and to drive me out from my paradise, to suffer again all I have suffered this last year."

"You mean that mad Sydney of whom you told me?"

"Yes. As soon as he hears of this good fortune to poor little Jean, he will hasten to mar it. He is my fate; I cannot escape him, and wherever he goes my friends desert me; for he has the power and uses it for my destruction. Let me go away and hide before he comes, for, having shared your confidence, it will break my heart to see you distrust and turn from me, instead of loving and protecting."

"My poor child, you are superstitious. Be easy. No one can harm you now, no one would dare attempt it. And as for my deserting you, that will soon be out of my power, if I have my way."

"How, dear Sir John?" asked Jean, with a flutter of intense relief at her heart, for the way seemed smoothing before her.

"I will make you my wife at once, if I may. This will free you from Gerald's love, protect you from Sydney's persecution, give you a safe home, and me the right to cherish and defend with heart and hand. Shall it be so, my child?"

"Yes; but oh, remember that I have no friend but you! Promise me to be faithful to the last—to believe in me, to trust me, protect and love me, in spite of all misfortunes, faults, and follies. I will be true as steel to you, and make your life as happy as it deserves to be. Let us promise these things now, and keep the promises unbroken to the end."

Her solemn air touched Sir John. Too honorable and upright himself to suspect falsehood in others, he saw only the natural impulse of a lovely girl in Jean's words, and, taking the hand she gave him in both of his, he promised all she asked, and kept that promise to the end. She paused an instant, with a pale, absent expression, as if she searched herself, then looked up clearly in the confiding face above her, and promised what she faithfully performed in afteryears.

"When shall it be, little sweetheart? I leave all to you, only let it be soon, else some gay young lover will appear, and take you from me," said Sir John, playfully, anxious to chase away the dark expression which had stolen over Jean's face.

"Can you keep a secret?" asked the girl, smiling up at him, all her charming self again.

"Try me."

"I will. Edward is coming home in three days. I must be gone before he comes. Tell no one of this; he wishes to surprise them. And if you love me, tell nobody of your approaching marriage. Do not betray that you care for me until I am really yours. There will be such a stir, such remonstrances, explanations, and reproaches that I shall be worn out, and run away from you all to escape the trial. If I could have my wish, I would go to some quiet place tomorrow and wait till you come for me. I know so little of such things, I cannot tell how soon we may be married; not for some weeks, I think."

"Tomorrow, if we like. A special license permits people to marry when and where they please. My plan is better than yours. Listen, and tell me if it can be carried out. I will go to town tomorrow, get the license, invite my friend, the Reverend Paul Fairfax, to return with me, and tomorrow evening you come at your usual time, and, in the presence of my discreet old servants, make me the happiest man in England. How does this suit you, my little Lady Coventry?"

The plan which seemed made to meet her ends, the name which was the height of her ambition, and the blessed sense of safety which came to her filled Jean Muir with such intense satisfaction that tears of real feeling stood in her eyes, and the glad assent she gave was the truest word that had passed her lips for months.

"We will go abroad or to Scotland for our honeymoon, till the storm blows over," said Sir John, well knowing that this hasty marriage would surprise or offend all his relations, and feeling as glad as Jean to escape the first excitement.

"To Scotland, please. I long to see my father's home," said Jean, who dreaded to meet Sydney on the continent.

They talked a little longer, arranging all things, Sir John so intent on hurrying the event that Jean had nothing to do but give a ready assent to all his suggestions. One fear alone disturbed her. If Sir John went to town, he might meet Edward, might hear and believe his statements. Then all would be lost. Yet this risk must be incurred, if the marriage was to be speedily and safely accomplished; and to guard against the meeting was Jean's sole care. As they went through the park—for Sir John insisted upon taking her home—she said, clinging to his arm:

"Dear friend, bear one thing in mind, else we shall be much annoyed, and all our plans disarranged. Avoid your nephews; you are so frank your face will betray you. They both love me, are both hot-tempered, and in the first excitement of the discovery might be violent. You must incur no danger, no disrespect for my sake; so shun them both till we are safe—particularly Edward. He will feel that his brother has wronged him, and that you have succeeded where he failed. This will irritate him, and I fear a stormy scene. Promise to avoid both for a day or two; do not listen to them, do not see them, do not write to or receive letters from them. It is foolish, I know; but you are all I have, and I am haunted by a strange foreboding that I am to lose you."

Touched and flattered by her tender solicitude, Sir John promised everything, even while he laughed at her fears. Love blinded the good gentleman to the peculiarity of the request; the novelty, romance, and secrecy of the affair rather bewildered though it charmed him; and the knowledge that he had outrivaled three young and ardent lovers gratified his vanity more than he would confess. Parting from the girl at the garden gate, he turned homeward, feeling like a boy again, and loitered back, humming a love lay, quite forgetful of evening damps, gout, and the five-and-fifty years which lay so lightly on his shoulders since Jean's arms had rested there. She hurried toward the house, anxious to escape Coventry; but he was waiting for her, and she was forced to meet him.

"How could you linger so long, and keep me in suspense?" he said reproachfully, as he took her hand and tried to catch a glimpse of her face in the shadow of her hat brim. "Come and rest in the grotto. I have so much to say, to hear and enjoy."

"Not now; I am too tired. Let me go in and sleep. Tomorrow we will talk. It is damp and chilly, and my head aches with all this worry." Jean spoke wearily, yet with a touch of petulance, and Coventry, fancying that she was piqued at his not coming for her, hastened to explain with eager tenderness.

"My poor little Jean, you do need rest. We wear you out, among us, and you never complain. I should have come to bring you home, but Lucia detained me, and when I got away I saw my uncle had forestalled me. I shall be jealous of the old gentleman, if he is so devoted. Jean, tell me one thing before we part; I am free as air, now, and have a right to speak. Do you love me? Am I the happy man who has won your heart? I dare to think so, to believe that this telltale face of yours has betrayed you, and to hope that I have gained what poor Ned and wild Sydney have lost."

"Before I answer, tell me of your interview with Lucia. I have a right to know," said Jean.

Coventry hesitated, for pity and remorse were busy at his heart when he recalled poor Lucia's grief. Jean was bent on hearing the humiliation of her rival. As the young man paused, she frowned, then lifted up her face wreathed in softest smiles, and laying her hand on his arm, she said, with most effective emphasis, half shy, half fond, upon his name, "Please tell me, Gerald!"

He could not resist the look, the touch, the tone, and taking the little hand in his, he said rapidly, as if the task was distasteful to him, "I told her that I did not, could not love her; that I had submitted to my mother's wish, and, for a time, had felt tacitly bound to her, though no words had passed between us. But now I demanded my liberty, regretting that the separation was not mutually desired."

"And she—what did she say? How did she bear it?" asked Jean, feeling in her own woman's heart how deeply Lucia's must have been wounded by that avowal.

"Poor girl! It was hard to bear, but her pride sustained her to the end. She owned that no pledge tied me, fully relinquished any claim my past behavior had seemed to have given her, and prayed that I might find another woman to love me as truly, tenderly as she had done. Jean, I felt like a villain; and yet I never plighted my word to her, never really loved her, and had a perfect right to leave her, if I would."

"Did she speak of me?"

"Yes."

"What did she say?"

"Must I tell you?"

"Yes, tell me everything. I know she hates me and I forgive her, knowing that I should hate any woman whom *you* loved."

"Are you jealous, dear?"

"Of you, Gerald?" And the fine eyes glanced up at him, full of a brilliancy that looked like the light of love.

"You make a slave of me already. How do you do it? I never obeyed a woman before. Jean, I think you are a witch. Scotland is the home of weird, uncanny creatures, who take lovely shapes for the bedevilment of poor weak souls. Are you one of those fair deceivers?"

"You are complimentary," laughed the girl. "I *am* a witch, and one day my disguise will drop away and you will see me as I am, old, ugly, bad and lost. Beware of me in time. I've warned you. Now love me at your peril."

Coventry had paused as he spoke, and eyed her with an unquiet look, conscious of some fascination which conquered yet brought no happiness. A feverish yet pleasurable excitement possessed him; a reckless mood, making him eager to obliterate the past by any rash act, any new experience which his passion brought. Jean regarded him with a wistful, almost woeful face, for one short moment; then a strange smile broke over it, as she spoke in a tone of malicious mockery, under which lurked the bitterness of a sad truth. Coventry looked half bewildered, and his eye went from the girl's mysterious face to a dimly lighted window, behind whose curtains poor Lucia hid her aching heart, praying for him the tender prayers that loving women give to those whose sins are all forgiven for love's sake. His heart smote him, and a momentary feeling of repulsion came over him, as he looked at Jean. She saw it, felt angry, yet conscious of a sense of relief; for now that her own safety was so nearly secured, she felt no wish to do mischief, but rather a desire to undo what was already done, and be at peace with all the world. To recall him to his allegiance, she sighed and walked on, saying gently yet coldly, "Will you tell me what I ask before I answer your question, Mr. Coventry?"

"What Lucia said of you? Well, it was this, 'Beware of Miss Muir. We instinctively distrusted her when we had no cause. I believe in instincts, and mine have never changed, for she has not tried to delude me. Her art is wonderful; I feel yet cannot explain or detect it, except in the working of events which her hand seems to guide. She has brought sorrow and dissension into this hitherto happy family. We are all changed, and this girl has done it. Me she can harm no further; you she will ruin, if she can. Beware of her in time, or you will bitterly repent your blind infatuation!' "

"And what answer did you make?" asked Jean, as the last words came reluctantly from Coventry's lips.

"I told her that I loved you in spite of myself, and would make you my wife in the face of all opposition. Now, Jean, your answer."

"Give me three days to think of it. Good night." And gliding from him, she vanished into the house, leaving him to roam about half the night, tormented with remorse, suspense, and the old distrust which would return when Jean was not there to banish it by her art.

VIII

Suspense

All the next day, Jean was in a state of the most intense anxiety, as every hour brought the crisis nearer, and every hour might bring defeat, for the subtlest human skill is often thwarted by some unforeseen accident. She longed to assure herself that Sir John was gone, but no servants came or went that day, and she could devise no pretext for sending to glean intelligence. She dared not go herself, lest the unusual act should excite suspicion, for she never went till evening. Even had she determined to venture, there was no time, for Mrs. Coventry was in one of her nervous states, and no one but Miss Muir could amuse her; Lucia was ill, and Miss Muir must give orders; Bella had a studious fit, and Jean must help her. Coventry lingered about the house for several hours, but Jean dared not send him, lest some hint of the truth might reach him. He had ridden away to his new duties when Jean did not appear, and the day dragged on wearisomely. Night came at last, and as Jean dressed for the late dinner, she hardly knew herself when she stood before her mirror, excitement lent such color and brilliancy to her countenance. Remembering the wedding which was to take place that evening, she put on a simple white dress and added a cluster of white roses in bosom and hair. She often wore flowers, but in spite of her desire to look and seem as usual, Bella's first words as she entered the drawing room were "Why, Jean, how like a bride you look; a veil and gloves would make you quite complete!"

"You forget one other trifle, Bell," said Gerald, with eyes that brightened as they rested on Miss Muir.

"What is that?" asked his sister.

"A bridegroom."

Bella looked to see how Jean received this, but she seemed quite composed as she smiled one of her sudden smiles, and merely said, "That trifle will doubtless be found when the time comes. Is Miss Beaufort too ill for dinner?"

"She begs to be excused, and said you would be willing to take her place, she thought."

As innocent Bella delivered this message, Jean glanced at Coventry, who evaded her eye and looked ill at ease.

A little remorse will do him good, and prepare him for repentance after the grand *coup,* she said to herself, and was particularly gay at dinnertime, though Coventry looked often at Lucia's empty seat, as if he missed her. As soon as they left the table, Miss Muir sent Bella to her mother; and, knowing that Coventry would not linger long at his wine, she hurried away to the Hall. A servant was lounging at the door, and of him she asked, in a tone which was eager in spite of all efforts to be calm, "Is Sir John at home?"

"No, miss, he's just gone to town."

"Just gone! When do you mean?" cried Jean, forgetting the relief she felt in hearing of his absence in surprise at his late departure.

"He went half an hour ago, in the last train, miss."

"I thought he was going early this morning; he told me he should be back this evening."

"I believe he did mean to go, but was delayed by company. The steward came up on business, and a load of gentlemen called, so Sir John could not get off till night, when he wasn't fit to go, being worn out, and far from well."

"Do you think he will be ill? Did he look so?" And as Jean spoke, a thrill of fear passed over her, lest death should rob her of her prize.

"Well, you know, miss, hurry of any kind is bad for elderly gentlemen inclined to apoplexy. Sir John was in a worry all day, and not like himself. I wanted him to take his man, but he wouldn't; and drove off looking flushed and excited like. I'm anxious about him, for I know something is amiss to hurry him off in this way."

"When will he be back, Ralph?"

"Tomorrow noon, if possible; at night, certainly, he bid me tell anyone that called."

"Did he leave no note or message for Miss Coventry, or someone of the family?"

"No, miss, nothing."

"Thank you." And Jean walked back to spend a restless night and rise to meet renewed suspense.

The morning seemed endless, but noon came at last, and under the pretense of seeking coolness in the grotto. Jean stole away to a slope whence the gate to the Hall park was visible. For two long hours she watched, and no one came. She was just turning away when a horseman dashed through the gate and came galloping toward the Hall. Heedless of everything but the uncontrollable longing to gain some tidings, she ran to meet him, feeling assured that he brought ill news. It was a young man from the station, and as he caught sight of her, he drew bridle, looking agitated and undecided.

"Has anything happened?" she cried breathlessly.

"A dreadful accident on the railroad, just the other side of Croydon. News telegraphed half an hour ago," answered the man, wiping his hot face.

"The noon train? Was Sir John in it? Quick, tell me all!"

"It was that train, miss, but whether Sir John was in it or not, we don't know; for the guard is killed, and everything is in such confusion that nothing can be certain. They are at work getting out the dead and wounded. We heard that Sir John was expected, and I came up to tell Mr.

Coventry, thinking he would wish to go down. A train leaves in fifteen minutes; where shall I find him? I was told he was at the Hall."

"Ride on, ride on! And find him if he is there. I'll run home and look for him. Lose no time. Ride! Ride!" And turning, Jean sped back like a deer, while the man tore up the avenue to rouse the Hall.

Coventry was there, and went off at once, leaving both Hall and house in dismay. Fearing to betray the horrible anxiety that possessed her, Jean shut herself up in her room and suffered untold agonies as the day wore on and no news came. At dark a sudden cry rang through the house, and Jean rushed down to learn the cause. Bella was standing in the hall, holding a letter, while a group of excited servants hovered near her.

"What is it?" demanded Miss Muir, pale and steady, though her heart died within her as she recognized Gerald's handwriting. Bella gave her the note, and hushed her sobbing to hear again the heavy tidings that had come.

> Dear Bella:
>
> Uncle is safe; he did not go in the noon train. But several persons are sure that Ned was there. No trace of him as yet, but many bodies are in the river, under the ruins of the bridge, and I am doing my best to find the poor lad, if he is there. I have sent to all his haunts in town, and as he has not been seen, I hope it is a false report and he is safe with his regiment. Keep this from my mother till we are sure. I write you, because Lucia is ill. Miss Muir will comfort and sustain you. Hope for the best, dear.
>
> Yours, G. C.

Those who watched Miss Muir as she read these words wondered at the strange expressions which passed over her face, for the joy which appeared there as Sir John's safety was made known did not change to grief or horror at poor Edward's possible fate. The smile died on her lips, but her voice did not falter, and in her downcast eyes shone an inexplicable look of something like triumph. No wonder, for if this was true, the danger which menaced her was averted for a time, and the marriage might be consummated without such desperate haste. This sad and sudden event seemed to her the mysterious fulfilment of a secret wish; and though startled she was not daunted but inspirited, for fate seemed to favor her designs. She did comfort Bella, control the excited household, and keep the rumors from Mrs. Coventry all that dreadful night.

At dawn Gerald came home exhausted, and bringing no tiding of the missing man. He had telegraphed to the headquarters of the regiment and received a reply, stating that Edward had left for London the previous day, meaning to go home before returning. The fact of his having been at the London station was also established, but whether he left by the train or not was still uncertain. The ruins were still being searched, and the body might yet appear.

"Is Sir John coming at noon?" asked Jean, as the three sat together in the rosy hush of dawn, trying to hope against hope.

"No, he had been ill, I learned from young Gower, who is just from town, and so had not completed his business. I sent him word to wait till night, for the bridge won't be passable till then. Now I must try and rest an hour; I've worked all night and have no strength left. Call me the instant any messenger arrives."

With that Coventry went to his room, Bella followed to wait on him, and Jean roamed through house and grounds, unable to rest. The morning was far spent when the messenger arrived. Jean went to receive his tidings, with the wicked hope still lurking at her heart.

"Is he found?" she asked calmly, as the man hesitated to speak.

"Yes, ma'am."

"You are sure?"

"I am certain, ma'am, though some won't say till Mr. Coventry comes to look."

"Is he alive?" And Jean's white lips trembled as she put the question.

"Oh no, ma'am, that warn't possible, under all them stones and water. The poor young gentleman is so wet, and crushed, and torn, no one would know him, except for the uniform, and the white hand with the ring on it."

Jean sat down, very pale, and the man described the finding of the poor shattered body. As he finished, Coventry appeared, and with one look of mingled remorse, shame, and sorrow, the elder brother went away, to find and bring the younger home. Jean crept into the garden like a guilty thing; trying to hide the satisfaction which struggled with a woman's natural pity, for so sad an end for this brave young life.

"Why waste tears or feign sorrow when I must be glad?" she muttered, as she paced to and fro along the terrace. "The poor boy is out of pain, and I am out of danger."

She got no further, for, turning as she spoke, she stood face to face with Edward! Bearing no mark of peril on dress or person, but stalwart and strong as ever, he stood there looking at her, with contempt and compassion struggling in his face. As if turned to stone, she remained motionless, with dilated eyes, arrested breath, and paling cheek. He did not speak but watched her silently till she put out a trembling hand, as if to assure herself by touch that it was really he. Then he drew back, and as if the act convinced as fully as words, she said slowly, "They told me you were dead."

"And you were glad to believe it. No, it was my comrade, young Courtney, who unconsciously deceived you all, and lost his life, as I should have done, if I had not gone to Ascot after seeing him off yesterday."

"To Ascot?" echoed Jean, shrinking back, for Edward's eye was on her, and his voice was stern and cold.

"Yes; you know the place. I went there to make inquiries concerning you and was well satisfied. Why are you still here?"

"The three days are not over yet. I hold you to your promise. Before night I shall be gone; till then you will be silent, if you have honor enough to keep your word."

"I have." Edward took out his watch and, as he put it back, said with cool precision, "It is now two, the train leaves for London at half-past six; a carriage will wait for you at the side door. Allow me to advise you to go then, for the instant dinner is over I shall speak." And with a bow he went into the house, leaving Jean nearly suffocated with a throng of contending emotions.

For a few minutes she seemed paralyzed; but the native energy of the woman forbade utter despair, till the last hope was gone. Frail as that now was, she still clung to it tenaciously, resolving to win the game in defiance of everything. Springing up, she went to her room, packed her few valuables, dressed herself with care, and then sat down to wait. She heard a joyful stir below, saw Coventry come hurrying back, and from a garrulous maid learned that the body was that of young Courtney. The uniform being the same as Edward's and the ring, a gift from him, had caused the men to believe the disfigured corpse to be that of the younger Coventry. No one but the maid came near her; once Bella's voice called her, but some one checked the girl, and the call was not repeated. At five an envelope was brought her, directed in Edward's hand, and containing a check which more than paid a year's salary. No word accompanied the gift, yet the generosity of it touched her, for Jean Muir had the relics of a once honest nature, and despite her falsehood could still admire nobleness and respect virtue. A tear of genuine shame dropped on the paper, and real gratitude filled her heart, as she thought that even if all else failed, she was not thrust out penniless into the world, which had no pity for poverty.

As the clock struck six, she heard a carriage drive around and went down to meet it. A servant put on her trunk, gave the order, "To the station, James," and she drove away without meeting anyone, speaking to anyone, or apparently being seen by anyone. A sense of utter weariness came over her, and she longed to lie down and forget. But the last chance still remained, and till that failed, she would not give up. Dismissing the carriage, she seated herself to watch for the quarter-past-six train from London, for in that Sir John would come if he came at all that night. She was haunted by the fear that Edward had met and told him. The first glimpse of Sir John's frank face would betray the truth. If he knew all, there was no hope, and she would go her way alone. If he knew nothing, there was yet time for the marriage; and once his wife, she knew she was safe, because for the honor of his name he would screen and protect her.

Up rushed the train, out stepped Sir John, and Jean's heart died within her. Grave, and pale, and worn he looked, and leaned heavily on the arm of a portly gentleman in black. The Reverend Mr. Fairfax, why has he come, if the secret is out? thought Jean, slowly advancing to meet them and fearing to read her fate in Sir John's face. He saw her, dropped his friend's arm, and hurried forward with the ardor of a young man, exclaiming, as he seized her hand with a beaming face, a glad voice, "My little girl! Did you think I would never come?"

She could not answer, the reaction was too strong, but she clung to him, regardless of time or place, and felt that her last hope had not failed. Mr. Fairfax proved himself equal to the occasion. Asking no questions, he hurried Sir John and Jean into a carriage and stepped in after them with a bland apology. Jean was soon herself again, and, having told her fears at his delay, listened eagerly while he related the various mishaps which had detained him.

"Have you seen Edward?" was her first question.

"Not yet, but I know he has come, and have heard of his narrow escape. I should have been in that train, if I had not been delayed by the indisposition which I then cursed, but now bless. Are you ready, Jean? Do you repent your choice, my child?"

"No, no! I am ready, I am only too happy to become your wife, dear, generous Sir John," cried Jean, with a glad alacrity, which touched the old man to the heart, and charmed the Reverend Mr. Fairfax, who concealed the romance of a boy under his clerical suit.

They reached the Hall. Sir John gave orders to admit no one and after a hasty dinner sent for his old housekeeper and his steward, told them of his purpose, and desired them to witness his marriage. Obedience had been the law of their lives, and Master could do nothing wrong in their eyes, so they played their parts willingly, for Jean was a favorite at the Hall. Pale as her gown, but calm and steady; she stood beside Sir John, uttering her vows in a clear tone and taking upon herself the vows of a wife with more than a bride's usual docility. When the ring was fairly on, a smile broke over her face. When Sir John kissed and called her his "little wife," she shed a tear or two of sincere happiness; and when Mr. Fairfax addressed her as "my lady," she laughed her musical laugh, and glanced up at a picture of Gerald with eyes full of exultation. As the servants left the room, a message was brought from Mrs. Coventry, begging Sir John to come to her at once.

"You will not go and leave me so soon?" pleaded Jean, well knowing why he was sent for.

"My darling, I must." And in spite of its tenderness, Sir John's manner was too decided to be withstood.

"Then I shall go with you," cried Jean, resolving that no earthly power should part them.

IX

Lady Coventry

When the first excitement of Edward's return had subsided, and before they could question him as to the cause of this unexpected visit, he told them that after dinner their curiosity should be gratified, and meantime he begged them to leave Miss Muir alone, for she had received bad news and must not be disturbed. The family with difficulty restrained their tongues and waited impatiently. Gerald confessed his love for Jean and asked his brother's pardon for betraying his trust. He had expected an outbreak, but Edward only looked at him with pitying eyes, and said sadly, "You too! I have no reproaches to make, for I know what you will suffer when the truth is known."

"What do you mean?" demanded Coventry.

"You will soon know, my poor Gerald, and we will comfort one another."

Nothing more could be drawn from Edward till dinner was over, the servants gone, and all the family alone together. Then pale and grave, but very self-possessed, for trouble had made a man of him, he produced a packet of letters, and said, addressing himself to his brother, "Jean Muir has deceived us all. I know her story; let me tell it before I read her letters."

"Stop! I'll not listen to any false tales against her. The poor girl has enemies who belie her!" cried Gerald, starting up.

"For the honor of the family, you must listen, and learn what fools she has made of us. I can prove what I say, and convince you that she has the art of a devil. Sit still ten minutes, then go, if you will."

Edward spoke with authority, and his brother obeyed him with a foreboding heart.

"I met Sydney, and he begged me to beware of her. Nay, listen, Gerald! I know she has told her story, and that you believe it; but her own letters convict her. She tried to charm Sydney as she did us, and nearly succeeded in inducing him to marry her. Rash and wild as he is, he is still a gentleman, and when an incautious word of hers roused his suspicions, he refused to make her his wife. A stormy scene ensued, and, hoping to intimidate him, she feigned to stab herself as if in despair. She did wound herself, but failed to gain her point and insisted upon going to a hospital to die. Lady Sydney, good, simple soul, believed the girl's version of the story, thought her son was in the wrong, and when he was gone, tried to atone for his fault by finding Jean Muir another home. She thought Gerald was soon to marry Lucia, and that I was away, so sent her here as a safe and comfortable retreat."

"But, Ned, are you sure of all this? Is Sydney to be believed?" began Coventry, still incredulous.

"To convince you, I'll read Jean's letters before I say more. They were written to an accomplice and were purchased by Sydney. There was a compact between the two women, that each should keep the other informed of all adventures, plots and plans, and share whatever good fortune fell to the lot of either. Thus Jean wrote freely, as you shall judge. The letters concern us alone. The first was written a few days after she came.

> "Dear Hortense:
>
> "Another failure. Sydney was more wily than I thought. All was going well, when one day my old fault beset me, I took too much wine, and I carelessly owned that I had been an actress. He was shocked, and retreated. I got up a scene, and gave myself a safe little wound, to frighten him. The brute was not frightened, but coolly left me to my fate. I'd have died to spite him, if I dared, but as I didn't, I lived to torment him. As yet, I have had no chance, but I will not forget him. His mother is a poor, weak creature, whom I could use as I would, and through her I found an excellent place. A sick mother, silly daughter, and two eligible sons. One is engaged to a handsome iceberg, but that only renders him more interesting in my eyes, rivalry adds so much to the charm of one's conquests. Well, my dear, I went, got up in the meek style, intending to do the pathetic; but before I saw the family, I was so angry I could hardly control myself. Through the indolence of Monsieur the young master, no carriage was sent for me, and I intend he shall atone for that rudeness by-and-by. The younger son, the mother, and the girl received me patronizingly, and I understood the simple souls at once. Monsieur (as I shall call him, as names are unsafe) was unapproachable, and took no pains to conceal his dislike of governesses. The cousin was lovely, but detestable with her pride, her coldness, and her very visible adoration of Monsieur, who let her worship him, like an inanimate idol as he is. I hated them both, of course, and in return for their insolence shall torment her with jealousy, and teach him how to woo a woman by making his heart ache. They are an intensely proud family, but I can humble them all, I think, by captivating the sons, and when they have committed themselves, cast them off, and marry the old uncle, whose title takes my fancy."

"She never wrote that! It is impossible. A woman could not do it," cried Lucia indignantly, while Bella sat bewildered and Mrs. Coventry supported herself with salts and fan. Coventry went to his brother, examined the writing, and returned to his seat, saying, in a tone of suppressed wrath, "She did write it. I posted some of those letters myself. Go on, Ned."

"I made myself useful and agreeable to the amiable ones, and overheard the chat of the lovers. It did not suit me, so I fainted away to stop it, and excite interest in the provoking pair. I thought I had succeeded, but Monsieur suspected me and showed me that he did. I forgot my meek role and gave him a stage look. It had a good effect, and I shall try it again. The man is well worth winning, but I prefer the title, and as the uncle is a hale, handsome gentleman, I can't wait for him to die, though Monsieur is very charming, with his elegant languor, and his heart so fast asleep no woman has had power to wake it yet. I told my story, and they believed it, though I had the audacity to say I was but nineteen, to talk Scotch, and bashfully confess that Sydney wished to marry me. Monsieur knows S. and evidently suspects something. I must watch him and keep the truth from him, if possible.

"I was very miserable that night when I got alone. Something in the atmosphere of this happy home made me wish I was anything but what I am. As I sat there trying to pluck up my spirits, I thought of the days when I was lovely and young, good and gay. My glass showed me an old woman of thirty, for my false locks were off, my paint gone, and my face was without its mask. Bah! how I hate sentiment! I drank your health from your own little flask, and went to bed to dream that I was playing Lady Tartuffe—as I am. Adieu, more soon."

No one spoke as Edward paused, and taking up another letter, he read on:

"My Dear Creature:

"All goes well. Next day I began my task, and having caught a hint of the character of each, tried my power over them. Early in the morning I ran over to see the Hall. Approved of it highly, and took the first step toward becoming its mistress, by piquing the curiosity and flattering the pride of its master. His estate is his idol; I praised it with a few artless compliments

> to himself, and he was charmed. The cadet of the family adores horses. I risked my neck to pet his beast, and he was charmed. The little girl is romantic about flowers; I made a posy and was sentimental, and she was charmed. The fair icicle loves her departed mamma, I had raptures over an old picture, and she thawed. Monsieur is used to being worshipped. I took no notice of him, and by the natural perversity of human nature, he began to take notice of me. He likes music; I sang, and stopped when he'd listened long enough to want more. He is lazily fond of being amused; I showed him my skill, but refused to exert it in his behalf. In short, I gave him no peace till he began to wake up. In order to get rid of the boy, I fascinated him, and he was sent away. Poor lad, I rather liked him, and if the title had been nearer would have married him.

"Many thanks for the honor." And Edward's lip curled with intense scorn. But Gerald sat like a statue, his teeth set, his eyes fiery, his brows bent, waiting for the end.

> "The passionate boy nearly killed his brother, but I turned the affair to good account, and bewitched Monsieur by playing nurse, till Vashti (the icicle) interfered. Then I enacted injured virtue, and kept out of his way, knowing that he would miss me. I mystified him about S. by sending a letter where S. would not get it, and got up all manner of soft scenes to win this proud creature. I get on well and meanwhile privately fascinate Sir J. by being daughterly and devoted. He is a worthy old man, simple as a child, honest as the day, and generous as a prince. I shall be a happy woman if I win him, and you shall share my good fortune; so wish me success.

"This is the third, and contains something which will surprise you," Edward said, as he lifted another paper.

> "Hortense:
>
> "I've done what I once planned to do on another occasion. You know my handsome, dissipated father married a lady of rank for his second wife. I never saw Lady H———d but

once, for I was kept out of the way. Finding that this good Sir J. knew something of her when a girl, and being sure that he did not know of the death of her little daughter, I boldly said I was the child, and told a pitiful tale of my early life. It worked like a charm; he told Monsieur, and both felt the most chivalrous compassion for Lady Howard's daughter, though before they had secretly looked down on me, and my real poverty and my lowliness. That boy pitied me with an honest warmth and never waited to learn my birth. I don't forget that and shall repay it if I can. Wishing to bring Monsieur's affair to a successful crisis, I got up a theatrical evening and was in my element. One little event I must tell you, because I committed an actionable offense and was nearly discovered. I did not go down to supper, knowing that the moth would return to flutter about the candle, and preferring that the fluttering should be done in private, as Vashti's jealousy is getting uncontrollable. Passing through the gentlemen's dressing room, my quick eye caught sight of a letter lying among the costumes. It was no stage affair, and an odd sensation of fear ran through me as I recognized the hand of S. I had feared this, but I believe in chance; and having found the letter, I examined it. You know I can imitate almost any hand. When I read in this paper the whole story of my affair with S., truly told, and also that he had made inquiries into my past life and discovered the truth, I was in a fury. To be so near success and fail was terrible, and I resolved to risk everything. I opened the letter by means of a heated knife blade under the seal, therefore the envelope was perfect; imitating S.'s hand, I penned a few lines in his hasty style, saying he was at Baden, so that if Monsieur answered, the reply would not reach him, for he is in London, it seems. This letter I put into the pocket whence the other must have fallen, and was just congratulating myself on this narrow escape, when Dean, the maid of Vashti, appeared as if watching me. She had evidently seen the letter in my hand, and suspected something. I took no notice of her, but must be careful, for she is on the watch. After this the evening closed with strictly private theatricals, in which Monsieur and myself were the only actors. To make sure that he received my version of the story first, I told him a romantic story of S.'s persecution,

> and he believed it. This I followed up by a moonlight episode behind a rose hedge, and sent the young gentleman home in a half-dazed condition. What fools men are!"

"She is right!" muttered Coventry, who had flushed scarlet with shame and anger, as his folly became known and Lucia listened in astonished silence.

"Only one more, and my distasteful task will be nearly over," said Edward, unfolding the last of the papers. "This is not a letter, but a copy of one written three nights ago. Dean boldly ransacked Jean Muir's desk while she was at the Hall, and, fearing to betray the deed by keeping the letter, she made a hasty copy which she gave me today, begging me to save the family from disgrace. This makes the chain complete. Go now, if you will, Gerald. I would gladly spare you the pain of hearing this."

"I will not spare myself; I deserve it. Read on," replied Coventry, guessing what was to follow and nerving himself to hear it. Reluctantly his brother read these lines:

> "The enemy has surrendered! Give me joy, Hortense; I can be the wife of this proud monsieur, if I will. Think what an honor for the divorced wife of a disreputable actor. I laugh at the farce and enjoy it, for I only wait till the prize I desire is fairly mine, to turn and reject this lover who has proved himself false to brother, mistress, and his own conscience. I resolved to be revenged on both, and I have kept my word. For my sake he cast off the beautiful woman who truly loved him; he forgot his promise to his brother, and put by his pride to beg of me the worn-out heart that is not worth a good man's love. Ah well, I am satisfied, for Vashti has suffered the sharpest pain a proud woman can endure, and will feel another pang when I tell her that I scorn her recreant lover, and give him back to her, to deal with as she will."

Coventry started from his seat with a fierce exclamation, but Lucia bowed her face upon her hands, weeping, as if the pang had been sharper than even Jean foresaw.

"Send for Sir John! I am mortally afraid of this creature. Take her away; do something to her. My poor Bella, what a companion for you! Send for Sir John at once!" cried Mrs. Coventry incoherently, and clasped her daughter in her arms, as if Jean Muir would burst in to annihilate the whole family. Edward alone was calm.

"I have already sent, and while we wait, let me finish this story. It is true that Jean is the daughter of Lady Howard's husband, the pretended clergyman, but really a worthless man who married her for her money. Her own child died, but this girl, having beauty, wit and a bold spirit, took her fate into her own hands, and became an actress. She married an actor, led a reckless life for some years; quarreled with her husband, was divorced, and went to Paris; left the stage, and tried to support herself as governess and companion. You know how she fared with the Sydneys, how she has duped us, and but for this discovery would have duped Sir John. I was in time to prevent this, thank heaven. She is gone; no one knows the truth but Sydney and ourselves; he will be silent, for his own sake; we will be for ours, and leave this dangerous woman to the fate which will surely overtake her."

"Thank you, it has overtaken her, and a very happy one she finds it."

A soft voice uttered the words, and an apparition appeared at the door, which made all start and recoil with amazement—Jean Muir leaning on the arm of Sir John.

"How dare you return?" began Edward, losing the self-control so long preserved. "How dare you insult us by coming back to enjoy the mischief you have done? Uncle, you do not know that woman!"

"Hush, boy, I will not listen to a word, unless you remember where you are," said Sir John, with a commanding gesture.

"Remember your promise: love me, forgive me, protect me, and do not listen to their accusations," whispered Jean, whose quick eye had discovered the letters.

"I will; have no fears, my child," he answered, drawing her nearer as he took his accustomed place before the fire, always lighted when Mrs. Coventry was down.

Gerald, who had been pacing the room excitedly, paused behind Lucia's chair as if to shield her from insult; Bella clung to her mother; and Edward, calming himself by a strong effort, handed his uncle the letters, saying briefly, "Look at those, sir, and let them speak."

"I will look at nothing, hear nothing, believe nothing which can in any way lessen my respect and affection for this young lady. She has prepared me for this. I know the enemy who is unmanly enough to belie and threaten her. I know that you both are unsuccessful lovers, and this explains your unjust, uncourteous treatment now. We all have committed faults and follies. I freely forgive Jean hers, and desire to know nothing of them from your lips. If she has innocently offended, pardon it for my sake, and forget the past."

"But, Uncle, we have proofs that this woman is not what she seems. Her own letters convict her. Read them, and do not blindly deceive yourself," cried Edward, indignant at his uncle's words.

A low laugh startled them all, and in an instant they saw the cause of it. While Sir John spoke, Jean had taken the letters from the hand which he had put behind him, a favorite gesture of his, and, unobserved, had dropped them on the fire. The mocking laugh, the sudden blaze, showed what had been done. Both young men sprang forward, but it was too late; the proofs were ashes, and Jean Muir's bold, bright eyes defied them, as she said, with a disdainful little gesture, "Hands off, gentlemen! You may degrade yourselves to the work of detectives, but I am not a prisoner yet. Poor Jean Muir you might harm, but Lady Coventry is beyond your reach."

"Lady Coventry!" echoed the dismayed family, in varying tones of incredulity, indignation, and amazement.

"Aye, my dear and honored wife," said Sir John, with a protecting arm about the slender figure at his side; and in the act, the words, there was a tender dignity that touched the listeners with pity and respect for the deceived man. "Receive her as such, and for my sake, forbear all further accusation," he continued steadily. "I know what I have done. I have no fear that I shall repent it. If I am blind, let me remain so till time opens my eyes. We are going away for a little while, and when we return, let the old life return again, unchanged, except that Jean makes sunshine for me as well as for you."

No one spoke, for no one knew what to say. Jean broke the silence, saying coolly, "May I ask how those letters came into your possession?"

"In tracing out your past life, Sydney found your friend Hortense. She was poor, money bribed her, and your letters were given up to him as soon as received. Traitors are always betrayed in the end," replied Edward sternly.

Jean shrugged her shoulders, and shot a glance at Gerald, saying with her significant smile, "Remember that, monsieur, and allow me to hope that in wedding you will be happier than in wooing. Receive my congratulations, Miss Beaufort, and let me beg of you to follow my example, if you would keep your lovers."

Here all the sarcasm passed from her voice, the defiance from her eye, and the one unspoiled attribute which still lingered in this woman's artful nature shone in her face, as she turned toward Edward and Bella at their mother's side.

"You have been kind to me," she said, with grateful warmth. "I thank you for it, and will repay it if I can. To you I will acknowledge that I am not worthy to be this good man's wife, and to you I will solemnly promise to devote my life to his happiness. For his sake forgive me, and let there be peace between us."

There was no reply, but Edward's indignant eyes fell before hers. Bella half put out her hand, and Mrs. Coventry sobbed as if some regret mingled with her resentment. Jean seemed to expect no friendly demonstration, and to understand that they forbore for Sir John's sake, not for hers, and to accept their contempt as her just punishment.

"Come home, love, and forget all this," said her husband, ringing the bell, and eager to be gone. "Lady Coventry's carriage."

And as he gave the order, a smile broke over her face, for the sound assured her that the game was won. Pausing an instant on the threshold before she vanished from their sight, she looked backward, and fixing on Gerald the strange glance he remembered well, she said in her penetrating voice, "Is not the last scene better than the first?"

Little Women *is undoubtedly Alcott's masterpiece. When in 1868 Thomas Niles of Roberts Brothers approached her about writing a girls' book, Alcott was unenthusiastic. But drawing upon her own and her sisters' experience, she managed to produce the first part of* Little Women, *all that she initially planned to write, in a matter of months. Both Niles and Alcott, who had feared the book might be dull, were more pleased with it than they had anticipated. And readers loved it. As soon as Alcott recognized the popular success that she had unwittingly achieved, she set to work on a sequel, determined not to marry Jo to Laurie as her readers demanded. The second volume, known as* Good Wives *in England, was published the next year to equal acclaim. Since then, the novel has never been out of print, and it has been beloved by generations of girls who, when grown, pass it on to their daughters. Although a few young readers have always found the book cloyingly sweet or relentlessly preachy,* Little Women *marked a departure from the didactic children's books of its own day, and many modern women credit tomboy Jo March with providing them with inspiration to write or follow unconventional careers. Scholars, too, in recent years have given the book serious critical attention, and it is regularly assigned in college courses.* Little Women *appears now in a dozen different editions, many edited by leading feminist scholars. The text for the following chapters is that of the Penguin Classic edited by Elaine Showalter. As Showalter explains, her text is based on the 1868 and 1869 editions, whereas most are reprints of the 1880 edition in which Alcott responded to criticisms of her slang and colloquial language by adopting a more genteel but less lively style.*

The two chapters presented here, from part 2, portray the literary career of Jo, which closely parallels that of her creator. In chapter 27, "Literary Lessons," Jo receives a one-hundred-dollar prize for a sensational story just as Alcott did in 1862 for "Pauline's Passion and Punishment." And as Alcott did with her first novel, Moods, *Jo edits her book to suit her publisher and receives conflicting reviews. Jo's defense of her book at the end of the chapter echoes Alcott's defense of* Moods *in her letters (see those to Moncure Conway and Mr. Ayer in this volume). In chapter 34, however, Jo's career begins to diverge from Alcott's. Fortunately for us, Alcott never had a "friend" like Professor Bhaer to persuade her to repudiate and destroy her sensation fiction. The fact that Alcott was continuing to market her sensation stories even as she penned the scene in which Jo burns hers forces us to question whether the narrator's approval reflects the author's.*

In response to the dictum of Jo's editor that "Morals don't sell nowadays," the narrator comments, "which was not quite a correct statement, by the way." Thus Alcott slyly suggests within the text of Little Women *itself that economics, not moral scruples, determined her choice of genres.*

Little Women

27

Literary Lessons

Fortune suddenly smiled upon Jo, and dropped a good-luck penny in her path. Not a golden penny, exactly, but I doubt if half a million would have given more real happiness than did the little sum that came to her in this wise.

Every few weeks she would shut herself up in her room, put on her scribbling suit, and "fall into a vortex," as she expressed it, writing away at her novel with all her heart and soul, for till that was finished she could find no peace. Her "scribbling suit" consisted of a black pinafore on which she could wipe her pen at will, and a cap of the same material, adorned with a cheerful red bow, into which she bundled her hair when the decks were cleared for action. This cap was a beacon to the inquiring eyes of her family, who, during these periods, kept their distance, merely popping in their heads semi-occasionally, to ask, with interest, "Does genius burn, Jo?" They did not always venture even to ask this question, but took an observation of the cap, and judged accordingly. If this expressive article of dress was drawn low upon the forehead, it was a sign that hard work was going on; in exciting moments it was pushed rakishly askew, and when despair seized the author it was plucked wholly off, and cast upon the floor. At such times the intruder silently withdrew; and not until the red bow was seen gaily erect upon the gifted brow, did any one dare address Jo.

She did not think herself a genius by any means; but when the writing fit came on, she gave herself up to it with entire abandon, and led a blissful life, unconscious of want, care, or bad weather, while she sat safe and happy in an imaginary world, full of friends almost as real and dear to her as any in the flesh. Sleep forsook her eyes, meals stood untasted, day and night were all too short to enjoy the happiness which blessed her only at such times, and made these hours worth living, even if they bore no other fruit. The divine afflatus usually lasted a week or two, and then she emerged from her "vortex" hungry, sleepy, cross, or despondent.

She was just recovering from one of these attacks when she was prevailed upon to escort Miss Crocker to a lecture, and in return for her virtue was rewarded with a new idea. It was a People's Course,—the lecture on the Pyramids,—and Jo rather wondered at the choice of such a subject for such an audience, but took it for granted that some great social evil would be remedied, or some great want supplied by unfolding the glories of the Pharaohs, to an audience whose thoughts were busy with the price of coal and flour, and whose lives were spent in trying to solve harder riddles than that of the Sphinx.

They were early; and while Miss Crocker set the heel of her stocking, Jo amused herself by examining the faces of the people who occupied the seat with them. On her left were two matrons with massive foreheads, and bonnets to match, discussing Woman's Rights and making tatting. Beyond sat a pair of humble lovers artlessly holding each other by the hand, a sombre spinster eating peppermints out of a paper bag, and an old gentleman taking his preparatory nap behind a yellow bandanna. On her right, her only neighbor was a studious-looking lad absorbed in a newspaper.

It was a pictorial sheet, and Jo examined the work of art nearest her, idly wondering what unfortuitous concatenation of circumstances needed the melodramatic illustration of an Indian in full war costume, tumbling over a precipice with a wolf at his throat, while two infuriated young gentlemen, with unnaturally small feet and big eyes, were stabbing each other close by, and a dishevelled female was flying away in the background, with her mouth wide open. Pausing to turn a page, the lad saw her looking, and, with boyish good-nature, offered half his paper, saying, bluntly, "Want to read it? That's a first-rate story."

Jo accepted it with a smile, for she had never outgrown her liking for lads, and soon found herself involved in the usual labyrinth of love, mystery, and murder,—for the story belonged to that class of light literature in which the passions have a holiday, and when the author's invention fails, a grand catastrophe clears the stage of one-half the *dramatis personæ,* leaving the other half to exult over their downfall.

"Prime, isn't it?" asked the boy, as her eye went down the last paragraph of her portion.

"I guess you and I could do most as well as that if we tried," returned Jo, amused at his admiration of the trash.

"I should think I was a pretty lucky chap if I could. She makes a good living our of such stories, they say;" and he pointed to the name of Mrs. S. L. A. N. G. Northbury, under the title of the tale.

"Do you know her?" asked Jo, with sudden interest.

"No; but I read all her pieces, and I know a fellow that works in the office where this paper is printed."

"Do you say she makes a good living out of stories like this?" and Jo looked more respectfully at the agitated group and thickly-sprinkled exclamation points that adorned the page.

"Guess she does! she knows just what folks like, and gets paid well for writing it."

Here the lecture began, but Jo heard very little of it, for while Professor Sands was prosing away about Belzoni, Cheops, scarabei, and hieroglyphics, she was covertly taking down the address of the paper, and boldly resolving to try for the hundred dollar prize offered in its columns for a sensational story. By the time the lecture ended, and the audience awoke, she had built up a splendid fortune for herself (not the first founded upon paper), and was already deep in the concoction of her story, being unable to decide whether the duel should come before the elopement or after the murder.

She said nothing of her plan at home, but fell to work next day, much to the disquiet of her mother, who always looked a little anxious when "genius took to burning." Jo had never tried this style before, contenting herself with very mild romances for the "Spread Eagle." Her theatrical experience and miscellaneous reading were of service now, for they gave her some idea of dramatic effect, and supplied plot, language, and costumes. Her story was as full of desperation and despair as her limited acquaintance with those uncomfortable emotions enabled her to make it, and, having located it in Lisbon, she wound up with an earthquake, as a striking and appropriate *dénouement.* The manuscript was privately despatched, accompanied by a note, modestly saying that if the tale didn't get the prize, which the writer hardly dared expect, she would be very glad to receive any sum it might be considered worth.

Six weeks is a long time to wait, and a still longer time for a girl to keep a secret; but Jo did both, and was just beginning to give up all hope of ever seeing her manuscript again, when a letter arrived which almost took her breath away; for, on opening it, a check for a hundred dollars fell into her lap. For a minute she stared at it as if it had been a snake, then she read the letter, and began to cry. If the amiable gentleman who wrote that kindly note could have known what intense happiness he was giving a fellow-creature, I think he would devote his leisure hours, if he has any, to that amusement; for Jo valued the letter more than the money, because it was encouraging; and after years of effort it was so pleasant to find that she had learned to do *something,* though it was only to write a sensation story.

A prouder young woman was seldom seen than she, when, having composed herself, she electrified the family by appearing before them with the letter in one hand, the check in the other, announcing that she had won the prize! Of course there was a great jubilee, and when the story came every one read and praised it; though after her father had told her that the language was good, the romance fresh and hearty, and the tragedy quite thrilling, he shook his head, and said in his unworldly way,—

"You can do better than this, Jo. Aim at the highest, and never mind the money."

"*I* think the money is the best part of it. What *will* you do with such a fortune?" asked Amy, regarding the magic slip of paper with a reverential eye.

"Send Beth and mother to the sea-side for a month or two," answered Jo promptly.

"Oh, how splendid! No, I can't do it, dear, it would be so selfish," cried Beth, who had clapped her thin hands, and taken a long breath, as if pining for fresh ocean breezes; then stopped herself, and motioned away the check which her sister waved before her.

"Ah, but you shall go, I've set my heart on it; that's what I tried for, and that's why I succeeded. I never get on when I think of myself alone, so it will help me to work for you, don't you see. Besides, Marmee needs the change, and she won't leave you, so you *must* go. Won't it be fun to see you come home plump and rosy again? Hurrah for Dr. Jo, who always cures her patients!"

To the sea-side they went, after much discussion; and though Beth didn't come home as plump and rosy as could be desired, she was much better, while Mrs. March declared she felt ten years younger; so Jo was satisfied with the investment of her prize-money, and fell to work with a cheery spirit, bent on earning more of those delightful checks. She did earn several that year, and began to feel herself a power in the house; for by the magic of a pen, her "rubbish" turned into comforts for them all. "The Duke's Daughter" paid the butcher's bill, "A Phantom Hand" put down a new carpet, and "The Curse of the Coventrys" proved the blessing of the Marches in the way of groceries and gowns.

Wealth is certainly a most desirable thing, but poverty has its sunny side, and one of the sweet uses of adversity is the genuine satisfaction which comes from hearty work of head or hand; and to the inspiration of necessity, we owe half the wise, beautiful, and useful blessings of the world. Jo enjoyed a taste of this satisfaction, and ceased to envy richer girls, taking great comfort in the knowledge that she could supply her own wants, and need ask no one for a penny.

Little notice was taken of her stories, but they found a market; and, encouraged by this fact, she resolved to make a bold stroke for fame and fortune. Having copied her novel for the fourth time, read it to all her confidential friends, and submitted it with fear and trembling to three publishers, she at last disposed of it, on condition that she would cut it down one-third, and omit all the parts which she particularly admired.

"Now I must either bundle it back into my tin-kitchen, to mould, pay for printing it myself, or chop it up to suit purchasers, and get what I can for it. Fame is a very good thing to have in the house, but cash is more convenient; so I wish to take the sense of the meeting on this important subject," said Jo, calling a family council.

"Don't spoil your book, my girl, for there is more in it than you know, and the idea is well worked out. Let it wait and ripen," was her father's advice; and he practised as he preached, having waited patiently thirty years for fruit of his own to ripen, and being in no haste to gather it, even now, when it was sweet and mellow.

"It seems to me that Jo will profit more by making the trial than by waiting," said Mrs. March. "Criticism is the best test of such work, for it will show her both unsuspected merits and faults, and help her to do better next time. We are too partial; but the praise and blame of outsiders will prove useful, even if she gets but little money."

"Yes," said Jo, knitting her brows, "that's just it; I've been fussing over the thing so long, I really don't know whether it's good, bad, or indifferent. It will be a great help to have cool, impartial persons take a look at it, and tell me what they think of it."

"I wouldn't leave out a word of it; you'll spoil it if you do, for the interest of the story is more in the minds than in the actions of the people, and it will be all a muddle if you don't explain as you go on," said Meg, who firmly believed that this book was the most remarkable novel ever written.

"But Mr. Allen says, 'Leave out the explanations, make it brief and dramatic, and let the characters tell the story,' " interrupted Jo, turning to the publisher's note.

"Do as he tells you; he knows what will sell, and we don't. Make a good, popular book, and get as much money as you can. By and by, when you've got a name, you can afford to digress, and have philosophical and metaphysical people in your novels," said Amy, who took a strictly practical view of the subject.

"Well," said Jo, laughing, "if my people *are* 'philosophical and metaphysical,' it isn't my fault, for I know nothing about such things, except what I hear father say, sometimes. If I've got some of his wise ideas jumbled up with my romance, so much the better for me. Now, Beth, what do you say?"

"I should so like to see it printed *soon,*" was all Beth said, and smiled in saying it; but there was an unconscious emphasis on the last word, and a wistful look in the eyes that never lost their childlike candor, which chilled Jo's heart, for a minute, with a foreboding fear, and decided her to make her little venture "soon."

So, with Spartan firmness, the young authoress laid her first-born on her table, and chopped it up as ruthlessly as any ogre. In the hope of pleasing every one, she took every one's advice; and, like the old man and his donkey in the fable, suited nobody.

Her father liked the metaphysical streak which had unconsciously got into it, so that was allowed to remain, though she had her doubts about it. Her mother thought that there *was* a trifle too much description; out, therefore, it nearly all came, and with it many necessary links in the story. Meg admired the tragedy; so Jo piled up the agony to suit her, while Amy objected to the fun, and, with the best intentions in life, Jo quenched the sprightly scenes which relieved the sombre character of the story. Then, to complete the ruin, she cut it down one-third, and confidingly sent the poor little romance, like a picked robin, out into the big, busy world, to try its fate.

Well, it was printed, and she got three hundred dollars for it; likewise plenty of praise and blame, both so much greater than she expected, that she was thrown into a state of bewilderment, from which it took some time to recover.

"You said, mother, that criticism would help me; but how can it, when it's so contradictory that I don't know whether I have written a promising book, or broken all the ten commandments," cried poor Jo, turning over a heap of notices, the perusal of which filled her with pride and joy one minute—wrath and dire dismay the next. "This man says 'An exquisite book, full of truth, beauty, and earnestness; all is sweet, pure, and healthy,' " continued the perplexed authoress. "The next, 'The theory of the book is bad,—full of morbid fancies, spiritualistic ideas, and unnatural characters.' Now, as I had no theory of any kind, don't believe in spiritualism, and copied my characters from life, I don't see how this critic *can* be right. Another says, 'It's one of the best American novels which has appeared for years' " (I know better than that); "and the next asserts that 'though it is original, and written with great force and feeling, it is a dangerous book.' 'Tisn't! Some make fun of it, some over-praise, and nearly all insist that I had a deep theory to expound, when I only wrote it for the pleasure and the money. I wish I'd printed it whole, or not at all, for I do hate to be so horridly misjudged."

Her family and friends administered comfort and commendation liberally; yet it was a hard time for sensitive, high-spirited Jo, who meant so well, and had apparently done so ill. But it did her good, for those whose opinion had real value, gave her the criticism which is an author's best education; and when the first soreness was over, she could laugh at her poor little book, yet believe in it still, and feel herself the wiser and stronger for the buffeting she had received.

"Not being a genius, like Keats, it won't kill me," she said stoutly; "and I've got the joke on my side, after all; for the parts that were taken straight out of real life, are denounced as impossible and absurd, and the scenes that I made up out of my own silly head, are pronounced 'charmingly natural, tender, and true.' So I'll comfort myself with that; and, when I'm ready, I'll up again and take another."

34

Friend

Though very happy in the social atmosphere about her, and very busy with the daily work that earned her bread, and made it sweeter for the effort, Jo still found time for literary labors. The purpose which now took possession of her was a natural one to a poor and ambitious girl; but the means she took to gain her end were not the best. She saw that money conferred power; money and power, therefore, she resolved to have; not to be used for herself alone, but for those whom she loved more than self. The dream of filling home with comforts, giving Beth everything she wanted, from strawberries in winter to an organ in her bedroom; going abroad herself, and always having *more* than enough, so that she might indulge in the luxury of charity, had been for years Jo's most cherished castle in the air.

The prize-story experience had seemed to open a way which might, after long travelling, and much up-hill work, lead to this delightful *chateau en Espagne.* But the novel disaster quenched her courage for a time, for public opinion is a giant which has frightened stouter-hearted Jacks on bigger beanstalks than hers. Like that immortal hero, she reposed a while after the first attempt, which resulted in a tumble, and the least lovely of the giant's treasures, if I remember rightly. But the "up again and take another" spirit was as strong in Jo as in Jack; so she scrambled up on the shady side, this time, and got more booty, but nearly left behind her what was far more precious than the money-bags.

She took to writing sensation stories—for in those dark ages, even all-perfect America read rubbish. She told no one, but concocted a "thrilling tale," and boldly carried it herself to Mr. Dashwood, editor of the "Weekly Volcano." She had never read Sartor Resartus, but she had a womanly instinct that clothes possess an influence more powerful over many than the worth of character or the magic of manners. So she dressed herself in her best, and, trying to persuade herself that she was neither excited nor nervous, bravely climbed two pairs of dark and dirty stairs to find herself in a disorderly room, a cloud of cigar smoke, and the presence of three gentlemen sitting with their heels rather higher than their hats, which articles of dress none of them took the trouble to remove on her appearance. Somewhat daunted by this reception, Jo hesitated on the threshold, murmuring in much embarrassment,—

"Excuse me; I was looking for the 'Weekly Volcano' office; I wished to see Mr. Dashwood."

Down went the highest pair of heels, up rose the smokiest gentleman, and, carefully cherishing his cigar between his fingers, he advanced with a nod, and a countenance expressive of nothing but sleep. Feeling that she must get through with the matter somehow, Jo produced her manuscript, and, blushing redder and redder with each sentence, blundered out fragments of the little speech carefully prepared for the occasion.

"A friend of mine desired me to offer—a story—just as an experiment—would like your opinion—be glad to write more if this suits."

While she blushed and blundered, Mr. Dashwood had taken the manuscript, and was turning over the leaves with a pair of rather dirty fingers, and casting critical glances up and down the near pages.

"Not a first attempt, I take it?" observing that the pages were numbered, covered only on one side, and *not* tied up with a ribbon—sure sign of a novice.

"No sir; she has had some experience, and got a prize for a tale in the 'Blarneystone Banner.' "

"Oh, did she?" and Mr. Dashwood gave Jo a quick look, which seemed to take note of everything she had on, from the bow in her bonnet to the buttons on her boots. "Well, you can leave it, if you like; we've more of this sort of thing on hand than we know what to do with, at present; but I'll run my eye over it, and give you an answer next week."

Now Jo did *not* like to leave it, for Mr. Dashwood didn't suit her at all; but, under the circumstances, there was nothing for her to do but bow and walk away, looking particularly tall and dignified, as she was apt to do, when nettled or abashed. Just then she was both; for it was perfectly evident from the knowing glances exchanged among the gentlemen, that her little fiction of "my friend" was considered a good joke; and a laugh produced by some inaudible remark of the editor, as he closed the door, completed her discomfiture. Half resolving never to return, she went home, and worked off her irritation by stitching pinafores vigorously; and in an hour or two was cool enough to laugh over the scene, and long for next week.

When she went again, Mr. Dashwood was alone, whereat she rejoiced. Mr. Dashwood was much wider awake than before,—which was agreeable,—and Mr. Dashwood was not too deeply absorbed in a cigar to remember his manners,—so the second interview was much more comfortable than the first.

"We'll take this" (editors never say "I"), "if you don't object to a few alterations. It's too long,—but omitting the passages I've marked will make it just the right length," he said, in a business-like tone.

Jo hardly knew her own MS. again, so crumpled and underscored were its pages and paragraphs; but, feeling as a tender parent might on being asked to cut off her baby's legs in order that it might fit into a new cradle, she looked at the marked passages, and was surprised to find that all the moral reflections,—which she had carefully put in as ballast for much romance,—had all been stricken out.

"But, sir, I thought every story should have some sort of a moral, so I took care to have a few of my sinners repent."

Mr. Dashwood's editorial gravity relaxed into a smile, for Jo had forgotten her "friend," and spoken as only an author could.

"People want to be amused, not preached at, you know. Morals don't sell nowadays;" which was not quite a correct statement, by the way.

"You think it would do with these alterations, then?"

"Yes; it's a new plot, and pretty well worked up—language good, and so on," was Mr. Dashwood's affable reply.

"What do you—that is, what compensation—" began Jo, not exactly knowing how to express herself.

"Oh, yes,—well, we give from twenty-five to thirty for things of this sort. Pay when it comes out," returned Mr. Dashwood, as if that point had escaped him; such trifles often do escape the editorial mind, it is said.

"Very well; you can have it," said Jo, handing back the story, with a satisfied air; for, after the dollar-a-column work, even twenty-five seemed good pay.

"Shall I tell my friend you will take another if she has one better than this?" asked Jo, unconscious of her little slip of the tongue, and emboldened by her success.

"Well, we'll look at it; can't promise to take it; tell her to make it short and spicy, and never mind the moral. What name would your friend like to put to it?" in a careless tone.

"None at all, if you please; she doesn't wish her name to appear, and has no *nom de plume,*" said Jo, blushing in spite of herself.

"Just as she likes, of course. The tale will be our next week; will you call for the money, or shall I send it?" asked Mr. Dashwood, who felt a natural desire to know who his new contributor might be.

"I'll call; good morning, sir."

As she departed, Mr. Dashwood put up his feet, with the graceful remark, "Poor and proud, as usual, but she'll do."

Following Mr. Dashwood's directions, and making Mrs. Northbury her model, Jo rashly took a plunge into the frothy sea of sensational literature; but, thanks to the life-preserver thrown her by a friend, she came up again, not much the worse for her ducking.

Like most young scribblers, she went abroad for her characters and scenery, and banditti, counts, gypsies, nuns, and duchesses appeared upon her stage, and played their parts with as much accuracy and spirit as could be expected. Her readers were not particular about such trifles as grammar, punctuation, and probability, and Mr. Dashwood graciously permitted her to fill his columns at the lowest prices, not thinking it necessary to tell her that the real cause of his hospitality was the fact that one of his hacks, on being offered higher wages, had basely left him in the lurch.

She soon became interested in her work,—for her emaciated purse grew stout, and the little hoard she was making to take Beth to the mountains next summer, grew slowly but surely, as the weeks passed. One thing disturbed her satisfaction, and that was that she did not tell them at home. She had a feeling that father and mother would not approve,—and preferred to have her own way first, and beg pardon afterward. It was easy to keep her secret, for no name appeared with her stories; Mr. Dashwood had, of course, found it out very soon, but promised to be dumb; and, for a wonder, kept his word.

She thought it would do her no harm, for she sincerely meant to write nothing of which she should be ashamed, and quieted all pricks of conscience by anticipations of the happy minute when she should show her earnings and laugh over her well-kept secret.

But Mr. Dashwood rejected any but thrilling tales; and, as thrills could not be produced except by harrowing up the souls of the readers, history and romance, land and sea, science and art, police records and lunatic asylums, had to be ransacked for the purpose. Jo soon found that her innocent experience had given her but few glimpses of the tragic world which underlies society; so, regarding it in a business light, she set about supplying her deficiencies with characteristic energy. Eager to find material for stories, and bent on making them original in plot, if not masterly in execution, she searched newspapers for accidents, incidents, and crimes; she excited the suspicions of public librarians by asking for works on poisons; she studied faces in the street,—and characters good, bad, and indifferent, all about her; she delved in the dust of ancient times, for facts or fictions so old that they were as good as new, and introduced herself to folly, sin, and misery, as well as her limited opportunities allowed. She thought she was prospering finely; but, unconsciously, she was beginning to desecrate some of the womanliest attributes of a woman's character.

She was living in bad society; and, imaginary though it was, its influence affected her, for she was feeding heart and fancy on dangerous and unsubstantial food, and was fast brushing the innocent bloom from her nature by a premature acquaintance with the darker side of life, which comes soon enough to all of us.

She was beginning to feel rather than see this, for much describing of other people's passions and feelings set her to studying and speculating about her own,—a morbid amusement, in which healthy young minds do not voluntarily indulge. Wrong-doing always brings its own punishment; and, when Jo most needed hers, she got it.

I don't know whether the study of Shakespeare helped her to read character, or the natural instinct of a woman for what was honest, brave and strong; but while endowing her imaginary heroes with every perfection under the sun, Jo was discovering a live hero, who interested her in spite of many human imperfections. Mr. Bhaer, in one of their conversations, had advised her to study simple, true, and lovely characters, wherever she found them, as good training for a writer; Jo took him at his word,—for she coolly turned round and studied him,—a proceeding which would have much surprised him, had he known it,—for the worthy Professor was very humble in his own conceit.

Why everybody liked him was what puzzled Jo, at first. He was neither rich nor great, young nor handsome,—in no respect what is called fascinating, imposing, or brilliant; and yet he was as attractive as a genial fire, and people seemed to gather about him as naturally as about a warm hearth. He was poor, yet always appeared to be giving something away,—a stranger, yet every one was his friend; no longer young,—but as happy-hearted as a boy; plain and odd,—yet his face looked beautiful to many, and his oddities were freely forgiven for his sake. Jo often watched him, trying to discover the charm, and, at last, decided that it was benevolence which worked the miracle. If he had any sorrow "it sat with its head under its wing," and he turned only his sunny side to the world. There were lines upon his forehead, but Time seemed to have touched him gently, remembering how kind he was to others. The pleasant curves about his mouth were the memorials of many friendly words and cheery laughs; his eyes were never cold or hard, and his big hand had a warm, strong grasp that was more expressive than words.

His very clothes seemed to partake of the hospitable nature of the wearer. They looked as if they were at ease, and liked to make him comfortable; his capacious waistcoat was suggestive of a large heart underneath; his rusty coat had a social air, and the baggy pockets plainly proved that little hands often went in empty and came out full; his very boots were benevolent, and his collars never stiff and raspy like other people's.

"That's it!" said Jo to herself, when she at length discovered that genuine good-will toward one's fellow-men could beautify and dignify even a stout German teacher, who shovelled in his dinner, darned his own socks, and was burdened with the name of Bhaer.

Jo valued goodness highly, but she also possessed a most feminine respect for intellect, and a little discovery which she made about the Professor added much to her regard for him. He never spoke of himself, and no one ever knew that in his native city he had been a man much honored and esteemed for learning and integrity, till a countryman came to see him, and, in a conversation with Miss Norton, divulged the pleasing fact. From her Jo learned it,—and liked it all the better because Mr. Bhaer had never told it. She felt proud to know that he was an honored Professor in Berlin, though only a poor language-master in America, and his homely, hard-working life, was much beautified by the spice of romance which this discovery gave it.

Another and a better gift than intellect was shown her in a most unexpected manner. Miss Norton had the *entrée* into literary society, which Jo would have had no chance of seeing but for her. The solitary woman felt an interest in the ambitious girl, and kindly conferred many favors of this sort both on Jo and the Professor. She took them with her, one night, to a select symposium, held in honor of several celebrities.

Jo went prepared to bow down and adore the mighty ones whom she had worshipped with youthful enthusiasm afar off. But her reverence for genius received a severe shock that night, and it took her some time to recover from the discovery that the great creatures were only men and women, after all. Imagine her dismay, on stealing a glance of timid admiration at the poet whose lines suggested an ethereal being fed on "spirit, fire, and dew," to behold him devouring his supper with an ardor which flushed his intellectual countenance. Turning as from a fallen idol, she made other discoveries which rapidly dispelled her romantic illusions. The great novelist vibrated between two decanters with the regularity of a pendulum; the famous divine flirted openly with one of the Madame de Staëls of the age, who looked daggers at another Corinne, who was amiably satirizing her, after out-manœuvreing her in efforts to absorb the profound philosopher, who imbibed tea Johnsonianly and appeared to slumber,—the loquacity of the lady rendering speech impossible. The scientific celebrities, forgetting their mollusks and Glacial Periods, gossipped about art, while devoting themselves to oysters and ices with characteristic energy; the young musician, who was charming the city like a second Orpheus, talked horses; and the specimen of the British nobility present happened to be the most ordinary man of the party.

Before the evening was half over, Jo felt so completely *désillusionnée,* that she sat down in a corner, to recover herself. Mr. Bhaer soon joined her, looking rather out of his element, and presently several of the philosophers, each mounted on his hobby, came ambling up to hold an intellectual tournament in the recess. The conversation was miles beyond Jo's comprehension, but she enjoyed it, though Kant and Hegel were unknown gods, the Subjective and Objective unintelligible terms; and the only thing "evolved from her inner consciousness," was a bad headache after it was all over. It dawned upon her gradually, that the world was being picked to pieces, and put together on new, and, according to the talkers, on infinitely better principles than before; that religion was in a fair way to be reasoned into nothingness, and intellect was to be the only God. Jo knew nothing about philosophy or metaphysics of any sort, but a curious excitement, half pleasurable, half painful, came over her, as she listened with a sense of being turned adrift into time and space, like a young balloon out on a holiday.

She looked round to see how the Professor liked it, and found him looking at her with the grimmest expression she had ever seen him wear. He shook his head, and beckoned her to come away, but she was fascinated, just then, by the freedom of Speculative Philosophy, and kept her seat, trying to find out what the wise gentlemen intended to rely upon after they annihilated all the old beliefs.

Now Mr. Bhaer was a diffident man, and slow to offer his own opinions, not because they were unsettled, but too sincere and earnest to be lightly spoken. As he glanced from Jo to several other young people attracted by the brilliancy of the philosophic pyrotechnics, he knit his brows, and longed to speak, fearing that some inflammable young soul would be led astray by the rockets, to find, when the display was over, that they had only an empty stick, or a scorched hand.

He bore it as long as he could; but when he was appealed to for an opinion, he blazed up with honest indignation, and defended religion with all the eloquence of truth—an eloquence which made his broken English musical, and his plain face beautiful. He had a hard fight, for the wise men argued well; but he didn't know when he was beaten, and stood to his colors like a man. Somehow, as he talked, the world got right again to Jo; the old beliefs that had lasted so long, seemed better than the new. God was not a blind force, and immortality was not a pretty fable, but a blessed fact. She felt as if she had solid ground under her feet again; and when Mr. Bhaer paused, out-talked, but not one whit convinced, Jo wanted to clap her hands and thank him.

She did neither; but she remembered this scene, and gave the Professor her heartiest respect, for she knew it cost him an effort to speak out then and there, because his conscience would not let him be silent. She began to see that character is a better possession than money, rank, intellect, or beauty; and to feel that if greatness is what a wise man has defined it to be,—"truth, reverence, and good-will,"—then her friend Friedrich Bhaer was not only good, but great.

This belief strengthened daily. She valued his esteem, coveted his respect, she wanted to be worthy of his friendship; and, just when the wish was sincerest, she came near losing everything. It all grew out of a cocked-hat; for one evening the Professor came in to give Jo her lesson, with a paper soldier-cap on his head, which Tina had put there, and he had forgotten to take off.

"It's evident he doesn't prink at his glass before coming down," thought Jo, with a smile, as he said, "Goot efening," and sat soberly down, quite unconscious of the ludicrous contrast between his subject and his head-gear, for he was going to read her the "Death of Wallenstein."

She said nothing at first, for she liked to hear him laugh out his big, hearty laugh, when anything funny happened, so she left him to discover it for himself, and presently forgot all about it; for to hear a German read Schiller is rather an absorbing occupation. After the reading came the lesson, which was a lively one, for Jo was in a gay mood that night, and the cocked-hat kept her eyes dancing with merriment. The Professor didn't know what to make of her, and stopped, at last, to ask with an air of mild surprise that was irresistible,—

"Mees Marsch, for what do you laugh in your master's face? Haf you no respect for me, that you go on so bad?"

"How can I be respectful, sir, when you forget to take your hat off?" said Jo.

Lifting his hand to his head, the absent-minded Professor gravely felt and removed the little cocked-hat, looked at it a minute, and then threw back his head, and laughed like a merry bass-viol.

"Ah! I see him now; it is that imp Tina who makes me a fool with my cap. Well, it is nothing; but see you, if this lesson goes not well, you too shall wear him."

But the lesson did not go at all, for a few minutes, because Mr. Bhaer caught sight of a picture on the hat; and, unfolding it, said with an air of great disgust,—

"I wish these papers did not come in the house; they are not for children to see, nor young people to read. It is not well; and I haf no patience with those who make this harm."

Jo glanced at the sheet, and saw a pleasing illustration composed of a lunatic, a corpse, a villain, and a viper. She did not like it; but the impulse that made her turn it over was not one of displeasure, but fear, because, for a minute, she fancied the paper was the "Volcano." It was not, however, and her panic subsided as she remembered that, even if it had been, and one of her own tales in it, there would have been no name to betray her. She had betrayed herself, however, by a look and a blush; for, though an absent man, the Professor saw a good deal more than people fancied. He knew that Jo wrote, and had met her down among the newspaper offices more than once; but as she never spoke of it, he asked no questions, in spite of a strong desire to see her work. Now it occurred to him that she was doing what she was ashamed to own, and it troubled him. He did not say to himself, "It is none of my business; I've no right to say anything," as many people would have done; he only remembered that she was young and poor, a girl far away from mother's love and father's care; and he was moved to help her with an impulse as quick and natural as that which would prompt him to put out his hand to save a baby from a puddle. All this flashed through his mind in a minute, but not a trace of it appeared in his face; and by the time the paper was turned, and Jo's needle threaded, he was ready to say quite naturally, but very gravely,—

"Yes, you are right to put it from you. I do not like to think that good young girls should see such things. They are made pleasant to some, but I would more rather give my boys gunpowder to play with than this bad trash."

"All may not be bad—only silly, you know; and if there is a demand for it, I don't see any harm in supplying it. Many very respectable people make an honest living out of what are called sensation stories," said Jo, scratching gathers so energetically that a row of little slits followed her pin.

"There is a demand for whiskey, but I think you and I do not care to sell it. If the respectable people knew what harm they did, they would not feel that the living *was* honest. They haf no right to put poison in the sugarplum, and let the small ones eat it. No; they should think a little, and sweep mud in the street before they do this thing!"

Mr. Bhaer spoke warmly, and walked to the fire, crumpling the paper in his hands. Jo sat still, looking as if the fire had come to her; for her cheeks burned long after the cocked-hat had turned to smoke, and gone harmlessly up the chimney.

"I should like much to send all the rest after him," muttered the Professor, coming back with a relieved air.

Jo thought what a blaze her pile of papers, upstairs, would make, and her hard-earned money laid rather heavily on her conscience at that minute. Then she thought consolingly to herself, "Mine are not like that; they are only silly, never bad; so I won't be worried;" and, taking up her book, she said, with a studious face,—

"Shall we go on, sir? I'll be very good and proper now."

"I shall hope so," was all he said, but he meant more then she imagined; and the grave, kind look he gave her, made her feel as if the words "Weekly Volcano" were printed in large type, on her forehead.

As soon as she went to her room, she got out her papers, and carefully re-read every one of her stories. Being a little short-sighted, Mr. Bhaer sometimes used eye-glasses, and Jo had tried them once, smiling to see how they magnified the fine print of her book; now she seemed to have got on the Professor's mental or moral spectacles also, for the faults of these poor stories glared at her dreadfully, and filled her with dismay.

"They *are* trash, and will soon be worse than trash if I go on; for each is more sensational than the last. I've gone blindly on, hurting myself and other people, for the sake of money;—I know it's so—for I can't read this stuff in sober earnest without being horribly ashamed of it; and *what should* I do if they were seen at home, or Mr. Bhaer got hold of them?"

Jo turned hot at the bare idea, and stuffed the whole bundle into her stove, nearly setting the chimney afire with the blaze.

"Yes, that's the best place for such inflammable nonsense; I'd better burn the house down, I suppose, than let other people blow themselves up with my gunpowder," she thought, as she watched the "Demon of the Jura" whisk away, a little black cinder with fiery eyes.

But when nothing remained of all her three months' work, except a heap of ashes, and the money in her lap, Jo looked sober, as she sat on the floor, wondering what she ought to do about her wages.

"I think I haven't done much harm *yet,* and may keep this to pay for my time," she said, after a long meditation, adding, impatiently, "I almost wish I hadn't any conscience, it's so inconvenient. If I didn't care about doing right, and didn't feel uncomfortable when doing wrong, I should get on capitally. I can't help wishing, sometimes, that father and mother hadn't been so dreadfully particular about such things."

Ah, Jo, instead of wishing that, thank God that "father and mother *were* particular," and pity from your heart those who have no such guardians to hedge them round with principles which may seem like prison walls to impatient youth, but which will prove sure foundations to build character upon in womanhood.

Jo wrote no more sensational stories, deciding that the money did not pay for her share of the sensation; but, going to the other extreme, as is the way with people of her stamp, she took a course of Mrs. Sherwood, Miss Edgeworth, and Hannah More, and then produced a tale which might have been more properly called an essay or a sermon, so intensely moral was it. She had her doubts about it from the beginning; for her lively fancy and girlish romance felt as ill at ease in the new style as she would have done masquerading in the stiff and cumbrous costume of the last century. She sent this didactic gem to several markets, but it found no purchaser; and she was inclined to agree with Mr. Dashwood, that morals didn't sell.

Then she tried a child's story, which she could easily have disposed of if she had not been mercenary enough to demand filthy lucre for it. The only person who offered enough to make it worth her while to try juvenile literature, was a worthy gentleman who felt it his mission to convert all the world to his particular belief. But much as she liked to write for children, Jo could not consent to depict all her naughty boys as being eaten by bears, or tossed by mad bulls, because they did not go to a particular Sabbath-school, nor all the good infants who did go, of course, as rewarded by every kind of bliss, from gilded gingerbread to escorts of angels, when they departed this life, with psalms or sermons on their lisping tongues. So nothing came of these trials; and Jo corked up her inkstand, and said, in a fit of very wholesome humility,—

"I don't know anything; I'll wait till I do before I try again, and, meantime, 'sweep mud in the street,' if I can't do better—that's honest, any way;" which decision proved that her second tumble down the beanstalk had done her some good.

While these internal revolutions were going on, her external life had been as busy and uneventful as usual; and if she sometimes looked serious, or a little sad, no one observed it but Professor Bhaer. He did it so quietly, that Jo never knew he was watching to see if she would accept and profit by his reproof; but she stood the test, and he was satisfied; for, though no words passed between them, he knew that she had given up writing. Not only did he guess it by the fact that the second finger of her right hand was no longer inky, but she spent her evenings down stairs, now, was met no more among newspaper offices, and studied with a dogged patience, which assured him that she was bent on occupying her mind with something useful, if not pleasant.

He helped her in many ways, proving himself a true friend, and Jo was happy; for while her pen lay idle, she was learning other lessons beside German, and laying a foundation for the sensation story of her own life.

It was a pleasant winter and a long one, for she did not leave Mrs. Kirke till June. Every one seemed sorry when the time came; the children were inconsolable, and Mr. Bhaer's hair stuck straight up over his head—for he always rumpled it wildly when disturbed in mind.

"Going home! Ah, you are happy that you haf a home to go in," he said, when she told him, and sat silently pulling his beard, in the corner, while she held a little levee on that last evening.

She was going early, so she bade them all good-by over night; and when his turn came, she said, warmly—

"Now, sir, you won't forget to come and see us, if you ever travel our way, will you? I'll never forgive you, if you do, for I want them all to know my friend."

"Do you? Shall I come?" he asked, looking down at her with an eager expression, which she did not see.

"Yes, come next month; Laurie graduates then, and you'd enjoy Commencement as something new."

"That is your best friend, of whom you speak?" he said, in an altered tone.

"Yes, my boy Teddy; I'm very proud of him, and should like you to see him."

Jo looked up, then, quite unconscious of anything but her own pleasure, in the prospect of showing them to one another. Something in Mr. Bhaer's face suddenly recalled the fact that she might find Laurie more than a best friend, and simply because she particularly wished not to look as if anything was the matter, she involuntarily began to blush; and the more she tried not to, the redder she grew. If it had not been for Tina on her knee, she didn't know what would have become of her. Fortunately, the child was moved to hug her; so she managed to hide her face an instant, hoping the Professor did not see it. But he did, and his own changed again from that momentary anxiety to its usual expression, as he said, cordially,—

"I fear I shall not make the time for that, but I wish the friend much success, and you all happiness; Gott bless you!" and with that, he shook hands warmly, shouldered Tina, and went away.

But after the boys were abed, he sat long before his fire, with the tired look on his face, and the *"heimweh,"* or homesickness lying heavy at his heart. Once when he remembered Jo, as she sat with the little child in her lap, and that new softness in her face, he leaned his head on his hands a minute, and then roamed about the room, as if in search of something he could not find.

"It is not for me; I must not hope it now," he said to himself, with a sigh that was almost a groan; then, as if reproaching himself for the longing that he could not repress, he went and kissed the two towzled heads upon the pillow, took down his seldom-used meerschaum, and opened his Plato.

He did his best, and did it manfully; but I don't think he found that a pair of rampant boys, a pipe, or even the divine Plato, were very satisfactory substitutes for wife and child, and home.

Early as it was, he was at the station, next morning, to see Jo off; and, thanks to him, she began her solitary journey with the pleasant memory of a familiar face smiling its farewell, a bunch of violets to keep her company, and, best of all, the happy thought,—

"Well, the winter's gone, and I've written no books—earned no fortune; but I've made a friend worth having and I'll try to keep him all my life."

In Work: A Story of Experience *(1873), Alcott returned to the earnest domestic realism of* Moods. *In fact, she had been working on the two adult novels simultaneously during the early 1860s until the mixed reception of* Moods *discouraged her from continuing with* Success, *as she then called the second novel. Her own success with* Little Women, *followed by* An Old-Fashioned Girl *(1870) and* Little Men *(1871), perhaps emboldened her to revise the early manuscript.* Work, *in its way, is as autobiographical as* Little Women. *In the latter, Alcott immortalized—and idealized—her family while dramatizing her adolescent conflicts and early literary career. In* Work, *Alcott presents a fictionalized account of her own work experience in Boston during the 1850s. But in the second part of* Work, *as in the second part of* Little Women, *she departs from her own experience by having her heroine, Christie Devon, fall in love and marry. Unlike Jo, however, Christie does play an active role in the Civil War, serving as a nurse while her husband, David Sterling, serves in the Union army. After his heroic death, Christie finds her life's work as an advocate for women's rights. Thus, after a brief marital interlude, during most of which she is separated from her husband, Christie, like her creator, uses her theatrical training to develop a public persona and career.*

"At Forty," the final chapter of Work, *is divided into three parts, the first and third of which are reprinted here. In the first, Christie discovers her true vocation as a mediator between working- and middle-class women. In the second, Christie counsels Bella, a rich woman, on the service she could render society. In the final section, Christie and Bella are surrounded by a circle of female friends that includes both Christie's daughter, Ruth, and her sister-in-law, Letty, a reclaimed "fallen woman." This scene, in which the heroine extends her arms to a mix of "old and young, black and white, rich and poor," invites comparison with the final chapter of* Little Women, *in which Marmee embraces her three surviving daughters. Both novels depict "a loving league of sisters," but "at forty," Alcott's concept of such a league has moved, like Christie's, beyond the personal to the political.*

Work: A Story of Experience

CHAPTER XX

At Forty

"Nearly twenty years since I set out to seek my fortune. It has been a long search, but I think I have found it at last. I only asked to be a useful, happy woman, and my wish is granted: for, I believe I *am* useful; I *know* I am happy."

Christie looked so as she sat alone in the flowery parlor one September afternoon, thinking over her life with a grateful, cheerful spirit. Forty to-day, and pausing at that half-way house between youth and age, she looked back into the past without bitter regret or unsubmissive grief, and forward into the future with courageous patience; for three good angels attended her, and with faith, hope, and charity to brighten life, no woman need lament lost youth or fear approaching age. Christie did not, and though her eyes filled with quiet tears as they were raised to the faded cap and sheathed sword hanging on the wall, none fell; and in a moment tender sorrow changed to still tenderer joy as her glance wandered to rosy little Ruth playing hospital with her dollies in the porch. Then they shone with genuine satisfaction as they went from the letters and papers on her table to the garden, where several young women were at work with a healthful color in the cheeks that had been very pale and thin in the spring.

"I think David is satisfied with me; for I have given all my heart and strength to his work, and it prospers well," she said to herself, and then her face grew thoughtful, as she recalled a late event which seemed to have opened a new field of labor for her if she chose to enter it.

A few evenings before she had gone to one of the many meetings of working-women, which had made some stir of late. Not a first visit, for she was much interested in the subject and full of sympathy for this class of workers.

There were speeches of course, and of the most unparliamentary sort, for the meeting was composed almost entirely of women, each eager to tell her special grievance or theory. Any one who chose got up and spoke; and whether wisely or foolishly each proved how great was the ferment now going on, and how difficult it was for the two classes to meet and help one another in spite of the utmost need on one side and the sincerest good-will on the other. The workers poured out their wrongs and hardships passionately or plaintively, demanding or imploring justice, sympathy, and help; displaying the ignorance, incapacity, and prejudice, which make their need all the more pitiful, their relief all the more imperative.

The ladies did their part with kindliness, patience, and often unconscious condescension, showing in their turn how little they knew of the real trials of the women whom they longed to serve, how very narrow a sphere of usefulness they were fitted for in spite of culture and intelligence, and how rich they were in generous theories, how poor in practical methods of relief.

One accomplished creature with learning radiating from every pore, delivered a charming little essay on the strong-minded women of antiquity; then, taking labor into the region of art, painted delightful pictures of the time when all would work harmoniously together in an Ideal Republic, where each did the task she liked, and was paid for it in liberty, equality, and fraternity.

Unfortunately she talked over the heads of her audience, and it was like telling fairy tales to hungry children to describe Aspasia discussing Greek politics with Pericles and Plato reposing upon ivory couches, or Hypatia modestly delivering philosophical lectures to young men behind a Tyrian purple curtain; and the Ideal Republic met with little favor from anxious seamstresses, type-setters, and shop-girls, who said ungratefully among themselves, "That's all very pretty, but I don't see how it's going to better wages among us *now.*"

Another eloquent sister gave them a political oration which fired the revolutionary blood in their veins, and made them eager to rush to the State-house *en masse,* and demand the ballot before one-half of them were quite clear what it meant, and the other half were as unfit for it as any ignorant Patrick bribed with a dollar and a sup of whiskey.

A third well-wisher quenched their ardor like a wet blanket, by reading reports of sundry labor reforms in foreign parts; most interesting, but made entirely futile by differences of climate, needs, and customs. She closed with a cheerful budget of statistics, giving the exact number of needle-women who had starved, gone mad, or committed suicide during the past year; the enormous profits wrung by capitalists from the blood and muscles of their employés; and the alarming increase in the cost of living, which was about to plunge the nation into debt and famine, if not destruction generally.

When she sat down despair was visible on many countenances, and immediate starvation seemed to be waiting at the door to clutch them as they went out; for the impressible creatures believed every word and saw no salvation anywhere.

Christie had listened intently to all this; had admired, regretted, or condemned as each spoke; and felt a steadily increasing sympathy for all, and a strong desire to bring the helpers and the helped into truer relations with each other.

The dear ladies were so earnest, so hopeful, and so unpractically benevolent, that it grieved her to see so much breath wasted, so much good-will astray; while the expectant, despondent, or excited faces of the work-women touched her heart; for well she knew how much they needed help, how eager they were for light, how ready to be led if some one would only show a possible way.

As the statistical extinguisher retired, beaming with satisfaction at having added her mite to the good cause, a sudden and uncontrollable impulse moved Christie to rise in her place and ask leave to speak. It was readily granted, and a little stir of interest greeted her; for she was known to many as Mr. Power's friend, David Sterling's wife, or an army nurse who had done well. Whispers circulated quickly, and faces brightened as they turned toward her; for she had a helpful look, and her first words pleased them. When the president invited her to the platform she paused on the lowest step, saying with an expressive look and gesture:

"I am better here, thank you; for I have been and mean to be a working-woman all my life."

"Hear! hear!" cried a stout matron in a gay bonnet, and the rest indorsed the sentiment with a hearty round. Then they were very still, and then in a clear, steady voice, with the sympathetic undertone to it that is so magical in its effect, Christie made her first speech in public since she left the stage.

That early training stood her in good stead now, giving her self-possession, power of voice, and ease of gesture; while the purpose at her heart lent her the sort of simple eloquence that touches, persuades, and convinces better than logic, flattery, or oratory.

What she said she hardly knew: words came faster than she could utter them, thoughts pressed upon her, and all the lessons of her life rose vividly before her to give weight to her arguments, value to her counsel, and the force of truth to every sentence she uttered. She had known so many of the same trials, troubles, and temptations that she could speak understandingly of them; and, better still, she had conquered or outlived so many of them, that she could not only pity but help others to do as she had done. Having found in labor her best teacher, comforter, and friend, she could tell those who listened that, no matter how hard or humble the task at the beginning, if faithfully and bravely performed, it would surely prove a stepping-stone to something better, and with each honest effort they were fitting themselves for the nobler labor, and larger liberty God meant them to enjoy.

The women felt that this speaker was one of them; for the same lines were on her face that they saw on their own, her hands were no fine lady's hands, her dress plainer than some of theirs, her speech simple enough for all to understand; cheerful, comforting, and full of practical suggestion, illustrations out of their own experience, and a spirit of companionship that uplifted their despondent hearts.

Yet more impressive than any thing she said was the subtle magnetism of character, for that has a universal language which all can understand. They saw and felt that a genuine woman stood down there among them like a sister, ready with head, heart, and hand to help them help themselves; not offering pity as an alms, but justice as a right. Hardship and sorrow, long effort and late-won reward had been hers they knew; wifehood, motherhood, and widowhood brought her very near to them; and behind her was the background of an earnest life, against which this figure with health on the cheeks, hope in the eyes, courage on the lips, and the ardor of a wide benevolence warming the whole countenance stood out full of unconscious dignity and beauty; an example to comfort, touch, and inspire them.

It was not a long speech, and in it there was no learning, no statistics, and no politics; yet it was the speech of the evening, and when it was over no one else seemed to have any thing to say. As the meeting broke up Christie's hand was shaken by many roughened by the needle, stained with printer's ink, or hard with humbler toil; many faces smiled gratefully at her, and many voices thanked her heartily. But sweeter than any applause were the words of one woman who grasped her hand, and whispered with wet eyes:

"I knew your blessed husband; he was very good to me, and I've been thanking the Lord he had such a wife for his reward!"

Christie was thinking of all this as she sat alone that day, and asking herself if she should go on; for the ladies had been as grateful as the women; had begged her to come and speak again, saying they needed just such a mediator to bridge across the space that now divided them from those they wished to serve. She certainly seemed fitted to act as interpreter between the two classes; for, from the gentleman her father she had inherited the fine instincts, gracious manners, and unblemished name of an old and honorable race; from the farmer's daughter, her mother, came the equally valuable dower of practical virtues, a sturdy love of independence, and great respect for the skill and courage that can win it.

Such women were much needed and are not always easy to find; for even in democratic America the hand that earns its daily bread must wear some talent, name, or honor as an ornament, before it is very cordially shaken by those that wear white gloves.

"Perhaps this is the task my life has been fitting me for," she said. "A great and noble one which I should be proud to accept and help accomplish if I can. Others have finished the emancipation work and done it splendidly, even at the cost of all this blood and sorrow. I came too late to do any thing but give my husband and behold the glorious end. This new task seems to offer me the chance of being among the pioneers, to do the hard work, share the persecution, and help lay the foundation of a new emancipation whose happy success I may never see. Yet I had rather be remembered as those brave beginners are, though many of them missed the triumph, than as the late comers will be, who only beat the drums and wave the banners when the victory is won."

. . . .

When Letty and her mother came in, they found a much happier looking guest than the one Christie had welcomed an hour before. Scarcely had she introduced them when voices in the lane made all look up to see old Hepsey and Mrs. Wilkins approaching.

"Two more of my dear friends, Bella: a fugitive slave and a laundress. One has saved scores of her own people, and is my pet heroine. The other has the bravest, cheeriest soul I know, and is my private oracle."

The words were hardly out of Christie's mouth when in they came;

Hepsey's black face shining with affection, and Mrs. Wilkins as usual running over with kind words.

"My dear creeter, the best of wishes and no end of happy birthdays. There's a triflin' keepsake; tuck it away, and look at it byme by. Mis' Sterlin', I'm proper glad to see you lookin' so well. Aunt Letty, how's that darlin' child? I ain't the pleasure of your acquaintance, Miss, but I'm pleased to see you. The children all sent love, likewise Lisha, whose bones is better sense I tried the camfire and red flannel."

Then they settled down like a flock of birds of various plumage and power of song, but all amicably disposed, and ready to peck socially at any topic which might turn up.

Mrs. Wilkins started one by exclaiming as she "laid off" her bonnet:

"Sakes alive, there's a new picter! Ain't it beautiful?"

"Colonel Fletcher brought it this morning. A great artist painted it for him, and he gave it to me in a way that added much to its value," answered Christie, with both gratitude and affection in her face; for she was a woman who could change a lover to a friend, and keep him all her life.

It was a quaint and lovely picture of Mr. Greatheart, leading the fugitives from the City of Destruction. A dark wood lay behind; a wide river rolled before; Mercy and Christiana pressed close to their faithful guide, who went down the rough and narrow path bearing a cross-hilted sword in his right hand, and holding a sleeping baby with the left. The sun was just rising, and a long ray made a bright path athwart the river, turned Greatheart's dinted armor to gold, and shone into the brave and tender face that seemed to look beyond the sunrise.

"There's just a hint of Davy in it that is very comforting to me," said Mrs. Sterling, as she laid her old hands softly together, and looked up with her devout eyes full of love.

"Dem women oughter bin black," murmured Hepsey, tearfully; for she considered David worthy of a place with old John Brown and Colonel Shaw.

"The child looks like Pansy, we all think," added Letty, as the little girl brought her nosegay for Aunty to tie up prettily.

Christie said nothing, because she felt too much; and Bella was also silent because she knew too little. But Mrs. Wilkins with her kindly tact changed the subject before it grew painful, and asked with sudden interest:

"When be you a goin' to hold forth agin, Christie? Jest let me know beforehand, and I'll wear my old gloves: I tore my best ones all to rags clappin' of you; it was so extra good."

"I don't deserve any credit for the speech, because it spoke itself, and I couldn't help it. I had no thought of such a thing till it came over me all at once, and I was up before I knew it. I'm truly glad you liked it, but I shall never make another, unless you think I'd better. You know I always ask your advice, and what is more remarkable usually take it," said Christie, glad to consult her oracle.

"Hadn't you better rest a little before you begin any new task, my daughter? You have done so much these last years you must be tired," interrupted Mrs. Sterling, with a look of tender anxiety.

"You know I work for two, mother," answered Christie, with the clear, sweet expression her face always wore when she spoke of David. "I am not tired yet: I hope I never shall be, for without my work I should fall into despair or *ennui*. There is so much to be done, and it is so delightful to help do it, that I never mean to fold my hands till they are useless. I owe all I can do, for in labor, and the efforts and experiences that grew out of it, I have found independence, education, happiness, and religion."

"Then, my dear, you are ready to help other folks into the same blessed state, and it's your duty to do it!" cried Mrs. Wilkins, her keen eyes full of sympathy and commendation as they rested on Christie's cheerful, earnest face. "Ef the sperrit moves you to speak, up and do it without no misgivin's. *I* think it was a special leadin' that night, and I hope you'll foller, for it ain't every one that can make folks laugh and cry with a few plain words that go right to a body's heart and stop there real comfortable and fillin'. I guess this is your next job, my dear, and you'd better ketch hold and give it the right turn; for it's goin' to take time, and women ain't stood alone for so long they'll need a sight of boostin'."

There was a general laugh at the close of Mrs. Wilkins's remarks; but Christie answered seriously: "I accept the task, and will do my share faithfully with words or work, as shall seem best. We all need much preparation for the good time that is coming to us, and can get it best by trying to know and help, love and educate one another,—as we do here."

With an impulsive gesture Christie stretched her hands to the friends about her, and with one accord they laid theirs on hers, a loving league of sisters, old and young, black and white, rich and poor, each ready to do her part to hasten the coming of the happy end.

"Me too!" cried little Ruth, and spread her chubby hand above the rest: a hopeful omen, seeming to promise that the coming generation of women will not only receive but deserve their liberty, by learning that the greatest of God's gifts to us is the privilege of sharing His great work.

A Modern Mephistopheles (1877) is Alcott's only work of sensation fiction known to have been written after the publication of Little Women, *and it is one of her best. A full-length novel, it appeared in Roberts Brothers No Name Series, which featured works by well-known authors published anonymously. The letters of Alcott's editor at Roberts, Thomas Niles, suggest that both he and Alcott enjoyed the idea of mystifying the reading public. And, according to Alcott's journal, she reveled in the return to her earlier style. Apparently, Alcott had first thought that she could revise a manuscript entitled "A Modern Mephistopheles," written and rejected during the 1860s; instead, she recycled elements from an earlier published story, "The Freak of a Genius," which had appeared serially in* Frank Leslie's Illustrated Newspaper *in October and November of 1866. The 1860s "Modern Mephistopheles" was finally published in 1995 by Random House under its subtitle* A Long Fatal Love Chase.

Critics have debated and will continue to debate the comparative merits of these three thematically related works. In both the novella "The Freak of a Genius" and A Modern Mephistopheles, *a beautiful youth with poetic aspirations but limited talent is befriended by an older, less attractive but much more gifted man. In both works, the young man becomes famous as the author of poems actually written by the older man, but in "The Freak of a Genius," Kent permits St. George to publish his poems out of mistaken kindness, whereas in* A Modern Mephistopheles, *Jasper Helwyze encourages Felix Canaris to appropriate his poems out of a fiendish curiosity and love of power. In both works, a character dies, but "The Freak of a Genius" otherwise ends happily; in* A Modern Mephistopheles, *on the other hand, four lives are devastated by the machinations of Helwyze. "The Freak of a Genius" resembles* A Modern Mephistopheles *in its concentration on four principal characters and the tangled relationships among them, but it is a much tamer piece.* A Long Fatal Love Chase *resembles* A Modern Mephistopheles *in that it, too, has a diabolic hero, but Philip Tempest's evil seems less subtle and sinister than that of Helwyze, who compares himself, obliquely, with Hawthorne's Chillingworth.* Love Chase *is, as its title suggests, a picaresque novel, loose and episodic, whereas* A Modern Mephistopheles *is one of Alcott's most tightly constructed works and almost claustrophobic in its confinement to a single setting. In addition to two modern reprints, several excellent analyses of* A Modern Mephistopheles *have been published, suggesting its literary merit and centrality in the Alcott canon.*

In the three chapters from A Modern Mephistopheles *reprinted here, we see Helwyze attempt what has been called an intellectual (and construed by one critic as an actual) rape of Gladys, the wife of his protégé Felix Canaris. Not content to bind Felix to him with their Faustian bargain, Helwyze blackmails him into marrying the innocent young woman to whom Helwyze is himself attracted. Virtually imprisoned in Helwyze's household, Gladys begins to succeed, despite Helwyze, in winning her husband's love and loyalty. In order to frustrate Gladys, Helwyze recalls his former mistress Olivia, with whom Felix earlier thought himself in love, and at the beginning of chapter 12 persuades her to attempt to seduce Felix. Then, in a succession of scenes that brings together a number of Alcott's favorite motifs—flower symbolism, drug-induced eroticism, literary allusion, and dramatic performance—Helwyze, like Chillingworth before him, attempts to "violate the sanctity of a human heart." In chapter 15, Gladys, pregnant with what she, at least, believes to be Felix's child and emboldened by three months' absence from Helwyze, discusses their triangular relationship in terms of Hawthorne's novel. In the chapters that follow this confrontation with Helwyze, Gladys does finally learn the secret of her husband's literary success, a secret that has been equated with Alcott's own double life as an author. Thus, in a series meant to prompt public speculation about authorship, Alcott dared to suggest that some of her own best work had yet to be acknowledged and that the author of her acclaimed work differed from the woman whom her readers thought they knew.*

XII

Olivia came before the swallows; for the three words, "I miss you," would have brought her from the ends of the earth, had she exiled herself so far. She had waited for him to want and call her, as he often did when others wearied or failed him. Seldom had so long a time passed without some word from him; and endless doubts, fears, conjectures, had harassed her, as month after month went by, and no summons came. Now she hastened, ready for any thing he might ask of her, since her reward would be a glimpse of the only heaven she knew.

"Amuse Felix: he is falling in love with his wife, and it spoils both of them for my use. He says he has forgotten you. Come often, and teach him to remember, as penalty for his bad taste and manners," was the single order Helwyze gave; but Olivia needed no other; and, for the sake of coming often, would have smiled upon a far less agreeable man than Canaris.

Gladys tried to welcome the new guest cordially, as an unsuspicious dove might have welcomed a falcon to its peaceful cote; but her heart sunk when she found her happy quiet sorely disturbed, her husband's place deserted, and the old glamour slowly returning to separate them, in spite of all her gentle arts. For Canaris, feeling quite safe in the sincere affection which now bound him to his wife, was foolhardy in his desire to show Olivia how heart-whole he had become. This piqued her irresistibly, because Helwyze was looking on, and she would win *his* approval at any cost. So these three, from divers motives, joined together to teach poor Gladys how much a woman can suffer with silent fortitude and make no sign.

The weeks that followed seemed unusually gay and sunny ones; for April came in blandly, and Olivia made a pleasant stir throughout the house by her frequent visits, and the various excursions she proposed. Many of these Gladys escaped; for her pain was not the jealousy that would drive her to out-rival her rival, but the sorrowful shame and pity which made her long to hide herself, till Felix should come back and be forgiven. Helwyze naturally declined the long drives, the exhilarating rides in the bright spring weather, which were so attractive to the younger man, and sat at home watching Gladys, now more absorbingly interesting than ever. He could not but admire the patience, strength, and dignity of the creature; for she made no complaint, showed no suspicion, asked no advice, but went straight on, like one who followed with faltering feet, but unwavering eye, the single star in all the sky that would lead her right. A craving curiosity to know what she felt and thought possessed him, and he invited confidence by unwonted kindliness, as well as the unfailing courtesy he showed her.

But Gladys would not speak either to him or to her husband, who seemed wilfully blind to the slowly changing face, all the sadder for the smile it always wore when his eyes were on it. At first, Helwyze tried his gentlest arts; but, finding her as true as brave, was driven, by the morbid curiosity which he had indulged till it became a mania, to use means as subtle as sinful,—like a burglar, who, failing to pick a lock, grows desperate and breaks it, careless of consequences.

Taking his daily walk through the house, he once came upon Gladys watering the *jardinière,* which was her especial care, and always kept full of her favorite plants. She was not singing as she worked, but seriously busy as a child, holding in both hands her little watering-pot to shower the thirsty ferns and flowers, who turned up their faces to be washed with the silent delight which was their thanks.

"See how the dear things enjoy it! I feel as if they knew and watched for me, and I never like to disappoint them of their bath," she said, looking over her shoulder, as he paused beside her. She was used to this now, and was never surprised or startled when below stairs by his noiseless approach.

"They are doing finely. Did Moss bring in some cyclamens? They are in full bloom now, and you are fond of them, I think?"

"Yes, here they are: both purple and white, so sweet and lovely! See how many buds this one has. I shall enjoy seeing them come out, they unfurl so prettily;" and, full of interest, Gladys parted the leaves to show several baby buds, whose rosy faces were just peeping from their green hoods.

Helwyze liked to see her among the flowers; for there was something peculiarly innocent and fresh about her then, as if the woman forgot her griefs, and was a girl again. It struck him anew, as she stood there in the sunshine, leaning down to tend the soft leaves and cherish the delicate buds with a caressing hand.

"Like seeks like: you are a sort of cyclamen yourself. I never observed it before, but the likeness is quite striking," he said, with the slow smile which usually prefaced some speech which bore a double meaning.

"Am I?" and Gladys eyed the flowers, pleased, yet a little shy, of compliment from him.

"This is especially like you," continued Helwyze, touching one of the freshest. "Out of these strong sombre leaves rises a wraith-like blossom, with white, softly folded petals, a rosy color on its modest face, and a most sweet perfume for those whose sense is fine enough to perceive it. Most of all, perhaps, it resembles you in this,—it hides its heart, and, if one tries to look too closely, there is danger of snapping the slender stem."

"That is its nature, and it cannot help being shy. I kneel down and look up without touching it; then one sees that it has nothing to hide," protested Gladys, following out the flower fancy, half in earnest, half in jest, for she felt there was a question and a reproach in his words.

"Perhaps not; let us see, in my way." With a light touch Helwyze turned the reluctant cyclamen upward, and in its purple cup there clung a newly fallen drop, like a secret tear.

Mute and stricken, Gladys looked at the little symbol of herself, owning, with a throb of pain, that if in nothing else, they *were* alike in that.

Helwyze stood silent likewise, inhaling the faint fragrance while he softly ruffed the curled petals as if searching for another tear. Suddenly Gladys spoke out with the directness which always gave him a keen pleasure, asking, as she stretched her hand involuntarily to shield the more helpless flower,—

"Sir, why do you wish to read my heart?"

"To comfort it."

"Do I need comfort, then?"

"Do you not?"

"If I have a sorrow, God only can console me, and He only need know it. To you it should be sacred. Forgive me if I seem ungrateful; but you cannot help me, if you would."

"Do you doubt my will?"

"I try to doubt no one; but I fear—I fear many things;" and, as if afraid of saying too much, Gladys broke off, to hurry away, wearing so strange a look that Helwyze was consumed with a desire to know its meaning.

He saw no more of her till twilight, for Canaris took her place just then, reading a foreign book, which she could not manage; but, when Felix went out, he sought one of his solitary haunts, hoping she would appear.

She did; for the day closed early with a gusty rain, and the sunset hour was gray and cold, leaving no after-glow to tint the western sky and bathe the great room in ruddy light. Pale and noiseless as a spirit, Gladys went to and fro, trying to quiet the unrest that made her nights sleepless, her days one long struggle to be patient, just, and kind. She tried to sing, but the song died in her throat; she tried to sew, but her eyes were dim, and the flower under her needle only reminded her that "pansies were for thoughts," and hers, alas! were too sad for thinking; she took up a book, but laid it down again, since Felix was not there to finish it with her. Her own rooms seemed so empty, she could not return thither when she had looked for him in vain; and, longing for some human voice to speak to her, it was a relief to come upon Helwyze sitting in his lonely corner,—for she never now went to the library, unless duty called her.

"A dull evening, and dull company," he said, as she paused beside him, glad to have found something to take her out of herself, for a time at least.

"Such a long day! and such a dreary night as it will be!" she answered, leaning her forehead against the window-pane, to watch the drops fall, and listen to the melancholy wind.

"Shorten the one and cheer the other, as I do: sleep, dream, and forget."

"I cannot!" and there was a world of suffering in the words that broke from her against her will.

"Try my sleep-compeller as freely as I tried yours. See, these will give you one, if not all the three desired blessings,—quiet slumber, delicious dreams, or utter oblivion for a time."

As he spoke, Helwyze had drawn out a little *bonbonnière* of tortoise-shell and silver, which he always carried, and shaken into his palm half a dozen white comfits, which he offered to Gladys, with a benign expression born of real sympathy and compassion. She hesitated; and he added, in a tone of mild reproach, which smote her generous heart with compunction,—

"Since I may not even try to minister to your troubled mind, let me, at least, give a little rest to your weary body. Trust me, child, these cannot hurt you; and, strong as you are, you will break down if you do not sleep."

Without a word, she took them; and, as they melted on her tongue, first sweet, then bitter, she stood leaning against the rainy window-pane, listening to Helwyze, who began to talk as if he too had tasted the Indian drug, which "made the face of Coleridge shine, as he conversed like one inspired."

It seemed a very simple, friendly act; but this man had learned to know how subtly the mind works; to see how often an apparently impulsive action is born of an almost unconscious thought, an unacknowledged purpose, a deeply hidden motive, which to many seem rather the child than the father of the deed. Helwyze did not deceive himself, and owned that baffled desire prompted that unpremeditated offer, and was ready to avail itself of any self-betrayal which might follow its acceptance, for he had given Gladys hasheesh.

It could not harm; it might soothe and comfort her unrest. It surely would make her forget for a while, and in that temporary oblivion perhaps he might discover what he burned to know. The very uncertainty of its effect added to the daring of the deed; and, while he talked, he waited to see how it would affect her, well knowing that in such a temperament as hers all processes are rapid. For an hour he conversed so delightfully of Rome and its wonders, that Gladys was amazed to find Felix had come in, unheard for once.

All through dinner she brightened steadily, thinking the happy mood was brought by her prodigal's return, quite forgetting Helwyze and his bitter-sweet bonbons.

"I shall stay at home, and enjoy the society of my pretty wife. What have you done to make yourself so beautiful to-night? Is it the new gown?" asked Canaris, surveying her with laughing but most genuine surprise and satisfaction as they returned to the drawing-room again.

"It is not new: I made it long ago, to please you, but you never noticed it before," answered Gladys, glancing at the pale-hued dress, all broad, soft folds from waist to ankle, with its winter trimming of swan's down at the neck and wrists; simple, but most becoming to her flower-like face and girlish figure.

"What cruel blindness! But I see and admire it now, and honestly declare that not Olivia in all her splendor is arrayed so much to my taste as you, my Sancta Simplicitas."

"It is pleasant to hear you say so; but that alone does not make me happy: it must be having you at home all to myself again," she whispered, with shining eyes, cheeks that glowed with a deeper rose each hour, and an indescribably blest expression in a face which now was both brilliant and dreamy.

Helwyze heard what she said, and, fearing to lose sight of her, promptly challenged Canaris to chess, a favorite pastime with them both. For an hour they played, well matched and keenly interested, while Gladys sat by, already tasting the restful peace, the delicious dreams, promised her.

The clock was on the stroke of eight, the game was nearly over, when a quick ring arrested Helwyze in the act of making the final move. There was a stir in the hall, then, bringing with her a waft of fresh, damp air, Olivia appeared, brave in purple silk and Roman gold.

"I thought you were all asleep or dead; but now I see the cause of this awful silence," she cried. "Don't speak, don't stir; let me enjoy the fine tableau you make. Retsch's 'Game of Life,' quite perfect, and most effective."

It certainly was to an observer; for Canaris, flushed and eager, looked the young man to the life; Helwyze, calm but intent, with his finger on his lip, pondering that last fateful move, was an excellent Satan; and behind them stood Gladys, wonderfully resembling the wistful angel, with that new brightness on her face.

"Which wins?" asked Olivia, rustling toward them, conscious of having made an impressive entrance; for both men looked up to welcome her, though Gladys never lifted her eyes from the mimic battle Felix seemed about to lose.

"I do, as usual," answered Helwyze, turning to finish the game with the careless ease of a victor.

"Not this time;" and Gladys touched a piece which Canaris in the hurry of the moment was about to overlook. He saw its value at a glance, made the one move that could save him, and in an instant cried "Checkmate," with a laugh of triumph.

"Not fair, the angel interfered," said Olivia, shaking a warning finger at Gladys, who echoed her husband's laugh with one still more exultant, as she put her hand upon his shoulder, saying, in a low, intense voice never heard from her lips before,—

"I have won him; he is mine, and cannot be taken from me any more."

"Dearest child, no one wants him, except to play with and admire," began Olivia, rather startled by the look and manner of the lately meek, mute Gladys.

Here Helwyze struck in, anxious to avert Olivia's attention; for her undesirable presence disconcerted him, since her woman's wit might discover what it was easy to conceal from Canaris.

"You have come to entertain us, like the amiable enchantress that you are?" he asked, suggestively; for nothing charmed Olivia more than permission to amuse him, when others failed.

"I have a thought,—a happy thought,—if Gladys will help me. You have given me one living picture: I will give you others, and she shall sing the scenes we illustrate."

"Take Felix, and give us 'The God and the Bayadere,'" said Helwyze, glancing at the young pair behind them, he intent upon their conversation, she upon him. "No, I will have only Gladys. You will act and sing for us, I know?" and Olivia turned to her with a most engaging smile.

"I never acted in my life, but I will try. I think I should like it for I feel as if I could do any thing to-night;" and she came to them with a swift step, an eager air, as if longing to find some outlet for the strange energy which seemed to thrill every nerve and set her heart to beating audibly.

"You look so. Do you know all these songs?" asked Olivia, taking up the book which had suggested her happy thought.

"There are but four: I know them all. I will gladly sing them; for I set them to music, if they had none of their own already. I often do that to those Felix writes me."

"Come, then. I want the key of the great press, where you keep your spoils, Jasper."

"Mrs. Bland will give it you. Order what you will, if you are going to treat us to an Arabian Night's entertainment."

"Better than that. We are going to teach a small poet, by illustrating the work of a great one;" and, with a mischievous laugh, Olivia vanished, beckoning Gladys to follow.

The two men beguiled the time as best they might: Canaris playing softly to himself in the music-room; Helwyze listening intently to the sounds that came from behind the curtains, now dropped over a double door-way leading to the lower end of the hall. Olivia's imperious voice was heard, directing men and maids. More than once an excited laugh from Gladys jarred upon his ear; and, as minute after minute passed, his impatience to see her again increased.

XIII

After what would have seemed a wonderfully short time to a more careless waiter, three blows were struck, in the French fashion, and Canaris had barely time to reach his place, when the deep blue curtains slid noiselessly apart, showing the visible portion of the hall, arranged to suggest a mediæval room. An easy task, when a suit of rusty armor already stood there; and Helwyze had brought spoils from all quarters of the globe, in the shape of old furniture, tapestry, weapons, and trophies of many a wild hunt.

"What is it?" whispered Canaris eagerly.

"An Idyl of the King."

"I see: the first. How well they look it!"

They did; Olivia, as

"An ancient dame in dim brocade;
And near her, like a blossom, vermeil-white,
That lightly breaks a faded flower-sheath,
Stood the fair Enid, all in faded silk."

Gladys, clad in a quaint costume of tarnished gray and silver damask, singing, in "the sweet voice of a bird,"—

"Turn, Fortune, turn thy wheel, and lower the proud;
Turn thy wild wheel through sunshine, storm, and cloud;
Thy wheel and thee we neither love nor hate.

"Turn, Fortune, turn thy wheel with smile and frown;
With that wild wheel we go not up nor down;
Our hoard is little, but our hearts are great.

"Smile and we smile, the lords of many lands;
Frown and we smile, the lords of our own hands;
For man is man and master of his fate.

"Turn, turn thy wheel above the staring crowd;
Thy wheel and thou art shadows in the cloud;
Thy wheel and thee we neither love nor hate."

There was something inexpressibly touching in the way Gladys gave the words, which had such significance addressed to those who listened so intently, that they nearly forgot to pay the tribute which all actors, the greatest as the least, desire, when the curtain dropped, and the song was done.

"A capital idea of Olivia's, and beautifully carried out. This promises to be pleasant;" and Helwyze sat erect upon the divan, where Canaris came to lounge beside him.

"Which comes next? I don't remember. If it is Vivien, they will have to skip it, unless they call you in for Merlin," he said, talking gayly, because a little conscience-stricken by the look Gladys wore, as she sung, with her eyes upon him,—

"Our hoard is little, but our hearts are great."

"They will not want a Merlin; for Gladys could not act Vivien, if she would," answered Helwyze, tapping restlessly as he waited.

"She said she could do *'any thing'* to-night; and, upon my life, she looked as if she might even beguile you, 'mighty master,' of your strongest spell."

"She will never try."

But both were mistaken; for, when they looked again, the dim light showed a dark and hooded shape, with glittering eyes and the semblance of a flowing, hoary beard, leaning half-hidden in a bower of tall shrubs from the conservatory. It was Olivia, as Merlin; and, being of noble proportions, she looked the part excellently. Upon the wizard's knee sat Vivien,—

"A twist of gold was round her hair;
A robe of samite without price, that more exprest
Than hid her, clung about her lissome limbs,
In color like the satin-shining palm
On sallows in the windy gleams of March."

In any other mood, Gladys would never have consented to be loosely clad in a great mantle of some Indian fabric, which shimmered like woven light, with its alternate stripes of gold-covered silk and softest wool. Shoulders and arms showed rosy white under the veil of hair which swept to her knee, as she clung there, singing sweet and low, with eyes on Merlin's face, lips near his own, and head upon his breast:—

"In Love, if Love be Love, if Love be ours,
Faith and unfaith can ne'er be equal powers;
Unfaith in aught is want of faith in all.

"It is the little rift within the lute
That by and by will make the music mute,
And ever widening, slowly silence all.

"The little rift within the lover's lute,
Or little pitted speck in garner'd fruit,
That, rotting inward, slowly moulders all.

"It is not worth the keeping: let it go:
But shall it? Answer, darling, answer 'No;'
And trust me not at all or all in all."

There Gladys seemed to forget her part, and, turning, stretched her arms towards her husband, as if in music she had found a tongue to plead her cause. The involuntary gesture recalled to her that other verse which Vivien added to her song; and something impelled her to sing it, standing erect, with face, figure, voice all trembling with the strong emotion that suddenly controlled her:—

"My name, once mine, now thine, is closelier mine,
For fame, could fame be mine, that fame were thine;
And shame, could shame be thine, that shame were mine;
So trust me not at all or all in all."

Down fell the curtain there, and the two men looked at one another in silence for an instant, dazzled, troubled, and surprised; for in this brilliant, impassioned creature they did not recognize the Gladys they believed they knew so well.

"What possessed her to sing that? She is so unlike herself, I do not know her," said Canaris, excited by the discoveries he was making.

"She is inspired to-night; so be prepared for any thing. These women will work wonders, they are acting to the men they love," answered Helwyze, warily, yet excited also; because, for him, a double drama was passing on that little stage, and he found it marvellously fascinating.

"I never knew how beautiful she was!" mused Canaris, half aloud, his eyes upon the blue draperies which hid her from his sight.

"You never saw her in such gear before. Splendor suits her present mood, as well as simplicity becomes her usual self-restraint. You have made her jealous, and your angel will prove herself a woman, after all."

"Is that the cause of this sudden change in her? Then I don't regret playing truant, for the woman suits me better than the angel," cried Canaris, conscious that the pale affection he had borne his wife so long was already glowing with new warmth and color, in spite of his seeming neglect.

"Wait till you see Olivia as Guinevere. I know she cannot resist that part, and I suspect she is willing to efface herself so far that she may take us by storm by and by."

Helwyze prophesied truly; and, when next the curtains parted, the stately Queen sat in the nunnery of Almesbury, with the little novice at her feet. Olivia *was* right splendid now, for her sumptuous beauty well became the costly stuffs in which she had draped herself with the graceful art of a woman whose physical loveliness was her best possession. A trifle *too* gorgeous, perhaps, for the repentant Guinevere; but a most grand and gracious spectacle, nevertheless, as she leaned in the tall carved chair, with jewelled arms lying languidly across her lap, and absent eyes still full of love and longing for lost Launcelot.

Gladys, in white wimple and close-folded gown of gray, sat on a stool beside the "one low light," humming softly, her rosary fallen at her feet,—

"the Queen looked up, and said,
'O maiden, if indeed you list to sing,
Sing, and unbind my heart, that I may weep.'
Whereat full willingly sang the little maid,

Late, late, so late! and dark the night and chill!
Late, late, so late! but we can enter still.
Too late! too late! ye cannot enter now.

No light had we; for that we do repent,
And, learning this, the bridegroom will relent.
Too late! too late! ye cannot enter now.

No light, so late! and dark and chill the night!
O let us in, that we may find the light!
Too late! too late! ye cannot enter now.

Have we not heard the bridegroom is so sweet?
O let us in, tho' late, to kiss his feet!
No, no, too late! ye cannot enter now."

Slowly the proud head had drooped, the stately figure sunk, till, as the last lament died away, nothing remained of splendid Guinevere but a hidden face, a cloud of black hair from which the crown had fallen, a heap of rich robes quivering with the stormy sobs of a guilty woman's smitten heart. The curtains closed on this tableau, which was made the more effective by the strong contrast between the despairing Queen and the little novice telling her beads in meek dismay.

"Good heavens, that sounded like the wail of a lost soul! My blood runs cold, and I feel as if I ought to say my prayers," muttered Canaris, with a shiver; for, with his susceptible temperament, music always exerted over him an almost painful power.

"If you knew any," sneered Helwyze, whose eyes now glittered with something stronger than excitement.

"I do: Gladys taught me, and I am not ashamed to own it."

"Much good may it do you." Then, in a quieter tone, he asked, "Is there any song in 'Elaine'? I forget; and that is the only one we have not had."

"There is 'The Song of Love and Death.' Gladys was learning it lately; and, if I remember rightly, it was heart-rending. I hope she will not sing it, for this sort of thing is rather too much for me;" and Canaris got up to wander aimlessly about, humming the gayest airs he knew, as if to drown the sorrowful "Too late! too late!" still wailing in his ear.

By this time Gladys was no longer quite herself: an inward excitement possessed her, a wild desire to sing her very heart out came over her, and a strange chill, which she thought a vague presentiment of coming ill, crept through her blood. Every thing seemed vast and awful; every sense grew painfully acute; and she walked as in a dream, so vivid, yet so mysterious, that she did not try to explain it even to herself. Her identity was doubled: one Gladys moved and spoke as she was told,—a pale, dim figure, of no interest to any one; the other was alive in every fibre, thrilled with intense desire for something, and bent on finding it, though deserts, oceans, and boundless realms of air were passed to gain it.

Olivia wondered at her unsuspected power, and felt a little envious of her enchanting gift. But she was too absorbed in "setting the stage," dressing her prima donna, and planning how to end the spectacle with her favorite character of Cleopatra, to do more than observe that Gladys's eyes were luminous and large, her face growing more and more colorless, her manner less and less excited, yet unnaturally calm.

"This is the last, and you have the stage alone. Do your best for Felix; then you shall rest and be thanked," she whispered, somewhat anxiously, as she placed Elaine in her tower, leaning against the dark screen, which was unfolded, to suggest the casement she flung back when Launcelot passed below,—

"And glanced not up, nor waved his hand,
Nor bade farewell, but sadly rode away."

The "lily maid of Astolat" could not have looked more wan and weird than Gladys, as she stood in her trailing robes of dead white, with loosely gathered locks, hands clasped over the gay bit of tapestry which simulated the cover of the shield, eyes that seemed to see something invisible to those about her, and began her song, in a veiled voice, at once so sad and solemn, that Helwyze held his breath, and Canaris felt as if she called him from beyond the grave:—

"Sweet is true love, tho' given in vain, in vain;
And sweet is death, who puts an end to pain;
I know not which is sweeter, no, not I.

Love, art thou sweet? then bitter death must be;
Love, thou art bitter; sweet is death to me,
O Love, if death be sweeter, let me die.

Sweet love, that seems not made to fade away,
Sweet death, that seems to make us loveless clay,
I know not which is sweeter, no, not I.

I fain would follow love, if that could be;
I needs must follow death, who calls for me:
Call and I follow, I follow! let me die!"

Carried beyond self-control by the unsuspected presence of the drug, which was doing its work with perilous rapidity, Gladys, remembering only that the last line should be sung with force, and that she sung for Felix, obeyed the wild impulse to let her voice rise and ring out with a shrill, despairing power and passion, which startled every listener, and echoed through the room, like Elaine's unearthly cry of hapless love and death.

Olivia dropped her asp, terrified; the maids stared, uncertain whether it was acting or insanity; and Helwyze sprung up aghast, fearing that he had dared too much. But Canaris, seeing only the wild, woful eyes fixed on his, the hands wrung as if in pain, forgot every thing but Gladys, and rushed between the curtains, exclaiming in real terror,—

"Don't look so! don't sing so! my God, she is dying!"

Not dying, only slipping fast into the unconscious stage of the hasheesh dream, whose coming none can foretell but those accustomed to its use. Pale and quiet she lay in her husband's arms, with half-open eyes and fluttering breath, smiling up at him so strangely that he was bewildered as well as panic-stricken. Olivia forgot her Cleopatra to order air and water; the maids flew for salts and wine; Helwyze with difficulty hid his momentary dismay; while Canaris, almost beside himself, could only hang over the couch where lay "the lily-maid," looking as if already dead, and drifting down to Camelot.

"Gladys, do you know me?" he cried, as a little color came to her lips after the fiery draught Olivia energetically administered.

The eyes opened wider, the smile grew brighter, and she lifted her hand to bring him nearer, for he seemed immeasurably distant.

"Felix! Let me be still, quite still; I want to sleep. Good-night, good-night."

She thought she kissed him; then his face receded, vanished, and, as she floated buoyantly away upon the first of the many oceans to be crossed in her mysterious quest, a far-off voice seemed to say, solemnly, as if in a last farewell,—

"Hush! let her sleep in peace."

It was Helwyze; and, having felt her pulse, he assured them all that she was only over-excited, must rest an hour or two, and would soon be quite herself again. So the brief panic ended quietly; and, having lowered the lights, spread Guinevere's velvet mantle over her, and reassured themselves that she was sleeping calmly, the women went to restore order to ante-room and hall, Canaris sat down to watch beside Gladys, and Helwyze betook himself to the library.

"Is she still sleeping?" he asked, with unconcealable anxiety, when Olivia joined him there.

"Like a baby. What a high-strung little thing it is. If she had strength to bear the training, she would make a cantatrice to be proud of, Jasper."

"Ah, but she never would! Fancy that modest creature on a stage for all the world to gape at. She was happiest in the nun's gown tonight, though simply ravishing as Vivien. The pretty, bare feet were most effective; but how did you persuade her to it?"

"I had no sandals as a compromise: I therefore insisted that the part *must* be so dressed or undressed, and she submitted. People usually do, when I command."

"She was on her mettle: I could see that; and well she might be, with you for a rival. I give you my word, Olivia, if I did not know you were nearly forty, I should swear it was a lie; for 'age cannot wither nor custom stale' my handsome Cleopatra. We ought to have had that, by the by: it used to be your best bit. I could not be your Antony, but Felix might: he adores costuming, and would do it capitally."

"Not old enough! Ah! what happy times those were;" and Olivia sighed sincerely, yet dramatically, for she knew she was looking wonderfully well, thrown down upon a couch, with her purple skirts sweeping about her, and two fine arms banded with gold clasped over her dark head.

Helwyze had flattered with a purpose. Canaris was in the way, Gladys might betray herself, and all was not safe yet; though in one respect the experiment had succeeded admirably, for he still tingled with the excitement of the evening. Now he wanted help, not sentiment, and, ignoring the sigh, said, carelessly,—

"If all obey when you insist, just make Felix go home with you. The drive will do him good, for he is as nervous as a woman, and I shall have him fidgeting about all night, unless he forgets his fright."

"But Gladys?"

"She will be the better for a quiet nap, and ready, by the time he returns, to laugh at her heroics. He will only disturb her if he sits there, like a mourner at a death-bed."

"That sounds sensible and friendly, and you do it very well, Jasper; but I am impressed that something is amiss. What is it? Better tell me; I shall surely find it out, and will not work in the dark. I see mischief in your eyes, and you cannot deceive me."

Olivia spoke half in jest; but she had so often seen his face without a mask, that it was difficult to wear one in her presence. He frowned, hesitated, then fearing she would refuse the favor if he withheld the secret, he leaned towards her and answered in a whisper,—

"I gave Gladys hasheesh, and do not care to have Felix know it."

"Jasper, how dared you?"

"She was restless, suffering for sleep. I know what that is, and out of pity gave her the merest taste. Upon my honor, no more than a child might safely take. She did not know what it was, and I thought she would only feel its soothing charm. She would, if it had not been for this masquerading. I did not count on that, and it was too much for her."

"Will she not suffer from the after-effects?"

"Not a whit, if she is let alone. An hour hence she will be deliciously drowsy, and to-morrow none the worse. I had no idea it would affect her so powerfully; but I do not regret it, for it showed what the woman is capable of."

"At your old tricks. You will never learn to let your fellow-creatures alone, till something terrible stops you. You were always prying into things, even as a boy, when I caught butterflies for you to look at."

"I never killed them: only brushed off a trifle of the gloss by my touch, and let them go again, none the worse, except for the loss of a few invisible feathers."

"Ah! but that delicate plumage is the glory of the insect; robbed of that, its beauty is marred. No one but their Maker can search hearts without harming them. I wonder how it will fare with yours when He looks for its perfection?"

Olivia spoke with a sudden seriousness, a yearning look, which jarred on nerves already somewhat unstrung, and Helwyze answered, in a mocking tone that silenced her effectually,—

"I am desperately curious to know. If I can come and tell you, I will: such pious interest deserves that attention."

"Heaven forbid!" ejaculated Olivia, with a shiver.

"Then I will *not*. I have been such a poor ghost here, I suspect I shall be glad to rest eternally when I once fall asleep, if I can."

Weary was his voice, weary his attitude, as, leaning an elbow on either knee, he propped his chin upon his hands, and sat brooding for a moment with his eyes upon the ground, asking himself for the thousandth time the great question which only hope and faith can answer truly.

Olivia rose. "You are tired; so am I. Good-night, Jasper, and pleasant dreams. But remember, no more tampering with Gladys, or I must tell her husband."

"I have had my lesson. Take Felix with you, and I will send Mrs. Bland to sit with her till he comes back. Good-night, my cousin; thanks for a glimpse of the old times." Such words, uttered with a pressure of the hand, conquered Olivia's last scruple, and she went away to prefer her request in a form which made it impossible for Canaris to refuse. Gladys still slept quietly. The distance was not long, the fresh air grateful, Olivia her kindest self, and he obeyed, believing that the motherly old woman would take his place as soon as certain housewifely duties permitted.

Then Helwyze did an evil thing,—a thing few men could or would have done. He deliberately violated the sanctity of a human soul, robbing it alike of its most secret and most precious thoughts. Hasheesh had lulled the senses which guarded the treasure; now the magnetism of a potent will forced the reluctant lips to give up the key.

Like a thief he stole to Glady's side, took in his the dimpled hands whose very childishness should have pleaded for her, and fixed his eyes upon the face before him, untouched by its helpless innocence, its unnatural expression. The half-open eyes were heavy as dew-drunken violets, the sweet red mouth was set, the agitated bosom still rose and fell, like a troubled sea subsiding after storm.

So sitting, stern and silent as the fate he believed in, Helwyze concentrated every power upon the accomplishment of the purpose to which he bent his will. He called it psychological curiosity; for not even to himself did he care confess the true meaning of the impulse which drove him to this act, and dearly did he pay for it.

Soon the passive palms thrilled in his own, the breath came faint and slow, color died, and life seemed to recede from the countenance, leaving a pale effigy of the woman; lately so full of vitality. "It works! it works!" muttered Helwyze, lifting his head at length to wipe the dampness from his brow, and send a piercing glance about the shadowy room. Then, kneeling down beside the couch, he put his lips to her ear, whispering in a tone of still command,—

"Gladys, do you hear me?"

Like the echo of a voice, so low, expressionless, and distant was it, the answer came,—

"I hear."

"Will you answer me?"

"I must."

"You have a sorrow,—tell it."

"All is so false. I am unhappy without confidence," sighed the voice.

"Can you trust no one?"

"No one here, but Felix."

"Yet he deceives, he does not love you."

"He will."

"Is this the hope which sustains you?"

"Yes."

"And you forgive, you love him still?"

"Always."

"If the hope fails?"

"It will not: I shall have help."

"What help?"

No answer now, but the shadow of a smile seemed to float across the silent lips as if reflected from a joy too deep and tender for speech to tell.

"Speak! what is this happiness? The hope of freedom?"

"It will come."

"How?"

"When you die."

He caught his breath, and for an instant seemed daunted by the truth he had evoked; for it was terrible, so told, so heard.

"You hate me, then?" he whispered, almost fiercely, in the ear that never shrank from his hot lips.

"I doubt and dread you."

"Why, Gladys, why? To you I am not cruel."

"Too kind, alas, too kind!"

"And yet you fear me?"

"God help us. Yes."

"What is your fear?"

"No, no, I will *not* tell it!"

Some inward throe of shame or anguish turned the pale face paler, knotted the brow, and locked the lips, as if both soul and body revolted from the thought thus ruthlessly dragged to light. Instinct, the first, last, strongest impulse of human nature, struggled blindly to save the woman from betraying the dread which haunted her heart like a spectre, and burned her lips in the utterance of its name. But Helwyze was pitiless, his will indomitable; his eye held, his hand controlled, his voice commanded; and the answer came, so reluctantly, so inaudibly, that he seemed to divine, not hear it.

"What fear?"

"Your love."

"You see, you know it, then?"

"I do not see, I vaguely feel; I pray God I may never know."

With the involuntary recoil of a guilty joy, a shame as great, Helwyze dropped the nerveless hands, turned from the mutely accusing face, let the troubled spirit rest, and asked no more. But his punishment began as he stood there, finding the stolen truth a heavier burden than baffled doubt or desire had been; since forbidden knowledge was bitter to the taste, forbidden love possessed no sweetness, and the hidden hope, putting off its well-worn disguise, confronted him in all its ugliness.

An awesome silence filled the room, until he lifted up his eyes, and looked at Gladys with a look which would have wrung her heart could she have seen it. She did not see; for she lay there so still, so white, so dead, he seemed to have scared away the soul he had vexed with his impious questioning.

In remorseful haste, Helwyze busied himself about her, till she woke from that sleep within a sleep, moaned wearily, closed the unseeing eyes, and drifted away into more natural slumber, dream-haunted, but deep and quiet.

Then he stole away as he had come, and, sending the old woman to watch Gladys, shut himself into his own room, to keep a vigil which lasted until dawn; for all the poppies of the East could not have brought oblivion that night.

XV

"Back again, earlier than before. But not to stay long, thank Heaven! By another month we will be truly at home, my Gladys," whispered Canaris, as they went up the steps, in the mellow September sunshine.

"I hope so!" she answered, fervently, and paused an instant before entering the door; for, coming from the light and warmth without, it seemed as dark and chilly as the entrance to a tomb.

"You are tired, love? Come and rest before you see a soul."

With a new sort of tenderness, Canaris led her up to her own little bower, and lingered there to arrange the basket of fresh recruits she had brought for her winter garden: while Gladys lay contentedly on the couch where he placed her, looking about the room as if greeting old friends; but her eyes always came back to him, full of a reposeful happiness which proved that all was well with her.

"There! now the little fellows sit right comfortably in the moss, and will soon feel at home. I'll go find Mother Bland, and see what his Serene Highness is about," said the young man, rising from his work, warm and gay, but in no haste to go, as he had been before.

Gladys remembered that; and when, at last, he left her, she shut her eyes to re-live, in thought, the three blissful months she had spent in teaching him to love her with the love in which self bears no part. Before the happy reverie was half over, the old lady arrived; and, by the time the young one was ready, Canaris came to fetch her.

"My dearest, I am afraid we must give up our plan," he said, softly, as he led her away: "Helwyze is so changed, I come to tell you, lest it should shock you when you see him. I think it would be cruel to go at once. Can you wait a little longer?"

"If we ought. How is he changed?"

"Just worn away, as a rock is by the beating of the sea, till there seems little left of him except the big eyes and greater sharpness of both tongue and temper. Say nothing about it, and seem not to notice it; else he will freeze you with a look, as he did me when I exclaimed."

"Poor man! we will be very patient, very kind; for it must be awful to think of dying with no light beyond," sighed Gladys, touching the cross at her white throat.

"A Dante without a Beatrice: I am happier than he;" and Canaris laid his cheek against hers with the gesture of a boy, the look of a man who has found the solace which is also his salvation.

Helwyze received them quietly, a little coldly, even; and Gladys reproached herself with too long neglect of what she had assumed as a duty, when she saw how ill he looked, for *his* summer had not been a blissful one. He had spent it in wishing for her, and in persuading himself that the desire was permissible, since he asked nothing but what she had already given him,—her presence and her friendship. It was her intellect he loved and wanted, not her heart; that she might give her husband wholly, since he understood and cared for affection only: her mind, with all its lovely possibilities, Helwyze coveted, and reasoned himself into the belief that he had a right to enjoy it, conscious all the while that his purpose was a delusion and a snare. Olivia had mourned over the moody taciturnity which made a lonely cranny of the cliffs his favorite resort, where he sat, day after day, watching, with an irresistible fascination, the ever-changing sea,—beautiful and bitter as the hidden tide of thought and feeling in his own breast, where lay the image of Gladys, as placid, yet as powerful, as the moon which ruled the ebb and flow of that vaster ocean. Being a fatalist for want of a higher faith, he left all to chance, and came home simply resolved to enjoy what was left him as long and as unobtrusively as possible; since Felix owed him much, and Gladys need never know what she had prayed *not* to know.

....

So the old life began again, at least in outward seeming; but it was impossible for it to last long. The air was too full of the electricity of suppressed and conflicting emotions to be wholesome; former relations could not be resumed, because sincerity had gone out of them; and the quiet, which reigned for a time, was only the lull before the storm.

Gladys soon felt this, but tried to think it was owing to the contrast between the free, happy days she had enjoyed so much, and uttered no complaint; for Felix was busy with his play, sanguine as ever, inspired now by a nobler ambition than before, and happy in his work.

Helwyze had flattered himself that he could be content with the harmless shadow, since he could not possess the sweet substance of a love whose seeming purity was its most delusive danger. But he soon discovered "how bitter a thing it is to look into happiness through another man's eyes;" and, even while he made no effort to rob Canaris of his treasure, he hated him for possessing it, finding the hatred all the more poignant, because it was his own hand which had forced Felix to seize and secure it. He had thought to hold and hide this new secret; but it held him, and would not be hidden, for it was stronger than even his strong will, and ruled him with a power which at times filled him with a sort of terror. Having allowed it to grow, and taken it to his bosom, he could not cast it out again, and it became a torment, not the comfort he had hoped to find it. His daily affliction was to see how much the young pair were to each other, to read in their faces a hundred happy hopes and confidences in which he had no part, and to remember the confession wrung from the lips dearest to him, that his death would bring to them their much-desired freedom.

At times he was minded to say "Go," but the thought of the utter blank her absence would leave behind daunted him. Often an almost uncontrollable desire to tell her that which would mar her trust in her husband tempted him; for, having yielded to a greater temptation, all lesser ones seemed innocent beside it; and, worse than all, the old morbid longing for some excitement, painful even, if it could not be pleasurable, goaded him to the utterance of half truths, which irritated Canaris and perplexed Gladys, till she could no longer doubt the cause of this strange mood. It seemed as if her innocent hand gave the touch which set the avalanche slipping swiftly but silently to its destructive fall.

One day when Helwyze was pacing to and fro in the library, driven by the inward storm which no outward sign betrayed, except his excessive pallor and unusual restlessness, she looked up from her book, asking compassionately,—

"Are you suffering, sir?"

"Torment."

"Can I do nothing?"

"Nothing!"

She went on reading, as if glad to be left in peace; for distrust, as well as pity, looked out from her frank eyes, and there was no longer any pleasure in the duties she performed for Canaris's sake.

But Helwyze, jealous even of the book which seemed to absorb her, soon paused again, to ask, in a calmer tone,—

"What interests you?"

" 'The Scarlet Letter.' "

The hands loosely clasped behind him were locked more closely by an involuntary gesture, as if the words made him wince; otherwise unmoved, he asked again, with the curiosity he often showed about her opinions of all she read,—

"What do you think of Hester?"

"I admire her courage; for she repented, and did not hide her sin with a lie."

"Then you must despise Dimmesdale?"

"I ought, perhaps; but I cannot help pitying his weakness, while I detest his deceit: he loved so much."

"So did Roger;" and Helwyze drew nearer, with the peculiar flicker in his eyes, as of a light kindled suddenly behind a carefully drawn curtain.

"At first; then his love turned to hate, and he committed the unpardonable sin," answered Gladys, much moved by that weird and wonderful picture of guilt and its atonement.

"The unpardonable sin!" echoed Helwyze, struck by her words and manner.

"Hawthorne somewhere describes it as 'the want of love and reverence for the human soul, which makes a man pry into its mysterious depths, not with a hope or purpose of making it better, but from a cold, philosophical curiosity. This would be the separation of the intellect from the heart: and this, perhaps, would be as unpardonable a sin as to doubt God, whom we cannot harm; for in doing this we must inevitably do great wrong both to ourselves and others.' "

As she spoke, fast and earnestly, Gladys felt herself upon the brink of a much-desired, but much-dreaded, explanation; for Canaris, while owning to her that there *was* a secret, would not tell it till Helwyze freed him from his promise. She thought that he delayed to ask this absolution till she was fitter to bear the truth, whatever it might be; and she had resolved to spare her husband the pain of an avowal, by demanding it herself of Helwyze. The moment seemed to have come, and both knew it; for he regarded her with the quick, piercing look which read her purpose before she could put it into words.

"You are right; yet Roger was the wronged one, and the others deserved to suffer."

"They did; but Hester's suffering ennobled her, because nobly borne; Dimmesdale's destroyed him, because he paltered weakly with his conscience. Roger let his wrong turn him from a man into a devil, and deserves the contempt and horror he rouses in us. The keeping of the secret makes the romance; the confession of it is the moral, showing how falsehood can ruin a life, and truth only save it at the last."

"Never have a secret, Gladys: they are hard masters, whom we hate, yet dare not rebel against."

His accent of sad sincerity seemed to clear the way for her, and she spoke out, briefly and bravely,—

"Sir, *you* dare any thing! Tell me what it is which makes Felix obey you against his will. He owns it, but will not speak till you consent. Tell me, I beseech you!"

"Could you bear it?" he asked, admiring her courage, yet doubtful of the wisdom of purchasing a moment's satisfaction at such a cost; for, though he could cast down her idol, he dared not set up another in its place.

"Try me!" she cried: "nothing can lessen my love, and doubt afflicts me more than the hardest truth."

"I fear not: with you love and respect go hand in hand, and some sins you would find very hard to pardon."

Involuntarily Gladys shrunk a little, and her eye questioned his inscrutable face, as she answered slowly, thinking only of her husband,—

"Something very mean and false *would* be hard to forgive; but not some youthful fault, some shame borne for others, or even a crime, if a very human emotion, a generous but mistaken motive, led to it."

"Then this secret is better left untold; for it would try you sorely to know that Felix *had* been guilty of the fault you find harder to forgive than a crime,—deceit. Wait a little, till you are accustomed to the thought, then you shall have the facts; and pity, even while you must despise, him."

While he spoke, Gladys sat like one nerving herself to receive a blow; but at the last words she suddenly put up her hand as if to arrest it, saying, hurriedly,—

"No! do not tell me; I cannot bear it yet, nor from you. He shall tell me; it will be easier so, and less like treachery. O sir," she added, in a passionately pleading tone, "use mercifully whatever bitter knowledge you possess! Remember how young he is, how neglected as a boy, how tempted he may have been; and deal generously, honorably with him,—and with me."

Her voice broke there. She spread her hands before her eyes, and fled out of the room, as if in his face she read a more disastrous confession than any Felix could ever make. Helwyze stood motionless, looking as he looked the night she spoke more frankly but less forcibly: and when she vanished, he stole away to his own room, as he stole then; only now his usually colorless cheek burned with a fiery flush, and his hand went involuntarily to his breast, as if, like Dimmesdale, he carried an invisible scarlet letter branded there.

Jo's Boys *(1886), published two years before her death, was Louisa May Alcott's last novel and the only one to be completed in the 1880s. Increasingly hampered by ill health, as well as by family responsibilities, she found the book difficult to write, and in her preface, she apologizes for its lack of liveliness. Yet it is actually one of her more interesting juvenile novels and important if for no other reason than that it provides readers with a last view of the now extended March family, including Alcott's most memorable creation, Jo. In* Little Men *(1871), the first sequel to* Little Women, *Alcott depicts life at Plumfield, the boarding school for boys founded by Jo and Professor Bhaer on the former estate of Jo's Aunt March. Jo, in this book, has given up writing altogether and is content to mother a dozen boys, including two of her own, and mentor the school's two girls, including Meg's daughter, Daisy. The novel is episodic, tracing the development of several of the children over the course of a year. It tends to focus, however, on two problem inmates of the school and their relationships with Jo: "Naughty Nan," a tomboy who aspires to be a doctor, resembles the young Jo in her determination to do everything her male peers do; Dan, the oldest boy, is a disruptive force and is never fully assimilated into Plumfield. Jo's championing of these two, often in opposition to Professor Bhaer, suggests the tensions in their marriage and the limitations of Plumfield, which some scholars have seen as representing Alcott's utopian vision and a feminist revision of her father's Fruitlands. Jo's poignant relationship with Laurie, the school's principal benefactor, further hints at a lack of complete fulfillment in Jo's life.*

In Jo's Boys, *published fifteen years later, we find that Jo has become a popular writer of children's books, that Laurence College now flourishes on the Plumfield campus, and that the widowed Meg, Laurie and Amy, and their children all live there, the Laurences in their elegant home, Parnassus. Nan, an ardent feminist, is studying medicine, Dan is seeking his fortune out West, Meg's younger daughter, Josie, is determined to become an actress, and Amy's daughter, Bess, is a talented sculptor. In the following pair of chapters from Alcott's last novel, we encounter two of her most characteristic scenes: amateur theatricals and "a league of sisters." In chapter 14, "Plays at Plumfield," Jo and Laurie collaborate on a play in which Meg and Josie win the approbation of a celebrated actress in the audience, Miss Cameron. But although Meg happily submerges her own theatrical triumph in that of her daughter, Jo cannot help yearning for the limelight of a wider stage. And in his tableaux "The Owlsdark Marbles," Laurie hints at the marital discord created by Jo's unfulfilled longings. Chapter 17, "Among the Maids," on the other hand, finds Jo in her element, leading discussions of literature, alternatives to marriage, and women's rights and reforms. Lady Ambercrombie's parting remark about "Penelope among her maids," however, seems an ambiguous comment on Jo's consciousness-raising circle, for although Homer's Penelope did succeed in outwitting her suitors and thus can be viewed as a model of female resistance, her labor was that of endless doing and undoing, her role the gendered one of passive waiting. In* Jo's Boys, *Jo's boys go west, to Europe, and to sea, but Jo and her girls remain at home. In the final chapter of the book, Alcott characterizes herself as a "weary historian" tempted to have an earthquake "engulf Plumfield and its environs . . . in the bowels of the earth." Instead, her final sentence reads like a valediction: "Let the music stop, the lights die out, and the curtain fall forever on the March family."*

Jo's Boys

CHAPTER XIV

Plays at Plumfield

As it is as impossible for the humble historian of the March family to write a story without theatricals in it as for our dear Miss Yonge to get on with less than twelve or fourteen children in her interesting tales, we will accept the fact, and at once cheer ourselves after the last afflicting events, by proceeding to the Christmas plays at Plumfield; for they influence the fate of several of our characters and cannot well be skipped.

When the college was built Mr. Laurie added a charming little theater, which not only served for plays, but declamations, lectures, and concerts. The drop curtain displayed Apollo with the Muses grouped about him; and as a compliment to the donor of the hall the artist had given the god a decided resemblance to our friend, which was considered a superb joke by everyone else. Home talent furnished stars, stock company, orchestra, and scene painter; and astonishing performances were given on this pretty little stage.

Mrs. Jo had been trying for some time to produce a play which should be an improvement upon the adaptations from the French then in vogue, curious mixtures of fine toilettes, false sentiment, and feeble wit, with no touch of nature to redeem them. It was easy to plan plays full of noble speeches and thrilling situations, but very hard to write them; so she contented herself with a few scenes of humble life in which the comic and pathetic were mingled; and as she fitted her characters to her actors, she hoped the little venture would prove that truth and simplicity had not entirely lost their power to charm. Mr. Laurie helped her, and they called themselves Beaumont and Fletcher, enjoying their joint labor very much; for Beaumont's knowledge of dramatic art was of great use in curbing Fletcher's too-aspiring pen, and they flattered themselves that they had produced a neat and effective bit of work as an experiment.

All was ready now; and Christmas Day was much enlivened by last rehearsals, the panics of timid actors, the scramble for forgotten properties, and the decoration of the theater. Evergreen and holly from the woods, blooming plants from the hothouse on Parnassus, and the flags of all nations made it very gay that night in honor of the guests who were coming, chief among them Miss Cameron, who kept her promise faithfully. The orchestra tuned their instruments with unusual care, the scene shifters set their stage with lavish elegance, the prompter heroically took his seat in the stifling nook provided for him, and the actors dressed with trembling hands that dropped the pins, and perspiring brows whereon the powder wouldn't stick. Beaumont and Fletcher were everywhere, feeling that their literary reputation was at stake; for sundry friendly critics were invited, and reporters, like mosquitoes, cannot be excluded from any earthly scene, be it a great man's deathbed or a dime museum.

"Has she come?" was the question asked by every tongue behind the curtain; and when Tom, who played an old man, endangered his respectable legs among the footlights to peep, announced that he saw Miss Cameron's handsome head in the place of honor, a thrill pervaded the entire company, and Josie declared with an excited gasp that she was going to have stage fright for the first time in her life.

"I'll shake you if you do," said Mrs. Jo, who was in such a wild state of dishevelment with her varied labors that she might have gone on as Madge Wildfire, without an additional rag or crazy elflock.

"You'll have time to get your wits together while we do our piece. We are old stagers and calm as clocks," answered Demi, with a nod toward Alice, ready in her pretty dress and all her properties at hand.

But both clocks were going rather faster than usual as heightened color, brilliant eyes, and a certain flutter under the laces and velvet coat betrayed. They were to open the entertainment with a gay little piece which they had played before and did remarkably well. Alice was a tall girl, with dark hair and eyes, and a face which intelligence, health, and a happy heart made beautiful. She was looking her best now, for the brocades, plumes, and powder of the Marquise became her stately figure; and Demi in his court suit, with sword, three-cornered hat, and white wig, made as gallant a Baron as one would wish to see. Josie was the maid, and looked her part to the life, being as pretty, pert, and inquisitive as any French soubrette. These three were all the characters; and the success of the piece depended on the spirit and skill with which the quickly changing moods of the quarrelsome lovers were given, their witty speeches made to tell, and the byplay suited to the courtly period in which the scene was laid.

Few would have recognized sober John and studious Alice in the dashing gentleman and coquettish lady who kept the audience laughing at their caprices; while they enjoyed the brilliant costumes, and admired the ease and grace of the young actors. Josie was a prominent figure in the plot, as she listened at keyholes, peeped into notes, and popped in and out at all the most inopportune moments, with her nose in the air, her hands in her apron pockets, and curiosity pervading her little figure from the topmost bow of her jaunty cap to the red heels of her slippers. All went smoothly; and the capricious Marquise, after tormenting the devoted Baron to her heart's content, owned herself conquered in the war of wits, and was just offering the hand he had fairly won when a crash startled them and a heavily decorated side scene swayed forward, ready to fall upon Alice. Demi saw it, and sprang before her to catch and hold it up, standing like a modern Samson with the wall of a house on his back. The danger was over in a moment, and he was about to utter his last speech when the excited young scene shifter, who had flown up a ladder to repair the damage, leaned over to whisper, "All right," and release Demi from his spread-eagle attitude; as he did so, a hammer slipped out of his pocket, to fall upon the upturned face below, inflicting a smart blow and literally knocking the Baron's part out of his head.

"A quick curtain" robbed the audience of a pretty little scene not down on the bill; for the Marquise flew to stanch the blood with a cry of alarm: "Oh! John, you are hurt! Lean on me"—which John gladly did for a moment, being a trifle dazed, yet quite able to enjoy the tender touch of the hands busied about him and the anxiety of the face so near his own; for both told him something which he would have considered cheaply won by a rain of hammers and the fall of the whole college on his head.

Nan was on the spot in a moment with the case that never left her pocket; and the wound was neatly plastered up by the time Mrs. Jo arrived, demanding tragically:

"Is he too much hurt to go on again? If he is, my play is lost!"

"I'm all the fitter for it, aunty; for here's a real instead of a painted wound. I'll be ready; don't worry about me." And catching up his wig, Demi was off, with only a very eloquent look of thanks to the Marquise, who had spoilt her gloves for his sake, but did not seem to mind it at all, though they reached above her elbows, and were most expensive.

"How are your nerves, Fletcher?" asked Mr. Laurie as they stood together during the breathless minute before the last bell rings.

"About as calm as yours, Beaumont," answered Mrs. Jo, gesticulating wildly to Mrs. Meg to set her cap straight.

"Bear up, partner! I'll stand by you whatever comes!"

"I feel that it ought to go; for, though it's a mere trifle, a good deal of honest work and truth have gone into it. Doesn't Meg look the picture of a dear old country woman?"

She certainly did, as she sat in the farmhouse kitchen by a cheery fire, rocking a cradle and darning stockings as if she had done nothing else all her life. Gray hair, skillfully drawn lines on the forehead, and a plain gown, with cap, little shawl, and check apron, changed her into a comfortable, motherly creature who found favor the moment the curtain went up and discovered her rocking, darning, and crooning an old song. In a short soliloquy about Sam, her boy, who wanted to enlist; Dolly, her discontented little daughter, who longed for city ease and pleasures; and poor "Elizy," who had married badly and came home to die, bequeathing her baby to her mother, lest its bad father should claim it, the little story was very simply opened, and made effective by the real boiling of the kettle on the crane, the ticking of a tall clock, and the appearance of a pair of blue worsted shoes which waved fitfully in the air to the soft babble of a baby's voice. Those shapeless little shoes won the first applause; and Mr. Laurie, forgetting elegance in satisfaction, whispered to his coadjutor:

"I thought the baby would fetch them!"

"If the dear thing won't squall in the wrong place, we are saved. But it is risky. Be ready to catch it if all Meg's cuddlings prove in vain," answered Mrs. Jo, adding, with a clutch at Mr. Laurie's arm as a haggard face appeared at the window:

"Here's Demi! I hope no one will recognize him when he comes on as the son. I'll never forgive you for not doing the villain yourself."

"Can't run the thing and act too. He's capitally made up, and likes a bit of melodrama."

"This scene ought to have come later; but I wanted to show that the mother was the heroine as soon as possible. I'm tired of lovesick girls and runaway wives. We'll prove that there's romance in old women also. Now he's coming!"

And in slouched a degraded-looking man, shabby, unshaven, and evil-eyed, trying to assume a masterful air as he dismayed the tranquil old woman by demanding his child. A powerful scene followed; and Mrs. Meg surprised even those who knew her best by the homely dignity with which she at first met the man she dreaded; then, as he brutally pressed his claim, she pleaded with trembling voice and hands to keep the little creature she had promised the dying mother to protect; and when he turned to take it by force, quite a thrill went through the house as the old woman sprang to snatch it from the cradle, and holding it close, defied him in God's name to tear it from that sacred refuge. It was really well done; and the round of applause that greeted the fine tableau of the indignant old woman, the rosy, blinking baby clinging to her neck, and the daunted man who dared not execute his evil purpose with such a defender for helpless innocence, told the excited authors that their first scene was a hit.

The second was quieter, and introduced Josie as a bonny country lass setting the supper table in a bad humor. The pettish way in which she slapped down the plates, hustled the cups, and cut the big brown loaf, as she related her girlish trials and ambitions, was capital. Mrs. Jo kept her eye on Miss Cameron, and saw her nod approval several times at some natural tone or gesture, some good bit of by-play, or a quick change of expression in the young face, which was as variable as an April day. Her struggle with the toasting fork made much merriment; so did her contempt for the brown sugar, and the relish with which she sweetened her irksome duties by eating it; and when she sat, like Cinderella, on the hearth, tearfully watching the flames dance on the homely room, a girlish voice was heard to exclaim impulsively:

"Poor little thing! She ought to have *some* fun!"

The old woman enters; and mother and daughter have a pretty scene, in which the latter coaxes and threatens, kisses and cries, till she wins the reluctant consent of the former to visit a rich relation in the city; and from being a little thundercloud Dolly becomes bewitchingly gay and good, as soon as her willful wish is granted. The poor old soul has hardly recovered from this trial when the son enters, in army blue, tells he has enlisted, and must go. That is a hard blow; but the patriotic mother bears it well, and not till the thoughtless young folks have hastened away to tell their good news elsewhere does she break down. Then the country kitchen becomes pathetic, as the old mother sits alone mourning over her children, till the gray head is hidden in the hands as she kneels down by the cradle to weep and pray, with only Baby to comfort her fond and faithful heart.

Sniffs were audible all through the latter part of this scene; and when the curtain fell, people were so busy wiping their eyes that for a moment they forgot to applaud. That silent moment was more flattering than noise; and as Mrs. Jo wiped the real tears off her sister's face, she said as solemnly as an unconscious dab of rouge on her own nose permitted:

"Meg, you have saved my play! Oh, why aren't you a real actress, and I a real playwright?"

"Don't gush now, dear, but help me dress Josie; she's in such a quiver of excitement I can't manage her, and this is her best scene, you know."

So it was; for her aunt had written it especially for her, and little Jo was happy in a gorgeous dress, with a train long enough to satisfy her wildest dreams. The rich relation's parlor was in festival array, and the country cousin sails in, looking back at her sweeping flounces with such artless rapture that no one had the heart to laugh at the pretty jay in borrowed plumes. She has confidences with herself in the mirror, from which it is made evident that she has discovered all is not gold that glitters, and has found greater temptations than those a girlish love of pleasure, luxury, and flattery bring her. She is sought by a rich lover; but her honest heart resists the allurements he offers and in its innocent perplexity wishes "mother" was there to comfort and counsel.

A gay little dance, in which Dora, Nan, Bess, and several of the boys took part, made a good background for the humble figure of the old woman in her widow's bonnet, rusty shawl, big umbrella, and basket. Her naïve astonishment, as she surveys the spectacle, feels the curtains, and smoothes her old gloves during the moment she remains unseen, was very good; but Josie's unaffected start when she sees her, and the cry, "Why, there's mother!" was such a hearty little bit of nature, it hardly needed the impatient tripping over her train as she ran into the arms that seemed now to be her nearest refuge.

The lover plays his part; and ripples of merriment greeted the old woman's searching questions and blunt answers during the interview which shows the girl how shallow his love is, and how near she has been to ruining her life as bitterly as poor Elizy did. She gives her answer frankly, and when they are alone, looks from her own bedizened self to the shabby dress, work-worn hands, and tender face, crying with a repentant sob and kiss, "Take me home, mother, and keep me safe. I've had enough of this!"

"That will do you good, Maria; don't forget it," said one lady to her daughter as the curtain went down; and the girl answered, "Well, I'm sure I don't see why it's touching; but it is," as she spread her lace handkerchief to dry.

Tom and Nan came out strong in the next scene; for it was a ward in an army hospital, and surgeon and nurse went from bed to bed, feeling pulses, administering doses, and hearing complaints with an energy and gravity which convulsed the audience. The tragic element, never far from the comic at such times and places, came in when, while they bandaged an arm, the doctor told the nurse about an old woman who was searching through the hospital for her son, after days and nights on battlefields, through ambulances, and among scenes which would have killed most women.

"She will be here directly, and I dread her coming; for I'm afraid the poor lad who has just gone is her boy. I'd rather face a cannon than these brave women, with their hope and courage and great sorrow," says the surgeon.

"Ah, these poor mothers break my heart!" adds the nurse, wiping her eyes on her big apron; and with the words Mrs. Meg came in.

There was the same dress, the basket and umbrella, the rustic speech, the simple manners; but all were made pathetic by the terrible experience which had changed the tranquil old woman to that haggard figure with wild eyes, dusty feet, trembling hands, and an expression of mingled anguish, resolution, and despair which gave the homely figure a tragic dignity and power that touched all hearts. A few broken words told the story of her vain search, and then the sad quest began again. People held their breath as, led by the nurse, she went from bed to bed, showing in her face the alternations of hope, dread, and bitter disappointment as each was passed. On a narrow cot was a long figure covered with a sheet, and here she paused to lay one hand on her heart and one on her eyes, as if to gather courage to look at the nameless dead. Then she drew down the sheet, gave a long shivering sigh of relief, saying softly:

"Not my son, thank God, but some mother's boy." And stooping down, she kissed the cold forehead tenderly.

Somebody sobbed there, and Miss Cameron shook two tears out of her eyes, anxious to lose no look or gesture as the poor soul, nearly spent with the long strain, struggled on down the long line. But her search was happily ended; for, as if her voice had roused him from his feverish sleep, a gaunt, wild-eyed man sat up in his bed, and stretching his arms to her, cried in a voice that echoed through the room:

"Mother, mother! I knew you'd come to me!"

She did go to him, with a cry of love and joy that thrilled every listener, as she gathered him in her arms with the tears and prayers and blessing such as only a fond and faithful old mother could give.

The last scene was a cheerful contrast to this; for the country kitchen was bright with Christmas cheer, the wounded hero, with black patch and crutches well displayed, sat by the fire in the old chair whose familiar creak was soothing to his ear; pretty Dolly was stirring about, gaily trimming dresser, settle, high chimneypiece, and old-fashioned cradle with mistletoe and holly; while the mother rested beside her son, with that blessed baby on her knee. Refreshed by a nap and nourishment, this young actor now covered himself with glory by his ecstatic prancings, incoherent remarks to the audience, and vain attempts to get the footlights, as he blinked approvingly at these brilliant toys. It was good to see Mrs. Meg pat him on the back, cuddle the fat legs out of sight, and appease his vain longings with a lump of sugar, till Baby embraced her with a grateful ardor that brought him a round of applause all for his little self.

A sound of singing outside disturbs the happy family, and, after a carol in the snowy moonlight, a flock of neighbors troop in with Christmas gifts and greetings. Much byplay made this a lively picture; for Sam's sweetheart hovered round him with a tenderness the Marquise did not show the Baron; and Dolly had a pretty bit under the mistletoe with her rustic adorer, who looked so like Ham Peggotty in his cowhide boots, rough jacket, and dark beard and wig, that no one would have recognized Ted but for the long legs, which no extent of leather could disguise. It ended with a homely feast, brought by the guests; and as they sat round the table covered with doughnuts and cheese, pumpkin pie, and other country delicacies, Sam rises on his crutches to propose the first toast, and holding up his mug of cider, says, with a salute, and a choke in his voice, "Mother, God bless her!" All drink it standing, Dolly with her arm round the old woman's neck, as she hides her happy tears on her daughter's breast; while the irrepressible baby beat rapturously on the table with a spoon, and crowed audibly as the curtain went down.

They had it up again in a jiffy to get a last look at the group about that central figure, which was showered with bouquets, to the great delight of the infant Roscius; till a fat rosebud hit him on the nose, and produced the much-dreaded squall, which, fortunately, only added to the fun at that moment.

"Well, that will do for a beginning," said Beaumont, with a sigh of relief, as the curtain descended for the last time, and the actors scattered to dress for the closing piece.

"As an experiment, it is a success. Now we can venture to begin our great American drama," answered Mrs. Jo, full of satisfaction and grand ideas for the famous play—which, we may add, she did not write that year, owing to various dramatic events in her own family.

The Owlsdark Marbles closed the entertainment, and, being something new, proved amusing to this very indulgent audience. The gods and goddesses on Parnassus were displayed in full conclave; and, thanks to Mrs. Amy's skill in draping and posing, the white wigs and cotton-flannel robes were classically correct and graceful, though sundry modern additions somewhat marred the effect, while adding point to the showman's learned remarks. Mr. Laurie was Professor Owlsdark, in cap and gown; and, after a high-flown introduction, he proceeded to exhibit and explain his marbles. The first figure was a stately Minerva; but a second glance produced a laugh, for the words "Woman's Rights" adorned her shield, a scroll bearing the motto "Vote early and often" hung from the beak of the owl perched on her lance, and a tiny pestle and mortar ornamented her helmet. Attention was drawn to the firm mouth, the piercing eye, the awe-inspiring brow, of the strong-minded woman of antiquity, and some scathing remarks made upon the degeneracy of her modern sisters who failed to do their duty. Mercury came next, and was very fine in his airy attitude, though the winged legs quivered as it was difficult to keep the lively god in his place. His restless nature was dilated upon, his mischievous freaks alluded to, and a very bad character given to the immortal messenger boy; which delighted his friends, and caused the marble nose of the victim to curl visibly with scorn when derisive applause greeted a particularly hard hit. A charming little Hebe stood next, pouring nectar from a silver teapot into a blue china teacup. She also pointed a moral; for the Professor explained that the nectar of old was the beverage which cheers but does not inebriate, and regretted that the excessive devotion of American women to this classic brew proved so harmful, owing to the great development of brain their culture produced. A touch at modern servants, in contrast to this accomplished table-girl, made the statue's cheeks glow under the chalk, and brought her a hearty round as the audience recognized Dolly and the smart soubrette.

Jove in all his majesty followed, as he and his wife occupied the central pedestals in the half-circle of immortals. A splendid Jupiter, with hair well set up off the fine brow, ambrosial beard, silver thunderbolts in one hand and a well-worn ferule in the other. A large stuffed eagle from the museum stood at his feet; and the benign expression of his august countenance showed that he was in a good humor—as well he might be, for he was paid some handsome compliments upon his wise rule, the peaceful state of his kingdom, and the brood of all-accomplished Pallases that yearly issued from his mighty brain. Cheers greeted this and other pleasant words, and caused the thunderer to bow his thanks; for "Jove nods," as everyone knows, and flattery wins the heart of gods and men.

Mrs. Juno, with her peacocks, darning needle, pen, and cooking spoon, did not get off so easily; for the Professor was down on her with all manner of mirth-provoking accusations, criticisms, and insults even. He alluded to her domestic infelicity, her meddlesome disposition, sharp tongue, bad temper, and jealousy, closing, however, with a tribute to her skill in caring for the wounds and settling the quarrels of belligerent heroes, as well as her love for youths in Olympus and on earth. Gales of laughter greeted these hits, varied by hisses from some indignant boys, who would not bear, even in joke, any disrespect to dear Mother Bhaer, who, however, enjoyed it all immensely, as the twinkle in her eye and the irrepressible pucker of her lips betrayed.

A jolly Bacchus astride of his cask took Vulcan's place, and appeared to be very comfortable with a beer mug in one hand, a champagne bottle in the other, and a garland of grapes on his curly head. He was the text of a short temperance lecture, aimed directly at a row of smart young gentlemen who lined the walls of the auditorium. George Cole was seen to dodge behind a pillar at one point, Dolly nudged his neighbor at another, and there was laughter all along the line as the Professor glared at them through his big glasses, and dragged their bacchanalian orgies to the light and held them up to scorn.

Seeing the execution he had done, the learned man turned to the lovely Diana, who stood as white and still as the plaster stag beside her, with sandals, bow, and crescent; quite perfect, and altogether the best piece of statuary in the show. She was very tenderly treated by the paternal critic, who, merely alluding to her confirmed spinsterhood, fondness for athletic sports, and oracular powers, gave a graceful little exposition of true art and passed on to his last figure.

This was Apollo in full fig, his curls skillfully arranged to hide a well-whitened patch over the eye, his handsome legs correctly poised, and his gifted fingers about to draw divine music from the silvered gridiron which was his lyre. His divine attributes were described, as well as his little follies and failings, among which were his weakness for photography and flute playing, his attempts to run a newspaper, and his fondness for the society of the Muses; which latter slap produced giggles and blushes among the girl graduates, and much mirth among the stricken youths; for misery loves company, and after this they began to rally.

Then, with a ridiculous conclusion, the Professor bowed his thanks; and after several recalls the curtain fell, but not quickly enough to conceal Mercury, wildly waving his liberated legs, Hebe dropping her teapot, Bacchus taking a lively roll on his barrel, and Mrs. Juno rapping the impertinent Owlsdark on the head with Jove's ruler.

While the audience filed out to supper in the hall, the stage was a scene of dire confusion as gods and goddesses, farmers and barons, maids and carpenters, congratulated one another on the success of their labors. Assuming various costumes, actors and actresses soon joined their guests, to sip bounteous draughts of praise with their coffee, and cool their modest blushes with ice cream. Mrs. Meg was a proud and happy woman when Miss Cameron came to her as she sat by Josie, with Demi serving both, and said, so cordially that it was impossible to doubt the sincerity of her welcome words:

"Mrs. Brooke, I no longer wonder where your children get their talent. I make my compliments to the Baron, and next summer you must let me have little 'Dolly' as a pupil when we are at the beach."

One can easily imagine how this offer was received, as well as the friendly commendation bestowed by the same kind critic on the work of Beaumont and Fletcher, who hastened to explain that this trifle was only an attempt to make nature and art go hand in hand, with little help from fine writing or imposing scenery. Everybody was in the happiest mood, especially "little Dolly," who danced like a will-o'-the-wisp with light-footed Mercury, and Apollo as he promenaded with the Marquise on his arm, who seemed to have left her coquetry in the greenroom with her rouge.

When all was over, Mrs. Juno said to Jove, to whose arm she clung as they trudged home along the snowy paths, "Fritz dear, Christmas is a good time for new resolutions, and I've made one never to be impatient or fretful with my beloved husband again. I know I am, though you won't own it; but Laurie's fun had some truth in it, and I felt hit in a tender spot. Henceforth I am a model wife, else I don't deserve the dearest, best man ever born." And being in a dramatic mood, Mrs. Juno tenderly embraced her excellent Jove in the moonlight, to the great amusement of sundry lingerers behind them.

So all three plays might be considered successes, and that merry Christmas night a memorable one in the March family; for Demi got an unspoken question answered, Josie's fondest wish was granted, and, thanks to Professor Owlsdark's jest, Mrs. Jo made Professor Bhaer's busy life quite a bed of roses by the keeping of her resolution. A few days later she had her reward for this burst of virtue in Dan's letter, which set her fears at rest and made her very happy, though she was unable to tell him so, because he sent her no address.

CHAPTER XVII

Among the Maids

Although this story is about Jo's boys, her girls cannot be neglected, because they held a high place in this little republic, and especial care was taken to fit them to play their parts worthily in the great republic which offered them wider opportunities and more serious duties. To many the social influence was the better part of the training they received; for education is not confined to books, and the finest characters often graduate from no college, but make experience their master and life their book. Others cared only for the mental culture, and were in danger of overstudying, under the delusion which pervades New England that learning must be had at all costs, forgetting that health and real wisdom are better. A third class of ambitious girls hardly knew what they wanted, but were hungry for whatever could fit them to face the world and earn a living, being driven by necessity, the urgency of some half-unconscious talent, or the restlessness of strong young natures to break away from the narrow life which no longer satisfied.

At Plumfield all found something to help them; for the growing institution had not yet made its rules as fixed as the laws of the Medes and Persians, and believed so heartily in the right of all sexes, colors, creeds, and ranks to education that there was room for everyone who knocked, and a welcome to the shabby youths from upcountry, the eager girls from the West, the awkward freedman or woman from the South, or the well-born student whose poverty made this college a possibility when other doors were barred. There still was prejudice, ridicule, neglect in high places, and prophecies of failure to contend against; but the faculty was composed of cheerful, hopeful men and women who had seen greater reforms spring from smaller roots, and after stormy seasons blossom beautifully, to add prosperity and honor to the nation. So they worked on steadily and bided their time, full of increasing faith in their attempt as year after year their numbers grew, their plans succeeded, and the sense of usefulness in this most vital of all professions blessed them with its sweet rewards.

Among the various customs which had very naturally sprung up was one especially useful and interesting to "the girls," as the young women liked to be called. It all grew out of the old sewing hour still kept up by the three sisters long after the little workboxes had expanded into big baskets full of household mending. They were busy women, yet on Saturdays they tried to meet in one of the three sewing rooms; for even classic Parnassus had its nook where Mrs. Amy often sat among her servants, teaching them to make and mend, thereby giving them a respect for economy, since the rich lady did not scorn to darn her hose and sew on buttons. In these household retreats, with books and work, and their daughters by them, they read and sewed and talked in the sweet privacy that domestic women love and can make so helpful by a wise mixture of cooks and chemistry, table linen and theology, prosaic duties and good poetry.

Mrs. Meg was the first to propose enlarging this little circle; for as she went her motherly rounds among the young women she found a sad lack of order, skill, and industry in this branch of education. Latin, Greek, the higher mathematics, and science of all sorts prospered finely; but dust gathered on the workbaskets, frayed elbows went unheeded, and some of the blue stockings sadly needed mending. Anxious lest the usual sneer at learned women should apply to "our girls," she gently lured two or three of the most untidy to her house, and made the hour so pleasant, the lesson so kindly, that they took the hint, were grateful for the favor, and asked to come again. Others soon begged to make the detested weekly duty lighter by joining the party, and soon it was a privilege so much desired that the old museum was refitted with sewing machines, tables, rocking chairs, and a cheerful fireplace, so that, rain or shine, the needles might go on undisturbed.

Here Mrs. Meg was in her glory, and stood wielding her big shears like a queen as she cut out white work, fitted dresses, and directed Daisy, her special aide, about the trimming of hats, and completing the lace and ribbon trifles which add grace to the simplest costume and save poor or busy girls so much money and time. Mrs. Amy contributed taste, and decided the great question of colors and complexions; for few women, even the most learned, are without that desire to look well which makes many a plain face comely, as well as many a pretty one ugly for want of skill and knowledge of the fitness of things. She also took her turn to provide books for the readings, and as art was her forte she gave them selections from Ruskin, Hamerton, and Mrs. Jameson, who is never old. Bess read these aloud as her contribution, and Josie took her turn at the romances, poetry, and plays her uncles recommended. Mrs. Jo gave little lectures on health, religion, politics, and the various questions in which all should be interested, with copious extracts from Miss Cobbe's *Duties of Women*, Miss Brackett's *Education of American Girls*, Mrs. Duffy's *No Sex in Education*, Mrs. Woolson's *Dress Reform*, and many of the other excellent books wise women write for their sisters, now that they are waking up and asking, "What shall we do?"

It was curious to see the prejudices melt away as ignorance was enlightened, indifference change to interest, and intelligent minds set thinking, while quick wits and lively tongues added spice to the discussions which inevitably followed. So the feet that wore the neatly mended hose carried wiser heads than before, the pretty gowns covered hearts warmed with higher purposes, and the hands that dropped the thimbles for pens, lexicons, and celestial globes were better fitted for life's work, whether to rock cradles, tend the sick, or help on the great work of the world.

One day a brisk discussion arose concerning careers for women. Mrs. Jo had read something on the subject and asked each of the dozen girls sitting about the room, what she intended to do on leaving college. The answers were as usual: "I shall teach, help mother, study medicine, art," etc.; but nearly all ended with, "Till I marry."

"But if you don't marry, what then?" asked Mrs. Jo, feeling like a girl again as she listened to the answers, and watched the thoughtful, gay, or eager faces.

"Be old maids, I suppose. Horrid, but inevitable, since there are so many superfluous women," answered a lively lass, too pretty to fear single blessedness unless she chose it.

"It is well to consider that fact, and fit yourselves to be useful, not superfluous women. That class, by the way, is largely made up of widows, I find; so don't consider it a slur on maidenhood."

"That's a comfort! Old maids aren't sneered at half as much as they used to be, since some of them have grown famous and proved that woman isn't a half but a whole human being, and can stand alone."

"Don't like it all the same. We can't all be like Miss Cobbe, Miss Nightingale, Miss Phelps, and the rest. So what can we do but sit in a corner and look on?" asked a plain girl with a dissatisfied expression.

"Cultivate cheerfulness and content, if nothing else. But there are so many little odd jobs waiting to be done that nobody need 'sit idle and look on,' unless she chooses," said Mrs. Meg, with a smile, laying on the girl's head the new hat she had just trimmed.

"Thank you very much. Yes, Mrs. Brooke, I see; it's a little job, but it makes me neat and happy—and grateful," she added, looking up with brighter eyes as she accepted the labor of love and the lesson as sweetly as they were given.

"One of the best and most beloved women I know has been doing odd jobs for the Lord for years, and will keep at it till her dear hands are folded in her coffin. All sorts of things she does—picks up neglected children and puts them in safe homes, saves lost girls, nurses poor women in trouble, sews, knits, trots, begs, works for the poor day after day with no reward but the thanks of the needy, the love and honor of the rich who make St. Matilda their almoner. That's a life worth living; and I think that quiet little woman will get a higher seat in Heaven than many of those of whom the world has heard."

"I know it's lovely, Mrs. Bhaer; but it's dull for young folks. We do want a little fun before we buckle to," said a western girl with a wide-awake face.

"Have your fun, my dear; but if you must earn your bread, try to make it sweet with cheerfulness, not bitter with the daily regret that it isn't cake. I used to think mine was a very hard fate because I had to amuse a somewhat fretful old lady; but the books I read in that lonely library have been of immense use to me since, and the dear old soul bequeathed me Plumfield for my 'cheerful service and affectionate care.' I didn't deserve it, but I did use to try to be jolly and kind, and get as much honey out of duty as I could, thanks to my dear mother's help and advice."

"Gracious! If I could earn a place like this I'd sing all day and be an angel; but you have to take your chance, and get nothing for your pains, perhaps. I never do," said the Westerner, who had a hard time with small means and large aspirations.

"Don't do it for the reward; but be sure it will come, though not in the shape you expect. I worked hard for fame and money one winter; but I got neither, and was much disappointed. A year afterward I found I had earned two prizes: skill with my pen, and—Professor Bhaer."

Mrs. Jo's laugh was echoed blithely by the girls, who liked to have these conversations enlivened by illustrations from life.

"You are a very lucky woman," began the discontented damsel, whose soul soared above new hats, welcome as they were, but did not quite know where to steer.

"Yet her name used to be 'Luckless Jo,' and she never had what she wanted till she had given up hoping for it," said Mrs. Meg.

"I'll give up hoping, then, right away, and see if my wishes will come. I only want to help my folks, and get a good school."

"Take this proverb for your guide: 'Get the distaff ready, and the Lord will send the flax,' " answered Mrs. Jo.

"We'd better all do that, if we are to be spinsters," said the pretty one, adding gaily, "I think I should like it, on the whole—they are so independent. My aunt Jenny can do just what she likes and ask no one's leave; but ma has to consult pa about everything. Yes, I'll give you my chance, Sally, and be a 'superfluum,' as Mr. Plock says."

"You'll be one of the first to go into bondage, see if you aren't. Much obliged, all the same."

"Well, I'll get my distaff ready, and take whatever flax the Fates send—single, or double-twisted, as the powers please."

"That is the right spirit, Nelly. Keep it up, and see how happy life will be with a brave heart, a willing hand, and plenty to do."

"No one objects to plenty of domestic work or fashionable pleasure, I find, but the minute we begin to study, people tell us we can't bear it, and warn us to be very careful. I've tried the other things, and got so tired I came to college; though my people predict nervous exhaustion and an early death. Do you think there is any danger?" asked a stately girl, with an anxious glance at the blooming face reflected in the mirror opposite.

"Are you stronger or weaker than when you came two years ago, Miss Winthrop?"

"Stronger in body, and much happier in mind. I think I was dying of ennui; but the doctors called it inherited delicacy of constitution. That is why mamma is so anxious, and I wish not to go too fast."

"Don't worry, my dear; that active brain of yours was starving for good food; it has a plenty now, and plain living suits you better than luxury and dissipation. It is all nonsense about girls not being able to study as well as boys. Neither can bear cramming; but with proper care both are better for it; so enjoy the life your instinct led you to, and we will prove that wise headwork is a better cure for that sort of delicacy than tonics, and novels on the sofa, where far too many of our girls go to wreck nowadays. They burn the candle at both ends; and when they break down they blame the books, not the balls."

"Dr. Nan was telling me about a patient of hers who thought she had heart complaint till Nan made her take off her corsets, stopped her coffee and dancing all night, and made her eat, sleep, walk, and live regularly for a time; and now she's a brilliant cure. Common sense versus custom, Nan said."

"I've had no headaches since I came here, and can do twice as much studying as I did at home. It's the air, I think, and the fun of going ahead of the boys," said another girl, tapping her big forehead with her thimble, as if the lively brain inside was in good working order and enjoyed the daily gymnastics she gave it.

"Quality, not quantity, wins the day, you know. Our brains may be smaller, but I don't see that they fall short of what is required of them; and if I'm not mistaken, the largest-headed man in our class is the dullest," said Nelly, with a solemn air which produced a gale of merriment; for all knew that the young Goliath she mentioned had been metaphorically slain by this quick-witted David on many a battlefield, to the great disgust of himself and mates.

"Mrs. Brooke, do I gauge on the right or the wrong side?" asked the best Greek scholar of her class, eyeing a black silk apron with a lost expression.

"The right, Miss Pierson; and leave a space between the tucks; it looks prettier so."

"I'll never make another; but it will save my dresses from inkstains, so I'm glad I've got it." The erudite Miss Pierson labored on, finding it a harder task than any Greek root she ever dug up.

"We paper stainers must learn how to make shields, or we are lost. I'll give you a pattern of the pinafore I used to wear in my 'blood-and-thunder days,' as we call them," said Mrs. Jo, trying to remember what became of the old tin kitchen which used to hold her works.

"Speaking of writers reminds me that my ambition is to be a George Eliot, and thrill the world! It must be so splendid to know that one has such power, and to hear people own that one possesses a 'masculine intellect'! I don't care for most women's novels, but hers are immense; don't you think so, Mrs. Bhaer?" asked the girl with the big forehead, and torn braid on her skirt.

"Yes; but they don't thrill me as little Charlotte Brontë's books do.

The brain is there, but the heart seems left out. I admire, but I don't love George Eliot; and her life is far sadder to me than Miss Brontë's, because, in spite of the genius, love, and fame, she missed the light without which no soul is truly great, good, or happy."

"Yes'm, I know; but still it's so romantic and sort of new and mysterious, and she *was* great in one sense. Her nerves and dyspepsia do rather destroy the illusion; but I adore famous people and mean to go and see all I can scare up in London someday."

"You will find some of the best of them busy about just the work I recommend to you; and if you want to see a great lady, I'll tell you that Mrs. Laurence means to bring one here today. Lady Ambercrombie is lunching with her, and after seeing the college is to call on us. She especially wanted to see our sewing school, as she is interested in things of this sort, and gets them up at home."

"Bless me! I always imagined lords and ladies did nothing but ride round in a coach and six, go to balls, and be presented to the Queen in cocked hats and trains and feathers," exclaimed an artless young person from the wilds of Maine, whither an illustrated paper occasionally wandered.

"Not at all; Lord Ambercrombie is over here studying up our American prison system, and my lady is busy with the schools—both very highborn, but the simplest and most sensible people I've met this long time. They are neither of them young nor handsome, and dress very plainly; so don't expect anything splendid. Mr. Laurence was telling me last night about a friend of his who met my lord in the hall, and owing to a rough greatcoat and a red face, mistook him for a coachman, and said, 'Now, my man, what do you want here?' Lord Ambercrombie mildly mentioned who he was, and that he had come to dinner. And the poor host was much afflicted, saying afterward, 'Why didn't he wear his stars and garters? Then a fellow would know he was a lord.' "

The girls laughed again, and a general rustle betrayed that each was prinking a bit before the titled guest arrived. Even Mrs. Jo settled her collar, and Mrs. Meg felt if her cap was right, while Bess shook out her curls, and Josie boldly consulted the glass; for they were women, in spite of philosophy and philanthropy.

"Shall we all rise?" asked one girl, deeply impressed by the impending honor.

"It would be courteous."

"Shall we shake hands?"

"No, I'll present you en masse, and your pleasant faces will be introduction enough."

"I wish I'd worn my best dress. Ought to have told us," whispered Sally.

"Won't my folks be surprised when I tell them we have had a real lady to call on us?" said another.

"Don't look as if you'd never seen a gentlewoman before, Milly. We are not all fresh from the wilderness," added the stately damsel who, having *Mayflower* ancestors, felt that she was the equal of all the crowned heads of Europe.

"Hush, she's coming! Oh, my heart, what a bonnet!" cried the gay girl in a stage whisper; and every eye was demurely fixed upon the busy hands as the door opened to admit Mrs. Laurence and her guest.

It *was* rather a shock to find, after the general introduction was over, that this daughter of a hundred earls was a stout lady in a plain gown, and a rather weather-beaten bonnet, with a bag of papers in one hand and a notebook in the other. But the face was full of benevolence, the sonorous voice very kind, the genial manners very winning, and about the whole person an indescribable air of high breeding which made beauty of no consequence, costume soon forgotten, and the moment memorable to the keen-eyed girls whom nothing escaped.

A little chat about the rise, growth, and success of this particular class, and then Mrs. Jo led the conversation to the English lady's work, anxious to show her pupils how rank dignifies labor and charity blesses wealth.

It was good for these girls to hear of the evening schools supported and taught by women whom they knew and honored; of Miss Cobbe's eloquent protest winning the protection of the law for abused wives; Mrs. Butler saving the lost; Mrs. Taylor, who devoted one room in her historic house to a library for her servants; Lord Shaftesbury, busy with his new tenement houses in the slums of London; of prison reforms; and all the brave work being done in God's name by the rich and great for the humble and the poor. It impressed them more than many quiet home lectures would have done and roused an ambition to help when their time should come, well knowing that even in glorious America there is still plenty to be done before she is what she should be—truly just, and free, and great. They were also quick to see that Lady Ambercrombie treated all there as her equals, from stately Mrs. Laurence to little Josie, taking notes of everything and privately resolving to have some thick-soled English boots as soon as possible. No one would have guessed that she had a big house in London, a castle in Wales, and a grand country seat in Scotland, as she spoke of Parnassus with admiration, Plumfield as a "dear old home," and the college as an honor to all concerned in it. At that, of course, every head went up a little, and when my lady left every hand was ready for the hearty shake the noble Englishwoman gave them, with words they long remembered:

"I am very pleased to see this much-neglected branch of a woman's education so well conducted here and I have to thank me friend Mrs. Laurence for one of the most charming pictures I've seen in America—Penelope among her maids."

A group of smiling faces watched the stout boots trudge away, respectful glances followed the shabby bonnet till it was out of sight, and the girls felt a truer respect for their titled guest than if she had come in the coach and six, with all her diamonds on.

"I feel better about the 'odd jobs' now. I only wish I could do them as well as Lady Ambercrombie does," said one.

"I thanked my stars my buttonholes were nice, for she looked at them and said, 'Quite workmanlike, upon my word,' " added another, feeling that her gingham gown had come to honor.

"Her manners were as sweet and kind as Mrs. Brooke's. Not a bit stiff or condescending, as I expected. I see now what you meant, Mrs. Bhaer, when you said once that well-bred people were the same all the world over."

Mrs. Meg bowed her thanks for the compliment, and Mrs. Bhaer said:

"I know them when I see them, but never shall be a model of deportment myself. I'm glad you enjoyed the little visit. Now, if you young people don't want England to get ahead of us in many ways, you must bestir yourselves and keep abreast; for our sisters are in earnest, you see, and don't waste time worrying about their sphere, but make it wherever duty calls them."

"We will do our best, ma'am," answered the girls heartily, and trooped away with their workbaskets, feeling that though they might never be Harriet Martineaus, Elizabeth Brownings, or George Eliots, they might become noble, useful, and independent women, and earn for themselves some sweet title from the grateful lips of the poor, better than any a queen could bestow.

PART III

MEMOIRS, JOURNALS, AND LETTERS

As indicated in the headnotes to other selections, much of Louisa May Alcott's fiction was autobiographical or at least based on her own experience. A chapter of her novella "Diana and Persis" (not published in her lifetime) consists entirely of her sister May's letters presented as those of Persis, one of the two artist heroines. The distinction between fact and fiction, often blurred in an author's work, is especially problematical in Alcott's case. In fact, the editors of Alcott's Selected Fiction *offer three memoirs in that volume, among them the selection that follows, "Transcendental Wild Oats." But though these editors perhaps rightly contend that " 'Transcendental Wild Oats' turns a disturbing, tragic experience into a humorous satire that ends in uplifting thought" (xliii), readers can nonetheless sense, beneath the burlesque treatment of the Fruitlands experiment, the real hardship and pain the family, including ten-year-old Louisa, endured. Would we be able to appreciate the full pathos of Louisa's Fruitlands diary entries if we did not also have the adult perspective offered by "Transcendental Wild Oats"? The editors of Selected Fiction (as well as Alcott's journals and letters) argue that her "character and life can be reconstructed far more accurately from letters and journals than from her fiction" (xlii), but because her father insisted that she and her sisters keep journals, and that these journals be open to parental scrutiny, she began almost immediately to construct in them a public persona. While the journals and letters may give us a more accurate account of the details of her life, the fiction may well have provided her, as theatricals provided her heroines, with a safer medium for expressing psychic truths (compare, for example, her Georgetown journal, the basis for Hospital Sketches, with her story "My Contraband," which also derives from her nursing experience).*

Perhaps because Alcott's journal writing began as a kind of command performance (see the note from her mother inscribed in the Fruitlands journal entries or her May 1850 entry), it tapered off as her fame and its demands grew. After the success of Little Women, *Alcott becomes increasingly terse and despondent in her journals (we can see the beginning of this process in her April 1869 entry, written after the completion of* Little Women, *part 2). Although she carried on a vigorous correspondence until shortly before her death, her journal dwindles into a succession of one-line and even single-word entries, mostly about the state of her health. Thus the journal entries reprinted here consist mainly of early ones. In the Boston journal entries, Alcott chides herself for "moods," lists her favorite books and authors (including those most frequently alluded to in her fiction), records her earnings, whether from stories or from stitching, and, years later, adds a cryptic gloss. In the entries for the late 1850s and early 1860s, Alcott describes many of the events immortalized in* Little Women, *including her sister Elizabeth's illness and death, her sister Anna's marriage, and the writing of her first published novel,* Moods. *She also describes the outbreak of the war and her family's intimacy with the John Browns. The Georgetown journal reveals how in one crucial instance she radically transformed her experience in writing* Little Women*: Alcott, not her father, goes to the war, falls ill, and has to be retrieved; unlike Jo, who heroically sells her hair, Alcott loses it to illness. Although a later entry claims "we really lived most of it," other entries enable us to see that Alcott lived more of it than Jo did.*

Unlike the sampling of journal entries, the letters reprinted here represent Alcott's entire life, but the majority were written after she became famous and a number of them were published in her lifetime. Early letters to her mother, father, and sister Anna reveal her family loyalty, youthful exuberance, desire for independence, and literary ambition. Three letters of the 1860s indicate her response to the reception of Moods. *To read Alcott's journal entries of the 1870s, one would think that her energy was flagging, but her letters of that decade express a lively interest in women's issues and a firm commitment to women's rights. A number of her letters to Lucy Stone, editor of* The Woman's Journal *(in which "Queen Aster" first appeared), were published, and both in public and in private she made it unmistakably clear that she could never " 'go back' on Womans [sic] Suffrage." Her letter to William Warland Clapp, Jr., is especially interesting in that she defends suffragists from the very charge leveled at Chow-chow's mother in "Cupid and Chow-chow"—that they "do not care for children and prefer notoriety to the joys of maternity." Alcott even tries to enlist her editor at Roberts Brothers, Thomas Niles, in the suffrage cause. Perhaps Alcott's most amusing (and possibly disingenuous) letter is one of literary advice to an aspiring author, but her most moving, self-revelatory correspondence, with Maggie Lukens, begins with similar advice to Maggie and her sisters. The depth of Alcott's love for her own dead sisters and for May's daughter, Lulu, who was left to her care, finds rare expression in her last letter to Maggie Lukens and suggests the biographical truth embodied in her most enduring legacy to us,* Little Women.

Those interested in reading a more extensive selection of Alcott's journal entries and letters should see The Journals of Louisa May Alcott *and* The Selected Letters of Louisa May Alcott, *edited by Joel Myerson, Daniel Shealy, and Madeleine B. Stern. The journal entries and many of the letters reprinted here were first published in Ednah Dow Cheney's* Louisa May Alcott *(1889).*

Transcendental Wild Oats

On the first day of June, 184-, a large wagon, drawn by a small horse and containing a motley load, went lumbering over certain New England hills, with the pleasing accompaniments of wind, rain, and hail. A serene man with a serene child upon his knee was driving, or rather being driven, for the small horse had it all his own way. A brown boy with a William Penn style of countenance sat beside him, firmly embracing a bust of Socrates. Behind them was an energetic-looking woman, with a benevolent brow, satirical mouth, and eyes brimful of hope and courage. A baby reposed upon her lap, a mirror leaned against her knee, and a basket of provisions danced about at her feet, as she struggled with a large, unruly umbrella. Two blue-eyed little girls, with hands full of childish treasures, sat under one old shawl, chatting happily together.

In front of this lively party stalked a tall, sharp-featured man, in a long blue cloak; and a fourth small girl trudged along beside him through the mud as if she rather enjoyed it.

The wind whistled over the bleak hills; the rain fell in a despondent drizzle, and twilight began to fall. But the calm man gazed as tranquilly into the fog as if he beheld a radiant bow of promise spanning the gray sky. The cheery woman tried to cover every one but herself with the big umbrella. The brown boy pillowed his head on the bald pate of Socrates and slumbered peacefully. The little girls sang lullabies to their dolls in soft, maternal murmurs. The sharp-nosed pedestrian marched steadily on, with the blue cloak streaming out behind him like a banner; the lively infant splashed through the puddles with a duck-like satisfaction pleasant to behold.

Thus these modern pilgrims journeyed hopefully out of the old world, to found a new one in the wilderness.

The editors of *The Transcendental Tripod* had received from Messrs.

Lion & Lamb (two of the aforesaid pilgrims) a communication from which the following statement is an extract:

"We have made arrangements with the proprietor of an estate of about a hundred acres which liberates this tract from human ownership. Here we shall prosecute our effort to initiate a Family in harmony with the primitive instincts of man.

"Ordinary secular farming is not our object. Fruit, grain, pulse, herbs, flax, and other vegetable products, receiving assiduous attention, will afford ample manual occupation, and chaste supplies for the bodily needs. It is intended to adorn the pastures with orchards, and to supersede the labor of cattle by the spade and the pruning-knife.

"Consecrated to human freedom, the land awaits the sober culture of devoted men. Beginning with small pecuniary means, this enterprise must be rooted in a reliance on the succors of an ever-bounteous Providence, whose vital affinities being secured by this union with uncorrupted field and unworldly persons, the cares and injuries of a life of gain are avoided.

"The inner nature of each member of the Family is at no time neglected. Our plan contemplates all such disciplines, cultures, and habits as evidently conduce to the purifying of the inmates.

"Pledged to the spirit alone, the founders anticipate no hasty or numerous addition to their numbers. The kingdom of peace is entered only through the gates of self-denial; and felicity is the test and the reward of loyalty to the unswerving law of Love."

This prospective Eden at present consisted of an old red farm-house, a dilapidated barn, many acres of meadow-land, and a grove. Ten ancient apple trees were all the "chaste supply" which the place offered as yet; but, in the firm belief that plenteous orchards were soon to be evoked from their inner consciousness, these sanguine founders had christened their domain Fruitlands.

Here Timon Lion intended to found a colony of Latter Day Saints, who, under his patriarchal sway, should regenerate the world and glorify his name for ever. Here Abel Lamb, with the devoutest faith in the high ideal which was to him a living truth, desired to plant a Paradise, where Beauty, Virtue, Justice, and Love might live happily together, without the possibility of a serpent entering in. And here his wife, unconverted but faithful to the end, hoped, after many wanderings over the face of the earth, to find rest for herself and a home for her children.

"There is our new abode," announced the enthusiast, smiling with a satisfaction quite undamped by the drops dripping from his hatbrim, as they turned at length into a cart-path that wound along a steep hillside into a barren-looking valley.

"A little difficult of access," observed his practical wife, as she endeavored to keep her various household gods from going overboard with every lurch of the laden ark.

"Like all good things. But those who earnestly desire and patiently seek will soon find us," placidly responded the philosopher from the mud, through which he was now endeavoring to pilot the much-enduring horse.

"Truth lies at the bottom of a well, Sister Hope," said Brother Timon, pausing to detach his small comrade from a gate, whereon she was perched for a clearer gaze into futurity.

"That's the reason we so seldom get at it, I suppose," replied Mrs. Hope, making a vain clutch at the mirror, which a sudden jolt sent flying out of her hands.

"We want no false reflections here," said Timon, with a grim smile, as he crunched the fragments under foot in his onward march.

Sister Hope held her peace, and looked wistfully through the mist at her promised home. The old red house with a hospitable glimmer at its windows cheered her eyes; and considering the weather, was a fitter refuge than the sylvan bowers some of the more ardent souls might have preferred.

The newcomers were welcomed by one of the elect precious—a regenerate farmer, whose idea of reform consisted chiefly in wearing white cotton raiment and shoes of untanned leather. This costume, with a snowy beard, gave him a venerable, and at the same time a somewhat bridal appearance.

The goods and chattels of the Society not having arrived, the weary family reposed before the fire on blocks of wood, while Brother Moses White regaled them with roasted potatoes, brown bread and water, in two plates, a tin pan, and one mug—his table service being limited. But, having cast the forms and vanities of a depraved world behind them, the elders welcomed hardship with the enthusiasm of new pioneers, and the children heartily enjoyed this foretaste of what they believed was to be a sort of perpetual picnic.

During the progress of this frugal meal, two more brothers appeared. One a dark, melancholy man, clad in homespun, whose particular mission was to turn his name hind part before and use as few words as possible. The other was a bland, bearded Englishman, who expected to be saved by eating uncooked food and going without clothes. He had not yet adopted the primitive costume, however; but contented himself with meditatively chewing dry beans out of a basket.

"Every meal should be a sacrament, and the vessels used beautiful and symbolical," observed Brother Lamb, mildly, righting the tin pan slipping about on his knees. "I priced a silver service when in town, but it was too costly; so I got some graceful cups and vases of Britannia ware."

"Hardest things in the world to keep bright. Will whiting be allowed in the community?" inquired Sister Hope, with a housewife's interest in labor-saving institutions.

"Such trivial questions will be discussed at a more fitting time," answered Brother Timon, sharply, as he burnt his fingers with a very hot potato. "Neither sugar, molasses, milk, butter, cheese, nor flesh are to be used among us, for nothing is to be admitted which has caused wrong or death to man or beast."

"Our garments are to be linen till we learn to raise our own cotton or some substitute for woollen fabrics," added Brother Abel, blissfully basking in an imaginary future as warm and brilliant as the generous fire before him.

"Haou abaout shoes?" asked Brother Moses, surveying his own with interest.

"We must yield that point till we can manufacture an innocent substitute for leather. Bark, wood, or some durable fabric will be invented in time. Meanwhile, those who desire to carry out our idea to the fullest extent can go barefooted," said Lion, who liked extreme measures.

"I never will, nor let my girls," murmured rebellious Sister Hope, under her breath.

"Haou do you cattle'ate to treat the ten-acre lot? Ef things ain't 'tended to right smart, we shan't hev no crops," observed the practical patriarch in cotton.

"We shall spade it," replied Abel, in such perfect good faith that Moses said no more, though he indulged in a shake of the head as he glanced at hands that had held nothing heavier than a pen for years. He was a paternal old soul and regarded the younger men as promising boys on a new sort of lark.

"What shall we do for lamps, if we cannot use any animal substance? I do hope light of some sort is to be thrown upon the enterprise," said

Mrs. Lamb, with anxiety, for in those days kerosene and camphene were not, and gas unknown in the wilderness.

"We shall go without till we have discovered some vegetable oil or wax to serve us," replied Brother Timon, in a decided tone, which caused Sister Hope to resolve that her private lamp should always be trimmed, if not burning.

"Each member is to perform the work for which experience, strength, and taste best fit him," continued Dictator Lion. "Thus drudgery and disorder will be avoided and harmony prevail. We shall arise at dawn, begin the day by bathing, followed by music, and then a chaste repast of fruit and bread. Each one finds congenial occupation till the meridian meal; when some deep-searching conversation gives rest to the body and development to the mind. Healthful labor again engages us till the last meal, when we assemble in social communion, prolonged till sunset, when we retire to sweet repose, ready for the next day's activity."

"What part of the work do you incline to yourself?" asked Sister Hope, with a humorous glimmer in her keen eyes.

"I shall wait till it is made clear to me. Being in preference to doing is the great aim, and this comes to us rather by a resigned willingness than a willful activity, which is a check to all divine growth," responded Brother Timon.

"I thought so." And Mrs. Lamb sighed audibly, for during the year he had spent in her family Brother Timon had so faithfully carried out his idea of "being, not doing," that she had found his "divine growth" both an expensive and unsatisfactory process.

Here her husband struck into the conversation, his face shining with the light and joy of the splendid dreams and high ideals hovering before him.

"In these steps of reform, we do not rely so much on scientific reasoning or physiological skill as on the spirit's dictates. The greater part of man's duty consists in leaving alone much that he now does. Shall I stimulate with tea, coffee, or wine? No. Shall I consume flesh? Not if I value health. Shall I subjugate cattle? Shall I claim property in any created thing? Shall I trade? Shall I adopt a form of religion? Shall I interest myself in politics? To how many of these questions—could we ask them deeply enough and could they be heard as having relation to our eternal welfare—would the response be 'Abstain'?"

A mild snore seemed to echo the last word of Abel's rhapsody, for brother Moses had succumbed to mundane slumber and sat nodding like a massive ghost. Forest Absalom, the silent man, and John Pease, the English member, now departed to the barn; and Mrs. Lamb led her flock to a temporary fold, leaving the founders of the "Consociate Family" to build castles in the air till the fire went out and the symposium ended in smoke.

The furniture arrived next day, and was soon bestowed; for the principal property of the community consisted in books. To this rare library was devoted the best room in the house, and the few busts and pictures that still survived many flittings were added to beautify the sanctuary, for here the family was to meet for amusement, instruction, and worship.

Any housewife can imagine the emotions of Sister Hope, when she took possession of a large, dilapidated kitchen, containing an old stove and the peculiar stores out of which food was to be evolved for her little family of eleven. Cakes of maple sugar, dried peas and beans, barley and hominy, meal of all sorts, potatoes, and dried fruit. No milk, butter, cheese, tea, or meat, appeared. Even salt was considered a useless luxury and spice entirely forbidden by these lovers of Spartan simplicity. A ten years' experience of vegetarian vagaries had been good for training for this new freak, and her sense of the ludicrous supported her through many trying scenes.

Unleavened bread, porridge, and water for breakfast; bread, vegetables, and water for dinner; bread, fruit, and water for supper was the bill of fare ordained by the elders. No teapot profaned that sacred stove, no gory steak cried aloud for vengeance from her chaste gridiron; and only a brave woman's taste, time, and temper were sacrificed on that domestic altar.

The vexed question of light was settled by buying a quantity of bayberry wax for candles; and, on discovering that no one knew how to make them, pine knots were introduced, to be used when absolutely necessary. Being summer, the evenings were not long, and the weary fraternity found it no great hardship to retire with the birds. The inner light was sufficient for most of them. But Mrs. Lamb rebelled. Evening was the only time she had to herself, and while the tired feet rested the skilful hands mended torn frocks and little stockings, or anxious heart forgot its burden in a book.

So "mother's lamp" burned steadily, while the philosophers built a new heaven and earth by moonlight; and through all the metaphysical mists and philanthropic pyrotechnics of that period Sister Hope played her own little game of "throwing light," and none but the moths were the worse for it.

Such farming probably was never seen before since Adam delved. The band of brothers began by spading garden and field; but a few days of it lessened their ardor amazingly. Blistered hands and aching backs suggested the expediency of permitting the use of cattle till the workers were better fitted for noble toil by a summer of the new life.

Brother Moses brought a yoke of oxen from his farm—at least, the philosophers thought so till it was discovered that one of the animals was a cow; and Moses confessed that he "must be let down easy, for he couldn't live on garden sarse entirely."

Great was Dictator Lion's indignation at this lapse from virtue. But time pressed, the work must be done; so the meek cow was permitted to wear the yoke and the recreant brother continued to enjoy forbidden draughts in the barn, which dark proceeding caused the children to regard him as one set apart for destruction.

The sowing was equally peculiar, for, owing to some mistake, the three brethren, who devoted themselves to this graceful task, found when about half through the job that each had been sowing a different sort of grain in the same field; a mistake which caused much perplexity, as it could not be remedied; but, after a long consultation and a good deal of laughter, it was decided to say nothing and see what would come of it.

The garden was planted with a generous supply of useful roots and herbs; but, as manure was not allowed to profane the virgin soil, few of these vegetable treasures ever came up. Purslane reigned supreme, and the disappointed planters ate it philosophically, deciding that Nature knew what was best for them, and would generously supply their needs, if they could only learn to digest her "sallets" and wild roots.

The orchard was laid out, a little grafting done, new trees and vines set, regardless of the unfit season and entire ignorance of the husbandmen, who honestly believed that in the autumn they would reap a bounteous harvest.

Slowly things got into order, and rapidly rumors of the new experiment went abroad, causing many strange spirits to flock thither, for in those days communities were the fashion and transcendentalism raged wildly. Some came to look on and laugh, some to be supported in poetic idleness, a few to believe sincerely and work heartily. Each member was allowed to mount his favorite hobby and ride it to his heart's content.

Very queer were some of these riders, and very rampant some of the hobbies.

One youth, believing that language was of little consequence if the spirit was only right, startled newcomers by blandly greeting them with "good morning, damn you," and other remarks of an equally mixed order. A second irrepressible being held that all the emotions of the soul should be freely expressed, and illustrated his theory by antics that would have sent him to a lunatic asylum, if, as an unregenerate wag said, he had not already been in one. When his spirit soared, he climbed trees and shouted; when doubt assailed him, he lay upon the floor and groaned lamentably. At joyful periods, he raced, leaped, and sang; when sad, he wept aloud; and when a great thought burst upon him in the watches of the night, he crowed like a jocund cockerel, to the great delight of the children and the great annoyance of the elders. One musical brother fiddled whenever so moved, sang sentimentally to the four little girls, and put a music-box on the wall when he hoed corn.

Brother Pease ground away at his uncooked food, or browsed over the farm on sorrel, mint, green fruit, and new vegetables. Occasionally he took his walks abroad, airily attired in an unbleached cotton *poncho,* which was the nearest approach to the primeval costume he was allowed to indulge in. At midsummer he retired to the wilderness, to try his plan where the woodchucks were without prejudices and huckleberry bushes were hospitably full. A sunstroke unfortunately spoilt his plan, and he returned to semi-civilization a sadder and wiser man.

Forest Absalom preserved his Pythagorean silence, cultivated his fine dark locks, and worked like a beaver, setting an excellent example of brotherly love, justice, and fidelity by his upright life. He it was who helped overworked Sister Hope with her heavy washes, kneaded the endless succession of batches of bread, watched over the children, and did the many tasks left undone by the brethren, who were so busy discussing and defining great duties that they forgot to perform the small ones.

Moses White placidly plodded about, "chorin' raound," as he called it, looking like an old-time patriarch, with his silver hair and flowing beard, and saving the community from many a mishap by his thrift and Yankee shrewdness.

Brother Lion domineered over the whole concern; for, having put the most money into the speculation, he was resolved to make it pay—as if anything founded on an ideal basis could be expected to do so by any but enthusiasts.

Abel Lamb simply revelled in the Newness, firmly believing that his dream was to be beautifully realized, and in time not only little Fruitlands, but the whole earth, be turned into a Happy Valley. He worked with every muscle of his body, for *he* was in deadly earnest. He taught with his whole head and heart; planned and sacrificed, preached and prophesied, with a soul full of the purest aspirations, most unselfish purposes, and desires for a life devoted to God and man, too high and tender to bear the rough usage of this world.

It was a little remarkable that only one woman ever joined this community. Mrs. Lamb merely followed wheresoever her husband led—"as ballast for his balloon," as she said, in her bright way.

Miss Jane Gage was a stout lady of mature years, sentimental, amiable, and lazy. She wrote verses copiously, and had vague yearnings and graspings after the unknown, which led her to believe herself fitted for a higher sphere than any she had yet adorned.

Having been a teacher, she was set to instructing the children in the common branches. Each adult member took a turn at the infants; and, as each taught in his own way, the result was a chronic state of chaos in the minds of these much-afflicted innocents.

Sleep, food, and poetic musings were the desires of dear Jane's life, and she shirked all duties as clogs upon her spirit's wings. Any thought of lending a hand with the domestic drudgery never occurred to her; and when to the question, "Are there any beasts of burden on the place?" Mrs. Lamb answered, with a face that told its own tale, "Only one woman!" the buxom Jane took no shame to herself, but laughed at the joke, and let the stout-hearted sister tug on alone.

Unfortunately, the poor lady hankered after the fleshpots, and endeavored to stay herself with private sips of milk, crackers, and cheese, and on one dire occasion she partook of fish at a neighbor's table.

One of the children reported this sad lapse from virtue, and poor Jane was publicly reprimanded by Timon.

"I only took a little bit of the tail," sobbed the penitent poetess.

"Yes, but the whole fish had to be tortured and slain that you might tempt your carnal appetite with that one taste of the tail. Know ye not, consumers of flesh meat, that ye are nourishing the wolf and tiger in your bosoms?"

At this awful question and the peal of laughter which arose from some of the younger brethren, tickled by the ludicrous contrast between the stout sinner, the stern judge, and the naughty satisfaction of the young detective, poor Jane fled from the room to pack her trunk, and return to a world were fishes' tails were not forbidden fruit.

Transcendental wild oats were sown broadcast that year, and the fame thereof has not yet ceased in the land; for, futile as this crop seemed to outsiders, it bore an invisible harvest, worth much to those who planted in earnest. As none of the members of this particular community have ever recounted their experiences before, a few of them may not be amiss, since the interest in these attempts has never died out and Fruitlands was the most ideal of all these castles in Spain.

A new dress was invented, since cotton, silk, and wool were forbidden as the product of slave-labor, worm-slaughter, and sheep-robbery. Tunics and trowsers of brown linen were the only wear. The women's skirts were longer, and their straw hat-brims wider than the men's and this was the only difference. Some persecution lent a charm to the costume, and the long-haired, linen-clad reformers quite enjoyed the mild martyrdom they endured when they left home.

Money was abjured, as the root of all evil. The produce of the land was to supply most of their wants, or be exchanged for the few things they could not grow. This idea had its inconveniences; but self-denial was the fashion, and it was surprising how many things one can do without. When they desired to travel, they walked, if possible, begged the loan of a vehicle, or boldly entered car or coach, and, stating their principles to the officials, took the consequences. Usually their dress, their earnest frankness, and gentle resolution won them a passage; but now and then they met with hard usage, and had the satisfaction of suffering for their principles.

On one of these penniless pilgrimages they took passage on a boat, and, when fare was demanded, artlessly offered to talk, instead of pay. As the boat was well under way and they actually had not a cent, there was no help for it. So Brothers Lion and Lamb held forth to the assembled passengers in their most eloquent style. There must have been something effective in this conversation, for the listeners were moved to take up a contribution for these inspired lunatics, who preached peace on earth and goodwill to man so earnestly, with empty pockets. A goodly sum was collected; but when the captain presented it the reformers proved that they were consistent even in their madness, for not a penny would they accept, saying, with a look at the group about them, whose indifference or contempt had changed to interest and respect, "You see how well we get on without money;" and so went serenely on their way, with their linen blouses flapping airily in the cold October wind.

They preached vegetarianism everywhere and resisted all temptations of the flesh, contentedly eating apples and bread at well-spread tables, and much afflicting hospitable hostesses by denouncing their food and taking away their appetites, discussing the "horrors of shambles," the "incorporation of the brute in man," and "on elegant abstinence the sign of a pure soul." But, when the perplexed or offended ladies asked what they should eat, they got in reply a bill of fare consisting of "bowls of sunrise for breakfast," "solar seeds of the sphere," "dishes from Plutarch's chaste table," and other viands equally hard to find in any modern market.

Reform conventions of all sorts were haunted by these brethren, who said many wise things and did many foolish ones. Unfortunately, these wanderings interfered with their harvest at home; but the rule was to do what the spirit moved, so they left their crops to Providence and went a-reaping in wider and, let us hope, more fruitful fields than their own.

Luckily, the earthly providence who watched over Abel Lamb was at hand to glean the scanty crop yielded by the "uncorrupted land," which, "consecrated to human freedom," had received "the sober culture of devout men."

About the same time the grain was ready to house, some call of the Oversoul wafted all the men away. An easterly storm was coming up and the yellow stacks were sure to be ruined. Then Sister Hope gathered her forces. Three little girls, one boy (Timon's son), and herself, harnessed to clothes-baskets and Russia-linen sheets, were the only teams she could command; but with these poor appliances the indomitable woman got in the grain and saved food for her young, with the instinct and energy of a mother-bird with a brood of hungry nestlings to feed.

This attempt at regeneration had its tragic as well as comic side, though the world only saw the former.

With the first frosts, the butterflies, who had sunned themselves in the new light through the summer, took flight, leaving the few bees to see what honey they had stored for winter use. Precious little appeared beyond the satisfaction of a few months of holy living.

At first it seemed as if a chance to try holy dying was also to be offered them. Timon, much disgusted with the failure of the scheme, decided to retire to the Shakers, who seemed to be the only successful community going.

"What is to become of us?" asked Mrs. Hope, for Abel was heartbroken at the bursting of his lovely bubble.

"You can stay here, if you like, till a tenant is found. No more wood must be cut, however, and no more corn ground. All I have must be sold to pay the debts of the concern, as the responsibility is mine," was the cheering reply.

"Who is to pay us for what we have lost? I gave all I had—furniture, time, strength, six months of my children's lives—and all are wasted. Abel gave himself body and soul, and is almost wrecked by hard work and disappointment. Are we to have no return for this, but leave to starve and freeze in an old house, with winter at hand, no money, and hardly a friend left, for this wild scheme has alienated nearly all we had. You talk much about justice. Let us have a little, since there is nothing else left."

But the woman's appeal met with no reply but the old one: "It was an experiment. We all risked something, and must bear our losses as we can."

With this cold comfort, Timon departed with his son, and was absorbed into the Shaker brotherhood, where he soon found that the order of things was reversed, and it was all work and no play.

Then the tragedy began for the forsaken little family. Desolation and despair fell upon Abel. As his wife said, his new beliefs had alienated many friends. Some thought him mad, some unprincipled. Even the most kindly thought him a visionary, whom it was useless to help till he took more practical views of life. All stood aloof, saying: "Let him work out his own ideas, and see what they are worth."

He had tried, but it was a failure. The world was not ready for Utopia yet, and those who attempted to found it only got laughed at for their pains. In other days, men could sell all and give to the poor, lead lives devoted to holiness and high thought, and after the persecution was over, find themselves honored as saints or martyrs. But in modern times these things are out of fashion. To live for one's principles, at all costs, is a dangerous speculation; and the failure of an ideal, no matter how humane and noble, is harder for the world to forgive and forget than bank robbery or the grand swindles of corrupt politicians.

Deep waters now for Abel, and for a time there seemed no passage through. Strength and spirits were exhausted by hard work and too much thought. Courage failed when, looking about for help, he saw no sympathizing face, no hand outstretched to help him, no voice to say cheerily:

"We all make mistakes, and it takes many experiences to shape a life. Try again, and let us help you."

Every door was closed, every eye averted, every heart cold, and no way open whereby he might earn bread for his children. His principles would not permit him to do many things that others did; and in the few fields where conscience would allow him to work, who would employ a man who had flown in the face of society, as he had done?

Then this dreamer, whose dream was the life of his life, resolved to carry out his idea to the bitter end. There seemed no place for him here—no work, no friend. To go begging conditions was as ignoble as to go begging money. Better perish of want than sell one's soul for the sustenance of his body. Silently he lay down upon his bed, turned his face to the wall, and waited with pathetic patience for death to cut the knot which he could not untie. Days and nights went by, and neither food nor water passed his lips. Soul and body were dumbly struggling together, and no word of complaint betrayed what either suffered.

His wife, when tears and prayers were unavailing, sat down to wait the end with a mysterious awe and submission; for in this entire resignation of all things there was an eloquent significance to her who knew him as no other human being did.

"Leave all to God," was his belief; and in this crisis the loving soul clung to his faith, sure that the All-wise Father would not desert this child who tried to live so near to Him. Gathering her children about her, she waited the issue of the tragedy that was being enacted in that solitary room, while the first snow fell outside, untrodden by the footprints of a single friend.

But the strong angels who sustain and teach perplexed and troubled souls came and went, leaving no trace without, but working miracles within. For, when all other sentiments had faded into dimness, all other hopes died utterly; when the bitterness of death was nearly over, when the body was past any pang of hunger or thirst, and soul stood ready to depart, the love that outlives all else refused to die. Head had bowed to defeat, hand had grown weary with too heavy tasks, but heart could not grow cold to those who live in its tender depths, even when death touched it.

"My faithful wife, my little girls—they have not forsaken me, they are mine by ties that none can break. What right have I to leave them alone? What right to escape from the burden and the sorrow I have helped to bring? This duty remains to me, and I must do it manfully. For their sakes, the world will forgive me in time; for their sakes, God will sustain me now."

Too feeble to rise, Abel groped for the food that always lay within his reach, and in the darkness and solitude of that memorable night ate and drank what was to him the bread and wine of a new communion, a new dedication of heart and life to the duties that were left him when the dreams fled.

In the early dawn, when that sad wife crept fearfully to see what change had come to the patient face on the pillow, she found it smiling at her, saw a wasted hand outstretched to her, and heard a feeble voice cry bravely, "Hope!"

What passed in that little room is not to be recorded except in the hearts of those who suffered and endured much for love's sake. Enough for us to know that soon the wan shadow of a man came forth, leaning on the arm that never failed him, to be welcomed and cherished by the children, who never forgot the experiences of that time.

"Hope" was the watchword now; and, while the last logs blazed on the hearth, the last bread and apples covered the table, the new commander, with recovered courage, said to her husband:

"Leave all to God—and me. He has done his part; now I will do mine."

"But we have no money, dear."

"Yes, we have. I sold all we could spare, and have enough to take us away from this snowbank."

"Where can we go?"

"I have engaged four rooms at our good neighbor, Lovejoy's. There we can live cheaply till spring. Then for new plans and a home of our own, please God."

"But, Hope, your little store won't last long, and we have no friends."

"I can sew and you can chop wood. Lovejoy offers you the same pay as he gives his other men; my old friend, Mrs. Truman, will send me all the work I want; and my blessed brother stands by us to the end. Cheer up, dear heart, for while there is work and love in the world we shall not suffer."

"And while I have my good angel Hope, I shall not despair, even if I wait another thirty years before I step beyond the circle of the sacred little world in which I still have a place to fill."

So one bleak December day, with their few possessions piled on an ox-sled, the rosy children perched atop, and the parents trudging arm in arm behind, the exiles left their Eden and faced the world again.

"Ah, me! my happy dream. How much I leave behind that never can be mine again," said Abel, looking back at the lost Paradise, lying white and chill in its shroud of snow.

"Yes, dear; but how much we bring away," answered brave-hearted Hope, glancing from husband to children.

"Poor Fruitlands! The name was as great a failure as the rest!" continued Abel, with a sigh, as a frost-bitten apple fell from a leafless bough at his feet.

But the sigh changed to a smile as his wife added, in a half-tender, half-satirical tone:

"Don't you think Apple Slump would be a better name for it, dear?"

Journals

FRUITLANDS

(1843)

September 1st.—I rose at five and had my bath. I love cold water! Then we had our singing-lesson with Mr. Lane. After breakfast I washed dishes, and ran on the hill till nine, and had some thoughts,—it was so beautiful up there. Did my lessons,—wrote and spelt and did sums; and Mr. Lane read a story, "The Judicious Father": How a rich girl told a poor girl not to look over the fence at the flowers, and was cross to her because she was unhappy. The father heard her do it, and made the girls change clothes. The poor one was glad to do it, and he told her to keep them. But the rich one was very sad; for she had to wear the old ones a week, and after that she was good to shabby girls. I liked it very much, and I shall be kind to poor people.

Father asked us what was God's noblest work. Anna said *men,* but I said *babies.* Men are often bad; babies never are. We had a long talk, and I felt better after it, and *cleared up.*

We had bread and fruit for dinner. I read and walked and played till supper-time. We sung in the evening. As I went to bed the moon came up very brightly and looked at me. I felt sad because I have been cross to-day, and did not mind Mother. I cried, and then I felt better, and said that piece from Mrs. Sigourney, "I must not tease my mother." I get to sleep saying poetry,—I know a great deal.

Thursday, 14th.—Mr. Parker Pillsbury came, and we talked about the poor slaves. I had a music lesson with Miss F. I hate her, she is so fussy. I ran in the wind and played be a horse, and had a lovely time in the woods with Anna and Lizzie. We were fairies, and made gowns and paper wings. I "flied" the highest of all. In the evening they talked about travelling. I thought about Father going to England, and said this piece of poetry I found in Byron's poems:—

"When I left thy shores, O Naxos,
Not a tear in sorrow fell;
Not a sigh or faltered accent
Told my bosom's struggling swell."

It rained when I went to bed, and made a pretty noise on the roof.

Sunday, 24th.—Father and Mr. Lane have gone to N. H. to preach. It was very lovely. . . . Anna and I got supper. In the eve I read "Vicar of Wakefield." I was cross to-day, and I cried when I went to bed. I made good resolutions, and felt better in my heart. If I only *kept* all I make, I should be the best girl in the world. But I don't, and so am very bad.

[Poor little sinner! *She says the same at fifty.*—L. M. A.]

October 8th.—When I woke up, the first thought I got was, "It's Mother's birthday: I must be very good." I ran and wished her a happy birthday, and gave her my kiss. After breakfast we gave her our presents. I had a moss cross and a piece of poetry for her.

We did not have any school, and played in the woods and got red leaves. In the evening we danced and sung, and I read a story about "Contentment." I wish I was rich, I was good, and we were all a happy family this day.

Thursday, 12th.—After lessons I ironed. We all went to the barn and husked corn. It was good fun. We worked till eight o'clock and had lamps. Mr. Russell came. Mother and Lizzie are going to Boston. I shall be very lonely without dear little Betty, and no one will be as good to me as mother. I read in Plutarch. I made a verse about sunset:—

Softly doth the sun descend
To his couch behind the hill,
Then, oh, then, I love to sit
On mossy banks beside the rill.

Anna thought it was very fine; but I didn't like it very well.

Friday, Nov. 2nd.—Anna and I did the work. In the evening Mr. Lane asked us, "What is man?" These were our answers: A human being; an animal with a mind; a creature; a body; a soul and a mind. After a long talk we went to bed very tired.

> [No wonder, after doing the work and worrying their little wits with such lessons.—L. M. A.]

A sample of the vegetarian wafers we used at Fruitlands:—

Vegetable diet
and sweet repose.
Animal food and
nightmare.

Pluck your body
from the orchard;
do not snatch it
from the shamble.

Without flesh diet
there could be no
blood-shedding war.

Apollo eats no
flesh and has no
beard; his voice is
melody itself.

Snuff is no less snuff
though accepted from
a gold box.

Tuesday, 20th.—I rose at five, and after breakfast washed the dishes, and then helped mother work. Miss F. is gone, and Anna in Boston with Cousin Louisa. I took care of Abby (May) in the afternoon. In the evening I made some pretty things for my dolly. Father and Mr. L. had a talk, and father asked us if *we* saw any reason for us to separate. Mother wanted to, she is so tired. I like it, but not the school part or Mr. L.

Eleven years old. *Thursday, 29th.*—It was Father's and my birthday. We had some nice presents. We played in the snow before school. Mother read "Rosamond" when we sewed. Father asked us in the eve what fault troubled us most. I said my bad temper.

I told mother I liked to have her write in my book. She said she would put in more, and she wrote this to help me:—

> DEAR LOUY,—Your handwriting improves very fast. Take pains and do not be in a hurry. I like to have you make observations about our conversations and your own thoughts. It helps you to express them and to understand your little self. Remember, dear girl, that a diary should be an epitome of your life. May it be a record of pure thought and good actions, then you will indeed be the precious child of your loving mother.

December 10th.—I did my lessons, and walked in the afternoon. Father read to us in dear Pilgrim's Progress. Mr. L. was in Boston, and we were glad. In the eve father and mother and Anna and I had a long talk. I was very unhappy, and we all cried. Anna and I cried in bed, and I prayed God to keep us all together.

> [Little Lu began early to feel the family cares and peculiar trials.—L. M. A.]

CONCORD

(1845–47)

CONCORD, *Thursday.*—I had an early run in the woods before the dew was off the grass. The moss was like velvet, and as I ran under the arches of yellow and red leaves I sang for joy, my heart was so bright and the world so beautiful. I stopped at the end of the walk and saw the sunshine out over the wide "Virginia meadows."

It seemed like going through a dark life or grave into heaven beyond. A very strange and solemn feeling came over me as I stood there, with no sound but the rustle of the pines, no one near me, and the sun so glorious, as for me alone. It seemed as if I *felt* God as I never did before, and I prayed in my heart that I might keep that happy sense of nearness all my life.

> [I have, for I most sincerely think that the little girl "got religion" that day in the wood when dear mother Nature led her to God.—L. M. A., 1885.]

HILLSIDE.

March, 1846.—I have at last got the little room I have wanted so long, and am very happy about it. It does me good to be alone, and Mother has made it very pretty and neat for me. My work-basket and desk are by the window, and my closet is full of dried herbs that smell very nice. The door that opens into the garden will be very pretty in summer, and I can run off to the woods when I like.

I have made a plan for my life, as I am in my teens, and no more a child. I am old for my age, and don't care much for girl's things. People think I'm wild and queer; but Mother understands and helps me. I have not told any one about my plan; but I'm going to *be* good. I've made so many resolutions, and written sad notes, and cried over my sins, and it doesn't seem to do any good! Now I'm going to *work really,* for I feel a true desire to improve, and be a help and comfort, not a care and sorrow, to my dear mother.

Sunday, Oct. 9, 1847.—I have been reading to-day Bettine's correspondence with Goethe.

She calls herself a child, and writes about the lovely things she saw and heard, and felt and did. I liked it much.

> [First taste of Goethe. Three years later R. W. E. gave me "Wilhelm Meister," and from that day Goethe has been my chief idol.—L. M. A., 1885.]

BOSTON
(1850–57)

BOSTON, *May,* 1850.—So long a time has passed since I kept a journal that I hardly know how to begin. Since coming to the city I don't seem to have thought much, for the bustle and dirt and change send all lovely images and restful feelings away. Among my hills and woods I had fine free times alone, and though my thoughts were silly, I daresay, they helped to keep me happy and good. I see now what Nature did for me, and my "romantic tastes," as people called that love of solitude and out-of-door life, taught me much.

This summer, like the last, we shall spend in a large house (Uncle May's, Atkinson Street), with many comforts about us which we shall enjoy, and in the autumn I hope I shall have something to show that the time has not been wasted. Seventeen years have I lived, and yet so little do I know, and so much remains to be done before I begin to be what I desire,—a truly good and useful woman.

In looking over our journals, Father says, "Anna's is about other people, Louisa's about herself." That is true, for I don't *talk* about myself; yet must always think of the wilful, moody girl I try to manage, and in my journal I write of her to see how she gets on. Anna is so good she need not take care of herself, and can enjoy other people. If I look in my glass,

I try to keep down vanity about my long hair, my well-shaped head, and my good nose. In the street I try not to covet fine things. My quick tongue is always getting me into trouble, and my moodiness makes it hard to be cheerful when I think how poor we are, how much worry it is to live, and how many things I long to do I never can.

So every day is a battle, and I'm so tired I don't want to live; only it's cowardly to die till you have done something.

I can't talk to any one but Mother about my troubles, and she has so many now to bear I try not to add any more. I know God is always ready to hear, but heaven's so far away in the city, and I so heavy I can't fly up to find Him.

FAITH.

Written in the diary.

Oh, when the heart is full of fears
And the way seems dim to heaven,
When the sorrow and the care of years
Peace from the heart has driven,—
Then, through the mist of falling tears,
Look up and be forgiven.

Forgiven for the lack of faith
That made all dark to thee,
Let conscience o'er thy wayward soul
Have fullest mastery:
Hope on, fight on, and thou shalt win
A noble victory.

Though thou art weary and forlorn,
Let not thy heart's peace go;
Though the riches of this world are gone,
And thy lot is care and woe,
Faint not, but journey hourly on:
True wealth is not below.

Through all the darkness still look up:
Let virtue be thy guide;

Take thy draught from sorrow's cup,
Yet trustfully abide;
Let not temptation vanquish thee,
And the Father will provide.

[We had small-pox in the family this summer, caught from some poor immigrants whom mother took into our garden and fed one day. We girls had it lightly, but Father and Mother were very ill, and we had a curious time of exile, danger, and trouble. No doctors, and all got well.—L. M. A.]

July, 1850.—Anna is gone to L. after the varioloid. She is to help Mrs.——with her baby. I had to take A.'s school of twenty in Canton Street. I like it better than I thought, though it's very hard to be patient with the children sometimes. They seem happy, and learn fast; so I am encouraged, though at first it was very hard, and I missed Anna so much I used to cry over my dinner and be very blue. I guess this is the teaching I need; for as a *school-marm* I must behave myself and guard my tongue and temper carefully, and set an example of sweet manners.

I found one of mother's notes in my journal, so like those she used to write me when she had more time. It always encourages me; and I wish some one would write as helpfully to her, for she needs cheering up with all the care she has. I often think what a hard life she has had since she married,—so full of wandering and all sorts of worry! so different from her early easy days, the youngest and most petted of her family. I think she is a very brave, good woman; and my dream is to have a lovely, quiet home for her, with no debts or troubles to burden her. But I'm afraid she will be in heaven before I can do it. Anna, too, she is feeble and homesick, and I miss her dreadfully; for she is my conscience, always true and just and good. She must have a good time in a nice little home of her own some day, as we often plan. But waiting is so *hard!*

August, 1850.—School is hard work, and I feel as though I should like to run away from it. But my children get on; so I travel up every day, and do my best.

I get very little time to write or think; for my working days have begun, and when school is over Anna wants me; so I have no quiet. I think a little solitude every day is good for me. In the quiet I see my faults, and try to mend them; but, deary me, I don't get on at all.

I used to imagine my mind a room in confusion, and I was to put it in order; so I swept out useless thoughts and dusted foolish fancies away, and furnished it with good resolutions and began again. But cobwebs get in. I'm not a good housekeeper, and never get my room in nice order. I once wrote a poem about it when I was fourteen, and called it "My Little Kingdom." It is still hard to rule it, and always will be I think.

Reading Miss Bremer and Hawthorne. The "Scarlet Letter" is my favorite. Mother likes Miss B. better, as more wholesome. I fancy "lurid" things, if true and strong also.

Anna wants to be an actress, and so do I. We could make plenty of money perhaps, and it is a very gay life. Mother says we are too young, and must wait. A. acts often splendidly. I like tragic plays, and shall be a Siddons if I can. We get up fine ones, and make harps, castles, armor, dresses, water-falls, and thunder, and have great fun.

1852.—*High Street, Boston.*—After the small-pox summer, we went to a house in High Street. Mother opened an intelligence office, which grew out of her city missionary work and a desire to find places for good girls. It was not fit work for her, but it paid; and she always did what came to her in the way of duty or charity, and let pride, taste, and comfort suffer for love's sake.

Anna and I taught; Lizzie was our little housekeeper,—our angel in a cellar kitchen; May went to school; father wrote and talked when he could get classes or conversations. Our poor little home had much love and happiness in it, and was a shelter for lost girls, abused wives, friendless children, and weak or wicked men. Father and Mother had no money to give, but gave them time, sympathy, help; and if blessings would make them rich, they would be millionnaires. This is practical Christianity.

My first story was printed, and $5 paid for it. It was written in Concord when I was sixteen. Great rubbish! Read it aloud to sisters, and when they praised it, not knowing the author, I proudly announced her name.

Made a resolution to read fewer novels, and those only of the best. List of books I like:—

Carlyle's French Revolution and Miscellanies.
Hero and Hero-Worship.
Goethe's poems, plays, and novels.
Plutarch's Lives.
Madame Guion.
Paradise Lost and Comus.

Schiller's Plays.
Madame de Staël.
Bettine.
Louis XIV.
Jane Eyre.
Hypatia.
Philothea.
Uncle Tom's Cabin.
Emerson's Poems.

1854.—*Pinckney Street.*—I have neglected my journal for months, so must write it up. School for me month after month. Mother busy with boarders and sewing. Father doing as well as a philosopher can in a money-loving world. Anna at S.

I earned a good deal by sewing in the evening when my day's work was done.

In February Father came home. Paid his way, but no more. A dramatic scene when he arrived in the night. We were waked by hearing the bell. Mother flew down, crying "My husband!" We rushed after, and five white figures embraced the half-frozen wanderer who came in hungry, tired, cold, and disappointed, but smiling bravely and as serene as ever. We fed and warmed and brooded over him, longing to ask if he had made any money; but no one did till little May said, after he had told all the pleasant things, "Well, did people pay you?" Then, with a queer look, he opened his pocket-book and showed one dollar, saying with a smile that made our eyes fill, "Only that! My overcoat was stolen, and I had to buy a shawl. Many promises were not kept, and travelling is costly; but I have opened the way, and another year shall do better."

I shall never forget how beautifully Mother answered him, though the dear, hopeful soul had built much on his success; but with a beaming face she kissed him, saying, "I call that doing *very well.* Since you are safely home, dear, we don't ask anything more."

Anna and I choked down our tears, and took a little lesson in real love which we never forgot, nor the look that the tired man and the tender woman gave one another. It was half tragic and comic, for Father was very dirty and sleepy, and Mother in a big nightcap and funny old jacket.

[I began to see the strong contrasts and the fun and follies in every-day life about this time.—L. M. A.]

Anna came home in March. Kept our school all summer. I got "Flower Fables" ready to print.

April, 1855.—I am in the garret with my papers round me, and a pile of apples to eat while I write my journal, plan stories, and enjoy the patter of rain on the roof, in peace and quiet.

[Jo in the garret.—L. M. A.]

Being behindhand, as usual, I'll make note of the main events up to date, for I don't waste ink in poetry and pages of rubbish now. I've begun to *live,* and have no time for sentimental musing.

In October I began my school; Father talked, Mother looked after her boarders, and tried to help everybody. Anna was in Syracuse teaching Mrs. S——'s children.

My book came out; and people began to think that topsey-turvey Louisa would amount to something after all, since she could do so well as housemaid, teacher, seamstress, and story-teller. Perhaps she may.

In February I wrote a story for which C. paid $5, and asked for more.

In March I wrote a farce for W. Warren, and Dr. W. offered it to him; but W. W. was too busy.

Also began another tale, but found little time to work on it, with school, sewing, and house-work. My winter's earnings are,—

School, one quarter $50
Sewing $50
Stories $20

if I am ever paid.

A busy and a pleasant winter, because, though hard at times, I do seem to be getting on a little; and that encourages me.

Have heard Lowell and Hedge lecture, acted in plays, and thanks to our rag-money and good cousin H., have been to the theatre several times,—always my great joy.

Summer plans are yet unsettled. Father wants to go to England: not a wise idea, I think. We shall probably stay here, and A. and I go into the country as governesses. It's a queer way to live, but dramatic, and I rather like it; for we never know what is to come next. We are real "Micawbers," and always "ready for a spring."

I have planned another Christmas book, and hope to be able to write it.

1855.—Cousin L. W. asks me to pass the summer at Walpole with her. If I can get no teaching, I shall go; for I long for the hills, and can write my fairy tales there.

I delivered my burlesque lecture on "Woman, and Her Position; by Oronthy Bluggage," last evening at Deacon G.'s. Had a merry time, and was asked by Mr. W. to do it at H. for money. Read "Hamlet" at our club,—my favorite play. Saw Mrs. W. H. Smith about the farce; says she will do it at her benefit.

May.—Father went to C. to talk with Mr. Emerson about the England trip. I am to go to Walpole. I have made my own gowns, and had money enough to fit up the girls. So glad to be independent.

> [I wonder if $40 fitted up the whole family. Perhaps so, as my wardrobe was made up of old clothes from cousins and friends.—L. M. A.]

June, 1857.—Read Charlotte Brontë's life. A very interesting, but sad one. So full of talent; and after working long, just as success, love, and happiness come, she dies.

Wonder if I shall ever be famous enough for people to care to read my story and struggles. I can't be a C. B., but I may do a little something yet.

July.—Grandma Alcott came to visit us. A sweet old lady; and I am glad to know her, and see where Father got his nature. Eighty-four; yet very smart, industrious, and wise. A house needs a grandma in it.

As we sat talking over Father's boyhood, I never realized so plainly before how much he has done for himself. His early life sounded like a pretty old romance, and Mother added the love passages.

I got a hint for a story; and some day will do it, and call it "The Cost of an Idea." Spindle Hill, Temple School, Fruitlands, Boston, and Concord, would make fine chapters. The trials and triumphs of the Pathetic Family would make a capital book; may I live to do it.

August.—A sad, anxious month. Betty worse; Mother takes her to the seashore. Father decides to go back to Concord; he is never happy far from Emerson, the one true friend who loves and understands and helps him.

September.—An old house near R. W. E.'s is bought with Mother's money, and we propose to move. Mother in Boston with poor Betty, who is failing fast. Anna and I have a hard time breaking up.

October.—Move to Concord. Take half a house in town till spring, when the old one is to be made ready.

Find dear Betty a shadow, but sweet and patient always. Fit up a nice room for her, and hope home and love and care may keep her.

People kind and friendly, and the old place looks pleasant, though I never want to live in it.

November.—Father goes West, taking Grandma home. We settle down to our winter, whatever it is to be. Lizzie seems better, and we have some plays. Sanborn's school makes things lively, and we act a good deal.

Twenty-five this month. I feel my quarter of a century rather heavy on my shoulders just now. I lead two lives. One seems gay with plays, etc., the other very sad,—in Betty's room; for though she wishes us to act, and loves to see us get ready, the shadow is there, and Mother and I see it. Betty loves to have me with her; and I am with her at night, for Mother needs rest. Betty says she feels "strong" when I am near. So glad to be of use.

December.—Some fine plays for charity.

CONCORD

(1858–62)

January, 1858.—Lizzie much worse; Dr. G. says there is no hope. A hard thing to hear; but if she is only to suffer, I pray she may go soon. She was glad to know she was to "get well," as she called it, and we tried to bear it bravely for her sake. We gave up plays; Father came home; and Anna took the housekeeping, so that Mother and I could devote ourselves to her. Sad, quiet days in her room, and strange nights keeping up the fire and watching the dear little shadow try to wile away the long sleepless hours without troubling me. She sews, reads, sings softly, and lies looking at the fire,—so sweet and patient and so worn, my heart is broken to see the change. I wrote some lines one night on "Our Angel in the House."

[Jo and Beth.—L. M. A.]

February.—A mild month; Betty very comfortable, and we hope a little.

Dear Betty is slipping away, and every hour is too precious to waste, so I'll keep my lamentations over Nan's [affairs] till this duty is over.

Lizzie makes little things, and drops them out of windows to the school-children, smiling to see their surprise. In the night she tells me to be Mrs. Gamp, when I give her her lunch, and tries to be gay that I may keep up. Dear little saint! I shall be better all my life for these sad hours with you.

March 14th.—My dear Beth died at three this morning, after two years of patient pain. Last week she put her work away, saying the needle was "too heavy," and having given us her few possessions, made ready for the parting in her own simple, quiet way. For two days she suffered much, begging for ether, though its effect was gone. Tuesday she lay in Father's arms, and called us round her, smiling contentedly as she said, "All here!" I think she bid us good-by then, as she held our hands and kissed us tenderly. Saturday she slept, and at midnight became unconscious, quietly breathing her life away till three; then, with one last look of the beautiful eyes, she was gone.

A curious thing happened, and I will tell it here, for Dr. G. said it was a fact. A few moments after the last breath came, as Mother and I sat silently watching the shadow fall on the dear little face, I saw a light mist rise from the body, and float up and vanish in the air. Mother's eyes followed mine, and when I said, "What did you see?" she described the same light mist. Dr. G. said it was the life departing visibly.

For the last time we dressed her in her usual cap and gown, and laid her on her bed,—at rest at last. What she had suffered was seen in the face; for at twenty-three she looked like a woman of forty, so worn was she, and all her pretty hair gone.

On Monday Dr. Huntington read the Chapel service, and we sang her favorite hymn. Mr. Emerson, Henry Thoreau, Sanborn, and John Pratt, carried her out of the old home to the new one at Sleepy Hollow chosen by herself. So the first break comes, and I know what death means,—a liberator for her, a teacher for us.

April.—Came to occupy one wing of Hawthorne's house (once ours) while the new one was being repaired. Father, Mother, and I kept house together; May being in Boston, Anna at Pratt Farm, and, for the first time, Lizzie absent. I don't miss her as I expected to do, for she seems nearer and dearer than before; and I am glad to know she is safe from pain and age in some world where her innocent soul must be happy.

Death never seemed terrible to me, and now is beautiful; so I cannot fear it, but find it friendly and wonderful.

May.—A lonely month with all the girls gone, and Father and Mother absorbed in the old house, which I don't care about, not liking Concord.

On the 7th of April, Anna came walking in to tell us she was engaged to John Pratt; so another sister is gone. J. is a model son and brother,—a true man,—full of fine possibilities, but so modest one does not see it at once. He is handsome, healthy, and happy; just home from the West, and so full of love he is pleasant to look at.

I moaned in private over my great loss, and said I'd never forgive J. for taking Anna from me; but I shall if he makes her happy, and turn to little May for my comfort.

> [Now that John is dead, I can truly say we all had cause to bless the day he came into the family; for we gained a son and brother, and Anna the best husband ever known.
>
> For ten years he made her home a little heaven of love and peace; and when he died he left her the legacy of a beautiful life, and an honest name to his little sons.—L. M. A., 1873.]

February, 1860.—Mr.——won't have "M. L.," as it is antislavery, and the dear South must not be offended, Got a carpet with my $50, and wild Louisa's head kept the feet of the family warm.

March.—Wrote "A Modern Cinderella," with Nan for the heroine and John for the hero.

Made my first ball dress for May, and she was the finest girl at the party. My tall, blond, graceful girl! I was proud of her.

Wrote a song for the school festival, and heard it sung by four hundred happy children. Father got up the affair, and such a pretty affair was never seen in Concord before. He said, "We spend much on our cattle and flower shows; let us each spring have a show of our children, and begrudge nothing for their culture." All liked it but the old fogies who want things as they were in the ark.

April.—Made two riding habits, and May and I had some fine rides. Both needed exercise, and this was good for us. So one of our dreams came true, and we really did "dash away on horseback."

Sanborn was nearly kidnapped for being a friend of John Brown; but his sister and A. W. rescued him when he was handcuffed, and the scamps drove off. Great ferment in town. A meeting and general flurry.

Had a funny lover who met me in the cars, and said he lost his heart at once. Handsome man of forty. A Southerner, and very demonstrative and gushing, called and wished to pay his addresses; and being told I didn't wish to see him, retired, to write letters and haunt the road with his hat off, while the girls laughed and had great fun over Jo's lover. He went at last, and peace reigned. My adorers are all queer.

Sent "Cinderella" to the "Atlantic," and it was accepted. Began "By the River," and thought that this was certainly to be a lucky year; for after ten years hard climbing I had reached a good perch on the ladder, and could look more hopefully into the future, while my paper boats sailed gaily over the Atlantic.

May.—Meg's wedding.

My farce was acted, and I went to see it. Not very well done; but I sat in a box, and the good Doctor handed up a bouquet to the author, and made as much as he could of a small affair.

Saw Anna's honeymoon home at Chelsea,—a little cottage in a blooming apple-orchard. Pretty place, simple and sweet. God bless it!

The dear girl was married on the 23d, the same day as Mother's wedding. A lovely day; the house full of sunshine, flowers, friends, and happiness. Uncle S. J. May married them, with no fuss, but much love; and we all stood round her. She in her silver-gray silk, with lilies of the valley (John's flower) in her bosom and hair. We in gray thin stuff and roses,—sackcloth, I called it, and ashes of roses; for I mourn the loss of my Nan, and am not comforted. We have had a little feast, sent by good Mrs. Judge Shaw; then the old folks danced round the bridal pair on the lawn in the German fashion, making a pretty picture to remember, under our Revolutionary elm.

Then, with tears and kisses, our dear girl, in her little white bonnet, went happily away with her good John; and we ended our first wedding. Mr. Emerson kissed her; and I thought that honor would make even matrimony endurable, for he is the god of my idolatry, and has been for years.

June.—To Boston to the memorial meeting for Mr. Parker, which was very beautiful, and proved how much he was beloved. Music Hall was full of flowers and sunshine, and hundreds of faces, both sad and proud, as the various speakers told the life of love and labor which makes

Theodore Parker's memory so rich a legacy to Boston. I was very glad to have known so good a man, and been called "friend" by him.

Saw Nan in her nest, where she and her mate live like a pair of turtle doves. Very sweet and pretty, but I'd rather be a free spinster and paddle my own canoe.

August.—"Moods." Genius burned so fiercely that for four weeks I wrote all day and planned nearly all night, being quite possessed by my work. I was perfectly happy, and seemed to have no wants. Finished the book, or a rough draught of it, and put it away to settle. Mr. Emerson offered to read it when Mother told him it was "Moods" and had one of his sayings for motto.

Daresay nothing will ever come of it; but it *had* to be done, and I'm the richer for a new experience.

September.—Received $75 of Ticknor "Cinderella," and feel very rich. Emerson praised it, and people wrote to me about it and patted me on the head. Paid bills, and began to simmer another.

February, 1861.—Another turn at "Moods," which I remodelled. From the 2d to the 25th I sat writing, with a run at dusk; could not sleep, and for three days was so full of it I could not stop to get up. Mother made me a green silk cap with a red bow, to match the old green and red party wrap, which I wore as a "glory cloak." Thus arrayed I sat in groves of manuscripts, "living for immortality," as May said. Mother wandered in and out with cordial cups of tea, worried because I couldn't eat. Father thought it fine, and brought his reddest apples and hardest cider for my Pegasus to feed upon. All sorts of fun was going on; but I didn't care if the world returned to chaos if I and my inkstand only "lit" in the same place.

It was very pleasant and queer while it lasted; but after three weeks of it I found that my mind was too rampant for my body, as my head was dizzy, legs shaky, and no sleep would come. So I dropped the pen, and took long walks, cold baths, and had Nan up to frolic with me. Read all I had done to my family; and Father said: "Emerson must see this. Where did you get your metaphysics?" Mother pronounced it wonderful, and Anna laughed and cried, as she always does, over my works, saying, "My dear, I'm proud of you."

So I had a good time, even if it never comes to any thing; for it was worth something to have my three dearest sit up till midnight listening with wide-open eyes to Lu's first novel.

I planned it some time ago, and have had it in my mind ever so long; but now it begins to take shape.

April.—War declared with the South, and our Concord company went to Washington. A busy time getting them ready, and a sad day seeing them off; for in a little town like this we all seem like one family in times like these. At the station the scene was very dramatic, as the brave boys went away perhaps never to come back again.

I've often longed to see a war, and now I have my wish. I long to be a man; but as I can't fight, I will content myself with working for those who can.

Sewed a good deal getting May's summer things in order, as she sent for me to make and mend and buy and send her outfit.

Stories simmered in my brain, demanding to be writ; but I let them simmer, knowing that the longer the divine afflatus was bottled up the better it would be.

John Brown's daughters came to board, and upset my plans of rest and writing when the report and the sewing were done. I had my fit of woe up garret on the fat rag-bag, and then put my papers away, and fell to work at housekeeping. I think disappointment must be good for me, I get so much of it; and the constant thumping Fate gives me may be a mellowing process; so I shall be a ripe and sweet old pippin before I die.

May, 1862.—School finished for me, and I paid Miss N. by giving her all the furniture, and leaving her to do as she liked; while I went back to my writing, which pays much better, though Mr. F. did say, "Stick to your teaching; you can't write." Being wilful, I said, "I won't teach; and I can write, and I'll prove it."

Saw Miss Rebecca Harding, author of "Margret Howth," which has made a stir, and is very good. A handsome, fresh, quiet woman, who says she never had any troubles, though she writes about woes. I told her I had had lots of troubles; so I write jolly tales; and we wondered why we each did so.

June, July, August.—Wrote a tale for B., and he lost it, and wouldn't pay.

Wrote two tales for L. I enjoy romancing to suit myself; and though my tales are silly, they are not bad; and my sinners always have a good spot somewhere. I hope it is good drill for fancy and language, for I can do it fast; and Mr. L. says my tales are so "dramatic, vivid, and full of plot," they are just what he wants.

GEORGETOWN

(1862–63)

November.—Thirty years old. Decided to go to Washington as nurse if I could find a place. Help needed, and I love nursing, and *must* let out my pent-up energy in some new way. Winter is always a hard and a dull time, and if I am away there is one less to feed and warm and worry over.

I want new experiences, and am sure to get 'em if I go. So I've sent in my name, and bide my time writing tales, to leave all snug behind me, and mending up my old clothes,—for nurses don't need nice things, thank Heaven!

December.—On the 11th I received a note from Miss H. M. Stevenson telling me to start for Georgetown next day to fill a place in the Union Hotel Hospital. Mrs. Ropes of Boston was matron, and Miss Kendall of Plymouth was a nurse there, and though a hard place, help was needed. I was ready, and when my commander said "March!" I marched. Packed my trunk, and reported in B. that same evening.

We had all been full of courage till the last moment came; then we all broke down. I realized that I had taken my life in my hand, and might never see them all again. I said, "Shall I stay, Mother?" as I hugged her close. "No, go! and the Lord be with you!" answered the Spartan woman; and till I turned the corner she bravely smiled and waved her wet handkerchief on the door-step. Shall I ever see that dear old face again?

So I set forth in the December twilight, with May and Julian Hawthorne as escort, feeling as if I was the son of the house going to war.

Friday, the 12th, was a very memorable day, spent in running all over Boston to get my pass, etc., calling for parcels, getting a tooth filled, and buying a veil,—my only purchase. A. C. gave me some old clothes; the dear Sewalls money for myself and boys, lots of love and help; and at 5 P.M., saying "good-by" to a group of tearful faces at the station, I started on my long journey, full of hope and sorrow, courage and plans.

A most interesting journey into a new world full of stirring sights and sounds, new adventures, and an ever-growing sense of the great task I had undertaken.

I said my prayers as I went rushing through the country white with tents, all alive with patriotism, and already red with blood.

A solemn time, but I'm glad to live in it; and am sure it will do me good whether I come out alive or dead.

All went well, and I got to Georgetown one evening very tired. Was kindly welcomed, slept in my narrow bed with two other room-mates, and on the morrow began my new life by seeing a poor man die at dawn, and sitting all day between a boy with pneumonia and a man shot through the lungs. A strange day, but I did my best; and when I put mother's little black shawl round the boy while he sat up panting for breath, he smiled and said, "You are real motherly, ma'am." I felt as if I was getting on. The man only lay and stared with his big black eyes, and made me very nervous. But all were well behaved; and I sat looking at the twenty strong faces as they looked back at me,—the only new thing they had to amuse them,—hoping that I looked "motherly" to them; for my thirty years made me feel old, and the suffering round me made me long to comfort every one.

January, 1863. *Union Hotel Hospital, Georgetown, D. C.*—I never began the year in a stranger place than this: five hundred miles from home, alone, among strangers, doing painful duties all day long, and leading a life of constant excitement in this great house, surrounded by three or four hundred men in all stages of suffering, disease, and death. Though often homesick, heartsick, and worn out, I like it, find real pleasure in comforting, tending, and cheering these poor souls who seem to love me, to feel my sympathy though unspoken, and acknowledge my hearty good-will, in spite of the ignorance, awkwardness, and bashfulness which I cannot help showing in so new and trying a situation. The men are docile, respectful, and affectionate, with but few exceptions; truly lovable and manly many of them. John Sulie, a Virginia blacksmith, is the prince of patients; and though what we call a common man in education and condition, to me is all I could expect or ask from the first gentleman in the land. Under his plain speech and unpolished manner I seem to see a noble character, a heart as warm and tender as a woman's, a nature fresh and frank as any child's. He is about thirty, I think, tall and handsome, mortally wounded, and dying royally without reproach, repining, or remorse. Mrs. Ropes and myself love him, and feel indignant that such a man should be so early lost; for though he might never distinguish himself before the world, his influence and example cannot be without effect, for real goodness is never wasted.

Monday, 4th.—I shall record the events of a day as a sample of the days I spend:—

Up at six, dress by gaslight, run through my ward and throw up the windows, though the men grumble and shiver; but the air is bad enough to breed a pestilence; and as no notice is taken of our frequent appeals for better ventilation, I must do what I can. Poke up the fire, add blankets, joke, coax, and command; but continue to open doors and windows as if life depended upon it. Mine does, and doubtless many another, for a more perfect pestilence-box than this house I never saw,—cold, damp, dirty, full of vile odors from wounds, kitchens, wash-rooms, and stables. No competent head, male or female, to right matters, and a jumble of good, bad, and indifferent nurses, surgeons, and attendants, to complicate the chaos still more.

After this unwelcome progress through my stifling ward, I go to breakfast with what appetite I may; find the uninvitable fried beef, salt butter, husky bread, and washy coffee; listen to the clack of eight women and a dozen men,—the first silly, stupid, or possessed of one idea; the last absorbed with their breakfast and themselves to a degree that is both ludicrous and provoking, for all the dishes are ordered down the table *full* and returned *empty;* the conversation is entirely among themselves, and each announces his opinion with an air of importance that frequently causes me to choke in my cup, or bolt my meals with undignified speed lest a laugh betray to these famous beings that a "chiel's amang them takin' notes."

Till noon I trot, trot, giving out rations, cutting up food for helpless "boys," washing faces, teaching my attendants how beds are made or floors are swept, dressing wounds, taking Dr. F. P.'s orders (privately wishing all the time that he would be more gentle with my big babies), dusting tables, sewing bandages, keeping my tray tidy, rushing up and down after pillows, bed-linen, sponges, books, and directions, till it seems as if I would joyfully pay down all I possess for fifteen minutes' rest. At twelve the big bell rings, and up comes dinner for the boys, who are always ready for it and never entirely satisfied. Soup, meat, potatoes, and bread is the bill of fare. Charley Thayer, the attendant, travels up and down the room serving out the rations, saving little for himself, yet always thoughtful of his mates, and patient as a woman with their helplessness. When dinner is over, some sleep, many read, and others want letters written. This I like to do, for they put in such odd things, and express their ideas so comically, I have great fun interiorally, while as grave as possible exteriorally. A few of the men word their paragraphs well and make excellent letters. John's was the best of all I wrote. The answering of letters from friends after some one had died is the saddest and hardest duty a nurse has to do.

Supper at five sets every one to running that can run; and when that flurry is over, all settle down for the evening amusements, which consist of newspapers, gossip, the doctor's last round, and, for such as need them, the final doses for the night. At nine the bell rings, gas is turned down, and day nurses go to bed. Night nurses go on duty, and sleep and death have the house to themselves.

My work is changed to night watching, or half night and half day,—from twelve to twelve. I like it, as it leaves me time for a morning run, which is what I need to keep well; for bad air, food, and water, work and watching, are getting to be too much for me. I trot up and down the streets in all directions, sometimes to the Heights, then half way to Washington, again to the hill, over which the long trains of army wagons are constantly vanishing and ambulances appearing. That way the fighting lies, and I long to follow.

Ordered to keep my room, being threatened with pneumonia. Sharp pain in the side, cough, fever, and dizziness. A pleasant prospect for a lonely soul five hundred miles from home! Sit and sew on the boys' clothes, write letters, sleep, and read; try to talk and keep merry, but fail decidedly, as day after day goes, and I feel no better. Dream awfully, and wake unrefreshed, think of home, and wonder if I am to die here, as Mrs. R., the matron, is likely to do. Feel too miserable to care much what becomes of me. Dr. S. creaks up twice a day to feel my pulse, give me doses, and ask if I am at all consumptive, or some other cheering question. Dr. O. examines my lungs and looks sober. Dr. J. haunts the room, coming by day and night with wood, cologne, books, and messes, like a motherly little man as he is. Nurses fussy and anxious, matron dying, and everything very gloomy. They want me to go home, but I *won't* yet.

January 16th.—Was amazed to see Father enter the room that morning, having been telegraphed to by order of Mrs. R. without asking leave. I was very angry at first, though glad to see him, because I knew I should have to go. Mrs. D. and Miss Dix came, and pretty Miss W., to take me to Willard's to be cared for by them. I wouldn't go, preferring to keep still, being pretty ill by that time.

On the 21st I suddenly decided to go home, feeling very strangely, and dreading to be worse. Mrs. R. died, and that frightened the doctors about me; for my trouble was the same,—typhoid pneumonia. Father, Miss K., and Lizzie T. went with me. Miss Dix brought a basket full of bottles of wine, tea, medicine, and cologne, besides a little blanket and pillow, a fan, and a testament. She is a kind old soul, but very queer and arbitrary.

Was very sorry to go, and "my boys" seemed sorry to have me. Quite a flock came to see me off; but I was too sick to have but a dim idea of what was going on.

Had a strange, excited journey of a day and night,—half asleep, half wandering, just conscious that I was going home; and, when I got to Boston, of being taken out of the car, with people looking on as if I was a sight. I daresay I was all blowzed, crazy, and weak. Was too sick to reach Concord that night, though we tried to do so. Spent it at Mr. Sewall's; had a sort of fit; they sent for Dr. H., and I had a dreadful time of it.

Next morning felt better, and at four went home. Just remember seeing May's shocked face at the depot, Mother's bewildered one at home, and getting to bed in the firm belief that the house was roofless, and no one wanted to see me.

As I never shall forget the strange fancies that haunted me, I shall amuse myself with recording some of them.

The most vivid and enduring was the conviction that I had married a stout, handsome Spaniard, dressed in black velvet, with very soft hands, and a voice that was continually saying, "Lie still, my dear!" This was Mother, I suspect; but with all the comfort I often found in her presence, there was blended an awful fear of the Spanish spouse who was always coming after me, appearing out of closets, in at windows, or threatening me dreadfully all night long. I appealed to the Pope, and really got up and made a touching plea in something meant for Latin, they tell me. Once I went to heaven, and found it a twilight place, with people darting through the air in a queer way,—all very busy, and dismal, and ordinary. Miss Dix, W. H. Channing, and other people were there; but I thought it dark and "slow," and wished I hadn't come.

A mob at Baltimore breaking down the door to get me, being hung for a witch, burned, stoned, and otherwise maltreated, were some of my fancies. Also being tempted to join Dr. W. and two of the nurses in worshipping the Devil. Also tending millions of rich men who never died or got well.

February.—Recovered my senses after three weeks of delirium, and was told I had had a very bad typhoid fever, had nearly died, and was still very sick. All of which seemed rather curious, for I remembered nothing of it. Found a queer, thin, big-eyed face when I looked in the glass; didn't know myself at all; and when I tried to walk discovered that I couldn't, and cried because my legs wouldn't go.

Never having been sick before, it was all new and very interesting when I got quiet enough to understand matters. Such long, long nights; such feeble, idle days; dozing, fretting about nothing; longing to eat, and no mouth to do it with,—mine being so sore, and full of all manner of queer sensations, it was nothing but a plague. The old fancies still lingered, seeming so real I believed in them, and deluded Mother and May with the most absurd stories, so soberly told that they thought them true.

Dr. B. came every day, and was very kind. Father and Mother were with me night and day, and May sang "Birks of Aberfeldie," or read to me, to wile away the tiresome hours. People sent letters, money, kind inquiries, and goodies for the old "Nuss." I tried to sew, read, and write, and found I had to begin all over again. Received $10 for my labors in Washington. Had all my hair, a yard and a half long, cut off, and went into caps like a grandma. Felt badly about losing my one beauty. Never mind, it might have been my head, and a wig outside is better than a loss of wits inside.

MOODS

(1864–65)

April.—At Father's request I sent "Moods" to T., and got a very friendly note from him, saying they had so many books on hand that they could do nothing about it now. So I put it back on the shelf, and set about my other work. Don't despair, "Moods," we'll try again by and by!

[Alas! we did try again.—L. M. A.]

September.—Mrs. D. made a visit, and getting hold of my old book of stories liked them, and insisted on taking "Moods" home to read. As she had had experience with publishers, was a good business woman, and an excellent critic, I let her have it, hoping she might be able to give the poor old book the lift it has been waiting for all these years. She took it, read it, and admired it heartily, saying that "no American author had showed so much promise; that the plan was admirable; the execution unequal, but often magnificent; that I had a great field before me, and my book must be got out."

Mrs. D. sent it to L., who liked it exceedingly, and asked me to shorten it if I could, else it would be too large to sell well. Was much disappointed, said I'd never touch it again, and tossed it into the spidery little cupboard where it had so often returned after fruitless trips.

October.—Wrote several chapters of "Work," and was getting on finely, when, as I lay awake one night, a way to shorten and arrange "Moods" came into my head. The whole plan laid itself smoothly out before me, and I slept no more that night, but worked on it as busily as if mind and body had nothing to do with one another. Up early, and began to write it all over again. The fit was on strong, and for a fortnight I hardly ate, slept, or stirred, but wrote, wrote, like a thinking machine in full operation. When it was all rewritten without copying, I found it much improved, though I'd taken out ten chapters, and sacrificed many of my favorite things; but being resolved to make it simple, strong, and short, I let everything else go, and hoped the book would be better for it.

[It wasn't. 1867.]

Sent it to L.; and a week after, as I sat hammering away at the parlor carpet,—dusty, dismal, and tired,—a letter came from L. praising the story more enthusiastically than ever, thanking me for the improvements, and proposing to bring out the book at once. Of course we all had a rapture, and I finished my work "double quick," regardless of weariness, toothache, or blue devils.

Next day I went to Boston and saw L. A brisk, business-like man who seemed in earnest and said many complimentary things about "Hospital Sketches" and its author. It was agreed to bring out the book immediately, and Mrs. D. offered to read the proof with me.

Was glad to have the old thing under way again, but didn't quite believe it would ever come out after so many delays and disappointments.

Sewed for Nan and Mary, heard Anna Dickinson and liked her. Read "Emily Chester" and thought it an unnatural story, yet just enough like "Moods" in a few things to make me sorry that it came out now.

On Mother's sixty-fourth birthday I gave her "Moods" with this inscription,—"To Mother, my earliest patron, kindest critic, dearest reader, I gratefully and affectionately inscribe my first romance."

A letter from T. asking me to write for the new magazine "Our Young Folks," and saying that "An Hour" was in the hands of the editors.

November.—Proof began to come, and the chapters seemed small, stupid, and no more my own in print. I felt very much afraid that I'd ventured too much and should be sorry for it. But Emerson says "that what is true for your own private heart is true for others." So I wrote from my own consciousness and observation and hope it may suit some one and at least do no harm.

I sent "An Hour" to the "Commonwealth" and it was considered *excellent.* Also wrote a Christmas Story, "Mrs. Todger's Teapot." T. asked to see the other fairy tales and designs and poems, as he liked "Nelly's Hospital" so much.

On my thirty-second birthday received Richter's Life from Nan and enjoyed it so much that I planned a story of two men something like Jean Paul and Goethe, only more every-day people. Don't know what will come of it, but if "Moods" goes well "Success" shall follow.

Sewed for Wheeler's colored company and sent them comfort-bags, towels, books, and bed-sacks. Mr. W. sent me some relics from Point Look Out and a pleasant letter.

December.—Earnings, 1864,—$476.

On Christmas Eve received ten copies of "Moods" and a friendly note from L. The book was hastily got out, but on the whole suited me, and as the inside was considered good I let the outside go. For a week whereever I went I saw, heard, and talked "Moods;" found people laughing or crying over it, and was continually told how well it was going, how much it was liked, how fine a thing I'd done. I was glad but not proud, I think, for it has always seemed as if "Moods" grew in spite of me, and that I had little to do with it except to put into words the thoughts that would not let me rest until I had. Don't know why.

By Saturday the first edition was gone and the second ready. Several booksellers ordered a second hundred, the first went so fast, and friends could not get it but had to wait till more were ready.

Spent a fortnight in town at Mary's, shopping, helping Nan, and having plays. Heard Emerson once. Gave C. "Mrs. Todger's Teapot," which was much liked. Sent L. the rest of his story and got $50. S. paid $35 for "An Hour." R. promised $100 for "Love and Loyalty," so my year closes with a novel well-launched and about $300 to pay debts and make the family happy and comfortable till spring. Thank God for the success of the old year, the promise of the new!

January, 1865.—The month began with some plays at the town hall to raise funds for the Lyceum. We did very well and some Scenes from Dickens were excellent. Father lectured and preached a good deal, being asked like a regular minister and paid like one. He enjoyed it very much and said good things on the new religion which we ought to and shall have. May had orders from Canada and England for her pretty pen-and-ink work and did well in that line.

Notices of "Moods" came from all directions, and though people didn't understand my ideas owing to my shortening the book so much, the notices were mostly favorable and gave quite as much praise as was good for me. I had letters from Mrs. Parker, Chadwick, Sanborn, E. B. Greene, the artist, T. W. Higginson and some others. All friendly and flattering.

Saw more notices of "Moods" and received more letters, several from strangers and some very funny. People seemed to think the book finely written, very promising, wise, and interesting; but some fear it isn't moral, because it speaks freely of marriage.

Wrote a little on poor old "Work" but being tired of novels, I soon dropped it and fell back on rubbishy tales, for they pay best, and I can't afford to starve on praise, when sensation stories are written in half the time and keep the family cosey.

Earned $75 this month.

I went to Boston and heard Father lecture before the Fraternity. Met Henry James, Sr., there, and he asked me to come and dine, also called upon me with Mrs. James. I went, and was treated like the Queen of Sheba. Henry Jr. wrote a notice of "Moods" for the "North American," and was very friendly. Being a literary youth he gave me advice, as if he had been eighty and I a girl. My curly crop made me look young, though thirty-one.

Acted in some public plays for the N. E. Women's Hospital and had a pleasant time.

L. asked me to be a regular contributor to his new paper, and I agreed if he'd pay beforehand; he said he would, and bespoke two tales at once, $50 each, longer ones as often as I could, and whatever else I liked to send. So here's another source of income and Alcott brains seem in demand, whereat I sing "Hallyluyer" and fill up my inkstand.

April.—Richmond taken on the 2d. Hurrah! Went to Boston and enjoyed the grand jollification. Saw Booth again in Hamlet and thought him finer than ever. Had a pleasant walk and talk with Phillips.

On the 15th in the midst of the rejoicing came the sad news of the President's assassination, and the city went into mourning. I am glad to have seen such a strange and sudden change in a nation's feelings. Saw the great procession, and though few colored men were in it, one was walking arm in arm with a white gentleman, and I exulted thereat.

Nan went to housekeeping in a pleasant house at Jamaica Plain, and I went to help her move. It was beautiful to see how Freddy enjoyed the freedom, after being cooped up all winter, and how every morning, whether it rained or shone, he looked out and said, with a smile of perfect satisfaction, "Oh, pretty day!"—for all days *were* pretty to him, dear little soul!

Had a fine letter from Conway, and a notice in the "Reader,"—an English paper. He advised sending copies to several of the best London papers. English people don't understand "transcendental literature," as they call "Moods." My next book shall have no *ideas* in it, only facts, and the people shall be as ordinary as possible; then critics will say it's all right. I seem to have been playing with edge tools without knowing it. The relations between Warwick, Moor, and Sylvia are pronounced impossible; yet a case of the sort exists, and the woman came and asked me how I knew it. I did *not* know or guess, but perhaps felt it, without any other guide, and unconsciously put the thing into my book, for I changed the ending about that time. It was meant to show a life affected by *moods,* not a discussion of marriage, which I knew little about, except observing that very few were happy ones.

LITTLE WOMEN

(1868–69)

May, 1868.—Father saw Mr. Niles about a fairy book. Mr. N. wants a *girls' story,* and I begin "Little Women." Marmee, Anna, and May all approve my plan. So I plod away, though I don't enjoy this sort of thing. Never liked girls or knew many, except my sisters; but our queer plays and experiences may prove interesting, though I doubt it.

[Good joke.—L. M. A.]

June.—Sent twelve chapters of "L. W." to Mr. N. He thought it *dull;* so do I. But work away and mean to try the experiment; for lively, simple books are very much needed for girls, and perhaps I can supply the need.

Wrote two tales for Ford, and one for F. L. clamors for more, but must wait.

July 15*th*.—Have finished "Little Women," and sent it off,—402 pages. May is designing some pictures for it. Hope it will go, for I shall probably get nothing for "Morning Glories."

Very tired, head full of pain from overwork, and heart heavy about Marmee, who is growing feeble.

> [Too much work for one young woman. No wonder she broke down. 1876.—L. M. A.]

August.—Roberts Bros. made an offer for the story, but at the same time advised me to keep the copyright; so I shall.

> [An honest publisher and a lucky author, for the copyright made her fortune, and the "dull book" was the first golden egg of the ugly duckling. 1885.—L. M. A.]

August 26*th*.—Proof of whole book came. It reads better than I expected. Not a bit sensational, but simple and true, for we really lived most of it; and if it succeeds that will be the reason of it. Mr. N. likes it better now, and says some girls who have read the manuscripts say it is "splendid!" As it is for them, they are the best critics, so I should be satisfied.

September.—Father's book ["Tablets"] came out. Very simple outside, wise and beautiful within. Hope it will bring him praise and profit, for he has waited long.

No girl, Mother poorly, May busy with pupils, Nan with her boys, and much work to be done. We don't like the kitchen department, and our tastes and gifts lie in other directions, so it is hard to make the various Pegasuses pull the plan steadily.

October 8*th*.—Marmee's birthday; sixty-eight. After breakfast she found her gifts on a table in the study. Father escorted her to the big red chair, the boys prancing before blowing their trumpets, while we "girls" marched behind, glad to see the dear old Mother better and able to enjoy our little fête. The boys proudly handed her the little parcels, and she laughed and cried over our gifts and verses.

I feel as if the decline had begun for her; and each year will add to the change which is going on, as time alters the energetic, enthusiastic home-mother into a gentle, feeble old woman, to be cherished and helped tenderly down the long hill she has climbed so bravely with her many burdens.

October 26th.—Came to Boston, and took a quiet room in Brookline Street. Heard Emerson in the evening. Sent a report of it to A. P. for the "Standard" at his desire.

Anna is nicely settled in her new house, and Marmee is with her. Helped put down carpets and settle things.

30*th.*—Saw Mr. N. of Roberts Brothers, and he gave me good news of the book. An order from London for an edition came in. First edition gone and more called for. Expects to sell three or four thousand before the New Year.

Mr. N. wants a second volume for spring. Pleasant notices and letters arrive, and much interest in my little women, who seem to find friends by their truth to life, as I hoped.

November 1st.—Began the second part of "Little Women." I can do a chapter a day, and in a month I mean to be done. A little success is so inspiring that I now find my "Marches" sober, nice people, and as I can launch into the future, my fancy has more play. Girls write to ask who the little women marry, as if that was the only end and aim of a woman's life. I *won't* marry Jo to Laurie to please any one.

Monday, 16*th.*—To the Club for a change, as I have written like a steam engine since the 1st. Weiss read a fine paper on "Woman Suffrage." Good talk afterward. Lunched with Kate Field, Celia Thaxter, and Mr. Linton. Woman's Club in P.M.

17*th.*—Finished my thirteenth chapter. I am so full of my work, I can't stop to eat or sleep, or for anything but a daily run.

29*th.*—My birthday; thirty-six. Spent alone, writing hard. No presents but Father's "Tablets."

I never seem to have many presents, as some do, though I give a good many. That is best perhaps, and makes a gift very precious when it does come.

December.—Home to shut up the house, as Father goes West and Mother to Anna's. A cold, hard, dirty time; but was so glad to be off out of C. that I worked like a beaver, and turned the key on Apple Slump with joy.

May and I went to the new Bellevue Hotel in Beacon Street. She doesn't enjoy quiet corners as I do, so we took a sky-parlor, and had a queer time whisking up and down in the elevator, eating in a marble café, and sleeping on a sofa bed, that we might be genteel. It did not suit me at all. A great gale nearly blew the roof off. Steam pipes exploded, and we were hungry. I was very tired with my hard summer, with no rest for the brains that earn the money.

January, 1869.—Left our lofty room at Bellevue and went to Chauncey Street. Sent the sequel of "L. W." to Roberts on New Year's Day. Hope it will do as well as the first, which is selling finely, and receives good notices. F. and F. both want me to continue working for them, and I shall do so if I am able; but my headaches, cough, and weariness keep me from working as I once could, fourteen hours a day.

In March we went home, as Mother was restless at Nan's, and Father wanted his library. Cold and dull; not able to write; so took care of Marmee and tried to rest.

Paid up all the debts, thank the Lord!—every penny that money can pay,—and now I feel as if I could die in peace. My dream is beginning to come true; and if my head holds out I'll do all I once hoped to do.

April.—Very poorly. Feel quite used up. Don't care much for myself, as rest is heavenly even with pain; but the family seem so panic-stricken and helpless when I break down, that I try to keep the mill going. Two short tales for L., $50; two for Ford, $20; and did my editorial work, though two months are unpaid for. Roberts wants a new book, but am afraid to get into a vortex lest I fall ill.

EMERSON'S DEATH

(1882)

Thursday, 27th.—Mr. Emerson died at 9 P.M. suddenly. Our best and greatest American gone. The nearest and dearest friend Father has ever had, and the man who has helped me most by his life, his books, his society. I can never tell all he has been to me,—from the time I sang Mignon's song under his window (a little girl) and wrote letters *à la* Bettine to him, my Goethe, at fifteen, up through my hard years, when his essays on Self-Reliance, Character, Compensation, Love, and Friendship helped me to understand myself and life, and God and Nature. Illustrious and beloved friend, good-by!

Sunday, 30th.—Emerson's funeral. I made a yellow lyre of jonquils for the church, and helped trim it up. Private services at the house, and a great crowd at the church. Father read his sonnet, and Judge Hoar and others spoke. Now he lies in Sleepy Hollow among his brothers, under the pines he loved.

I sat up till midnight to write an article on R. W. E. for the "Youth's Companion," that the children may know something of him. A labor of love.

Letters[1]

TO ABIGAIL MAY ALCOTT

20 Pinckney Street, Boston, Dec. 25, 1854.

Dear Mother,—Into your Christmas stocking I have put my "first-born" [*Flower Fables*], knowing that you will accept it with all its faults (for grandmothers are always kind), and look upon it merely as an earnest of what I may yet do, for, with so much to cheer me on, I hope to pass in time from fairies and fables to men and realities.

Whatever beauty or poetry is to be found in my little book is owing to your interest in and encouragement of all my efforts from the first to the last, and if ever I do anything to be proud of, my greatest happiness will be that I can thank you for that, as I may do for all the good there is in me, and I shall be content to write if it gives you pleasure.

Jo is fussing about;
My lamp is going out.

To dear mother, with many kind wishes for a happy New Year and merry Christmas.

I am your ever loving daughter
Louy.

TO AMOS BRONSON ALCOTT[2]

Boston, Nov. 29, 1856.

Dearest Father,—Your little parcel was very welcome to me as I sat alone in my room, with snow falling fast outside, and a few tears in (for birthdays are dismal times to me), and the fine letter, the pretty gift, and, most of all, the loving thought so kindly taken for your old absent daughter, made the cold, dark day as warm and bright as summer to me.

And now, with the birthday pin upon my bosom, many thanks on my lips, and a whole heart full of love for its giver, I will tell you a little about my doings, stupid as they will seem after your own grand proceedings. How I wish I could be with you, enjoying what I have always longed for,—fine people, fine amusements, and fine books. But as I can't, I am glad you are; for I love to see your name first among the lecturers, to hear it kindly spoken of in papers and inquired about by good people here,—to say nothing of the delight and pride I take in seeing you at last filling the place you are so fitted for, and which you have waited for so long and patiently. If the New Yorkers raise a statue to the modern Plato, it will be a wise and highly creditable action.

. . . .

I am very well and very happy. Things go smoothly, and I think I shall come out right, and prove that though an *Alcott* I *can* support myself. I like the independent feeling; and though not an easy life, it is a free one, and I enjoy it. I can't do much with my hands; so I will make a battering-ram of my head and make a way through this rough-and-tumble world. I have very pleasant lectures to amuse my evenings,—Professor Gajani on "Italian Reformers," the Mercantile Library course, Whipple, Beecher, and others, and, best of all, a free pass at the Boston Theatre. I saw Mr. Barry, and he gave it to me with many kind speeches, and promises to bring out the play very soon. I hope he will.

My farce is in the hands of Mrs. W. H. Smith, who acts at Laura Keene's theatre in New York. She took it, saying she would bring it out there. If you see or hear anything about it, let me know. I want something doing. My mornings are spent in writing. C. takes me one a month, and I am to see Mr. B., who may take some of my wares.

In the afternoons I walk and visit my hundred relations, who are all kind and friendly, and seem interested in our various successes.

Sunday evenings I go to Parker's parlor, and there meet Phillips, Garrison, Scherb, Sanborn, and many other pleasant people. All talk, and I sit in a corner listening, and wishing a certain placid gray-haired gentleman was there talking too. Mrs. Parker calls on me, reads my stories, and is very good to me. Theodore asks Louisa "how her worthy parents do," and is otherwise very friendly to the large, bashful girl who adorns his parlor steadily.

Abby is preparing for a busy and, I hope, a profitable winter. She has music lessons already, French and drawing in store, and, if her eyes hold out, will keep her word and become what none of us can be, "an accomplished Alcott." Now, dear Father, I shall hope to hear from you occasionally, and will gladly answer all epistles from the Plato whose parlor parish is becoming quite famous. I got the "Tribune," but not the letter, and shall look it up. I have been meaning to write, but did not know where you were.

Good-by, and a happy birthday from your ever loving child,

LOUISA.

TO ANNA ALCOTT PRATT

[DATE UNCERTAIN][3]

My Lass,—This must be a frivolous and dressy letter, because you always want to know about our clothes, and we have been at it lately. May's bonnet is a sight for gods and men. Black and white outside, with a great cockade boiling over the front to meet a red ditto surging from the interior, where a red rainbow darts across the brow, and a surf of white lace foams up on each side. I expect to hear that you and John fell flat in the dust with horror on beholding it.

My bonnet has nearly been the death of me, for, thinking some angel might make it possible for me to go to the mountains, I felt a wish for a tidy hat, after wearing an old one till it fell in tatters from my brow. Mrs. P. promised a bit of gray silk, and I built on that, but when I went for it I found my hat was founded on sand; for she let me down with a crash, saying she wanted the silk herself, and kindly offering me a flannel petticoat instead. I was in woe for a spell, having one dollar in the world, and scorning debt even for that prop of life, a "bonnet." Then I roused myself, flew to Dodge, demanded her cheapest bonnet, found one for a dollar, took it, and went home wondering if the sky would open and drop me a trimming. I am simple in my tastes, but a naked straw bonnet is a little too severely chaste even for me. Sky did not open; so I went to the "Widow Cruise's oil bottle"—my ribbon box—which, by the way, is the eighth wonder of the world, for nothing is ever put in, yet I always find some old dud when all other hopes fail. From this salvation bin I extracted the remains of the old white ribbon (used up, as I thought, two years ago), and the bits of black lace that have adorned a long line of departed hats. Of the lace I made a dish, on which I thriftily served up bows of ribbon, like meat on toast. Inside put the lace bow, which adorns my form anywhere when needed. A white flower A. H. gave me sat airily on the brim,—fearfully unbecoming, but pretty in itself, and in keeping. Strings are yet to be evolved from chaos. I feel that they await me somewhere in the dim future. Green ones *pro tem.* hold this wonder of the age upon my gifted brow, and I survey my hat with respectful awe. I trust you will also, and see in it another great example of the power of mind over matter, and the convenience of a colossal brain in the primeval wrestle with the unruly atoms which have harassed the feminine soul ever since Eve clapped on a modest fig-leaf and did up her hair with a thorn for a hairpin.

I feel very moral to-day, having done a big wash alone, baked, swept the house, picked the hops, got dinner, and written a chapter in "Moods." May gets exhausted with work, though she walks six miles without a murmur.

It is dreadfully dull, and I work so that I may not "brood." Nothing stirring but the wind; nothing to see but dust; no one comes but rose-bugs; so I grub and scold at the "A" because it takes a poor fellow's tales and keeps 'em years without paying for 'em. If I think of my woes I fall into a vortex of debts, dishpans, and despondency awful to see. So I say, "every path has its puddle," and try to play gayly with the tadpoles in *my* puddle, while I wait for the Lord to give me a lift, or some gallant Raleigh to spread his velvet cloak and fetch me over dry shod.

L. W. adds to my woe by writing of the splendors of Gorham, and says, "When tired, run right up here and find rest among these everlasting hills." All very aggravating to a young woman with one dollar, no bonnet, half a gown, and a discontented mind. It's a mercy the mountains are everlasting, for it will be a century before *I* get there. Oh, me, such is life!

Now I've done my Jeremiad, and I will go on twanging my harp in the "willow tree."

You ask what I am writing. Well, two books half done, nine stories simmering, and stacks of fairy stories moulding on the shelf. I can't do much, as I have no time to get into a real good vortex. It unfits me for work, worries Ma to see me look pale, eat nothing, and ply by night. These extinguishers keep genius from burning as I could wish, and I give up ever hoping to do anything unless luck turns for your

LU.

TO ANNIE MARIA LAWRENCE[4]

My Dear Miss Lawrence.

I have a vague recollection of some little girl who was Lizzie's friend in the old Still River days, but do not recal the name though very glad to welcome any one who knew & loved our Lizzie.

Those *were* jolly times, & I never think of them without a laugh. The Gardeners were our mates then, & I remember being married to Walter by Alfred Haskell with a white apron for a veil & the old wood shed for a church. We slapped one another soon after & parted, finding that our tempers didn't agree. I rather think my prejudices in favor of spinsterhood are founded upon that brief but tragical experience.

I am glad if my scribbles amuse you & thank my friend "Mrs Podgers" for bringing me another expression of good will. "Moods" wont suit you so well I suspect, for in it I've freed my mind upon a subject that always makes trouble, namely, Love. But being founded upon fact, & the characters drawn from life it may be of use as all experiences are & serve as a warning at least.

I also have been a schoolmarm for ten years, but I dont like it & prefer pen & ink to birch & book, for my imaginary children are much easier to manage than living responsibilities.

My little nephew, Annie's son, is calling "Aunty Wee-wee" to come & take him for his daily constitutional, & the young lord of the house must be obeyed. Please remember me to the Gardeners, & believe me

Very truly your friend
L. M. Alcott.

Concord Feb 3rd/65.

TO MONCURE DANIEL CONWAY[5]

My Dear Mr Conway.

Mr Sanborn offers me a place in his parcel & I want to do myself the pleasure of sending you a copy of my little book because you were so kindly interested in the other one.

"Moods" is not what I meant to have it, for I followed bad advice & took out many things which explained my idea & made the characters more natural & consistent. I see my mistake now for I find myself accused of Spiritualism, Free Love, Affinities & all sorts of horrors that I know very little about & dont believe in.

Perhaps I was over bold to try the experiment of treating an old theme in a new way. But out of my own observation & experience I ventured to say what I thought to the young people whom I see so often making blunders that mar their whole lives, & then blaming God or fate, & becoming dismal martyrs when they should be cheerful workers.

Self abnegation is a noble thing but I think there is a limit to it; & though in a few rare cases it may work well yet half the misery of the world seems to come from unmated pairs trying to live their lie decorously to the end, & bringing children into the world to inherit the unhappiness & discord out of which they were born. There is discipline enough in the most perfect marriage & I dont agree to the doctrine of "marry in haste & repent at leisure" which seems to prevail. I onor [sic] it too much not to want to see it all it should be & to try to help others to prepare for it that they may find it life's best lesson not its heaviest burden.

The book has been sharply criticised & I am glad of it, though I wish I had done better justice to my own idea. I heartily believe it, am willing to be blamed for it, & am not sorry I wrote it, for it has not only cleared & fixed many things in my own mind, but brought me thanks & good wishes from many whom I find I have served better than I knew.

Pardon my egotistical note, but I did want to set myself right before you if I could, as it is too late to do it here before others, & with all its imperfections "Moods" is an honest, well meaning, little book.

Please remember me to Mrs Conway, & with affectionate regards from us all believe me

Very truly yours
L. M. ALCOTT.

Concord Feb 18/65.

TO MR. AYER

Mr Ayer.

I do not usually reply to the letters of strangers, having barely time to answer my friends, but you so entirely misunderstand Moods that I am anxious to set you right as far as I can in a hasty letter.

Your first question concerns the relations between Sylvia, Moor & Warwark [sic]. I know them to be *possible* as I have seen them more than once; they are *natural* though not common, for peculiar minds demonstrate their thoughts & feelings in peculiar ways; they are *desirable* only so far as they help men & women to understand themselves & each other.

You think that Moods teaches that marriage should be founded on some indefinable feeling or attraction not upon respect or esteem. Now if there is any thing that I heartily detest it is the theory of Affinities, also Spiritualism & Free Love, though I am grieved to find myself accused of all three. I honor marriage so highly that I long to see it what it should be life's best lesson not its heaviest cross. It has so great an influence upon us all that it should be held in greater reverence, prepared for carefully entered upon solemnly, & kept holy by being kept true. Respect & esteem must be the foundation, but above & beyond must be an abiding love that makes all things possible & without which no marriage is a true one, no household a home.

Half the misery of our time arises from unmated pairs trying to live their legal lie decorously to the end at any cost. Better a few cases of open infidelity that warn & shock than many hidden tragedies that doom the innocent children as well as guilty parents.

If you read carefully the 17th & 18th Chapters you will see that Sylvia did try to be all she should to Moor, did give up love for duty, & resist temptation, trying to do right through all delusions & mistakes although it cost her life. Warwick has been pronounced an impossible character, but as he was drawn from life he must stand for what he is worth. Not a base nor treacherous man, but one possessing great faults as well as virtues & like better men most inconsistent, unwise & blind when in love. He too makes his mistakes, endeavors to amend them, & is true to his belief of what is right in defiance of the world's opinion. He asked Sylvia to be true to herself & not decieve Moor, & in time she saw the worth of this advice, found Warwick upright even when most tempted to claim her after Moor knew all & was helped to see her way out of the dark by his plain dealing.

These latter chapters were more carefully written than any others, & as the book has been underway for six years there has been no occasion for haste any where. In justice to myself I want to say that by the advice of my publisher I took out ten chapters in order to shorten it; this I find was very unwise for these chapters explained much that now is obscure & made the whole story more natural & consistent. I shall know better another time, & do not blame my critics for failing to understand what I have not fully explained.

The design of Moods was to show the effect of a moody person's moods upon their life, & Sylvia, being a mixed & peculiar character, makes peculiar blunders & tries to remedy them in an uncommon manner. I had no desire to settle or unsettle any question, to convince or convert any one to any theory whatever, but wrote straight out of my own observation, experience & instinct.

Others beside yourself have made the same mistakes regarding my purpose, & perhaps it is well for me that they have as it will teach me that even a little romance has some influence for good or evil & make me careful in what I write hereafter. I think Moods will do no harm to the pure hearted & for them alone was it written. That it has done some good I already have proofs in the letters I receive from good women who have tried to do their duty & become meek martyrs instead of happy workers in God's world; young girls thank me for the warning I have unconsciously given them, & more than one minister has assured me that with all its faults the book has has taught a lesson that many needed to learn.

Pardon my seeming egotism, but when thoughtful men or women honor me with sincere praise or blame I desire to show that I am grateful for both by an equal sincerity on my part.

Respectfully Yours
L. M. ALCOTT.

Concord Mar. 19th/65.

TO THE LUKENS SISTERS[6]

CONCORD SEPT. 4TH [1873]

Dear Sisters,

You ask about little stories. Well, D. Ford of the Companion pays $50 apiece for them. Much more than they are worth of course, but he says he pays for the name, & seems satisfied with his bargain. I write for nothing else except a tale for the Independent now & then, which brings $100. This winter I shall write for Scribner at their request, as I have no book on the stacks.

For you I will, if I have time, write a tale or sketch now & then for love not money, & if the name is of any use you are very welcome to it.

I remember the dear little Pickwick Portfolio of twenty years ago & the spirit of an editor stirs within me promoting me to lend a hand to a sister editor.

I like to help women help themselves, as that is, in my opinion, the best way to settle the Woman question. Whatever we can do & do well we have a right to, & I dont think any one will deny us.

So best wishes for the success of Little Things & its brave young proprietors.

yrs truly L. M. ALCOTT.

P.S.

I did not like the suicide in "Work," but as much of that chapter was true I let it stand as a warning to several people who need it to my knowledge, & to many whom I do not know. I have already had letters from strangers thanking me for it, so I am not sorry it went in. One must have both the dark & the light side to paint life truly.

I'll write from imagination not cuts. I send you the last style of photo I have. Not very good but you can't make a Venus out of a tired old lady. Let me see yours by all means.

TO LUCY STONE[7]

CONCORD, MASS., OCT. 1, 1873.

Dear Mrs. Stone:—I am so busy just now proving "Woman's Right to Labor" that I have no time to help prove "Woman's Right to Vote." When I read your note aloud to the family, asking "What shall I say to Mrs. Stone?" my honored father instantly replied: "Tell her you are ready to follow your leader, sure that you could not have a better one." My brave old mother, with the ardor of many unquenchable Mays shining in her face, cried out: "Tell her I am seventy-three, but I mean to go to the polls before I die, even if my three daughters have to carry me." And two little men already mustered in added the cheering words: "Go ahead, Aunt Weedy, we will let you vote as much as you like." Such being the temper of the small convention of which I am now President, I can not hesitate to say that though I may not be with you in the body I shall be in spirit, and I am, as ever, hopefully and heartily yours,

LOUISA MAY ALCOTT.

TO MARIA S. PORTER[8]

[1874]

I rejoice greatly therat, and hope that the first thing that you and Mrs. Sewall propose in your first meeting will be to reduce the salary of the head master of the High School, and increase the salary of the first woman assistant, whose work is quite as good as his, and even harder; to make the pay equal. I believe in the same pay for the same good work. Don't you? In future let woman do whatever she can do; let men place no more impediments in the way; above all things let's have fair play,—let *simple justice* be done, say I. Let us hear no more of "woman's sphere" either from our wise (?) legislators beneath the State House dome, or from our clergymen in their pulpits. I am tired, year after year, of hearing such twaddle about sturdy oaks and clinging vines and man's chivalric protection of woman. Let woman find out her own limitations, and if, as is so confidently asserted, nature has defined her sphere, she will be guided accordingly; but in heaven's name give her a chance! Let the professions be open to her; let fifty years of college education be hers, and then we shall see what we shall see. Then, and not until then, shall we be able to say what woman can and what she cannot do, and coming generations will know and be able to define more clearly what is a "woman's sphere" than these benighted men who now try to do it.

TO LUCY STONE[9]

Dear Mrs. Stone:—One should be especially inspired this Centennial year before venturing to speak or write. I am not so blest, and find myself so busy trying to get ready for the good time that is surely coming, I can only in a very humble way, help on the cause all women should have at heart.

As reports are in order, I should like to say a word for the girls, on whom in a great measure, depends the success of the next generation.

My lines fell in pleasant places last year, and I looked well about me as I went among the young people, who unconsciously gave me some very cheering facts in return for very poor fictions.

I was both surprised and delighted with the nerve and courage, the high aims and patient persistence which appeared, not only among the laborious young women whose teacher is necessity, but among tenderly nurtured girls who cherished the noblest ambitions and had learned to earn the happiness no wealth could buy them.

Having great faith in young America, it gave me infinite satisfaction to find such eager interest in all good things, and to see how irresistably the spirit of our new revolution, stirring in the hearts of sisters and daughters, was converting the fathers and brothers who loved them. One shrewd, business man said, when talking of Woman Suffrage, "How *can* I help believing in it, when I've got a wife and six girls who are *bound* to have it?"

And many a grateful brother declared he could not be mean enough to shut any door in the face of the sister who had made him what he was.

So I close this hasty note by proposing three cheers for the girls of 1876—and the hope that they will prove themselves worthy descendants of the mothers of this Revolution, remembering that

> *"Earth's fanatics make*
> *Too often Heaven's saints."*

L. M. ALCOTT.

Concord, June 29 [1876].

TO JOHN PRESTON TRUE[10]

CONCORD, OCTOBER 24 [1878].

J. P. True

Dear Sir,—I never copy or "polish," so I have no old manuscripts to send you; and if I had it would be of little use, for one person's method is no rule for another. Each must work in his own way; and the only drill needed is to keep writing and profit by criticism. Mind grammar, spelling, and punctuation, use short words, and express as briefly as you can your meaning. Young people use too many adjectives to try to "write fine." The strongest, simplest words are best, and no *foreign* ones if it can be helped.

Write, and print if you can, if not, still write, and improve as you go on. Read the best books, and they will improve your style. See and hear good speakers and wise people, and learn of them. Work for twenty years, and then you may some day find that you have a style and place of your own, and can command good pay for the same things no one would take when you were unknown.

I know little of poetry, as I never read modern attempts, but advise any young person to keep to prose, as only once in a century is there a true poet; and verses are so easy to do that it is not much help to write them. I have so many letters like your own that I can say no more, but wish you success, and give you for a motto Michael Angelo's wise words: "Genius is infinite patience."

Your friend, L. M. ALCOTT.

P.S.—The lines you send me are better than many I see; but boys of nineteen cannot know much about hearts, and had better write of things they understand. Sentiment is apt to become sentimentality; and sense is always safer, as well as better drill, for young fancies and feelings.

Read Ralph Waldo Emerson, and see what good prose is, and some of the best poetry we have. I much prefer him to Longfellow.

TO THOMAS NILES

FEBRUARY 12, 1881.

Dear Mr. Niles,—Wendell Phillips wrote me a letter begging me to write a preface for Mrs. Robinson's "History of the Suffrage Movement;" but I refused him, as I did Mrs. R., because I don't write prefaces well, and if I begin to do it there will be no end. . . .

Cannot you do a small edition for her? All the believers will buy the book, and I think the sketches of L. M. Child, Abby May,[11] Alcott, and others will add much to the interest of the book.

Has she seen you about it? Will you look at the manuscripts by and by, or do you scorn the whole thing? Better not; for we are going to win in time, and the friend of literary ladies ought to be also the friend of women generally.

We are going to meet the Governor, council, and legislature at Mrs. Tudor's next Wednesday eve and have a grand set-to. I hope he will come out of the struggle alive.

Do give Mrs. R. a lift if you can, and your petitioners will ever pray.

Yours truly, L. M. A.

TO THOMAS NILES

FEBRUARY 19, 1881.

Dear Mr. Niles,—Thank you very much for so kindly offering to look at Mrs. R.'s book. It is always pleasant to find a person who can conquer his prejudices to oblige a friend, if no more.

I think we shall be glad by and by of every little help we may have been able to give to this reform in its hard times, for those who take the tug now will deserve the praise when the work is done.

I can remember when Anti slavery was in just the same state that Suffrage is now, and take more pride in the very small help we Alcotts could give than in all the books I ever wrote or ever shall write.

"Earth's fanatics often make heaven's saints," you know, and it is as well to try for that sort of promotion in time.

If Mrs. R. does send her manuscripts I will help all I can in reading or in any other way. If it only records the just and wise changes Suffrage has made in the laws for women, it will be worth printing; and it is time to keep account of these first steps, since they count most.

I, for one, don't want to be ranked among idiots, felons, and minors any longer, for I am none of the three, but very gratefully yours,

L. M. A.

TO WILLIAM WARLAND CLAPP, JR.[12]

Editor Boston Daily Journal.

My attention having been called to the fact that a letter of mine sent to the annual Woman Suffrage meeting, has been entirely misunderstood by the opponents of the cause, I wish to set the matter right, being as anxious as Mrs Howe to have it clearly understood that, though "a well-descended woman" I am heart and soul on the unpopular side of the question.

Those to whom the letter was addressed made no mistake in its meaning, knowing well that while home duties kept me from a festival where I was not needed, nothing but the most pressing care or calamity would prevent me from discharging the duties I owe the cause. I had no time for *pleasure,* but when our Town Meeting comes I shall be there, glad of a chance to help secure good schools for my neighbours' children. Surely this will be as feminine and worthy an act as standing behind a stall at a charity fair, or dancing in a ball-room.

The assertion that suffragists do not care for children and prefer notoriety to the joys of maternity is so fully contradicted by the lives of the women who are trying to make the world a safer and a better place for both sons and daughters, that no defense is needed. Having spent my own life from fifteen to fifty, loving and laboring for children, as teacher, nurse, story-teller and guardian, I know whereof I speak, and value their respect and confidence so highly that for their sakes, if for no other reason, I desire them to know that their old friend never deserts her flag.

So far from losing interest in this question, every year gives me greater faith in it, greater hope of its success, a larger charity for those who cannot see its wisdom, and a more earnest wish to use what influence I possess for its advancement. LOUISA MAY ALCOTT.

Concord,
Mar 6, 1883

TO MAGGIE LUKENS

BOSTON JAN. 14TH [1884]

Dear Maggie.

I have *not* forgotten my five sisters, & was glad to hear from them again, though sincerely grieved to learn that one of the dear group had gone.

I know how hard it is to spare these dear sisters, having lost two, & how empty the world seems for a long time. But faith, submission & work sustain, cheer & help so much that after the first sharpness of the loss is over, we often find a very sweet & precious tie still binds us even more tenderly together than when the visible presence was here.

Beth & May are always mine, though twenty five years have passed since we laid the poor shadow of one under the pines at Concord, & the dust of the other sleeps far away in Paris. Both are young, & bright, & live so always in my mind, for the pain & the parting, the years & sea are all as nothing, & I see them safe with Marmee waiting for the rest to come.

May's blooming baby, which she gave me with all her lovely pictures, is a great comfort to me, & promises to be as full of courage, talent & nobility as her gifted mother. I am so busy helping little Louisa May Nieriker live her own sweet story that I find no time to write others, & am settling down to be a cosy old Granny with my specks & knitting.

My dear old father, now 84, is quite helpless & feeble in mind, but serene & happy as a child, suffering little but waiting cheerfully to slip away in God's good time after a long & blameless life.

You speak of "breaking away;" if it can be dutifully & wisely done I think girls *should* see a little of the world, try their own powers, & keep well & cheerful, mind & body, because life has so much for us to learn, & young people need change. Many ways are open now, & woman can learn, be & do much if they have the will & opportunity.

I hope to see you if you take flight from the nest. With much love & sympathy to all I am, dear Maggie,

Your friend as always
L. M. ALCOTT.

TO MAGGIE LUKENS

FEB. 5TH [1884]

My Dear Maggie.

I hope I never shall be too busy or too old to answer letters like yours as far as I can, for to all of us comes this desire for something to hold by, look up to, & believe in. I will tell you my experience & as it has stood the test of youth & age, health & sickness, joy & sorrow, poverty & wealth I feel that it is genuine, & seem to get more light, warmth & help as I go on learning more of it year by year.

My parents never bound us to any church but taught us that the love of goodness was the love of God, the cheerful doing of duty made life happy, & that the love of one's neighbor in its widest sense was the best help for oneself. Their lives showed us how lovely this simple faith was, how much honor, gratitude & affection it brought them, & what a sweet memory they left behind for, though father still lives his life is over as far as thought or usefulness are possible.

Theodore Parker & R. W. Emerson did much to help me to see that one can shape life best by trying to build up a strong & noble character through good books, wise people's society, an interest in all reforms that help the world, & a cheerful acceptance of whatever is inevitable. Seeing a beautiful compensation in what often seems a great sacrifice, sorrow or loss, & believing always that a wise, loving & just Father cares for us, sees our weakness & is near to help if we call. Have you read Emerson? He is called a Pantheist or believer in Nature instead of God. He was truly *Christian* & saw God *in* Nature, finding strength & comfort in the sane, sweet influences of the great Mother as well as the Father of all. I too believe this, & when tired, sad, or tempted find my best comfort in the woods, the sky, the healing solitude that lets my poor, weary soul find the rest, the fresh hope, or the patience which only God can give us.

People used to tell me that when sorrow came I should find my faith faulty because it had no name, but they were wrong, for when the heavy loss of my dear, gifted sister found me too feeble to do anything but suffer passively, I still had the sustaining sense of a love that never failed even when I could not see why this lovely life should end when it was happiest.

As a poor, proud, struggling girl I held to the belief that if I *deserved* success it would surely come so long as my ambition was not for selfish ends but for my dear family, & it did come, far more fully than I ever hoped or dreamed tho youth, health & many hopes went to earn it. Now when I might enjoy rest, pleasure & travel I am still tied by new duties to my baby, & give up my dreams sure that something better will be given me in time.

Freedom was always my longing, but I have never had it, so I am still trying to feel that this is the discipline I need & when I am ready the liberty will come.

I think you need not worry about any name for your faith but simply try to be & do good, to love virture [sic] in others & study the lives of those who are truely worthy of imitation. Women need a religion of thier own, for they are called upon to lead a quiet self sacrificing life with peculiar trials, needs, & joys, & it seems to me that a very simple one is fitted to us whose hearts are usually more alive than heads, & whose hands are tied in many ways.

Health of body helps health of soul, cheerful views of all things keep up the courage & brace the nerves. Work for the mind *must* be had, or daily duty becomes drudgery & the power to enjoy higher things is lost. Change of scene is sometimes salvation for girls or women who out grow the place they are born in, & it is thier duty to go away even if it is to harder work, for hungrey minds prey on themselves & ladies suffer for escape from a too pale or narrow life.

I have felt this, & often gone away from Concord to teach, (which I never liked) because there was no food for my mind in that small conservative town, especially since Mr Emerson died.

Food, fire & shelter are not *all* that women need, & the noble discontent that asks for more should not be condemned but helped if possible.

At 21 I took my little earnings ($20) & a few clothes, & went to seek my fortune tho I might have sat still & been supported by rich friends. All those hard years were teaching me what I afterward put into the books, & so I made my fortune out of my seeming *mis* fortunes; I speak of myself because what one has *lived* one really knows & so can speak honestly. I wish I had my own house (as I still hope to have) so that I might ask the young women who often write to me as you do, to come & see me, & look about & find what they need, & see the world of wise, good people to whom I could introduce them as others did me thirty years ago. I hope to have it soon, & then you must come & have our talk, & see if any change can be made without neglecting duty.

When one cannot go away one can travel in spirit by means of books. Tell me what you read & like, & perhaps I can send you a key that will at least open a window through which your eyes can wander while the faithful hands & feet are tied by duty at home.

Write freely to me, dear girl, & if I can help in any way be sure I gladly will. A great sorrow often softens & prepares the heart for a new harvest of good seed, & the sowers God sends are often very humble ones, used only as instruments by him because being very human they come naturally & by every day ways to the help of those who are passing through trials like thier own.

I find one of the compensations for age in the fact that it seems to bring young people nearer to me, & that the experiences so hard to live through now help me to understand others. So I am always glad to do what I can, remembering how I wrote to my father for just such help as you ask, & how he answered as I have tried to answer you.

Let me know if it does comfort you any.

With love to my other girls

I am always your friend
L. M. A.

TO MAGGIE LUKENS

FEB. 14TH [1884]

Dear Maggie.

I am glad that my letter pleased you, & though always busy I at once answer your last because if by word or act one can help a fellow creature in the care or conduct of a soul that is one's first duty.

About the great Hereafter I can only give you my own feeling & belief, for we can *know* nothing, & must wait hopefully & patiently to learn the secret.

Death never seemed terrible to me, the fact I mean, though the ways of going & the sad blow of a sudden end are of course hard to bear & understand.

I feel that in this life we are learning to enjoy a higher, & fitting ourselves to take our place there. If we use well our talents, opportunities, trials & joys here when we pass on it is to the society of nobler souls, as in this world we find our level inevitably.

I think immortality is the passing of a soul thro many lives or experiences, & such as are *truly* lived, used & learned help on to the next, each growing richer higher, happier, carr[y]ing with it only the real memories of what has gone before. If in my present life I love one person truly, no matter who it is, I believe that we meet somewhere again, though where or how I dont know or care, for genuine love is immortal. So is real wisdom, virtue, heroism &c. & these noble attributes lift humble lives into the next experience, & prepare them to go on with greater power & happiness.

I seem to remember former states before this, & feel that in them I have learned some of the lessons that have never been mine here, & in my next step I hope to leave behind many of the trials that I have struggled to bear here & begin to find lightened as I go on.

This accounts for the genius & the great virtue some show here. They have done well in many phases of this great school & bring into our class the virtue or the gifts that make them great & good.

We don't remember the lesser things, they slip away as childish trifles, & we carry on only the real experiences. Some are born sad, some bad, some feeble, mentally & morally I mean, & all thier life here is an effort to get rid of this shadow of grief, sin, weakness in the life before. Others come as Shakespere, Milton Emerson &c. bringing thier lovely reward with them & pass on leaving us the better for thier lives.

This is my idea of immortality. An endless life of helpful change, with the instinct, the longing to rise, to learn, to love, to get nearer the source of all good, & go on from the lowest plane to the highest, rejoicing more & more as we climb into the clearer light, the purer air, the happier life which must exist, for, as Plato said "The soul cannot imagine what does not exist because it is the shadow of God who knows & creates all things."

I dont believe in spiritualism as commonly presented. I dont want to see or feel or hear dead friends except in my own sense of nearness, & as my love & memory paint them. I do believe that they remember us, are with us in a spiritual sense when we need them, & we feel thier presence with joy & comfort, not with fear or curiosity.

My mother is near me sometimes I am sure, for help comes of the sort she alone gave me, & May is about her baby I feel, for out of the innocent blue eyes sometimes come looks so like her mother's that I am startled, for I tended May as a child as I now tend Lulu. This slight tie is enough to hold us still tenderly together, though death drops a veil between us, & I look without doubt or fear toward the time when in some way we shall meet again.

About books. Yes, I've read "Mr Isaacs" & "Dr C." & like them both. The other "To Leeward" is not so good. "Little Pilgrim" was pretty, but why try to paint Heaven? Let it alone, & prepare for it whatever it is, sure that God knows what we need & deserve.

I will send you Emerson's Essays. Read those marked & see what you think of them. They did much for me, & if you like them you shall have more. Ever yr. friend L. M. A.

Love to the girls & respects to Papa.

TO THE WOMAN'S JOURNAL

CONCORD, MASS., MAY 8, 1884.

Editors Woman's Journal:

There is very little to report about the woman's vote at Concord Town Meeting, as only eight were there in time to do the one thing permitted them.

With the want of forethought and promptness which shows how much our sex have yet to learn in the way of business habits, some dozen delayed coming till the vote for school committee was over. It came third on the warrant, and a little care in discovering this fact would have spared us much disappointment. It probably made no difference in the choice of officers, as there is seldom any trouble about the matter, but it is to be regretted that the women do not give more attention to the duty which they really care for, yet fail, as yet, to realize the importance of, small as it is at present.

Their delay shows, however, that home affairs are *not* neglected, for the good ladies remained doubtless to give the men a comfortable dinner and set their houses in order before going to vote.

Next time I hope they will leave the dishes till they get home, as they do when in a hurry to go to the sewing-society, Bible-class, or picnic. A hasty meal once a year will not harm the digestion of the lords of creation, and the women need all the drill they can get in the new duties that are surely coming to widen their sphere, sharpen their wits, and strengthen their wills, teaching them the courage, intelligence and independence all should have, and many sorely need in a world of vicissitudes. A meeting should be called before the day for action comes, to talk over matters, to get posted as to time, qualifications of persons, and the good of the schools, then the women can act together, know what they are doing, and keep up the proper interest all should feel in so important a matter.

"I come, but I'm lukewarm," said one lady, and that is the spirit of too many.

"We ought to have had a meeting, but you were not here to call it, so no one did," said another, as if it were not a very simple thing to open any parlor and ask the twenty-eight women voters to come and talk an hour.

It was a good lesson, and we hope there will be energy and foresight enough in Concord to register more names, have a quiet little caucus, and send a goodly number of earnest, wide-awake ladies to town-meeting next year.

LOUISA M. ALCOTT.

Concord, May 8, 1884.

TO LUCY STONE[13]

AUG. 31 [1885]

My Dear Mrs Stone.

I should think it was hardly necessary for me to write or to say that it is impossible for me ever to "go back" on Womans Suffrage. I earnestly desire to go forward on that line as far & as fast as the prejudices, selfishness & blindness of the world will let us, & it is a great cross to me that ill health & home duties prevent my devoting heart, pen & time to this most vital question of the age.

After a fifty years acquaintance with the noble men & women of the Anti slavery cause, & the sight of the glorious end to their faithful work, I should be a traitor to all I most love, honor & desire to imitate, if I did not covet a place among those who are giving their lives to the emancipation of the white slaves of America.

If I can do no more let my name stand among those who are willing to bear ridicule & reproach for the truth's sake, & so earn some right to rejoice when the victory is won.

Most *heartily* yours for *Woman's Suffrage* & all other reforms,

LOUISA MAY ALCOTT.

Concord Mass.

TO THOMAS NILES

SUNDAY, [JUNE?] 1886.

Dear Mr. Niles,—The goodly supply of books was most welcome, for when my two hours pen-work are over I need something to comfort me, and I long to go on and finish "Jo's Boys" by July 1st.

My doctor frowns on that hope and is so sure it will do mischief to get up the steam that I am afraid to try, and keep Prudence sitting on the valve lest the old engine run away and have another smash-up.

I send you by Fred several chapters, I wish they were neater, as some were written long ago and have knocked about for years, but I can't spare time to copy, so hope the printers won't be in despair.

I planned twenty chapters and am on the fifteenth. Some are long, some short, and as we are pressed for time we had better not try to do too much.

. . . I have little doubt it will be done early in July, but things are so contrary with me I can never be sure of carrying out a plan, and I don't want to fail again; so far I feel as if I could, without harm, finish off these dreadful boys.

Why have any illustrations? The book is not a child's book, as the lads are nearly all over twenty, and pretty pictures are not needed. Have the bas-relief if you like, or one good thing for frontispiece.

I can have twenty-one chapters and make it the size of "Little Men." Sixteen chapters make two hundred and sixteen pages, and I may add a page here and there later,—or if need be, a chapter somewhere to fill up.

I shall be at home in a week or two, much better for the rest and fine air; and during my quiet days in C. I can touch up proofs and confer about the book. Sha'n't we be glad when it is done?

Yours truly,

L. M. A.

NOTES TO THE LETTERS

1. Unless otherwise indicated, the letters in this section were first published in Ednah Dow Cheney's *Louisa May Alcott: Her Life, Letters, and Journals* (1889). Dates appearing in brackets are supplied by Myerson and Shealy's *Selected Letters*, in which all of the following letters appear. Alcott's letters to Lucy Stone, Maria S. Porter, William Warland Clapp, Jr., and the *Woman's Journal* were also reprinted in Madeleine B. Stern's "Louisa Alcott's Feminist Letters," *Studies in the American Renaissance 1978*, ed. Joel Myerson (Boston: Twayne, 1978).
2. Ellipses in this letter appear in Cheney and are retained in Myerson and Shealy's *Selected Letters*.
3. This letter, undated in Cheney, is tentatively dated by Myerson and Shealy as August 1860.
4. This letter first appeared in Annie M. L. Clark, *The Alcotts in Harvard* (1902).
5. Alcott's letters to Moncure Daniel Conway and to Mr. Ayer first appeared in Myerson and Shealy's *Selected Letters* and are reprinted here with the kind permission of the Estate of Theresa W. Pratt.
6. The letters to the Lukens sisters and to Maggie Lukens were first published by Edward W. Bok in "Louisa May Alcott's Letters to Five Girls," *Ladies Home Journal* 13, no. 5 (April 1896).
7. This letter to Lucy Stone appeared in the *New York Daily Tribune* (15 October 1873), and was reprinted in *History of Woman Suffrage*, edited by Elizabeth Cady Stanton.
8. This letter first appeared in Maria S. Porter's "Recollections of Louisa May Alcott," *New England Magazine* (March 1892).
9. This letter was first printed in the *Woman's Journal* 7 (15 July 1876).
10. Alcott's letter to True first appeared in *St. Nicholas* 15 (May 1888).
11. The comma between Abby May and Alcott may be a misprint, either introduced or reproduced by Cheney and preserved by Myerson and Shealy. Although it is possible that Alcott is referring to her mother by her maiden

name and her father by his surname, it seems more likely that she is referring only to her mother, Abigail May Alcott.

12. Alcott's letter to Clapp was first published in the *Boston Morning Journal* (8 March 1883) and the *Woman's Journal* 14 (10 March 1883).
13. This letter to Stone first appeared in the *History of Woman Suffrage*.

SELECTED BIBLIOGRAPHY

PRIMARY WORKS

Behind a Mask: The Unknown Thrillers of Louisa May Alcott. Ed. Madeleine B. Stern. New York: Avenel, 1975. New York: Morrow, 1997.

"Diana and Persis." *Alternative Alcott.* Ed. Elaine Showalter. American Women Writers Series. New Brunswick: Rutgers University Press, 1988, 383–441.

A Double Life: Newly Discovered Thrillers of Louisa May Alcott. Ed. Madeleine B. Stern with Joel Myerson and Daniel Shealy. Boston: Little, Brown, 1988.

Eight Cousins; or, The Aunt-Hill. Boston: Roberts Brothers, 1875. New York: Dell, 1986.

Freaks of Genius: Unknown Thrillers of Louisa May Alcott. Ed. Daniel Shealy with Joel Myerson and Madeleine B. Stern. Contributions to the Study of Popular Culture 28. New York: Greenwood, 1991.

From Jo March's Attic: Stories of Intrigue and Suspense. Ed. Madeleine B. Stern and Daniel Shealy. Boston: Northeastern University Press, 1993.

Hospital Sketches. Boston: James Redpath, 1863. Reprinted in *Alternative Alcott,* 3–93.

The Inheritance. New York: Dutton, 1997.

Jo's Boys and How They Turned Out. A Sequel to "Little Men." Boston: Roberts Brothers, 1886. New York: Grosset and Dunlap, 1949.

The Journals of Louisa May Alcott. Ed. Joel Myerson and Daniel Shealy with Madeleine B. Stern. Boston: Little, Brown, 1989.

Little Men: Life at Plumfield with Jo's Boys. London: Samson Low, 1871. New York: Grosset and Dunlap, 1947.

Little Women or Meg, Jo, Beth, and Amy. Boston: Roberts Brothers, 1868; Part Second. Boston: Roberts Brothers, 1869. Ed. Elaine Showalter. New York: Viking Penguin, 1989.

A Long Fatal Love Chase. New York: Random House, 1995.

Louisa May Alcott on Race, Sex, and Slavery. Ed. Sarah Elbert. Boston: Northeastern University Press, 1997.

Louisa May Alcott: Selected Fiction. Ed. Daniel Shealy, Madeleine B. Stern, and Joel Myerson. Boston: Little, Brown, 1990.

Louisa May Alcott's Fairy Tales and Fantasy Stories. Ed. Daniel Shealy. Knoxville: University of Tennessee Press, 1992.

A Modern Mephistopheles. No Name Series. Boston: Roberts Brothers, 1877. Reprinted in *A Modern Mephistopheles and Taming a Tartar.* Ed. Madeleine B. Stern. New York: Praeger, 1987.

Moods. Boston: Loring, 1864. Revised edition. Boston: Roberts Brothers, 1882. Ed. Sarah Elbert. American Women Writers Series. New Brunswick: Rutgers University Press, 1991.

Norna or, the Witch's Curse. Ed. Juliet McMaster. Edmonton: Juvenilia Press, 1994.

An Old-Fashioned Girl. Boston: Roberts Brothers, 1870. New York: Viking Penguin, 1996.

Plots and Counterplots: More Unknown Thrillers of Louisa May Alcott. Ed. Madeleine B. Stern. New York: Avenel, 1976. Reprinted as *A Marble Woman: Unknown Thrillers of Louisa May Alcott.* New York: Morrow, 1995.

Rose in Bloom, A Sequel to "Eight Cousins." Boston: Roberts Brothers, 1876. New York: Dell, 1986.

The Selected Letters of Louisa May Alcott. Ed. Joel Myerson and Daniel Shealy with Madeleine B. Stern. Boston: Little, Brown, 1987.

"Transcendental Wild Oats." *Independent* 25 (December 18, 1873). Reprinted in *Alternative Alcott*, 364–79, and *Louisa May Alcott: Selected Fiction*, 447–60.

Work: A Story of Experience. Boston: Roberts Brothers, 1873. New York: Viking Penguin, 1994.

Works of Louisa May Alcott. Ed. Claire Booss. New York: Avenel, 1982.

SECONDARY WORKS: BOOKS

Bedell, Madelon. *The Alcotts: Biography of a Family.* New York: Charles N. Potter, 1980.

Cheney, Ednah D. *Louisa May Alcott: Her Life, Letters, and Journals.* Boston: Roberts Brothers, 1889. Reprinted as *Louisa May Alcott.* Introduction by Ann Douglas. American Men and Women of Letters Series. New York: Chelsea House, 1980.

Critical Essays on Louisa May Alcott. Ed. Madeleine B. Stern. Boston: G. K. Hall, 1984.

Elbert, Sarah. *A Hunger for Home: Louisa May Alcott and "Little Women."* Philadelphia: Temple University Press, 1984. Revised edition. *A Hunger for Home: Louisa May Alcott's Place in American Culture.* New Brunswick: Rutgers University Press, 1987.

Keyser, Elizabeth Lennox. *"Little Women": A Family Romance.* Twayne's Masterwork Studies. New York: Twayne, 1999.

———. *Whispers in the Dark: The Fiction of Louisa May Alcott.* Knoxville: University of Tennessee Press, 1993.

"Little Women" and the Feminist Imagination. Ed. Janice M. Alberghene and Beverly Lyon Clark. New York: Garland, 1998.

MacDonald, Ruth K. *Louisa May Alcott.* Twayne United States Authors Series, no. 457. Boston: Twayne, 1983.

Marsella, Joy A. *The Promise of Destiny: Children and Women in the Short Stories of Louisa May Alcott.* Contributions to the Study of Childhood and Youth, no. 2. Westport, CT: Greenwood, 1983.

Saxton, Martha. *Louisa May: A Modern Biography of Louisa May Alcott.* New York: Avon, 1978.

Stern, Madeleine B. *Louisa May Alcott.* Norman: University of Oklahoma Press, 1950, 1978. Revised edition. *Louisa May Alcott: A Biography.* New York: Random House, 1996.

Strickland, Charles. *Victorian Domesticity: Families in the Art and Life of Louisa May Alcott.* Foreword by Robert Coles. University, Alabama: University of Alabama Press, 1985.

SECONDARY SOURCES: ARTICLES AND CHAPTERS IN BOOKS

Armstrong, Frances. " 'Here Little, and Hereafter Bliss': *Little Women* and the Deferral of Greatness." *American Literature* 64 (1992): 453–74.

Auerbach, Nina. "Waiting Together: Two Families." *Communities of Women: An Idea in Fiction.* Cambridge: Harvard University Press, 1978, 35–73.

Bassil, Veronica. "The Artist at Home: The Domestication of Louisa May Alcott." *Studies in American Fiction* 15 (1987): 187–97.

Bernstein, Susan Naomi. "Writing and *Little Women*: Alcott's Rhetoric of Subversion." *American Transcendental Quarterly* n.s. 7 (1993): 25–43.

Brodhead, Richard H. "Starting Out in the 1860s: Alcott, Authorship, and the Postbellum Literary Field." *Cultures of Letters: Scenes of Reading and Writing in Nineteenth-Century America.* Chicago: University of Chicago Press, 1993.

Campbell, Donna M. "Sentimental Conventions and Self-Protection: *Little Women* and *The Wide, Wide World.*" *Legacy* 11 (1994): 118–29.

Carpenter, Lynette. " 'Did They Never See Anyone Angry Before?': The Sexual Politics of Self-Control in Louisa May Alcott's 'A Whisper in the Dark.' " *Legacy* 3 (1986): 31–41.

Chapman, Mary. "Gender and Influence in Louisa May Alcott's *A Modern Mephistopheles*." *Legacy* 13 (1996): 19–37.

Clark, Beverly Lyon. "Domesticating the School Story, Regendering a Genre: Alcott's *Little Men*." *New Literary History* 26 (1995): 323–42.

———. "A Portrait of the Artist as a Little Woman." *Children's Literature* 17 (1989): 81–97.

Cowan, Octavia. Introduction. *A Modern Mephistopheles.* By Louisa May Alcott. Toronto: Bantam, 1987.

Crisler, Jesse S. "Alcott's Reading in *Little Women*: Shaping the Autobiographical Self." *Resources for American Literary Study* 20 (1994): 27–36.

Dalke, Anne. " 'The House-Band': The Education of Men in *Little Women*." *College English* 47 (1985): 571–78.

Donovan, Ellen. "Reading for Profit and Pleasure: *Little Women* and *The Story of a Bad Boy*." *Lion and the Unicorn* 18 (1994): 143–53.

Estes, Angela M., and Kathleen Margaret Lant. "Dismembering the Text: The Horror of Louisa May Alcott's *Little Women*." *Children's Literature* 17 (1989): 98–123.

———. "The Feminist Redeemer: Louisa May Alcott's Creation of the Female Christ in *Work*." *Christianity and Literature* 40 (1991): 223–53.

———. " 'We Don't Mind the Bumps': Reforming the Child's Body in Louisa May Alcott's 'Cupid and Chow-chow.' " *Children's Literature* 22 (1994): 27–42.

Fetterley, Judith. "Impersonating 'Little Women': The Radicalism of Alcott's *Behind a Mask*." *Women's Studies* 10 (1983): 1–14.

———. "*Little Women*: Alcott's Civil War." *Feminist Studies* 5 (1979): 369–83.

Foster, Shirley, and Judy Simons. "Louisa May Alcott: *Little Women*." *What Katy Read: Feminist Re-Readings of "Classic" Stories for Girls.* Iowa City: University of Iowa Press, 1995.

Gaard, Greta. " 'Self-Denial Was All the Fashion': Repressing Anger in *Little Women*." *Papers on Language and Literature* 27 (Winter 1991): 3–19.

Gehrman, Jennifer A. " 'I am half-sick of shadows': Elizabeth Stuart Phelps's Ladies of Shalott." *Legacy* 14 (1997): 123–28.

Griswold, Jerry. "Bosom Enemies: *Little Women*." *Audacious Kids: Coming of Age in America's Classic Children's Books.* New York: Oxford University Press, 1992.

Habegger, Alfred. "Precocious Incest: First Novels by Louisa May Alcott and Henry James." *Massachusetts Review* 26 (1985): 233–62.

Halttunen, Karen. "The Domestic Drama of Louisa May Alcott." *Feminist Studies* 10 (1984): 233–54.

Hollander, Anne. "Reflections on *Little Women*." *Children's Literature* 9 (1981): 28–39.

James, Henry. "Miss Alcott's *Moods*." *North American Review* 101 (July 1865): 276–81. Reprinted *Moods* by Louisa May Alcott. Ed. Sarah Elbert. American

Women Writers Series. New Brunswick: Rutgers University Press, 1991, 219–24.

Kaledin, Eugenia. "Louisa May Alcott: Success and the Sorrow of Self-Denial." *Women's Studies* 5 (1878): 251–63.

Keyser, Elizabeth Lennox. " 'Playing Puckerage': Alcott's Plot in 'Cupid and Chow-chow.' " *Children's Literature* 14 (1986): 105–22.

Langland, Elizabeth. "Female Stories of Experience: Alcott's *Little Women* in Light of *Work.*" *The Voyage In: Fictions of Female Development.* Ed. Elizabeth Abel, Marianne Hirsch, and Elizabeth Langland. Hanover, NH: University Press of New England, 1983, 112–17, 333–34.

May, Jill P. "Spirited Females of the Nineteenth Century: Liberated Moods in Louisa May Alcott's *Little Women.*" *Children's Literature in Education* 11 (Spring 1980): 10–20.

Minadeo, Christy Rishoi. "*Little Women* in the 21st Century." *Images of the Child.* Ed. Harry Eiss. Bowling Green: Bowling Green State University Popular Press, 1994, 119–214.

Murphy, Ann B. "The Borders of Ethical, Erotic, and Artistic Possibilities in *Little Women.*" *Signs* 15 (Spring 1990): 562–85.

O'Brien, Sharon. "Tomboyism and Adolescent Conflict: Three Nineteenth-Century Case Studies." *Woman's Being, Woman's Place: Female Identity and Vocation in American History.* Ed. Mary Kelly. Boston: G. K. Hall, 1979, 351–72.

Patterson, Mark. "Racial Sacrifice and Citizenship: The Construction of Masculinity in Louisa May Alcott's 'The Brothers.' " *Studies in American Fiction* 25 (1997): 147–66.

Reardon, Colleen. "Music as Leitmotif in Louisa May Alcott's *Little Women.*" *Children's Literature* 24 (1996): 74–85.

Rosenfeld, Natania. "Artists and Daughters in Louisa May Alcott's *Diana and Persis.*" *New England Quarterly* 64 (1991): 3–21.

Sanderson, Rena. "*A Modern Mephistopheles:* Louisa May Alcott's Exorcism of Patriarchy." *American Transcendental Quarterly* n.s. 5 (1991): 41–55.

Showalter, Elaine. "*Little Women:* The American Female Myth." *Sister's Choice: Tradition and Change in American Women's Writing.* Oxford: Clarendon Press, 1991, 42–64, 183–85.

Sicherman, Barbara. "Reading *Little Women*: The Many Lives of a Text." *U.S. History as Women's History: New Feminist Essays.* Ed. Linda K. Kerber, Alice Kessler-Harris, and Kathryn Kish Sklar. Chapel Hill: University of North Carolina Press, 1995, 245–66, 414–24.

Stimpson, Catharine R. "Reading for Love: Canons, Paracanons, and Whistling Jo March." *New Literary History* 21 (1990): 957–76.

Vallone, Lynne. "The Daughters of the Republic: Girls' Play in Nineteenth-Century Juvenile Fiction." *Disciplines of Virtue: Girls' Culture in the Eighteenth and Nineteenth Centuries.* New Haven: Yale University Press, 1995, 106–34, 192–200.

Van Buren, Jane. "*Little Women*: A Study in Adolescence and Alter Egos." *The Modernist Madonna: Semiotics of the Maternal Metaphor.* Bloomington: Indiana University Press, 1989, 96–123, 192–97.

Yellin, Jean Fagan. "From *Success* to *Experience*: Louisa May Alcott's *Work*." *Massachusetts Review* 21 (1980): 527–39.

Young, Elizabeth. "A Wound of One's Own: Louisa May Alcott's Civil War Fiction." *American Quarterly* 48 (1996): 439–74.

Zehr, Janet S. "The Response of Nineteenth-Century Audiences to Louisa May Alcott's Fiction." *American Transcendentalist Quarterly* n.s. 1 (1987): 323–42.

Zwinger, Linda. "*Little Women*: The Legend of Good Daughters." *Daughters, Fathers, and the Novel: The Sentimental Romance of Heterosexuality.* Madison: University of Wisconsin Press, 1991, 46–75, 1146–49.

Printed in the United States
by Baker & Taylor Publisher Services